1635
THE DREESON INCIDENT

The Ring of Fire series:

1632 by Eric Flint

1633 by Eric Flint & David Weber

1634: The Baltic War by Eric Flint & David Weber

Ring of Fire ed. by Eric Flint

1634: The Galileo Affair by Eric Flint & Andrew Dennis

1634: The Ram Rebellion by Eric Flint with Virginia DeMarce et al.

1634: The Bavarian Crisis by Eric Flint & Virginia DeMarce

1635: The Cannon Law by Eric Flint & Andrew Dennis

Ring of Fire II ed. by Eric Flint

1635: The Dreeson Incident by Eric Flint & Virginia DeMarce

Grantville Gazette ed. by Eric Flint

Grantville Gazette II ed. by Eric Flint

Grantville Gazette III ed. by Eric Flint

Grantville Gazette IV ed. by Eric Flint

Time Spike by Eric Flint & Marilyn Kosmatka

**For a complete list of
Baen Books by Eric Flint,
please go to www.baen.com.**

1635
THE DREESON INCIDENT

ERIC FLINT AND
VIRGINIA DEMARCE

1635: The Dreeson Incident

This is a work of fiction. All the characters and events portrayed in this book are fictional, and any resemblance to real people or incidents is purely coincidental.

A Baen Books Original

Baen Publishing Enterprises
P.O. Box 1403
Riverdale, NY 10471
www.baen.com

ISBN 10: 1-4165-5589-7
ISBN-13: 978-1-4165-5589-6

Cover art by Tom Kidd
Maps by Gorg Huff

First printing, December 2008

Distributed by Simon & Schuster
1230 Avenue of the Americas
New York, NY 10020

Library of Congress Cataloging-in-Publication Data

Flint, Eric.
1635 : the Dreeson incident / Eric Flint and Virginia DeMarce.
p. cm. — (Ring of fire series)
"A Baen books original"—T.p. verso.
ISBN 1-4165-5589-7
1. Thirty Years' War, 1618–1648—Fiction. 2. Time travel—Fiction. 3. Europe—History—17th century—Fiction I. DeMarce, Virginia Easley, 1940– II. Title.
PS3556.L548A61865 2008
813'.54—dc22

2008035303

10 9 8 7 6 5 4 3 2 1

Pages by Joy Freeman (www.pagesbyjoy.com)
Printed in the United States of America

To the memory of
Dr. Caroline Emma Edith Hartwig (1899-1990)
and Priscilla Mailey (1918-1995).
Two extraordinary high school history teachers.

Contents

Maps ix

Family Trees xii

1635: The Dreeson Incident 1

Cast of Characters 583

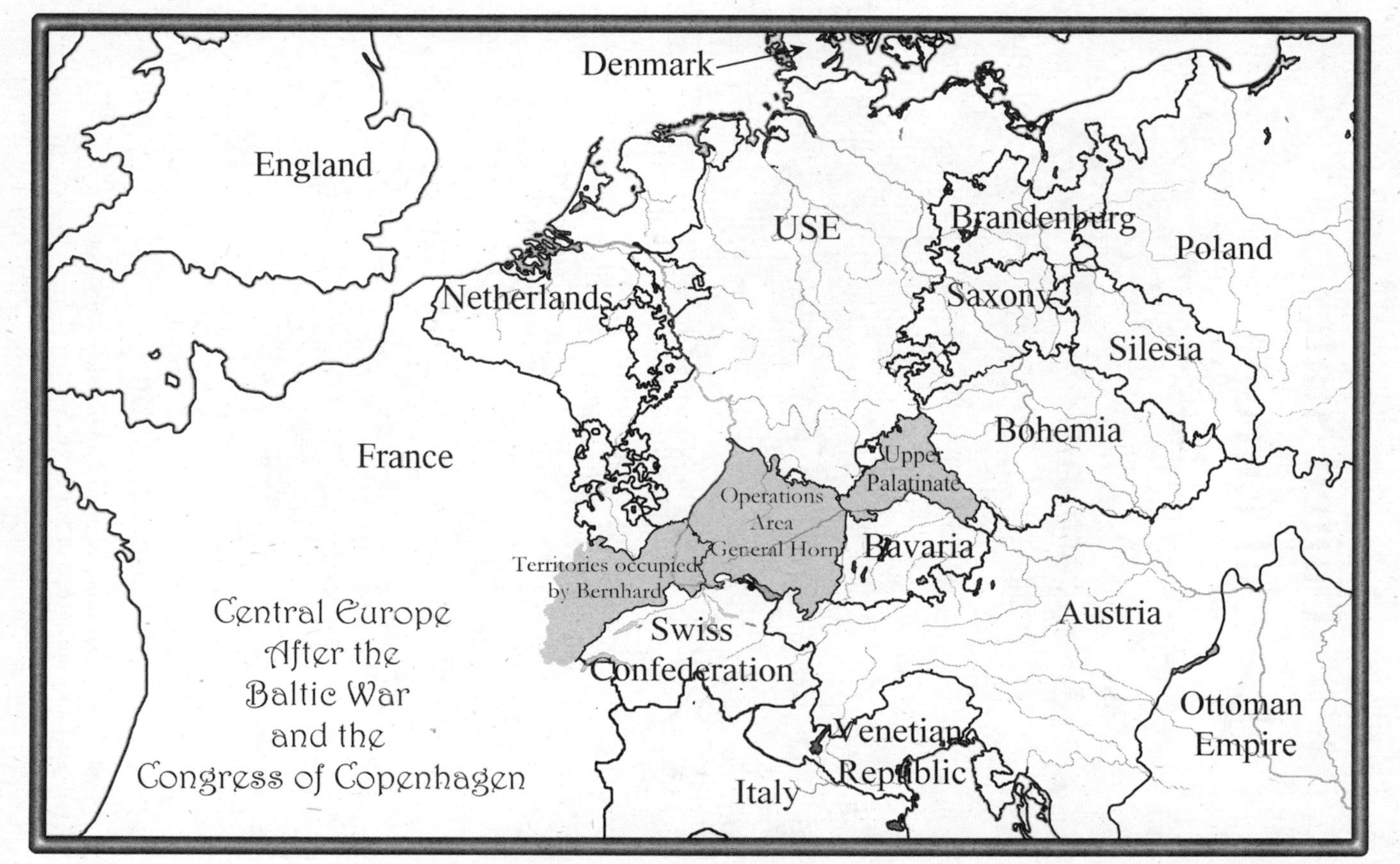
Denmark
England
USE
Brandenburg
Poland
Netherlands
Saxony
Silesia
Bohemia
France
Upper Palatinate
Operations Area General Horn
Bavaria
Territories occupied by Bernhard
Austria
Swiss Confederation
Central Europe After the Baltic War and the Congress of Copenhagen
Ottoman Empire
Venetian Republic
Italy

*Swabia is still under direct imperial administation and not yet a self-governing province as of March 1635

Brunswick
Nordhausen
Kassel
Hesse-
Kassel
Halle
Mulde
Elbe
Mulhausen
Merseburg
Leipzig
Saale
Saxony
Eisenach
Weimar
Erfurt
Jena
Suhl
See detail
below
Chemnitz
Fulda
State of
Thuringia-
Franconia
Schweinfurt
Bohemia
Bamberg
Bayreuth
Wurzburg
Main
Rothenburg
Nuremberg
Oberpfalz
Swabia
Badenburg
Rudolstadt
Saxony
Grantville
Saalfeld

Descendants of John Charles Jenkins

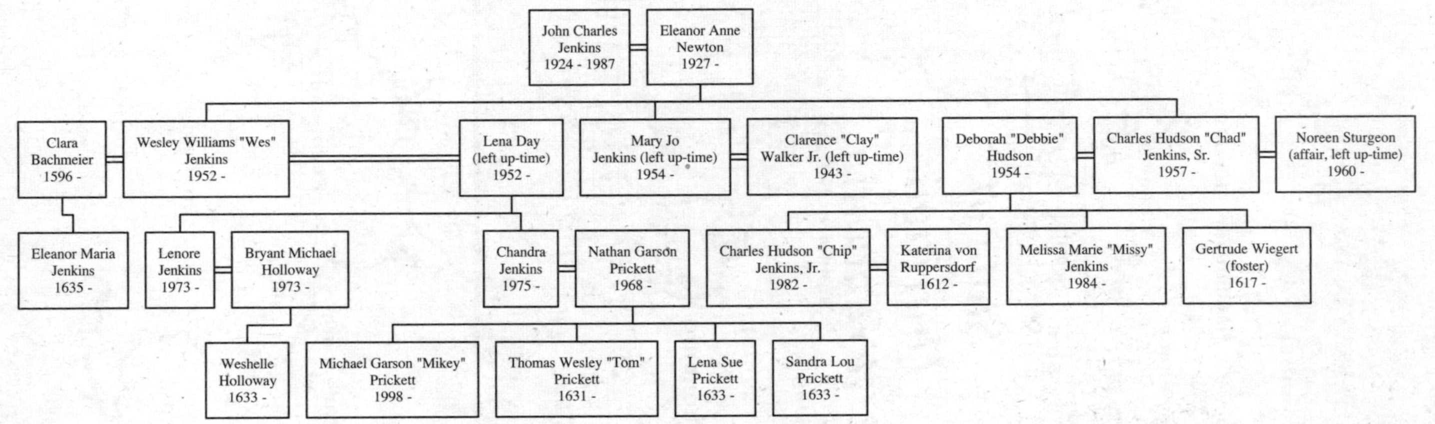

Descendants of Willie Ray Hudson

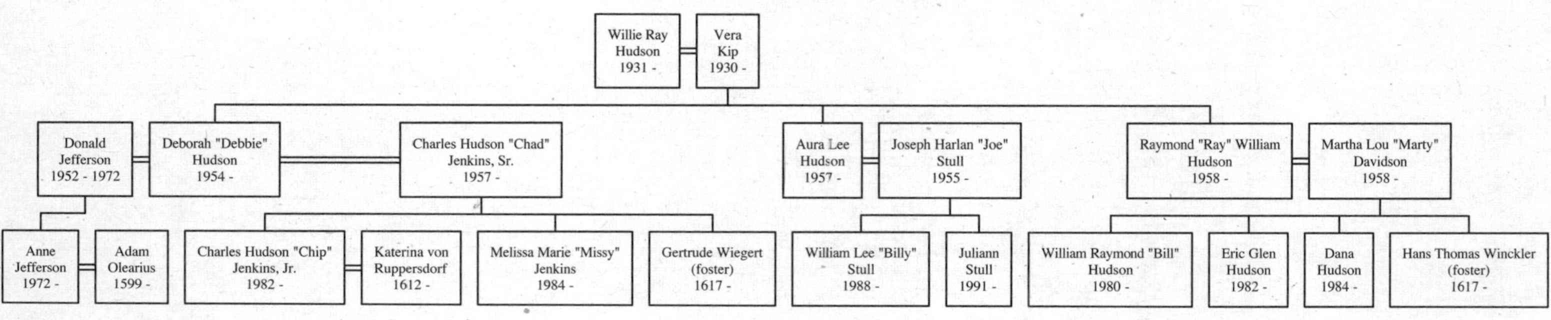

Prologue

August 1634

Magdeburg
United States of Europe

Don Francisco Nasi, spymaster for the United States of Europe, pushed his glasses up his nose. "Michel Ducos moved on quickly, even before Peter Appel notified the Frankfurt authorities. He'd been gone a couple of days before they got the news to me. We can't just move in and arrest his lieutenant Guillaume Locquifier, partly because then we'd lose the trail, but jurisdictionally because the crime didn't happen on USE soil and we don't have an arrest on sight and extradite agreement with the Papal States. It's better just to keep Locquifier under surveillance. Frankfurt says that he isn't doing anything active right now—just huddling in the back parlor of an inn with a few other men."

Ed Piazza scowled. Once a high school principal in Grantville, he was now the president of the State of Thuringia-Franconia. The SoTF, whose capital was Grantville, was one of the largest and most populous provinces of the United States of Europe. Ed was in Magdeburg for a few days consulting with Mike Stearns, the prime minister of the USE. "It's your call, I guess. Personally,

I'd be happier if they were in jail, considering that mess at the Galileo hearing."

Sitting behind his desk not far away, Mike Stearns shrugged. "Mazarini cleaned up the mess around the assassination attempt on the pope very efficiently. Politically speaking, I mean—he didn't wash the blood off the floor of the church or dig the bullets out of the plaster himself, of course. Frank, Ron and Gerry Stone were all in big trouble right after the assassination attempt and things could have turned out a lot worse if he hadn't put in the fix."

"Nevertheless," said Nasi, "once they realized that Ducos was not really a member of the Committees of Correspondence, but had been using them for his own purposes, the Stone boys acted decisively. The assassination might very well have succeeded had it not been for them. Therefore they interest me."

"Tom Stone told me that his son Frank and his new wife Giovanna are staying in Venice," added Mike. "Frank's going to keep working with the Committee of Correspondence there. Maybe try to develop some in other places in Italy. In the *Italies*, I should say. It's as bad as 'the Germanies.' A patchwork of little duchies and principalities, the Papal States in the middle and the Spanish in the south in Naples."

Piazza shook his head. "Where's Garibaldi when we need him?"

"Not born yet. Never will be, in this universe," Nasi said practically.

"Tom and Magda are staying in Italy, too. His lectures at the Padua medical school are really catching on, and she's done very well negotiating the purchase of a lot of things we need for industrial development in the USE. But Tom's other two sons, Ron and Gerry, are coming back to Grantville when Simon Jones does. They're traveling with him and with the mother of Jabe McDougal's girlfriend. The painter. Artemisia Gentileschi. The mother, I mean—not the girlfriend."

Nasi smiled and looked at Ed. "I would appreciate an opportunity to speak with Signora Gentileschi, should one arise. She has been living in Naples, working for the Spanish. Her father is in England. She has ties to both the Barberini and the Tuscan court in Florence. Let me know when they get to Grantville. If she isn't coming to Magdeburg, I believe such a conversation would be worth my while, even if I need to make the trip to Grantville to have it. Jabe goes back and forth, I believe."

"Will do. I'll radio you as soon as she shows up. What about the boys?"

"How old are they, exactly?"

"Ron graduated from high school on the accelerated program, right before they all left for Venice. He'd turned seventeen the December before that, so that would make him eighteen, now. Eighteen and a half. Gerry . . ." Piazza stopped and thought a minute. "He should be turning sixteen this month. Gus Heinzerling was supposed to be tutoring him while they were in Venice, so he didn't fall behind. But I'm told that he's not coming back to high school in Grantville. He's decided to finish up at the boys' school in Rudolstadt. I'm not sure why. But if they're willing to admit him over there, it means that Gus really did keep his nose to the grindstone, at least as far as Latin was concerned."

"Too young for my work, and he will be too busy. Gerry, that is," Nasi said. "Would the older one have anything to contribute?"

"You can debrief him, of course. If he's willing to talk to you. He's a legal adult, so he can make his own decision on that. Tom Stone's always been a little . . . antiauthoritarian. More than a little. Magda's a straight arrow, though, and she has that incredible Lutheran sense of duty. Well, she grew up in Jena, with all those theology professors in the town. She's been their stepmother for close to three years now, and they like her. So maybe . . . I can't make any promises on his behalf."

Nasi dug into his briefcase and drew out a sheaf of papers. "He submitted a written report to me. Voluntarily, sent in the diplomatic pouch from Venice. Detailing all of their contacts with Michel Ducos while he was posing as a member of the Venice Committee of Correspondence. It's retrospective, of course. Written with all the benefits of hindsight. He does not spare himself or his brothers. Perhaps he is even too harsh in his judgment of them. We sent them out with very little training and with no expectation that they would encounter the developments that occurred. Bedmar, d'Avaux, Ducos. The boys were, as your baseball commentators would say, 'way out of their league.' But, the self-condemnation aside, his analysis of what happened is certainly competent. More than competent."

"Tom and Magda seem to agree with you," said Mike. "On

the competence issue, that is. Karl Jurgen Edelman will stay available for consultation—Magda's father has a keenly honed sense about the importance of following the money—but he has his own businesses to run and he's tired of being on the train between Jena and Grantville every week and sometimes twice a week. So Ron's going to be managing Lothlorien for them when he gets back. Not just the Farbenwerke, but the pharmaceuticals end of it, too."

Piazza nodded. "I'll keep an eye on him."

Padua

"Signora Gentileschi and her daughter arrived from Rome last night," the doorman reported. "They send a message that they are prepared to leave for Grantville as soon as the rest of you can pack up. Unless there is some delay here, they do not plan to unpack more than they will need for a night or two."

Simon Jones stood up, taking the note from the porter's hand. "Please let them know that all I still have to do is put the clothes I wore yesterday into my saddlebags. The rest of the stuff is ready for the men to put on the pack horses any time."

Magda smiled. "I think the boys are ready, too. More than ready."

The doorman bowed slightly and backed out of the room. They'd never been able to break him of that habit.

Simon looked at the note again and frowned. "Sometimes I wish that Larry and Gus hadn't had to stay in Rome. Who's Joachim Sandrart, and why is he with the Gentileschis? Why is he traveling with us, that is?"

Magda shrugged.

"Who would know?" Simon frowned. "If he's someone who could be a problem, I should warn Ron and Gerry to keep their lips zipped when he's around."

"Signora Gentileschi is an artist. Perhaps he is another one. An . . . associate?"

Simon had no trouble interpreting Magda's disapproving tone. Cardinal Antonio Barberini, by way of Mazzare, had warned them. By the standards of a respectable Lutheran from Jena, Artemisia Gentileschi's past was as colorful as her canvases. It was by no means certain that her younger daughter, the one she was bringing with her, was the child of her husband.

"Not a lover, probably, if you're worried about bad influences on the boys. This," Simon waved the note in the air, "says he's in his twenties. She's fortyish and the little girl she has with her is only ten or eleven, I think. Probably some ambitious young artist who's finished putting in his practically mandatory time in Italy and is ready to go home and launch himself into a hopefully lucrative career of putting paint on canvas."

Magda snorted. "I will ask someone. I do have responsibilities, after all."

Lausanne
Switzerland

Duke Henri de Rohan put down his pen. He had finished today's letter to his brother Benjamin in England, but hadn't signed it yet, in case something else came to mind. He re-read. *After his assassination attempt on the pope was foiled, Michel Ducos was last seen escaping by boat down the Tiber, presumably to take ship from Ostia. I predict that he will not go back to d'Avaux. In any case, Mazarini is ensuring that d'Avaux will have only minimal chances to foment mischief in the future. I am afraid that Ducos has become the head of a small group of unpredictable fanatics. Keep an eye out in England for any sign of him and his followers. Though, of course, he may be headed for Holland. Or Scotland. Or . . .*

He picked up the pen again. *I am also writing to our agent in Frankfurt am Main. If necessary, please be prepared to make a rapid trip to Frankfurt. You should find the burden of this bearable, since to a considerable extent our associates there are also members of a network of international wine merchants.* He paused a moment, then signed his name.

The duke moved on, to finish his outgoing correspondence for the day. Happily, his new assignment from Venice, attempting to reconcile the feuding Swiss cantons, significantly reduced the time it took for his letters to reach their destinations. Instructions for his wife in France; a shorter note to his father-in-law, also in France; another one to his brother Benjamin, in care of Isaac de Ron in Frankfurt; a letter to Hugo Grotius, another to the mathematician Descartes. One to the city council of the Most Serene Republic of Venice, which was dithering about whether or not to renew his employment contract.

And one to Cardinal Richelieu, assuring him, with the monotonous regularity he brought to such reassurances, that he remained a loyal and faithful subject of the French monarchy.

The duke missed his long and faithful correspondence with his mother, who had died three years earlier. If he was not concentrating, Rohan often still found himself thinking that he should mention something to her.

Now, a letter to his daughter Marguerite, in France with her mother. Marguerite had been born almost fifteen years after the wedding and was now seventeen years old. Of the nine children of his marriage, only she had survived. When he finished it, he started to put down his pen and then picked it up again.

One to Duke Bernhard of Saxe-Weimar. After Bernhard's successes this summer, it was time to consider the possibility that he might make a suitable son-in-law. He was thirty. It was time for him to be getting married. Marguerite had the splendid advantage that she was already old enough to bear children and still young enough to bear a lot of children, God willing.

The Austrians would probably try to pick Bernhard off with some minor Habsburg bride, of course, to protect their interests in Vorarlberg and the other territories dotted across southern Swabia to the Breisgau. But it would be a terrible pity, in Rohan's opinion, to waste a successful Protestant prince on a Catholic wife.

True, Bernhard was Lutheran, not Calvinist as was the duke himself. But Lutherans counted as Protestants, at least from the political perspective, the same way that members of the Church of England did. If not, quite, theologically. After all, the Lion of the North himself was a Lutheran. German-language Catholic popular pamphleteers, an imprecise group of people sadly lacking in perception where the nuances of doctrinal distinction among their opponents were concerned, tended to refer even to Calvinists and Anabaptists as *Lutheraner*.

Even the city council of Venice had been known to refer to Duke Henri de Rohan himself as a "Lutheran." The most prominent Huguenot in contemporary France shuddered slightly at such a lack of theological precision.

A match between Marguerite and Bernhard would not make

King Louis XIII of France and Cardinal Richelieu at all happy, of course. But then neither would a match between Marguerite and young Turenne, which was also an attractive possibility. The only thing that would make Louis and Richelieu happy would be for Marguerite to convert to Catholicism and marry one of Richelieu's relatives.

Which wasn't going to happen. At least not as long as Henri de Rohan was alive.

Then he wrote directly to Isaac de Ron in Frankfurt, telling him to expect the arrival of Henri's brother Benjamin (letter to him enclosed) from England any day now.

Please take out a lease on a suitable town house and have it furnished and staffed with reliable people by the time he arrives, charging the cost to my account with the banker Milkau.

Benjamin liked his comforts. He accomplished more when he was comfortable.

Now for the inbox. On top of it, the latest report from Leopold Cavriani. A delightful man. He'd had a really fascinating summer. Leopold did not suffer from the constraints that were an inevitable part of having been born into the high nobility.

Occasionally, Henri de Rohan envied him.

But only occasionally.

Somewhere in Switzerland

"If he pontificates at me one more time," Ron Stone said, "I think I'll gag. I don't see how Gerry can stand to listen. Hour after hour, after hour."

Artemisia Gentileschi smiled patiently. "Your brother isn't listening, really. He's just . . . not bothering to avoid Joachim."

"How much more do we need to know about him? Hell, we already know more than enough." Ron grabbed onto the reins with one hand and waved the other in the air. "Talk, talk, talk, talk, talk, talk, jabber, pontificate, talk some more. We've already heard that he was born in Frankfurt, that his family are Calvinists who fled from the Spanish Netherlands because of religious persecution, that he apprenticed with Soreau and Stoskopff in Hanau and can't face a future limited to still-lifes so he'll probably have to work for Catholic patrons mostly, that he learned print making in Nürnberg, that the engraver he worked for in Prague advised him to specialize in painting, that he learned to paint from Gerard van Honthorst in Utrecht, that he toured Holland with Pieter Paul Rubens, that he worked at the English court for a while with Honthorst, that he has not only seen Florence, Rome, and Naples, but also Messina and Malta, that he thinks the war has ruined the career prospects of most German artists, that . . ." He stopped. "If I hear one more word about the trials, troubles, and travails of the 'Frankenthal exiles,' I think I'll spit. What's worse, the guy talks in capital letters." He groaned with disgust.

Simon Jones, riding on his other side, laughed out loud. Joachim Sandrart *did* talk in capital letters. He didn't speak, he orated.

He was doing it now.

"Time and again Queen Germania has seen her Palaces and Churches, decorated with splendid Painting, go up in Flames, and her Eyes are so darkened with Smoke and Weeping that she no longer has the Desire or the Strength to pay Heed to this Art: Art that now seems to want only to enter into a long and eternal Night and there to sleep. Perhaps a man may find a short Contract with one Ruler. But as the Scene of War moves, so, perforce, does he, leaving his Efforts unfinished. And so such Things fall into Oblivion, and those that make Art their Profession fall into Poverty and Contempt. They put away their Palettes and Easels. They must take up the Pike, the Sword, or the Beggar's Staff instead of the Paintbrush, while the Gently Born are ashamed to apprentice their Children to such despicable Persons."

Are you planning to do anything about it, man? Ron thought sourly. *Like maybe try to end the war? Or do you just plan to complain and complain and complain?*

"Gently born?" Ron asked Artemisia Gentileschi. "Is the guy noble?"

"No." She twisted her lips. "Joachim is far more gently born than I, to be sure. The family was Walloon, certainly one of the more prominent commoner lineages in Hainaut. His father was—is, if he is still alive, but I haven't heard recently—a merchant. Very wealthy, but still a merchant. His mother was from a merchant family, also. Joachim's a cousin of Michel le Blon. Still, even in Frankfurt Laurentius Sandrart achieved some status. Certainly among the Walloons, if not among the native-born. Even though he was an immigrant into a city where the Lutheran council does not precisely make Calvinists welcome—they refused to grant permanent resident to Sebastian Stoskopff, which is why he went to Paris when he left Hanau.

"However, I'm sure that Joachim would not object if, some time in the future, a ruler chose to ennoble him for his many services to the cause of Art. Services which he has yet to perform, though I don't really doubt that he is capable of performing them. If he hadn't decided to return with me, Count Vincenzo Giustiniani in Rome had made him a very generous offer to manage his collection. So he should do well as an art dealer and promoter, at least, even if his own canvases do not display an immense amount of promise. Merely a high level of workmanlike competence. Both of my brothers, after all, have made their way quite successfully as dealers and agents. As has Hainhofer in Augsburg. The art world needs its intermediaries.

"Nor, I'm sure, would Joachim object if a ruler who employs him as a painter should also choose to utilize him as a diplomat, as the rulers of the Spanish Netherlands have done with Rubens. Everybody knows that his cousin le Blon—he's an engraver and goldsmith, a good twenty years older than Joachim, I think—operates out of Amsterdam as an agent for Oxenstierna." Artemisia frowned. "Of course, le Blon is a religious nut, too, quite taken with the writings of that Silesian, Jacob Böhme. Just because a man is successful in one field, it doesn't necessarily follow that he has common sense in any other.

"Joachim is an ambitious man. He is unlikely to become as great an artist as Rubens, but he doesn't lack high aspirations."

Grantville

"Denise!"

There were several Denises in town. She kept going.

"Denise Beasley, hey there!"

She slowed down, then stopped her motorcycle. Someone was running after her.

"Denise, if you're going downtown, can you give me a lift? Drop me off at the middle school. I'm going to be late for practice." It was Missy Jenkins, who worked in the "State Library" part of the libraries housed in the high school these days.

"What are you practicing?"

"I'm not. I'm coaching recreation league girls' soccer. I don't usually mind the run; it's only a couple of miles and good for me. But we had a VIP tour this afternoon and I got away a half hour after I should have."

"Sure. Climb on behind."

Missy did. "There are days that I would give my eyeteeth to be able to ride one of these. If I had one, that is."

Denise was a little surprised. "Compared to horses?" A lot of the girls her own age were totally horse crazy. A lot of the older ones, too, for that matter.

"Horses don't speak to me," Missy said.

"I can see that. Horses don't speak to me, either. I don't speak to them, if I can avoid it. Do you mind if we stop at the funeral home first, for a second? I'll take you all over and get you there on time."

"No problem. But why?"

"Minnie Hugelmair garages her cycle there, behind the hearse. It's more secure than the old shed behind Benny's house. They had a few problems. Some vandalism and at least once somebody tried to break in and steal it, we think. At the funeral home, there's always someone up and around, every day, all around the clock. It's safer, and Jenny doesn't charge much."

They headed down Route 250 in silence.

Until Missy, the wind whipping through her hair since she didn't have a helmet, asked, "Would you teach me to drive this thing? We could figure out the costs of the lessons. Your time, the fuel, wear and tear, all that."

Joe Pallavicino sat in the principal's office at the middle school, cleaning his fingernails while he waited to talk to Archie Clinter about their common problems. Denise Beasley had gone on to high school this fall. There had already, less than a month into the academic year, been trouble in regard to a boy who tried to hit on her after she told him to beat it. Senior on freshman. He'd recover.

It looked like Minnie Hugelmair would probably finish sixth grade by Thanksgiving, according to Tina Sebastian. By spring, at this rate, she would get her eighth grade diploma—earlier, if she tested out. Then, if she went to summer school and Denise didn't, she'd finish ninth grade in August of '35 and they'd both be sophomores the fall of 1636. In the class of '38.

There was no question that Minnie did her own school work. She wasn't in English for Speakers of Other Languages classes at all any more. She seemed to regard textbooks as obstacles on a course she was running and scaled them with determination.

There was no question that she still attracted trouble like a magnet.

Especially . . .

Especially given the increasing level of "anti-Kraut" muttering here and there around Grantville. Considering that she was still best friends with Denise Beasley. Considering that Denise's uncle Ken owned the 250 Club, which was the center of most of the muttering.

High school was one of the ages that started a lot of the trouble, with up-time and down-time boys competing for the attention of the same girls.

Minnie was not a beauty. She probably hadn't been before the riot in Jena. With the addition of the scar and the slightly mismatched artificial eye, she never would be.

But Denise was. She always would be. At the age of ninety, if she lived that long. Somehow, she managed to combine her mother Christin's delicate build and brunette vividness with Buster's sheer vigor. Trouble also, if a different kind of trouble. With Minnie there to take her part, next year. And there were too many up-time kids who would classify any retaliation by Minnie as "Kraut trouble."

Minnie wasn't likely to be as gentle as Denise herself had been. As a rule, Denise never did more than was necessary to make her point.

Of course, any boy who wasn't a total idiot knew that she would, in a pinch, call on her father for backup. Buster Beasley was an ex-biker whose seventeen-inch biceps were only partly obscured by the tattoos that covered them. He constituted significant backup for a girl.

Some boys, on the other hand, were total idiots.

Joe decided he'd better talk to a few people besides Archie. Benny and Buster. Preston Richards at the police department. Lisa Dailey and Vic Saluzzo at the high school. Henry Dreeson and Enoch Wiley. Mary Ellen Jones, maybe. If they had some lead time, maybe they could arrange things so that Denise and Minnie could finish high school without triggering some kind of mudslide.

✧ ✧ ✧

Words and music came wafting up the high school corridor.

"You know," Victor Saluzzo said, leaning against the library circulation desk. "I could have lived my life a lot more happily if Benny Pierce hadn't decided to teach Minnie Hugelmair that old turkey of a song and she hadn't spread it to our incoming freshmen."

> *"School days, school days,*
> *Dear old Golden Rule days.*
> *Reading and writing and 'rithmetic,*
> *Taught to the tune of a hickory stick . . ."*

Missy Jenkins giggled. She was there on temporary loan from the state library for a couple of weeks while the school went through the agonies of starting a new semester. "I hope you know that Minnie herself has every intention of finishing sixth grade the first semester and showing up on your doorstep before Christmas."

Pam Hardesty, also on loan from the state library, grinned. "Then you'll have both of them, Victor. Not just Denise, but Minnie, too. They do sort of have a tendency to cut out of school on the slightest excuse, don't they?"

Victor shook his head. "The real problem is that they're both bright enough to do it without really hurting their grades. But a lot of other kids aren't that smart, so it's a bad example." The high school principal paused. "Maybe we should try providing them with mentors." He pushed himself upright. "If anybody comes looking for me, I'll be down in the guidance counseling office."

Pam watched him go and sighed.

"What's the matter?"

"Reproaching myself, I guess. When he mentioned Minnie, what hit me first was *Schadenfreude*. And that's terrible. Taking pleasure in somebody else's troubles. But, honest to God, Missy, the great Velma Hardesty soap opera continues. Given the way Mom's been behaving lately, hanging around with that gorgeous garbage man . . . You've seen him, haven't you? Jacques-Pierre Dumais? I guess it's sort of comforting to realize that other people have troubles, too."

"Yeah. Like Winnie the Pooh called honey. 'Sustaining.' You're not alone, though. Neither is Mr. Saluzzo. Think of what Mr. Dreeson has to deal with, every single day."

Part One

August 1634

He with his horrid crew

Chapter 1

Frankfurt am Main
Independent imperial city
United States of Europe

"We could do it, you know," Gui Ancelin said. He threw the newspaper down on the table in the private parlor at Isaac de Ron's inn. "The woman, this Dreeson's wife, has turned up in Basel, it says. Logically, to return to the USE, she will shortly be traveling right through Frankfurt. An old woman. How hard could it be to intercept her?"

"We will not violate the trust Michel has placed in us!" Guillaume Locquifier said forcefully. He even went so far as to make a fist at the other man.

Mathurin Brillard blinked. That was not part of Guillaume's usual repertoire of gestures, but he was unusually furious this morning. Possessed by all of the classical furies. Even more immovable and stubborn than usual.

The table was covered with newspapers, and their headlines. Headlines about the new king in the Netherlands and the prospect that Frederik Hendrik, the Calvinist prince of Orange, would betray his Protestant allies by compromising with the Spaniard—formerly the cardinal infante. Headlines about airplanes. Headlines about the archduchess Maria Anna of Austria, who was going to marry that Spanish conqueror after having fled from her intended husband, the duke of Bavaria, on the eve of her wedding.

There were also headlines about the up-time woman, Simpson's wife. Headlines about Admiral Simpson, who apparently had plans to install a major naval facility within the lands surrounded by those that the Spanish conqueror had already occupied.

There were even headlines about the Grantville mayor's wife, Veronica Richter, who had accompanied Simpson's wife and the former Austrian archduchess in their adventures.

Admittedly, it was maddening. So far, Michel Ducos had not given the people he left behind in Frankfurt permission to do anything at all. Brillard sometimes suspected that Michel was trying to hog all the glory for himself.

But Ducos and Antoine Delerue had placed Guillaume Locquifier in charge of the group in Frankfurt—and as far as Locquifier was concerned, Michel Ducos was The Great Leader. A brilliant leader; an inspiring leader. If seeing him that way would not amount to idolatry, almost a semi-divine leader.

Not to mention a somewhat intimidating leader.

In Brillard's personal opinion, Ducos was also a leader who was more than halfway to becoming insane. He never mentioned that to Guillaume, of course.

So, no matter how furious Locquifier became at the news in the papers, he would wait. Which was precisely what he was proclaiming now.

"Michel has never mentioned this woman. We do not have time to get his permission by way of Mauger's commercial contacts before she will have come and gone. She may not be part of his greater plan. We do not *know* all the details of his greater plan. He has not chosen to impart them to us."

Fortunat Deneau reached over and picked the paper up. "She will have guards around her if she comes on a Rhine boat. There are still so many different jurisdictions along the Rhine that no one would let her travel without guards. If she travels by river at all, of course. Once she reaches Mainz, however, it is all within the USE to Frankfurt. Is she important enough that any of them would be detailed to accompany her to Frankfurt?"

"We cannot initiate anything without Michel's approval," Guillaume insisted. "Nothing. We will do nothing. *Absolutement!*"

Robert Ouvrard looked a little mutinous. "If and when we

know for certain that she will follow this route, are we to sit around all winter, then, doing nothing but talk? Then maybe talk some more?"

"We may watch her," Locquifier conceded. "Once we know that she has left Basel, if she is coming this way, some of us may go down to Mainz. When she arrives there, we can observe her land. See where she stays. Find out how many people are in her party. Surely she will not be traveling entirely without companions for the rest of her trip, though she is unlikely to have bodyguards." He turned to Ancelin. "You and"—he looked around the room—"Deneau. Get on the same boat on which she comes to Frankfurt. Observe her. Hear anything useful that is to be heard. But . . . Do . . . Nothing."

"Why don't we at least write to Michel?" Ancelin picked up the paper again. "Ask for a sort of blanket approval that we can make some decisions here. Get his agreement that we can take out easy targets if and when we identify any, if they fit in with the prospect of destabilizing Richelieu. We wouldn't have to mention this particular woman. Just ask for something general."

"*Non!*" Ouvrard shook his head. "Tell Michel who this woman is. She makes a good example. Point out what a splendid opportunity we may be missing because of our obedience to his directives." He stood up, waving his hands in the air. "Michel is the leader, Guillaume, but he simply isn't *here*. Since we don't have, and won't have, one of the almost magical radios, not any time soon, we can't afford to wait for his approval of every single action. Even our Lord Christ, when he sent out the seventy to convert the world, did not reserve unto himself approval of every minor thing they decided to do."

"I will write him," Locquifier said finally. "But I will not do any more than ask. I will not urge. Remember what he told me in Italy. 'Don't be stupid, Guillaume. Do you propose to curse every soldier who stands against us? Divert ourselves at each instant in order to punish lackeys?' I, personally, have no intention of letting him call me 'stupid' again."

Brillard shrugged. It was more than he had expected Ancelin and Ouvrard to accomplish. Michel Ducos was not a man to be pushed. Guillaume Locquifier was not a man to try.

Chapter 2

Switzerland

"Sandrart, what the . . . heck?" Simon Jones frowned.

"What he means is 'what the hell,'" Ron Stone interpreted. "We're supposed to be going straight home. Not taking scenic detours."

"But it's important to us." Artemisia Gentileschi started to wave her hands. "Joachim sent the messenger more than a week ago. Almost ten days ago. Telling him that if the duke agreed, he should meet us at the inn here and let us know. And Rohan *has* agreed."

"One more jumped-up nobleman," Jones muttered.

"Duke Henri de Rohan is the most important Protestant patron in France. Well, not *in* France, since he's in exile, but the most important French Protestant patron of the arts. If Joachim can possibly find a permanent position under the de Rohan/Sully-Bethune umbrella, don't you see, then he won't have to spend most of his life doing commissions for Catholics."

Artemisia's hands stopped for a moment then started up again. "Not that I see that as a problem. Many Catholic artists work for Protestant patrons, such as the king of England, as I have done myself. And vice versa. It won't be a really major problem for Joachim, either. Even someone like Maximilian of Bavaria is inclined to make temporary exceptions to the rules when it comes to the painters and sculptors in his employ. As long as they paint exactly the subjects that he wants them to, of course. But still." Her hands flew out like two birds taking flight. "We're so *close*!"

"A week," Jones said. "A week, at least. Two days to get there, a day for the two of you to talk to the man, and two days back to this road. That's if he sees you right away and isn't so puffed up with his own importance that he keeps you hanging around in his waiting room for a while."

Joachim Sandrart looked at Ron. "He is a high military commander in the service of Venice. Your father, being at the University of Padua, is now, also, in a way in the service of Venice. Although I understand, of course, that he is an independent docent, not a salaried member of the faculty at the medical school. Given the popularity of his lectures, he's probably making more money that way. But if he, or your stepmother, should some day encounter any more difficulties, it would be all to the good if they could call on Rohan's good will. Which they are much more likely to be able to do if you have paid your courtesies to him."

Ron looked at Sandrart, then over to his brother Gerry, who was sitting in a corner of the inn by himself.

"Okay, then. We've been making pretty good time. A lot better than we did on the way down to Venice last year, but that was winter. I guess you deserve your chance. Though you could have asked the rest of us first, before you sent the messenger out. If the duke guy doesn't start playing games with us. Is that all right with you, Simon? We can ride over. If he sees Artemisia and Joachim the day we get there or the next, fine. If he doesn't, we're outta there. Or if Joachim wants to wait for him, he can stay behind."

Lausanne, Switzerland

The duke kissed Artemisia's hand in a very courtly manner. She was delighted, having begun to suspect that she was getting beyond the years when a man might think of kissing her hand outside of a formal public reception.

Rohan welcomed Sandrart briefly and immediately sent him upstairs with his private secretary and some other factotum to look at architectural drawings of his various residences, requesting that he submit a proposal for improving their interior decoration before he left or, if that was not possible, as soon as possible thereafter.

Then he told Gerry and Ron that he had heard their father, Herr Thomas Stone, the great chemist, speak. Several times. He had heard one of their father's public lectures during his last visit to Venice and deliberately delayed his return to Switzerland by a week in order to be a guest at his presentations at the medical school in Padua. True, he should have returned at once to engage in one more round of negotiations to bring peace between the Catholic and Protestant cantons. However, since they had now gone several years without achieving peace, he had doubted that a week would make much difference to the rate of progress.

Gerry mumbled, "We're glad you enjoyed it." He obviously wasn't going to say anything else. Ron realized that he would have to take over the conversation.

"It is my hope that your father found pleasure in reading the book I presented to him. Renee of Ferrara advocated some very bold religious ideas."

Ron swallowed hard. "He didn't say anything. Ah, he's been very busy this summer, Your Grace."

Henri de Rohan smiled. "So I have heard. You have scarcely been idle, yourself."

"None of the stuff that happened in Rome was boring. Yeah. A person could really say that. We actually got to see Galileo."

The duke stroked his chin with his finger. Far from preening himself upon his achievements in averting the assassination, the boy seemed to be more inclined to discount them. Modesty or dissembling? Or a prudent concern that a Huguenot leader might not have been averse to the death of Urban VIII?

In any case, it would be a good idea to learn more about Ron Stone.

After dinner, Rohan indicated, perfectly politely, that everyone but Ron was free to withdraw.

Resisting an urge to wriggle along the floorboards and out through a knothole somewhere, Ron stood up, bowed to Artemisia, and resumed his place.

A servant came up behind him, offering to refill his wine glass.

Ron thought about the ghost of conversation yet to come. "Well-watered, please."

The servant complied.

Rohan picked up a small leather-bound volume. "I have a book for you, too, young Monsieur Stone. You may find it interesting. *Le Parfait Capitaine*, which I completed a few years ago. It discusses Caesar's *Gallic Wars* and the applicability of their lessons to contemporary warfare. A historical essay, if you will. I attempted to trace the true foundations of the military art from its ancient origins until our own day."

"Thanks. Thanks a lot, really. But I don't know how much I'll get out of reading it. I'm not a soldier, Your Grace. I'm not planning to be one. I'm . . . an embryonic businessman, perhaps."

"Ah, that interests me. Scarcely the thing that a French merchant would say to a representative of the ancient nobility. They all make at least some pretense to gentility, no matter how transparent that pretense may be."

Ron swallowed again. "I really do believe in what Thomas Jefferson wrote, Your Grace. Maybe I'm not as sophisticated about it as someone like Ms. Mailey. But . . ."

"Ah, yes. Your 'Declaration of Independence . . . that all men are created equal, and endowed by their creator . . .' The grounds it adduced to justify the American Revolution made fascinating reading, given how many years my brother and I were in armed revolt against our duly constituted monarch. I thoroughly enjoyed the biography of George Washington that Leopold Cavriani sent me, as well. It is in a way humbling to think that a mere member of the rural gentry was so much more successful than my brother and I. Or, indeed, that some few years from now in England, Cromwell, of much the same class in society, would also succeed far better than we did. Such events serve to remind us that all outcomes are in the hand of God."

"Oh." Ron had a feeling he was running out of acceptable things to say to a French duke. Even an exiled ex-revolutionary Protestant French duke.

Rohan turned to a small chest on the floor next to his chair. He opened it and drew out a sheaf of papers tied with red tape. "If not the *Parfait Capitaine*, then perhaps this would interest you more. I finished it this spring. The manuscript is at the printer's now. This is an extra copy completed by my secretary. It contains many of my thoughts in regard to the administration of Cardinal Richelieu."

"I . . . well . . . do you have much in common?"

"A surprising amount. He and I both agree that the public interest, the *raison d'état*, must always be the ruling force in government affairs. Our differences are more a matter of how we interpret what the public interest is. But still. A ruler may deceive himself. His advisers may become corrupt. Even men of good will may misunderstand what the public interest is. But that interest itself, whether it is understood well or badly, can never be at fault. And the king, in the long run, in the last resort, remains responsible for his own actions, and those of his subordinates, before God. If he chooses his delegates poorly or does not supervise them thoroughly . . ."

Ron's next, panicked, thought was, *no nobleman is going to speak this kind of treason to a foreign kid unless the kid's next scheduled stop is having his head chopped off.* Then he pulled himself together. Rohan had already said he was having the book printed. So he must be willing to stand behind it, unless . . .

And he and his brother had fought against Louis XIII at least as long as Washington had fought against George III. "Are you having this printed under your own name, Your Grace?"

Rohan smiled again. "Ah, then you are not politically insensitive. Yes. Under my own name. But in Geneva, not in France. Most certainly not in Paris."

Ron nodded.

"You will not find it surprising, perhaps, that as a Protestant I believe that France's public interest lies in opposition to the Spanish monarchy. You probably, if you have thought of it, find it more surprising that Richelieu allied with the Protestant English and Danes in the League of Ostend. However, the interests of France remain the interests of France. Note which navy bore the brunt of the Battle of Dunkirk. At this point, an equilibrium in Europe can only be to France's advantage. The recent change in the balance of power among the various branches of the Habsburg dynasty, especially the developments in the Netherlands . . ."

"Did you come to bed at all, last night?" Gerry asked.

"Yeah, but it must have been two or three o'clock in the morning."

Joachim Sandrart looked at him questioningly.

"The duke was in a talkative mood."

Chapter 3

Grantville
State of Thuringia-Franconia

Henry Dreeson, Grantville's mayor, stood on the sidewalk outside City Hall leaning heavily on his cane, watching the garbage collection wagon rumble by on its iron-rimmed wheels. Yesterday's parade had generated even more trash than usual. People had been in a pretty exuberant mood because of the final peace settlement reached with the Spanish in the Netherlands, especially coming on top of the thorough trashing that the USE had given the League of Ostend still earlier in the year.

The marching band had stepped out to "Hey, Look Me Over." Henry liked that song. Peppy. There'd been a couple of down-time tunes then, that Marcus Wendell had worked over to make them marchable, so to speak. Finished up with "High Hopes." He liked that one, too. They'd stopped still and stepped in place to play the SoTF anthem. Marching along to "Jerusalem, *Du Hochgebaute Stadt*" would take a miracle as big as the Ring itself. Not that the "Star Spangled Banner" had been any better, when it came to rhythm. Not if they sang it right and didn't mangle it.

The Jerusalem song fit in well enough with American history, though, Mary Kat Riddle said. Something about a city on a hill. Henry looked around. "Down in the Valley" would make more sense for Grantville.

Not Riddle now. Well, probably still Riddle. Mary Kat had gotten married last winter, to Lisa Dailey's brother, but girls were mostly keeping their maiden names these days, just like the down-time women did. What was Mary Kat's husband's name? Utt. Derek Utt. He was over at Fulda.

There had been a float made to look like one of the ironclads. One with Benny Pierce fiddling and Minnie Hugelmair singing. They'd labeled another one "Narnia," with costumed characters from the books and a girl representing Princess Kristina. The folks at St. Mary's were so dizzy with joy over Larry Mazzare's being made a cardinal that they'd managed to build a float that looked like a big red hat. It had been the biggest parade since the Ring of Fire.

He wondered if the folks at St. Mary's—the up-timers, at least—would still be feeling so joyful once they realized that Larry's new honor meant that he likely wouldn't be coming back from Italy to be their parish priest again. He'd be going to Magdeburg. Ed Piazza had pointed that out to Henry. It would be one more upset to smooth over. Sometimes it seemed like every success they had brought along its own set of new problems and the changes never stopped.

Henry glanced back, up at the door he had just come through. Sometimes it seemed like every time he had to go up and down these steps, it took a little more out of him than it had the time before. He prayed that his wife Ronnie, wherever she was, was safe. He wished really hard that Ronnie would come home pretty soon. Sometimes, he admitted to himself, he wished even harder that she had never gone off on this trip with Mary Simpson. They'd have been able to get by without her first husband's money, whatever was left of it.

If, of course, there had not been the problem of college tuition for Annalise. He'd said to Enoch Wiley more than once that Ronnie had piled too much on Annalise's shoulders this summer, between trying to manage Gretchen's orphan collection, some of them nearly as old as she was herself, and running the St. Veronica's Academy schools. She was barely seventeen. Idelette Cavriani, the Genevan girl staying with the Wileys, was the same age and had agreed to help her, but Henry was not certain that two heads were better than one when each of the heads was seventeen years old. The theory seemed to be that adding a Calvinist to be Annalise's assistant, even with the bookkeeping part, would prevent people from seeing the academies as Catholic parochial schools.

That thought made Enoch rather grumpy. Enoch did not approve of the ecumenical movement. He was quite as sure that the pope was the anti-Christ as any seventeenth-century Scots Presbyterian in Grantville. But Henry had married a Catholic—sort of a Catholic, so to speak. Ronnie and Inez had become friends, which had led to Annalise and Idelette becoming friends. So Enoch made the best of it.

Gretchen made Henry feel a bit grumpy himself. She ought to come back, too. Generously adopting a crew of orphans during the stress of war was one thing. *Life-affirming*, he guessed his daughter Margie would have said back before the Ring of Fire. What had Melissa Mailey called her? *A chooser of the living.*

Well, Gretchen had chosen those kids. Much as he hated to say it, choosing to stay home and bring them up appeared to be something else again. First, she got involved with those Committees of Correspondence. Then, off she went to Paris and Amsterdam. Sure, the kids were better off at his house than they would have been in a mercenary army. They were clean, dry, and well fed. They were going to school.

But he had to work, Annalise had to go to school herself and work, Gretchen and Jeff had been gone for over a year, and now Ronnie was away. He didn't see that they were getting much parenting staying home with a housekeeper and the cook. He'd said so to Enoch.

"Parenting" had been one of Margie's words, too. Some days he missed Margie and her kids more than others. This was one of them.

Stress, Enoch called it. He'd learned that word from Henny de Vries, the Dutch nurse. Back before the Ring of Fire, she'd specialized in nut cases. It was one of her words.

When Denise's father, Buster Beasley, caught Minnie and Denise starting to teach Missy Jenkins and Pam Hardesty to ride the hogs—not that catching them was hard, since they made no attempt to hide the project and started the experiment by having their pupils ride around the rental storage units on Buster's lot on the little dirt bikes—he announced that anything worth doing was worth doing well, intervened, and took over the instruction.

But he made sure to tell the girls that they had been doing a good job considering their own level of experience, and they should assist him so that eventually they would be fully capable of teaching others.

Considering that Missy and Pam didn't have cycles of their own and only had time to come out to the lot two or three times a week, he told Denise, they were making pretty good progress. Though neither of them would ever be the kind of pip she was.

Father and daughter smiled at one another in close harmony.

Pam Hardesty looked up from her perch on a high three-legged stool. Since she had taken this job, the sign over her head had been changed from "National Library of the New United States" to "State Library of Thuringia-Franconia."

It was the same library, of course, in the same part of the high school building. But when their little "nation" confederated with the CPE had become one more province in the United States of Europe last winter, the congress had prudently demoted the library's title, just in case the word "national" might give the USE's ruler, who was something of a cultural imperialist, the idea of removing it to Magdeburg. Or even Stockholm.

Gustavus Adolphus had removed quite a few books to Stockholm during the years he had been campaigning in Germany. And a couple of whole libraries, like the one in Würzburg. As the boss, Elaine Bolender, had said in her recommendation to the SoTF congress, it paid to be careful when you were dealing with that man. Not quite in those words, of course.

Pam had started at the library as a page, in the spring of 1633. Before that, she'd been an aide for English for Speakers of Other Languages at the middle school. She had kept on ESOL-aideing in her spare time, of course. They always needed people and when a girl was entirely on her own it was sometimes hard to make ends meet.

This fall, she was starting training to manage the circulation desk some day. She'd already "interned" here at the state library, at the public library, and at the high school. With a week or so each at the elementary school and the middle school, to give her a "taste" of librarianship at that level, Elaine Bolender had said. Then Elaine had given her a choice between specializing in circulation and training for reference. Well, and staying a page, of course, which was what she'd been doing before. She'd picked the desk. She liked meeting all the new people who came in and seeing who was interested in what better than she did wandering through the closed stacks looking things up.

She grinned at Missy Jenkins.

Missy, now, she was the reverse. She liked looking things up, even though she was a few years younger, eighteen to Pam's twenty-one. Pam had been in the same class as Missy's older brother Chip.

When Missy graduated from high school on the accelerated schedule they'd set up after the Ring of Fire for the kids who could hack it, of course her mom had stuck her right into teacher training and ESOL-aideing at the middle school. With no universities or colleges that took girls and Missy definitely not wanting to be a nurse, Debbie Jenkins had regarded teaching school as the only game in town.

This year, a couple of new games were starting to be developed out of town, if you looked at it that way. A women's college in Quedlinburg that would open this fall; the Roths' co-ed university way over in Prague that was getting organized.

That was this year. Missy had graduated in August a year ago. Pam suspected that with Chip in Jena, her folks wouldn't have been thrilled to have her go off to school somewhere else anyway. Her dad kept trying to get her interested in his businesses, and she did quite a bit of office work for him, but she seemed to shy away from getting really involved with it. She'd never said why, at least not to Pam.

Then, the middle of Missy's first year in the teacher training program, her mom took over running it. Missy had groaned dramatically.

Pam thought, a little wistfully, that it might be nice to have a mom who ran a teacher training program. Instead of . . . Velma.

Maybe it looked different from Missy's perspective. The end of the year, last spring, Missy had transferred out of teacher training and ESOL-aideing, over here to the state library.

She was training to be an information librarian. What they used to call a reference librarian, Pam suspected.

Anyway, Missy had turned out to be a good friend.

Chapter 4

Grantville
State of Thuringia-Franconia

Jacques-Pierre Dumais did not care for garbage, as such. However, the Garbage Guys did not merely collect Grantville's garbage. Even this long after the Ring of Fire, a fair number of people still tossed out things for which other people might have some conceivable use, not even going to the trouble of taking them to the recycling center themselves. So the people who worked for Garbage Guys separated the trash themselves, as soon as possible after collecting it, in order to find as many items as possible that they could resell for a profit. Very little of Grantville's garbage was sent to the incinerator.

Objectively, Jacques-Pierre did not find the collection of garbage to be a desirable task. The separation of garbage, however, he found to be very helpful to his goals.

He had heard someone describe a device called a paper shredder. That invention was enough to make a man shudder. It was most fortunate that few of the Grantvillers had owned such a thing at the time of the Ring of Fire. It was too bad that one of them had been owned by the Kellys, the would-be aircraft manufacturers, who still used it and thus made it unnecessarily difficult for Jacques-Pierre to access information about their technology.

But a spy could scarcely hope for life to be full of free gifts, after all.

Like almost every other French Huguenot descended from members of the diaspora that had spread across Europe during the Wars of Religion of the preceding century, Jacques-Pierre had found the widely circulated accounts of the revocation of the Edict of Nantes that had occurred—

—or would have occurred, or will occur—

—some verb tense, in any case—

—in the year 1685 fascinating. Absolutely fascinating. As, of course, did Duke Henri de Rohan.

It turned out, according to the American history books, that the Edict of Nantes issued in the year 1598 by the French king Henry IV, which established many religious and civil freedoms for France's Protestants, would be revoked less than a century later by the still-unborn Louis XIV, son of the currently reigning French monarch, Louis XIII. That would happen in October of 1685, a half century in the future. Thereafter, almost all of France's Protestants—usually called Huguenots—emigrated from the country.

So when Laurent Mauger, from a Huguenot family but now a merchant in Haarlem, had approached Jacques-Pierre about the possibility of going to Grantville to gather further information that could be used to benefit the Protestant cause in France, he had agreed with only the most perfunctory raising of difficulties. Only enough difficulties to improve the remuneration that Mauger first offered. Not to have done so would have raised Mauger's suspicions immediately.

After the two of them had reached an agreement, of course, Jacques-Pierre immediately notified Duke Henri. The duke was Jacques-Pierre's real employer and he knew that Rohan had already, for some time, been seriously concerned about what some of the Huguenot extremists might do. In which, God only knew, he was justified, considering the information that had come from Venice during the spring in regard to the activities of Michel Ducos and his gang of fanatics. Not to mention the news that had come from the duke's Venetian contacts in Rome earlier in the summer: that it was Ducos who had attempted to assassinate the pope.

Duke Henri de Rohan did not care for assassinations. Or

assassins. His father-in-law had been a close friend as well as a counselor of the late, most unfortunately assassinated, King Henri IV of France. Sully had been one of those who had advised the Huguenot Henri de Navarre that Paris was worth a mass, thus possibly contributing to the circumstances that had led the madman to storm the royal carriage with his knife. It bore on his conscience.

Although he had so advised his friend, Sully had never brought himself to make such a . . . transition . . . in the practice of his faith. At the king's wish, he had married his daughter to Rohan who, himself, like his mother, his brother, his wife, and his father-in-law, remained a Calvinist.

This time, perhaps, history would be different. At the parade, everyone in Grantville had been celebrating the overwhelming defeat of the forces of the League of Ostend. Jacques-Pierre smirked. Most of them didn't bother to think that they were celebrating the overwhelming defeat of the French regiments under the command of that idiot de Valois, with only the Huguenot Turenne coming out of the campaign with any glory at all. That would do a lot to undermine the position of Richelieu. Richelieu, the villain who had so strengthened the French crown at the expense of the Estates that in another half-century a French king had been able to revoke the Edict of Nantes.

That was the first and prime goal, Mauger had assured him—to undermine Richelieu. To prevent the centralization of all political power in France in the crown, to the point that the next king could revoke the Edict of Nantes. It didn't matter much how they did it, Mauger claimed. Even that idiot, the king's brother and heir presumptive, Monsieur Gaston, could be a tool. Getting the royal forces out of La Rochelle and returning the city to its pre-1628 status as a bastion of French Protestantism would be a triumph, if they could achieve it.

Mauger even argued that if the Huguenots, ordinary people, had some successes, it might encourage Henri de Rohan to return to a more active leadership role. It might at least allow him to return from his years of exile in Venice and the Swiss cantons.

Wouldn't the duke be surprised to hear that?

That had been months ago, long before Turenne's successful cavalry raid on the oil fields of the United States of Europe at Wietze. Now . . . Ah, if it should happen that the Protestant

Turenne was the *only* effective military leader the king of France could rely upon, that would be superb.

But Mauger was only an agent. He admitted that himself, when Dumais pressed him on the subject. His own contact—rather, the mysterious employer of his own contact—needed information. Must have information. So Jacques-Pierre had agreed to go to Grantville.

Even more, Henri de Rohan needed information about Mauger's mysterious employer. So, in Grantville, Jacques-Pierre had become a garbage collector. In life, there were few free gifts.

Madame Haggerty—now she was a free gift. To have such a woman as the mother of one of his employers was far more than he could have reasonably hoped for, he reflected, as he jogged along next to the garbage wagon.

Later that day, Dumais collected his mail, regretting that Venice and the Swiss had not yet joined the new International Postal Union that made use of pre-paid stamps. If it had, Duke Henri would be paying the postage, not himself.

Ah, well. Even if Jacques-Pierre could rent a post office box, it wouldn't keep him from having to appear at the post office fairly regularly. That wasn't something ordinarily expected of a garbage collector. Luckily, the Grantvillers were, as a whole, so eccentric themselves that they did not find it notably unusual or peculiar for a trash man to receive letters with international postmarks.

Dumais could have tried to pass for a Walloon instead of a Frenchman, he supposed, but there were too many Walloons working at USE Steel down around Saalfeld and Kamsdorf. Some one of them might have tried to look him up. Bad idea. Simpler was better, particularly since so many of the Grantvillers were convinced that all Frenchmen were incompetent—aside from Richelieu, of course. In a pinch, he identified himself as Rochellais, which was perfectly true, too.

There was a letter from Henri de Rohan today. As soon as Dumais was outside the post office, he opened it and began reading.

The duke was worried about Ducos. He speculated that Ducos had, from Rome, headed for the south coast of France, gone up the Rhone, crossed over to the upper Rhine, taken it as far of the mouth of the Main, and would probably soon be meeting with his henchmen and cohorts in Frankfurt am Main. The duke would make arrangements in Frankfurt, through his contacts with the Huguenot colony there, to have people on the alert for Locquifier and the others.

Dumais nodded. That was not his problem. What was this leading up to?

He read on. Of course. A Grantville connection. Rohan had also learned that the one Roman confederate of Ducos who had been apprehended was caught due to the rapid action and thinking of a boy named Ron Stone and his brothers. Stone was now reported to be in transit from Padua to Grantville. Should he appear there, Dumais should attempt to contact him.

Dumais shook his head, wryly. There were times the duke's exalted position made him blind to certain realities. He seemed to think that a lowly garbage collector could easily contact the son of the owner of Lothlorien Farbenwerke, who was now probably the wealthiest man in Grantville.

Pas du tout, monsieur le duc!

True, it would be easier for Jacques-Pierre to make Stone's acquaintance in Grantville than in most other places. But easier did not necessarily mean easy.

Rohan, de Ron, Ron Stone. All for his mind to keep track of on one assignment. Sometimes he suspected that the Lord God had a perverse sense of humor.

Chapter 5

Grantville

"Thanks for letting us use your living room, Chad." Henry Dreeson sank gratefully into Charles Jenkins' comfortably upholstered leather recliner. "My place is too much of a madhouse to do any serious talking, with all those kids around, and it's getting so that in the middle of the noise level at the Gardens, I can't hear myself think."

"Just can't hear, is more like it," Enoch Wiley said. "It's getting to be the same way for me. None of us are getting any younger."

"Or spryer." Henry leaned his cane against the chair arm. "I hate seeing Tom Riddle in a wheel chair, even if he does look like he's having a good time being pushed all over the place by his students. Seems like he sort of enjoys law professing."

"Gets him out of the house and away from Veleda. That woman is downright strenuous."

The rest of them nodded while they were sorting themselves out onto the couch and other chairs. Veleda Riddle was a good woman and no one could say a word against her, but she did tend to take the bit between her teeth when she got one of her enthusiasms. Like founding the League of Women Voters. Or, now, reopening and restoring the old Episcopalian church and getting hold of a minister for it.

Missy Jenkins came in through the archway in hostess mode.

"Hi, Dad. Hi, everybody. Mom's at a meeting over at the middle school—teacher training stuff." She kissed her father on the cheek and smiled at the rest of them.

"Coffee, tea, hot chocolate, beer, or wine from Winzerla up by Jena," she said, giving her best impression of a waitress. In a more normal voice, she added, "The coffee's fresh-roasted from Sternbock's and I just ground it. The cocoa beans are from Sesma's. I'll strain the hot chocolate through cheesecloth if anyone wants it, to get out those little granules that get stuck in the back of your throat."

After taking orders she disappeared through the dining room and swinging doors to the kitchen to produce two coffees, one hot chocolate, and three beers.

"Where were we?" Joe Stull rocked back on the hind legs of the straight chair he had chosen.

Ed Piazza stretched. "Trying to think of some tactful way to tell Mike Stearns that the Fourth of July Party here in West Virginia County can't really afford to have Becky as our senator in the SoTF House of Lords any more. Nothing against her. We all like the girl. But, face it, she's been gone for a year and a half on this embassy to Paris and Amsterdam. No end to it in sight right away, and now she's going to have another baby in a couple of months. We can't afford not to have a real, effective, voice speaking for us. Either she's got to come home—come back here, make Grantville her real residence, and attend the sessions of the congress—or she's got to resign, so we can run another candidate. The election's not that far off."

Tony Adducci shook his head. "Personally, I don't think she's going to come home. Come back. Her home's wherever Mike is, and Mike's going to be staying in Magdeburg, I expect, even if he loses to Wettin. He'll still be in Parliament and he'll be the head of the opposition to the Crown Loyalists. I don't think she'll be willing to move away from him again, once they get this peace in place. If you want my opinion, she'll come down here long enough to collect Sephie and Balthazar and then settle down in Magdeburg. They might even take Mike's mom with them."

Enoch Wiley shook his head. "Don't think Jean'll be willing to go. She's one of those women who positively enjoy ill health."

Joe reached up, taking a beer from the tray that Missy brought in. "It's an awfully big house for one woman and a home health aide to be rattling around in, but I can't see Jean taking in boarders. Just can't. Becky'll take Sephie's nanny pair along to Magdeburg, probably. She's almost bound to. She has that little boy she adopted in Amsterdam and now a new baby coming."

Tony shook his head. "She might not need a nanny. She's not had the kind of problems having babies that Aura Lee did, Joe. Becky bounced right back, after Sephie."

Henry cleared his throat. "Bounced back and hared off to Paris, not six months later. When she does get home, that little baby will be over two years old. Sephie won't have the slightest idea who she is. Not any more than Will and Joey will remember Gretchen. Ah, Will maybe can remember her, a little. But Joey not at all. He was only three months old when she left."

Arnold Bellamy reached up for one of the coffees. "Natalie would not be pleased to hear us making disparaging remarks about women who are trying to combine motherhood with a career."

Chad shook his head. "They're not criticizing, Arnold. They're just telling the truth. No matter how grateful we are to those two girls for what they've done for Grantville, and for the USE, and for anything in between, the fact remains that neither of them has exactly been a homebody. And, in Becky's case, since she's a government official, we've got to deal with this and have some kind of a plan in place before the next election." He took the last beer and looked at the tray. "Who's the second hot chocolate for?"

"Me," Missy answered cheerfully, plopping the tray down on the coffee table. " 'Train up a child in the way he should go.' 'She,' if you want to be picky. Maybe even, 'the laborer is worthy of his hire.' Or 'her hire.' "

She sat down on the second straight chair she had brought in from the dining room. "Think of me as a politician in training. Dad served a term as county commissioner back before the Ring of Fire. Why can't I, someday?"

"You're a librarian-in-training, Miss Missy," Ed Piazza said.

She nodded agreeably. "That, too. It's always a good thing to have a fallback position. Local politics doesn't exactly pay well. Have you guys heard anything about setting a date? That's an odd thing about this parliamentary system, for most Americans—that elections don't come on a regular schedule, but whenever Mike decides to call them."

Piazza leaned back and started to talk. Finally, he wound up.

"So, to Mike's surprise as much as Wettin's, coming out of the military and naval victories this spring, it started to look like Mike actually could, and *would*, win the election. Which wasn't what he'd expected, and it damn sure wasn't what Wettin expected. So as soon as the Congress of Copenhagen was over, Wettin and the Crown Loyalists started maneuvering to get the election postponed to as late in the year as possible. Don't forget that while we've got a cease-fire in place in the Netherlands, the war isn't over yet. Look what Nils Brahe managed across the Rhine once Bernhard of Saxe-Weimar pulled his cavalry back from around Mainz. It worked, but it could have gone wrong. Wettin and his people figure that the more time between the battles of Ahrensbök and Luebeck and the election, the more time for the war gloss to rub off Mike. The more time for him and his people to administer a thousand little cuts about every minor thing that does go wrong."

"What does that amount to as far as setting a date goes?"

"I don't think it's going to happen before the end of this year. It's the first national election the USE will be running, after all. Think of what it was like doing the SoTF election last spring—setting up polling places, training poll workers, getting the ballots printed and distributed. And now, with the war, Gustav has annexed a whole lot of entirely new territory that hadn't even started to get ready because it wasn't in the country. He sure doesn't want to tick off Frederik of Denmark by not letting his new Province of Westphalia vote. Or Nils Brahe, by offending the people in Upper Rhine now, after Brahe managed to do a Florida on it. So there's a bunch of stuff to be done. Offhand, I'd say early next year. February or March, probably. But I don't know anything for sure."

Joe rocked his chair forward. "Let's figure that it'll be February, then, for this year's election. Next year's election, if you want to be picky. February worked out pretty well in the SoTF when we used it this year. It's easy for people living in villages to get to the polling place, even in winter. And in the slack season, for farmers, they have time to read the newspapers and statements and such. If it turns out to be a little earlier, we can cope. If it's a little later, we'll have that much more time to cope." The chair went back again.

Tony Adducci changed the subject. "Chad, have you heard

anything from Wes about the way he sees things going around Fulda?"

"I've heard from him, and passed his letter on to Ed. He's had a chance to talk to Constantin Ableidinger's people over there. And I know Ed's talked to Ableidinger himself. Franconia's pretty much in agreement with Thuringia as far as what has to go on the state ballot is concerned. It's mainly restructuring the SoTF constitution to handle the results of the Ram Rebellion. An amendment to bring the margraves of Bayreuth and Ansbach into the House of Lords. And the biggie."

The conversation dwindled into silence for the next couple of minutes.

The biggie. The elephant in Chad Jenkins' living room. The invisible elephant on the coffee table, occupying a lot of space right next to the tray of sliced cheese and pretzels that Missy had brought in. The real reason why six up-timers were having this meeting without bringing any down-timers into it this evening.

The choice of a permanent state capital for the State of Thuringia-Franconia.

Nobody ever voted for Grantville to be the capital. It happened by default, right after the Ring of Fire, when the SoTF was still the New United States, and the NUS was a half-dozen little towns and principalities in south central Thuringia. A long time before it had turned into a province of the USE with nearly a million people.

The congress of the SoTF, in its collective wisdom, had passed a bill to put the issue on the ballot in the next election.

The problem of a permanent capital had been stewing around for a while. The candidates would be Grantville, Weimar, Erfurt, Würzburg, and Bamberg. Suhl had been nominated, but the city council declined. A suspicion existed that the gun makers of Suhl really didn't want all that many resident bureaucrats looking over their shoulders.

Of course, Suhl would have had the same main problem that Grantville did. Because of the geography of the place, it really didn't have a lot of room to grow, if the state capital started to become a big city. Grantville had maybe twenty thousand people in it now, give or take the ones who were moving in or out almost every day. It wasn't ever going to have more, because the narrow valley of Buffalo Creek, and the shale slate rock of the hills that went close to straight up from the flood plain meant there wasn't any place to put them. They could spill over the edges of the Ring of course, and they did. Grantville had suburbs, now. But by the time folks were living halfway to Rudolstadt or Saalfeld or Badenburg, they weren't really in Grantville.

So something was on the mind of everyone in the room. Uppermost on the mind of Henry Dreeson, who had called the meeting in the first place. How were the up-timers—mainly the ones who still lived in town, but maybe some of the ones who were off in places like Magdeburg or Swabia—going to react if Grantville didn't win this vote? They started to scope out ways to handle it. All the possible reactions there might be, from "those ingrates, after all we've done for them" right up to "man the barricades, boys—the barbarians are coming."

"What, exactly, do they want?" Annabelle Piazza stood in her kitchen, holding a piece of paper against the wall next to the phone while she tried to scribble notes with a worn-down pencil.

"I thought I'd better call Ed at home," Henry Dreeson repeated for the third time. "I wasn't sure that it's really SoTF state business and I know he's trying to keep civil service and politics separate. Which is good and right, I suppose, but pretty hard to do when a man has to get elected. Anyway, what I think it amounts to is that Wes Jenkins and Harlan Stull think it would do the Fourth of July Party some good in Buchenland County in these upcoming elections for me to come over on a politicking trip some time this fall. Buchenland County—that's what we used to call Fulda. Because they're having some fallout from this Ram Rebellion that's going on down in Franconia and all. I'll call Joe, too, since Harlan's his nephew. And Chad, since Wes is his brother. Maybe they've heard something about what's up."

"I'll pass it on. It could be legitimate SoTF business though, it sounds like. So maybe you *should* call him at the office."

"Seems to me more like Fourth of July Party business. I can't go anyway, of course. Ronnie's still among the missing and I can't go haring off and leave Annalise to watch over the rest of Gretchen's orphans all by herself. Not even with a cook and a sort of nanny in the house. There has to be somebody who's in charge. Gretchen's had more than a year to organize the Committee of Correspondence in Amsterdam. You'd think that she'd be getting herself organized by now and come home and take care of those kids. Especially with Ronnie still down in Bavaria, somewhere, as far as we know. The shooting war's been over for nearly three months. Why's Gretchen still in Amsterdam, anyhow? But maybe somebody else could go over to Fulda. Can you ask Ed that, to do me a favor?"

He was about to put down the phone, when the doorbell rang. Annabelle was saying something about Ronnie and Mary Simpson, though, so he kept hold of the receiver. "Annalise," he called. "Can you answer that?"

She came scurrying from somewhere at the back of the house, opened the door, and stood there talking for a couple of minutes to someone outside. Just as he finished up with Annabelle, she turned back into the front hall leading by the hand another girl who looked so much like her that she could have been her sister. "It's my cousin Dorothea and her fiancé. From Grafenwöhr. Oma sent them here so they can get married. She's Catholic. He's not. They can't get married in the Upper Palatinate. They've been on the road ever since Oma got kidnapped."

She pulled the girl into the living room, turned her head, and waved at the couch. "Sit down, Dorothea, for goodness sake!"

Dorothea sat.

Pregnant, Henry thought. Annie sat down that way when she was carrying Margie. Margie sat down that way when she was carrying all three of her kids. A kind of bottom-heavy thump, like her rear end couldn't wait to meet the chair.

"Hell," he said. "Let me call Jenny Maddox. I'll waive the waiting period for the license and we can take care of it after supper, over at city hall. Run into the kitchen, will you, Annalise, like a good girl, and tell Martha that we're going to have two more at the table, so she can set places. Then come back and explain about civil wedding ceremonies to them." He grabbed his cane and stumped back out into the hall to use the phone again before she could object.

When he got back into the living room after he'd gotten Jenny to agree to go back to the Bureau of Vital Statistics as soon as she had finished eating and fetch a marriage license, the girl—Dorothea? Yep, Dorothea—had slid off the sofa down onto the floor. She was rolling a ball back and forth with Gretchen's two-year-old Joey. Annalise and the boy—all right, young man, somewhere in his mid-twenties, probably, but he had one of those eternally boyish faces—were talking a mile a minute about civil weddings. He was a Calvinist, not a Lutheran, and Calvin had originally been in favor of having weddings be civil, it seemed, because marriages were legal contracts. It was all right with him.

Henry looked at Dorothea on the floor. She was Catholic, Annalise had said, but it didn't look like she was the kind to argue with her future husband. *After* he'd gotten the two of them good and tightly married, Annalise could call someone over at St. Mary's, explain it all, and let them worry about fixing the situation up with the priests. Seemed to him that this was one of those *better to beg forgiveness than ask permission* situations. If they could fix it up. He wasn't sure what the Catholic church rules were, either up-time or down-time. Jesuits were supposed to be good at figuring the angles, though.

Dorothea was still rolling the ball with Joey. Will came in from the back yard. He watched a couple of minutes, walked over, and leaned against her shoulder, his blond hair falling against hers. She kept rolling the ball with her left hand and put her right arm around the older boy's waist.

Family. Annalise's cousin, so Gretchen's cousin, too. Knew how to deal with kids.

"I'd like to invite the pair of you to stay with us, here at the house," Henry said. "Not for just a few days, but until Nicholas here finds a job and the two of you have a chance to look around and get settled permanently. No hurry about that. You're welcome to stay as long as you like. It's a big old house. We've got plenty of room."

Laurent Mauger climbed down from the wagon. The driver had set out the set of portable folding steps he took along when he traveled, so Mauger managed it with considerable dignity. He stretched his legs, crooked a finger at the porter outside the Higgins Hotel, and walked in.

It was such a wonderful world in which a man's dutiful service to the Huguenot cause had the side effect of allowing him to stay in the Higgins Hotel in Grantville on quite legitimate business, which he could expense to the company.

Quite legitimate business. He was a wine merchant. While the local wines grown around Jena weren't bad, and the Franconian wines were really superb if one liked a dry white, there was a lot of money in Grantville now. Some of that money belonged to people who were convinced that Rhine wines, Moselle wines, sometimes even Italian red wines, but above all French wines, were better. Or, if not better, at least more impressive when a man served them to his dinner guests.

Down-timer money, mostly, when it came to wine marketing. Most of the up-timers preferred beer. The men, at least.

Money to be made. That was how he had come to know Isaac de Ron in Frankfurt. Money to be made quite honestly, along with the thrill of doing something a little devious, perhaps, for his fellow religionists. And a town with a class structure so peculiar that nobody thought it odd to see a wine merchant talking to a garbage collector as long as they had made it known to anyone who cared to listen that they shared a common church affiliation.

He huffed his way up the steps. In deference to the local creek's tendency to flood, the ground floor of the Higgins Hotel was devoted to service area. The splendid reception room was on the first floor, some distance above the street.

All this, and a hot tub, too.

Mauger felt no obligation to identify "my contact" as the host of *Zum Weissen Schwan* in Frankfurt. Then his own mouth betrayed him by speaking the name. "De Ron." *Merde!* Conspiracy wasn't as easy as it might be. He might as well keep going, now that Dumais knew who the intermediary was.

Paranoia. What a wonderful word. A wonderful thing, too. It made the life of a field agent so much simpler. Jacques-Pierre Dumais stretched out on his pallet, propped his feet up on his trunk, and started a mental diagram. It didn't look quite like a spider web. More like two webs, blown together by a strong wind, not meshing, but intersecting in certain areas.

Henri de Rohan, the duke, in the center of one. For whom Isaac de Ron in Frankfurt worked and for whom Jacques-Pierre worked himself. Not via de Ron, but directly. Two different threads. However, he had, in that trunk right under his feet, well hidden in a secret compartment, authorization letters that would permit him to call upon de Ron if he should need him.

Ducos, the madman, in the center of the other. Well, Ducos and

Delerue both. Dumais counted down on his fingers. For whom Guillaume Locquifier worked. For whom in turn de Ron worked, or at least pretended to. For whom Laurent Mauger worked—at least he worked for "de Ron in his guise as Locquifier's man" but not for "de Ron in his guise as Rohan's agent." For whom Jacques-Pierre Dumais worked. Or pretended to.

Their own rampant and paranoid security had broken a link in the chain that would have enabled Ducos' men to make the critical connections. With any luck at all, Locquifier would never learn that Jacques-Pierre was Laurent Mauger's Grantville informant. So neither Locquifier in Frankfurt nor Ducos nor Delerue, wherever they might be by now, would have a chance to connect one Jacques-Pierre Dumais, a garbage collector, with the Jacques-Pierre Dumais who was otherwise known to them as one of Henri de Rohan's footmen.

One hoped, at least, that the link was well and completely broken. It would be unfortunate if Ducos found out. Potentially quite dangerous, also. Ducos and his fanatics were a murderous lot.

Ducos might find out, of course. It was not beyond the realm of the possibility that he would. Ah, well. *C'est la vie!*

Part Two

September 1634

Under amazement of their hideous change

Chapter 6

Grantville

Ed Piazza looked at the packet of papers that Martin Wackernagel had just dropped directly into his hands.

Wes Jenkins was very conscientious. He hadn't sent them by SoTF government pouch. Like Henry Dreeson, he thought of this project as a "politicking trip," Ed supposed.

And he wouldn't have wanted to put them in the mail. That was probably prudent. The mail was a great thing for inquiring after the health of your great-aunt Gladys. But the fact remained that under the postmastership of Johan van den Birghden, the USE postal system was not exactly impermeable to snooping, any more than the imperial system under the Thurn und Taxis family was impermeable to snooping.

So Wes had paid a private courier, like almost everybody else who wanted to be as sure as possible that confidential or sensitive information got from here to there without an intermediate detour into the hands of someone else's spies.

"He paid you at the other end?"

Wackernagel nodded and smiled.

Ed thought that he'd never let that smile anywhere near his daughter. How the man had managed to remain a bachelor this long, in a world that didn't have effective contraceptives and did have shotgun weddings . . .

Ed might be as straight as a ruler himself, but that didn't mean he couldn't recognize a guy with the masculine equivalent of *come hither* when he saw one.

The courier waved and walked out the door. Ed waved absent-mindedly in return.

Now all they had to do was talk Henry into going on a tour of Buchenland and coaxing it into a solidly pro-Fourth of July Party stance before Mike called new elections. Which they should be able to do. The news had arrived a couple of days ago that Mary and Veronica had reached Basel and were safely in the USE embassy with Diane Jackson.

Plus, the word from Franconia was that the Ram Rebellion had pretty much wound to its end with the face-down of Freiherr von Bimbach by Anita Masaniello.

Which left the problem that some group of unknown recalcitrants had kidnaped more than half of the SoTF administrators in Fulda, including Wes Jenkins himself.

Which was where Henry would be going.

Wes must have sent the paperwork before they got him.

Ed got up and walked over to the window.

Nothing he could do about Wes and the others from here. Anyway, the folks over in Fulda had already managed to get Harlan Stull and Roy Copenhaver back. They'd radioed that in yesterday. Plus Fred Pence and Johnny Furbee. That had come in this morning, barely in time for him to get a news release out.

Ed would have to work on faith that they'd do as well with Orville and Mark. And Wes and Clara. And the abbot. He'd spent a lot of time these last few years doing that—working on the faith that the people he'd sent out to do an impossible job would accomplish it.

If Derek Utt and his people didn't find the others. Well, then Buchenland would need something like a visit from Henry Dreeson more than ever.

He picked up the phone. "Chad, can you get hold of Joe, Tony, and the rest of the crew? See if we can meet with Henry for lunch? Somewhere quiet, so not the Gardens. Not Cora's. See if the back room at Tyler's is free."

"Basel's better than 'somewhere in Bavaria,'" Henry admitted. "But it's still not exactly 'right here in Grantville.'"

Arnold Bellamy, who was twirling his knife in his fingers, said, "You're weakening."

"I've talked to Tony Jr.," Tony Sr. said. "Well, we've sent a lot of Morse Code back and forth since he first raised up Bernadette and told her that the ladies were there."

"Not a little bit proud of that boy of yours, are you?" Joe Stull grinned.

"Not a 'little bit,' no," Tony answered agreeably. "He's pretty sure we'll be able to get them out of Basel. So I figure," he looked at Henry, "that we might as well go ahead and do the planning for your trip. Then, when we get the actual news that Horn or somebody else on our side has collected them, you'll be ready to go ahead and start out."

Henry pushed his plate back and leaned forward, elbows on the table and fingers steepled. "I've still got that house full of kids to deal with. Jeff and Gretchen are still in Amsterdam and I don't mind saying that I'm getting sort of exasperated by the whole thing. Not that Will and Joey and the older ones aren't pretty well behaved as kids go, but they're her job. Not mine. Not Annalise's. And really not Ronnie's." He leaned back. "Now that I've gotten that off my chest . . ."

"How're you going to handle it?"

"Well, with Ronnie's niece staying with us now, it's a different kettle of fish than it was a couple of months ago. Thea and Nicol are grown-ups. In their twenties and married and expecting a baby. So they can house sit. Babysit. Plus, I've talked to Enoch and Inez. They've agreed to supervise. Sort of at a distance, with Nicol and Thea on the spot. Since the Cavriani girl staying with them is Annalise's best friend, they'll have plenty of excuses to drop by and sort of cast an eye over the way things are going."

Arnold started twirling his knife in the opposite direction. "Knew you were going, didn't you?"

"Yep." Henry nodded. "Even before I admitted it to myself, I guess. Haven't done any traveling since the Ring of Fire—never been farther than Jena—and it's sort of a pity to waste what amounts to my first and only trip to Europe, I suppose. I'd better go see something outside West Virginia County and the middle of Thuringia before this hip gives out, if I want to see it at all."

✧ ✧ ✧

"Good news about Orville Beattie and Mark Early."

Ed smiled broadly. "I really enjoyed that phone call I made to Lisa this morning. And I have to admit that I stood right there while Tanya radioed it into Mike Stearns' office in Magdeburg, pretending that I could hear Susan stand up and shout. I was principal when Mark and Susan graduated. Three years apart, but my stint covered them both. And all three of Orville and Lisa's kids. Shane—he's the youngest—was finishing his sophomore year the spring that the Ring of Fire hit and I had to turn things over to Len Trout."

He paused a minute.

Arnold raised an imaginary glass. "Absent friends."

Ed nodded. "So, yeah, it felt real good." He looked at Arnold. "Real, real, good. Thanks for coming down from Magdeburg to back me up on handling this. Did Tanya get the press release out?"

"First thing. And I phoned Henry. Any word about Wes and Clara? Or the abbot?"

Ed shook his head. "No. Well, not yet."

"Do you think we really ought to let Henry go if things don't calm down over there in the next couple of days? The people who did this—some of them, at least—could still be in Buchenland County. Could make another try. The mayor of Grantville would make a tempting target."

"Right now, I don't think we could stop him. He's gone into his old-fashioned stump speaker mode. Even . . ."

"Even what?"

"Tried to talk young Muselius from over at Countess Kate's into going along to translate for him. Henry's not one to overestimate the quality of his German. Muselius can't go. The beginning of the school year is too busy. But he's persuaded one of Kastenmayer's sons, Cunz, the one who's about to finish up his law degree at the University of Jena, into doing it. Muselius also talked the boy's exam committee into accepting a paper analyzing the trip as his honors thesis in constitutional law under Arumaeus, so he won't have wasted a semester."

Bellamy shook his head. "I'm not surprised. I've met Muselius, several times. Golden-tongued, that young man."

"Is young Kastenmayer?"

"What?"

"Golden-tongued?"

"The boy knows a half-dozen different languages, they say. That wouldn't mean he's a good public speaker, necessarily. But going into law, with his dad a preacher . . . he might be. The way they do the schools here, he's at least bound to have had a lot of debate practice. Disputations, they call them."

Ed nodded. "If so, he can double up as the PR man. Run the press conferences."

Johann Conrad Kastenmayer, generally known as Cunz for all purposes other than his formal, legal, signature, was surprised that he had been invited to this meeting.

He had met Charles Jenkins the Younger, of course. He was the one who was always called Chip, much as he himself was called Cunz. Chip was also a law student at Jena. The law school was not really very large. All the students knew one another.

Now he was in Chip's father's parlor, with Chip's sister holding out a tray and offering him a choice between coffee, hot chocolate, tea, and beer. He thought a moment. She was named Melissa, like the famous Ms. Mailey, but everyone seemed to call her Missy.

Really, he would prefer beer. Probably.

However, he had never tasted oriental tea and might not get another chance to taste it for quite some time. It was very expensive. The Kastenmayer household in the rectory at St. Martin's in the Fields could not afford to *do* expensive, as the up-timer young people expressed it. Neither could the Kastenmayer sons in Jena afford to *do* expensive. So, in the interest of furthering his liberal education . . . He reached out and took a cup of tea.

In some ways, visiting Grantville was almost like taking a miniature grand tour. Which he would also never be able to afford to do, he supposed. As soon as he got his degree, he would have to find a job—take some of the burden off his father and start making a positive contribution. It was noble of his oldest brother Matthaeus to follow a vocation into the pastorate like their father. But it didn't pay very much. Martin's position as an assistant city clerk didn't pay much more. And with Andrea's elopement, which meant that this year the parish was going to have to pay for a second teacher in the primary grades, there was no prospect that Papa was going to get a raise. But this . . . Visiting Erfurt and Frankfurt didn't precisely constitute a grand tour, but maybe a mini-tour. They were larger cities than he'd ever seen before.

One thing you could say for going into law, it usually paid pretty well. Cunz pulled his mind back to the conversation swirling around him. Only to discover that someone was asking him what *he* thought about it. Which was certainly not something for which he had prepared himself. It was much more surprising than his being invited in the first place.

What was the *it* about which he had been asked?

He uttered a few reasonably coherent sentences on the theme that Mayor Dreeson's trip to Buchenland should have great value in making the former Franconian territories feel themselves more of an integral part of the State of Thuringia-Franconia. He added a few comments in regard to the outcome of the Ram Rebellion. He prayed that he hadn't made a total fool of himself.

Apparently not. The man who had asked, Herr Stull, nodded and turned to someone else, who said, "He'll do."

Missy Jenkins, who had astonished him by sitting down between him and her father as soon as she had distributed the beverages, leaned over and whispered, "Good save."

He made a resolution to be attentive at all times for the remainder of this tour.

"There's no reason at all to make that big a deal out of it." Henry Dreeson, being a small town American at heart, with the resulting conviction that he really didn't need any such thing as a bodyguard, or whatever the military types wanted to call it, was taking a stand. "I don't need a fancy escort to make the trip over to Fulda. All I'm going to do is talk to a few city councils about my experiences in local government. The government of West Virginia County has agreed to loan me an ATV—one of those four-wheeled dune buggy things—and they'll provide enough fuel to get me there and back, as long as the party's willing to reimburse them for the expense. I'll need to find a driver. My hip's not up to driving any distance on these down-time roads. I won't get lost, either. For one thing, we'll be sticking to the main roads. In case we have to detour, I'm going to take Wackernagel, the courier, along with me in the ATV. He makes the circuit all the time, so he knows the roads well, and I'm pretty sure that he'll have a hoot riding in a car rather than riding a horse for a change." He smiled at everyone else in the room. "Why, Wackernagel might even enjoy learning to drive."

"Henry, what the hell!" Joe Stull practically exploded. "They've been taking our people over there prisoner!"

"Then Utt can give me a bodyguard once we get there. He's got a whole regiment at Fulda. No point in dragging a bunch of people from here all the way over there."

"Two ATVs," Ed Piazza said. "It's a rough road and if the one you're riding in breaks down, we don't want you stranded. The schedule's too tight. The SoTF will provide the second one and pay for the fuel. And since it's going, it might as well have people in it. The driver, you, Cunz, and Wackernagel in the first one. The driver and three other guys in the second one. And the army picks the guys."

Henry eyed him. "What kind of guys?"

"Mechanics. Really *tough* mechanics."

"You've got that 'I'm the principal' look on your face, Ed."

"I am the principal. Or, at least, the president, even if that doesn't give me quite as much authority." Ed grinned. "Two ATVs or you don't go, important politics or not."

"Still no word about the abbot?" Annabelle passed over a dish of sliced pears.

Ed shook his head. "He seems to have dropped off the map. We don't question people under torture, of course, in the SoTF. But Derek and his people sure have *questioned* those guys, the imperial knights like von Schlitz who were involved in the conspiracy. Up one side and down the other. They think that they genuinely don't know where he is. But, probably, not in Fulda any more. The guys who took him were probably Irish mercenaries. Who knows who was paying them?"

"At least you got to spread tidings of comfort and joy about Wes Jenkins and Clara Bachmeier. Or are they Mr. and Mrs. Jenkins, now?"

"Bachmeierin."

"What?"

"She insists on the feminine form of her surname. On the grounds that she is not male. Trust me. I still remember my first interview with her very well. She's as stubborn as Veleda Riddle. Just as ladylike and just as stubborn."

"That's . . . Well, I'm glad she's on our side, in that case."

"I think that the word you want is 'daunting.' Or maybe 'dauntless.' She's dauntless herself and it's very daunting to everyone who gets on her bad side."

"Odd sort of woman for Wes to marry."

"Guess he managed to get on her good side."

"It doesn't sound like she's even a little bit like Lena was."

Ed thought a minute before he answered that one. "Maybe he learned something, the first time."

Chapter 7

Grantville
State of Thuringia-Franconia

Dear Nathan,

Chandra Prickett wished that she still had a pencil with an eraser on it. She still had plenty of pencils. There had been a lot of pencils around the house when the Ring of Fire hit. A whole ceramic pot full of pencils of various lengths. Plus a hand-cranked pencil sharpener, which still worked and didn't show any signs of quitting. And, when she had looked around and made an inventory of their stuff, a lot more pencils here and there. Like two in the kitchen, one fastened to the refrigerator with a magnet and one tied onto a hook screwed into the wall by the sink where she kept her grocery list.

She wasn't going to run out of pencils any time soon.

Ball point pens were another story.

None of the pencils had erasers any more, though. Since Nathan went down to Suhl last year, she had chewed them all off while she was trying to write letters to him.

Dear Nathan,

No. She'd already written that.

What could she say, if she didn't want to sound whiny? She hated sounding whiny.

> *Dad got married again over in Fulda, which is why I'm writing an extra letter, in spite of what postage costs. She's Clara Bachmeierin from Badenburg. She's a widow and has been over there for eighteen months or so, helping the administration handle the abbot, after he went back.*

Deflect what she could deflect.

> *So they've known each other quite a while and they've been working together. Mom's been gone three years, now.*

The metal band on the top of this pencil had tooth marks. Doc Sims had told her not to bite on those any more, after she went in to have a chipped tooth smoothed down.

> *We'd been sort of wondering if he'd ever take the big step again, so Lenore and I are both real happy for him. I hope that you will be, too. Bryant's in Magdeburg, of course, so Lenore doesn't know what he thinks about it. Weshelle is getting to be a big girl, now. She's already pulling herself up on the furniture.*
>
> *Dad's going to transfer back to Grantville, to take over the SoTF consular service for Ed Piazza. Clara will be coming back with Dad. Maybe you could take a couple of weeks off, over the holidays, and come meet her, especially since I hear that you're being transferred to Frankfurt.*

That was okay. It didn't say, "Our little twin girls are now nine months old and you haven't been home to see them yet." It didn't sound whiny.

> *We all hope and pray that the war will be over pretty soon.*

That was safe enough.

Mikey has started all-day kindergarten and I've put Tom into preschool three mornings a week this year. The money you're having put into our bank account every month is plenty to cover that. I'm sending him to the St. Veronica's school that Mayor Dreeson's wife Ronnie runs. We all hope that she gets home safe after the problems this summer. I sort of decided about the school at the last minute, after I talked to Paige. She thinks it's better for the kids to start learning German right away, these days.

That was good. That would tell him that she expected to be here in Grantville the whole school year. That she wasn't going to do something he didn't want her to, like packing up all four kids and going off on her own to wherever he was working.

I hope that the guys who have their wives in Suhl now invite the rest of you over for home cooking every now and then.

Your Uncle Simon will be home from Italy, pretty soon. Aunt Mary Ellen says they should be here early next month. He's coming back with Ron and Gerry Stone. He must have had an exciting time there with Father Mazzare, especially in Rome this summer. I wonder what it's like to meet a pope.

Well, anyway, that's the news this week. I guess I'd better quit, since I'm coming to the end of this page and don't want to start another one, what with paper and postage costing what they do these days.

Love from all of us,
Chandra

She'd drop it at the post office on her way to pick up Tom from St. Veronica's.

So she wouldn't cry, because she didn't want Pam or Bernita to see tears on her cheeks.

She didn't have a job that was keeping her in Grantville. She was a plain vanilla housewife. Why was Nathan so dead set against having her join him?

Suhl

Dear Chandra,

Nathan Prickett sighed. He didn't want to write this.

I know I'm not much of a correspondent. But look, we've been married for going on ten years now, and I can see through you like a pane of glass.

He looked down at Chandra's latest letter again. Transparent, all right. Hint, hint, hint. Why couldn't she leave it be?

He wanted another beer, but he wasn't going to have one. He was strict with himself about that, come what may. Some guys claimed that a man couldn't become a drunk on beer, but it wasn't true. A mug with lunch and a mug with supper. That was going to be it, Ring of Fire or no Ring of Fire. As far as that went, it was twice as much as he used to drink, back home.

He'd had his life planned. Graduate from high school, go into the army for four years, go to college. It hadn't worked quite that way, but pretty close. He'd come out after three years with a skilled trade; joined the Army Reserves, gotten a job in manufacturing in Fairmont, and concentrated on making foreman as fast as possible. He'd done it, too, all the while living with his parents in Grantville, saving his money, going to church regularly, playing baseball for fun. Baseball was pretty cheap fun. Girlfriends, but only one really serious.

He hadn't planned on Chandra. She just happened to him. He must have seen her now and then when she was a kid, but he hadn't noticed her. Then all of a sudden, one day, there she was. It had been sort of like finding a sinkhole in his front yard. The size sinkhole that can swallow a man's car whole and then start working on the house.

No, he sure hadn't planned on Chandra. He'd done his best to fit her into his plans, though. By the time he was close to making foreman, he started dating her, which her parents did not like much, since he was seven years older and she was still in high school. But his folks were good Methodists too, like Wes and Lena, and nobody could say that he wasn't a responsible churchgoing man.

After he proposed and she accepted, the fall of her senior year, Wes Jenkins had a talk with them about being willing to go ahead and pay for her to go to college after they married, if Nathan was willing for her to commute to Fairmont—no big problem, since Nathan worked there anyway.

Chandra had gotten a bit antsy. The "go to college while married" idea had appealed to her some. He'd had to get up on his high horse about "I'm able to support my own wife" and say "no way, José." After all, now he was planning for Chandra to work for four or five years after they married, which should cover the extra expense of buying their own place instead of living with their respective parents, and by that time, he should have enough ahead to start his own business.

She'd almost backed out of the engagement after that, so he started putting on a bit of steam in the sex area and like the good little girl she was, she wasn't about to let him go even a half inch further in any direction than they had already gone until she actually had a wedding ring on the third finger of her left hand. And that was the kind of girl he had wanted as a wife, really. So she went along with his ideas and they got married right after she graduated.

Putting on the steam hadn't been a bit of a problem, the way he had reacted to her then. He still did now, for that matter, every time he laid eyes on her, every time he laid hands on her, every time he laid her, which was what had caused the current mess.

Mikey arrived four and a half years after they got married, right on schedule. They'd saved every cent Chandra earned up to that point and had enough for a really good down payment on a house in Grantville. It wouldn't have gone nearly as far in Fairmont.

When the Ring of Fire came, Chandra was five months along with Tom. She was being a stay-at-home mom, the way they'd planned. He'd put enough money in the bank to leave the factory and go out on his own. Then it happened and everything fell in. He didn't care for unplanned events and you had to say that the Ring of Fire was as unplanned as things came. Well, everything collapsed except that Tom was a second boy, so they had the perfect family, exactly what he had hoped for.

He'd found work right away, with the Mechanical Support Division, but it didn't pay anything like what he was earning before, and the mortgage on the house was on contract with the seller who made it through the Ring of Fire too, so they didn't have any windfall there. They had to keep paying. And it looked like he wouldn't ever have a business of his own, even though he at least had the savings account in the Grantville bank, so he didn't lose the money.

They seemed to be doing okay, not losing ground, at least, but then, hell, he couldn't keep his hands off her when they were right there in the same house and bed, so she got pregnant again. Unplanned.

Probably what he said when she told him hadn't been the best comment he could have come up with. "How could you possibly do anything so stupid?" Especially considering that it took two to tango. He was ashamed of himself later, but couldn't make himself apologize, so they sort of jogged along until he got the chance to buy into this new firm in Suhl and took it. She'd been six months along, then.

The third pregnancy turned out to be twins. Girls.

It had been nice of her to name them for both of their moms, and the "Sue" and "Lou" rhyme for the middle names was sort of cute. He wished . . .

Damn it, he was staying out of Grantville and Chandra was staying in Grantville; that was the end of it. He didn't have to worry that she would start fooling around on him, not the kind of girl she was. The business in Suhl was doing well. They were opening up the new branch in Frankfurt. He'd already gone back and forth a couple of times because he was in charge of training the militia there on how to use the new weapons. He was making a lot more money here than he ever could have again if he had stayed at home and he liked all the guys he was working with. The down-timers had as much energy and smarts as any up-timer he had ever met. But he wasn't going to give in to her whining about wanting to come and join him. No way was he going to end up fathering a dozen children like some backwoods redneck hillbilly, digging his own grave with his penis, never being able to better himself. He was supporting her and the kids, wasn't he? The two extras as well as Mikey and Tom? What more could she reasonably ask?

I've told you my reasons. You know yourself that schools for the kids are better in Grantville. They can have real teachers, not home schooling, and I'm not about to start in on health care again.

Give it up, honey. I'm working out of town now and you're staying put. And I don't have the time or money to come running back and forth to Grantville on vacation, the stage the business is in now. Not even when I'm on my way from here to Frankfurt. I go down the other way, south of the Thuringenwald.

But I will write Mom and Dad oftener. Promise.

Say Hi! to Wes and the new bride for me. I hope, given the way it happened, that the old biddies like Veda Mae Haggerty aren't giving you and Lenore too much grief. That could get embarrassing. I guess I'll meet her when I meet her, more or less.

Love to all of you,
Nathan

That was about all there was to say.

He picked up another sheet of paper.

Dear Don Francisco,

He always felt like it wasn't very polite of him to write to the don that way, but the don said himself that it was correct and "Don Nasi" would be the wrong form, even though a lot of people in Grantville used it because they were trying to be polite themselves.

Nathan sighed. A guy could get himself into the damnedest things, without even trying. Just because he'd already been working in Suhl and knew Ruben Blumroder when that "selling arms to the enemy" thing blew up eighteen months ago . . .

Somehow or other—he still couldn't quite figure how it had happened—Nathan had gotten talked into becoming Nasi's agent in Frankfurt. Or one of his agents. Nathan was pretty sure he wasn't the only one. Don Francisco was the kind of guy for whom the saying "have a second string to your bow" came automatically.

Grantville

"Thanks for coming over, Paige. I didn't want to embarrass you but . . . I guess I was to the point where I had to ask."

"It's okay, Chandra." Paige Modi picked up her cup. "You were bound to be thinking about it, I guess, considering that some of the other Grantville guys who've spent so much time out of town are ditching their first wives. But honestly, there's not a shred of anything. Not so much as a whisper that Nathan has been seeing some other woman down in Suhl. Or over in Frankfurt, when he goes there for Blumroder."

Chandra stirred some honey into her herbal tea. She didn't really like the taste all that much, but that was what she had. There wasn't a lot of point in spending money for sugar. It was a lot more expensive than honey. The down-time sugar tasted a little funny, too, and was sort of a tannish-gold color.

"What's weird," she said, "is that I don't know whether that makes me feel better or worse. I know that it makes me feel more up in the air. If Nathan *was* seeing someone else . . . Well, at least I'd know why this is happening."

Chapter 8

Magdeburg

"Come on in. Good lord, Ed. You're sopping wet." Claire Hudson, Mike Stearns' executive assistant and all-around handywoman, threw a towel at him.

Ed Piazza started patting himself dry. "Evening, Claire. How's Duke? How are Stoffel and the girls? It's not cold out and I was nice and dry till a half hour ago, so don't worry. The roof of the litter that I hired at the train station had a leak that collected the water and poured it down on the seat through a little hole. Looked to me like someone had tried to stub a cigarette out on the canvas. The world is full of assholes. Before I go up and change, what's the word from Amsterdam? Considering that I've been on the train all day."

"Nothing exciting this evening. I told the operator that if he got word on army radio and he didn't send a runner right over to tell me, I'd make him sorry. So I guess Rebecca hasn't had the baby yet."

"Mike must be wearing out the floors, pacing back and forth."

"Wearing Becky out too, I expect. She's probably thinking that she had it easy with Sephie, him being off fighting a battle when she went into labor. Talk about a worrywart. You'd think she's the only woman in the world who ever had a baby."

"He's not in love with the rest of them." Ed yawned. "I'll go up and change into something dry before we eat. Same room?"

"Same room, and your clean stuff is in the trunk. Put the wet clothes in the bin at the top of the stairs. Trina will take it down to the kitchen. That's one of her chores."

"Any hint about names yet?"

"He's been so closemouthed you can't believe it. National security has absolutely nothing on how tight he's been playing this to his chest."

Ed put down the tote bag he was carrying. "Here's something for you from Annabelle."

"Orange carrots! God bless the woman. The white and purple ones I can buy here taste pretty much the same, but I can't convince myself that they look right on my plate. It's weird to get carrot flavor when you're looking at a vegetable that resembles a turnip. Kiss her for me when you get home."

"Be glad to."

Ed put down his fork. "It's not as if everyone hadn't expected it. Constantin Ableidinger is definitely running for the USE Parliament from Bamberg district on the Ram Platform. He's coming through Grantville on his way back from Fulda, to work on developing a common slate of candidates in the upcoming election. We want to have one worked out and ready to go the minute Mike names the date."

Arnold Bellamy scribbled something on the clipboard lying next to his plate. "Are Ableidinger and his people going to merge into the Fourth of July Party?"

"They'd rather keep some level of independence. 'Closely allied' and agreeing not to ever run candidates against each other in the same race is good enough for me. I sure wouldn't want to see the Crown Loyalists picking up a seat on a plurality because we split the vote between us. Mostly, I guess, they'll run their people south of the Thuringenwald and we'll run ours north of it. One thing we'll have to work out is what will be happening around Suhl and thereabouts. Not to mention Buchenland. I expect that's one reason he's going up there, touring around with Henry. Sounding things out."

"Who are we putting up for Becky's seat if she's willing to bow out?" Claire asked. "I swear that I haven't heard anything. Not a word. Or don't we know yet?"

"Well, we haven't approached Becky and Mike about it yet.

That's one of the reasons I'm headed to Amsterdam next. But a lot of the up-timers would like to run Chad Jenkins if the seat opens up."

"We could do a lot worse. He supported Simpson in 1631, so he might appeal to some of the conservative-side-of-the-middle-of-the-road types who are skittish about Mike. He's pretty conservative himself. In fact, I was always surprised that he wasn't a Republican, up-time."

Ed chuckled. "Given his druthers, I'm sure he would have been. But Chad knew better to think that being a Republican would help him much in the middle of Bobby-Byrd-Land."

"How would it go over with the new majority in Grantville, though, having an up-timer succeed to a down-timer's seat?"

"Chad's good at schmoozing. And there's no really suitable down-timer in West Virginia County who's both available and willing to run. They're . . ."

"All still too busy making money. Recouping their war losses." Arnold put a word into the conversation. "Give it five years before one of them starts to eye Becky's seat. What about the House?"

"Don't know yet. I want to float a few possibilities past Mike while I'm here."

"UMWA people?" Claire asked.

Ed shook his head. "Actually, they're all down-timers I've been working with. I don't know if Mike has even met any of them. He sure hasn't worked with them, not closely at least. I was talking to Chad and Henry the other day. Henry said, 'You know, my grandpa used to have a saying. *Sometimes I feel like I've been hung out on a line to dry and then plumb forgot.*' That's the way it is, this year. Even looking at it from the province-wide level, sometimes I feel like Grantville's been hung out on a line to dry and plumb forgot. All the Fourth of July Party bigwigs are in Magdeburg now, busy with Gustav, busy with national politics. International politics, when it comes to things like the Congress of Copenhagen. They don't even have time to think about the town long enough to give Henry and the others the okays that they need to move on."

Claire sighed. "Henry has a point, you know. As mayor. Before the Ring of Fire, our town was dying. Slower than the other little towns around Fairmont, but dying. All the ambitious kids leaving after high school—well, the way Duke did, and our older kids.

That's why they were left up-time. We came back when Duke retired. Then it came back to life after the Ring of Fire, and he got to oversee that. Now it looks to me like it's dying again. The ambitious people, a lot of them, moving out. Turning into a backwater. He's having to watch that happen, too. He's got to be hurting."

"He has a point about getting the okays. We talk a lot about politics from the bottom up. But the truth is, as far as the party is concerned, Mike and the UMWA have kept it pretty tightly buttoned up from the top down, when it comes to nominations and such. He just . . ." Arnold's voice trailed off.

Claire finished the sentence. "Wants to work with people he trusts. Can't blame him for that."

Things went on from there.

"And that's the last I've heard from Steve Salatto about the way things are falling out in Franconia."

Someone knocked on the door. Francisco Nasi glanced up, pushing his glasses back to their proper place on the bridge of his nose. "What is it?"

Samantha Burka poked her head into the room. "You and Mr. Piazza have to finish up now, Sir. The Gustav taking him to Amsterdam will be leaving in less than two hours."

Chapter 9

Grantville

"I'll get it."

Annalise jumped up from the dinner table and dashed for the front hall. "Hello. Yes, Mrs. Piazza? They're *out*! They're out of Basel? They're okay? Really all right? Not hurt or anything. You're sure? Just a minute."

She left the receiver on the telephone stand and ran back into the dining room. "They're out of Basel. Oma and Mrs. Simpson and the archduchess. They're okay. Absolutely okay. Henry, can you come to the phone?"

She turned right around and dashed again, so she could pick up the receiver again as fast as possible. She didn't want Mrs. Piazza to think that she'd hung up before Henry could get there. "Don't go away. He's coming right now. Thea had to get his cane for him."

Denise Beasley spread out the morning newspaper on the kitchen table in her father Buster's trailer. Her best friend Minnie Hugelmair read over her shoulder. "Isn't that a hoot? Mary Simpson and the archduchess getting into a plane with the new king in the Netherlands so Jesse Wood could fly them off to Amsterdam." The girl's very pretty face twisted into a half-scowl. "I've never flown. I bet I would have, by now, if the Ring of Fire hadn't happened. Maybe we still can, someday."

"Oh, sure," Minnie commented. "I can see it now. We get so famous that a plane lands out in your dad's storage lot to take us someplace exciting. Not likely. Just *not*. How about checking my algebra homework before we leave for school?"

The noise in the Thuringen Gardens was deafening. But on the evening of a day that most people had spent talking about this kind of news, Henry felt like he had to show up. Flying the flag, or something. The Gardens were a kind of symbol for Grantville by now, he supposed. If you really had something to celebrate, you celebrated it at the Gardens. Not to mention—this was where he'd met Ronnie, in the first place.

"Veronica's still with Horn's army, then?" Tony Adducci waved at Thecla to bring him another beer.

"She'll be on her way home by the end of the week, they tell me. Horn's sending her by boat as soon as he can arrange to get her on one with all the necessary safe-conducts and such for passing through the region held by Bernhard of Saxe-Weimar. Down the Rhine and then up the Main."

Chad Jenkins nodded. "Bernhard's being cooperative, they say."

"Just hope that it lasts."

Joe Stull grinned. "So, Henry, are you going to climb into that ATV to make the tour of the towns in Buchenland before the snow flies?"

"Yep."

"We got a new message in from Fulda right before I left the office," Ed Piazza said.

"What?"

"They're suggesting that since Veronica will be landing at Frankfurt, you ought to extend the tour. Go on down the Kinzigtal and meet her there. There are bits and pieces of Buchenland County along the route until you get as far as Hanau."

Martin Wackernagel finished chewing a bite of pretzel. "Not a bad idea. It's a pretty trip. Not a very good road, but a really pretty trip, especially in the fall when the leaves are turning. I go that road all the time. The *Reichsstrasse*."

"What a hellish racket." Missy clamped her hands over her ears. "Maybe they should have waited and not had last month's parade until they got Mrs. Simpson and Mrs. Dreeson back. That would have made for a few more floats."

"It would have saved a lot of beer, too." Denise smirked. "Most of the guys are going to end up just as drunk tonight as they did after the parade. First they strut and then they swill. It's not as if any of them here had anything to do with what was going on in Basel, but to hear them talk, you'd think that the SoTF Reserves rode into the city with Don Fernando—the king in the Netherlands, whatever he's called at the moment—and raised the siege at the embassy."

"Maybe we should go home early. It's not as if there's anyone here we're interested in, and we're not close enough to Dad and Mayor Dreeson to overhear anything political." Missy turned around and tapped Pam Hardesty's shoulder. "Pam? Are you ready to go?" Then, "Pam? Is something wrong?"

Pam shook her head, eyes narrow. "No. Not really. I just spotted one of Velma's less pleasant old boyfriends, over there. Take a sighting past Wackernagel, then a little to the left and four tables toward the door. I don't want to walk past him. Is there enough room, anywhere, that we could get out one of the other doors?"

Minnie stood up, swiveling her head. "Not right now. We'd better wait a bit."

Missy frowned at Pam. "He didn't . . . ?"

"He didn't. But not for lack of trying. Talk about a nasty, nasty, man. Fish bait."

Denise's nouns and adjectives were considerably more colorful than that, ending up with, "Maybe you'd better let Daddy give you some lessons in dirty fighting. You ought to see what Mom can do."

"Benny's a good man," Minnie said slowly. "His sister Betty's husband seems to be a good man, too, but he's been so sick ever since we came to Grantville that it's hard to tell what he'd be like if he wasn't coughing all the time. Betty likes him, though. Her son David's nice, and so is Louise's husband, but they're both about fifty, I guess. How do you tell if someone young is going to turn out to be a good man?"

"Wait until they're old," Missy suggested.

"Where's the fun in that?" Denise asked. "Just arrange things so you're in the driver's seat."

Pam looked at Minnie. "Reputation, I guess. Pay attention to what other girls say. Sometimes it does pay to listen to gossip."

"Hell," Denise said. "Listen to what the guys say. Oh, sure, men say they don't gossip. They do, though. They just call it 'shooting the breeze.' There were a bunch out in Daddy's welding shop the other day. Older guys, not our age, but it's all the same. One of them asked, 'Who did Bobby Fitz marry, anyway?' That's what they called Austin O'Meara's brother—it wasn't his name, but everyone called him that. I don't know why. None of you probably ever met him, since he moved away a dozen or so years before the Ring of Fire. But you remember Austin—the one who got killed in a fight here at the Gardens last year. Well, first one of them said it was Obie Conway's sister down in Kentucky and then they started talking about the job corps and when Bobby Fitz met her and how her folks interfered and she married someone from her dad's snake handler church instead, but after he died, Obie dropped a word to Bobby Fitz and he gave notice at his job that same afternoon and headed for Pikeville with everything he owned in his pickup."

Missy raised her eyebrows. "So?"

"There wasn't a one of them who doubted that when Bobby Fitz tore out of town, he had a respectable marriage on his mind, even if it did come with three half-grown stepsons attached. Or that he'd be good to Sandy Jo and her kids. There's a lot to be said for listening to guys who work with a man. They know how he acts if it's one of those days that started by dropping an anvil on his big toe and ended by having a big weld go wrong at the last minute."

"Yeah, maybe. But Buster's friends are old enough to tell the difference. I don't think guys our age really are." Missy looked at Minnie. "My advice is that you don't even try to tell the difference now. Just hold back for a while. I'm not planning to get serious for another ten years, at least. Not until I've finished all my education and worked for a while. Maybe not until I've traveled some, if things settle down."

Denise grinned. "No fun and games along the way."

Missy shook her head. "I don't need that kind of complication in my life right now." She looked at them solemnly. "Neither do the rest of you."

Minnie stood up. "Thecla and her flying squad of waitresses have cleared a path along the wall, on the other side of the room from where Pam's nasty man is sitting. Let's get out of here while we can."

Fulda

"A welcoming parade," Andrea Hill said. "We've got Wes and Clara back." She waved toward the head of the table. "Henry's coming. We ought to put on the biggest parade this town's ever seen. Kids from the schools. Captain Wiegand and his city militia. The whole Fulda Barracks Regiment."

Orville Beattie shook his head. "It won't fly, Andrea. We've got Wes and Clara back, but the *Stift* is missing its abbot and we don't even know where he is or if he's still alive. 'Hearts and minds' stuff. We've got to do something more subdued. We can't ignore the way the monks have got to be feeling."

Mark Early scratched his chin. "Maybe Henry could review the militia and the regiment out at Barracktown."

"Not a bad idea," Derek Utt said. "That way, we can pretty well secure the perimeter while Henry's up on the reviewing stand. Not that I'm expecting the farmers to try anything. The Ram Rebellion never really got violent over here, the way it did at Miltitz, and anyway, they're on our side. But we haven't caught the kidnappers and we don't know if the guys who hauled Schweinsberg away were the only ones that the archbishop of Cologne sent into our territory."

"Did he send them because he's archbishop of Cologne or did he send them because he's the brother of the duke of Bavaria?" Harlan Stull asked.

"I'm not even sure he could separate those two things in his own mind." Clara frowned. "If he wasn't Maximilian's brother, he wouldn't be an archbishop."

Wes took his glasses off and started to polish them with his handkerchief. "Is he in any position to do anything after the Essen War?"

"He's on the run," Derek conceded. "Or, at least, out of Bonn and lurking somewhere over on the other side of the Rhine. But if we've still got some of the guys he hired running around loose . . . And I don't know that we don't. It doesn't seem likely, but I can't be sure. A closed perimeter looks good to me."

"Make sure there's a chair for him on the reviewing stand. George Chehab says Henry's having problems with that hip again."

Derek nodded. "Sure. He can go through the new school building, too, while he's out at Barracktown. The roof is on, now, and there's glass in the windows. We can set up the lunch in the larger schoolroom. He can eat with the teachers. We've hired a second teacher for next year."

"That's that, then," Wes said, putting his glasses back on. "How are you planning to get Henry out to all the small towns and villages, Orville?"

Amsterdam

"What is it about men whose wives have just had babies that makes them look insufferably smug and oh-so-pleased with themselves?" mused Ed Piazza. "I mean, it's not as if the man did anything except get his rocks off months ago."

Mike Stearns' grin never wavered. "And you didn't?"

"Oh, sure," said Ed. "I'm just quoting my wife's none-too-admiring words addressed at me, back when."

Francisco Nasi, the only single man in the trio, shook his head. "I'm simply glad that Rebecca is well. And the girl also."

"What are you going to name her?" asked Ed.

"Kathleen," said Mike. "We decided that a long time ago. In fact, it was supposed to have been the name we gave Sephie, except we decided in the end that 'Sepharad' would be better for our first child."

The term *Sepharad* was the word used by Europe's Sephardic Jews to refer to the Iberian homeland from which they had been driven almost two centuries earlier. As always, Nasi was struck by the name, used as the name of a child—and, still more so, by the complexities of the gentile father who had chosen that name. Complexities which had, in the end, produced something as simple and clear-cut as Nasi's own firm allegiance to the man.

But it was a complex world, after all. And there was always this, too—working for Michael Stearns was invariably an interesting experience. Sometimes, even an exhilarating one.

"Kathleen," said Ed, rolling the name. "After a relative?"

Mike's grin got a bit crooked. "Uh, no. It was my ex-fiancée's name."

Ed looked a bit startled. Nasi, who knew the story, said: "The woman who died in the car crash. In California."

Ed was still looking startled. "And Becky didn't mind?"

"It was her suggestion, in fact," said Mike.

That led Francisco to reflect on the complexities of the woman Rebecca Abrabanel. With some regrets, even. Had she not married Mike Stearns, she might have wound up marrying Francisco himself.

Possibly. That had been his family's plan, at least. But what was done, was done, and Nasi was not a man given to fretting over the past.

Speaking of which—complexities, that is . . .

"Is it possible to speak to her?" he asked. "Or is she maintaining seclusion?"

Mike's grin got very crooked, now. "Yeah, sure. We'll have to manage something discreet, though. Becky maintains most of the rituals and customs, but not all of them, especially the ones she thinks are—her words, not mine—'stupid and pointless leftovers from tribal pastoralism.' But she tries not to rub anybody's nose in it."

Nasi chuckled. "Especially in Amsterdam, whose rabbis are notoriously rigid."

"'Reactionary scoundrels,' is the phrase Becky herself uses to describe them." Mike shrugged. "She doesn't care at all what *they* think. Still, most Jews in the city are religiously very conservative, if not always politically, and she doesn't see any point in needlessly irritating them. So, although she's not maintaining the forty days of seclusion, she's not flaunting the fact either. Come by our place tonight, after dark."

Nasi nodded. Mike cocked his head quizzically.

"What do you need to talk to her about? If it's something personal, of course, you can ignore the question."

"No, it's political," said Ed. "And you should be part of the discussion anyway. The problem is with Becky's seat in the SoTF Congress. She's been gone for a long time, Mike. Is she planning to come back to Grantville? If so, we'll figure on running her again as the candidate of the Fourth of July Party. But, if she's not coming back—or not coming back soon—we really need to run somebody else. We just can't keep that seat held for somebody in absentia."

Mike scratched his jaw. "Yeah, I understand. Becky and I have talked about it, but—what with this and that and this and that—"

"It's been a hectic few months," Ed said, chuckling.

"—we never came to any conclusions. And, yes, I can see where it'd be a problem for the party in Thuringia."

"We'll be by tonight, then. In the meantime . . ." Ed winced. "I suppose we may as well go see Gretchen."

Mike frowned. "What's the problem? She's not hard to talk to—at least, if you can pry yourself through the small mob of CoCers who are usually surrounding her." He glanced at his watch. "And, this time of day, that's where you'll usually find her. At the CoC headquarters downtown."

"Well . . . this is a personal matter. Henry Dreeson asked us to talk to her while we were here. He's wondering—and he's getting pretty damn dyspeptic about it—when Gretchen's planning to come home and start taking care of that mob of kids of hers. She's been gone just as long as Becky, you know."

"Oh." Now Mike made a face. "Yeah. Good luck. The old saw comes to mind. 'Better you than me.' "

That made his grin reappear.

"That's really a pretty disgusting grin," Ed observed.

In the event, though, Gretchen wasn't belligerent. In fact, she looked downright shamefaced when Ed finished passing on the message from Henry.

"Well, yes, I know. But . . . we've been very busy . . ." She made a fluttery sort of gesture, very out of character for Gretchen. "The struggle against reaction . . ."

Ed just waited. Under the circumstances, that seemed the wisest course.

Eventually, Gretchen stopped muttering and mumbling about the needs of the struggle and started muttering and mumbling noises on the subject of returning to Grantville. After a couple of minutes or so, Ed decided he could excavate enough of those vague phrases to mollify Henry.

For a while, anyway. But, by then, all sorts of things might happen. The newly arrived cousin might turn into the reincarnation of Mary Poppins or . . . Whazzername, the great governess played by Julie Andrews in *The Sound of Music*. The one who wound up marrying von Trump. Von Trapp?

Or, horses might learn to sing. Or, Gretchen might actually tear herself away from the struggle against reaction and the forces of darkness long enough to come home to Grantville and do something with that gaggle of kids.

Who was to say? All Ed had agreed to do was pass on the message. Which, he'd done.

"I'll tell Henry," he said stoutly.

Rebecca seemed a bit shamefaced herself, that night, after Ed raised the problem of her seat in the SoTF Congress.

"Yes, I understand. You may tell our people back in Grantville that I think it would be best if I simply resigned from the seat." She glanced at her husband. "Michael and I . . . well, we do not wish to be parted again. And he must remain in Magdeburg. Even if he loses the election, as we expect, he will have to lead the opposition."

She looked back at Ed. "So, we have decided. I will go to Magdeburg also. And if my father is willing, we will ask him to move in with us."

Ed nodded. He didn't ask about Mike's mother, since he knew full well she'd be quite unwilling to leave Grantville even if she wasn't an invalid. But that wouldn't be a major problem, he didn't think, with all the support she had in the town.

And it was none of his business anyway. The political issue had been resolved. "All right," he said. "You might consider becoming active politically in Magdeburg."

Mike and Rebecca both smiled. "As it happens," Mike said, "Gunther Achterhof has been pestering us for weeks now to agree to let Becky run for the House of Commons from one of Magdeburg's districts."

Ed's eyes widened. "The *USE* Parliament?"

"Yup."

"But . . ."

"Exactly what I said!" exclaimed Rebecca. Her hands fluttered much the way Gretchen's had earlier than day. "I've never lived in the city—anywhere in the province. Only even visited just a few times. I could just manage to move there in time for the election. The idea seems absurd."

Mike, on the other hand, was looking smug again. "Who cares? Gunther sure doesn't—and he says nobody else will either. If we run Becky, he says she'll win in a landslide."

Nasi cleared his throat. "I have to say, I agree with Achterhof.

Magdeburg province is even more . . . ah, I will say 'July-Fourthish' rather than 'radical,' just to avoid haggling, than the State of Thuringia-Franconia." His eyes got a little unfocused. "I'm quite familiar with the subject, you know. I estimate she'd get at least two-thirds of the vote, in any district in the province. If she ran in the city itself, she'd almost certainly go unopposed. The Crown Loyalists have given up there, for all practical purposes."

"I'll be damned," said Ed. He realized, not for the first time, that because he'd always remained in Grantville since the Ring of Fire that he had a tendency to underestimate the impact that the time-transplanted Americans were having on the seventeenth century. In some places, at any rate.

"Anything else?" asked Mike.

"No. Unless you'd like to hear the latest Grantville gossip."

"Oh, horrors," said Becky, leaning forward. "But start with something pleasant."

"Pleasant, it is—at least, if you enjoy the exploits of rambunctious girls. You know Denise Beasley, don't you?"

"Such a sprightly lass," said Becky. "What did she do now?"

On the Reichsstrasse between Arnstadt and Erfurt

Wackernagel was doing explanations at the front of the first ATV. Cunz Kastenmayer was doing explanations at the back of the rear ATV. The drivers were standing by the doors, pointing at first one thing and then another. The soldiers, who were standing around, trying to look casual, were surrounded by a lot of boys and a few girls who had already had their turn in the vehicles but wanted to know more about how they worked.

Henry Dreeson was on a bench, leaning back against a tree, enjoying the shade and letting them have at it.

There hadn't been this much excitement when they stopped in Badenburg, even though they'd done a press conference. The people in Badenburg saw various kinds of motorized this-and-that almost every day. Beyond there, though, even on the way up to Arnstadt, the first day out, this had happened every time Wackernagel called a stop. Which he did at about every good-sized village.

Henry didn't mind admitting that he appreciated the frequent stops. Not just because his hip ached, even though it did. The prostate gland wasn't what it used to be, either. Who used to sing that song? Rosemary Clooney. "This ole house . . ."

He hummed a couple of lines. That must have been fifty years ago, give or take a couple. Right about the time he and Annie got married. Before he understood in his bones what it was about.

Over by the ATVs a boy, ten years old maybe, blew the horn and let out a whoop of delight.

Henry had been surprised at how much interest there was in his tour. Wackernagel said that if he was doing a goodwill tour, he might as well do it right from the start and all the way over. People in the villages, both between Badenburg and Erfurt and on the Imperial Road from Erfurt to Fulda, had all seen up-time vehicles going back and forth before. Lots of times. They had *not*, very often, seen one of them stopped, where they could take a closer look, with a driver who was willing to explain how things worked. Much less passengers who were willing to vacate the premises and let them climb in and out, let the boys put their hands on the steering wheel and go *vroom* for a while, or anything else of the sort.

It was sort of restful, as long as people were more interested in the cars than they were in him. He had a feeling that was going to stop once they got over into Buchenland.

Tonight they'd be staying in Erfurt. Probably no curious kids there—Erfurt had a lot of trucks, being the central supply depot for the army—but the city council was giving a dinner for him tonight and then he'd promised to do an interview for the newspaper. Newspapers. There were three, but Cunz had told them that they all had to come to the same interview.

The difference between an interview and a press conference seemed to be that at an interview, everyone sat around a table. At a press conference, he stood up in front and the reporters sat in a row.

Tomorrow morning, Wackernagel wanted them to make a stop at a little village called Bindersleben right outside the city limits. It didn't make much driving sense to stop that soon after they got started, but apparently he knew people there and had promised some kids they could have a good look at the cars.

It was probably a good idea to do it this way, with all the stops. He was glad Wackernagel had come up with the idea. Good PR.

Cunz was writing up a kind of trip diary saying what they did at every village and sending it back to the Grantville papers. It listed the names and everything of the kids who came to look at the ATVs. The *Times* had promised to send copies of the those issues to the villages, so parents could buy copies of the Grantville paper with their children's names in it. Ed Piazza would like that. It would make people who didn't have the time or money to visit the Grantville Fair to see machinery feel more connected to the government. That sort of stuff. It was a lot more personal than watching a truck on the road or looking up and seeing an airplane flying overhead, or even having a crystal set and hearing about it on the radio. Ed believed in personal.

Of course, Ed was thinking about the election.

And his driver was waving. On the road, again.

Someone had told him that Cardinal Richelieu had hemorrhoids. So bad that five or six years ago, when the king of France took down La Rochelle, they'd had to put some kind of a stretcher between the seats in a carriage so he could ride to the siege lying down on his stomach. Made that sort of *pained* expression on the man's face in all the portraits people had looked up in the encyclopedias a little more understandable, he guessed.

He was going to have the same kind of expression on his own face before he got into a bed tonight. Even with an ATV that had padded seats to ride in. It was a hell of a good thing that he wasn't trying to make this trip sitting on a hard wagon bench.

He grabbed his cane and heaved himself up.

Vacha, on the Reichsstrasse

His driver was slowing down and the car behind, the one with the mechanics riding in it, was pulling around, ahead of them. Henry looked more closely. There were a half-dozen men hanging around the little guardhouse. Those weren't kids interested in looking at cars.

Wackernagel cussed something in German. Must have been a good one, because Henry hadn't ever heard it before.

"It's a divided town," the driver said. "The crossing's always been a bone of contention between the abbots of Fulda—that's the SoTF now—and the landgraves of Hesse-Kassel, so they say.

But I know for damn sure that our people cleared this motorcade with their people in advance."

"But Hesse-Kassel is *in* the USE. *Verdammt!*" One of the reasons Cunz Kastenmayer said he was glad that he'd gone into law rather than theology, aside from the money he expected to earn, was that he was free to indulge in the occasional profanity. If not in his father's hearing. "And don't think that Wilhelm V isn't making the most of it. Think how much extra acreage he grabbed for himself last spring, all the way over to the Rhine. Under color of doing a good deed for Gustav."

Henry understood them, which he felt pretty good about, considering that when the Ring of Fire happened, his German had been limited to the title of "*Auf Wiederseh'n*, Sweetheart." "California was in the United States of America too, up-time. That didn't stop them from searching cars crossing into the state and telling people they couldn't bring in any fresh fruits or vegetables."

The driver looked at him, surprised.

"I don't care what they tell you in citizenship class. We weren't perfect. No country ever has been. No country ever will be. The thing to aim at is to get it as good as you can for as many of your people as you can. We had as many arrogant assholes up-time as you have down-time. We just made a little more effort to get a grip on them, most of the time."

Kastenmayer nodded. "The greatest happiness of the greatest number," he said in English. "We covered that in the history of political philosophy class I took last year."

Henry nodded. "I hadn't ever heard it put quite that way. But it pretty much sums up the idea. But without a tyranny of the majority. Hard to pull off."

The two sets of soldiers were still arguing. But it looked like it was going to turn into a paper war rather than a shooting war.

"Can you walk a quarter of one of your up-time miles?" Wackernagel asked. "I know a family here. I stay with them overnight every trip. It's cheaper than a room in the inn. We can go over there and get something to drink. The street's wide enough that when they finish up with this"—he leaned his head in the direction of the disputing-the-right-of-way critters—"the driver can bring the car down and pick you up. He can turn around using the alley."

Henry nodded. "Sounds good to me. I can make it that far. I make it that far from the house to City Hall and back home every day, still. The hip's going bad, but I don't want all the rest of my joints to stiffen up, too. Counterproductive."

He smiled a little. That had been one of his daughter Margie's words, too.

Hesse-Kassel's head honcho yelled something when they opened the car doors. He had an accent Henry had never heard before, thick enough to cut with a knife. Not one word in four came through. That seemed to happen every time he started to think he had a handle on the language, finally. Wackernagel yelled back in the same lingo. Whatever he said, the Hessian soldiers let them walk away without any more fuss.

But they'd already held the drivers up for a couple of hours, splitting hairs. Trying to featherbed by arguing that even if an ATF didn't need to hitch up extra horses from the Hessian teamsters to help it handle these hills, they were still obliged to pay the mandatory fee for the extra team of horses. Which, since there were two ATVs, meant that they owed the fee for two teams.

Which meant that even if they left right now, which it sure didn't look like they were going to, they wouldn't be able to reach Fulda before dark. So they might as well plan to stay the night in Vacha. Nobody in his right mind would try to drive through these hill roads with nothing but headlights to see by.

Henry intended to have Wes file an official complaint with the landgrave once they got to Fulda. He wasn't a man to let himself be pushed around.

And it wasn't just him they were trying to push around. Hesse-Kassel was a Crown Loyalist, really close to Wettin, and he was insulting the SoTF. Just to see if they'd let him get away with it, probably. He wasn't exactly farting in the face of Mike Stearns in person, but that's what this kind of idiocy amounted to.

Hesse-Kassel's nose was probably out of joint because Mary Simpson and Ronnie had gotten so much publicity in the newspapers this summer while they were kiting around Bavaria with the Austrian archduchess. Which amounted to publicity for the SoTF.

Wackernagel said they could all spend the night at this family's house, where he stayed, but it would be crowded. Henry could have a bed, but he and Cunz, the drivers, and the mechanics would have to sleep on the floor.

A couple of hours before dark, though, three companies of

orange-uniformed men on horses, led by Derek Utt himself, showed up in Vacha. The Fulda Barracks Regiment was thoroughly spooked by what had happened to the civilian administrators and doubly determined that it wasn't going to happen again. They'd been camping five miles or so outside of town all week and kept a couple of lookouts in an inn on the Fulda side of the town.

The lookouts had spotted the problem. One of them had slipped out, picked up his horse from a farmer's stall, and gone down to collect the whole troop.

Sergeant Hartke was now having a few words with Hesse-Kassel's border guards.

Derek moved Henry from the outside picnic table in the friendly woman's yard over to an inside parlor in the Fulda-side inn where the scouts had been staying.

Wackernagel said he'd spend the night at the house like usual and meet them at the ATVs in the morning.

Henry nodded. He supposed the woman counted on having the income from her regular customers and Wackernagel knew it. She had three little kids, that he'd seen.

That night he didn't just have the three soldiers from Grantville staying at the same motel with him. These roadside inns were really motels, when you came right down to it. He had two orange-colored guards inside his room and a couple more standing outside his door all night.

He felt a little bit ashamed that he'd kicked up such a big fuss when Piazza insisted on sending the second ATV. Utt seemed to take the problem seriously. Real seriously.

Chapter 10

Frankfurt am Main

Ron Stone wiggled his legs around. There wasn't a lot of leg room on the barge that the crew was slowly poling up the Main River.

Joachim Sandrart, sitting next to him, had a dreamy expression on his face. Joachim had been mentally counting his future money all the way down the Rhine, since their visit to Duke Henri de Rohan.

In other words, Rohan had turned out to be a reasonable man. A reasonable man who was interested in art. A reasonable man who was interested in art and had money. The ambitious young painter's dream patron, perhaps.

"When are we going to get there?" Ron's brother Gerry asked from the narrow single seat at the back of the barge.

Ron twisted around. "Haven't you outgrown that by now?"

"Nah. It was the first thing I learned to say in German. And Italian. Well, the second, I guess. The first thing was, 'What's for supper?' "

"A couple more hours," the crew captain answered.

Gerry subsided back into silence.

"I don't suppose we have reservations," Reverend Jones said ironically. Down-time travel did not lend itself to advance reservations.

"Rohan's secretary recommended a place. The host's name is de Ron and the inn's called *Zum Weissen Schwan*."

Sandrart shook his head. "Don't stay at an inn. After you were so cooperative about letting me go over to meet with the duke, the least I can do is extend the hospitality of my father's house. We've got plenty of room."

"Vengeance," Ouvrard said. "We have this wonderful chance to avenge the failure of Ducos' plot to assassinate the pope in Rome. It has fallen to us, into our laps like a ripe plum. We did nothing to seek it out. The Stone brothers. Two of the three culprits are right here! To think that Antoine Delerue predicted that we were unlikely to encounter them again."

"Antoine is scarcely a prophet. Certainly not an infallible one. Count your lucky stars that they're staying at Sandrart's house," Brillard said. "And keep your face out of public view. Maybe they wouldn't recognize any of us, and wouldn't remember having ever seen us talking to Michel anywhere in Italy. But then again, one of them might. Talk about good luck. If the Sandrart son hadn't invited them, they'd be right here at the *Swan* and we'd be huddling in the sleeping chambers all day to avoid them."

"Another heaven-sent, predestined, foreordained, clearly God-given opportunity wasted because of Michel's . . ." Ouvrard shut up before Guillaume could tell him to.

"Working within the limitations that our leader has placed upon us is an exercise in humility," Locquifier said. He didn't look at his hands. These past two days, he had chewed his own fingernails down to the quick in frustration.

"At least tell Michel about it. Why did he and Antoine have to go as far away as Scotland? What can they possibly be trying to accomplish in Scotland, of all places?"

"Robert." Locquifier paused. "I will send another letter to him, explaining what has happened. After that, all we can do is wait for his further directions."

There were musicians at one end of the room. A sort of string quartet. Lots of candles in sconces reflecting off the window panes, of which there were also a lot. Downtown Frankfurt mostly looked sort of Gothic in its architecture, but it was clear that Sandrart's father had remodeled this house not too long ago, modernized it.

There was a buffet table at the other end of the room. A big one, loaded with more food than Ron had seen in one place since the last reception he'd attended at the Barberini mansion. Off in a corner by himself, behind the table, Gerry was eating a plate of fruit and cheese and keeping one eye on Artemisia's little girl, who was standing right by the table, eating everything sweet that she could identify by the sugar crystals sprinkled on the top. That was okay.

There were polished blue and white tiles under foot. They had to be marble. Marble was a rock, when you came right down to it, and these were as hard as rocks. Joachim Sandrart's mother would start the dancing up in a few minutes, he expected, and he'd be expected to punish his feet on them. She'd be dancing with the *Bürgermeister*. He'd be dancing with whatever girl they told him to dance with. He'd gone to a depressing number of fancy parties since that first one in Venice, and was getting, in his own opinion, depressingly good at doing what he was supposed to do at them. Bourgeois, his dad would say.

Overhead—Ron took another surreptitious glance upward. Woodcarvings and murals. The murals were a bit amateurish. He wondered it Sandrart had painted them on the ceiling in his own father's house. Maybe for practice, when he was a teenager?

Simon was sitting down, talking to a middle-aged man garbed in what Ron had come to think of as the Calvinist preacher's uniform. A Geneva gown, they called it. Black pleats and a white collar. He thanked his lucky stars that Simon still had diplomatic credentials, in case the other guy took offense at some of his theological opinions.

Joachim was—he looked toward the big fireplace with its ornamental mantel—over there. Ron had met the man he was talking to, earlier in the evening. He was a banker, another Calvinist refugee from somewhere, named Philipp Milkau. The girl next to Artemisia was his daughter Johanna. Milkau's only daughter and sole heiress. Fräulein Walking-pots-of-money. The girl that Sandrart was going to marry, most likely. She was exactly the kind of wife that a promising young artist with ambitions to enter the diplomatic service needed. Paying for a reception like this a couple of times every week wouldn't even start to drain the exchequer she would bring along as a dowry.

She seemed nice enough. Pleasant looking. Good manners. Couldn't be more than about sixteen. Of course, Joachim hadn't ever met her until this week, but his relatives and her father had reached a sort of preliminary arrangement. Nothing legal, like a betrothal. An understanding that was contingent on the main parties to the agreement not taking a dislike to each other on first sight and developing an even greater loathing on longer personal acquaintance.

But they seemed to be getting along fine. She had her hand on Joachim's arm. He was sort of sniffing at her hair. Which was a good thing, Ron supposed. Sandrart said that his own family could only afford to put on a party like this once a month or so.

The Stone brothers left the city the next day. Mathurin Brillard and Robert Ouvrard made one last effort to persuade Guillaume Locquifier to allow them to go in pursuit. But Locquifier was adamant.

Michel has given us no such instructions!

It was enough to drive a man insane. Michel Ducos was far distant—they had no idea where, precisely—so how could his "instructions" possibly cover any eventuality that might develop?

Brillard and Ouvrard did not share Locquifier's adulation of Michel Ducos. Both men thought Ducos' grasp on reality was shaky, in fact. Still, they were not prepared to wage an outright rebellion. True, Ducos' "authority" was mostly a matter of prestige, nothing formal. Insofar as the organization of Huguenot zealots had an officially recognized leader, it was Antoine Delerue and not Ducos. But Ducos' force of personality was such that any dispute with him almost invariably became ferocious.

As much as Mathurin and Robert would have enjoyed getting their revenge on the Stone brothers, they didn't feel strongly enough about the issue to risk getting into a brawl with Ducos. So, off the brothers went. Not touched, not even pursued.

On the Reichsstrasse between Frankfurt and Hanau

"Philipp Milkau is being blackmailed," said Artemisia Gentileschi.

The part of the *Reichsstrasse* they were following this morning was headed generally uphill, a steeper grade than a person would think unless he looked back to see what he'd already climbed, so they were going slowly to spare the horses. That gave them plenty of time to talk, but the sentence that she'd just dropped on him wasn't Artemisia's ordinary horse-riding conversation.

"He is?" Ron hoped that he didn't sound too dumb.

"By some Huguenot extremist group."

Ron groaned inwardly. The last time that he'd met a Huguenot extremist, it had been at the hearing for Galileo. He didn't really want to meet any more of them.

"Why's he being blackmailed?" If the man turned out to be a pedophile or something, he definitely didn't want to get involved.

"Something involving real estate. Buying an estate called Stockau. It's over near Ingolstadt, somewhere. In Pfalz-Neuburg."

"Didn't that belong to the abominable Wolfgang Wilhelm? Before he got himself killed in the Essen War last summer?"

"That's the one. If you can think of a triangle between Augsburg, Munich, and Neuburg, it's in there."

"The south side of the river?"

Artemisia nodded. "It's noble land. So it's tax exempt, for all practical purposes. Plus being a way for Milkau to lever his family up into the nobility, if he played his cards right. But somewhere along the way, he bribed the wrong person, or didn't bribe the right person, or . . . something."

"Like he maybe told Wolfgang Wilhelm something that amounted to treason to get him to approve the sale?"

"You are young to be so suspicious, my friend Ron. The problem, I think, is that the purchase would have made him *landsässig* to an ally of Bavaria. It's a bit moot, now that General Banér has occupied Pfalz-Neuburg south of the Danube for Gustav Adolf and it's in the USE, or soon will be. But in any case, whatever the specifics, during the negotiations it was enemy territory. If the Frankfurt council finds out what he did, or was prepared to do, he will be tossed out of the city, bank and all. These . . ."

" 'Fanatics' is probably the right word."

"Fanatics. Yes. *Zeloti.* These zealots are using their knowledge to force him to finance their projects. Whatever their projects are. He is not sure. But he believes that he is probably not alone. That they are extorting money from other prominent members of the Calvinist diaspora."

"And I need to know this . . . why?"

"Your father is important. And rich. Therefore, you have ties to influential men in the State of Thuringia-Franconia, and through them into the highest circles of the USE. He thought that you might be able to bring the problem to the attention of the appropriate persons, since you are a friend of his future son-in-law. Discreetly, of course, naming no names, but letting someone know of the existence of the zealots and that they have established themselves in Frankfurt."

Ron had never thought of himself as having ties into the highest circles of the USE. But if Frank could get married in the Sistine Chapel . . . The only important man he knew was Mr. Piazza. That was because Mr. Piazza used to be the high school principal, so everybody in Grantville knew him, pretty much. But he did know him, and Piazza was as thick as thieves with Mike Stearns. Whom he'd also actually met. Once. In a bunch of other people at the Thuringen Gardens. Everybody knew that Francisco Nasi worked for Stearns.

"I'll see what I can do."

Chapter 11

Frankfurt am Main

Nathan Prickett figured he'd done his duty to common courtesy already by looking up the other Grantvillers in Frankfurt and saying Hi, letting them know where he was staying. He hadn't expected that he'd have much in common with them, except for being from Grantville, and he didn't.

Jason Waters was a newspaperman. He was here to establish an American-style newspaper. If he could get permission from the city council, that was. And from Magdeburg, since the guy who was publishing the big paper in Frankfurt now had a kind of grandfathered-in imperial monopoly that went back to the days before the Ring of Fire.

The USE Parliament hadn't gotten around to abolishing monopolies yet. They probably would, but the country had only existed for less than a year and a good portion of that time, there'd been a war on. It looked like there'd be a war on a good portion of next year, too, if Gustav decided to take on Saxony and Brandenburg.

Waters was from Charlestown and only settled down in Grantville to start with because he'd married a local girl. Nathan had no idea why he'd brought Ernest Haggerty with him, unless to be a gofer.

Wayne Higgenbottom was studying the post office system.

Wayne was here because the Grantville post office had sent him. None of them were likely to stay long. It wasn't as if Nathan had ever gone to school with any of them. Haggerty did belong to the same church—Methodist—but he was married to a Catholic and didn't attend regularly. Ernest was some kind of a cousin of Gary Haggerty and them, but not close.

Odd, but by now, after all the time he'd lived in Suhl, Nathan had more in common with Ruben Blumroder than he did with some of the guys from back home.

He picked up his pen.

Dear Don Francisco,

He didn't have a lot to report. He'd only been here a week. But he owed the don a letter.

Johann Wilhelm Dilich, who is in charge of Frankfurt's fortifications, knows a lot more about city defenses than I do, or probably ever will.

I expect you already know that way back before Grantville arrived, the father of the guy who's now the landgrave of Hesse put Dilich's father in jail. And, I sort of think from what I've been picking up, it was for unfair reasons. As soon as the father got out in 1623, he went to work for the elector of Saxony. That's John George. He's still working there, and he's famous.

I guess that worked out fine in the world we came from, because Frankfurt and Hesse and Saxony were all on the side of Gustavus Adolphus.

Well, sort of, at least. Seems like John George was always a bit iffy, to put the best face possible on it.

What with the war coming up next spring, though, I thought I'd at least better remind you that the guy in charge of the fortifications at Frankfurt, which is a really important city (province, I guess, since the Congress of Copenhagen) for the USE and smack on the Main River, is the son of the guy who's in charge of the fortifications for John George.

Just in case.

The militia captain told me all this. He's an old friend

of a gunsmith named Heinrich Dilles. He—Dilles, that is—has been dead for almost ten years, but Blumroder used to know him pretty well and said that the captain could tell me a lot. Blumroder gave me a few other names of men to look up beyond the ones I've already talked to on my sales trips over here. Kolb and Mohr. Hung and Rephun. And Schmidt. I don't exactly have high hopes of finding the right person named Schmidt. It's a good-sized town and they don't have street numbers.

Otherwise, Simon Jones, the minister of my church back home, came through town, with that hippie Tom Stone's two younger boys and an Italian woman painter, on his way back to Grantville. Funny company for him to be keeping. But I expect you've already heard that.

Best wishes,
Nathan Prickett

"I'm not here to tell you how to put your men through drill," Nathan said firmly. The Frankfurt militia officers were a touchy bunch, a lot of them. Not the captain, who was the head guy, but several of the lieutenants.

"I'm a veteran, yeah. One three-year enlistment from 1986 through 1989. Not an officer. I went in right out of high school, because I couldn't afford to start college right away. We were in the middle of an economic bust in Grantville, the year I graduated."

Someone asked a question.

"College? I guess you'd call it your 'arts faculty' at a university like Jena. Or a 'philosophy faculty.' But I'd planned to major in engineering, or something technical."

The man nodded. "Leiden," he said.

Nathan didn't catch the reference, so he kept going. "Never did get to college. By the time I got out of the army, I'd decided to start my own business, so I took a job to start saving money." He looked around the room. "Any questions? Is that clear?"

No more questions.

"Okay, one three-year enlistment. 'That's all, folks,' just like the cartoons say. I've been in the National Guard ever since, but that's weekend warrior stuff."

More technical terms to explain.

"Look, the main point is. You keep on teaching your troops to fight. I teach them how to take care of the new guns the city council has paid out their good tax money to buy." He looked around the room again. "Any questions? Is that clear?"

He'd learned the hard way, his first few trips over to Frankfurt for Ruben Blumroder, that "Any questions?" and "Is that clear?" were his best friends.

He hadn't expected Jason Waters to come tracking him down at the tavern where he ate dinner, but here he came. So he nodded. The two of them consumed stew and bread in silence for a while. Waters broke it.

"Ever run across a guy named Wackernagel?"

"The courier?"

"Um-hmmn. Guess you have, if you know his name."

"Read it in the paper. He's being the friendly local guide for Henry Dreeson's trip this fall."

"Yeah, that one."

"Never actually met him. Haven't gotten back to Grantville much these last couple of years."

"He works out of Frankfurt."

They both went back to dipping rye bread in the stew juice. That was about the only way to make the bread chewable, once it got stale.

Waters broke the silence again. "He's got a brother-in-law who runs a print shop here. Name's Neumann."

"Haven't met him." Nathan figured that he had the home court advantage and wasn't about to give it up. If Waters wanted something, he'd have to come right out and ask for it.

"Higgenbottom's run into him several times."

"Haven't seen much of Wayne since I got here."

"You run across some pretty odd people in Frankfurt. It's big enough that they can sort of keep themselves under the radar, if they're careful. Not like a village, where you've only got a couple hundred people and they all know each other."

"Odd, as in peculiar? Or odd, as in this could get to be a problem?"

"Plenty of the first around. Harmless religious nuts of various persuasions. Wayne's thinking that there's some of the second kind. Religious nuts of the ayatollah persuasion."

Nathan nodded.

"Jessica—sister of Bill Porter over at the power plant—divorced Wayne last year. He worked in Morgantown all his life. Managed the campus mail system for WVU. Doesn't belong to a church in Grantville. Wasn't born there. Didn't go to school there."

"So?" Nathan hated having to put that question mark at the end of his words. It amounted to giving up points. But Waters was a reporter. A word professional, so to speak. He'd probably had whole classes in turning conversations around on the people he talked to.

"There's at least one of the ayatollah bunches that's gotten hold of their own duplicating machine, Neumann says. One of the Vignelli machines. Got it used from Freytag when he bought a new model. They've been on the market for more than a year now—the machines, I mean. A trickle at first. Now it's a pretty wide stream. They're coming out of Tyrol, mostly, but there are already some knock-offs on the market."

Nathan gave up and asked a straight question. "What does that mean?"

"It means they're funded. The group of would-be ayatollahs, I mean. And well-funded. Even second-hand, a Vignelli will set you back a couple thousand dollars. The price will be coming down, of course, but for now, it's almost entirely print shops that are buying them. For small runs, they're cheaper than setting type."

"And?"

"Higgenbottom thinks somebody ought to know. And since you're Wes Jenkins' son-in-law and he's still the grand pooh-bah over in Fulda and since they had a problem with those pamphlets a while back . . ."

"You're nominating me for the fall guy."

"That's pretty much it."

At least they'd picked on him because of Wes and didn't know anything about his relationship to Francisco Nasi. Nathan picked up his pen.

Dear Don Francisco.

He'd better write to Wes, too. Just in case Waters or Higgenbottom asked about it, some day. CYA. Always.

Grantville

Jacques-Pierre Dumais decided that he would talk to Velma Hardesty at the 250 Club, sitting at a table right out in the open. Why not? Veda Mae Haggerty had introduced them to one another in public. Madame Hardesty was upon occasion a waitress there. Duck and Big Dog drank there; he worked for them. It was natural enough for him to come in with them, at first, and then to come back. The regulars didn't object, because the Garbage Guys had all vouched for him.

If you went slinking around, someone was eventually bound to notice that you were slinking.

As far as Jacques-Pierre was concerned, Grantville's greatest contribution to the education of seventeenth-century spies was that delightful couple, Boris Badenoff and Natasha. He had transcribed every episode of the tapes featuring the Russian pair, the squirrel, and the moose, listening to them over and over. With sketches of the best scenes, after he had learned to use the "pause" button. He sent them back to Henri de Rohan for use in training. A splendid object lesson in how not to gather intelligence. Himself, he preferred to go places where he had some reason to be and speak openly with people who also had some logical reason to be there.

He stopped to examine the place carefully on his way in. The 250 Club had missed out on most of Grantville's ongoing redevelopment. The building itself backed up to a rise. Above it, the hill rose fairly high. There wasn't really anything behind the building except a narrow walkway, because it was too close to the slope. That cut had been made, Duck had told him, nearly a half-century before the Ring of Fire.

The front of the building was a dull red. The back was painted in a faded dark green, a kind of paint that weathered, but did not peel. Part of the walkway had always been kept open to allow the beer delivery man to run his hand truck to the back door. It was hard to tell the color in places. Before the Ring of Fire, everywhere there wasn't junk, generations of beer deliverymen and meter readers had rubbed against the paint and sworn over damaging their clothes. The rest of the walkway used to be blocked by a pile of old refrigerators, broken bar furniture, and other miscellaneous junk that eventually merged into the former scrapyard if a person went that far. The junk was gone now. The Garbage Guys had paid Ken Beasley enough to make it worth his while to let them have it. The color of the paint was a little brighter where the junk had protected it.

Redevelopment had hit the area around it. Dumais had seen historical photographs at the museum. Before the Ring of Fire, facing the 250 Club from the road, on the right, there had been a small scrapyard with a few dead cars—not really a wrecking yard, just random accumulation—with a fence made of wired-up pieces of sheet-iron roofing. The Garbage Guys had bought up everything there, also, the owner being too cheap to donate it to recycling. Now there were new buildings and new businesses. On the left, the road curved away, and the parking still went around to that side of the building, not that anyone needed a parking lot any more. The next thing in that direction was—once upon a time—a failed gas station, with a rusty brown 1971 Mercury with a torn vinyl top and the right-front wheel missing parked under the portico. The car was long gone for parts. A down-time blacksmith had bought the building and stripped it. Now it was a butcher shop.

After a full evening of Madame Hardesty's conversation, Jacques-Pierre was tempted to give up the trade of espionage for good. He was suffering from *la migraine*. Getting any sound information out of the woman would be hopeless. She was utterly indifferent to anything that did not affect her directly.

She was stupid. She was spiteful. She was frivolous. She believed in astrology and who knew what other superstitions. She spouted platitudes that she found in her horoscope.

She was also a first cousin of the prime minister of the United States of Europe. True, Mike Stearns avoided claiming the relationship as much as possible—and had, by all accounts, long before he became the prime minister. A prime minister and a waitress in a tavern? Cousins? It would not be possible in a well-ordered world. But Stearns *was* an upstart and he did acknowledge the relationship in a minimal sort of way. At least, the woman had been invited to his wedding. Jacques-Pierre had confirmed that.

So.

If he could put ideas *into* that hennaed head? Ideas that she could drop into her normal conversation? It wouldn't work in a larger community, but there were really so few of the up-timers. A comment here. An innuendo there. A veiled criticism here. A barbed jab there. Each of them the kind of thing that people who knew the woman might expect her to say, but with the added little fillip that well, she *was*, after all, Mike Stearns' first cousin. Even if it was on the Lawler side of the family and they weren't that close.

Jacques-Pierre set out to flatter Madame Hardesty while, at the same time, seeding her mind with comments that would cultivate enough mild dissatisfaction in Grantville about the USE's policy in regard to Louis XIII and Richelieu to persuade Mauger that it was worthwhile to keep employing him. But not so much dissatisfaction as to cause really major problems, since that was not what Henri de Rohan wanted, not at all.

He must encourage her to undertake a self-improvement project. How? What would she understand? Ah, yes—the practice of transcendental meditation. Reduced to words she might at least pretend to understand.

The woman was not only lazy but also not known to be interested in public affairs. So he would be careful. Of the subjects that he gave her, "new insights" she should share with others to impress them, only about one in three, maybe fewer, would have any possible political implications. Most of the positive ones would involve the need for up-timers to harbor warm, fuzzy thoughts about French Huguenots and the Calvinist exiles from the Spanish Netherlands. The negative ones would target Gustavus Adolphus' treaty proposals. The remainder would be platitudes such as *A Discontented Heart Breeds a Discontented Life*. He could easily plagiarize most of them from Seneca, which the Grantvillers would soon realize, if they read Seneca.

But they didn't. So.

Chapter 12

Grantville

"Hey, Veda Mae. Can I share your table?"

She looked up. The dining room at the Willard Hotel was crowded for lunch and it was Bryant Holloway. She had known him all his life and he was her cousin somehow through the Cunninghams, so she couldn't very well say no. Therefore, she cleared her purse off the other side where it had been staking her claim and said, "Sure. Haven't seen you for a while."

"I've been in Magdeburg since the middle of last winter. I'm just back for a month or so now for a fire prevention training conference."

"What's Magdeburg like?"

"Start with this. The Fire Marshal of our wonderful United States of Europe is that prick from Baltimore, Archie Stannard. One of the Masaniellos' relatives who got caught in the Ring of Fire because of Vince and Carla's fortieth anniversary party over at Pray Your Rosary Catholic Church, or whatever they're calling it these days."

"What's wrong with him?"

"From the minute the Grantville fire department chief Steve Matheny picked him up as assistant chief, Stannard's been trying to make us more 'professional.' Sometimes I thought that if I heard the word 'professional' one more time, I would gag. Steve kept us right up to the mark on equipment and training, but he didn't preach about it. Stannard does. I guess I could have lived with that, though. Since the Ring of Fire, we'd all been on call 24/7 and that wears you out, so I sort of put it down to stress. But then in the fall of '32, Stearns made this agreement with What's His Name, the captain general you know, and Stannard started on this kick of expanding modern fire prevention into the rest of the New United States. It's one thing to work your ass off for Grantville. It's something else when they expect you to do it for a bunch of foreigners."

Sensing a kindred spirit, Veda Mae actually smiled. "You didn't have anyone in Magdeburg back then, did you?"

"No. But they sent me over to Rudolstadt, right off the bat, as soon as Steve insisted that he needed me to go full-time rather than volunteer. Which I agreed to do, even though, with overtime, I was sure making more at Ollie's than the government pays us. The count over there speaks some English, at least, even though he sounds like one of those Shakespeare plays that Lisa Dailey tried to make us read in high school."

"Shakespeare's not so bad. We even read some of his stuff back in my day, and he sounded a lot like the King James Version. Which the Reverends Jones never should have gotten rid of and put in one of these so-called modern translations of the Bible." Veda Mae veered off on a tangent, pursuing one of her favorite grievances. By the time she ran down, Bryant had finished half of his lunch.

"Anyway, you asked what Magdeburg is like. We're trying to prevent all of the wonderful Emperor Gustavus Adolphus' Kraut allies from turning themselves into krispy kritters, which, if you ask me, most of them deserve. They're the ones who messed up and caused the disaster at Underwood's coal gas company. And now Quentin's dead himself, poor guy. None of the Krauts up at Wietze went running to help him, as far as I've ever heard.

"I'm not even at the Navy Yard, which might make some sense. I drew Station Number One. With Bibi Blackwood, of all people, as Captain and Officer in Charge. I never did hold with women 'firefighters' and I still don't. They even had to change the word from 'firemen.'"

"I never heard anyone complain that Bibi couldn't handle it. She's a big woman."

Bryant couldn't argue with that. Bibi was a big woman, all right. He nodded, then said, "At least her boys are grown and Sara stayed back here in Grantville with Dean and his new wife, so she's not distracted by having to find child care and schools. I'll give her that much."

"Kraut woman."

"Bibi?"

"Dean's new wife. Would you believe that her name is Krapp?"

Bryant laughed so loud that people stared at them.

"The whole town is going to pot," Veda Mae said. "You can't believe how many decent Americans are marrying these Kraut whores. There must be a half dozen or so who are actually taking classes at that Kraut church out on what used to be Route 250 on the way to Rudolstadt so they can marry them in Kraut ceremonies. And it won't be any too soon for Ryan Baker and his girlfriend if you know what I mean, believe me. Little slut. She works in Cora Ennis' kitchen at the cafe."

"I can see that it's getting to be a problem. Hell, Veda Mae. Have you heard what Lenore's dad did?"

"Wes? Not a word. Not since he and the other people we sent over to Fulda were kidnapped by a bunch of ungrateful Krauts. That was in the paper a while back. I don't have time to read the papers much, though."

"Well, the rest of our people over there got them back, including Wes. Anyway, he celebrated his delivery from the dungeon, or wherever he was, by marrying a Kraut woman himself. Sister of that Dietrich Bachmeier from Badenburg who's a sort of cousin of the guy who's Birdie Newhouse's partner these days. That farmer up at Sundremda. Same last name."

"At his age, he should have known better. Wes, I mean. Stearns and Piazza must be nuts to have appointed someone as chief civilian administrator in one of our Kraut territories who would behave like that. He ought to have kept his distance, so they would respect him. What did they call it after World War II? 'Nonfraternization policy.' That's it. Not that it worked the way it should have. Arnold Bellamy's own mother was one of those Kraut war brides. He's not from here, of course; he was from someplace in New Jersey when Natalie Fritz married him. So he's half-Kraut himself. And Curtis Maggard's mother, too. The woman's as crazy as a coot. Well, of course, Stearns . . . Becky's a Kraut, no matter what people say. Sometimes it seems to me that half of this town is going native. Thank god he's no relative of mine. Neither one of them is, Stearns nor Jenkins.

"Nor, thank heavens, the daughter of that idiot Pat Murphy. Did you hear that she's back in town again, with that Kraut named Junker she works with? Junk's a good name for him. Back from whatever it was she's been doing down in Franconia. Probably up to no good. She's working for Carol Unruh at the Department of Economic Resources, did you know. With that name, Carol's likely a Kraut herself. I know her husband is, that Koch. She met him in Germany, up-time, for all he tells people that he was actually born in Greece."

It got to be sort of a habit for Bryant. He certainly didn't want to eat lunch with all of the people who had come for the training conference. It was bad enough having to spend the rest of the day with them, listening to mostly German, even if it was peppered full of English words about firefighting equipment, without trying to talk it when he was trying to relax a bit.

And Veda Mae had lunch at the Willard every day.

"As I said, the first time that they sent me out of town, it was over to Rudolstadt. Fall of 1632, that was. I ran into Lenore again, there. She was taking some kind of class at the chancery. I knew perfectly well that her family was a little bit out of my league, but she was the only American girl in town, so we started to see one another. What with one thing and another, I proposed. Not right away, but pretty near to it. What do they call it?"

Veda Mae thought a minute. "Propinquity."

"Yeah, that's it."

"I saw a program about it on TV once, before we got ourselves stuck here. Oprah or somebody. You were right about 'out of your league,' though, if I do say so myself. That's why I stuck my oar in when Laurie wanted to go to nursing school. And I was right, wasn't I? Just her wanting to go and get herself above Gary led to a divorce."

"And Lenore accepted. I didn't pretend to myself that I was her 'Mr. Right.' Lenore was getting close to thirty and, God knows, she's no beauty. String bean with a horse face just about sums it up. How she can be so hellishly sexy is beyond me. I was her 'Mr. Good Enough.' Maybe even her 'Mr. The Best I Can Do.' Hell, maybe I was even 'Mr. It Looks Like He's All I'm Going To Get So If I Ever Want Children I Had Better Take Him.'

"So we got married in January 1633. She wanted to go to premarital counseling at First Methodist, but I told her I didn't want to. Certainly not sit through a bunch of 'holier than thou' from Mary Ellen Jones, calling herself a minister when the Bible forbids it. So we went to Brother Green, at his home. With 'obey' in the ceremony, like it should be. At least they had sent her prissy stick of a father off to Fulda by then, so he wasn't around to interfere."

Bryant looked down. "Maybe I should have broken it off right after I proposed. Do you know what she said? 'I hope you don't expect to be deflowering a virgin on your wedding night. No history of social diseases. Just for informational purposes.' Then she wouldn't explain any more than that when I asked her to. All she would say was that according to Dear Abby, that was plenty and I could take it or leave it.

"I should have realized then that she was a bitch, before it was too late. I should have left it. If a woman's been somewhere else before she marries, who's to say she won't go there again afterwards?

"Anyhow, we moved back to Grantville a couple of months later, after I finished up in Rudolstadt. Then we had the kid. And Lenore invented a stupid name, so she could call a girl after her father. I'd said that I didn't care what name she chose if it was a girl. Hell, I was so tired all the time right then that I didn't even want to think about baby names. But I'd been expecting her to pick something normal. Jessica, maybe. Or Caitlin. Or after one of our mothers. Something like that."

"I don't think I've ever heard of any other little girl named Weshelle," Veda Mae said. "But at least it isn't a Kraut name. Some of the men around here are letting their Kraut wives give Kraut names to babies that are half-American."

"I'd hated it in Rudolstadt, being off in a foreign town. Not very far, but too far to go back and forth every day. Then for the two months after the kid was born, she squalled her lungs out day and night, whenever I was trying to get some sleep between calls, so coming back to Grantville was actually worse in some ways. Given the way that kid yelled, I wouldn't actually have minded being sent to Magdeburg all that much, even if I do have to deal with another batch of foreigners all the time, if it hadn't been for having Stannard as my boss."

Veda Mae thought for a minute. "Weshelle should be beyond that crying stage now. She's almost a year old."

"Yeah. Instead, she's starting to walk and gets into everything if Lenore doesn't keep her penned up. Smears food all over her face and into her hair. And all over me, if I let her get near. A whole handful of mashed squash on my good blue shirt."

Veda Mae nodded solemnly. "Sometimes kids that age can get to be a real pain. Now take Alden Junior's kid, my great-grandson, he's just a couple of months older and the way Alden Junior's wife Kim lets him get away with things . . ."

Bryant rearranged the silverware on his plate, pushing the last of the food to the side. "Roasted turnips are not the same as baked potatoes, no matter what the menu here claims. Sometimes I wish that I could get drunk."

"Well, don't. I'm proud of you for sticking to the Baptist teetotalling line. I do myself, for the Methodists. Even though they're getting slack, these days."

"Damn kid. Here, I've been gone for nine months and it's pretty clear that Lenore didn't miss me much. Stays in the nursery until Weshelle is sound asleep. Jumps up out of bed in the middle of the night and goes to sleep on the cot in the nursery if she hears the least little bit of fussing."

"You're right about that. It's nothing but spoiling. If the child goes to the bad, it will be Lenore's fault. Just like Alden Junior's wife Kim. I could tell you—" Veda Mae stopped, annoyed, because Bryant was interrupting her again.

"She probably said 'yes' because she was far too proper to have a baby in anything but marriage. If not too proper to have sex outside it beforehand. Boy, but that grated on me. I'd been around a bit, myself, had a few girlfriends, but it's different for a man."

"Ummn." Veda Mae frowned. "I've sort of always thought that what's sauce for the goose is sauce for the gander."

Bryant ignored her. "And after we got married, I thought, she would obey me, at least. We left that in the ceremony. I thought that after she agreed to be married by Brother Green, she'd change over to Baptist, but she won't. Just because, she says, I hardly ever go myself, so why should she change?"

"Well," Veda Mae said, "I'm Methodist myself, so I don't think that you should really complain about that. After all, Methodist is really the right church. The others just sort of try. And it's teetotal too, like the Baptists, or it should be. Though I have my doubts about the Reverends Jones. Maybe you could change."

Bryant glared at her.

"Get that expression off your face, Bryant Holloway," Veda Mae said. "I'm your cousin and old enough to be your grandmother, so I can say what I please. Especially when it's the truth. There's no reason for her to change churches."

"Plus, now she wants to go back to work. She has more education than I do and wants to show it off, I suppose."

"Maybe that's why she doesn't want to sleep with you," Veda Mae suggested. "Having another baby would interfere. But I already told you what I think of women who have more schooling than their husbands. I know what it leads to. I went through it myself."

"So I'm stuck, I guess. She'll never do anything to give me a reason to divorce her, now that we're married. Well, probably not. She acts as prim and prissy as old Wes Jenkins himself, but... You know. She wouldn't ever have been to my taste, up-time. I would never even have asked her out. The only reason I did was that she was the only American woman that I could date in Rudolstadt that fall."

Veda Mae nodded. "There's this guy here in Grantville," she said. "He's a foreigner, but not a Kraut. He's working for Gary. His name is Jacques-Pierre Dumais, and he's pretty nice. A good listener, as Oprah would have said. Maybe it would help if you could talk some of these things out with him."

She felt pretty pleased with herself, for a change. Jacques-Pierre was always so grateful for introductions. He was anxious to get to know more Americans, he said, to improve himself and get to understand how they did things. That was a really proper attitude for an immigrant to take.

Humble.

Part Three

October 1634

Innumerable force of spirits armed

Chapter 13

Fulda

"There's not a place to stay anywhere in Fulda." Simon Jones' voice was very glum. "One of those 'no room at the inn' situations. We should have thought ahead. It's been in all the papers, after all. Henry Dreeson's little motorcade arrived early this afternoon. All the bright lights and would-be bright lights of Buchenland County have crammed themselves into town."

"Aw, shit." Okay, that might not be elegant. But it was exactly how Ron Stone felt. They'd been riding up and down hills all day. "I'm pooped. What next? Any place to camp?"

"There's not any place to hang by your fingernails, the way it looks. We'd better plan on going to the next village and hope someone has a spot. I sort of feel like we should try to say hello to Henry, but I don't think we could get anywhere near him."

"That probably means that his tour is a big success. I hope it is. You can say hello to him when he gets back to Grantville. To Ronnie and him both. Has anybody heard anything about the abbot yet?"

"Not a clue. Not one single everlovin' clue."

"Oh, well. Too bad we don't have an ATV. We'd be getting home a lot sooner than we will riding these poor beaten-down rental horses."

Gerry Stone just kept plodding along, not paying any real

attention to the conversation. Artemisia Gentileschi and her daughter followed him, their heads drooping.

Suddenly, Ron pulled on the reins. His horse stopped, so everyone behind him stopped, too. They didn't have much choice. "Just a minute."

The Reverend Jones frowned slightly. He knew what happened when that gleam appeared in Ron's eye. It wasn't a new phenomenon. When Ron was in the lower grades, Jones had heard all about it from his brother David, who was principal of the elementary school. When Ron was in middle school . . . When Ron was in high school . . . And then, these last months in Venice and Rome, he'd seen the results for himself. He opened his mouth. "Whatever you're thinking—"

"We're not going on past Fulda, hoping to find an inn with space somewhere farther along. It's already late and we're worn out, all of us. By the time we get around the city, the places on the other side will already be full with people coming from the other direction who know there won't be places to stay in Fulda itself and pulled over early. Everybody turn around. We'll backtrack a little."

"We've already checked with every inn along here," Simon protested.

"Yeah. That's right. Follow me."

"Barracktown?" Simon Jones exclaimed.

"It's obvious, when you think about it. All those orange uniforms out guarding VIPs means a whole batch of empty bunks in the barracks."

"We can't."

"Sure we can. You're a preacher from Grantville." He pointed his thumb. "She's a famous artist from Italy." He grinned. "The obligation of hospitality. Down-timers take it seriously. Just let me nose around and find someone I knew before we left for Venice last winter. Leave it to 'Stone the Golden-Tongued' or whatever some poet in a heroic epic might call me. If I didn't learn anything else from Sandrart—actually, to be honest, I learned quite a bit from him—he really improved my schmooze quotient."

"Hell, if that doesn't look like an Old West general store! What's it doing in Barracktown? Hold up, everyone." Ron dismounted with something of a groan and tossed his reins to Gerry. He was back ten minutes later with a young down-time woman following him. With something of a flourish, he bowed to Jones. "We're in luck. It's the sutler's cabin. The new guy remodeled. Everybody left in Barracktown seems to be shopping. Reverend Jones, may I have the privilege of presenting to you Antonia Kruger. She's married to Sergeant Johnny Furbee, who goes to your church in Grantville."

Antonia produced something that might have been a curtsey, if curtseys only involved a two-inch bob rather than a sweeping bend of the knees, and averred that she was honored by the privilege. She also took Signora Gentileschi and Signorina Constantia off to her own cabin, after having hauled a couple of half-grown boys out of the store, one to take the horses to the stables and the other to take the men to the barracks.

"Told you," Ron said, as they tucked into ham sandwiches. "Piece of cake."

Gerry looked at him. "It's rye bread."

"Whatever."

Buchenland

"Y'know," Mark Early remarked. "If Freiherr von Schlitz wasn't in jail again for plotting against the government of the SoTF, he'd hate this. Absolutely hate it."

Orville Beattie grinned. "Yup. Henry's holding up real well. Rip-roarin' job of stumping. God, what a stroke of luck that we managed to get Constantin Ableidinger to come at the same time. The newspapers are eating it up. 'Handing on the torch'—ain't that how the Magdeburg paper put it? I've got to say that Jason Waters in Frankfurt has been earning his keep, too." He looked at the back of the wagon bed that Henry was standing on. "What do they call it—what the Kastenmayer boy is doing?"

"Simultaneous translation."

"I thought that was sign language."

"They do it from one language to another, too. Gets the words out in the second language while the audience can still hang onto the tone of voice that the speaker was using when he said them in the first language."

"Then when Henry gets tired, Ableidinger booms at them for a while."

"We ought to get some great publicity when Henry goes down to Frankfurt to meet Ronnie."

"If we don't, Wes wasted a lot of money on flyers. Wackernagel wangled the printing contract for his brother-in-law. Jason Waters promised to get it into the Frankfurt papers. We'll send a messenger down when the motorcade reaches Gelnhausen. We're pacing ourselves. Mainz is going to radio through when Ronnie gets onto the Main barge there, so we can stage an impressive reunion."

"Like, 'Dr. Livingstone, I presume'?"

"Sort of. But I don't think there were any reporters at that one."

"At least one's bound to have been there. It wouldn't be so famous if someone hadn't covered it."

Wes Jenkins took his glasses off and put them safely on the nightstand. *On your face or in the case*, he recited under his breath. The optometrist had taught him that when he was six years old. Jim McNally would be proud of him for remembering it, he expected, but it was really sheer self-interest. He could get new frames down-time, if he had to. There were people in Grantville right now, jewelers' journeymen, mainly, studying how to make hinges, so people didn't have to wear those things that were expected to stick on the bridge of your nose by themselves, whatever they were called. But they wouldn't be lightweight titanium.

He picked up the conversation again. "I'm worried about them both, Lenore and Chandra. Bryant Holloway was never the man I'd have picked for Lenore at all, not that I had anything to say about it at the time. And Nathan's been so . . . standoffish, lately. Like for the past year, at least, from what I can pick up from her letters. They're both out of town all the time. It's hard on a young woman to have to bring up her children alone, to be mother and father both."

"You can't live their lives for them. Especially not at ten o'clock in the evening when you are in Fulda and they are in Grantville." Clara slipped under the comforter. "Think about the good things. How well your idea for the speaking tour is working out."

"I didn't really expect people to be quite so impressed with

Henry. After all, he's just a small town mayor. Not some dramatic or charismatic political figure."

She curled up and tucked her head under his chin. "That's why he impresses them."

"You've lost me."

"The people who come to hear him are village and small town mayors and councilmen too, mostly. And their wives. Or ordinary people who aren't even on the councils. Almost all of them. It's important that he *isn't* some remarkable and alien hero. What you would call a superman. He's average size. Short and a little scrawny, for an up-timer, but average size for the seventeenth century. He isn't as young as he used to be. He walks with a cane. He faces a lot of the same problems that they do, such as tight budgets and people who constantly complain to the point that there's no pleasing them. He doesn't pretend that he has all the answers. He just says that he does his best and keeps on trying."

Wes snuggled her in a little closer and kissed the top of her ear.

"No, don't distract me. I'm not done yet."

"Finish up, then."

"For people like these, Mike Stearns or Hans Richter may be an inspiration, yes. Constantin Ableidinger is an inspiration, too. But Mr. Dreeson is a comfort. They know, most of them, in their own hearts, that they will never be heroes. He shows them that they don't have to be, to be good citizens. To be a valuable part of the USE that we're trying to build."

"I hear you."

"He doesn't glorify what he has done in Grantville. He doesn't say anything about being part of a great miracle. He just talks about local government—says that he was mayor before the Ring of Fire and he's kept on being mayor. Doing the same job to the best of his ability. Nothing fancy. Nothing new and special. The same man, doing the same job. That is what he shows them."

"Sometimes, maybe, that's all a man can do."

Chapter 14

Scotland

The news of an official peace treaty between Gustavus Adolphus and the king in the Netherlands had not improved Antoine Delerue's mood. The arrangements between the Swede and Denmark the previous summer had been bad enough, but this was appalling.

The simultaneous arrival of two letters from Guillaume Locquifier had ruined the day altogether. Their arrival was simultaneous because the first one had been delayed in transit, waiting in a bin in the office of that fool Mauger in Haarlem until he had a wine shipment ready to go out to Glasgow.

"Locquifier is an idiot. Can't he make up his own mind about anything?"

Michel Ducos shook his head. "I did, very specifically, instruct him not to take any action without my consent."

Delerue frowned. The problem here was that Michel's personality was so forceful and intimidating that people tended to overdo his instructions. But it was an old problem, and not one for which he'd ever found a good solution. Michel was simply too valuable to the cause for Delerue to be willing to risk a sharp clash with him.

He looked around the room. André Tourneau was arguing with Levasseur and the other two Lyonnais silk weavers. Mademann, the Alsatian, was, as usual, off by himself.

"The time is not yet ripe for us to act," Ducos said firmly. "And in Frankfurt, of all ridiculous places. What kind of symbolism would Frankfurt bring to our great undertaking?"

Delerue decided he was probably right. The situation in France still needed to mature. Gaston needed to consolidate his base of support. Although Delerue wasn't sure how much success the king's brother would have, given the naturalization of that very capable Italian Mazarini. The one who, after the debacle in Rome, had moved to France and was now throwing his diplomatic talents behind Richelieu. And his talents were not inconsiderable.

Delerue picked up what he had been saying earlier. "The proposed treaty terms . . ."

Tourneau, who had once been a steward for the de Beauharnais family, broke off from his argument with Levasseur and waved a hand. "Are very unsatisfactory! Why hasn't Henri de Rohan at least issued a public condemnation of any idea that France might accept them?"

Delerue shook his head. "As for Rohan, *pah!* He is a weakling and Richelieu's lackey. I have written a new pamphlet explaining it all. I will be sending the manuscript to Mauger by the next packet so he can arrange to have it printed."

Abraham Levasseur focused his eyes on Tourneau. "There is no possible treaty between the Swede and France that we could describe as satisfactory. Not so much because the Swede is the Great Satan—that is what the *dévots*, Père Joseph's Catholic fanatics in France, are calling him. So we must not. But—"

Delerue intervened again. "But because peace in France, any peace on any terms, means that Richelieu will get a second chance to entrench his rule. Even if Stearns prevails on Gustav Adolf to offer France more lenient terms, we will be opposed."

"What we need," Ducos announced a few hours later, "is a coordinated operation. Europe-wide. One that will backlash on Richelieu, since everyone will blame him for it."

"That's going to take money."

"In that matter, at least, Guillaume has shown himself to be effective. Our treasury is refilling rapidly."

"Other than persuading wealthy men to contribute, by whatever means, what can he do though? In Frankfurt, that is?"

"I will tell him what to do."

Enough time had passed since Ducos first read Locquifier's letters that he had managed to interpret them to his own satisfaction. "Guillaume has demonstrated his unswerving loyalty by adhering faithfully to the orders I gave him before we left. He should be rewarded for this, not condemned. I shall appoint him as my coordinator for all actions within the United States of Europe."

"Guillaume?" Tourneau emitted a disbelieving hiss, half under his breath.

Ducos heard it. "Unquestioning obedience, especially when it goes contrary to a man's own instincts, is a rare quality. It should be rewarded."

Tourneau glanced at Delerue, but saw that Antoine was not inclined to dispute the point with Michel.

So, he nodded. What else could he do?

"Antoine."

"Yes, Michel?"

"You must write to Guillaume. You must explain to him that while his decision concerning the Dreeson woman and the Stone boys was correct, we must conduct another assassination. Several assassinations, probably."

Delerue scratched notes on the back of Locquifier's second letter.

Ducos kept talking. "But they must be major actions, of true political significance, designed in such a way that Richelieu will be blamed for them. Assassinations that will destroy any prospect for peace. A wave of assassinations, flooding across the map of Europe. No. Wait. Stop. Scratch that out. One massive assassination.

"Assure him that he and the other men in Frankfurt will play a major role in regard to the portion of our great plan that will unfold in the United States of Europe. They will have the honor of planning and carrying out the deaths of Michael Stearns and Rebecca Abrabanel."

He paused a moment. "And of Gustavus Adolphus and Princess Kristina." He paused again. "And of Wilhelm Wettin. All on the same day, for maximum effect. In Magdeburg, the so-called 'imperial capital.' In front of one of the spectacular, if as yet unfinished, new buildings. There is no reason for us to carry out picayune little actions against people who are, in the great picture, insignificant. As for the Stones . . . Yes, in Rome, they did us a great disservice. But their time will come. After we have achieved our greater goals."

Tourneau cleared his throat. "That's very . . . ambitious, Michel."

Fortunately, Ducos interpreted the comment as a compliment. And, unfortunately, Antoine was still not inclined to dispute the matter. Not for the first time in the history of their organization, Michel Ducos' force of personality would drive a decision that was perhaps not wise on its own merits.

Delerue sent his letter containing Ducos' instructions out on the next packet boat to the Netherlands. It would take some time, even with the most favorable weather. To Laurent Mauger in Haarlem, then to Isaac de Ron at the inn *Zum Weissen Schwan* the next time Mauger had cause to travel to Frankfurt, for they had given de Ron the strictest orders not to trust the postal system. De Ron would turn them over to Locquifier.

De Ron was a reliable man. Laurent Mauger was also reliable, he supposed. But, at the very least, not overcurious. That in itself was a virtue.

Haarlem, Netherlands

Laurent Mauger surveyed his warehouse with pride.

Excusable pride, he thought. He had built a business that supported his entire family. Supported it well. Not to mention, employed most of it.

His sons were learning the business. Barendt and Jan Willem, the only survivors of the nine children born to his late wife. Barendt was twenty-two already. Time flew. He'd need to start looking for a wife pretty soon. Jan Willem at eighteen could afford to wait a few more years before worrying about such weighty matters.

Neither was home. Barendt was observing wine-making in the Moselle Valley. Jan Willem had accompanied his cousin Pierre Guillaume de Grasse to Italy on a buying trip.

Which brought Laurent to those who had finished learning the business and now helped him run it. Pierre Guillaume was his chief buyer. He was the younger son of his widowed half-sister, Marie, who ran his household here in town. Her older son, Laurent, called Lolo by the family, was his chief accountant. Her daughters, both unmarried, lived at home.

A slight shadow passed over his face. The girls should be married by now, but their brothers were reluctant to let the dowry money bequeathed by Marie's late husband out of their own hands.

Then there were the sons of his deceased half-sister Louise. Jan Dircksen Pieterz was, unfortunately, as improvident as his late father had been. Mauger kept looking for some avenue by which Jan might display his talents. Thus far, none had appeared, and the boy was . . . um . . . thirty-six years old now, it must be. Still, he was family, so he must be fed—and luckily, he hadn't married. For the time being, he was in charge of arranging shipping contracts. Somebody else always double-checked the arrangements he made, of course. Usually his younger brother, who was cautious and careful, if not particularly resourceful.

They couldn't have dowered their sisters if they wanted to. Dirck had died bankrupt. So both Alida and Madeleine were, to put it plainly, upper servants. Ladies-in-waiting to the wives of wealthy merchants. Not chambermaids, but not far above that status, either. They fetched, carried, read out loud, made lace.

He had offered to dower them, but they were both too proud. Or ashamed that he had needed to make the offer. Alida had been in her teens when Dirck went bankrupt and killed himself. Madeleine was old enough to remember that time.

All six of those boys, his own sons and the sons of his half-sisters, had a remarkable sense of entitlement where the business was concerned. They thought of it as already theirs, although he was far from dead yet.

Nowhere close to dead. How surprised they would be if they knew that his sedate business trips also involved secret work for the Huguenot cause!

His greatest affection was reserved for his younger sister Aeltje. She wasn't here. Widowed like Marie, she had chosen not to depend on him when Louis died. Rather, she had remained in Leiden, where she had turned her large house into a residence for a dozen or so students. Both of her sons were attending the university. Mauger liked the boys, too. Jean-Louis was studying science and engineering. He said that the chemistry, at least, would be of use in the wine business if he some day joined the firm. The younger boy had started classes this semester. Aeltje was no longer young, but now she had the help of her daughter Marte, who had a quite respectable dowry.

With any luck, Marte would soon find a husband in the form

of one of her brothers' friends. University towns were useful, that way. They provided a pool of promising young men, preselected for a certain minimum level of intelligence and ambition.

Aeltje was not stupid. That might be why she was his favorite sister.

Mauger spent three days reviewing the business developments that had occurred while he was gone. Then he couldn't put it off any longer. He would be made to regret it if he postponed it any farther.

It was time to face the villa.

He had bought the villa after Adriaantje had died. His late wife. A saint. Not in the idolatrous Catholic sense of the word, of course. Rather, a saint as in "a woman of noble character."

The "girls" had lived with them throughout their marriage. Not one of them had been willing to assume responsibility for the household after Adriaantje died. They said that, never having married, they had no experience in the matter.

So he had asked Marie. Who came and, a scant three months later, proclaimed: "Either they go or I go."

He needed Marie in his Haarlem townhouse. So he bought the villa. Hired a steward and a housekeeper. It was a truly lovely country home.

The door opened. They emerged like a flock of crows. His oldest half-sister, Catherine. She was seventy-two now. Followed by his three older sisters.

Not an Arminian among them. Surely that consistency of theological opinion in his family was something of which a man could be proud.

But he would prefer to be away on a business trip.

Grantville

"Perhaps he is interested in you." Veda Mae pursed her lips. "Personally, I mean."

Velma Hardesty shook her head. She might not be a brain, but one thing was always perfectly clear to her. "Look, Veda Mae. I can *tell* when a man's interested in me."

"You've certainly had enough chances to practice that skill."

"Thanks for the compliment. But, what I mean is—Jacques-Pierre isn't. Interested in me, I mean. Except for teaching me to Meditate. Which must have been Meant. By the Stars, you know. It's sort of too bad. He's in great condition."

Veda Mae cocked her head to the side. "Spending every day trotting alongside a wagon and heaving the contents of garbage cans into it will do that for the old biceps and triceps and abs, I suppose. Several of the orderlies at the assisted living center—why don't they tell the plain truth and call it an old folks home or a nursing home, the way people used to?—are in really good shape, too."

Velma raised her eyebrows. "Window shopping?"

"I'm a widow," Veda Mae said righteously. "It's perfectly proper, as long as all I do is look."

Chapter 15

Frankfurt am Main

"*Solch eine Schlamperei!*" Johann Wilhelm Dilich was screaming at the top of his lungs.

Nathan Prickett wasn't quite certain that there was one word that could translate all thc nuances into English. It was carelessness combined with messiness combined with filthiness. Filthiness like dirt, not filthiness like porn. Maybe even a little recklessness, combined with quite a bit of fecklessness.

The militia captain was looking horrified.

The people who prepared bodies for burial had already come and gone.

The demo was supposed to have been a showpiece. Showing off all the nice new gun-shaped toys the militia had been practicing with.

It had been quite a bang. Amideutsch had coined a word. *Boomenstoff.* Stuff that went boom. Or bang. Or bam-bam-bam. Or blam. Most of the words that used to come with exclamation points after them in comic books.

They'd been storing a lot of *Boomenstoff* in the bunker.

That was a really big hole in the redoubt now.

The bright spot was that they were south of the river, in Sachsenhausen. At least it hadn't happened right downtown.

Who in hell had taken a candle down into the bunker where the guys were loading? They weren't even supposed to go down there wearing any iron, for fear of striking a spark. Dusty air was dangerous, even if the dust wasn't gunpowder. Once, once when he was a kid, he'd managed a pretty good boom just by throwing a canister of his mom's flour up into the air. Everybody knew about grain elevators. Well, the down-timers didn't have grain elevators.

But it was all spelled out in the manual. Line by line, word for word.

Fat lot of good that had done.

Seven men dead. For a couple of them, they wouldn't find enough to bury. That included the guy with the candle, whoever he'd been. They could probably identify him by a process of elimination. Figure out who everyone else was, alive and dead. He'd be the one they couldn't account for. Forty-three injured, including two officers from patrician families.

The muttering in taverns throughout Frankfurt had started the evening after the catastrophe at the Sachsenhausen redoubt.

There was always some level of resentment of the ghetto in the city, because of its size. Except for possibly Nürnberg, Frankfurt had the largest Jewish population of any city in the Germanies. The last time it really boiled over had been twenty years before, during the so-called Fettmilch revolt.

The Jews. It must have been the Jews.

It didn't make any sense. Nathan ran his hand through his hair. There had not been a single Jew involved.

They must have contaminated the powder.

How in hell could they have done that? It was kept in the magazine in Sachsenhausen.

They changed the instructions in the manual on how to handle it somehow. Left out a step. Or added one, maybe, so the next one didn't work right. Just enough that our sons and brothers would have to suffer.

The manual was perfectly good. What's more, the militia captain had promised to have all the men read it. That he would drill them in the procedures.

And he had kept his promise.

It had been plain, ordinary, contrary, human stupidity. Pilot error, as people said.

The up-timer. He is called Nathan. His name is Jewish.

Nathan had a suspicion that they wouldn't be a bit more pleased when they found out that he was Methodist. He picked up his pen.

Dear Don Francisco.

You won't believe what is going on here. Or, maybe you would.

This was going to be a long letter.

On the Reichsstrasse between Fulda and Steinau

The two drivers and three mechanics were patching a tire on the rear ATV. Again. This time, it had taken a sharp rock.

About fifty or sixty men from the Fulda Barracks Regiment were watching with great interest. It was taking a while. The patch kit had been sitting on a shelf in someone's garage ever since inner tubes went out of style, up-time. The patches weren't for this kind of tire. The goop wasn't what it had once been.

Henry Dreeson was sitting on a different rock, waiting for them to finish. Margie and her husband had taken a trip to Europe once, back up-time. A package tour. Afterwards, the next time she came home to Grantville for a visit, she'd brought a video for her parents to watch. *If It's Tuesday, This Must Be Belgium.* That was the title, or something like it.

He was beginning to understand what his daughter's excursion must have been like.

"Where are we?" he asked Martin Wackernagel.

"About five miles northeast of Steinau an der Strasse. On the *Reichsstrasse*, that is. That's where we'll be spending the night."

"Wackernagel, I hate to tell you this, but if by the word *Reichsstrasse* you folks mean something like 'superhighway,' the follow-through on construction leaves something to be desired."

Cunz Kastenmayer, always the peacemaker, said, "You have to admit that it is much better than some of the rural roads we have traveled during the past two weeks in Buchenland County."

Dreeson nodded a little reluctantly. "Yep. Some of them were worse than anything I'd seen since about, oh, 1950 or 1960 in up-time West Virginia. Before the War on Poverty. Thank God for four-wheel drive."

A couple of horses came in sight around the bend behind them. The riders stopped suddenly. They had planned to lag back far enough that the motorcade never spotted them.

Derek Utt was looking back. "Jeffie," he yelled. "Jeffie, what in hell?"

Jeffie Garand—Sergeant Garand now, Henry reminded himself—was moving up to face his commander.

"Ah. Um. Well, Gertrud and her stepmother wanted to come along to see the sights in Frankfurt, since the rest of us are going. I know you always say 'no camp followers,' but that's not exactly it. They're going to find a different inn to stay at, everywhere we stop, and they're paying their own way."

Utt looked around again. "Sergeant Hartke, did you know about this?"

Helmuth Hartke, father of Gertrud and husband of Dagmar, came forward. Dragging his feet a bit. "No, sir." He cleared his throat. "I understand the problem, sir. Dagmar really shouldn't be riding right now. In her condition."

Utt groaned and looked at Henry Dreeson.

He didn't have to ask. "Sure," Henry said. "We'll be glad to give her a place in the car. I'm sure Martin won't mind riding her horse the rest of the way into Frankfurt. He rides the *Reichsstrasse* all the time. It's his job."

Jeffie looked at Gertrud. Then at Wackernagel. He'd picked up a couple of rumors about the courier, when it came to girls. That's all they were, rumors, but . . .

Gertrud was *his* girl. He looked at Derek Utt.

"Maybe Gertrud oughta ride in the car with Dagmar? In case that she has, you know, female troubles, or something. Cunz can ride the other horse."

Derek sighed, waved one hand, and proclaimed, "So be it."

Frankfurt am Main

"Michel has gone mad," Mathurin Brillard said, almost snarling the words. "Stark, raving mad. Assassinate *Stearns*?"

Guillaume Locquifier glared at him. But not even Locquifier, with his near-adulation of Ducos, was prepared to argue the matter straight out. Instead, all he said was: "We will have to give Michel's orders some thought. Hard thought."

Those thoughts came to a consensus without much difficulty. It didn't take long, either. Two bottles of wine, at most.

Nobody said out loud that Michel Ducos really *must* have already heard about the group of Yeoman Warders whom the now-fabled Captain Lefferts had brought with him out of England—and who now served the USE's prime minister as a bodyguard. Or that, if not, he really should have. Ducos should have realized that Stearns would be almost impossible to assassinate, at least with the resources at their disposal.

True, the pope's guards had been as ferocious—but there, they'd had the advantage of surprise. Nobody had really expected anyone to make a serious assassination attempt on the pope. Whereas no one in Europe, down to village idiots, had any difficulty imagining the multitude of enemies who might wish to assassinate Michael Stearns.

No, it was simply out of the question to assassinate the USE's prime minister. Or his wife, for that matter. The protection of the Yeomen Warders extended to her also.

Robert Ouvrard shook his head. "Security is too tight around Gustavus Adolphus and Princess Kristina, too. The Swedes and Finns who guard them really mean business. If it comes to dying for them, those men will do so."

Locquifier chewed his upper lip. "Who does that leave, then? Wettin?"

Ouvrard shook his head. "Wettin doesn't have Yeoman Warders, but he does have bodyguards who take their jobs really seriously. Almost the only place we could reach him would be when he attends church. I am afraid that we all still have unfortunate memories of the last time Michel tried an assassination in a church."

"And what would be the point, even if we could kill him?" asked Brillard. "There is at least a logic to Michel's proposal to assassinate Wettin *along with* the USE's emperor and prime minister. But without them, simply killing Wettin will accomplish nothing. Let us not forget that the purpose of all this is to prevent the signing of a peace treaty—on any terms—between France and the USE. How does killing Wettin by himself advance that goal by so much as one step?"

Carefully, he did not refer openly to the significance of what was actually the single most important word in his statement. The term *proposal,* as applied to Ducos' instructions.

Not to his surprise, no one in the room chose to challenge the term. Not one of them, not even Locquifier, was as enthusiastic about martyrdom for the cause as Michel and Antoine were. Michel in practice; Antoine in theory.

"Do we inform Michel that we can't do it, then?" Ouvrard asked.

Locquifier shook his head. "Ah, no. Not a good idea."

They looked at one another. It was always a possibility that some member of the group held secret instructions to exert a very final sort of discipline against any others who appeared to be wavering. It was even possible, theoretically, that the one of them who held such instructions might also act as a provocateur, expressing dissenting opinions to see if anyone else was prepared to agree with them. Even Jesus Christ had his Judas.

Locquifier leaned back. "Instead, let suggest some softer targets. Chose someone for whom the security level is not so high."

Ouvrard nodded. "Ableidinger? That would certainly sow confusion in Franconia. And he's a Lutheran, so it would be plausible to blame it on Richelieu."

Locquifier was still chewing his lip. "No 'lackeys,' remember? Michel is adamant about that. The Richter woman? The one they call Gretchen?"

Ouvrard shook his head. "She's hardly a 'softer target.' She has Committee of Correspondence security coming out of her big tits."

"The up-time admiral and his wife?"

"Possibly," Brillard said, "if we could get close to them while they are in the Netherlands. In Magdeburg, Achterhof and his men have them, also, under a very tight watch."

Locquifier frowned. "But Michel's instructions say that the assassinations must occur in Magdeburg. Just as the death of the pope had to occur in Rome. A country villa somewhere, when Urban VIII was on vacation, would not have done at all. Because of the symbolism. Antoine also emphasizes that it must be Magdeburg. Because it is the new imperial capital. All on the same day. To demonstrate how weak these 'leaders' really are."

"And does Antoine suggest how we should persuade these several people to gather together for us in a convenient group?" Brillard's tone was sarcastic. "Just as one would scarcely expect Stearns' Jewish wife to attend church with William Wettin, I truly do not expect to see all of our possible 'soft targets' in one place at one time, either. Not to mention another small problem."

Locquifier raised his eyebrows.

"Of all of us whom he left behind in Frankfurt," said Mathurin, "I am the only one with enough skill with a rifle to carry out an actual assassination. From any distance, at least. I suppose that either of you, or Gui or Fortunat once they are back with us, might have the same luck with a knife as the man who killed Henri IV. I don't see how we could get that close. Certainly not to the whole group at a public event, which is the only time they are all likely to appear together. Not that I have any qualms about the action itself. I served as a sniper long enough. As a practical matter, having only one competent shot places limits on the grandiosity of our ambitions. Something which Michel and Antoine seem to have forgotten about."

"That's what I managed to overhear," Isaac de Ron finished. He glanced out the window. "I had best be going, my lord. I have been here, supposedly in your cellars talking to the butler, for much longer than I would need to stay for even the most complex delivery of fine wines. Someone might notice."

"I suppose you would not want me to ruin your reputation by having the butler complain in public that you delivered inferior goods and he was rebuking you?"

Benjamin de Rohan, duke of Soubise, was trying to be jocular, but de Ron jerked his head up. "Never!"

"Very well then. I will let my brother know of your fears that Ducos is planning additional assassinations." Soubise stood up.

De Ron withdrew. He recognized permission to depart when he saw it.

On the Main River

Ancelin and Deneau sat quietly in the back of the barge.

Locquifier's assumptions had been wrong. The old woman had no maid or steward or driver. None of the ordinary attendants of a traveling gentlewoman.

She did have a bodyguard, which was unexpected. When she left the Rhine packet at Mainz, the commander of a detachment of guards wearing Bernhard of Saxe-Weimar's livery—guards who were accompanying a young girl—detached four of them to go with "Mrs. Dreeson."

That was presumably because she was the grandmother of Hans Richter. She had no real distinction of her own, but even Frankfurt by now had renamed a square in honor of the "hero of Wismar."

The girl had hugged her. Hard.

Why, they could not imagine.

Nils Brahe, Gustav Adolf's commander in Mainz, had met her in person. She had immediately addressed several complaints to him. She had no information she had not gotten from newspapers. Nobody had sent her any information about her schools. Was Annalise all right? What about the other children? If one of them had died during the summer, she was sure no one had thought to tell her. She had not had a word from Amberg. Had those young idiots Thea and Nicol starved to death when they went off without a bank draft? Where was Elias Brechbuhl? Had Hieronymus Rastetter been in touch? She had no expectations that those Jesuits were any more cooperative now than they had been last spring. Had Cavriani arrived in Geneva safely with his son? Well, of course not—they had probably been set upon by bandits along the way. What about Mary Ward and the English Ladies? Had they all been raped by mercenaries between Neuburg and Grantville? Why was everybody else in the world too busy to tell her *anything*?

She had continued to make similar comments ever since they got on the barge. Directed, now, not to Brahe, but rather to a young German officer, the head of her bodyguard. She spoke quite clearly. Of course, her false teeth were famous, now. Almost as famous as Wallenstein's jaw. Several newspaper reports covering her escape from Bavaria in company with the "wheelbarrow queen" and the admiral's wife had mentioned the effective way she used them.

Ancelin almost felt sorry for the archduchess Maria Anna, if she had to put up with this for what must have seemed like two very long months.

The conversation of Veronica Schusterin, *verw*. Richter, *verh*. Dreeson, was an apparently unending paean to the concept "cranky." That was all they had learned from their observations.

"I wonder what Guillaume expected us to learn?" Deneau whispered. "Or did he just want to get us out of the way? Do you suppose the others have planning something while we've been gone? Are they going to exclude us from some new project?"

Ancelin shook his head. "It was exactly what he said, probably. A concession to our desire to actually *do* something. Not just sit in de Ron's back room and talk. Now be quiet. I'm trying to listen."

"Why? Nothing important is going to happen on this stupid boat. I don't think I've ever come across such a pessimistic old lady."

In addition to the two of them, the bodyguards, and old woman, there were several other passengers. One man, dressed in black riding clothes, sitting by himself at the far front, had been escorted to the pier by a couple of Nils Brahe's Swedes.

A courier, probably, Ancelin thought.

Frankfurt am Main

As soon as the barge tied up, the man in black got off. He walked up to the lanky, freckled redhead who was commanding a group of sickly-shade-of-salmon-pinkish-orange-uniformed soldiers. That had to be Utt, the commander of the Fulda Barracks Regiment. Ancelin could figure out that much from the newspaper reports he had read in Mainz. *And doesn't that color clash with the man's hair*? he thought. *Terrible. No sense of style at all. If he had chosen a rich brown, or even a deep shade of rust . . .*

Before he became a conspirator, Gui Ancelin had been a tailor.

But that had been another world. Before Richelieu's siege of La Rochelle, he had also been a man with a wife and three children. A father and two sisters. Before the starvation and the plague brought by the siege. Louis XIII's siege. Richelieu's siege.

The newcomer was waving a sheaf of papers. Utt turned and told off a half-dozen mounted soldiers. They moved away, one of them calling for a water boy to bring up one of the remounts.

A courier, then. Nothing to get excited about. Couriers came and went all the time.

Then the bodyguards debarked. Followed by Frau Dreeson in full spate.

An elderly man limped down the quay to meet her.

"Henry, what were they *thinking* of, sending you on such a strenuous trip? What if you had fallen? Remember what Doctor Nichols told you. Hip replacements are a thing of the past. Or of the far future, depending upon how a person looks at it. Or the ATV had an accident and you were thrown out? You could have been killed. What good would a hip replacement have done you then, even if you could have one?

"What were *you* thinking, for that matter, going off and leaving Annalise alone with the children.

"No, it does not matter that Thea and Nicol are there. It is just as well they didn't die, I suppose, but being alive is no remedy for being fools. They were alive when I met them in Grafenwöhr and fools there, already. Just one more expense for you, I suppose. It would be too much to hope that they are paying their own way."

By this time, she was halfway up the pier, the bodyguards closed in behind her. Ancelin and Deneau stayed at the rear of the other debarking passengers, but they could still hear her voice, ranting away.

Then she reached the head of the pier, where the formal reception party was waiting. Stopped. Lifted her head and smoothed her face.

"I am honored to make the acquaintance of the *Bürgermeister* and councilmen of Frankfurt and their gracious wives."

The *Bürgermeister* turned to another man. "Permit me to present you to *Monsieur le duc de Soubise*, a guest in our city."

The wrinkled old harridan curtsied quite properly.

Ancelin couldn't quite believe it.

Of course, he had never encountered the abbess of Quedlinburg.

The *Bürgermeister* had turned to his prominent guest again. "*Monsieur le duc*, may I present Mayor Henry Dreeson of Grantville. Herr Wesley Jenkins, the State of Thuringia-Franconia's administrator in Fulda. His wife. Major Derek Utt." He proceeded through the litany, having carefully memorized the list that his secretary had given him the evening before.

Soubise inclined his head. "It is my pleasure. My brother, the duke of Rohan, has already met one of your fellow-countrymen, Monsieur Thomas Stone. In Padua, where he presented him with an autographed copy of his translation of the life of Duchess Renee of Ferrara. He was very favorably impressed with Monsieur Stone's lectures and delighted to extend hospitality to his son Elrond at his current headquarters in Switzerland. He finds him to be a very promising young man."

The Grantville contingent blinked but, all things considered, bore up well under this rather startling information.

Occasionally, the newspapers did miss something.

Chapter 16

Frankfurt am Main

"Angry people are, mostly, just angry people," said Henry Dreeson. "It's their nature. Solve one of their problems and they'll find something else to be angry about. Maybe because you solved it and took away their gripe."

Henry figured that this ceremonial banquet with the Frankfurt bigwigs was going fine. Shop talk was shop talk, wherever you found it. Names kept floating past his ears. Günderrode. Zum Jungen. Both of them named Hector, which was sort of peculiar. He hadn't met any Germans in Grantville named Hector. Maybe they were relatives. Stalburger. A couple of men with a "von" in front of their names, though he didn't understand why nobles would be city councillors. But "Baur von Somewhere" didn't actually sound very much like he descended from some medieval knight in shining armor, and neither did "Weiß von Somewhere Else." Recent promotions, maybe—guys who had bought the farm, or at least the estate, in the most literal sense of the word.

Down the table, past the *Bürgermeister*, one of the councilmen was starting to rant about the dangers of popular revolution. Sounded like Tino Nobili going full tilt. He turned his head a little to direct his good ear toward the man. "Popular election to choose the council is the worst idea I've ever heard. And I've heard it before. If you let these CoC rabble into the city government . . . Why, the last time, twenty years ago, it took us two years to get the movement under control."

As usual. The municipal equivalent of generals fighting the last war.

"The gates of the ghetto are barricaded. The main difference from twenty years ago is that this time the defenders are armed, as well." The printer Crispin Neumann finished his report. He was known to have connections in Frankfurt's Jewish ghetto, although most people were too polite to specify what they were—namely, that his grandfather had been a convert to Lutheranism; he still had relatives who lived there.

The members of the Frankfurt city council looked at one another.

"Isn't there any way you can head it off?" Henry figured that maybe he wasn't expected to talk, him not being a citizen of Frankfurt; but, what the hell, the *Bürgermeister* had invited him to come to the meeting. He looked at the militia captain. "I mean, this town can't be that different from Grantville. Our police know to keep an eye on the 250 Club when certain sorts of things come up. Don't your watchmen do the same thing? Have a sort of list of trouble spots, that is? Even if it's in their own heads and not written down anywhere?"

The captain nodded; started to say something.

In the back of the room, someone stood up. Henry peered through his glasses. Sergeant Hartke's wife? The Danish woman, Dagmar?

"It is work righteousness to attack the Jews!"

Everyone in the room blinked.

"These men in the taverns are not good Lutherans! Think, only think!"

Her German was beginning to fray a little at the edges, but she clearly had something to say. Cunz Kastenmayer slid, as inconspicuously as possible, away from his post. He had been standing behind Mayor Dreeson's left shoulder, translating whenever a conversation between the Grantvillers and the leading lights of Frankfurt politics became too complex for either the councilmen's limited English or Dreeson's less limited, but still far from fluent, German.

"Think of the words of Paul Speratus!"

Every Lutheran in the room, obediently, thought of the words of Paul Speratus. They could do that effortlessly, of course. The hymn "Salvation Unto Us Has Come" had been a staple of the Lutheran liturgy for a century. They all knew it by heart.

"Think!" Dagmar boomed again. She started reciting in Danish, but Cunz repeated the German after her.

"It is a false, misleading dream
That God his law has given
That sinners can themselves redeem
And by their works gain heaven.
The law is but a mirror bright
To bring the inbred sin to light
That lurks within our nature.

"See!" Dagmar proclaimed. "These men who attack the poor Jews. Like little Riffa's parents, who are the sutlers at Barracktown now. Or her husband, David Kronberg, at the post office. Who has an aunt and uncle who have adopted him . . ." She paused for effect. ". . . and who live *right here in Frankfurt!*" Her voice, deep and stentorian at most times, rose to a shrill dramatic screech. "They are trying to earn heaven by their works, these anti-Semites, as you call them. But, remember—

"Christ came and has God's anger stilled,
Our human nature sharing.
He has for us the law obeyed
And thus the Father's vengeance stayed
Which over us impended.

"It is Christ's atonement that saves us. Not actions such as killing usurers. Which means," she concluded triumphantly, "that these men, these mutterers against the Jews, are *doctrinally unsound!*"

Cunz would have been struck dumb with admiration if it hadn't been his duty to keep translating. No one could possibly have come up with a condemnation of attacking the ghetto that would have a deeper resonance in a Lutheran city. Anti-Semitism as "doctrinally unsound" work righteousness. How . . .

Inspired.

Dagmar sat down. Cunz returned to his assigned place at Mayor Dreeson's shoulder.

✧ ✧ ✧

"What are you planning to do then?" the militia captain asked. "Create what Nathan Prickett would call a 'thin blue line' around the ghetto?"

He hadn't been in the planning meeting. He had been off getting his lieutenants to agree to go along with the program. Whatever the program might prove to be.

"*Ach, nein.*" The *Bürgermeister* gestured expansively. "There are not enough of us in the city government to surround it if there is a coordinated attack. Besides, since the ghetto is armed this time, not to mention reinforced . . ."

The militia captain nodded. A fair number of Frankfurt's CoC members had somehow managed to be inside the ghetto when the elders of the Jewish community barricaded the gates.

". . . we might be caught in crossfire. Which would be stupid of us. Dreeson, the Grantviller, mentioned that his daughter had many favorite words. One of them was *proactive*. This means that we do not wait for the mutterers to finish getting organized. We will not wait for an attack on the ghetto."

The captain was pretty sure that he would not like what came next. "So, then . . ."

"We shall be *proactive*. We march on the taverns where the mutterers gather. Tonight."

"Your cane will slip on a cobblestone wet with this mist. You will break your hip."

Henry Dreeson shook his head. "Nonsense, Ronnie. Anyway, if the hip has to go one of these days, at least it'll be going in a good cause. And 'march' doesn't mean 'be carried along in a litter.' Anyway, there'd be just as much chance that one of the litter bearers would slip on a wet cobblestone, fall, and throw me out. That would be a longer way down and a harder landing than if I trip myself."

Veronica glared at him. "Then," she said, "I am marching with you. Only to hold your other arm, mind you. Only to steady you if your cane should not be enough. Not for some stupid heroic cause such as the one that led Hans to his death."

Frankfurt's militia officers were, by order of the council, in full ceremonial uniform. The type of uniform that they normally wore only to awards banquets. With sashes, satin trousers, lace collars, and polished boots. Items that were both difficult and expensive to clean.

The militia captain gave his instructions. He had a loud and booming voice that carried well, too. Not in the Ableidinger league, but plenty loud enough. "One company surrounds each of the target taverns right after the bells toll. Ensure that no one leaves. Those who resist will be shot. Those who surrender will be arrested."

As usual, Nathan Prickett noted a bit cynically, seventeenth-century notions of legitimate police work diverged sharply from twentieth. Granted that they were a bunch of loudmouthed anti-Semites, the men in the taverns who were about to be set upon by the city militia hadn't actually *done* anything illegal. They weren't even drunk and disorderly yet.

Fat lot of good it would do them.

The militia lieutenants nodded firmly at their captain's instructions.

"Ensure it. You have the best of the guns from Blumroder. Your men know how to use them. No one leaves."

The captain looked around. On the average, the militiamen looked more enthusiastic about the evening's proposed project than the lieutenants did. That was Nathan's assessment, anyway, and it seemed the captain shared it.

"If anyone tries to leave a tavern," he bellowed, "the man who shoots him will succeed to the lieutenancy of the company. If more than one man tries to leave at the same time, every man in the company who shoots will receive a substantial reward."

That ought to stiffen everyone's back a bit. Not to mention encouraging the lieutenants to do a little shooting themselves. It wasn't an empty threat. Judging from their own vigorous nodding, the council had already agreed to the provision.

"In the front row with the *Bürgermeister*." The city council secretary had a list, by which he was lining up the order of march.

"I have never entered some of these neighborhoods in my life," one of the councilmen muttered.

"Maybe it will do you some good. You can learn how the other half lives."

He started to sputter; then decided that sputtering at the grandmother of the "hero of Wismar," right at this moment, was not the best idea.

The Grantville mayor was on the left hand of the *Bürgermeister*. On his right hand—the unhappy councilman grimaced—was the Danish woman who had disrupted the council hearing. And, behind the civic officials, the orange uniforms of the Fulda Barracks Regiment.

Henry looked around and yelled, "Jeffie?"

Jeffrey Garand looked rather anxiously at Derek Utt. "Derek? Uh? I mean, Major Utt?"

"Go on."

Jeffie ran to the front line.

"Is that your flute, you've got there in your hand?"

"Ah, yeah, Mr. Dreeson. It's not standard, I know, for one of the sergeants to double as a piper, but, well, I've got it, and we're not quite fully staffed, so . . ."

"You were in the marching band, weren't you? In high school?"

"Um-hmmn."

"Can you still play 'Hey, Look Me Over'?"

Jeffie sighed. "In my sleep."

"Then get on up here with the drums. We're stepping out."

The Frankfurt municipal drum corps was good. They caught on to Jeffie's rhythm in no time.

Soubise and Sandrart, watching the preparations, made particular note of the three companies of orange uniforms at the rear of the procession.

"Pour encourager les autres, I presume," the brother of the duke of Rohan remarked.

Nathan Prickett felt obliged to march with one of the militia companies, seeing as how he'd provided the arms for most of them. On the other hand, since he wasn't actually a member of the militia, he didn't feel obliged to march in the front rank. So he more or less hung around in the third rank. Close enough to "show the flag," not close enough to get hurt—well, not likely—in case the would-be pogromists in the taverns decided to fight back.

Some of them did fight, in fact, including the ones in the tavern that Nathan's company marched against. But it was a pretty lame sort of thing. You might almost call it desultory, except there was nothing desultory about the man dying in the doorway of the tavern. He'd been the first one shot, as he came rushing out with an old musket, and it took a while before he stopped howling in agony. He'd been shot three times, all the wounds coming low down in his hips and abdomen. One of the militiamen might have shot him again just to put him out of his misery, but the other anti-Semites in the tavern had chosen to pour out of a side door and that had distracted the company.

The first three of them got shot dead, too, but they were killed almost instantly.

The rest surrendered. One of them, it seemed, had piled up a few too many grudges over the years. The militia company just plain refused to accept his surrender and shot him about half a dozen times. The others got off with nothing worse than a fair-to-middling beating with gun butts before they were marched down to the city's jail. Well, what passed for a jail. Back up-time, the SPCA would have screamed bloody murder if you'd stuffed rats in that hole.

After checking around later—Henry Dreeson had a really good eye for these things and so did Sandrart, oddly enough—Nathan concluded that the experience of his militia company was about standard. Middle of the road experience, anyway. Some company had a tougher fight, but some didn't run into any opposition at all. Their targets just ran off.

"Maybe we ought to hold off on the popular revolution for a little while," the chief theorist of the Frankfurt CoC said the next day. "Pay a little more attention to some of the stuff that Spartacus is publishing. Maybe we can work out a *modus vivendi* with the council. After all, Gretchen Richter's own grandmother marched with members of the city council . . . not against them."

The others nodded, including the chairman.

There was no way for them know why Veronica had marched. Or that Gretchen hadn't known anything about the plan, much less approved her grandmother's participation in the activity.

It was impressive, Soubise wrote to his brother.

> *I have been, to some extent, surprised by the effectiveness of the Grantville mayor during this political tour. It was, after all, no more than a provincial town before the Ring of Fire. Not even a provincial capital. Nonetheless, he, in cooperation with Constantin Ableidinger, has proven to*

be effective in encouraging the successful integration of the former Franconian territories into the SoTF.

His wife, of course . . .

After that paragraph, he stopped to think again.

De Ron has not managed to gather any additional information in regard to what Locquifier may be planning. I still have hopes that continued observation of the men staying at the inn Zum Weissen Schwan *will provide us with information as to where Ducos has gone to ground.*

Dear Ruben, Nathan Prickett wrote to Blumroder in Suhl.

I expect you'll already have heard about all the excitement last night before this letter gets to you, so I'll stick to what's important. The new guns that the firm provided to the militia performed really well. I was real pleased with the results. Even though it was damp, and toward the end of the evening it started to drizzle, there were hardly any misfires.

Two of the militia lieutenants lost their jobs over it, but since we've been working through the city council and the captain, that shouldn't affect sales.

He figured that it wasn't worth wasting postage on a letter to Don Francisco. He was bound to hear all about it from a lot of other people. But someone else was sure going to expect a personal report from Johnny-on-the spot. He picked up another piece of paper.

Dear Chandra.

Erfurt

Simon Jones spread the various newspapers out on the table, sorting them by date. "I've got to say," he commented, "that it seems to have played really well in Copenhagen."

It certainly had.

Any reporter worth his wages could see the drama of a Danish woman, a Danish commoner, showing the way to the patricians of an imperial city; more, showing the way to the up-timers; to the officials of the United States of Europe, even. Jason Waters was worth his wages, and more.

Headlines, and then more headlines.

It didn't quite salve the pride of Denmark for having been forced into a second Union of Kalmar. But it sure helped.

Christian IV would present a medal to Dagmar Nilsdotter, wife of Sergeant Helmuth Hartke of the State of Thuringia-Franconia's own Fulda Barracks Regiment.

More headlines.

The same regiment that had, a short while before, heroically rescued Wesley Jenkins, the State of Thuringia-Franconia's civilian administrator of Buchenland, and his wife, his *down-timer* wife, from durance vile. (No need to mention that the jailers had already fled, leaving them nothing to do but unlock the door. Picayune details remained picayune details).

Even more headlines.

Christian IV would award the medal as soon as Dagmar could travel to Copenhagen, that was. She was expecting a baby in November.

The heroine was not a virago, not a masculinized Amazon, but an honest Lutheran wife and mother.

Gustavus Adolphus, not to be outdone or upstaged, would award a medal as soon as Dagmar Nilsdotter could travel to Magdeburg.

Christian IV announced that he would travel to Barracktown bei Fulda and present the medal in person as soon as the mother-to-be had recovered from the travails of childbirth.

Gustavus Adolphus, very busy but always alert to a good PR opportunity, announced that Princess Kristina would travel to Barracktown bei Fulda and present the medal in person.

Christian IV announced that he and his future daughter-in-law would fly to Fulda together and present the medals simultaneously.

Derek Utt and Wes Jenkins, after contemplating the topography of the immediate region, sent off a brief radio message that said, in essence, "not unless they intend to parachute out of the damned plane, they won't." To the distress of the politicians, the pilots agreed with their assessment.

Erfurt, then. Christian IV and Kristina would fly to Erfurt and proceed the rest of the way in a motorized vehicle.

That was where things stood at the moment the latest of the papers had gone to press. The reporter's breathless prose ended with: "Stand by for further announcements."

Ron Stone nodded his head. "Ain't radio communication grand?"

Chapter 17

Frankfurt am Main

Guillaume Locquifier pinched the candle out and lay on his pallet, thinking.

They should have taken out the Stone brothers when they had the chance. Lackeys or not. Everything that had gone wrong in Rome had been the fault of those . . . He couldn't think of a suitable epithet. The sons of Tom Stone were in a category beyond epithets, whatever Michel said regarding their insignificance.

The woman Veronica. The security surrounding her in Frankfurt had not been tight, except during the march itself. That had only been an artifact of the security surrounding the important civic officials.

In one way, though, Antoine was perfectly correct. She was only important because of her relatives. There was no reason on earth for Richelieu to order her assassination. No reason for anyone to order her assassination.

Except, perhaps, her own family. If the reports that Gui and Fortunat had given about her general temperament, as they had observed it on the barge from Mainz to Frankfurt, were correct, then it would seem quite possible that almost any near relative might wish to see the end of her. But that would be personal, not political.

Symbolism. Antoine wanted symbolism. When Antoine wanted it, Michel ordered it.

Richelieu, once, had sent the Croats against Grantville.

An assassination in Grantville itself? Everyone would blame that on Richelieu at once. Which would be . . . very satisfactory.

Symbolism.

Piazza perhaps? He was their president. The same office that Stearns had previously held, which would be a clear symbolic link.

Or a down-timer? Ableidinger when he was *in* Grantville. He came, occasionally, to consult with Piazza.

Or . . .

He fell asleep.

"It is clear to me now."

The other four men looked at Locquifier.

"It came to me in a dream a few days ago. The riot against the Jews. The riot here in Frankfurt that did not happen. That is something we can do."

"Here in Frankfurt?" Deneau looked puzzled.

"We have a guest." Locquifier opened the door and beckoned to de Ron, who showed another man in. "I would like to introduce Vincenz Weitz. He has a proposal for us."

Brillard knew the man. By reputation, at least. Weitz was a teamster. He spent most of his time going back and forth from Frankfurt into the little jigsaw puzzle that Nils Brahe had turned into the Province of the Upper Rhine the previous summer, hauling wine. He and a half-dozen or so like-minded friends had been prominent among the anti-Semitic mutterers after the explosion at the Sachsenhausen redoubt. Not from Frankfurt, most of them—other haulers of heavy freight. A useful occupation. They were men who were regularly on the move from place to place. It did not attract any special attention from city authorities when they came or when they left.

At Locquifier's invitation, Weitz began talking. He was arguing that it would be a major propaganda coup if they could destroy the synagogue in Grantville, thus demonstrating that the up-timers were either unable (too weak) or unwilling (thus hypocritical) to maintain in practice, right in the center of their power, the religious freedom that they advocated putting into the proposed constitution for the entire United States of Europe.

"This will destabilize Richelieu how?" Brillard asked.

Locquifier smiled. "By angering Stearns so much that he drops his opposition to the more punitive aspects of the treaty that Gustavus Adolphus intends to impose on the French."

Brillard blinked. That was . . . really quite good.

Ancelin nodded. "Such an attack would enable us to take propaganda advantage of the entire controversy going on between the Fourth of July Party and the Crown Loyalists on the topic of the level of religious toleration and the issue of a state church."

Ouvrard jumped up. "He is right. Everyone has heard of the Grantville's synagogue. Of their anarchist 'freedom of religion.' We must destroy that synagogue. Wipe out the ghetto that exists like a worm in the heart of their little radish."

Brillard stifled a smile. Clearly, Robert had not forgotten an unfortunate event that had marked the previous evening's supper. It was rare for de Ron to serve bad produce. He bought through a local grocery wholesaler name Peter Appel. Yesterday night, however . . . After Robert's experience, the rest of them had used their knives to cut their radishes in half before eating them. Which had proven to be a prudent precaution. Clearly, a field somewhere had an infestation of worms. Which was not immediately relevant, other than to the production of bad metaphors and similes, perhaps.

"They don't have a ghetto," Ancelin said. "The synagogue is right out on an open street in the heart of the town. Close to the meeting of two bridges, which is the closest thing they have to a decent market square. I've seen it marked on my map of the Croat Raid."

Weitz spoke up again. "So much the better. We will show that the up-timers cannot even protect their own pet Jews. They have built no palisade for them, leaving them open to random attacks."

"Their lack of city walls was not precisely a problem during the Croat Raid," Ancelin pointed out.

Brilliard leaned back, chewing on his upper lip. Neither Ducos nor Delerue had anything against the Israelites. Nor did he, himself. Clearly, God, for some incomprehensible reason, did not want the Jews to become Christian. If He wanted them to, they would scarcely have an option, no matter how stubborn and hard-hearted they might be. God was, after all, omnipotent.

Still, Weitz was right about one basic fact. There was a synagogue in Grantville. That might work as a starting point.

"There are five of us," Deneau said. "Five. One, two, three, four, five. I've organized riots and demonstrations before. How can our small group possibly attack such a major target, Weitz? At least, with any hope of success. We could, I suppose, lie down in front of the buildings and offer ourselves to be arrested on a matter of principle."

"The attack will succeed this time. I will plan better than the Croat leader did. We will . . ." Weitz paused.

"We?"

"I have allies. Aschmann, from Hesse; Meininger, from Schleusingen; Heft from Bamberg; others. All of whom have their own ties. You will only need to provide a distraction somewhere else. Draw their police forces away from the synagogue. Only then will my men advance."

Once Weitz had left, Ouvrard frowned. "I still don't like it. There are so few of us."

"We can give ourselves time to bring in some of our other men from La Rochelle," Ancelin said.

"So we write to Chalifour. Who will he send? Not Marin Girard—in her last letter, Jeanne said he had gone out of town with Etienne Lorion. Olivier won't part with Piquet or Marchant. Who does that leave? Léon Boucher. Georges Turpin, perhaps. Why would we want them?" Deneau threw his hands up in the air. "Even if he sent Plante and Baudin also—so we have nine men instead of five. How much does that help?"

"Jeanne shouldn't be writing about whether they are in town or out. It's none of her business," Ouvrard griped.

"How can she keep from knowing? They sleep in her attic. They eat in her kitchen. When Chalifour doesn't have jobs for them, they work in her brother's knife-grinding shop."

"Even if she knows, she doesn't have to tell you about it."

"I'm her husband."

Locquifier stood up. "We can hire others for the distraction. They don't need to know what is going on. Ordinary street thugs. Mauger has an informant in place in Grantville. He can organize that."

"Not the school. The Croats failed in their attack on the school, because . . ." Ancelin started to unroll his map. He truly loved his map of the Croat Raid on Grantville. He spent hours studying it.

"We must not let Mauger's man in Grantville know about the synagogue." Locquifier shook his head. "That would make it necessary for us to let him, whoever he is, know too much about our overall goals and purposes. We will use hired thugs for only one. Only for the distraction, but Mauger's man must not know that it is a distraction. He must think it is all we are planning. Fortunat and Vincenz must take direct responsibility for the synagogue."

"Is it a good idea to keep Mauger's agent so far out of the loop?" Ancelin asked.

"We must," Locquifier said. "It is policy."

Mathurin Brillard leaned against the wall, remembering Delerue's "Do not let your right hand know what your left hand is doing." It was pretty hard to argue with that one. Although given the complexity of what Guillaume was now planning, the "wheels within wheels" of Ezekiel 1:15–17 might be more appropriate.

Ouvrard looked over Ancelin's shoulder. "What should we tell him to target, then, if not the school? "

"There are three schools." Ancelin pointed. "But the building they call the 'middle school' is very near the synagogue, so it would not be of any use at all. The police could easily see from one to the other and move to the second disturbance."

Not any of the schools. For one thing, somewhere during the discussion, they had decided on March 4. A Sunday. In the morning. The schools would be empty.

Ancelin studied the map for a few minutes more. "The hospital. The one with the famous Moorish surgeon. It's far enough away. Since the other attack is to be on the synagogue, it is all to the good that they permit Balthazar Abrabanel to practice there, since he is Jewish. And the father of Stearns' wife." He moved his finger. "Perhaps we can actually do them enough damage to please Michel."

"Laurent Mauger must know nothing of what we plan. We must use him as a courier only. I emphasize this as strongly as I can." Locquifier tapped on the table.

"Are you sure we can rely on him? That he won't open our instructions?" Ouvrard was a congenital pessimist.

"The only sure things are death and taxes. So far, though, there haven't been any leaks from the letters we have sent to Michel through his firm." Deneau looked at Robert. "Just have de Ron flatter him a little. Congratulate him on his prudence and forethought in having someone in place."

"Do we know who his local informant is? If we're planning to use the man to organize a demonstration, not just as a source of information, maybe we should find out more about him. After all, he isn't one of ours."

"No, I don't think so, Robert. We can't control every single detail. As long as we strictly limit what information we send via Mauger, it should be safe enough." Locquifier paused in his finger tapping. "All he needs to know is that he is to find a pretext and, on the specified date, carry out a demonstration against the Leahy Medical Center."

"True. Not one word to him about the synagogue. That, we will manage ourselves."

"There should be some pamphlets," Locquifier said. "Something disseminating a sense of growing discontent. So the demonstration at the hospital will not come as a complete surprise, totally disconnected from the 'will of the people' of which the up-timers claim to be so fond."

Laurent Mauger had begun to wonder whether or not keeping an informant in place in Grantville, full time on the ground, was worth the expense, since the real center of political action in the USE had moved to Magdeburg. Now, however, he was reassured. De Ron said that his employer was pleased. That Mauger was to make sure he had an agent in place there, and to prepare that person to conduct an important propaganda blitz.

He was not only reassured. He could (and did) congratulate himself on his wisdom in not having transferred Jacques-Pierre Dumais somewhere else. In spite of the extra cost he had absorbed by hiring someone else in that someplace else.

The thought of hauling crates of pamphlets from Frankfurt to Grantville did not please him. He rarely rode. Because of his bulk, it was too hard on all but the largest and strongest of horses. But he preferred a lightweight wagon, a cart, really. He only hauled enough wine for his personal use, and let teamsters move the commercial loads. That's what freight companies were for. Pamphlets would be too heavy. He would just get Dumais his own duplicating machine.

At least he now had a good reason to visit Grantville again. The Higgins Hotel. The hot tub. Aahhh.

Grantville

"It is part of the 'destabilization' campaign against Richelieu."

"What is the connection?"

Mauger frowned. The truth was that he could not perceive much connection between demonstrating against the hospital in Grantville and undermining Richelieu's position in the French government.

Dumais laughed. "Ah, well. They have a poem, these up-timers, from a war in the Crimea that, now, will probably never happen. 'Ours not to reason why, ours but to do or die.' If they want a demonstration, they shall have one. I assure you. But why, specifically, on the fourth of March?"

"They simply had to pick a date, I presume. It is far enough away that you will have plenty of time to make arrangements. Now, as for money . . ."

Jacques-Pierre poured another glass of wine.

Yes. There were possibilities associated with his dinner companions.

Laurent Mauger was a lonely man. He had talked quite a lot during the course of their association. While he was grieving after the death of his wife, his sons and nephews had extracted a pledge from him that he would not remarry and beget a second family. They didn't want to see their inheritances dispersed. Not just a promise. A legally binding contract.

As far as he knew, Mauger's pledge had not contained any proviso about remarriage to a woman beyond childbearing age. Any widow required some provision for her support, of course, but was a temporary thing that reverted to her husband's family after her death. Not the same thing as shares allotted to additional children.

Madame Velma Hardesty, in addition to being Michael Stearns' cousin, was not a bad-looking woman—for a sleazy floozy. Silently, Jacques-Pierre rolled the English words on his tongue; he appreciated their euphony. She must *sans doute* be beyond childbearing age. He could scarcely confirm it, of course, since it would not be tactful for him to ask and would be most out of character for him to investigate that at the Bureau of Vital Statistics. Doing things that were out of character drew attention to oneself: something to be scrupulously avoided. But the oldest daughter, he had ascertained, was past twenty. And there had been a first marriage, which had produced the hopefully-to-become-a-valuable-contact son in the army. With the up-timer women it was hard to judge from their appearance, but presuming that she had married at the normal age, even a little young . . . She had to be fifty, at least.

Mauger was taking a good look. Madame Hardesty was talking about money again. Money, Jacques-Pierre knew, was something that Laurent Mauger had plenty of.

Jacques-Pierre poured more wine. Mauger had brought plenty of that, too.

Madame Hardesty said that It Was Meant to Be.

Jacques-Pierre had missed something while he was thinking about Mauger. He nodded his head solemnly. When Madame Hardesty said that something was Meant to Be, it was usually followed by a quotation from her most recent horoscope. Nodding seemed safe enough.

Madame Hardesty was certainly Meant to leave Grantville. Preferably before her conversation drove him insane.

Mauger leaned far enough forward that he could look down Madame Hardesty's yellow-eyelet-ruffle outlined cleavage.

Velma went to bed feeling pretty good about things.

Mauger went to bed thinking about Madame Hardesty's beauty. Particularly her lack of a corset.

Jacques-Pierre went home to unpack his new Vignelli duplicating machine. At least the Dutchman had brought quite a few useful things this time. Plus instructions.

Nothing about Ducos or Locquifier. Mauger never mentioned their names, but that was not surprising. Mauger's awareness didn't go beyond Isaac de Ron. Behind de Ron, in the background, there was some wealthy Huguenot patriot whom he represented, as far as Mauger was concerned.

Jacques-Pierre's own belief was that after the debacle associated with the failed attempt to assassinate the pope in Rome the previous summer, Ducos and his closest associates had somehow managed to find a hiding place in England, so it made sense that his directives would be coming through the Netherlands and Frankfurt now.

Interesting instructions. And the wonderful provision of a genuine duplicating machine. Jacques-Pierre drummed his fingers on the table. Propaganda and planning. The coming winter would not be dull.

If only he could get rid of Velma Hardesty before he succumbed permanently to *la migraine*.

"I tell you, Veda Mae, I grinned when I looked in the mirror." Velma gestured dramatically, to draw attention to her nails. She was getting a lot of good, now, from the fact that back up-time she hadn't been able to walk into a drugstore without buying cosmetics. She still had nail polish. Today, her nails featured an azure undercoat with white tips and a little glitter on each one.

"What do you have to grin about?"

"Just look at me! Jacques-Pierre comes over to the trailer and talks to me for an hour or two at least three or four times a week. He's giving me ideas that I'm supposed to Meditate on. Mental Enlightenment and Spiritual Comfort. It's done wonders. I have to admit it."

"You're about as able to meditate as . . . as . . . an ostrich."

"I *do* try to meditate, just like he says. A whole five minutes, twice a day. And to share my new insights. He gives me Themes. For each one of them, I'm supposed to walk around town every day until I've talked to at least four people. I'm supposed to Share Words of Enlightened Wisdom."

"Have people started to run when they see you coming?"

"Well, of course not. I'm supposed to share each Theme with four different people. I don't bother with that, most of the time. Whenever he gives me a new one, I share it with the receptionist at the probate court and the receptionist in Maurice Tito's office, since I have to go talk to them about Susan's money and the custody of Susan, anyway. Dropping off papers and things like that."

"Captive audiences, then. Figures."

"But I have to do extra walking to find enough people to share the rest of the Themes. By now, I know almost every place in town where I can be sure of finding several all at once. The checkout line at the grocery store. The line for the circulation desk at the public library. I figure that even if I just *say* it to the person behind the counter, I've *shared* it with everyone in line. Don't you think so?"

"More captive audiences."

"With all the extra walking, I've lost four pounds. If the bathroom scale is right, which I can't guarantee. It's ancient. Really, having someone who listens to me—really listens—has made *so* much difference in my life. So I owe you."

Veda Mae blinked.

"I can see what you were trying to tell me, now. It really does have to be Meant that Jacques-Pierre came to Grantville. He agrees that I ought to have custody of Susan. Or, least, take care of her money. He promised to help me. At least, he nodded his head the other evening, when I said it was Meant to Be."

"Mummph."

"So now I'll pay even more attention to his other suggestions in regard to Mental Enlightenment and Spiritual Comfort."

"I bet there isn't a single soul in Grantville who believes that the only comfort he's offered you is spiritual."

"Hell, Veda Mae. I scarcely believe it myself. But let me tell you something, Even if Jacques-Pierre isn't interested, his friend Laurent Mauger definitely is. A girl can tell that kind of thing."

As soon as Mauger left town again—his comings and goings served more or less as punctuation marks for the sentences that Jacques-Pierre's experiences in Grantville were writing in the story of his life—it was time to send another report to Henri de Rohan.

Dumais passed on what Mauger brought him in the way of new instructions from de Ron. Exactly and precisely as he had received them. Since de Ron would also be sending a report to the duke, the duke could worry about the question of whether Mauger had manipulated or misinterpreted anything.

In response to a question he had received from the duke himself, Jacques-Pierre confirmed his belief that that Henry Dreeson and his wife Veronica had, during this autumn, become some sort of symbols—icons or "morale builders" as the up-timers described it—of significance beyond the town of Grantville itself. Even beyond the borders of West Virginia County. Possibly even beyond the borders of the State of Thuringia-Franconia. He included things he'd heard various people say about Dreeson's "your local government in action" tour over in the Fulda and Frankfurt region.

✧ ✧ ✧

"When are you going back to Magdeburg?" Jacques-Pierre asked. He didn't mind having a sandwich with Bryant Holloway here at the Willard Hotel in the evenings. The food was awful, true. But otherwise it was more pleasant than the 250 Club. It certainly smelled better.

"Not right away. I guess Steve has some inkling that Stannard and I aren't the best of pals. He's sending me over to Frankfurt, on a temporary assignment, to work with the militia on getting fire prevention up to standard there. Actually, even though Frankfurt is Kraut country too, this won't be bad."

"In what way?"

"Well, for one thing, it will let me save some money. Nathan Prickett—he's married to my wife's sister—is over there, working on getting the city militia used to the new weapons systems that Suhl is delivering to the USE. I can stay with him; not pay rent. I should be back about the middle of December. Before Christmas, anyhow."

"Ah. This man Prickett. He is your brother-in-law?"

"No. That would be the relationship if he was married to my sister Lola. Or if I had married his sister. I'm not exactly sure myself what you call someone who's married to your wife's sister. If you're interested in finding out, I could introduce you to some of the ladies in the Genealogy Club. They know that sort of stuff."

"I would appreciate it." Jacques-Pierre meant that quite sincerely. Whenever he received a new introduction, to find out the answer to some question that he was legitimately asking, it gave him wonderful entree into more of Grantville. From some member of this genealogy club, perhaps he really could come to have a reason to go places like the Bureau of Vital Statistics. With all of its files that were guarded so protectively by the formidable Ms. Jenny Maddox.

"Actually," Bryant was saying. "Prickett's mom belongs to that club. I'll introduce you to her. And he might have been my brother-in-law if things had turned out different. He dated Lola for a while, before he started going out with Chandra Jenkins and Lola married Latham Beckworth. Grantville was a pretty small town, after all, before the Ring of Fire. Everybody knew everybody else, just about, and a lot of us are related to each other. He and Lola got into a big fight about politics and broke up. She was pretty much a left wing Democrat and he sure wasn't. It added a certain something to their relationship. They'd done it three or four times before—fought and broken up. I was sort of surprised when the last time turned out to be permanent."

"This Beckworth, then, is your brother-in-law."

"Not any more. They're divorced and both looking, sort of. They've been stuck at that level for five years, though, so I'm not holding my breath that either one of them will get married again. She caught his eyes wandering while she still hadn't quite gotten her figure back from the second kid. Well, more than his eyes wandering. She caught him and this other gal doing the horizontal tango, ten toes up and ten toes down."

"She initiated the divorce procedure, then?"

"Damn tootin'. Hell, but she was mad. Called Mom and Dad, who drove over from Clarksburg. Called me—I was working in Fairmont then. Called Latham's father. It's got to be humiliating for a woman when her husband goes out and diddles a woman a dozen years older than she is. The stuff she said about Velma, you would hardly believe."

"Velma?" Jacques-Pierre asked tentatively.

"Velma Hardesty," Bryant answered. "You know her. I've seen you talking to each other."

"Yes, I do know her. We were introduced by Veda Mae Haggerty."

"Just like us, huh?" Bryant commented.

Jacques-Pierre nodded. He was thinking that Velma Hardesty could become a liability. More than merely a cause of *la migraine*. When Mauger got back . . .

Jacques-Pierre did not particularly like the fat Netherlander, but the man was rich. Certainly rich enough to attract Madame Hardesty. Certainly, if all went well, rich enough to remove her from this town.

That wasn't part of his assignment, of course. But in some things, a man had to look out for his own welfare. Take the initiative. Much more of Madame Hardesty's conversation and he would run out into the night, screaming.

Mauger had not tried to lay a hand on Madame Hardesty. When he left town the morning after their introduction, though, she had come to the hotel to tell him good-bye. He had assured her that he would be back in a few weeks.

That was a possibility with some potential. If properly managed, it might even offer some hope.

Chapter 18

Grantville

Simon Jones stood at the livery stable next to the still-under-construction St. Thomas the Apostle Lutheran Church, right outside the Ring of Fire, on the main road to Badenburg. Really the not-yet-much-more-than-a-foundation St. Thomas the Apostle church. With winter coming on, it would probably keep that status until next spring.

They had come into Grantville from the west. The trip back had been shorter. The Duchy of Tirol had granted them safe-conducts. It seemed that among the changes in the political picture, the duchess-regent there, who was Italian, was sending out feelers to the USE. Probably nervous about Maximilian of Bavaria.

Coming through Bavaria would not have been prudent. Not at all. Swabia was still really uneasy, too. So they'd gone northwest through Switzerland, and then down the Rhine. Whatever else Bernhard of Saxe-Weimar might be up to, he was keeping the river open for commercial traffic. Then, up the Main to Frankfurt, the Imperial Road to Erfurt, and then the Erfurt-Badenburg-Grantville route.

The crews had done a lot to improve the Badenburg-Grantville road since the embassy left for Venice last winter. Of course, Thuringia had been through another prime road-improvement season since then. Now the road was not only graded and ditched, with a single wagon-width of gravel for bad weather, but macadamized on a double track, starting right where Route 250 came to an end and going all the way to Badenburg. Same thing from there up to the trade route.

After he had transferred the Gentileschis' luggage, he looked down toward the trolley stop just inside the Ring of Fire's border. He was very glad to be getting off a horse and onto a trolley. Very. He understood the priorities that were pushing the railroad north past Magdeburg. It would be great when a spur went west. It would be worth a big detour not to have to travel from Erfurt by horseback.

Pushing it south was so far off that there wasn't even any point in dreaming. He'd probably be dead before people could get on the train in Nürnberg and get off again in Grantville.

Ron and Gerry Stone, ignoring the trolley, were starting off for Lothlorien on foot. He looked after them, a little wistfully. Thirty or forty years ago, he would have had that much energy, too. At the age of fifty-two, he welcomed a seat on the trolley. A seat in which he could sit and worry about Gerry until he got home and finally saw his wife and kids again.

The trolley station had a pay phone. Not one that accepted coins. You paid the station attendant and got to use his phone. Simon called Mary Ellen and told her that he was on the very final leg of the trip back.

She said that she would let everyone at First Methodist know. And call the Nobilis and let Prudentia know that her mother was on her way.

He would really rather have gotten a good night's sleep before facing a reunion at First Methodist. He had been a minister for years, though. He realized that it wasn't feasible. He would say hello to everyone at church, eat a potluck dinner, and sleep later. Or, maybe, be too tired to sleep. Or, with better luck, not be too tired to sleep. He had really missed Mary Ellen.

Ron and Gerry left the hired horses they had ridden in on at the livery stable. They left most of the baggage there, too, in the lockup. Ron told the manager that he'd send a cart for it in the morning. The shouldered their backpacks and headed up the road to Lothlorien.

"Are you going to get a horse of your own now?" Gerry asked.

"I won't need one, in Rudolstadt, and I can always take the train back and forth between school and home. But to get back and forth between the dye works and town, you might need one."

Ron shook his head. "I hadn't really thought about it. There's no hurry and I really don't like to ride, just for its own sake. It's really almost as fast to walk back and forth, and if I have things to carry, I can always hitch a ride on a delivery wagon if I remember to schedule my meetings right."

"Look, Minnie!" Denise yelled over the sound of the motors. "It's Gerry! He's back."

"Gerry?"

"Stone. Well, maybe you didn't know him. You didn't start school until the fall of '33 and you were over in the ESOL classes then. He left for Italy with his folks the next January. But it's impossible to miss him when you do see him. Carrot top. Freckles."

"Should I run over him for you?"

"No! He's almost the only boy who was ever nice to me, back in elementary school. Polite nice, I mean. He was one year behind me, before I got sick and lost a grade—had to do it over, I mean. Since then, we've been in the same class. And he stayed nice. Not trying to grope me after I got into middle school and started to develop. Sort of absentminded about it. I don't know whether he meant to be nice to me but, he's not a pain. And he knows more chemicals to play pranks with than the average person would ever dream of. Picked the right targets. Not afraid of a fight if someone tries to hassle him. He isn't afraid of guns, either, but he's not a very good shot. You can't have everything, though. I want to offer him a lift up to Lothlorien. You can haul the other guy."

Minnie considered the matter. She did recognize the Lothlorien name. The dyes; the medications. All she had heard about the old hippie man and his three sons.

She nodded. If Denise thought this Gerry counted as a friend, or even as "not a pain," she was willing to haul the other fellow along, whoever he was.

The other fellow, who turned out to be Gerry's brother Ron, didn't have the carrot top. He was just sort of there. Not at all in the category of, "impossible to miss him when you do see him." Nothing remarkable, nothing dashing, nothing piratical.

As the hero of a ballad, Minnie thought, he would have been a total loss. He seemed to be polite nice, too, which was good in everyday life but didn't get a hero far in a ballad, either. She lost what little interest she might have had if he had been more like Denise's friend.

Pastor Ludwig Kastenmayer of St. Martin's in the Fields Lutheran Church was finding the conversation somewhat confusing.

But one point was clear. The youngest of the three sons of Herr Thomas Stone, the now-wealthy proprietor of the well known dye works, had chosen, with the consent of his father, to attend the Latin School in Rudolstadt rather than the high school in Grantville. He now, at the age of sixteen, wished Pastor Kastenmayer's assistance in being admitted in the midst of the current semester, with perhaps tutoring for some remedial work he would need to do to qualify.

While in Italy with his father and stepmother for the past nine months, he had devoted himself to private preparatory study under the guidance of two Roman Catholic priests, one of them a Jesuit.

In order to enter a Lutheran school? With the intention of further study at the university of Jena, also a Lutheran institution? Preparatory study which, apparently, the two priests had willingly provided to him?

"Actually, though," Gerry said, "they didn't know that I was going to study Lutheran theology. Because I didn't know it myself, until the very end."

Pastor Kastenmayer's little piece of the earth stopped shaking under his feet.

"You may change your mind yet, before you get that far," the other young man said. That was his older brother, Ron.

Gerry ignored him. "Not until after I shot Marius while Ducos and his people were trying to assassinate the pope. He was one of them. He had a gun. I was right in front of Marius. I shot him in the throat. Blood splattered everywhere. His head almost came off in my arms. I didn't really mean to do it, but I killed him. Marius wasn't normal. Not quite right in the head. He had a gun and he was dangerous, but mentally he wasn't all there. If I hadn't done it, he would have killed the pope. Yeah, I get that. He was a little simpleminded, but he would have killed the pope.

Now he's the one who's dead instead, and I'm the one who killed him. Did I say that his head almost came off in my arms? And I knew there was nothing I could ever do to make up for it. Until Magda explained that I didn't have to, because God already had. Atonement. It was the greatest thing I ever heard of."

Kastenmayer shook his head and fastened on one clear fact. "Magda?"

"Our stepmother," the older brother said. "She's the daughter of Herr Karl Jurgen Edelman in Jena."

Kastenmayer knew Edelman. The small piece of firm ground under his feet expanded a bit.

"She'd already baptized us," the red haired boy was saying. "Right after she married Dad, when she found out that nobody ever had done it."

A third of them are heathen rang through Kastenmayer's brain. That's what Jonas had said about gathering converts from among the up-timers. *A third of them are heathen.*

"And she's Lutheran, so I guess that she meant to baptize us as Lutherans."

"A valid baptism is a valid baptism," Kastenmayer said firmly. "For any variant of Christianity, whether truth or heresy, orthodox or heterodox." Some points of doctrine might be in dispute among Germany's Lutherans, but he would have given that reply if total strangers had roused him from a sound sleep at three o'clock in the morning and demanded to know the answer.

"She used water. And she said, 'I baptize you in the name of the Father and of the Son and of the Holy Spirit.'"

"It was Magda," Ron said grumpily. "In the greenhouse. With the garden hose."

Pastor Kastenmayer, whose acquisition of knowledge about up-time culture had not yet reached the game of Clue, ignored him. "That would be quite sufficient. But I really should get it recorded in the church registers. When did this sacramental act take place?"

The two young men agreed that it had been the spring of 1632. That was before Kastenmayer had been appointed as first pastor of St. Martin's in the Fields. Before the parish had been established. He would have to get Rothmaler in Rudolstadt to enter the three baptisms into the registers there. He made a note.

"But after I killed Marius by accident and felt so awful about it, then she told me about all of the rest of it. She had this book with her. It's called *Luther's Small Catechism*."

"I've heard of it," Kastenmayer admitted.

"Through it, I have come to understand the doctrine of salvation by grace alone. To accept all that I owe to the overwhelming mercy of God. I am certain that I have a vocation to the ordained Lutheran ministry."

Kastenmayer stared at the boy's freckles. All of his efforts to obtain "payback" for the up-timer who had married his daughter Andrea by converting other up-timers to Lutheranism paled before this opportunity. This young up-timer, of wealthy family, coming to him. Voluntarily.

God was humbling him, he knew. *Man proposes, God disposes.*

The older of the two cleared his throat. "It's awfully early for Gerry to be making a final decision. Really, all that we're sure of is that he wants to go to school this winter in Rudolstadt instead of here. We thought that if, maybe, you could give him a letter of recommendation to the school there . . ."

"My mind is made up. All the way."

"Look, Gerry. You can't study to be a Lutheran preacher until, at least, you're a Lutheran. Magda said that herself. She could baptize you, but she couldn't confirm you. Theologically, you're still somewhere out in left field."

This was confusing. "Your father does not consent to theological study?"

"He didn't say no. He'll pay for it," the younger boy said. "Magda thinks it's a fine idea. And she said that I could get confirmed at the school."

"Many men do not make an immediate decision in regard to their life work," Kastenmayer said soothingly. "Consider Dean Gerhard at Jena. He completed two years of the university medical curriculum before committing himself to another path." He prudently did not add that the other path had led Gerhard to the deanship of the theological faculty, since that appeared to be a matter of some contention between the two brothers.

Kastenmayer had spoken, over the past decade and a half, with many decent young men, scarcely more than boys, who had been dragged as soldiers into these incessant wars. Some became brutes. Others could be redeemed, keeping their consciences in the face of the things they had done. This was familiar ground. "Come into my study. I'll prepare a letter to the rector in Rudolstadt for you." He paused. "While *you*," he said to the other one, "may and will remain out here."

God had never promised him that things would be simple.

Ron was thinking much the same thing, in a more secular manner. Sometimes, since the events of last summer, his younger brother Gerry had seemed more alien to him than Mork from Ork. Before, he'd at least been able to understand adolescent testosterone overload. This religious kick . . .

After hearing Kastenmayer's summary that evening, Jonas Justinus Muselius chuckled and wrote to Pastor Johann Rothmaler in Rudolstadt, with an additional quick note to the rector of the Rudolstadt Latin School along the general lines of "we've got us a hot prospect here, so don't do anything to mess it up."

Some days were definitely better than others. Occasionally Jonas felt very tired and started to worry that he was the only person around Grantville who had really faced up to the challenge that assimilating these new immigrants from up-time was going to present for the Evangelical Lutheran Church of Schwarzburg-Rudolstadt.

It would probably be even more difficult, in the long run, than absorbing the Austrian exiles into Bayreuth or the Bohemian exiles into Saxony had been, even though there were far fewer of them. What was the English word? Oh, yes. "Diverse." They were far more diverse.

He was so glad that Ronella Koch was already a Lutheran. Not that anyone of her status would ever be allowed to marry a crippled schoolteacher. But nevertheless, he was glad.

Ron heard motorcycles coming up behind him, which meant Denise and Minnie of course. Or probably. Not many motorcycles appeared on the road out to Lothlorien.

"Want a ride?"

"Sure. Thanks."

She pulled off her helmet.

Not . . .

The other girl also. Not Denise and Minnie. Pam Hardesty. Tina Logsden's half-sister. He'd been in class with Tina until he'd been accelerated. Then he came back and heard that she'd drowned at the graduation party last spring, while he was in Italy. And—of all people to be on a Harley!—Missy Jenkins. Chip's sister.

Ron hadn't seen much of Chip the last few years. He knew in theory that Chip had gotten involved in the Committees of Correspondence and done a bunch of stuff in Jena, but in Ron's mind he was still a high school jock. Enemy of the people, in so far as the people were geeks, nerds, and hippies—categories which included the three Stone brothers, in varying proportions.

Not to mention that the Stones had been a family of disreputable hippies and the Jenkins family was about as close as a West Virginia town like Grantville ever got to aristocracy.

"I'm stopping here, Missy," Pam said. "I've got a cramp in my leg that I need to walk off. Then I'll go back. I'll tell Christin that you went on up to Lothlorien, so she'll know about when to expect you."

"Why don't you wait for me here? I won't stop; just drop Ron off and do a turnaround. I'm scheduled to work evening shift."

Missy pulled her helmet back on. "You'll have to ride behind. Buster doesn't think we've gotten good enough to try balancing with the sidecars on yet."

"Not exactly where I would have expected to see you perched, Dumpling," Ron said.

"Call me that again and I'll put you back down on the ground." Missy was noticing, really noticing, that his arms were around her. Not doing anything improper; just there, holding on.

"All right. You haven't really deserved to be called 'Dumpling' since you were in sixth grade. Whatever you did that summer between sixth and seventh was a big improvement."

"It was called puberty and included a waistline." The same waistline, she thought, that he was holding on to. Not a particularly slender or dainty one, but functional for dividing her body into an upper half and a lower half. "Why don't these things come equipped with riding whips? Useful for putting impertinent people in their place and things like that."

"Why the motorcycle?"

"I figured it couldn't hurt to learn. Not since the Ring of Fire. We're having to stretch a lot, all of us, or there isn't going to be enough to go around. Horses don't speak to me. There aren't that many full-size cycles in town, but maybe some day I can get a dirt bike of my own. And anyway . . ."

"What?"

"It's the people who are trying to keep things exactly the way they used to be who are having most trouble getting along with the way things are now. And also . . ."

"Yeah?"

"Once I had my first ride, behind Denise, I had to. Talk about a rush!"

"Do you suppose they would give me lessons? I'm not that fond of horses either. It's more fun here on the pillion than it was in the sidecar with Minnie. Did you say that dirt bikes are for sale?"

"You have to keep your eyes peeled, but every now and then there's one available. Mickey Simmons sold Kevin's after he died in that horseback riding accident last spring. I didn't have the money to buy it, though. And it wasn't the kind of thing I could ask my parents for."

Chapter 19

Grantville

"I think, Nani, that before you repeat that story, you had better correct it."

Everyone at the Jenkins dinner table looked at Missy, who was looking at her maternal grandmother.

"I had it directly from someone who had it from someone who saw the whole thing," Vera Hudson said indignantly.

"Very few of someone's 'facts' are accurate."

Missy turned. "Gertrude, now pay attention, because they'll probably be repeating it at school, too." She looked back. "Nani, there's one pretty major problem with what that person thought he saw. Or she saw. Minnie and Denise didn't take the cycles out this afternoon. Pam and I did."

Vera opened her mouth, then closed it.

"That leads logically," Missy continued, "to the fact that Minnie did not pick up Ron Stone and give him a lift out to Lothlorien. This leads logically to the fact that when Ron got off the cycle and kissed the driver, the driver was not Minnie Hugelmair."

She paused. "That's how far your narrative got, Nani. Please note that the last fact that I just provided leads logically to the conclusion that Minnie is not a down-time Lolita and Ron Stone is not a dirty old man planning to commit statutory rape, which is, I think, the direction in which your narrative was tending."

"Mother," Debbie said. "Missy. Uh. Both of you."

Willie Ray said, "Vera."

"Nani, when you consider repeating that story, if you would run through it substituting 'Missy' for 'Minnie' as a kind of preliminary, it might sound a bit different to your ears. What I don't understand is how anyone could confuse the two of us. About the only thing we have in common, as far as looks are concerned, is light brown hair. Even then, hers is straight and mine is wavy."

"Maybe someone just assumed . . ." Debbie said, a bit lamely.

Missy laughed. "For informational purposes, Mother, Ron and I were born in the same month and I think that he's somewhere between one day and two weeks younger than I am. As the evidence upon which I base this conclusion, I would adduce the monthly birthday lists that graced the classrooms we shared between kindergarten and fourth grade, when our names always came up together and his always followed mine. Since I was born on the sixteenth of December, he must have arrived in the world somewhere between the seventeenth and the thirty-first."

"That's nicely pedantic," Chad said. "You may make a reference librarian yet. Would you care to share with us the sequence of events that gave rise to this, ah . . ." He spared a sly glance for his mother-in-law. "Misunderstanding."

"Pam and I like to use that road for practice runs. It's good for our level of experience. They've improved the surface to get things in and out of the dye works, but that's the only place it goes, so there isn't a lot of traffic."

So far, so good, thought Chad. At least his daughter had avoided using the word "motorcycle," which acted on Vera like a red flag on a bull.

"We caught up with Ron. I offered him a lift and Pam decided to wait there. We were talking on the way up. It's the first time we had seen each other for, well, since they left last January. That's quite a while. I asked him if he had learned any suave Italian phrases while they were down there. He said that he'd picked up a lot of the profanity used by workers at the arsenal in Venice. Things like that. Just talking. Then when he got off, he said, '*Mille grazie, signorina,*' and performed a really flourishing bow. Then he took my hand and kissed it. That was followed by Nani's version of the significant event. I would like to point out that I was straddling the cycle, he was standing on the ground, and there was about six inches of clear air in between everything except our lips and the hand he was holding."

She took a deep breath. "We were also in full view of half of the employees of Lothlorien Farbenwerke, I think. It must have been break time or something, so you don't have to rely on Nani's informant as the sole eyewitness. Then I took Minnie's motorcycle back to the lot."

"Thank you," Chad said, thinking that she had used the word "motorcycle." Still, it was probably better to spend the rest of the meal listening to Vera on the topic of motorcycles than listening to Vera on the topic of Missy kissing Ron Stone.

"Plus, he'll be coming by in about fifteen or twenty minutes because we're going to the library this evening since I'm working tonight. The public library. Where your cousin Marietta can watch our every move."

"Oh." That, Chad thought, was definitely a curve ball. Or a slider.

"Not that one cousin or another doesn't watch every move I make in my life. I think I'll wait out on the porch."

Ron looked up the steps. Missy was sitting on the glider, wearing a sweatshirt and a glum expression on her face.

"I think," he said, "that we disturbed the cosmic rhythm this afternoon. Or the karmic balance. Or something that Dad believes in."

He climbed the steps, stopped with his hand on the banister, and looked at her again. He felt a little queasy. Up till now the girls he had seriously wanted to kiss had mostly been . . . pretty. Preferably gorgeous, but cute was the bottom cut-off and "pretty" covered most of them.

Missy Jenkins wasn't ugly. She wasn't even unattractive. She just wasn't . . . pretty.

Missy looked back at him. Ron Stone seemed more or less like he always had been. He was a little more adult-shaped than she remembered. Thicker in the chest. He didn't really look like a kid any more. But he was still himself. Straight hair, darkish blond. Medium. Medium height, width, face. Ordinary, except for the hazel eyes which proclaimed "brighter than your average bear." She knew that from being in school with him, anyway. So what had happened?

They had disturbed something, all right.

Her.

Missy didn't have anything against Ron, but she had *sooooo* not wanted to respond like that to a kiss from any guy in the world for another five years. Ten years. Until she got herself organized and had real life down pat.

"Yeah," she said. "Maybe."

"I figure it this way," Ron said. "We performed the deed that upset the equilibrium in front of my place. So we ought to be able to reverse the process if we kiss again in front of your house. That will put everything right back where it always was."

She looked around. "Interesting hypothesis. Nice persuasive tone of voice, too. You're talking to the daughter of a car salesman, though. If you think I'm going to add another chapter to Nani's story by standing here on the porch and kissing you again—rethink the program."

"Hmmn. We did it in the daylight, there, and it's still barely dusk. In order to achieve karmic balance, let's figure that the reverse process will work better if we do it in front of your house after dark. I'll accept the sidewalk if you have a quibble about the porch. Library now, kiss me again later."

In spite of herself, Missy laughed.

They weren't walking very fast. For one thing, the public library wasn't far from her house.

"What do you mean, you're studying to be a librarian?"

That really startled Ron. He'd figured that Missy had picked "library" as a place to spend what amounted to their first non-date on the theory that it was safe. Neutral. Noncommittal. A part-time job, since she had said she had to work.

Not that it was her own personal turf.

If it was, though, it sort of made sense. She was trying to put herself in charge of whatever was going on. Playing on the home field.

That kiss this afternoon had been weird.

"There weren't that many options when I graduated. Well, when you graduated, too. You knew that it was either the army or pharmaceuticals, though, and everyone knew that even Frank Jackson wanted you to work with your dad, like your brother Frank was doing—not waste the preparation you already had.

What was there for me? I didn't want to join the army. Definitely not nursing or medicine. I didn't really want to devote my life to manufacturing steel or dealing with methanol or being a radio operator. Dad could use me as an assistant for his office work, but . . . So Mom stuck me into teacher training, which wasn't bad. And being an ESOL aide at the same time was fine. I'd had the experience, in a way, with Gertrude living with us. I did that until this spring. You were off in Venice with the embassy by then. That's when Marietta talked to me."

"Marietta?"

"Ms. Fielder to you."

"The Sherman tank of Grantville Public Library."

Missy gave him a sour look. "She's Dad's first cousin and what you've been undressing with your eyes is my version of the 'Newton body.' My half-sister Anne Jefferson got Mom's shape, with her father's height. Elegant. I got this. Before the Ring of Fire, Dad was headed in an expansive direction, too. Gran doesn't have it, herself. She's paper thin, like most of the Williamses were, but she passed it on to Dad and Chip and me. It's one of my annual New Year's resolutions—never to let myself blossom to the extent that Marietta and Great-aunt Elizabeth have. It's what I've inherited, but at least I'll keep it pared down. In order to do that, though, I have to exercise regularly. Which I do, even though it's boring. I'm actually in very good shape."

Ron eyed her again, from head to toe. He repeated the scan focusing on neck to knee. The sweatshirt was not a lot of help. "Way to go."

She gave him a shove and started to talk about data and information gathering. How important they were becoming to Grantville; the role of the different libraries and the research center. That her real apprenticeship, if that was what you wanted to call it, was out at the high school under Elaine Bolender, but that she spent time in every library inside the Ring of Fire, from the grade school to the power plant. That was the first year. By third year, she would need to be learning about down-time libraries. The University of Jena, for example. By then, there would be an exchange system set up, Elaine expected, sort of like the one the medical school would have between Leahy Medical Center here in Grantville and Jena. There were down-time librarians coming to Grantville fairly regularly now, especially to study cataloging.

By the time they got there, she had given him a virtual tour of how the configuration of the town's various libraries had changed while he was in Italy, with special attention to the way their resources, as they were being developed, would be of use to an enterprise like Tom Stone's.

In turn, Ron had taken her on the same kind of procession through what Lothlorien Farbenwerke was turning into under the management of Magda's father, which no longer bore much resemblance to a decrepit hippie commune. Aside from the manufacturing areas, which dwarfed the greenhouses, the original geodesic dome was now only an annex to a quite respectable house. The Stones hadn't wanted to get rid of the dome. Sentiment, Ron said.

Then they spent three hours talking to Marietta Fielder about cross-indexing and information retrieval systems, specifically as they applied to facilitation of pharmaceutical research.

Missy gave an extra special smile of thanks to the other student assistant on evening shift, who had ended up carrying a very heavy load of circulation and reference questions.

A monk in full habit? Ron shrugged to himself. Grantville sure wasn't what it had been when he and Missy were growing up. But if there had to be some guy working one-to-one with Missy on evening shift, Ron thought a monk was a really good choice. He smiled warmly also, trying to project a few thoughts at the guy while he did it. Thoughts about a really enthusiastic embrace of lifelong celibacy.

On the way home, they talked about what had happened in Venice and Rome during the so-called Galileo Affair. The CoC printing press and the Phillips screwdriver. Joe Buckley, murdered by the French Protestant fanatic, Michel Ducos—the same guy who'd almost engineered the pope's assassination. Sharon Nichols and Feelthy Sanchez. Father Mazzare. Cardinal Mazzare, now.

Ron was pleased to discover that Missy had no sympathy for Billy Trumble. He'd been a year ahead of her in school and had once tried out the "lordly senior jock" approach. Ron found her frankly expressed wish that some day Trumble would make an even worse fool of himself satisfying. At some level, Ron was still holding a grudge against him in regard to the escape of Ducos.

Shortly thereafter, they tested the Stone Hypothesis. By then, on the way back from the library, they had refined the proposed procedural rules. In front of her house, on the sidewalk, in the dark, clasping the opposite hands to the ones they had been holding that afternoon, and, upon Ron's strong urging, without six inches of air separating them.

"I don't think that worked quite the way we intended," Ron said. "As far as restoring karmic balance and getting things back to the *status quo ante*, all I can say is that it was a real bummer. Otherwise, it was a great success."

"This is strange." *Strange* didn't even begin to cover it, Missy thought. Little impish electrons seemed to have taken up residence in both of her kneecaps and both of her hip sockets, from which locations they kept shooting sparks at one another. Diagonally.

"Yeah. It is, sort of."

"I wonder why we never kissed each other earlier? All those years going through middle school or high school together? Almost everyone kisses everyone else, somewhere along the line."

"The forces that manage Dad's beloved cosmic rhythm knew we weren't old enough to handle it? Maybe I ought to toss them a bit of incense for that."

Missy stood there thinking that she *sooooo* did not want this kind of complication in her life right now. Maybe never. Definitely not right now.

She hadn't really given a thought to religion since she got old enough to tell her mother that she wasn't going to Sunday School at First Methodist any more and made it stick. Her name was still on the rolls, she supposed, if only because she had never had any incentive to have it removed. But if Ron's cosmic forces existed and they had kept this from happening four or five years ago, she owed them. A lot.

"Give them an extra handful, while you're at it. Pat Bonnaro down at the gift shop still carries the stuff. I'll pay for my share."

Part Four

November 1634

Sublimed with mineral fury

Chapter 20

Magdeburg

"When you agreed to delay the national election, Prime Minister," said Francisco Nasi, "I think you played into Wilhelm Wettin's hands. We would have done better to insist on the earliest election possible."

Frank Jackson, sitting in another chair in Mike Stearns' office, nodded his head. "He's right, Mike. I told you at the time that coming right off our victory at Ahrensbök would be the best time to have the election. Instead, you gave Wettin months to start working on peoples' fears and insecurities again. *Months,* dammit. Now, Ahrensbök is half a year in the past. These days, that's not much different from a decade. Nobody remembers."

Being one of Mike's oldest and closest friends, Frank was blunter and cruder than Francisco would have been. But everything he said was true, in Nasi's opinion.

Stearns simply looked patient. Almost serene, even.

"And I told both of you at the time—I was right then, and I'm right now—that you were missing the forest for the trees. Sure, I know that a lot of people straddling the fence, and even some of Wettin's supporters, think I make a better war president than he will. Who knows? If I'd pushed it, and insisted on a quick election, we might even have won. Gotten a big enough plurality, anyway, and then we could have formed a coalition government with one or another of the smaller parties." Mike smiled thinly. "Now that would've been a barrel of laughs, wouldn't it? Spend half our waking hours squabbling over crossing t's and dotting i's."

Nasi couldn't help but wince. None of the small political parties in the USE was inclined in the least toward political practicality and they all viewed the term "compromise" as being a synonym for "treason."

That was one of the reasons they were small, of course.

He looked out the window. Since he wasn't sitting near it and the prime minister's office was in the palace's top floor, there was nothing to see but sky.

Gray sky. What you'd expect, of course, in November. That dull, sullen, somber month. The battle of Ahrensbök, where the USE army under Torstensson's command had won its great victory over the French, had taken place in May.

Bright, sunny, cheerful May. As Frank Jackson said, though, that might as well have been a decade in the past. In the six months since, Wilhelm Wettin and his Crown Loyalist party—coalition, rather; as a "party" the CLs were ramshackle—had spent every waking hour working on every fear and doubt and insecurity that any German might have concerning Mike Stearns and his Fourth of July Party—which was also a coalition, being honest, if not as ramshackle—and their supposed "radicalism."

Well. His *actual* radicalism, in the case of Stearns himself if not every member of his party. By the standards of the seventeenth century, certainly.

The end result . . .

Stearns said it aloud. "Look, guys, face it. We're going to lose the election. I've always known we would"—here he leaned forward in his chair and his tone hardened—"just as I knew at the time that winning the election by taking advantage of Ahrensbök would be a fool's paradise. Once the glow wore off, the fact is that the majority of people in the United States of Europe simply aren't ready—not yet—for my political program. And a politician who tries to obtain office for any reason *other* than carrying through his program is either a scoundrel or a fool. Often enough, both."

He leaned back in his seat and clasped his hands over his belly. It was a belly which was perhaps a bit larger than the one he'd carried into the office of prime minister a little over a year ago, but not much. Even with his incredibly heavy work load, Stearns always managed to exercise for at least a half hour each day.

"Here's what would have happened," he continued. "At best. We might have won, although we'd almost certainly not have won an outright majority. That means a government that can't rule very effectively. Then, squabbling and bickering all the while, we'd have tried to shove a program down the throats of a nation that really wasn't ready for it. Not enough of its people, at any rate. The result? Sooner or later, Wilhelm forces a vote of confidence, there's another election, and we're out and he's in anyway. Only, this time, after having discredited ourselves."

He unclasped his hands and sat up straight again. "No, gentlemen, there are times when taking the high road is not only the right thing to do, it's the smart thing to do. So we lose an election. Big deal. In the meantime—swords have two edges, don't forget—we've been able to take advantage of this long election campaign to solidify our own political base and clarify our own political program. You both know as well as I do what the realities are in the seventeenth century, when it comes to political activity. Most people are farmers and they work like dogs nine months out of the year. They have very little time for politics, and when they do they just want to get something *done,* not sit around and jabber. That means that winter is the only time of year you can talk to most people about politics—not to mention *listen* to them—and really hammer out a solid program that your electorate understands. Politics is education, before it's anything else."

Frank Jackson's scowl had never left his face. By temperament, Jackson was simply not given to patient explanation and elucidation.

Nasi looked at the window again. Neither was he, really. But at least he could understand clearly what Stearns was saying.

And . . . the man might very well be right, after all. If there was one thing Francisco Nasi had learned very thoroughly in the many months since he'd become the head of USE intelligence and one of the prime minister's closest advisers, it was not to underestimate the political acumen and shrewdness of Mike Stearns. A "radical," the man might be—well, surely was—but he did not have a trace of the airy impracticality of so many political radicals.

"I did not bring up the matter to thrash a dead horse, Michael,"

Francisco said mildly. "Whether you were right or not, we may never know. What we *do* know—can be almost certain about, anyway—is that come February twenty-second the Crown Loyalists will win the election. On a national level. Not in every province, of course."

Frank shook his head. "Christ, that's not much more than two months from now."

"Well, that's the day the election happens," said Nasi, shrugging. "But in a country as big as the USE, and with the facilities we have available, it will take several weeks for the results to come in and be tabulated. We're not living in your old United States of America up-time where the winner of a national election was usually known by the following day. I don't expect a winner in our upcoming election to be definitely announced until mid-March. Then, given the realities of travel in the here and now, I can't see any realistic way the change in government can happen before June."

"True enough," said Mike. "Even in the late twentieth century, it took us two and a half months to go from a presidential election to inauguration day. When the republic was first founded, the time between election and inauguration was four months. We'll actually be doing quite well if we can inaugurate a new government less than four months after an election on February twenty-second."

"How sure are you, Francisco?" asked Frank. "It's not as if we have the kind of polling capabilities that we Americans had up-time."

"No. But the methods and techniques we do have available are not so bad. Not when the results are going to be so lopsided."

"What's your estimate?" Mike asked.

"We will win no more than forty percent of the vote. Perhaps as little as one-third, although not any less. Wettin's party will win a majority. Not much of a majority—somewhere in the low fifty percentile range—but a clear majority. All the small parties put together will get somewhere between five and ten percent of the vote. Most of those votes, however, will be concentrated in a few provinces."

Mike simply nodded. "That's about what I figure, too, just using my own stick-my-thumb-in-the-wind hunches. How about our strongholds?"

"Well, that's the good news. The same strident campaign being waged by the Crown Loyalists that is stirring up fears and uncertainties in most of the provinces is having the opposite effect in regions where we are solidly rooted. It's just making our supporters angry."

Nasi glanced down at his notes. That was just ingrained reflex. By now, he could have recited all of that material in his sleep.

"The State of Thuringia-Franconia is solid as the proverbial rock. Whatever shakiness might have existed in Thuringia is being offset—more than offset—by the continuing political ramifications of the Ram Rebellion in Franconia."

"Ableidinger?" asked Mike, referring to the man generally considered to have been the Ram Rebellion's principal leader. Even its "mastermind," according to those hostilely inclined.

"He'll run for a seat in the USE Congress from the SoTF. There's not much doubt in my mind or anyone else's that he'll win by a landslide."

"About what I figured. And Magdeburg province is probably even more solid than the SoTF. It doesn't have as big a population, of course, but it's still one of the bigger provinces in the USE. So we'll have very solid bases in at least two of the major provinces. And three imperial cities, at least: Magdeburg itself, of course, along with Hamburg and Luebeck."

Jackson looked a bit skeptical. "Are you sure about Magdeburg? The city, I mean. Otto Gericke's the mayor, which means he'll be sitting in the Senate for it, thanks to these idiot rules we set up. He's always struck me as pretty stodgy."

"We didn't 'set up' those idiot rules, Frank," Mike said mildly. "We grudgingly agreed to them in the course of a three-way compromise between us and Wettin and the emperor—*with* the understanding that if we won the election one of the things we'd be pushing for was broadening the Senate and making it more democratic."

The USE's Senate was a peculiar institution, as things presently stood. Something of a cross between a "senate" as normally understood—by Americans, at any rate—and a House of Lords. Each province and imperial city got one seat in the Senate, but the seat *had* to be taken by whoever was that province or city's "head of state." That meant, for instance, that Ed Piazza sat in the national Senate by virtue of having been elected president of the

State of Thuringia-Franconia. But, of course, since most of the provincial heads of state in the USE were hereditary positions, that meant the Senate was a heavily aristocratic institution.

Just to add the icing to the cake—and the cherry—there was the charming twist that Gustav II Adolf, in addition to being the emperor of the United States of Europe, was *also* two of its senators. Two, not one. He was officially the heads of state of both Pomerania and Mecklenburg, having appointed himself the duke of both provinces when he conquered them.

"As for Otto," Mike continued, "in some ways, he is pretty stodgy. All other things being equal, he'd normally be more inclined toward the Crown Loyalists. But all thing are not equal, not even close. First and foremost, Otto's an architect and he positively adores this city, now that Gustav Adolf gave him free rein to build it up as he likes."

"So?"

Francisco and Mike chuckled simultaneously. "Hell, figure it out, Frank. Magdeburg was sacked less than five years ago. It was only rebuilt this quickly because of us. And who do you think Otto has the most confidence will keep it from being sacked again? Us—or that feckless pack of squabbling noblemen and guildmasters around Wilhelm Wettin? The same people who didn't do squat to protect the city last time around."

Mike swiveled his chair and gazed out the window. "Have you given any thought to your own situation, after the election, Francisco?"

"Yes, of course." Nasi hesitated, then chuckled. "Amazingly, though—I am hardly what you'd call indecisive, as a rule—I haven't been able to come to any conclusions."

Mike smiled, still looking out the window. "Hard to give it up, isn't it?"

"Excuse me?"

"Power. Influence." Stearns waggled his hand. "And—at least for people like you and me—I think what's probably even harder is giving up the game itself."

He swiveled his chair around. "Fortunately, however, the game itself is one thing the loser in an election does *not* have to concede. Keep in mind, though, that all this may be irrelevant in your case. Wilhelm may want to keep you on in your current position."

Francisco shook his head. "You don't really believe that. I

certainly don't. And it doesn't matter, in any event. Even if Wettin offered to retain me in my current post, I would decline."

"Why?"

Nasi looked at Stearns squarely. "It is perhaps finally time to say this aloud. I have become quite loyal to you, Michael. Even to your political program, although most of my allegiance is personal. I would find it difficult—impossible, really—to serve Wilhelm Wettin in this same capacity. I don't dislike the man. I don't even distrust him, within limits. He's simply . . . not you."

Jackson grinned. "He has that effect on people, doesn't he?" He hooked a thumb at Stearns. "It's why I soldiered on as his secretary-treasurer after he got elected president of our mine local."

"Well, thanks," Mike said. "But you don't need to feel any obligation, Francisco."

Nasi laughed. "'Obligation' is not really the word. The truth is, I *enjoy* working for you. First, because I've discovered that I am quite good at this work. Second, because I've eventually concluded—*quite* to my surprise—that I think the work itself is worth doing. No small leap of faith, that, I assure you. Not for a man like me, raised in the environs of the Ottoman court."

Mike smiled. "It must have been a switch, going from a prospective courtier in the Turkish empire to the spymaster of a rabble-rouser."

"Yes. On the other hand, it's a lot less dangerous."

Jackson looked startled. "Since when is being a rabble-rouser less dangerous than being part of the establishment?"

"When the establishment in question is that of Istanbul, a lot safer," said Nasi. "I hate to think what percentage of the sultan's advisers wind up at the bottom of the sea with a garrote around their neck. The odds of surviving are no better than our odds in the upcoming election—and no one expects us to actually lose our heads as a result."

"No—but it's not a possibility to overlook, either," said Mike. "In this day and age, politics is very much a contact sport. About the only difference here in the USE is that we wear gloves. It can still get very rough."

He sat erect and leaned over the desk, planting his hands in front of him. "Francisco, I think we need to give some consideration to your safety. After the election, I mean, when you're back to being a private citizen."

It was Nasi's turn to look startled. He hadn't really considered that matter, he realized.

"You've made enemies in your position," Mike continued. "And what's worse, some of them are not what you'd call casual enemies."

"Well . . . yes. But so have you, Michael." He nodded at Jackson. "Even Frank, for that matter."

Jackson snorted. "Big deal. I'm in the army. I've got soldiers around me every day. Very well armed soldiers. As for Mike . . ."

He snorted again. "First, as long as he stays in Magdeburg, he's got Gunther Achterhof's CoC people watching over him. You know what *they're* like."

Gunther Achterhof was perhaps the most ruthless of all the CoC leaders—which was saying something, in an organization that had Gretchen Richter as one of its leaders. He more or less ran the Committee of Correspondence in the USE's capital city, and he had what you might call "proactive" notions when it came to security issues. That there were enemies' spies in Magdeburg, no one doubted. What no one also doubted was that those spies worked very, very, very carefully—and stayed well away from any activities which the city's CoC might perceive as a direct threat to its people or those they supported.

Mike stirred in his chair. "I probably won't be staying in Magdeburg, though. I'm almost certain, by now, that once I lose the election Gustav Adolf is going to ask me to become a general in the army."

Frank shook his head. "That still seems just plain nuts to me. Meaning no offense, old buddy, but you've got as many qualifications to be an army general as I do to be a brain surgeon. Zip. You served exactly three years in the army, back up-time—as a grunt. That's it."

But Nasi agreed with Mike's estimate. "It doesn't matter, Frank. You even have the same tradition in your own history, if you go back far enough."

"Huh?"

Francisco still found it amazing how many Americans—even otherwise intelligent ones like Jackson, holding important positions—knew practically nothing even of their own nation's history. Much less the history of the rest of the world.

Mike provided the explanation. "In the twentieth century, generals in the American army were almost all professional soldiers. But if you go back to the Civil War, Frank, you'll find that Abe Lincoln appointed lots of civilians to generalships. In some cases, men with no military experience at all. The most famous is probably Ben Butler. He had a post as an officer in one of the state militias, but that didn't mean squat in military terms. He just got the post because he was a prominent politician. When the war started, Lincoln made him a major general in the U.S. Army."

"In God's name, why?"

Mike shrugged. "Pretty much the same reason that Gustav Adolf is going to offer me a position as general. Ben Butler was a very prominent Democrat, but one who stuck with the North when the South seceded. He supported Lincoln's prosecution of the war. So Lincoln made him a general."

"You could refuse," pointed out Nasi. "You even have a good excuse, since you'll be the leader of the opposition."

"It'd be stupid for me to do that. If we were in peacetime, yes. But we're going to be at war again next summer. You know it, I know it, everybody knows it. Gustav Adolf is coldly furious with Saxony and Brandenburg and come hell or high water he's going to bring them to heel for their treachery in the Baltic War. They'll put up a fight and he'll overrun them."

For the first time, Mike's placid countenance became somber. "Mind you, if I thought I could persuade the emperor to leave it at that, I'd stay a civilian. But I don't. The Poles and the Austrians are bound to come in on the other side. In and of itself, that wouldn't be a problem. But Gustav Adolf thinks—and so do I—that he's going to hammer all of them on the battlefield. And that being so, unfortunately, I'm almost certain he's going to try to conquer Poland itself. Big chunks of it, anyway. And then all hell's going to break loose. A smallish and self-contained war—really, more in the way of suppressing a rebellion—is going to turn into an ongoing nightmare. Gustav Adolf is simply biting off more than he can chew, even if he won't accept the fact."

Jackson looked at Nasi. "You agree with him?"

"Oh, yes. On both counts. First, that the emperor will make the mistake of turning the war into a full-scale war with Poland. Second, that the Polish resistance will be ferocious." He made a face. "Unfortunately, the Poles are so feckless in their politics that people tend to forget what they're like on the battlefield. Especially when they have a Grand Hetman with the military skills of Stanislaw Koniecpolski."

Jackson looked back at Stearns. "All the more reason, that would seem to me, to stay the hell out of it."

Mike spread his hands. "I can't, Frank. Agree with the emperor or disagree with him, it doesn't matter. If I was just a private citizen, it'd be different. But I'm not. I'm trying to lead a revolution—all across Europe, not just here. Under the circumstances, if Gustav Adolf offers me a post as general in the army on the eve of a new major war for the USE and I refuse, I'll just marginalize myself politically. Besides . . ."

He paused, for a moment. "Being cold-blooded about it, I expect Wilhelm to screw up as the new prime minister. Screw up badly, in fact. On his own, he might not. But he's made too many promises and owes too many favors to too many people, many of whom are stone reactionaries and dumber than bricks. So I think there's likely to be some real political explosions after he takes office. Which, being blunt about it, is fine with me—especially if I'm not around where people can try to force me to play fireman."

"Oh." Frank pursed his lips. "To put it another way, you figure the CoCs are going to be running amok sooner or later, and you'd just as soon not be around when they do."

"Not . . . exactly. I want to be close enough—hopefully—to be able to guide the thing a bit. Turn an explosion into a shaped charge, you might say. But, yes, not so close that Gustav Adolf or anybody else can expect me to squelch anything right away." He leaned back, his complacent expression returning. "I figure a military camp somewhere on the Polish border is about right."

Frank shook his head. "God, you're a scheming bastard."

Mike smiled. "Speaking of which—to get back to the topic—even assuming I leave Magdeburg, I'll still have plenty of protection. And it won't just be 'well-armed soldiers' in the abstract. I'm quite sure I can get Gustav Adolf to let me bring all the Warders into the army with me, as . . . oh, we'll call them some sort of 'special unit,' just like we do with Harry Lefferts and his wrecking crew. But what they'll actually be is my bodyguards."

He swiveled the chair to face Nasi squarely. "None of which will apply to you, Francisco. Not if you leave Magdeburg, at any rate—which I imagine you'd like to be able to do, at least from time to time."

"Actually, I've been thinking of moving to Prague. Leaving the USE altogether."

"Why?" asked Frank.

"Various reasons. Some of them, purely personal." Francisco hesitated. But . . . these two men were good friends, in addition to everything else. "If nothing else, I am getting to the age where I need to get married. And where better to look for a wife than Prague? It has the largest Jewish community in Europe—probably the whole world—and, even better for me, its most cosmopolitan and sophisticated. Well, except for, in some ways, the Jewry of Istanbul. But I think the Ottoman Empire is now too dangerous for me."

"Okay, I can see that. You'll need a real bodyguard, then."

Nasi winced. "Please, Frank! The nature of my work—which I will certainly continue, even in Prague, even as a private citizen—does not lend itself well to having great hulking brutes shuffling along after me."

Mike laughed. "God, the Warders would love to hear *that* description of them!"

"Oh, I admit the Warders are different. But how many bodyguards of that caliber are available?"

"Warders, none," said Frank. "But I have somebody who'd probably suit you even better."

Nasi cocked an eye at him.

"Cory Joe Lang," said Jackson. "Know the fellow?"

"His name, yes. I don't believe I've ever met him, though. He's one of the military intelligence people attached to your . . . ah . . ."

"Special unit," supplied Frank, smiling. "Which means, among other things, that I can assign him to do pretty much anything, anywhere, for any length of time—and neither General Torstensson nor anyone else is going to ask me any questions or raise any objections."

Francisco thought about it. It was certainly true that having a man familiar with intelligence work as a bodyguard would solve some of the problems involved. On the other hand, "intelligence work" covered a lot of ground. For all practical purposes, most "spies" were really just clerks. In many cases, what the Americans would call "outright geeks." Hardly suitable for the possible ramifications of the job of being a bodyguard.

"Ah . . . that would leave the issue of this Cory Joe Lang's . . . ah . . ."

"Physical qualifications?" said Frank, grinning. "Don't worry about it."

Stearns was back to his very comfortable, slouched-back-in-his-chair, hands-clasped-over-his-belly posture. "Yeah," he said. "Really don't worry about it."

Francisco looked from one to the other. "What are you not telling me?"

"Let's put it this way. Harry Lefferts was known to say that the one man in or around Grantville he'd cross the street to avoid getting into a fight with was Cory Joe Lang. Not—he'd always add this, right off—that he and Cory Joe didn't get along just fine so it was all a moot point anyway."

"Ah." Nasi reviewed what he knew of the record of Harry Lefferts. Which was a great deal.

The very sanguinary record.

"Ah," he repeated. "Yes, that should work quite nicely."

Frank nodded. "I'll give him his new marching orders in a few days, when he comes back to Magdeburg. Right now, he's in Grantville."

The down-time lieutenant in the tavern was petrified. His face, literally, was as pale as a sheet.

"Look, Cory Joe, I'm *sorry.* I didn't know—"

The man sitting across from him at the table in the Thuringen Gardens nodded. "Yeah, I understand. Different last names. My last name 'Lang' comes from my dad. 'Hardesty' is my mother's maiden name, and it's the one she goes by these days."

Lang raised one hand and, with the other, began counting off the fingers. As he did so—as surreptitiously as possible—the other three young officers at the table began sliding their chairs back. If Cory Joe's fury cut loose, they wanted to be as far as possible from the coming victim.

"I'll explain the family relationships involved, just so you're not confused any longer. I'm the oldest of Velma Hardesty's kids. Born on January 14, 1979, up-time calendar." The first finger was counted off.

All the more so because "fury" did not accurately describe the intelligence officer's likely behavior. There would be no insensate and unfocused explosion here. If ever there lived a man who exemplified the old American saw, *don't get mad, get even*, it was Cory Joe Lang. If he decided—and this seemed to be the direction things were going—to take Lieutenant Stammler's characterization of Velma Hardesty as a "whore" as a personal insult, then who could say how far he thought the insult extended? Perhaps the idiot Stammler's companions were guilty also.

"She was only married to my dad for a year or so, before she broke it off," Lang continued. "Lucky for him. Then she screwed around for a few years with God knows how many guys. My half-sister Pam—she goes by 'Pam Hardesty,' not having much choice in the matter—was one of the byproducts. She was born on May 11, 1982, and she's the one outright bastard in the family. Nobody actually knows for sure who her father was. Including Velma. Might have been any one of several guys."

The second finger was counted off. Throughout, Cory Joe's tone had remained as level and even as an iron bar. Lieutenant Stammler's face somehow managed to get paler still; his three fellows slid their chairs back just a little farther.

"Eventually, though, she got married again. To a logger—poor stupid fuck must have dropped one on his own head—by the name of Carney Logsden. That didn't last much longer than her marriage to my dad, but it did last long enough to produce my other two half-sisters, Tina and Susan."

Two more fingers were counted off, leaving only the thumb sticking up. It wasn't a particularly large thumb, as these things go. But Cory Joe Lang's reputation didn't stem from his size. He was perhaps a bit larger and more muscular than average, but not extraordinarily so. His reputation stemmed from the fact that nobody sitting at that table had any trouble at all envisioning that thumb gouging out an eye or two. Or four or five. Wolverines aren't particularly large, either.

"They both go—or went, in the case of Tina, since she's dead now—by the last name of 'Logsden.' That was probably true enough, in the case of Tina, but me and just about everybody else has their doubts whether it really applies to Susan. She's the youngest of Velma's kids—born on December 11, 1986, almost eight years younger'n me—and by then Velma was back to fucking everything in pants. 'Course, that probably started happening the day after Carney was dumb enough to marry her."

He lowered the hand. "The point, though, is this." That calm, level, even tone was quite frightening to anyone who knew the man. "It's fair enough to call my mother a slut or a tramp or a roundheels. But 'whore'? Well, that's pushing it. At least, I've never heard anybody claim my mother took money to screw. Gifts, presents, anything like that, sure. She's about as avaricious as they get. But I think 'whore' goes beyond the pale."

Lieutenant Stammler managed to choke out a few more words. "I apologize, Cory Joe. I didn't *know*—"

"Yeah, sure. I know you didn't realize I was her son when you called her a whore, right in front of me. But so what? I mean, I really think a man owes it to himself to be a bit more careful how he uses words. 'Less he wants to wind up a cripple, or dead before his time."

There was silence, for a moment. Then, Cory Joe leaned back in his seat a little. "Ah, hell, Fritz, you don't need to shit a brick. The truth is, I could care less personally. My dad raised me, not that worthless bitch. I've seen as little of my mother as I possibly could, my whole life. Happily for me, she returns the sentiment."

Stammler swallowed. It seemed he would live to see another dawn. Perhaps even intact.

Lang waved his hand. "It's my sisters. Okay, half-sisters. I don't see too much of them, but I like 'em. Nice girls. I always remember their birthdays, whatever else I screw up. And either one of them might get a little upset if they heard their mother casually referred to as a 'whore' in public by a drunk soldier—not that they'd really dispute the charge too strongly, anymore than I would—so I really feel obliged to discourage that sort of thing."

"Never do it again!"

There was silence, again, for a few seconds.

"Well, okay, then. We'll leave at that. But you'd better not forget."

"Never do it again."

Chapter 21

Grantville

"When I sent them to Grantville last spring, I had no intention that they would batten on you forever, Henry."

Veronica Dreeson was steaming with wrath. Truly with wrath, because during the months she had been gone, Henry's health had worsened noticeably. The trip back, even in the ATV, with its seats so much softer than a wagon, had been hard on him.

Why had he been so inconsiderate of himself as to make that trip to Fulda and Frankfurt? Why had he been so inconsiderate of her? Didn't he realize that she had already been a widow once? Once was enough. He should not have gone.

She should not have gone to Amberg. She should have remained in Grantville to care for him. She had accomplished nothing at all during that trip to the Upper Palatinate in any case. Except to provide him with one more burden.

Officially, therefore, she was wrathful this morning because after her late husband Johann Stephan's niece Dorothea and her lover Nicholas Moser had arrived here, Henry had not only performed a civil marriage ceremony for them, but had also found a job for Nicholas as a clerk with the SoTF court system. And, since the job was very junior and did not pay enough that they could rent their own apartment, had permitted them to live in one of the rooms of his house ever since.

"Now, Ronnie," he said mildly. "Dorothea has taken some of the burden off Annalise. It is her senior year in high school, after all. Dorothea is here when the other children leave, when they come home. She was a big help when Ed Piazza asked me to go over to Buchenland. I think I'd have said no if she and Nicholas hadn't been available to Annalise for backup."

That was the wrong thing to say. So it was really Nicol and Thea's fault that Henry had risked his health on that strenuous trip. "What does she do here?" Veronica asked suspiciously.

"Reads novels, mostly," Henry admitted. "When she isn't playing with Will and Joey. But don't blame Annalise. Thea already knew about Harlequin Romances when she arrived."

"I know." Veronica's sigh was disgusted.

"It makes the housekeeper feel better to have an adult member of the family present, whether she does anything at all." That, Henry thought, was perfectly true.

Possibly the best thing was that she had arrived home to find that the rest of the household appeared to be well and happy. It was the worst thing, too. They had gotten along fine without her. She was just a useless old woman.

"What is that book?" Veronica asked suspiciously.

Thea looked up, apprehensively. She knew perfectly well that her aunt, aunt-by-marriage, widow-of-her-father's-half-brother, was not pleased to have her in the house.

"It's called *Where's Waldo*. I found it in that chest under the bay window. Henry said that one of Margie's kids left it behind. Joey is really too young, but Will loves it." She clambered up from the floor to the sofa. "Sit next to me, *Tante*. See, in each of the pictures, there is a little monkey hidden."

Veronica didn't want to take the book away from Will and Joey. It took some time to locate another copy and quite a few USE dollars to buy it from Chandra Prickett, who said, "I guess, since you want to send it out of town, to Becky, for the baby, I'll sell it. I can always check it out of the library for my kids, since it doesn't look like we're going anywhere."

She did send the book to Becky.

In the same packet as a letter to Gretchen, who now claimed that her political obligations to the CoC and Mike Stearns required that she had to go campaigning for Fourth of July Party candidates between now and the February elections, instead of coming home to collect her many and varied offspring, natural and adopted.

A rather tart letter, headed with the words:

Where's Gretchen?

She slipped her hand into the pocket tied under her skirt. It held the disintegrating remains of a makeshift rosary, constructed of a piece of Bavarian grapevine and with snips of hollowed-out twigs for the beads. Perhaps the summer had not been entirely wasted, after all. She had learned a lot about this "guilt tripping" from Mary Ward and Archduchess Maria Anna. She couldn't do it quite as deftly as they did, yet, and the technique was hard to combine with her abbess of Quedlinburg face, but perhaps she could alternate.

"Good to see you back, Ronnie."

"Good morning, Enoch. Is Idelette here? I have a package for her that Leopold sent from Rheinfelden, and a letter from Marc. Probably telling her how crazy he is about that little seamstress, Susanna."

"Actually, she's over at St. Veronica's with your girl. Catching up the bookkeeping. Come in and sit down for a spell. Inez is just making coffee."

"The bookkeeping's in good shape. I was surprised. I suppose I owe her something for the work . . ."

"No, no. Consider it part of her apprenticeship. Leopold sent her to Grantville to learn how to run a business. Helping Annalise is part of that. Aura Lee Hudson and Carol Koch—she's gone back to using Carol Unruh as her professional name, I suppose you'd call it—are mentoring them, I guess you'd say. It's working out pretty well."

"Hummph." Ronnie snorted. "Everyone knows that children will pay more attention to outsiders than to their own families. That's one of the reasons we apprentice them in the first place."

Inez nodded. "It's not just what they're learning. It's the willingness. That's what my mother used to say. 'You'll always get a lot more help around the house from a hired girl than you will from your own daughter. And the woman who hires your daughter will get a lot more help from her than from any of her own.'"

"But there's still a lot that Annalise has to learn. The trip to Amberg was a complete waste. At least, from all I can figure out so far. Well, we're getting the books that Annalise negotiated for. That's something, I suppose."

"You can't bring yourself to say it, but you're as pleased by the way Annalise managed the schools while you were gone as you've ever been by anything in your life."

"I suppose."

Inez poured a little milk into her coffee. "You ought to tell her so. She worked really hard."

"Ronnie doesn't want to give her the big head."

"Enoch! Don't encourage Ronnie to hold it all in. Annalise deserves a pat on the back. She's earned it."

"What she deserves is to go to college," said Ronnie firmly. "But I don't see how. The Jesuits are paying a little rent for the site in Amberg where the print shop used to be, and the normal school a little more, but it has to be split five ways, since Johann Stephan's girls in Nürnberg have a right to their shares. A fifth of it isn't going to pay Annalise's tuition at Quedlinburg, or even come close to it. Brechbuhl hasn't managed to break the Grafenwöhr property out of probate yet. By the time he does, it will be too late for Annalise. I can predict that right now."

After Inez saw her out, she came back laughing. "That was a really classic Veronica grump."

Enoch nodded. "She's got a point, though."

"As far as Grantville is concerned," Henry Dreeson said, "Jarvis Beasley's wife is not a bigamist. Judge Tito will explain."

Maurice Tito, not speaking from the bench but rather acting as a consultant, explained in painstaking detail that the law of West Virginia, as brought from up-time and still fully applicable within Grantville itself and West Virginia County as a whole, did not consider a betrothal to be a binding contract that prohibited the fiancé or fiancée from entering into marriage with a different person. He had a lot of citations to precedents.

The delegate who represented Saxony in the former House of

Lords of the New United States and current Senate of the State of Thuringia-Franconia (in right of Saxony's status as co-administrator of the territories of the extinct county of Henneberg south of the *Thueringerwald*), pointed out in equal detail that under the law which prevailed there, a betrothal was indeed a binding contract. He seemed almost regretful. Nonetheless, in a case in which a young woman had entered into a betrothal, and her fiancé subsequently went to be a soldier and disappeared, she could not remarry until such time as the marriage court declared a presumption of death or dissolved the betrothal. He stated that it was rare for a presumption of death to be granted less than seven years after the person's disappearance, and then only if the surviving partner to the contract could document a good faith effort to locate the other. Occasionally, indeed, such decrees had been issued after as little as three years, if there appeared to be good reason to assume death. On the other hand, there was no requirement that it be issued at all. It could take ten years, a dozen, or never be issued, particularly if there was some evidence that the partner who left was living elsewhere.

In that event, of course, the abandoned partner could re-petition to have the betrothal dissolved upon the ground of desertion.

The fact remained, however, that Hedwig Altschulerin, the daughter of a man who prior to his death had been a subject of Duke John George of Saxony, had not even sought a dissolution of her prior betrothal. She merely, upon meeting this soldier named Jarvis Beasley while she was working in Meiningen, had left that city. She had accompanied him to Grantville, had married him there, and currently was residing with him there. Wherefore she was, in the eyes of the laws of Saxony, a bigamist.

Saxony, he pointed out, administered the Henneberg village of her birth under a valid inheritance agreement, which was why it had a seat in the House of Lords. Consequently she was properly subject to Saxon law. He respectfully requested her extradition to appear before the Saxon *Ehegericht* in the Henneberg territories to answer for her transgression.

Mayor Dreeson equally respectfully refused.

The session adjourned. The Saxon delegate left a lot of paperwork for someone to file.

Maurice Tito strongly, if privately and informally, advised Hedwig Altschulerin, aka Hedy, now wife of Jarvis Beasley, that if she knew what was good for her, she would stay inside West Virginia County for the foreseeable future. Which meant no shopping trips in Rudolstadt. No fairs in Badenburg, although, at least, Grantville had a wonderful fair of its own.

Hedy nodded. Jarvis had taken her to it last fall.

Tito kept going. And, unfortunately, no going to church at either St. Martin's in the Fields or St. Thomas the Apostle, since both, while in the State of Thuringia-Franconia, were part of the County of Schwarzburg-Rudolstadt. While he certainly didn't *think* that Count Ludwig Guenther and his consistory would be likely to approve her extradition to Saxony, but neither could he guarantee that they would refuse.

Hedy nodded unhappily. She was causing Jarvis a lot of trouble. Maybe more than she was worth.

And she wanted to go to church. Hedy liked to go to church. Where she grew up, church was the most interesting thing that happened all week.

"I think," Maurice Tito said after she and Jarvis left, "that we really ought to do something. At a minimum, the law should be the same all the way across the State of Thuringia-Franconia. But Congress hasn't gotten around to passing matrimonial legislation, so for the time being, we're stuck with what we have. Saxony will appeal to the Supreme Court, of course, so it'll land in Chuck Riddle's lap, eventually.

"There's no point in waiting for Congress to get off its ass. It has too much else on its plate. Much less the USE Parliament, considering everything that's going on in Magdeburg. See if you can get the Bureau of Consular Affairs to look into this. Let's start some kind of an initiative. We can't have people stuck here in Grantville, after all, unable to put their noses across the border, because of things like this. There ought to be some kind of reciprocal agreement."

"Full faith and credit." Tito nodded. "But we'll have to be careful. It might be a trap we could fall into, if we had to give full faith and credit to Saxony's laws about betrothals when our own citizens apply for marriage licenses. In any case, it's a statewide or nationwide problem, not just a Grantville problem."

Henry Dreeson nodded. "I'll ask Ed Piazza about it, anyway. I'll check with Chad Jenkins, too. Now that his brother Wes has come back and taken over consular affairs, it seems to me that he'd be the person to head up the project, but I don't want to do anything that might step on Chad's toes—not with the campaign coming up."

Mary Ellen Jones decided that she'd better go over and talk to Simon. She had her office in the rectory; he had his in the church.

Wes Jenkins, on the theory that his marriage to Clara had been, at best, a civil ceremony, had requested a church wedding. If he just wanted a church blessing, that would be one thing. But he wanted the whole thing. Having, perhaps, a few private doubts of his own about the do-it-yourself version.

Now that she had slept on it . . . Private. An utterly private ceremony to salve Wes' conscience would be best. Considering Clara's possible—probable—pregnancy, which Simon really didn't need to know about yet either, the Methodist church certainly shouldn't do anything that would throw any doubt on the legal validity of what the two of them had done while they were in Freiherr von Schlitz's lockup.

She and Simon wouldn't have to involve anybody but the principals and the witnesses. Simon could perform the ceremony. She'd be the first witness, since she already knew about it. Jenny Maddox could issue the license, be the second witness, and file the certificate herself. Keep it out of the list published in the papers.

There would be no cause for gossip. None. As far as the rest of Grantville would ever know or need to know, Wes and Clara were properly married in Fulda last August.

Chapter 22

Frankfurt am Main

"I was having a drink with Ernie Haggerty," said Bryant Holloway.

"You're drinking way too much. Ever since you got here."

"What business is it of yours, Nathan the Prick?"

Nathan Prickett had not liked that nickname when he was in high school and he still didn't like it.

"The places where Haggerty spends his time aren't on anybody's five-star list."

"That's what he's here for. Waters dresses up, plays 'gentleman publisher who hasn't forgotten his days as a front-line reporter,' and hobnobs with all the best people in Frankfurt. Ernie gets the dirt on low-lifes who hang out in low places."

"Look, Bryant."

"Don't 'Look, Bryant' me. Don't fucking 'Listen, Bryant' me, either. I don't know why the hell I'm staying with you, anyway."

"Because you're too cheap to pay for your own room. I know damned well that the fire department is paying you a per diem that's calculated to cover rent. Rent you're not paying, which is why you can afford to drink so much."

"It doesn't affect me. I've never missed a training session." Bryant Holloway banged his fist down on the table. "Have I?"

Reluctantly, Nathan shook his head. Bryant had never missed a training session. No matter how obnoxious he could be, he worked hard. The Frankfurt fire watch hadn't made any complaints about him. Not a single one.

"He's an up-timer."

"I heard him, though," Gui Ancelin said. "He was in a tavern with another up-timer. The one who works for Waters. Muttering against Dreeson."

"A plant," Locquifier said. "A would-be spy."

"I don't think so. Not after his sixth cider. Not beer. Cider, and he really drank them all. I'm not that simpleminded, Guillaume, not to watch out for such things. It's not as if he had come here to *Zum Weissen Schwan* to drop his hints and innuendoes under our noses. That would be suspicious. They were in a dingy little tavern in Sachsenhausen. I've only been there once before, myself. By the time he left, he smelled like Robert's grandfather's orchard during pressing season."

"I don't understand," Ouvrard said. "Why would he be complaining about Dreeson? The man is long gone from Frankfurt."

"His resentment was not against Dreeson, only. He also dislikes Prickett, the arms merchant from Suhl, even though he is staying at Prickett's house. He was complaining even more against Jenkins, the former administrator in Fulda. Who is also gone from Fulda, now. Even more against Jenkins' daughter. It appears that he is married to one of Jenkins' daughters. She isn't as deferential to him as a wife should be. Or so he thinks."

"Who knows how 'deferential' may be defined by the up-timers? Does she refuse to arise and greet him at the door when he returns home? Does she refuse to look up from the book she is reading and smile at him when he enters the room? Does she go around in public with her *forearms bare*?"

Ancelin managed not to grin. Fortunat Deneau had domestic problems of his own with Jeanne, back in La Rochelle. "I still think that we should approach him. Tentatively, at least."

Locquifier shook his head. "Don't approach him. Not now. Not yet." He paused. "But do watch him. If he continues to be a discontented man, a man with grievances . . . We can file the information away. He isn't someone we could take into our confidence, but the day may come when we can find a use for him."

Brillard usually didn't talk. Just listened. But . . . "Not Gui. Not any of us. We shouldn't watch him ourselves. We're foreigners.

Not Germans. Just five men. Even some slattern of a waitress might notice if one of us shows up too often and tell it to someone else who'll tell it to a watchman. They're nervous after last month. Weitz managed to elude last month's militia dragnet. Get him to keep an eye on this Holloway. His connections are mostly with the kind of people who normally spend their leisure time sitting in cheap taverns and grousing about something. They'll look right at home."

"I don't want to get a reputation for being seen in low taverns," Joachim Sandrart protested.

Soubise waved one hand airily. "Ah, but you are an artist. A painter who has been in Italy and spent time in the artists' quarter of the city of Rome itself. Nude models. Carousing during carnival. All that. The sister of some rival for your hand is certain to have told your little Johanna about it already. It hasn't caused her to throw a glove in your face so far."

"'All that' was a long way from here. Before I knew I would have a chance to marry the daughter of a wealthy banker. It could just be 'out of sight, out of mind' for her. What you're asking me to do is right here and right in front of her. Or in front of people who will tell other people who will make it their business to be sure she knows about it. I don't want the Milkaus to get any idea that I'm . . . unstable."

Soubise narrowed his eyes. "I want to include some paintings of low tavern types in my collection."

"What?"

"They're becoming very popular in the Netherlands, you know. As odd as it may seem. I suppose they are seen as a fresh, modern alternative to all those classical gods floating around on pink clouds. Men in everyday working clothes. Card players. Smokers so poor they have to share a pipe. The painters still get to include some very impressive atmospheric effects. Tobacco smoke is as effective as clouds, if you catch it right. Your earliest training, under the Soreaus in Hanau, was in still life painting, so you can do it, easily enough. Reflections in the glass of cheap goblets on the table. Chipped earthenware, with little bubbles in the cheap glaze. Wood grain, old and weathered, if the table is bare. Wrinkles in the linen, if there is a cloth."

Soubise leaned back. "I'll tell Milkau, myself, that I have

commissioned you to do such a series and intend to display it prominently." He smiled. "That will account nicely for as many low taverns as you find it necessary to visit."

"Yes, Your Grace."

"I do intend to receive the paintings, you know." Soubise stood up. "Make sketches while you are listening. Talk to my steward about costs and delivery schedules."

"Holloway's hooking up with some pretty nasty types, Jason. I think maybe you ought to clue Nathan Prickett in."

Jason Waters grinned. "Nasty types by my standards or nasty types by your standards? Don't forget I'm a newspaper reporter."

Ernie Haggerty grinned back. "Both. But the second variety is the one you need to worry about. Not just rough characters. Any town that has a main highway going through it and a river port is going to have plenty of those. Not just stevedores and roustabouts and freighters. A half dozen or so of Vincenz Weitz's cronies, to start with."

"Weitz? I don't think I know the name."

Ernie shook his head. "Too much time in high society, man. Last month—the ghetto thing?"

The newspaper reporter came sharply to attention.

"The militia had enough companies to march on just so many taverns without splitting them up, so that's how many they marched on. It doesn't mean they marched on every single place that guys sit and mutter about Jews and Nasi and Becky Stearns and stuff. They missed some. This Weitz, I think, might be the biggest fish they missed."

Dear Don Francisco,

Nathan paused a minute, trying to decide which piece of information he had would be more important to the don.

A man has recently arrived in Frankfurt who might be doing something important here. His name is William Curtius and he is staying with Benjamin de Rohan—they call him Soubise, not Rohan—who is a brother of the duke of Rohan. He, the brother that is, could be a duke himself. I'm not sure how these things work with noble titles, but I've at least figured out that it isn't like England. All four of those Saxe-Weimar brothers are dukes. Or were, until the oldest one stopped duking it out and ran for the House of Commons. So Rohan's brother could be a duke, too.

Anyway, Benjamin de Rohan has rented a town house and Curtius is staying with him. He's maybe thirty-five years old, or so. Curtius, that is (Rohan's about fifty, I'd say). He went to college in Germany for several years and speaks the language like a native. Jason Waters found out from a newspaper guy he's met here that Curtius studied at a place called Herborn and his professor was named Johann Heinrich Alstedt. Alstedt is still alive. Curtius is a diplomat, or wants to be, at least. He's angling for a job with Gustavus Adolphus, so you might want to keep an eye on him. Maybe warn Nils Brahe down in Mainz, since he's the one doing the hiring for Gustav around here. Well, the hiring for Mr. Oxenstierna, I suppose. The emperor probably doesn't spend his time reading resumes.

He stopped a minute. The nib on the damned quill was going blunt. He pulled out his pocket knife. Now he understood why some of the old people used to call them pen knives.

As soon as he got his next paycheck, he was going to buy one of the new pens. Not a fountain pen—he couldn't afford that. But the other day, over at Neumann's, he'd seen Merga using one of the new steel-nibbed dipping pens, which looked to be a mile and a half more practical.

Not to mention that they had plain stems and you wouldn't have to feel foolish watching a feather wiggle while you wrote. The stupid quill always made him feel like he was an illustration in a book about Benjamin Franklin or something. He'd had to do a report about Benjamin Franklin, back in sixth grade.

Like they'd say in Star Wars, I have a really bad feeling about what Bryant Holloway is getting up to. Even though he's from Grantville and is married to my wife's sister Lenore and is staying with me here while he's doing training exercises with the Frankfurt fire department.

The report on Holloway took up all the rest of the piece of paper. Right at the bottom, he squeezed in:

> *I'm sending this to you by Martin Wackernagel, the courier. If you have any more questions, ask him. His brother-in-law is a printer here in town and knows a lot of the people involved, including a lot of the Jews.*
>
> *With all best wishes,*
> *Nathan Prickett*

Joachim Sandrart wasn't on corresponding terms with Don Francisco Nasi—not that he wouldn't have liked to be. So, in addition to reporting to Soubise, he sent a letter to Ron Stone. The son of such a prominent merchant house was bound to have contacts in the intelligence community.

Sandrart had every intention of cultivating his connection to the Stones, now that he had established it. The Rohan commissions were good, true—very, very good. But an artist in search of patronage should never put all his eggs in one basket. Ron's father undoubtedly had the most important quality that any potential patron could possess.

Money. Lots and lots of money.

Chapter 23

Magdeburg

Francisco Nasi found Cory Joe Lang, his new assistant and bodyguard, to be a more interesting fellow than he'd expected.

First impressions, admittedly, had not been promising. Being fair, though, that was mostly because of Cory Joe's improbably blond hair, which he emphasized by keeping very long and usually tied back in a pony tail.

When Francisco commented on the matter to Jackson, the American general smiled.

"Yeah, I know. He looks like a faggot hairdresser who uses more peroxide than Marilyn Monroe. More muscular than most, but that's about it. Don't let appearances deceive you, though. The hair color's real—you should see his half-sister Pam Hardesty, if you want an even more outlandish head of genuine blond hair. And, like Pam, he's a lot smarter than he looks."

Jackson shook his head. "It's always amazed people, the way Velma Hardesty—who's about the most worthless tramp who ever infested Marion County—managed to produce such good kids. Even Tina, the one who got drowned at a graduation celebration party, wasn't any worse than reckless. And what teenager isn't?"

Nasi hated to ask for translations, because doing so always made him feel mildly foolish. Unfortunately, where his boss Mike Stearns was almost preternaturally acute when it came to such things and always provided Francisco with internal cues, Frank Jackson was obtuse.

Faggot? Peroxide? Marilyn Monroe? The term "tramp" seemed clear enough, but Francisco went ahead and asked anyway. Since he was already making a fool of himself.

At the moment, Cory Joe, sitting in a small chair at the very back of the conference room in the palace, looked bored and half-asleep. In point of fact, Francisco had already learned, Lang had a phenomenal memory and would be able to recite back all of the important details of this meeting, if asked.

"—about the way it looks," concluded Mike Stearns. "As you can see, Wettin's not making any attempt to sugarcoat anything."

Ed Piazza and Melissa Mailey had come up to Magdeburg for this meeting. They'd brought Chad Jenkins with them, too, since he'd be running for Rebecca's vacated seat, as well as Constantin Ableidinger.

Piazza had his lips pursed, contemplating Mike's summary. Ableidinger's face was expressionless. Jenkins was scowling. Melissa was shaking her head.

"Stupid," she pronounced. "Why is he doing this, do you think?"

Ed snorted. "They want to win the election? Look, Melissa, you might think and I might think—everybody in this room might think—that the platform of Wilhelm and his Crown Loyalists is stupid, but don't kid yourself. It's also very popular, in most places in Germany."

"With the upper crust," Frank Jackson qualified. "I doubt if people farther down the food chain are that crazy about it."

By up-time standards, Jackson shouldn't have been attending the meeting, since it was a purely partisan political affair and he was an actively serving general in the USE army. But cultural influences worked both ways. By seventeenth-century standards and customs, it would be ridiculous *not* to include Jackson in a strategy session like this one. Frank had been one of Mike Stearns' closest friends and advisers since before the Ring of Fire, and still was.

Piazza shrugged. "Sure—and so what? Most provinces in Germany are still firmly under the thumbs of their upper classes."

Mike Stearns waggled his hand. "That's putting it too strongly,

Ed. Much too strongly, in most places. 'Under their thumb,' yes. 'Firmly under their thumb?' Not really. The truth is, I think the only major provinces in the USE whose established rulers have a solid hold on their populations are Brunswick and Hesse-Kassel. In the case of Brunswick, because the new oil revenues allow the duke to finance lots of popular projects. And in the case of Hesse-Kassel, because William V—not to mention his wife Amalie—is unusually smart for a provincial ruler. *And* unusually moderate. Odd as it may be, the Landgrave and Landgravine of Hesse-Kassel are the left wing of the Crown Loyalists."

"Insofar as the term 'left wing' applies in the seventeenth century," Chad Jenkins said stiffly.

Mike and Melissa grinned. Back up-time, before the Ring of Fire, you couldn't have found the terms "Chad Jenkins" and "left wing" in the same room. But whether the man was comfortable with the fact or not, in the year 1634 in central Europe, Chad Jenkins was a flaming radical. Even Grantville's most reactionary prominent individual, Tino Nobili—a man who'd been regularly described as "to the right of Genghis Khan"—was, in most ways, a "left-winger" in the here and now. At least, with regard to strictly political matters if not theological ones.

Luckily, Jenkins had a sense of humor. After a moment, he chuckled and leaned back in his chair. "Okay, okay, old habits die hard. I guess I might as well resign myself to the fact that I'm part of this revolutionary cabal."

Now it was Melissa's turn to get a little stiff. "It's hardly a 'cabal,' Chad. Most of us here *are,* after all, elected officials."

"So?" His grin was more in the way of a jeer. "And since when did being an of-fi-cial cut any mustard with *you,* Melissa? I can remember at least one speech you gave, back during the miners' strike, when you referred to the entire U.S. government as a conspiracy on the part of the rich and mighty to downtrod the masses."

"'Downtrod' is not a verb, and I'm sure I didn't use it that way," Melissa said primly. "I know. I'm a schoolteacher. Other than that . . ." She returned the jeering grin with a cool smile. "Fine. *Touché.*"

"If the two of you will quit squabbling over terminology," Ed said mildly, "I'd like to return to the subject. My point was that in most provinces in the USE, most people will let the upper crust determine how they vote. And for the nobility and the town gentry, the Crown Loyalist platform pushes all the right buttons. Especially the two big ones."

He stuck up his thumb. "First, of course, they want to reestablish a state church. On a national level, not simply a provincial level."

"They have not much choice," said Constantin Ableidinger, "if they want an established church. Most of the CL leaders are Lutherans, and the few who aren't are Calvinists. They know perfectly well that if they let each province determine its own established church, some of them—certainly the SoTF and Magdeburg—would flat refuse. And if they forced the issue, Thuringia and Franconia would probably decide to split the difference and let Franconia choose Catholicism."

Melissa shook her head. "It's insane! The problem isn't simply Lutheran versus Calvinist versus Catholic. Even if they get their damn established Lutheran church, then what? There are two major factions among the Lutherans, the Philippists and the Flacians. There's no way the same pigheaded idiots who insist on a state church aren't also going to insist that it has to have the right theology. And there we are, back in the soup. Philippists and Flacians squabbling all over Germany, with everybody else—Calvinists, Catholics, Anabaptists, Jews, everybody else—out in the cold."

"The emperor and Wettin himself will lean heavily in favor of the Philippists," said Ed. "Which means the Flacians will go berserk. What a mess."

"Not to mention the Committees of Correspondence," said Chad. "Speaking of 'going berserk.' Setting up an established church will have the same effect on them as waving a red flag in front of bull."

Mike seemed a little exasperated. "Unfortunately, I'm afraid you're right."

Chad looked at him quizzically. "I thought you were dead set against established churches yourself."

"In theory, yes. In practice . . . it depends how it's done. Back in the universe we came from, several advanced industrial nations still had established churches, formally speaking. But if the English or the Danes were groaning under theological tyranny, somehow it slipped our attention."

Melissa frowned. "Well, yeah, but . . . Mike, it took *centuries* for that to evolve."

"I understand that—which is exactly why I advocate a complete separation of church and state. I'm just saying that I wouldn't lose much sleep if we wound up having to settle for a compromise. As long as nonestablished churches aren't persecuted, I can live with an established church." He leaned forward in his chair. "For sure and certain, better than I could live with what the Crown Loyalists propose to do with the *other* central political issue in the campaign. The question of citizenship."

Ed nodded. "Yes, that's really the big one."

"Can somebody explain this one to me?" asked Chad. "I have a grasp of the issue—sort of—but it's still fuzzy around the edges. We don't seem to have to deal with this problem much in our neck of the woods."

Ableidinger grinned. "That's because, between you Americans and we Ram folk, the issue got pretty well settled in practice in Thuringia and Franconia."

"It's not much of an issue in Magdeburg province either," said Gunther Achterhof. His grin was a lot thinner than Ableidinger's. "And it won't be, no matter who wins the election."

"The essence of the matter is this, Charles," said Rebecca. "In the world you came from—I speak of your old United States of America—being a 'citizen' of the nation was quite straightforward. If you were born in America, or became a naturalized citizen, that was the end of it. You were a citizen, pure and simple."

Chad nodded. "Pretty much. A lot of states had a provision to take away your citizenship—your right to vote, I should say—if you got convicted of a felony. But, other than that, yes."

"Here in the Germanies, on the other hand, it is far more complicated. To begin with, there is nothing equivalent to national citizenship. Insofar as 'citizenship' is concerned, it is a local matter. A man may reside and work in a given city or province, and yet not be a citizen. In practice, that means that he does not enjoy a great number of protections—residency rights, for instance—nor is he entitled to charity or other support."

"Most Germans in the here and now," Mike interrupted, "are not really citizens of anything. They are 'German' in terms of language, custom, what have you. But they are not 'German' in any meaningful political sense of the term. And, if the Crown Loyalists have their way, that won't change in the future."

"I still don't get it," said Chad. "They have the right to *vote* in the coming national election. So how can they not be 'citizens'?"

Becky smiled. "Being a 'voter' and a 'citizen' are not the same thing. It's far more complicated. Let's take a lower class man—an apprentice carpenter, let's say—in . . . oh, Hamburg, for example. He can vote in the coming election for whichever candidate he wants for his House of Commons district. But that's it. He cannot vote for any of the officials of the city itself. That's because Hamburg is one of the half-dozen or so free imperial cities in the United States of Europe. For most purposes, it is a province of its own—of which he is not a citizen. He has no rights in Hamburg, not even residency rights. He is there on sufferance, essentially."

Jenkins scratched his head. "It's sort of like Jim Crow, then?"

Mike made a face. "Well . . . there are differences. At least in many towns, the spirit is closer to up-time laws about out-of-state tuition for going to state colleges and universities. But, yes, it's a lot closer to Jim Crow than we'd like. In some ways, in fact, it's even worse. At least black people in the Jim Crow south had the theoretical right to vote, even if exercising the vote was stifled in practice. Here, though, a lot of people in Germany won't even theoretically be citizens, if the Crown Loyalists get their whole program enacted."

"Will they be able to?" asked Chad.

Ed shrugged. "Hell, who knows? Ask that question again after the election. It'll depend how many seats they wind up winning in the House of Commons. They'll completely dominate the Chamber of Princes, of course."

"Ed's fudging," said Mike. "This question of citizenship is the one big issue on which all the small parties are in solid agreement with the CLs. There are other issues—an established church, for instance, since some of the small parties are heavily Calvinist—that I think we might be able to block. But unless we win an outright majority in the Commons, which none of us expects to happen, then Wettin and his CLs will get that citizenship legislation passed."

"At which point," said Gunther Achterhof, "all hell breaks loose."

He didn't say that threateningly, or even with a scowl. Just . . . matter-of-factly.

Chad Jenkins looked alarmed. "Hey, Gunther, we have to obey the law here."

Achterhof gave him a calm, level look. "'Obey the law' has very little to do with it, Mr. Jenkins. Once that legislation is enacted, then the informal freedoms and rights that many lower class persons all across the Germanies have come to expect while he"—he nodded toward Mike—"was prime minister, will start vanishing. Be assured that every petty nobleman and town council and guildmaster in the USE will immediately take advantage of the situation to reimpose their authority and restrict the rights of the lower classes as much as possible. And nowadays, several years after the Ring of Fire—you may be assured of this also—*that* will trigger off an explosion."

For all that Achterhof's depiction had the air of a neutral observation by an unbiased observer, Francisco Nasi knew perfectly well that when the time came Gunther—certainly Gretchen Richter—and every Committee of Correspondence in the Germanies would be leading the protests.

Protests? It might very well come down to an outright rebellion. Nasi knew that Mike Stearns didn't think there was any realistic prospect of avoiding violence. Mike's concern, at the moment, was simply to find ways to channel the upcoming explosion in the hopes that it might produce some positive results instead of simply a bloodbath.

Easier said than done, of course. Gunther Achterhof was quite right in his analysis. Even the short time Mike Stearns had wielded power in the USE as prime minister had been enough to produce a revolution of rising expectations in Germany's lower classes. Many if not all of them would find a return to the old dispensation intolerable.

And what made the whole situation so utterly perilous—looking at it now from the standpoint of the upper crust, whom Nasi thought were outright imbeciles—was . . .

Stearns said it bluntly.

"You may as well swallow the whole thing, Chad, whether you like it or not. The kicker in all this is that the factor that most ruling classes in history rely on to impose their will on the population is the army. And in the United States of Europe in the year 1635, that army will be leaning heavily in favor of us—not the establishment."

Jenkins was looking even more alarmed. "Jesus, Mike! You can't seriously be proposing a mutiny!"

"Oh, cut it out, Chad," interrupted Frank Jackson brusquely. "We're not living any longer in a nice, polite, well-ordered and comfortable political situation where political parties make 'propositions' and everybody waits patiently to see who wins the vote." He jerked a thumb toward Mike. "It doesn't matter whether he advocates or proposes a mutiny. I guarantee you that if the Crown Loyalists order the regular army—just to give an example—to march into Magdeburg and suppress a demonstration—hell, even an outright armed rebellion—the regiments will flat refuse. And if Wettin's government tries to force the issue, the soldiers will start shooting at him instead."

Jenkins stared at him. Francisco cleared his throat. "General Jackson's assessment is almost certainly correct, Mr. Jenkins. I know for a fact that General Torstensson is deeply concerned over the matter and has warned the emperor several times that Wettin's recklessness—"

"The Crown Loyalists' recklessness, really," Mike interrupted. "I don't think, left to his own devices, Wilhelm would be pushing the issue this hard."

Nasi nodded his agreement and continued. "Torstensson has warned Gustav Adolf that he can't rely on the army for suppression of internal dissent. Not the regular USE army, at least. And if the emperor or anyone else tries to use other units, either Swedish troops or mercenary forces, it's quite possible that would trigger off a rebellion on the part of the regular army."

"Jesus." Chad shook his head, as if clearing away confusion. "I didn't realize things were that tense." He gave Ed Piazza and Constantin Ableidinger a sly smile. "I guess, down there in the SoTF, I've gotten used to the way these two firebrands keep everything under control."

"And will keep things under control," Ed said, smiling just as slyly. "Not even the most rabid Crown Loyalist proposes the imposition of any sort of national citizenship requirement. The whole matter will be left to each province to decide for itself—and for us in Thuringia-Franconia, it's a done deal. Nothing will change, so far as citizenship is concerned."

Jenkins looked back at Nasi. "And what did Gustav Adolf say? In response to Torstensson's warning?"

Nasi's smile was serene. "You understand, of course, that I am not officially privy to any private conversations between the emperor and the top commander of the USE's armed forces."

"Yeah, sure. Butter doesn't melt in your mouth and all that. What'd he say?"

"Alas, our esteemed emperor is far too preoccupied at the moment with foreign affairs to pay sufficient attention to domestic matters. So his responses have been terse—being honest—to the point of vacuity. The gist of his attitude seems to be that it will all prove to be a moot point, since by the time the Crown Loyalists are able to enact their citizenship legislation, Gustav Adolf and Lennart Torstensson and the entire USE regular army will be somewhere in Brandenburg or Saxony—perhaps even Poland—dealing mighty blows to the unrighteous cohorts of the wicked."

Jenkins stared at him. "That . . . seems a little foolhardy."

Mike snorted. "A 'little'? Here's the truth, Chad. Gustav Adolf is just too absorbed—hell, call it 'obsessed' and you won't be far off—with settling accounts with the French and the Danes and chomping at the bit to pile onto the Saxons and Brandenburgers next year to be thinking much at all about the domestic situation in the USE. So it apparently hasn't dawned on him yet that if any sort of major rebellions break out while the regular army is fighting in the east, then the various provincial forces in the USE will be hard-pressed to squash them."

"Yeah," said Frank. "Squash them with what? They can't use Swedish forces without the emperor's permission—and even if he was inclined to give it, he'll have all those forces with him fighting the war anyway. So that means they have to use provincial troops and city militias. And while that might have been good enough a few years back, it ain't now. Just to name one example, nobody much doubts that if a civil war breaks out again in Hamburg that it'll be won hands-down by the city's CoC. For that matter, the same's likely to be true in five out of the USE's seven imperial cities, because the CoC is also strong in Luebeck, Frankfurt and Strassburg. The only 'moderate' imperial cities are Augsburg and Ulm."

"There are two provinces where the same's true, also," added Mike. "The Upper Palatinate and Mecklenburg."

"Hesse-Kassel's provincial forces are quite substantial," Nasi said. "But Hesse-Kassel won't see any major upheavals anyway—and there's very little chance that the landgrave would agree to send his troops to the aid of the establishment in any other province."

Ed Piazza cleared his throat. "Especially after I send him a stiff note, as president of the SoTF, explaining that if Hesse-Kassel starts sending its troops into other provinces, Thuringia-Franconia will start doing the same. On the other side."

Now, Jenkins was *really* looking alarmed. "For Christ's sake, Ed! The SoTF's so-called 'provincial troops' don't amount to squat. They're just small garrisons—a police force more than anything else."

"Sure—and so what? If the situation goes to hell in a handbasket, we'll call for volunteers. We'll get 'em, don't think we won't. The CoCs are strong in Thuringia and—"

Ableidinger chimed in. "And the Ram will call for volunteers in Franconia. They'll come, too."

Piazza shrugged. "Push comes to shove, the State of Thuringia-Franconia has the largest population of any province in the USE and we've got a far better industrial base than any other except—in some industries—Magdeburg. And Magdeburg will be doing the same thing anyway."

Jenkins was looking a little haggard, now. "Jesus H. Christ."

"Let's hope it doesn't come to that," said Mike. "But we've wandered into speculation here, people. I think we need to get back to the nuts and bolts of the coming campaign. That's starting immediately, where this other—if it happens at all—is months down the road."

After the meeting was over and everyone had left the conference room except Stearns, Nasi and Lang, Mike turned to Francisco.

"The one thing we really *don't* want is any kind of premature confrontation with the Crown Loyalists. I don't know whether it'll come to a civil war of sorts next summer or fall, but what I know for sure is that if it does I want all our ducks lined up in a row, not scattered all over East Jesus because they got disorganized during some second-rate squabble in the spring."

Nasi nodded. "Yes, I understand."

"So. Are there any flash points you can see? If there are, I'd like to make sure they're squelched ahead of time."

"Outside of the usual problems . . ." Francisco turned to look at Lang. "There is the matter of whatever those Huguenot fanatics may be up to. The ones around Michel Ducos—his followers, I should say. We don't know the current whereabouts of Ducos. Cory Joe?"

Lang's sleepy look didn't quite vanish. But he certainly didn't look as alert as his ensuing words indicated him to be. "The don asked me to pull all that information together, Mike. So far, though, it's pretty ragged. Bits and pieces from Nathan Prickett in Frankfurt, which is where they've had a cell for a few months. And a few odds and ends from elsewhere."

"What does it all add up to?"

"Hard to say," replied Nasi. "The problem is that whatever the Huguenots are involved with here in the USE does not directly involve us. Or, it might be better to say, we are simply a means to an end. Their real target is Cardinal Richelieu."

"And why is that a problem—for us?"

"Because it makes it hard to predict exactly what they might do *here.* Since their aim is on Richelieu, they might do something that makes sense in a French political context but makes no sense at all from our standpoint."

"I'm not quite following you."

Cory Joe spoke up. "Here's an example, Mike. From the latest items we've gotten, it seems as if the Huguenots in Frankfurt may be getting involved with some of our own anti-Semitic groups. Yet there doesn't seem to be any logical reason for that. As fanatical as they may be, Ducos' Huguenots are not anti-Semitic themselves. Actually, that's part of the fanaticism, in a way, since they're extreme Calvinist predestinationists, if that's a real word."

Mike chuckled. "I don't think so, but I get the point. If there are Jews in the world it's because God wants them here and who the hell are you to question His judgment?"

Nasi shook his head. "Of course, one might wonder why the same principle doesn't apply to their political concerns. If Cardinal Richelieu is running France it's because God wants him to and who are you to question His judgment?"

"And it's still more complicated," Cory Joe added, "because it seems that we might be dealing with *two* different Huguenot outfits, not just Ducos and his people."

Mike cocked an eye. "And the other being . . ."

"Duke Henri de Rohan," said Nasi. "Probably France's most prominent Huguenot political figure. Now residing in Besançon, it seems. And the duke's younger brother Benjamin, the duke of Soubise."

"And to make things *still* more complicated," said Cory Joe, "we're beginning to suspect that some of the agents on the ground are working for both parties. If so, obviously, one of those parties is getting suckered by a double-agent. But we have no idea which one is which or who's suckering who."

Mike shook his head much the way Chad Jenkins had earlier, as if clearing away confusion. "Boy, I'm glad it's the two of you trying to keep track of this spaghetti instead of me." He scratched his chin for a minute. "All right, I think I get at least as much of the picture as there is to get right now. If so, it sounds as if things have developed enough that maybe Cory Joe should start going down to Grantville on a regular basis. Francisco, you don't really need his services as a bodyguard so long as you're residing in Magdeburg."

"No, I don't. As for the other"—here he smiled, very coolly—"I believe that expression you're overfond of applies here."

Mike chuckled. "'Don't teach your grandmother how to suck eggs.'"

"Yes, that one. We've already set up the premises, with Frank Jackson's cooperation. Cory Joe's heading down to Grantville the day after tomorrow."

For the first time, Cory Joe seemed to come wide awake. "You got any messages you want me to pass on to anybody, Mike? Like, y'know, to your favorite cousin my mother."

Mike made a face. Cory Joe laughed. "Just as well, since I woulda refused anyway. I haven't seen the worthless bitch in months and I'd just as soon keep the streak going." His hard face softened a little. "It'll be nice to see my sisters again, though."

Chapter 24

Grantville

"Well, if you want an honest answer . . ." Count Ludwig Guenther of Schwarzburg-Rudolstadt raised his eyebrows.

"I very definitely do," said Tony Adducci.

"I don't think Duke Albrecht wanted to run against Piazza for president of the State of Thuringia-Franconia. At all. So don't hold it against him once the election is over. I know that he's William Wettin's brother, but he's really not a political type. He's perfectly happy, really, managing their property—finding new leaseholders and trying to bring it back into maximum production. But someone among the Crown Loyalists noticed that there's no prohibition in the SoTF constitution against a nobleman running for president—which would have been governor, up-time, if I understand what I have read concerning the structure of your government."

Adducci started to cuss a blue streak, which finally dwindled into, "Hell, it's like John and Bobby Kennedy, more than anything else, I guess. Brother act."

Mary Kat Riddle shook her head. "I wish Ms. Mailey was here. Or Mr. Piazza. But I'll do what I can to sort it out for you all." She pushed her hair behind her ears, a little nervously.

"Let's start at the beginning. William Wettin isn't 'running for prime minister.' That's not the way it works in a parliamentary system. Wettin's running for the lower house of the USE parliament from the Duchy of Saxe-Weimar—which is now actually one of the counties in the SoTF, just like we are."

She looked at Count Ludwig Guenther's wife Emelie, who was going to have a baby . . . just any minute now, it looked like. She was due this month. They'd gotten to be friends. "Or you are, in Schwarzburg-Rudolstadt."

"Okay."

"If the Crown Loyalists win a majority of the seats in the USE House of Commons in this election, they'll pick Wettin to be prime minister. Or, technically, send his name to the emperor, who will have to agree, pretty much, the way things are set up now. Gustav won't just be able to appoint someone, right out of the blue, the way he did with Mike last year. There's an actual system in place."

Count Ludwig Guenther nodded his approval.

Mary Kat looked back at Tony. "Let me back up a bit. Since Wettin is a commoner now, Duke Ernst is away working for Gustav, and Duke Bernhard is a loose cannon, Duke Albrecht has been representing Saxe-Weimar in the SoTF House of Lords."

Tony nodded. "Okay."

"The USE doesn't have a House of Lords, exactly, even though its Parliament is designed on the British model. In the CPE, its upper house used to be called the Chamber of Princes. We carried over the title but added the provision that if the head of state or a province was an elected or appointed official, then that official represented the province in the Chamber of Princes." She smiled. "That's why our very own unassuming Ed Piazza will wind up being not just the SoTF president, but also the SoTF 'prince' in the Chamber of Princes."

"I don't like this mixing the executive and legislative branches together," Joe Stull muttered. "We learned about checks and balances in civics. There's supposed to be three branches of government and they're supposed to be separate."

"We all know, Joe," Tony said. "We've heard your opinion before. My wife says that Montesquieu would be proud of you."

"Who?"

Mary Kat looked at Count Ludwig Guenther, got a cue, and went on. "The reason Wettin's a commoner is that when they wrote the USE constitution, they put in a requirement that the prime minister had to be from the lower house—the House of Commons, not the Chamber of Princes. So he abdicated."

She sighed, pushing her hair back again.

Count Ludwig Guenther smiled. "Do you have a problem?"

"I honestly don't understand this one, myself. I mean, we'd already 'slid' Saxe-Weimar out from under him. He wasn't a *ruling* prince any more. Being a duke was just a kind of personal title—not political, any more. If they'd had the constitution written up then . . ." She frowned. "I hadn't thought of this before, but Mike was the president of the NUS then. He'd have been serving in the Chamber of Princes then, just like Ed is now."

"Yes." Count Ludwig Guenther rather enjoyed watching the young up-time lawyer think.

"But Gustavus Adolphus just sort of arbitrarily appointed Mike the prime minister of the new USE, before they got the new constitution written. Ed succeeded him as president. Oh. This is baaaaad! Once he was president, since they weren't able to have elections, then Ed appointed Mike to the House of Commons from one voting district in Thuringia, making him eligible to be prime minister under the new constitution. Sort of *ex post facto*."

She looked at the count again. "Believe me, for the USA in the twentieth century, and ever since the American constitution was adopted, *ex post facto* was forbidden. Bad stuff. No *ex post facto* laws. But what else could Ed have done?"

He nodded. "I am familiar with the platitude that hard cases make bad law."

"Okay. But things were really crazy those few weeks right after the Battle of Wismar, so they had to do something sort of . . . retroactive . . . to fix the situation. Also, because Mike and Wettin had made a sort of gentlemen's agreement, Ed appointed Wettin to the House of Commons from another voting district in Thuringia. And . . . stuff happened."

"Scads of bad stuff," Joe Stull muttered. "I know all about it. It was all over West Virginia, up-time, like slime. Horace Bolender and his cronies down-time, too. 'One hand washes the other.'"

"Okay." Mary Kat looked around the room. "This is what I really don't understand. Only about a dozen people were eligible to serve in the Chamber of Princes back then. Two of those were Gustavus Adolphus being the duke of Mecklenburg and Gustavus Adolphus being the duke of Pomerania. Brunswick. Hesse-Kassel. Ed. The governor of Magdeburg Province, who's elected, like Ed.

"Now, since, the Congress of Copenhagen, there are several more, and a bunch of them are the provincial administrators that Gustavus Adolphus appointed—his own guys in Westphalia, Upper Rhine, and Mainz. There will be another appointed member of the upper house from Swabia once things settle down there, but it doesn't look like that will happen in time for this election. Those appointed administrators may or may not get elected as the heads of those provinces in this election. I'm not even sure if Gustavus is planning to throw them open for election this time around."

Nobody else had anything to contribute on that issue, so after a pause, Mary Kat continued.

"But, since Copenhagen, there actually already are more elected members of the upper house—the mayors of the new expanded imperial city-provinces like Hamburg and Frankfurt am Main. But none of those elected members can ever be prime minister, any more than Ed can, because the constitution says that the prime minister has to come from the House of Commons, the lower house."

"Your analysis is admirably succinct," Count Ludwig Guenther said. "And correct."

"I never really thought about this before." Mary Kat looked at the count. "Where does this leave, uh, guys like you? Nobles who hang onto their titles but aren't princes? You don't get to be in the Chamber of Princes and you don't get to be in the House of Commons."

"If they are my age? They may resign themselves to exerting local political influence only, at the level of the provinces. Or they may accept appointive positions in the USE executive branch, as Wilhelm of Hesse-Kassel's brother Hermann has done."

Mary Kat nodded. "He's secretary of state. And Wettin's brother, Duke Ernst, is regent in the Upper Palatinate."

"If they are younger? Why, in my opinion, they should think of abdicating their titles, so they can enter the House of Commons." Count Ludwig Guenther smiled wryly. "That, I believe, was in large part the point of it all."

Joe Stull shook his head. "Sure does make a man understand the proverb about not watching anyone make laws or sausages.

But you're off on a tangent. Way out in left field. Can we get back to Duke Albrecht of Saxe-Weimar running against Ed Piazza?"

Mary Kat checked where she was on the outline she had brought to the meeting. At least they'd warned her a couple of days ahead of time that they wanted a briefing. She wasn't coming in cold.

"Way back when we—well, not me as a part of 'we' because I sure wasn't on the committee—but when the constitutional subcommittee of the Emergency Committee drew up the NUS constitution, back in 1631, Grantville wasn't setting up a parliament. Our constitution sets up a congress. It's turned into a state legislature for all practical purposes, now that we're a province of the USE, but we're still calling it 'Congress' and it's still organized pretty much the same. With a 'House and Senate' structure, except—"

"How many 'excepts' are there going to be?" Joe asked.

"A lot. If you'll just let me finish what I'm saying now . . ." Mary Kat sighed. "Sorry, Joe. I'm getting frazzled."

"I'm the one frazzling you. Sorry, go ahead. I'll keep my mouth shut."

"In the deal that Mike and Gustavus Adolphus cut after the Croat Raid in 1632, Gustavus Adolphus, back when he was the captain general and not the emperor yet, made Mike agree that the NUS had to have a House of Lords. Except not like the English House of Lords, where guys got to come just because they had titles. That would never have worked, because the German noble houses don't use primogeniture."

Joe broke his promise and opened his mouth. "What the hell's that?"

"Oldest son takes it all. That's too simple, but not-too-simple would take all night to explain. In England, just the one guy was noble. In the Germanies, all the sons and daughters are noble. We'd have ended up looking like Poland or someplace if we'd let them all into the NUS House of Lords. So the House of Lords that Ms. Mailey—it was her, really—designed was more like the Chamber of Princes. Not every noble in the NUS had a seat in it. If the place being represented had a ruling count or duke or something, he was automatically in it."

She waved across the room. "Like Count Ludwig Guenther for Schwarzburg-Rudolstadt when it joined the NUS, or Margrave Christian of Bayreuth, now, after the Ram Rebellion. But for Grantville, and Badenburg, and other places without lords that joined the NUS, the person elected to the House of Lords could be a commoner and was called a senator. Like Becky. Didn't have to be a noble. Plus, nobles who weren't rulers didn't have a seat in the House of Lords. Just the ones who used to be in the *Reichstag*."

"Okay," Tony Adducci said.

Joe Stull shook his head. "Not okay by me. I'm getting a headache already."

Mary Kat stood up. "And, now, here's the point, so pay attention, Joe. Sort of the reverse, and it's never been amended—just got carried over to the SoTF without change. The constitution that the Emergency Committee drafted didn't say that the president of the NUS had to be a commoner. Just a citizen."

Tony brought his chair forward so hard that the front legs skidded on the hardwood floor of Chad Jenkins' living room. "Oh, God. Why not?"

Chad Jenkins shrugged. "Because it damned well didn't occur to the constitutional subcommittee. We were flying by the seat of our pants, back then, all of us. It just didn't occur to anybody to put in a requirement that the president had to be a commoner."

Missy Jenkins frowned. "Not even to Ms. Mailey?"

Her father shook his head. "Nope. Who dreamed, back then, that any noble was ever going to want to run for president of the NUS?"

Tony's next contribution was, "Flying, fucking, triple-damn."

Mary Kat looked at Countess Emelie a little apologetically. "So. Duke Albrecht's got a grandfathered seat in the SoTF House of Lords. He doesn't have to run for that. Then the Crown Loyalists figured out that he can run for president against Ed, too. Without resigning from the House of Lords, unless he gets elected."

Count Ludwig Guenther nodded. "Which he doesn't have a prayer of doing. The Piazza-Ableidinger ticket is going to win the SoTF in a landslide and the Crown Loyalists know it. Which is why they aren't wasting a viable candidate running against Ed Piazza."

Missy giggled. "Or against Dad, for Becky's seat."

"I am sure," Count Ludwig Guenther said a little sententiously, "that they seriously regret having nominated Marcus von Drachhausen just two weeks before he was arrested for attempted rape. Not to mention the subsequent charges brought against him in the Bolender scandal. They've been playing catch-up ever since, trying to find someone with the sheer gall to accept a belated special nomination."

Joe Stull reached for another beer. "I really can't say that I wish them luck."

In the carriage on the way back to Rudolstadt, Count Ludwig Guenther looked at his wife a little anxiously. "Do you think I should have made my point more forcefully, dear? I meant my statement that I don't think Duke Albrecht wants to run against Piazza for president of the State of Thuringia-Franconia. At all. I am honestly afraid that many of the up-timers are likely to hold it against him personally once the election is over. That will make things much more difficult in the House of Lords, and possibly spill over into the SoTF's ability to influence measures in the USE Parliament. Because of the relationship with Wettin. While it's true enough that Albrecht isn't a viable candidate in his own right, his name on the ballot will help with name recognition for Wettin."

Emelie leaned her head against his shoulder. "Why on earth would they hold it against him?"

"Because so many of them, in their hearts, have contempt for the art of government. The art of politics that is, in its essence, compromise. The ability to see that the other side may also have a point. They want a world that comes in black and white; absolute good or absolute evil. They find multiple shades of gray frustrating.

"It is, I think, one of the reasons that I am able, and Gustavus Adolphus, for that matter, is able, to work with Stearns. He, very refreshingly, came to us as an experienced negotiator. In the odd environment of these 'unions,' to be sure, but still with what amounts to extensive experience in diplomacy. He realizes that after the negotiations are over, life must continue. That it is the attitude of 'either we smash them utterly or they will smash us utterly' that drew the Germanies into this disastrous war."

His voice trailed off. "Not to mention the Lutheran theological negotiations of last spring."

Emelie shifted her head, so she could look up. "You mean Stearns understands that a victory, to be secure, must lead to a peace that both sides can bear."

"Precisely. That it is unwise to demonize the other side. Except, of course, in those rare cases when the other side is utterly demonic. But Albrecht of Saxe-Weimar is by no means a demon. Not even an enemy of the Fourth of July Party. Merely, for the duration of this campaign, an opponent."

"But if Prime Minister Stearns understands all this . . . ?"

"There is no way that Stearns can be omnipresent, my dear. He is now an actor on the national—even the international—stage. But we must somehow make sure that the scenes being acted in our provincial theater . . . I am far from sure how to phrase this."

"Remain in harmony with the overall theme of the larger play?"

"Excellent, dearest. Excellent."

"I think the carriage is coming to a halt. We are home."

The count nodded absentmindedly. "I must speak with Piazza. He also, of course, understands negotiations. School boards. Parent-teacher associations. Such a plethora of training grounds for an aspiring participant in the 'great game.' It's a pity that so many of them were politically apathetic."

Emelie smiled as the footman handed her down from the coach. "The 'great game.' Kipling. I have read Kipling, too."

Chapter 25

Grantville

Pam Hardesty looked at the newspaper. Blinked, and looked again.

That's what it said, all right. Under the column headed MARRIAGES:

> *MAUGER, Laurent, of Haarlem, Netherlands, and HARDESTY, Velma, of Grantville, at City Hall.*
>
> *The groom wore a scarlet satin suit with a lace collar and black patent leather boots. The bride wore a lavender vinyl wrap dress and matching backless, toeless high-heeled slip-on sandals. They exchanged rings. Official witnesses were Jacques-Pierre Dumais, formerly of La Rochelle, now of Grantville, and Veda Mae Haggerty, of Grantville. The groom is a wine merchant well-known as a frequent visitor to our town. The bride was most recently employed as a waitress at the 250 Club.*

"Goddam her," she hissed, half under her breath. It would be just like her mother Velma to get remarried without even bothering to mention it to her own children.

Pam grabbed the telephone. There was no way to reach her half-brother Cory Joe Lang quickly, but she could at least reach her half-sister Susan Logsden. That was more important anyway, since Susan was still a teenager.

"Grandpa Ben," she wailed. "Have you seen the *Times*? Page three, column four. I'm at work, so I'm going to check in Principal Saluzzo's office for her class schedule, find Susan, and tell her before some spiteful little bitch does. In the meanest way possible, of course. High school is the pits. You and Grandma Gloria better come, too. Yeah, I know it's too far for her to walk. Take the trolley; everybody else does."

"I could scarcely believe she wore that dress. And talk about a pair of slut shoes." Veda Mae swallowed the last of her spinach pudding.

Jacques-Pierre had scarcely been able to believe the dress at all. Much less that anyone would wear it. However, who was he to question Madame Hardesty's sartorial preferences? They had served their purposes—and, more to the point, his purposes. The happy couple had already departed for the Netherlands. With even the slightest amount of luck, he would never be obliged to speak with Velma Hardesty again.

"Mauger seemed to have a favorable enough view of her choice."

"How would he know what's good taste or not? Satin and lace on a man. I remember those clothes people wore when Schmidt from Badenburg married Delia Higgins' daughter Ramona. Stupid little whore. Trousers blown up like balloons. They have to have stuffing inside. What is he, a fag?"

Jacques-Pierre reviewed the progress of the match he had initiated, from introduction to, presumably, consummation. "I seriously doubt it."

Veda Mae snorted.

"Mauger and his first wife had several children."

"What does that tell anybody? You have no idea how many politicians they used to catch, back up-time, with perfectly nice wives and children, from the pictures that the papers published afterwards, doing what they shouldn't in men's restrooms at truck stops or lay-byes on the highways."

He nodded.

"This so-called emperor of the USE. Have you *seen* some of the clothes he wears? Purple. Silver embroidery. Ruffles on his cuffs.

And he's left his wife up there in Sweden by herself for years at a time, now. That tells you something, doesn't it?"

Jacques-Perre sipped his coffee, thinking rather abstractedly that Madame Haggerty was in rare form, tonight. As loquacious as always and spiteful to boot. Now, what more fruitful topic might he introduce into the conversation?

"I have heard that one of the Kelly Aviation planes has been taken on a test flight."

"By Lannie Yost, that stupid sot. With Keenan Murphy, who can't shoot at all. And Buster Beasley's kid, Denise. Bob Kelly has to be nuts to send up a crew like that."

"There are some rumors that he didn't approve the flight in advance."

"Probably too henpecked."

"His wife approved it?"

"Not that I know of. Kelly and his wife are outsiders, you know. He was here in Grantville working on a construction project. They got stuck. And stuck-up is what Kay Kelly is. Serves her right to have to spend the rest of her life in some little hick town. Which is how she sees it, I'm sure. That's probably why she accepted the nomination."

"What nomination?"

"To run against Chad Jenkins on the Crown Loyalist ticket. For the seat that Kraut wife of Mike Stearns is giving up. Talk about scraping the bottom of the barrel—they managed to find someone lower than von Drachhausen. Bottom of the barrel for both parties. When Chad served a term as county commissioner, up-time, he was a real fizzle."

"Oh?"

"But I suppose there's one bright spot. No matter which of them wins, at least it won't be a Kraut."

He could scarcely ask Madame Haggerty to give him a good reason for someone to demonstrate against the Grantville hospital.

She gave him one, without his asking. Truly, the woman was a free gift.

It came in the course of a long recitation of her quasi-medical grievances against what he had learned was called "the establishment." In this case, "the medical establishment" and the physicians whose diagnoses had denied her late husband's right to receive certain benefits for "black lung disability" prior to the Ring of Fire. Madame Haggerty was quite certain that he had been entitled to them, no matter what the doctors claimed that the X-rays showed.

Her specific complaint in this matter escalated into resentment of the medical profession as a whole. Particularly the portion of it that managed the Bowers Assisted Living Center, where she worked.

It would not have occurred to Jacques-Pierre that such a manifest benefit as the prevention of smallpox would have been controversial among the up-timers. However, she brought him a group of "alternative medicine" pamphlets she had found stuffed into the drawer of a lamp table in the vestibule of the assisted living center. By, Madame Haggerty said, somebody who obviously understood "what those quacks who call themselves doctors are up to."

The pamphlets had been very valuable in allowing him to develop the medical rationale that would be used by the protesters at Leahy Medical Center.

He wondered what the Canadian Chiropractic Association had been. Canada, to the best of his knowledge, was very sparsely populated by French settlers, but these pamphlets had been printed in English. The members of the organization had, in any case, been vociferous in their opposition to vaccinations, inoculations, and immunizations. Since the up-time doctors, through the new medical school in Jena, were at the forefront of a campaign to introduce these ways of warding off smallpox, the discovery that there had been up-time opposition to the practice was a delight.

Yes, given his current assignment from Mauger, it was a delight and a comfort to learn that not all up-time influence would be pulling in the same direction. After some questioning, he had discovered that there were a few, though not many, Grantvillers who shared this philosophy.

He took the pamphlets to the Grantviller who called himself a chiropractor. That did not turn out to be very rewarding. The man did not agree with their contents. But his usual presentation of himself as a humble seeker of enlightenment had been quite successful. The man had shown him other materials of the same type that he had collected at "conventions." These appeared to be equivalent to diets or parliaments, but conducted by "professional associations," which were not the same as guilds, but in some ways comparable. The materials had confirmed the existence of differences of opinion.

He notified Mauger.

And Duke Henri, of course, although the duke had never displayed the slightest interest in the topic of vaccinations, pro or con.

He duplicated a couple hundred copies of the anti-vaccination pamphlets for use in central Thuringia. Mauger wrote, saying that he should mail a couple of copies to Frankfurt for printing and distribution from there.

They would soon be circulating quite widely throughout the USE. No one would be surprised when protesters inspired by their contents appeared in Grantville.

"I'm not sure," Pam Hardesty said, "that it would be so bad."

"What?" asked Missy Jenkins.

"Having a mom who's . . . well, sort of maternal. What you're complaining about, Missy. A mom who takes an interest in what you're doing. Doesn't want you to get hurt. What do you think, Ron?"

Ron's feelings were ambivalent. Debbie's strong interest in where her daughter Missy was, when, and with whom, tended to have a sort of hamstringing effect on where Missy went and when. The "with whom" had not, so far, kept her from being with him, though.

Ron's own mother had been primarily notable for her absence. So . . .

"Magda's actually a pretty cool stepmother. And she can cook."

Both of the girls looked at him. It must have slipped Pam's mind that the Stone boys, until their father married Magda a couple of years ago, hadn't had a mother at all.

He realized that Pam might be feeling a little bad for having asked him.

"That's okay," he told her. "We were used to it. Making do on our own. It was probably better than having the kind of mom you had to put up with."

Oh, no, Stone. You did not say that. You did not. She's Missy's friend. You're sunk.

"You could," Pam said, "have a point there. You have no idea how happy I was to get the news that she was marrying a foreigner and going away. I'll probably never have to see her again. Never have to be embarrassed again by the slutty things she did. I was sixteen when . . ."

Her voice trailed off, then started up again. "That was when I left home. Never again to wake up to get ready for school and find out that she came home drunk and vomited on the shoes in my closet. Inside them. All of them, so I'm standing there in my socks knowing that either I'll be late for school to run the sneakers through the laundromat or go to school stinking.

"Now I'll never have to fend off any more guys who think I'll be like her if they push a little harder. She's gone. She's actually *gone*."

Missy listened, astonished by Pam's tone of voice. Not to mention by her statements in regard to shoes.

Obviously, the range of maternal variants included mothers who were far worse than her own.

Which didn't mean that her own wasn't behaving like a pain right now. That was true, too. Compared to the way Nani Hudson was behaving, though, Mom wasn't so bad. Mellow, almost.

Ron stood, watching the end of practice. As a coach, Missy was fierce. Ferocious. Aggressive. Not harsh with the kids, but pulling the best out of those girls and getting them to play their hearts out on a day that even the boys' high school team would have considered a little too cold.

He recognized some of the kids. Most of them appeared to be up-timers. Didn't the down-time parents want their daughters to play, or didn't they have time?

An idea dawned. The Farbenwerke needed its own soccer teams. Boys and girls both. With the idea gotten across that it was really a good thing for the parents to send their little girls out to play.

Missy watched as the girls ran into the building. Then she ran to the edge of the field where Ron was waiting and kissed him. She made sure to do that now. Every time they met. Right out in public. Just so Nani would hear about it.

Well, maybe not *just* so Nani would hear about it. It sort of put all the other girls in Grantville on notice that they would be trespassing if they so much as thought about kissing Ron Stone at present or any time in the immediate future.

She felt a little guilty about that, occasionally. He hadn't given her any right to put a brand on him. But he didn't seem to have any objection to the procedure.

It occurred to her that this particular kiss was going on for several seconds longer than absolutely necessary to make a point. Maybe she should demand her money back from the cosmic forces for that incense. If they had preserved her from this in the past, they were trying to double-time it now. They made it way too convenient to kiss Ron. He was only an inch or two taller than she was, which meant that no contortions were necessary. She gave herself a little shake and pulled away from the arm he had put around her waist.

It didn't occur to her that he might regard the procedure as an effective hands-off notification to other guys. Not even when he put the arm back and kissed her again. She was too busy trying to keep the impish electrons subdued.

Cunz Kastenmayer saw the kiss. He wondered if he might have averted it, if he hadn't been away for so many weeks, going to Fulda and Frankfurt and back with Mayor Dreeson. Had his mini-tour been worth it?

Then he told himself firmly not to be a fool. All that had happened, once, was that Herr Jenkins' daughter had sat down next to him at a meeting. Only in romances did the daughters of wealthy merchants fall in love with the sons of impecunious pastors, much less marry them. That was one of life's truths. The only kind of girl likely to marry the son of an impecunious pastor was the daughter of another impecunious pastor.

The likelihood that any of the Kastenmayer offspring would ever marry serious money and bring relief to the parental budget was really, to be honest, nonexistent. He pulled his cloak closer around his neck and walked on down the shortcut to catch the trolley that would take him to St. Martin's in the Fields.

Missy wasn't sure she ought to do it.

Her parents knew that she was seeing Ron regularly.

He came to the house to pick her up. So far, he had not come inside.

She'd been fine with that. Really, really, fine with that. She hadn't wanted him to. Somehow, if he was not laying eyes on her parents and her parents were not laying eyes on him, that made it a little less-so.

Made *him* a little less-so.

He was getting to be way-too-much-so. He was occupying a lot of her personal space.

Missy opened her mouth and invited Ron and Gerry to Thanksgiving dinner *chez* Jenkins on the excuse that they didn't have family in town.

Then she waited for him to turn it down.

He accepted.

She went home and told her mother that they were coming. The way that Mom had been sniping at her about Ron the last few weeks, it served her right.

Although it might make him even-more-so.

Ron went home and told the facilities manager at the Farbenwerke that he wouldn't have to worry about sending a meal up to the house from the cafeteria Thursday, because he and Gerry would go to the house of Herr Charles Jenkins for the holiday.

Then Ron mentioned the manager's son Lutz, who was in seventh grade at the middle school. The manager was very gratified that Herr Ron remembered.

"Come spring," Ron said, "when the weather allows, we'll be setting up soccer teams out here at the dye works to play in the recreation league. That will mean that the kids can practice near home rather than having to stay in town late. I'll coach the boys myself. Missy Jenkins has agreed to coach the girls."

The manager nodded.

"Missy says that equipment is tight in most sports below high school level, now that Grantville has five times the kids it used to. So as soon as you can, please get in touch with the sheltered workshop they've set up next to the Tech Center. There's a guy who works there a couple of days each week who is sewing leather skins for soccer balls. He only completes about one per week and we'll need at least a half dozen of them. If we want modern valves, we have to corner the market on deflated balls and transfer them. Any old inflatable balls like kids use in splash pools. Those can work for linings, too, if we find the right size. Check with Missy. She can tell you want to look out for."

The facilities manager happily told every other employee, not only about the sports teams the dye works would soon sponsor but also about the dinner.

Especially about the dinner.

The employees at the Farbenwerke had all naturally been concerned about the long-term future of the business when Herr Stone's oldest son had married in Italy the previous summer and appeared likely to remain there. So it had been a great relief to all the employees when, so soon after his return, Herr Ron had kissed Fräulein Jenkins right in front of the main building for all to see.

A very suitable choice, everyone agreed. Ron Stone and Missy Jenkins were quite young, of course. But the families in question, both fathers being such prosperous merchants, could certainly afford to have their heirs marry young.

Herr Ron was shouldering his responsibilities very well. Even though he wanted people to call him "Ron" without any form of address, which made several of the older employees quite uncomfortable.

The officials of the employees' union started to give thought to an appropriate celebration once the betrothal was officially announced.

Ron asked himself why he had accepted that invitation? Why he was getting involved with Missy Jenkins? The strong preferences in favor of it expressed by cosmic rhythm and karmic balance aside, of course. Those two obviously thought that getting involved with Missy in every way he could manage was a splendid idea and had started to bring along an associate named primal instinct every time he set eyes on her. That one insisted that if any other guy ever so much as looked at Missy that way, Ron would be obliged to turn him into toast. If any other guy tried to touch her, there would be burnt toast on the menu.

Not that he had any right to feel possessive, of course. They were, ummm, well, something. Friends. Friends plus. That would do for the time being. Definitely not *MineMineMineMine.*

In grade school, they'd gotten along fine. But in high school, Missy had been the sister of a jock, and Ron and his brothers had usually been on the outs with the jocks. Sure, maybe he had called her "Miss Cheerleading Ditz" a few times, but what could a girl whose parents gave her the totally ridiculous nickname of "Missy" expect? It was barely less absurd than Muffy and Buffy. Not that he had any right to make comments about ridiculous names, given that his own official monicker was Elrond.

Then the high school had stuck them into the accelerated schedule, the one that dumped a half dozen kids abruptly into the real world after summer school. She really hadn't been a ditz, he now realized. That had just been his own prejudices at work. She'd been a cheerleader because everyone expected Chip Jenkins' sister to be one. She'd been one of those four girls every squad needed. The indispensable ones who made up the base of the pyramid. The ones who held up six perky, bouncy girls. Without wobbling.

He'd thought of her as "Miss Utterly Bourgeois." Her father had been a businessman; Ron's father had been a hippie. Now his father was a businessman, too . . . a successful one. In point of fact, a very wealthy one, now. And, uh, really . . . Ron was a businessman himself. Probably also wealthy, if he sat down and figured it out.

This could all get very confusing.

Once Ron asked himself the question, he had to admit to himself that he actually was getting involved with Missy. Beyond the mutually enjoyable experience of making out until he ached, every chance they got (which he deemed to be insufficiently frequent) and as far as she would let him go (which he deemed to be nowhere near far enough). That was the "plus" in "friends plus."

Sometimes it seemed closer to "friends minus." Missy had picked up a very clear understanding of the limited reliability of down-time birth control. Some of it, he was sure, came from the health classes during their last two years of high school. He'd sat through those himself. More of it, she said, was based upon advice from Jewell Johnson, the retreaded home economics teacher at the middle school where she had worked as an ESOL aide. Mrs. Johnson had felt quite free to dispense certain types of practical advice to the girls working in the ESOL program, since they had already graduated and attained legal adulthood, advice that perhaps even the health teacher at the high school might have flinched at.

"In my day," Mrs. Johnson would say cheerfully. She made no bones about the fact that she had been born in 1934. "Her day" had been the era before the pill—the great generation gap between the 1950s and the 1960s. Another world. One in which Grantville couples, when they went up to the quarry to neck, took along a length of clothesline to tie the girl's ankles together.

Or didn't, which had led to quite a few hurried weddings.

Missy pushed Ron's hand away. "Right now, I am definitely not interested in human reproduction. Or, at least, not in personal participation in the process. Live with it, or leave."

"Leave?" Ron asked cheerfully. "We're at my house." But he removed the hand.

Unfortunately, he *knew* that she was right. The various things that people were using for birth control were better than nothing, but . . . not all that good. Birth control now meant, as his dad put it, that over ten years, a well nourished fertile couple on good terms with one another would probably have a statistical two or three kids rather than a statistical four or five kids. If they were consistent and determined.

That was useful from a Malthusian perspective, but it was not exactly fail-safe in any one month.

Or convenient.

Or elegant.

Except, of course, for the method Missy was using. Reliable old standby. Keeping her legs firmly crossed and his hands off sensitive spots. Exactly what, during those last two years of high school, the recalled retired teachers who remembered life before the pill had drilled into the girls and Mrs. Johnson had reinforced. In this fourth year after the Ring of Fire, there were a lot of ways that life in Grantville didn't resemble the twentieth century any more.

"It's almost funny," Missy said. "Nobody talks about it, but you can practically look around town and see which couples opted for a permanent method up-time, once they had as many kids as they wanted. And which ones didn't. Which guys have had it done since the Ring of Fire, once an unexpected addition to the family showed up. And which ones apparently won't, no matter how hard the doctors and midwives push it." She giggled. "When my cousin Bill was detailed here by the army to get his EMT training last year, he was calling Susannah Shipley 'Dr. Snipley.' "

Ron nodded. In spite of everything the medical types had thought up, there were a lot more babies coming along now than there used to be. One thing he had noticed right away when he got back from Italy was that businesses had nursery rooms almost automatically. Private offices were furnished with portable cribs. It was that or lose your female employees.

As for "morning after?" There was only one possibility, now.

"I guess I could go through with an abortion, "Missy said. "If I was raped by Croats or something, and absolutely had to. But I don't want to. I sure don't intend to get myself into a pickle where I even have to think about it."

As for voluntary participation in human reproduction, her motto was, "No way do I want to go through the rest of my life barefoot and pregnant. Well, especially not pregnant."

She wiggled her toes against his feet. Shoes and socks were among the few items of clothing she thought they could dispense with. The rest were all in the category of parkas and mittens.

He wouldn't try to put his hand back.

At least not this time. Not right now.

Why did he even want to put it on her sturdy, square-ish body? When she was seven or eight, he remembered, she'd had plump cheeks and dimples. The plumpness was long gone. Missy wasn't elfin, like a gymnast, nor graceful, like a figure skater. Very definitely female, almost maddeningly female sometimes. But a guy could see why, when a larger, masculine version of the build turned up on her brother, Chip had played football much better than basketball.

Grantville had quite a few girls who were prettier than Missy Jenkins. Up-timers and down-timers, both. The little Gertrude from Jena who was living with her family and going to school here was a lot cuter, objectively speaking.

But until and unless Ron managed to stabilize that upset karmic balance, the rest of them might as well be made of cardboard. That was fairly disgusting in its own right.

His hand went out again, tracing a line about three or four inches above her body, from neckline to groin.

"What on earth are you doing?"

"Confirming something I suspected."

"What?"

"I'd still be lying here wanting to put my hand on those parts of you if you'd never stopped being a dumpling or had already turned into a Sherman tank."

"Ron, that's gross."

"I think it's pretty basic data."

Chapter 26

Rudolstadt

"It is 'Thanksgiving' today in Grantville, isn't it?" Count Ludwig Guenther asked at breakfast. "A holiday. That's why there are so few up-timers here, going about their business, even though it is a Thursday."

His wife nodded. "*Dankfest. Erntedankfest*, more precisely. Mary Kat says that it is a harvest festival. Or began as one. But religious, not a fair, not a *Kirmess*. Though surely *Kirmess* and *Messe*, as in the Frankfurt *Buchmesse*, must derive from the same origin as *Messe* as a worship service, don't you think? In any case, in Magdeburg last spring, Caroline Platzer, Princess Kristina's lady companion, told me that it was the most intensely familial of their holidays. She hated it so much, the first couple of years after the Ring of Fire. Not that she was alone, because someone always invited her to dinner. But because it reminded her so much that her own family was gone that sometimes she would rather have been alone in her room rather than with someone else's relatives, pretending that she was all right."

Countess Emelie stood up. "Oh, how my back aches. I don't believe that I am hungry after all, dearest. There must be some tie to the liturgy. I'll go check in the library."

Grantville

"I'd expected the girl to come with you, but I suppose that it makes sense, since they have tomorrow off from school too, that Gertrude took the chance to go to see her sister." Eleanor Jenkins got up and looked out the living room window. "And, in a way, it will be nice to have just family for Thanksgiving dinner. Here they come."

"Who?" asked her daughter-in-law Debbie. "And, uh, it's not going to be 'just family,' Mom. Not even near-family, like Chip's Katerina."

"Wes and Clara. I see them coming around the corner. And what do you mean, 'not just family'?"

"Missy asked Ron Stone and his little brother. That was when we thought the dinner would be at our place; before we decided to have it here with you. Gerry's come down from Rudolstadt for the holiday. They're out in your side yard, talking to Chip, right now. When they saw that Missy was heading straight for the kitchen, they sort of ducked around coming inside and having to talk to the grownups."

Eleanor frowned, mentally identifying and classifying the Stone boys, and then looked around. "What do you think about it, Chad?" she asked her son. "Really. About Wes' getting married again."

Charles Jenkins got up and looked over her shoulder. "Big brother? We couldn't have expected him not to, I suppose. By nature, he's inclined to go out of his way to be a happily married man. I know that you and Dad had more than a few doubts about Lena, too, at first, when he fixated on her when he was barely seventeen. I was five years younger, but even at age twelve I was old enough to figure that much out. That one certainly lasted. Clara seems okay, I guess. At least they didn't rush into it." He grinned. "Except right at the end."

Eleanor looked out through the curtain again. Her older son and his new wife had paused on the sidewalk. Clara looked up at Wes' face and gave a little skip; he put his arm around her shoulder.

"I worried about Lena," she said. "More than I did about Wes, really. When he started going out with her, she used to look at him more like a startled doe caught in the headlights than a girl in love. As if she were hypnotized but barely conscious enough to realize that something odd was going on. It didn't strike me as the best foundation . . . But Wes isn't . . . Never mind. As you say, it certainly lasted and they were happy together. At least it's pretty clear that Clara does love him dearly, his little foibles and all. Which is just as well."

"Wes isn't what?"

Eleanor was still looking out the window. "Callous, I suppose. I guess that would be the best word. He never has been."

"Why 'just as well' for Clara?"

"I don't want to criticize Lena now that she's gone, but she was always very willing to let Wes make up her mind for her. All those years. This time . . . I have a feeling, Chad, that he has acquired about as much woman as he is likely to be able to handle." She chuckled. "It will be good for him, I think."

One of the cooks was also looking out the window. "Here's Dad and Clara," Chandra said.

"I get to run and hug Grandpa." Mikey was proud of his status as oldest grandchild, which brought him privileges, such as running outdoors by himself, that the younger ones had not yet earned.

"Coat, mittens, hat. Okay." Chandra opened the kitchen door.

"You really like Clara, don't you?" her aunt asked. "No problems that your dad married her."

Chandra grinned. Smirked, more precisely. "I sent her to Ed Piazza to apply for the job in Fulda in the first place."

Deborah Jenkins looked up, startled. "I didn't know that. Neither did Chad."

"I didn't exactly announce the plan with trumpets. I couldn't be sure that it would 'take.' I was beginning to think that it wouldn't, until Kortney Pence came home after last Christmas and reported that there was definitely a mutual attraction in place. Clara had qualms because she didn't have kids during her first marriage, Kortney told us. She thought Dad deserved a second wife who could give him sons. Kortney did a gyne exam while she was over there in Fulda and told Clara there wasn't anything obviously wrong, so if Dad ever got around to making a move, she could do what came naturally with a clear conscience. Lenore said that Dad would be utterly, totally, completely, and abysmally humiliated if he knew that we were sitting there discussing his prospective sex life with Kortney, but we both said that neither of us was ever going to tell him that we had, so that only left her as a possible tattletale."

"And now," her Aunt Debbie giggled, "us. 'Two can keep a secret' and all that. Talk about the blackmail possibilities when I need help from my nieces."

"Why did you pick Clara?" Missy asked.

"Well, because she's different from Mom. At least, she's as different from Mom as a woman could be and still get Dad interested in her."

"What do you mean by that?"

"Well, not just that they don't look alike. Though that's true enough, and I didn't think it would be a good idea to try for a rerun. Mom was so 'West Virginia' if you know what I'm trying to say. Lanky, nearly as tall as Dad, straight sandy blond hair, light blue eyes, oblong face. And Clara . . ."

Missy laughed. "Is seven or eight inches shorter than he is with curly dark brown hair and a round face. Generally rounded. Yep. Differences duly noted."

"I'd make it nine or ten inches shorter. My knee-length skirts are floor-length on her. But they're also enough alike. People may go around saying that 'bad girls have all the fun,' but they sure aren't going to have any of it with Dad. He may see bad girls in the sense that he perceives that they exist, but he's just not interested. He wants 'everything nice,' like in the rhyme. Mom was really nice, and so is Clara. But . . ."

"But what?"

"On the rest of it, sugar and spice, Mom was really heavy on the sugar in the mix. Clara's got a lot more spice, I think." Chandra winked.

"Not exactly," Gerry answered Chip. "I do expect to go to the university of Jena, yeah. That's why I decided to attend high school in Rudolstadt rather than here in Grantville, really. I'm not interested in law or medicine. I'm interested in theology. For that, the Latin School in Rudolstadt is head and shoulders better preparation than anything the high school here has yet, even if it did hire several Latin teachers. I want to become a Lutheran minister."

For a minute, Chip stared at him. Then he remembered that Gerry's stepmother Magda was from Jena, and things sort of clicked. He looked at Ron's little brother with considerably more interest.

"I'm going to have to take instruction about becoming Lutheran in order to marry Katerina 'properly,'" he said. "When you come right down to it, in order to marry Katerina at all. There are a few things that seem to be nonnegotiable. Exactly what's involved in it?"

All of a sudden, Gerry's expression changed. Intent. With his red hair, Chip thought, in spite of the round face, it made him look like a setter on the point.

"Before you go back to Jena, you ought to talk to Teacher Muselius. He and Pastor Kastenmayer here have more experience than anyone else in providing instruction to up-timers. Saint Martin's is right on the road outside town leading to Rudolstadt. When are you leaving, you can stop and see them on the way. I'll go with you."

Gerry's description of what he would be expected to do didn't seem too bad. A little tedious maybe, but not bad. Chip listened for a while; then started to retaliate with an equal amount of sententious advice for Gerry.

"You really ought to take at least a few law courses," he said. "Lutheran pastors have to sit on consistorial courts, sometimes. I expect that will keep on happening as long as any of the territories in the USE continue to have state churches. You might as well resign yourself to learning this sort of stuff as well as theology."

Gerry groaned dramatically.

"I mean it," Chip said. He waved his hand toward the sidewalk. "Look there. When Uncle Wes married Clara over in Fulda, I looked up some of the background, and it can get really complicated. Up-time, one day you weren't married; then you got married; the next day you were married all the way, so to speak. Here, there are centuries of accumulated laws, some of them civil, some of them canon, some of them customary. And at least a half-dozen different stages of being married, depending on the jurisdiction. When couples start fighting, the marriage courts—and there are pastors serving on those, too—have to sort the tangles out."

"So that's where the negotiations stand on the marriage contract right now," Chad was saying to his mother. "Dieter von Thierbach has brought up a lot of issues I never would have thought of. Sometimes I long for the 'good old days' when two people just went out and got married."

His wife Debbie shook her head. "They didn't, quite. There was 'going steady.' Letter jackets. Class rings. 'Engaged to be engaged.' There was a song that Dad used to play. 'Me and my girl are goin' steady, We're not married, but we're gettin' ready.' Maybe we didn't notice it, didn't think of them as 'betrothal rituals,' because we were used to it all."

She turned, hearing a sound at the door, to see Katerina, the other half of Chip's future marriage contract in person, coming down late. "Why don't you go on into the kitchen," Debbie suggested. "It will be more fun for you with the younger women."

"Hey, Katerina, come in," Missy called from her perch among the pie crusts. "I can use some company. This is our cousin Chandra. Lenore is over at Bryant's sister's." Missy proceeded with the pie crusts.

About fifteen minutes later, Debbie shooed Katerina outside to join Chip. "Go out with the guys," she said. "This kitchen isn't all that big to start with, and it's getting crowded. They're around in the side yard."

"Poor kid," Missy said. "I sort of like her, but talk about a fish out of water."

"They're not likely to settle in Grantville. The kind of career that Chip's aiming at, she'll be in her normal habitat ninety percent of the time, at least. And, as your dad says, a real asset to him."

"Hey, Katerina, come on," Chip called. "I've got more family for you. Meet my uncle, Wes Jenkins, and his new wife, Clara. And Mikey, he's Chandra's oldest. She managed to get the other three down for naps right after she got here, or they would all be out here running us ragged. Plus Ron and Gerry Stone. Ron's sort of informally attached to Missy and Gerry is his brother. Uncle Wes, this is my just-about-to-be-a-fiancée Katerina."

Wes smiled. "I would offer to shake hands," he said, "except that I am carrying two dozen eggs."

Chip turned to the older woman. "I guess you're my Aunt Clara now, aren't you."

She smiled. "Oh, yes. Though I have been someone's Aunt Clara for many years, already." Clara stood on her tiptoes, kissed Wes on the cheek, took the eggs from his hands, and said, "Have fun with Mikey. I'm going to run in and help Debbie and the girls."

Chandra looked out the window, noticed that Mikey had diverted Grandpa as well as the boys for a visit to the swing set and that Katerina had found them. Then she sighed.

"Aunt Debbie?"

"Yes."

"Have you noticed anything different about Lenore, lately?"

"Like what?"

"Lenore's quite a bit like Mom, you know. She's never been right up front when it comes to expressing her own opinion about anything."

"Yes." Debbie sighed. "Every Thanksgiving, when we were deciding who would bring what, Lena would always say, 'everybody else pick and I'll bring whatever is left on the list.'"

"That was Mom. Sometimes, at dinner, Dad would ask her questions for fifteen or twenty minutes trying to find out if she actually had a preference about where we were going on vacation or what color car they should buy. He was always awfully patient about it. More than I was, once I got into my teens," Chandra admitted.

"So?"

"So Bryant isn't patient like that with Lenore, Aunt Debbie. And he doesn't care at all what she wants, as far as I can tell. He was sort of *squashing* her between when he got back from Magdeburg and when he left for Frankfurt. At least, he was trying to. Lenore doesn't ever really want to speak up for herself. She's like Mom that way, but this time, she dug in her heels. He wasn't listening. I'm not looking forward to having him get back from Frankfurt next month."

There was a tap, or a light kick to be more precise, at the back door. Missy, hands still sticky, opened up. Clara was waiting. "Hello Debbie, Chandra, Missy. Sorry, my hands are full, but it is eggs, because I promised to show you how to make the egg-glazed flatbreads we always had for the autumn *Kirmess*."

Missy took the eggs so that Clara could get her cloak off, without interrupting the preceding conversation. "Like you said, Bryant isn't even in town most of the time, any more," she protested to

Chandra. "He's off working on these big fire prevention projects. Lenore pretty much *has* to cope on her own."

"That doesn't keep him from trying to boss her. This time, she honestly doesn't want to do what Bryant is telling her she has to. Not one little bit. I sort of like being a stay-at-home mom, but she went to all the trouble of learning how to read the German handwriting and stuff. She liked what she was doing at work and she doesn't want to give it up permanently. Lenore didn't mind staying home for a while after Weshelle was born. Well, she did, really, even though she went along with him on it, but Weshelle is completely weaned now, old enough that she doesn't have to be an 'office baby.' I can keep her along with my kids."

"What is this leading up to?" Debbie asked.

Chandra looked around from where she was chopping onions for the stuffing. "Lenore's going to go back to work after New Year's. She's already set things up with the judge."

"Isn't that going to cause major problems?" Debbie frowned.

"I don't know if they'll get to be 'major' as long as Bryant is out of town. All he can do from someplace like Frankfurt or Magdeburg is write letters complaining about it. But she hasn't told him. She's trying to evade. That's what bothers me. I'm getting nervous about what might happen when he comes back later on and finds out that she is working again, if she doesn't tell him that she's going to first. Or if someone who doesn't realize how touchy things are right now happens to mention that she's going to while he's here over Christmas. And now that Dad's back, she's likely to ask him to back her up against Bryant."

"Oh." Missy frowned, glancing over at Clara, who was constructing the pastries. Uncle Wes had a temper, sometimes. She wondered if Clara knew that, yet. Probably. They'd worked together long enough.

"You're smart to be taking the librarian training," Chandra said. "Dad would have been happier, you know, if we had both gone through college. Not Lenore taking a few courses here and there and me not going at all because I married Nathan right out of high school. I wasn't really thinking about it, then. Mom only finished high school, after all, and Nathan thought that I needed to work. But since he's been out of town on this armaments business, I'm beginning to think that Dad was right."

"Any change in that argument?" Missy asked.

"No, Nathan still doesn't want me to come to Frankfurt. He's still saying that health care and schools for the kids are so much better here in Grantville, and that's true enough. But he's been gone more than a year and a half. Other guys in other cities have their wives with them, now. And their kids. And he's only come home once. Suhl wasn't that far away, but he's never even seen Lena Sue and Sandra Lou. They're a year old, now. It's scarcely worth making a cake for the first birthday, is it? Sugar is so expensive. They don't really know what's going on, yet, and it's not as if we can take snapshots any more. And he's not coming for Christmas. I took the kids to that new old-fashioned photography shop downtown and got their picture taken together, to send him for a present. But if . . ."

"If what?"

"If he hasn't come by spring, I'm going to Frankfurt, whether he wants me to or not. Just to see what's going on. That was one thing that I wanted to ask you, Aunt Debbie. If I go to Frankfurt in the spring, could you and Missy keep the kids for a few weeks? Even though you're managing the teacher training now and she's going to school?"

"I'm sure we can."

Chandra looked down at the onions again, blaming them for the tears in her eyes. "Don't skimp on the teacher training program, though. If, well, if things don't work out with Nathan in the long run, I may need it. Or something."

Tom, up from his nap, came wandering down the hall barefoot.

Missy looked up. "Who's on babysitting patrol?"

"You take it, honey," Chandra said. "Get all three of them up, will you, and then take them out where Katerina and the guys are to run off some steam before we start eating.

"And talk to Katerina. She's bound to be feeling a little out of it. Keep her company."

"Nani and Pop are having dinner with Aura Lee and Joe. Ray's family will be there, too. They all decided to go to Aura Lee's when we decided not to have dinner at home but come over to Gran's instead." Missy's tone was very neutral.

"Presumably," Chip said, "Nani has her nose a bit out of joint because the rest of us are here."

"She was expecting a formal presentation of Katerina."

"There's time after dinner. Katerina and I can walk over there and I'll introduce her to everyone else."

"You two," Missy said, "certainly do have an unending store of excuses to go for walks." She gave him a wink. Not only she but everyone else at the table could make a pretty good guess as to what they spent some of their time doing on those walks.

Then she turned. "I'm sure this is exactly how you wanted to spend your first visit to Grantville, isn't it, Katerina? Meeting more and more apparently endless bunches of Chip's relatives, most of whom are going to give you that 'is she really suitable?' look. You'll survive. Clara had to go through it last month and she's flourishing. Aren't you?" She waved to Clara at the other end of the table, who waved back.

Missy turned back to Katerina. "But, of course, she didn't have to face up to inspection by Nani. That's Mom's side of the family."

Chapter 27

Grantville

Ron Stone was feeling rather paralyzed in the presence of Missy's grandmother. Not so much her parents. Chad and Debbie Jenkins weren't so bad. He'd seen them often enough when he was in high school. But as the conversation progressed, it was slowly dawning upon him that, necessarily, Missy had as many relatives as Chip did. All of whom probably took as much interest in her activities as they did in Chip's. This was just one grandmother. There was another one, somewhere out in the woodwork. A grandfather. More aunts and uncles.

He advised himself to be cool. Yes, that was the word. Cool, Stone, cool. If you are totally casual, maybe they will all be so preoccupied with Chip's girl that they won't notice you. What was that word in the poem they had studied in English literature? Hecatombs? Yes, that was it. Missy didn't just have cousins. She had hecatombs of cousins, most of whom trailed spouses and children along with them.

In the poem, hecatombs had involved broken hearts. Broken dreams. Something broken.

The grandmother was discussing the history of the serving dishes on the table. Each bowl and tray, none of which matched any of the rest, had apparently been passed down in some branch of her mother's family for several generations.

For a guy who had never exactly met his mother, since she had taken off from Lothlorien Commune for parts unknown before he was old enough to remember, this was a little disconcerting. Ron looked a little warily at Gerry, sitting close to the other end of the table, who had never exactly met his mother either. He hoped that Gerry would keep his mouth shut on the subject of mothers.

The old lady asked his opinion on the design of the gravy boat.

To the best of his knowledge, this was the first time he had ever seen a gravy boat.

"Well," he said, "it's bourgeois." Then clearing his throat, "But it's *good* bourgeois."

Missy was trying not to giggle. Chandra wasn't even trying not to.

Ron had a feeling that he should sink down right through the floor.

Missy's uncle was looking at the gravy boat with a critical eye. "I think," Wes said, "that that's a fair enough assessment."

Missy's grandmother glared at Missy's uncle.

Ron analyzed his feelings and decided that they clearly fell under the label of "immense, deep, profound gratitude." He could, he thought, get to like Missy's Uncle Wes.

He looked toward the other end of the table again. Gerry was talking to Missy's Aunt Clara. Since their conversation was entirely in German, it was more or less sliding in and out among the rest of the dialogue at the table.

At least until Clara looked up to the end of the table where he was and said, "Wesley, how interesting. This young man Cherry plans to study theology at Jena."

Wes looked down toward her, smiling. The soft "g" sound, along with occasional tangles with the past tenses of irregular verbs, was almost Clara's only concession to the fact that English was not her first language. She had even mastered the English "w"—an uncommon achievement for an adult whose native language was German. Though, as she had once whispered into the ear she was tickling, her desire to be able to say "Wesley" correctly as soon as she had the chance had provided an uncommonly strong motivation.

He'd have to ask her, some time, if she had written "Wesley

and Clara" on her note paper and drawn hearts and daisies around the names. If she hadn't, it was probably because it hadn't occurred to her.

The boy didn't seem to be offended by "Cherry."

Wes said, "Yes, that is interesting." Because it was. And smiled at her again.

"Actually," Ron said. "He's young enough that he still has a lot of options. Nothing's set in concrete, yet."

"Give it up, Ron," Gerry said. "I *am* going to be a Lutheran pastor."

Ron groaned to himself. Gerry had not indicated in any way at all that his plans were confidential. He had proclaimed them right out loud. By this time next week, it would be all over town.

He sat there, thinking about his brother Faramir—Frank, to Grantville—and Giovanna's two weddings. One Catholic, performed by a cardinal, in the Sistine Chapel, believe it or not; the other by way of his father's mail-order credentials as a minister in the Universal Church of Life in . . . whatever . . . and . . . stuff. His older brother would probably end up Catholic, no matter how socialist and atheist the rest of the Marcolis were. After all, Giovanna had promised the pope himself that she would do all that was in her power to convert Frank. He had a feeling that Giovanna was the kind of girl who kept her word. Plus Frank was chums with Father Gus Heinzerling. Catholic on one side of him, Lutheran on the other. Himself . . .

Ron was never likely to be "any of the above." His mind didn't work that way.

That was how he lost track of what people were talking about. Only to come back to reality and find out that Missy's father was telling everyone about that ultimately improbable and utterly unfortunate mechanical event, back before the Ring of Fire, in the days when there were car lots in Grantville and his brother had been dating Missy.

Ron had sort of hoped that Chad Jenkins had forgotten that those two had ever dated. It hadn't been for long. Six weeks, maximum.

Why did we come here? he asked himself. *We could have gotten a meal from the staff cafeteria out at the plant.*

✧ ✧ ✧

"Mom has quite a display up, doesn't she?" Chad stopped next to his new sister-in-law, who was looking at a wall full of framed family photographs in the rec room.

"I am always fascinated by photographs," Clara answered. "If the Ring of Fire had happened earlier, we in Badenburg, ordinary people, could have had pictures of our grandparents. Not only wealthy people who can afford to have portraits painted. Though my brother Dietrich does have a drawing of my grandfather Pohlmann, who lived in Arnstadt, made by a student at the Latin School. He was no great artist, but it is said to be a good likeness. It is in pen and ink, though, so it does not tell us the color of his hair and eyes any more than these 'black and white' ones."

She looked at the wall critically. "Though, mostly, they are shades of gray, and some are more tan or brown. Wes says that we will have our photograph made and give a copy to your mother for Christmas. And to my father."

"Your family is okay with having you marry an up-timer?"

"Yes. Maybe they would not have been 'okay with it' two years ago, but there has been enough time now. In any case, I did not ask them. I did not request their permission."

It was an oddity in her English, Chad thought. A tendency to say the same thing, or almost the same thing, two or three ways in succession, as if she were trying out different model sentences from a conversation manual to see how they fit.

Clara turned back to the wall. "Who are all the people?"

Chad toured her through the Jenkins and Newton families, with a side trip through the five Williams sisters.

"A violinist," she said, looking at Joe Newton's picture. "That is interesting. And this man is your other grandfather, Hudson Jenkins?"

"A fiddler more than a violinist. On the other, Hudson Jenkins, yes. He died young and Grandma Mildred married again. This is her second family, with Clarence Walker, taken right after World War II. That's Dad, over in the corner, at the end of the back row."

Clara looked back and forth, from Hudson Jenkins to his son standing in a far corner of the Walker family photo, then to Joe Newton with his wife and daughters.

"Perhaps," she said slowly, "it is as well that we do not all keep photographs of our families."

Chad raised an eyebrow. "Meaning?"

Clara frowned at the photos she had been examining. "I knowed—knew—already that Debbie was a widow when she married you." She pointed. "There is the photograph for her first wedding, to the soldier who was killed. Don Jefferson. You said that this child"—she pointed to a snapshot of a little girl about six years old—"is her daughter, Anne, the nurse who has gone to Amsterdam. But there is no first husband for your mother."

She pointed to the wedding photograph of John Charles Jenkins and Eleanor Anne Newton, the date in an ornamental garland at the top. Then to a family picture, taken shortly before Wes and Lena married, the two of them standing in back, one on each side of their sister Mary Jo, who had been left up-time, with their parents sitting in front, drawing the downward slant from Wes' height to Chad's, the shape of each face and hairline, on the glass with her fingernail. "Where did Wesley come from?"

Chad looked at her, considering what he should say. Fresh eyes . . .

"Never mind," she added, before he had said anything. "It makes no difference."

"Things happen," he said. "Dad did the right thing."

Clara, he decided, was not only "okay" but also no slouch.

She was looking at Wes' and Lena's wedding photo now, then one with Lenore about ten and Chandra about eight, both long legged and gawky. "Those little apples did not fall very far from the tree," she commented.

"I expect that Wes has copies of most of those newer ones. You'll have to ask him to dig out the albums."

"I wish that Lenore could have come today," Eleanor Jenkins said.

"Too many places for her to be, Gran," Missy said. "Bryant wrote her. The letter made a fuss that she should have noon dinner with his sister Lola, and then the Days wanted her and Weshelle for supper. Maybe she can run in here for an hour or so between two Thanksgiving dinners, the way Chandra is going to do for the Pricketts, before she goes to the Days'. Well, Chandra's really going over to David Jones' house, since Nathan's mom is Mr. Jones' sister and they're having Thanksgiving there. I can phone Lenore at Lola's and ask, but I wouldn't count on her being able to get away soon enough."

"Jasper Day isn't even in town. He's up in Magdeburg, still, so she doesn't have grandparents there. Believe me, at Thanksgiving a grandmother outranks three aunts. If she had to be at Lola's for dinner, she could have dropped in on the Days this afternoon and come here for leftovers for supper." Eleanor's voice was very firm.

"They guilt-trip her, Grandma. Because Aunt Lena and Sarah and Diana and Di's girls had gone to the movies together and were left up-time, now Janice and Nell and Cassandra are putting pressure on Chandra and Lenore and Sarah's kids to hang tight with them as a family group. Which goes triple now that Ed Monroe and Chauncey Wilson as well as Uncle Wes have all remarried. Plus, they're pushing even harder since Janice and Ross adopted five kids and Nell and Fenton have adopted two kids. Replacements for the ones they lost. They're trying to focus on them, I guess. Bonding and all that kind of stuff. Make them feel that they are really part of the family. Plus, with Cassie remarrying to a German guy this month and bringing in three stepchildren . . . and the Nazarenes lost almost their whole church congregation and their minister. The Days were hit really hard by the Ring of Fire."

"You're sounding very grown up, littlest granddaughter."

"Teacher training. Child psychology as well as library science. I'm not 'littlest' any more, really," Missy said. "You'll have to promote one of the great-granddaughters to spoil in that spot. Or leave it vacant for a while, considering that Chandra's girls are twins, which might cause sibling rivalry. Wait and see what Chip and Katerina produce once they get themselves organized."

"Missy, where are you going?" Debbie hurried out into the hall.

"Home. Gran brought up 'good bourgeois' and started saying things about Ron's dad. He and Gerry left."

Debbie winced. Her mother-in-law's talent for disguising catty remarks as polite comments was one of the banes of her life. It occurred to her that Ron Stone might not be so bad to have around if he had an antenna that picked it up too.

"I'm sorry, hon. But you can't go straight home. You've got to stop by Aura Lee's. You can't not go see Nani and Pop on Thanksgiving. Everyone's feelings will be hurt if you don't."

"Sometimes," Missy said. "Sometimes I wish that people would collect all the things they get hurt feelings about and put them out in a garbage can."

"Sorry I put you through that," Ron said, lounging on his dad's favorite bean bag chair.

"No problem," Gerry answered. "Dinners like that are part of what pastors have to learn to do."

Ron stared a minute. More alien than Mork from Ork.

Then he got up and looked in the mirror. Missy. Miss Utterly Bourgeois. That meant that she knew, without thinking about it, where her body, her face, her hair, every bit of her, came from. What did he know about himself? Looking at his reflection, he had to admit that it would probably have been sort of hard to tell the origin of any of the component parts, even if he had known his mother at all and his father for sure, given how . . . average . . . the whole ensemble was that looked back at him.

For the first time in his life, it occurred to him that even though his biological paternity was a bit optional, so to speak, Dad had at least known his mother. In every sense of the word. They'd been acquainted. In his next letter to Italy, he would ask what she had looked like. Even if the answer was "sort of all-round unimpressive," that would be something. And his school records should have a copy of his birth certificate. He could ask for a copy of it to back file with the Bureau of Vital Statistics. Maybe he ought to do that for all three of them. It wasn't a bad idea to make sure that your paperwork was in order.

"It can't be serious, Chad. Can it?" Debbie took off her shoes and propped her feet up on a hassock. It had been quite a day. "They can't be serious?"

"No idea," Chad answered sleepily, tilting his recliner backwards before folding his hands across his chest.

"Surely not. Oh, surely not. They're only eighteen."

"Nineteen next month. Both of them. Out of high school for quite a while now, when you think about it."

"She was just being nice because their father and stepmother are still in Italy. If they hadn't come here, where would they have eaten?"

"With somebody else, I expect. Or done something at their place with chicken. Based on the way she was looking at him, wherever he was, she would be too. Seemed rather taken by him. Vice versa. Both trying hard to keep anyone else from noticing. Success level with that project measurable at roughly zilch. Very taken with him. Can't imagine where she gets it," he yawned.

That was probably the best tack to take, he thought, remembering that Debbie had been seventeen and still in high school when she married Don Jefferson, who was only a year older. She was eighteen when Anne was born and Don was killed in Vietnam. Willie Ray had used every ounce of political clout at his disposal to get the school board to let her come back the next year and graduate. Willie Ray had once told him that Debbie would have run off with Don if he hadn't given his consent at the time. Debbie had been a rather determined young lady herself, Chad mused. *Nope. Absolutely can't imagine where Missy gets it.*

"Charles Hudson Jenkins!"

He assured himself that Debbie hadn't been reading his thoughts. "It's not as if Tom Stone is a social pariah any more. He's made a ton of money legally and his father-in-law's not too shabby when it comes time to bargain either."

"Well, I'm going to call Mother. If Missy came straight home rather than stopping by Aura Lee's, I might as well hear about it now as later."

She reached for the phone extension, listened a moment, and put the receiver down again. "It's busy."

Chad raised an eyebrow.

"Missy and Ron. Dissecting the dinner events." She frowned. "Missy has a sharper tongue than I ever realized. I wish that I weren't such an honorable mom. I might have learned a lot from eavesdropping longer."

"What did you learn in fifteen seconds?"

"That Gerry called the Lutheran minister out at St. Martin's as soon as they got home from here. About Chip's needing to take instructions, I mean."

"That's not exactly revolutionary news. Chip broke it to us a long time ago. And they *are* Protestants. Lutherans, I mean. I looked that up after Vera said . . ."

Debbie would rather not talk about her mother right now. "According to Ron, this school teacher out there, the one who is going with the Kochs' daughter, is practically keeping a prize list under the heading of 'up-time converts we have caught.' With Chip, at the moment, as a candidate for the blue ribbon."

"One hand washes the other. We can't expect all the influence to run one way. Doesn't the Koch girl count as a prize?"

"The Kochs were Lutheran already. Before."

"Oh. I guess I never knew that. Our paths didn't cross much."

Chapter 28

Grantville

The plane banked and came down neatly on the landing field just outside the edge of the Ring of Fire.

The walls weren't as smooth and sharp as they had been in the spring of 1631. Where there was soil above the rock, they were starting to erode.

"I still don't like using a government plane for what's really a private trip," Mike Stearns groused.

"Travel is dangerous for babies," came his wife Becky's firm response. "Baruch is barely two and I am still nursing. It is a miracle that they didn't catch something deadly on the trip from Amsterdam to Magdeburg. It will be a miracle if they don't catch something deadly on this trip."

"Gustav ordered a plane to bring us to Magdeburg, too. What are they likely to catch, spending a couple of hours in the air with their parents and one pilot, that they might not catch at home? It's not as if you were dragging them around on wagons and barges for weeks. Or even on a truck for a couple of days, stopping at inns at night."

The plane taxied to a stop. Chocks. Steps. A government truck.

"Damn, I hate these perks of office," Mike said. "They're bound to come back and bite us on the campaign trail. No matter what Gustavus Adolphus says about down-time standards being different,

I'm not a down-timer, so Wettin's propagandists will be all over me for using government resources for personal trips. And not just Wettin's people. Some of our own, like Joe Stull, when he hears about it. There's just no 'give' to that man."

A couple of young men from the ground crew scrambled into the plane and started unloading.

"The next time," Woody said to Emil. "The next time, *you* fly them. Okay, I know the calculations. Two babies weigh a lot less than one adult, so we can transport four people plus the pilot when it's the prime ministerial family. But it's not just two babies. It's two babies and all that gear. And ear problems, so there I am, flying the whole way with one of them whining and the other one squalling. Next time . . ."

Opa had explained all about it. Sepharad's daddy was bringing her mommy this time. With a brother for her to play with, and a new baby.

She believed it, but that was very different from seeing it.

Daddy came to Grantville every couple of months. Sometimes oftener. Sephie knew him. She adored him. He came and when he came, he was hers.

She knew he was coming.

She was waiting by the door. Opa told her when he saw the plane coming. He took her out in the yard to watch. She knew that after the plane landed, Daddy would come.

He did.

With a strange woman, whose hand was resting on his elbow. He was holding the hand of a little boy about her size. Carrying a baby against his chest. Bringing them into her house.

Sephie knew how to handle this. It was a time for courage. Bravery. Spunk, Daddy called it. He told her on every visit that she was a little girl with a lot of spunk.

This was not a moment to hide behind her grandfather.

Sephie marched out onto the front steps and said it plainly.

"You can take them back, now."

"It's her age," Balthazar said to his devastated daughter. "The books of the up-timers call it 'the terrible twos.'"

✧ ✧ ✧

"There's an acronym for the way Sephie's behaving today," Mike said to Balthasar. "Or, at least, there was up-time. But I don't think that Becky needs to know what it was."

Grantville, Dreeson Household

Veronica stood at the train station. Henry had decided to wait at home, since it would be nearly supper time when the train got in. The early dark of winter was closing down already. The wind was chilly and his hip was aching.

Annalise waited next to her, holding Will by the hand; Nicol on the other side, holding his other hand. Thea had decided to wait at home, too. Which made sense. The girl was as big as a house by now.

All the children came down, cold evening or no cold evening. Martha was seventeen now, the same age as Annalise. The oldest, the most damaged by the war. A good girl. She was holding Joey, wrapped up as warmly as they could wrap him, in her arms.

Hans Balthasar—the up-time children called him "Baldy," partly from his name and partly from the scar on his scalp, she supposed. He didn't seem to mind the nickname. He left school this year and took an apprenticeship at the Kudzu Werke. Henry and Nicol talked to the owners; they would see to it that he learned enough to make him into a good craftsman.

Karl and Otto, who'd been ten and nine years old at the Battle of the Crapper. Now they were teenagers, stretching out tall. Sue and Chris, also both with up-time nicknames. Little Johann was long since back with his own family in Jena; the rest of them hardly ever saw him.

The train was late. Of course, the train would be late. The first time they had seen Gretchen and Jeff in nearly two years and the wonderful, splendid, industrial, rapid, so-great-a-modern-improvement train was late.

How late? She stomped over to the stationmaster's office for what seemed like the tenth time, but in fact was only the fourth.

"Fifteen minutes? That's what you said a half hour ago."

She stomped back to the waiting group.

No matter how cold it was, she almost begrudged the fact that this time, in fact, the stationmaster was right.

✧ ✧ ✧

They jumped off together. Of course Gretchen would not wait for someone to hand her down. Annalise let go of Will's hand and ran forward. Veronica waited; then greeted them with, "It's a miracle you are not both dead like Hans, the things you have done. This is your cousin Dorothea's husband, from back home."

Nicol came forward, leading Will. He was four, now. Nicol and Thea had spent a lot of time explaining to him that his Mutti and Vati were coming to visit him. Tall for his age, blond, blue-eyed, serious. Before Gretchen could kneel down to hug him, he reached up and solemnly shook her hand. And said, "I am very pleased to meet you."

Jeff laughed, but Gretchen gasped.

At least, Veronica thought, they wouldn't be able to find fault with his manners.

Martha came up with Joey. He turned away from the strangers, burying his face in her neck. "He's cold," she said apologetically. "He doesn't want to put his face out in the wind."

The others, old enough to remember, wanted hugs.

After dinner, warm and fed, Joey was happy enough to play with the visitors. Until bedtime. When Jeff started to pick him up, he yelled for Martha. She took him and started upstairs. Gretchen got up to come along. Then he yelled for Thea. Until he got Thea.

Jeff and Gretchen sat down at the supper table again.

"He's just a baby," Will said. "You can't expect him to be polite, yet."

Will was very nice about letting Jeff and Gretchen help Annalise put him to bed.

"Joey'll start warming up to you in a few days," Henry remarked while the womenfolk were upstairs seeing to baths and bedtime stories for the rest of the bunch.

Jeff looked up, startled. "Didn't Gretchen tell you? We can't stay that long. We've been on the train all day. I only have a four-day pass and we'll need another whole day to get back to Magdeburg. Two days. That's all we have. I have to get back to work and she has to hit the campaign trail again."

"Until the election," Veronica said. "Until the election, and no longer."

"There is no way we can move everyone to Magdeburg." Gretchen shook her head. "Rents are out of this world. We're living in two rooms. We can't afford a house with room for eight more. Nine more, if you're intending to throw Annalise out, too."

"Gretchen, don't be . . ." Jeff put his hands out, palms up. "You can see for yourself that Henry's a lot more feeble than he was when we left for Paris."

Part of the problem was that Gretchen could. See it, that was. Which made her a little sharp tongued.

"Well, don't say that in front of him," Veronica said tartly. "He knows it, but he doesn't have to know that other people notice. And of course I am not intending to throw Annalise out. She's going to college."

"We can't take them all back with us. Not now. Not at Christmas."

Veronica grimaced. "Not as far as the eye can see, perhaps?"

"We can probably hang on here a while longer," Henry said to Jeff. "Just letting things ride. But not forever. That's the simple truth of it. I know it and Ronnie knows it. I'm watching a lot of my contemporaries, couple by couple or one by one, get to the point where they have to give up their houses and go into assisted living. Extended care, if something really goes wrong. The longer Gretchen procrastinates, the crankier Ronnie is going to get about it. She's younger than I am by quite a few years, but this is one thing where you have to make your decisions on the basis of the 'weaker vessel,' No matter what the Bible says, this time it's not the woman."

Jeff shifted in his chair. "If Gretchen's grandma thinks that *she's* short on cash, she ought to look at *our* budget. Being a political organizer has its rewards, I guess, but they don't come in the form of money. What do they call them? 'Psychic compensation?' Something like that. In Paris and Amsterdam, we were living on the embassy's dime. We had to pay for our clothes and stuff, which we covered out of my army salary—whenever that got delivered through the siege lines; we had to borrow a lot—but Becky provided our room and food. Covered the travel expenses, too. That's gone now. We're on our own, and while I'm at least getting my army pay regularly now, the fact is that the pay sucks. After the election, Henry. I'll try to get something organized so we can take the kids with us after the election. That's the best I can do. And, honestly, Gretchen hadn't let me know that Ronnie was so upset."

"—college tuition. And that's just for Annalise. Martha's only a year behind her in school; Henry's already paying for Hans Balthasar. You should leave him here, at least, and not take him away from his master. They'll let him board. Then four more who are between fourteen and twelve now, three of them boys. To be apprenticed or kept in school." Nicol shook his head. "Honestly, Jeff. What was Gretchen thinking?"

"When she adopted them? That, with any luck, she could keep them alive. In a way, this argument's showing me, better than anything else could, how far we've come in how short a time. The day I met Gretchen, even the day I married her, she wasn't thinking about schools and apprenticeships for these kids. She just hoped she could find food for them, one day at a time. Talk about a 'revolution of rising expectations.' The problem is that our income isn't keeping pace. Especially since they're so bunched up in age, except for Will and Joey. If it was just Will and Joey, we'd have a break, another twelve or fifteen years for me to get promotions and raises before we had to worry about paying college tuition."

"—Quedlinburg, if I can just find the tuition."

"Quedlinburg isn't the only choice, Oma," Annalise said. "I know you like the abbess, but there's the new university in Prague, too."

"It's a lot longer way to travel." Veronica looked stern. "Who knows what Wallenstein will get up to next? And they don't have dormitories. Quedlinburg does. Supervised dormitories. Plus, Mrs. Nelson is teaching there. You know her. She used to be at the middle school here."

"I know Mrs. Roth, too, and she's in Prague. And other Grantvillers. We could find someplace for me to stay, if I went there. Anyway, by the time I graduate, they should have the new women's college in Franconia started up, too. The one that Bernadette Adducci is founding. I think I might like it better."

"Why?" Gretchen asked.

"Well, it's in the SoTF. And it's Catholic. Quedlinburg is Lutheran."

"Saint Elisabeth's won't be a state college," Veronica pointed out. "The tuition isn't going to be any cheaper than Quedlinburg. And they won't have dormitories ready next year."

Gretchen was prepared to ignore the dormitory issue, though it was obviously near and dear to her grandmother's heart. "Do you mean to say you would choose a school because . . . because . . . because of a confessional allegiance?"

Annalise shook her head. "Well, not just that. No, don't go all hostile and CoC on me. I'm not a bigot. Idelette Cavriani is my best friend, and she's a Calvinist. But I'm Catholic, Gretchen. You can believe whatever you like. Or not believe anything, as you choose. But I am a Catholic. It makes a difference to me."

Veronica looked at them grimly. "Quedlinburg. If I can find the tuition, of course."

Some one walked up quietly and sat down on the floor next to his recliner. Henry lifted his head and blinked a couple of times to clear his eyes.

"Henry . . ."

"Yep. Evenin', Martha."

She did that sometimes. Just came and sat there, like she needed a little company.

"I'm sorry if I'm disturbing you."

"No, no. Just resting my eyes for a bit. You're always welcome."

"Henry?"

"Yes."

She put one hand on the arm of his chair. "Do I have to go? If they take the others?"

"Of course not, Margie. Sorry, I mean Martha. You're always welcome to stay here."

"I owe Gretchen so much. I ought to be willing to go, whenever she wants me to, and help her with the younger ones. But I want to finish high school here. I want to learn to be a librarian, like Missy Jenkins and Pam Hardesty. Mrs. Bolender says I can, if I do well in school this year and next. I help Ms. Fielder at the public library, already. I don't want to go off wandering to every place in Europe that needs a Committee of Correspondence organized."

"Don't blame you. I was glad to get home myself, this fall."

"It seems so selfish of me."

"Just because she pretty much saved your life, and your sanity, that doesn't mean you owe her unpaid nannydom forever and a day. Which is what it would amount to."

"Okay."

She sat there quietly for a few more minutes.

"Do I have to say so, right now?"

"Naw. Leave it till Jeff and Gretchen actually make some move to take the kids. To be perfectly honest, I'll be awfully surprised if they turn up the week after the election and say they're all set to go with the rest of them."

"—couldn't believe what Annalise said. And that Thea! Cousin or not, she has the brains of a peahen."

"C'mon Gretchen," Jeff said. "Settle down and go to sleep. We've got blessings to be thankful for."

Chapter 29

Grantville

Susan Logsden was happy at Thanksgiving dinner. Grandpa Ben Hardesty, Grandma Gloria, Pam, Cory Joe briefly back from Magdeburg on leave. All with her; all at Cory Joe's dad's cousin Gerrie's. She was Gerrie Bennezet now. Her husband was a Walloon Huguenot who had come to work at USE Steel and then set up his own blacksmith operation here in Grantville.

When they went around the table saying what each of them was thankful for, Grandma Gloria said that she was grateful to Gerrie that she didn't have to cook the dinner this year.

Susan suspected that she was also grateful not to be at her daughter Betty's, this year since things were still a bit strained between Aunt Betty and them—Velma's kids. Grandma and Grandpa weren't at Aunt Betty's because Aunt Betty and Uncle Monroe Wilson had gone to Fulda last month to be Mormon missionaries. Joe and the two adopted children had gone with them.

Grandpa and Grandma would be having pizza for supper with the other Wilsons, the Nisbets, and the Sterlings, leaving the three of them on their own.

Most of the people here were Gerrie's family. Her daughter Paige was married to Derek Modi. She was here, with the kids. Derek had gone to Luebeck. Paige said she was thankful that he had arrived safely.

Gerrie's daughter Marlo worked at Cora's as a cashier. She had married a Scot, a guy named Malcolm Finlay, back in February. She was going to have a baby. Marlo said that she was thankful for the baby.

Cora Ennis might be Grantville's worst gossip, but Marlo was catching up to her fast. Before dinner, she and Paige had been talking about the fact that Chandra Prickett's husband hadn't even stopped by in Grantville on his way from Suhl to Frankfurt. That he wasn't seeing anyone in Suhl, though.

And Paige didn't think it was likely that he would be seeing anyone in Frankfurt, either. Paige said that if Nathan Prickett ever went straying off the straight and narrow, it wouldn't be with some German woman. It would be with Bryant Holloway's sister Lola. He'd been dating her before either of them ever got married. But Lola, like Chandra, was right here in Grantville. She worked as an assistant in the optician's office, she had been working there ever since she divorced Latham Beckworth back before the Ring of Fire, and she sure hadn't been going down to Suhl and she wasn't going to Frankfurt for visits.

Actually, Marlo pointed out, since Bryant was married to Chandra's sister Lenore now, Lola was part of that family, in a funny kind of way.

Mr. Bennezet and Sergeant Finlay had been talking about Huguenots, spies, and other topics of common interest. Pam and Cory Joe had been listening to that, since their mother Velma had married a Huguenot. Then Cory Joe asked whether Bennezet had experienced much in the way of anti-immigrant sentiment among the up-timers. Bennezet said that it varied. He did quite a lot of specialized work for Grantville-Saalfeld Foundries and Metalworks. Some of the people there were very friendly. The boss was not, but although two of the men had married down-time women, he had not fired them. But Bennezet understood from conversation that several of the friendliest up-timers working there would not be averse to finding other employment if an opportunity arose. The main obstacle was that none of them wished to uproot their families by leaving Grantville.

Now they were talking about the same things again. Susan listened to the grownups for a while and began to wish that she had brought a CD player and earphones along.

She was mostly glad that her mother was somewhere in the

Netherlands instead of here. It hadn't been much fun growing up as Velma Hardesty's daughter. Maybe she could be thankful for that, but she had a feeling that it would be better not to say so when her turn came. Grandma Gloria thought tact was important.

She'd say that she was thankful that she would have Cory Joe and Pam to herself this evening. That was true enough.

The Jones family always had Thanksgiving dinner late, because Simon and Mary Ellen were busy with the services at the Methodist church in the morning. For the same reason, they had it at his brother's house, since David's wife was a teacher and always had the day off, so she could do the cooking. And she had the next day off, for that matter, so she could clean up. Nobody ever asked Susan what she thought of this arrangement. The rest of them took it as a given.

David Jones, the assistant principal of Grantville's elementary school, looked around the table. At the other end, his wife. All three of their children were home. Austin with Alison and little Susie, the new baby due next month. Ceci's husband Harry Ennis—and they just got married earlier in the month—was already back in Magdeburg with the army. Ceci had already been over to Cora's, her home, not the café, for lunch with his mom and Melinda, his brother Joe's wife. And Steve and Phoebe.

It wouldn't be long, probably, before Ceci went to Magdeburg herself. As soon as Harry found a place for them to live.

He wasn't so happy with Caroline's pick, Trent Dorrman. Less education, fifteen years older than she, divorced, a grown son, what had to be a dead end job at Grantville-Saalfeld Metalworks and Foundries, Baptist rather than Methodist. Not what he had hoped for his older daughter.

When he'd brought it up before the marriage, she had answered a little bitterly, "Are you fishing? Pushing? What do you want me to say? That I left it too long, up-time? That the pickings are slim these days for a woman my age?" Since then, he had kept his mouth shut.

Dorrman was a quiet type. The two of them had been married a little over a year. Caroline was pregnant now; she planned to keep on working at the accounting firm after the baby was born. She and Trent seemed to be getting along with one another well enough. The less said the better, probably.

Next to Ceci, his sister Sandra Prickett and her husband. Their son Nathan was in Frankfurt now, of course. Their daughter-in-law Chandra had run in with the four grandchildren earlier in the afternoon before going over to her mother's family for supper.

His brother and wife, the Reverends Simon and Mary Ellen Jones, with children. Though, of course, Vanessa's husband, Jake Ebeling, was down in the Upper Palatinate with the army. He laughed to himself. While Simon was away in Italy, the Reverend Mary Ellen had unabashedly started a campaign for ensuring the future of Methodism in a time line in which John Wesley had never been born and never would be born by matchmaking among the church's younger generation. She had done more weddings in those nine months than First Methodist normally held in three years.

Then Mary Ellen's whole crew of Sebastian relatives. Well, except that Allan Sebastian's two girls by his first marriage had both gone up to Erfurt to spend a long weekend with their husbands, who couldn't get away to come to Grantville.

Finally, his sister Laura Ann had been left up-time, but her son Bill and family and Bill's Furbee grandparents were here. Bill's brother Johnny was out of town, gone back to his station with the army over in Fulda, where he had married a German girl. He'd brought Antonia to meet the family earlier in the fall. Their baby had been born and died last spring.

It was odd, in a way. Of all the families in Grantville, theirs had about the least marrying back and forth with down-timers. Only Johnny, of all of them, and that while he was stationed away for so long.

Even Jarvis Beasley had remarried to a German girl; he met her while he was in the army. That had sort of given his father Ken and the others who haunted the 250 Club a black eye. Jarvis wasn't welcome there any more.

So many people were more or less permanently out of town, now, because of the war effort.

First Methodist had done a lot of charity work among the refugees, of course. But it hadn't done much in the way of outreach, so far. Not much evangelism. A couple of down-time wives, like Farley Utt's Maggie, had joined the church, but most of them hadn't.

Maybe he ought to talk to Simon and Mary Ellen about evangelism. Being ecumenical had been all well and good in the twentieth century. If they relied entirely on growing their own in the seventeenth century, though, Methodism would be doomed to remain a minority sect. A tiny minority sect, if you looked at Europe as a whole.

Minnie Hugelmair had received her promotion from sixth grade to seventh the day before Thanksgiving break started. She was determined to have that eighth-grade diploma by next spring. She didn't see any reason why she couldn't finish the other two grades of middle school in six months. School stuff wasn't exactly hard. All she had to do was read the books, fill out the assignments, and turn them in.

She owed Benny. She ate her Thanksgiving dinner with the Pierce and Coffman families like a proper lady, as Louise would put it.

Then she went up to the storage lot. Denise's dad had faith in her and she owed him for it, too. Denise had gone off somewhere, flying in a plane with those losers Lannie Yost and Keenan Murphy, chasing after defectors. Which had to be hard on Buster and Christin, not having their daughter here on a big, important, up-timer holiday.

So she ate Thanksgiving dinner again.

Rudolstadt

Count Ludwig Guenther of Schwarzburg-Rudolstadt, aged fifty-three, looked proudly on the son he had never, during his long bachelorhood, expected to have.

Countess Emelie, aged twenty, smiled up at him, beatifically exalted in the realization of a job well done, a duty superbly performed, and having made her kindly husband possibly, at this moment, the happiest man in the USE. In addition to which, of course, she had a baby. The most wonderful baby ever born.

"What are you going to call him?" his widowed sister-in-law asked.

"Albrecht, I think, for our father. And Karl, for my brother."

Anna Sophia of Anhalt-Zerbst smiled. She was the widow of the late Count Karl Guenther. "And, of course, naming him for your father will also provide a suitable opportunity to reach out to the Crown Loyalists by inviting Duke Albrecht of Saxe-Weimar to lift him from the font. An excellent choice of godfather, by the way."

"No Ludwig?" Emelie asked. Then with a little laugh, "No Guenther to join the forty or more previous Guenthers who have been counts in Schwarzburg?"

He smiled again. "Not this time, I think. God willing, there will be other sons to bear those names." He leaned over and placed the baby back in her arms. "But, I think, it is an opportune moment for a little 'cultural borrowing,' as they call it. I shall proclaim that this day of the year will henceforth be a *Dankfest* in Schwarzburg-Rudolstadt, too."

Part Five

December 1634

Hovering on wing under the cope of hell

Chapter 30

Frankfurt am Main

"The anti-vaccination pamphlets are excellent. Perhaps we should make the effort to find out who Mauger's informant is. He appears to have some talent." Fortunat Deneau was actually smiling.

"The increased virulence of the criticism of Stearns and his allies by the Crown Loyalists is also opening up marvelous propaganda opportunities. Splendid ones." Ancelin was also smiling as he read the paper. "How opportune of those Grantvillers to defect to Austria at this time."

"How are Vincenz Weitz's contacts developing?" asked Locquifier.

"He will be able to provide us with sufficient practical assistance," Deneau answered. "He will continue to explore his various contacts until he has, I hope, a few hundred people who are willing to conduct demonstrations and start minor riots whenever and wherever he tells them to. Once he has reached that point, and actually conducted some preliminary agitation in other Thuringian towns—Arnstadt, Badenburg, Stadtilm, Ilmenau—not villages, but small cities—I will be in a position to set up the attack in Grantville itself."

"March fourth, you realize. Coordination is important. It must be the fourth of March, precisely. Weitz is very insistent on that point."

"Yes, Guillaume," Ancelin said. "I know."

Locquifier frowned. There would necessarily be so many people involved in the synagogue attack that there was an extremely high danger of leaks. Still, there were some measures that they could take in advance. It was not as if Weitz were the only anti-Semite in the Germanies. Someone else had written the pamphlets directed against Rebecca Abrabanel. Someone else was producing the worst of the slanders against Francisco Nasi. They were not coming out of Frankfurt. So . . .

"Robert."

Ouvrard looked up from the newspaper.

"You need to write several pamphlets, short ones, in the style of those attacking the wife of Stearns and the spymaster. Those pamphlets will . . ." He slowed down a little, thinking on his feet. ". . . at least make some references, not direct threats but references, to those Jews who have settled within the State of Thuringia-Franconia, even within the Ring of Fire itself, and think themselves secure there. Thus, if there are some leaks from among the people Deneau and Weitz are recruiting, there will be several false leads already out in public. That will divert attention from us."

"What about Antoine and Michel? They might not like us doing that."

Ancelin interrupted before Locquifier could continue. "Don't say anything about strategy or policy, purposes or goals. Nothing about us. You will be writing in the name of others, making comments that purport to come from others. Antoine can't complain about that. Well, he can, I suppose, being Antoine. If he finds out. But I don't see any reason to tell him. If we are lucky, he'll never need to know that we are the source of these little diversions."

Deneau, who liked to have all of his ducks in a row when he was organizing a riot, asked, "What about the hospital?"

"Mauger has assured de Ron that his agent feels confident of organizing a demonstration against the hospital that, if you give it a couple of hours of advance time, will be large enough to draw away the Grantville police—almost all of the police force—before the attack on the synagogue begins."

Switzerland

Henri de Rohan felt pretty good about the perceptiveness and intelligence of his agent on the scene in Grantville. Although, as he remarked in his next letter to his wife, that does tend to be the reaction when someone agrees with you—especially when that person has been reared in your own household. It only confirmed his belief that talent should be cultivated to its fullest, even when it blossomed in the humblest of worldly circumstances.

Jacques-Pierre Dumais' father was among the poorest. He still earned his living as a bootblack in La Rochelle; the boy's mother had worked as a fishmonger on the docks. A Walloon refugee had brought the talented child to the attention of the Rohan family.

To Dumais, he sent an alarm and a warning.

I am preparing to withdraw from my present location—probably to Geneva, but possibly to Besançon—not feeling myself secure any longer in either the Grisons or Sondrio. Richelieu is of a suspicious nature and wary of my enduring friendship with Bernhard of Saxe-Weimar. In spite of the repeated entreaties of the duchess, he refuses absolutely to permit me to return to Venice. Still, never doubting the justice of the Protestant cause, I continue to act in the assured belief that God has predestined me to save his churches, wherefore I will not lose my composure in the face of the greatest adversity.

Have a care. Michel Ducos is a dangerous man and I am having you play a dangerous game for us. Do not become overconfident. Always prepare for a fall when fortune puffs you up, for it is then that peril comes closest.

For the time being, you can reach me through Soubise in Frankfurt; should you hear that he has left the city, through de Ron.

Chapter 31

Grantville, December 1634

"I hadn't expected Lannie to crash the damned plane."

Victor Saluzzo, elbows on his desk, steepled his fingers. That was pretty much a picture-book perfect Concerned Principal's pose.

"Well, I hadn't. This time it's not my fault that I missed a bunch of school." Denise Beasley stuck her chin out and looked at her father Buster for support.

She hated parent-teacher conferences. Especially when they involved the principal. And the guidance counselor. And . . .

She looked across the room. The police.

Not that Preston Richards hadn't been pretty reasonable, but he was still the police.

"I expected that we'd fly down there, following the Saale, try to spot where the defectors were, turn around, and come back. I expected to be here for school the next morning. Honest, I did."

Honest, she hadn't. She hadn't thought about school at all. But that didn't seem to be quite the thing to say, right here and right now.

"They're giving her a hard time at school."

Saluzzo raised his eyebrows at Buster.

"Lots of hassling, needling, teasing. Even some significantly nasty threats. She's handled it pretty maturely, I think, for a sixteen-year-old."

Buster could play the game, if he had to. Denise hadn't killed any of the creeps. Or even done them significant bodily damage.

"Unfortunately," Joe Pallavicino said, "it isn't the first time that she has missed a block of school." Or the second, or even the fifth, but it didn't seem he was inclined to bring that up unless he had to. "I've been thinking that, perhaps, a mentoring program . . ."

Denise didn't stick her tongue out, and gave herself points.

"I have spoken to some of Denise's friends . . ."

Denise frowned. She didn't have any friends, except for Minnie.

"Tom Stone's youngest boy . . ."

Denise's forehead smoothed out. Yeah. Gerry actually was her friend. Unfortunately, he was going to school in Rudolstadt this year. Boarding over there.

". . . spoke to his brother. Ron suggested . . ." Pallavicino looked at Buster. ". . . since they already know one another, that perhaps Missy Jenkins and Pam Hardesty would be willing to act as big sisters for Denise and Minnie. On a more formal basis."

Denise nodded. That wouldn't be so bad. She liked Missy.

". . . with some adult supervision, of course."

That didn't sound so good.

"So Gerry talked to Pastor Kastenmayer's wife . . ."

Denise grinned. The mental picture of the redoubtable Salome Piscatora dancing in seven veils to get Herod to chop off John the Baptist's head had amused and occupied her mind through several tedious visits to St. Martin's in the Fields in the company of Gerry and Minnie. Even if Frau Kastenmayer did insist she was named for another Salome, the one who had stood at the foot of the cross. She jerked her mind back to this . . . hearing.

". . . who suggested that, in the interest of cross-cultural understanding, it might be best if one of the adult mentors was an up-timer and the other a down-timer."

Principal Saluzzo was nodding.

"I am happy to say that Mrs. Wiley and Mrs. Dreeson have agreed."

Denise stared at him, horror dawning upon her face.

Buster was grinning.

Daddy had known about this. The *traitor*. Denise resigned herself to her fate. Until she could figure some way to wiggle out of it.

✧ ✧ ✧

"I suppose it's consular work, in a way." Wes Jenkins looked a little dubious. "The mission of the Bureau of Consular Affairs, the way it's written, is to assist SoTF citizens when they run into difficulties outside our borders. Jarvis Beasley's wife is clearly inside our borders."

"Physically," Henry Dreeson said. "She's here, all right."

"Jurisdictionally, then," Wes went on imperturbably, "the first question to resolve is whether or not Hedy Beasley's problems count as being outside our borders. Physically, as you say, she is here. Geographically, her home village is certainly inside the borders of the SoTF. Now. On the other hand, when she was born in that same place, she was undoubtedly born as a citizen of Saxony. Then."

"Has she ever been naturalized?" Noelle Stull asked.

"Naturalized?" Wes blinked.

"Yeah, like we set up for refugees coming into the RoF, way back when."

"So long ago," Dreeson said. "Not yet four years and it's 'way back when.'"

"No, no, pay attention." Noelle jumped up. "I'm thinking, guys. I was working for Deborah Trout back then. I know we've sort of lost focus on it since, what with annexations, like up around Remda, and places like Badenburg voluntarily joining, and then the whole Franconia thing. The only naturalizations I see listed in the *Times* these days are real foreigners."

"And a 'real' foreigner is . . . ?" Eddie Junker raised an eyebrow.

"Drat it, Eddie. Behave yourself. You know what I mean. Walloons or Poles or—"

"Hungarians." He gave her a teasing smile.

"Not people from the USE. Definitely not people from the rest of the SoTF. But Saxony's backed out of being part of the USE. That means that if John George's delegate is right, and Hedy's actually Saxon, not just born in a piece of the SoTF south of the Thuringenwald where Saxony has administrative jurisdiction, I mean—"

Noelle stopped before her grammar got into a hopeless tangle; then started fresh. "If those old laws are still on the books . . ." She looked at Wes. "Those old laws *are* still on the books, aren't they? Nobody's taken them off in a fit of efficiency?"

"As far as I know, they're still on the books." Wes picked up the phone. "Let me check with Maurice Tito."

"Well, if they are, let's just naturalize her. Problem solved. Or, at least, we turn her into 'entirely our problem' instead of 'partly their problem.' Don't we? What do you think, Mr. Dreeson? Saxony couldn't extradite a citizen of West Virginia County, could it?"

"Those naturalization laws were written when the NUS was a country of its own. They may still be on the books, but . . . I'm not actually sure that a county can naturalize somebody."

"Then why are we still naturalizing Walloons, and Poles, and—"

"—and the occasional passing Hungarian?" Eddie raised up the arm with a cast on it. "Hey, no fair attacking an injured man. Injured in the course of duty, no less. *Noelle!*"

Wes looked up from the phone. "Hey, kids. Cut that out. This is a government office and you are both civil servants. Not a couple of first graders squabbling on the playground."

"I thought it was a fair enough question. Why are we still doing naturalizations, Maurice?" Henry Dreeson picked up a cup of coffee. "Thanks, Missy."

"The sheer force of inertia, I suppose. We were doing them and nobody thought to challenge it. I did call the Genealogy Club last night. They had some pamphlets about the history of naturalization. Put out for people to use who were looking up their ancestors, trying to figure out where they came from before they stepped off the boat. In the nineteenth century, in the back-time of the up-time so to speak, American naturalizations did run through the state courts and sometimes even the county courts. Not the federal courts. So we could claim precedent."

"So we could go ahead and naturalize her," Chad Jenkins said. "Just not as a NUS citizen or a SoTF citizen or a Grantville citizen or a West Virginia County citizen, but as a USE citizen."

"It could work," Maurice Tito said. "Maybe. Since Parliament hasn't gotten around to passing any nationwide citizenship law. At the very least, that little village down in Henneberg would have to appeal it to the SoTF Supreme Court, for a judgment as to whether one county in the SoTF can naturalize someone born in another county in the SoTF. And, I suppose, once that decision came down, someone could appeal to the *Reichsgericht* in Wetzlar. It would eventually issue a decision. If it decided that it had jurisdiction, of course."

Tom Riddle sipped his glass of wine. "By which time Hedy and Jarvis will have grandchildren playing around their feet."

"Assuming that I get elected," Chad asked, "should I try at least to introduce statewide legislation, do you think? Get every county and county-equivalent in the SoTF on the same page when it comes to the question of what's a valid marriage? Or do you think that Parliament ought to do it? Ed, since as president you're automatically the SoTF member in the Chamber of Princes, would you be introducing it there?"

Tom Riddle shook his head. "Matrimonial legislation was a state matter up-time. No telling how the Crown Loyalists in parliament would weigh in on it. Personally, I don't want to see the USE overcentralize. The SoTF Congress would be a better place to handle it. In my humble opinion, of course.

"Citizenship should, probably, eventually, end up being in Parliament's hands. When they get around to it. Which won't be before the election, certainly. It's not even in session. Everybody's out campaigning. But Ed could introduce citizenship legislation. Probably should. We need to produce a draft we'd be happy with."

Ed Piazza shifted in his chair. "Maybe we ought to let Wes look into this for a while before we make up our minds about introducing marriage legislation in the SoTF Congress, even. Make sure that we have a majority of the delegates who see it our way. It could take a considerable amount of logrolling to be sure of coming up with the kind of statute we can live with. Or want to live with."

Henry Dreeson nodded. "Sometimes it really is smarter to let sleeping dogs lie. But as for Hedy, specifically. Yep. She's been living here plenty long to meet the residency requirements we put on the books. Get Noelle to give her the little citizenship class. I'll administer the oath of allegiance myself. Take that, John George!"

Henry Dreeson sighed. Thea hadn't made it to the hospital. She'd produced her baby in the back downstairs bedroom of his house, which she and her husband Nicholas were still occupying, not having been able to find an apartment they could afford.

She'd probably dragged her feet deliberately, waiting till it was too late to leave the house even when the hospital was just a few blocks away, not telling anybody. Down-time women didn't like to go to Leahy Medical Center to have their babies. They wanted to have them at home, with midwives. That was probably just as well in a way. Given the size of Grantville these days, if all the women wanted to have their babies in the hospital with up-time physicians officiating, the deliveries would spill over into the parking lot and the town's three doctors would be working nonstop.

It caused a bit of tension, sometimes, between the doctors and the German midwives. Sometimes even between the doctors and the nurse-midwives whom Beulah MacDonald was training. Maybe he ought to talk to Kortney Pence, and Beulah the next time she came up from Jena . . .

He brought his mind back to the tension right here. Nicholas was hovering next to Dorothea.

On one side of the bed, the Reverend Enoch Wiley for the Calvinists. On the other side of the bed, Father Athanasius Kircher for the Catholics. *In this corner, wearing a black suit; in the opposite corner, wearing a clerical collar . . .*

He'd married Nicholas Moser and Dorothea Richter himself, at city hall, to avoid the question of which kind of church ceremony they might have to pick between, so to speak.

He didn't think that even Grantville had a provision for anything you might call civil baptism.

The way things were starting to sound, it might be a useful idea, though. He could suggest it to the county board. Maybe Jenny Maddox could do them at the funeral home. The chapel there was pretty nondenominational.

A sort of generic baptism for those who wanted it, not committing the baby to anything specific in the long run. It could be filed with the birth certificate instead of in a church. That would be convenient, since the Bureau of Vital Statistics was still in the funeral home.

Enoch advanced, defending the ecclesiastical allegiance of the father; Kircher countered, championing the faith of the mother.

The proud parents were doing their best to bury their heads in the sand. Dorothea, literally, her head in the pillow. They didn't deal with problems like this very well.

Maybe it wasn't the sort of thing that he really needed to run by the county board. He left the room, picked up the phone, and called Jenny.

Mike Stearns and the "total separation of church and state" radicals in the CoC might want to haul him in front of a firing squad for this. At a minimum, there would be a lively controversy in the newspapers after it was announced. But Mike was in

Magdeburg these days, and the CoC didn't have the responsibility for keeping life in Grantville on an even keel.

"Thea's worn out," he said firmly. "I don't want to be inhospitable, but everybody except Nicol ought to get out of the room. There's coffee and cookies in the living room. Then, the rest of you, go home. She doesn't need this right now."

"He didn't," Chad Jenkins said.

"He did," Ed Piazza answered. "Right after supper, once he'd gotten rid of the rest of them, Henry had Ronnie bring a basin of water in from the kitchen and he baptized the baby himself."

"Oh, Lord."

"It's a valid baptism. I've checked with everyone. Kircher, Kastenmayer, Jones, Wiley. All the ministers agree. Well, not Green, or old Joe Jenkins, of course, but that's only because they don't believe in infant baptism at all and insist on total immersion of adults. She wasn't even a day old and Henry just dribbled some water on her forehead. The rest of them, though, except the Baptists and Curtis at the Church of Christ, figure that the kid is now a properly saved Christian until such time as she reaches the age of reason. That gives Nicol and Thea another, oh, seven to ten years to decide which direction she's going, ecclesiastically speaking. He named her, too, while he was at it, since Nicol and Thea couldn't agree on a name, either."

"What did he pick?"

"Anna Elisabetha. For Annalise. He said that Annalise deserved a tribute, the way she bore up under everything last summer."

Chad picked up his notebook. "Well, let's start laying out how we're going to play it as far as the campaign is concerned. Annalise was a good idea for a name, because we can bring in Hans . . . At least Henry doesn't have any significant opposition. The Crown Loyalists, the few we have locally, thought they ought to run someone. Their caucus picked a down-timer, a guy named Hartmuth Frisch. He's a friend of Tino Nobili and already on the county board, but he's mostly known in town as Count August von Sommersburg's factor. Henry should win in a walk, even if he has introduced 'civil baptism' sort of off the top of his head."

Henry Dreeson pursed his lips and wished for the nine hundred ninety-ninth time in the past five hours—which was how long this county board meeting had been dragging on—that sixteen fewer people had voted for Tino Nobili. Or seventeen more people had come to the polls and voted for Orval McIntire. Or some combination of the above that would have kept Tino out of office.

Henry was still the mayor, but it wasn't a city council, any more. It was a county board, now. When the SoTF went to the county system, they'd decided that the make-do of a slightly expanded Grantville city council being the governing body of the whole RoF circle plus everything it had annexed since 1631 had to be scrapped. So they'd scrapped it and turned the whole area into an urban county. He was still the mayor. Partly because he'd been the mayor to start with. Partly because the down-timers had a good grasp on what a mayor did and hanging on to the familiar, when you could, wasn't a bad idea. So instead of mayor/council or chairman/board, they had a mayor/board system now.

For which Tino ran. And won. And just at this moment sat in a chair at the other end of the table. Bringing as many complications with him as the vain little Maizie bird in Dr. Seuss had stuck artificial feathers in her tail to make herself prettier. Till she had so many that they overbalanced her.

The time when Tino's pretensions overbalanced him and he fell flat on his face couldn't come too soon. Right now . . . Well, it got complicated. What happened to having a world in which you could tell your players if you did have a scorecard? It was getting to the point that a man needed a cat's cradle with diagrams on it to figure out the way things worked.

Some ways, Tino was a good guy. A family man. Hospitable. The daughter of that Italian artist woman who'd come into town with Simon Jones and the Stone boys had been staying with them for quite a while, and the girl was going to marry Pete McDougal's son.

Pete was Fourth of July Party, of course. Good friend of Mike Stearns. Which you'd think might tilt things one way.

But politically, on the board, Tino had hooked up with Hartmuth Frisch, who was running for mayor.

Now Frisch, you'd think, wouldn't be running on the other ticket. Not in a logical world. He came from the Palatinate—the one over by the Rhine, not the one over by Bohemia. A pretty reasonable man. He'd come into town at the end of a long, long, trip that had taken him all over the northern half of Germany, following the trail of his dead brother and trying to track his kids. Found them here, adopted by Orval and Karin McIntire a couple years before he caught up with them. Hadn't made a fuss—Orv and Karin were Presbyterian, Calvinists like Frisch was, and the kids were happy. A lot happier than they would have been spending those years in an orphanage, somewhere. Frisch was a widower; he was happy just to be an uncle. He'd taken a job as a factor for Count August von Sommersburg's slate quarries. Good businessman. Ed's friend Cavriani had brought his daughter Idelette to town; she was living with Enoch and Inez Wiley and working for the guy.

Sommersburg was Mike's ally; Orv was Mike's ally; Cavriani . . . well, he was friends with Ed Piazza and Ronnie liked him fine.

So you'd think maybe that Frisch would join the Fourth of July Party.

Naaaah!

Frisch didn't usually say much, himself. He didn't need to. He had Tino, who was willing to say it all. Tino was a really conservative sort of Catholic. He thought that what Henry had done when he baptized Thea's baby was an awful thing. Frisch was a really conservative sort of Calvinist. He thought that what Henry had done when he baptized Nicol's baby was an awful thing.

It was the same baby, of course. They seemed to forget that, from time to time.

The only thing that ever shut Tino up was an emergency at the pharmacy. Then he forgot all about strutting in his artificial peacock plumage and dashed off to do what he did best.

That was probably why Henry hadn't ever strangled him.

Chapter 32

Grantville

"So that's what we did, Daddy," Denise said.

Buster looked at her, twisting his thin reddish beard around in his fingers.

"Keenan Murphy, you said?"

"He was one of them. Egging the rest of them on, for the first part of it."

"I thought ol' Keenan had been playing the hero lately. Chasing down Francis when he shot at Dennis Stull. Chasing after Noelle when those guys grabbed her."

"He's not a hero, Daddy. He's not a villain, either. Mostly he's just dumb. He chased down Francis because his grandma told him to and chased after Noelle because they have the same mother. But he's dumb. Most of his friends are even dumber."

"Who else was with him? Names?"

"Mitchell Kovacs. Bubba."

"Not a surprise." Buster looked at his daughter. "Out with the rest of it."

"And Jermaine."

"Not a kids' fight, then."

"There were a couple of kids with them, I guess. Not kids the same age as Gerry and Minnie and me, though. Not fifteen or sixteen. More like eighteen or nineteen."

"Names." Buster was starting through his checklist.

"Bill Sanabria. Dustin Acton. I saw those two, at least. I didn't see Nino. He used to run with Bill, but he seems to have straightened out a lot since their mom married Ronnie Bawiec. So has Olivia."

"She's Pat's cousin," her mother Christin inserted into the conversation. "Bill's mom, that is. She's a cousin of Keenan and Noelle's mother. Fitzgeralds, both of them. That's how Bill connects to Keenan."

Buster let that pass, still focusing on Denise. "Arguments?"

"When we came out of Marcantonio's, the usual sort of thing," Denise said. "Gerry's home for a couple of weeks, for the holidays. Gerry Stone. Because he's going to school in Rudolstadt, they said he's 'going native.' Bill and Justin started to hassle him. Were hassling us, I should say, calling Minnie names too. Gordy Fritz and Dane Stevenson, Dane Junior, were with them to start with, but backed off right after it started, so they don't really count. We got out of it clean and wouldn't have bothered anyone else about it, except that Dustin said something about 'another job at the fairgrounds' that Jermaine was doing. So we followed them."

"Carefully?"

"They never knew we were there."

"You're a pip."

"Jermaine and the others tried to corner Jarvis and Hedy when they were walking home from the laundry. While they were crossing the fairgrounds, by the community center, going over to the bridge, Jermaine came up to Jarvis and said something about Hedy."

"Tried to?"

"Jarvis had heard about the plan. He still has some friends who hang out at the 250 Club, even though Uncle Ken won't have him there any more since he married Hedy. So he had friends shadowing them, too. Enough to persuade the guys with Jermaine to stay out of it, so just the two of them fought. And that's why Jermaine and Jarvis had a fight last night."

"Who won?"

"A draw, more or less. Jarvis was pretty mad and gave Jermaine as good as he got. Except that in a way, Jarvis won, because Hedy got home okay. That was what they planned to do. Take Jarvis down and then take Hedy away and beat her up good. Try to make her lose the baby. Then they were going to take her back to where she came from, so she could be prosecuted for being a bigamist for marrying Jarvis. And in the election campaign, say that when Mayor Dreeson married the two of them, he knew she was a bigamist."

"So then you went to see your Uncle Ken?"

"Yeah. I thought it was a bit much. After all, Jarvis and Hedy's kid is going to be his grandchild."

"And that's what he said?"

"Ummhmmh. That he wished that they *had* beat her up. That he'd rather see her and the kid dead than have a half-Kraut grandchild."

"You know," Buster said, "I think Ken is going overboard. I'm going to have to cogitate on all this for a while."

"Okay. Then, after that, we went over to Benny's and wrote up a story about it all and we sent copies to all of the papers. That's what we did. Minnie and me. English and German, both. Naming names. Remains to be seen if they'll publish it. The *Freie Presse* probably won't, they're so righteous, but the *Daily News* probably will. And maybe Rodger Rude's column in the *Times*. I sure hope the *National Inquisitor* doesn't. That would ruin everything. Nobody else would believe a word of it." She picked up her jacket.

"Where are you going?"

"Over to see Eddie Junker. See how his arm's doing. With Minnie and Gerry. Then we're going to a play at the church—St.Martin's in the Fields." She zipped out the door of the trailer.

Buster looked after her blankly. "Church?"

"Gosh, Mom, sorry I'm late. Let me get a quick shower." Missy headed for the stairs.

"Where have you been?"

"Out at Lothlorien. Christmas Eve. Children's presents. Well, we also sang 'Happy Birthday' to Ron. Do you know that he's never actually had a birthday party in his life?"

The bathroom door slammed behind her.

It opened again. "Uh, he and Gerry are coming to dinner tomorrow, if I forgot to tell you before. I didn't even invite them for tonight. I was afraid that Christmas Eve at Gran's would be a bit much for them. Considering Thanksgiving. Anyway Gerry is going to a children's play out at St. Martin's. With Minnie Hugelmair and Denise Beasley. And Eddie Junker."

Another slam and the sound of rushing water.

Chad put his arm around Debbie. "Experience teaches us that she really can shower and dress in fifteen minutes."

She made it in thirteen, pulling a ski cap over her wet hair as she ran down the stairs. The three of them headed toward the family party.

"Is Ron going with Gerry?" Debbie asked.

"No. He's working evening shift in the lab so that a couple of other people who have kids in the play can go to it."

Then, apparently out of a clear blue sky, Missy added, "Ron looked up his birth certificate out at the high school. His mother's name was Mary Beth Shaw. Otherwise known as Dreamcatcher. It says that she was born in Illinois, for what it's worth."

Just before they got to Gran's, she added, "He says that's going to be it in the way of a family tree. Fairly shallow roots."

"Oh, well," Debbie said. "I'm sure that he actually has as many ancestors as anyone else. Everybody does, after all. It's unavoidable. He may not know who they were, but that's a different question."

"Oh! They are beautiful, Lenore. Really they are. Thank you so much."

Clara was looking at a set of framed drawings.

"I saw you yearning over the photos one day, Clara. It used to be easy to copy old ones, pretty much, but even if someone could figure out how to do it now and get the chemicals, it would probably cost the earth and the sky. But I've always had a knack for sketching, so . . ."

"I didn't even know you could do this, honey child," Wes said.

Lenore glanced over at her grandmother, who was sitting on the other side of the room talking to Uncle Chad and Chandra. They were looking at something else. She wiggled a little uncomfortably. "I got it from Gran, I suppose. She knew that I liked to draw, back when I was in school, but she never really encouraged me. Not the way she encouraged Chip to play violin, later on. The reverse, if anything. She sure made a fuss when I said once that I might like to go to a school of design rather than to a regular college. I found out later—a lot later—that she actually went over to the high school and asked my counselor to tell me that it was a bad idea, if I brought it up."

Now Wes looked across toward his mother, frowning.

Lenore didn't notice. "So don't make a big production about these, please. I sneaked over and made the sketches from the photos while she was out doing her Red Cross stuff, on the excuse that I was checking the tops of her cupboards and other stuff she can't really reach any more. She wanted to be sure the maid was cleaning them. 'Trust but verify.'"

"This, though . . ." Clara drew her index finger along some fine cross-hatching. "This is not—not a 'knack' as you say. You have been taught. Did you apprentice with someone?"

"Well, I took college classes at Fairmont State off and on. Over six or seven years, I got about four semesters worth of classes in, I guess. None the first couple of years after I finished high school, but after that, since my schedule at work was pretty flexible, I took a couple of courses every now and then. And if I was on campus anyway for something I should take for work, like retailing or business applications, and there was an art class, or an art history class, available that day, I would take one." She looked a little defiant. "I was working and paying the tuition myself. It isn't as if I was wasting Dad's money."

"I'd have *liked* you to finish college," Wes said. "In anything. Underwater basket weaving would have been fine. I had a savings account for it in your name, ever since you were tiny." He laughed. "For that matter, it's still there in the bank if you ever need it. One for Chandra, too. I wouldn't have minded if you chose a design school. There were good ones, up-time. It wouldn't have been wasting anything."

"Yeah, I guess. But Gran said . . . well, that she had majored in art and then never used it, really. She said that only genius pays you back if you get a degree in art, not just a little flair like hers or mine. And Mom went along with her. She didn't think it was practical, even though commercial art actually paid pretty well, back up-time, if a person was good at it. I couldn't really see spending the money if I didn't know what I wanted to do with a degree when I got it. Not nursing, for sure. Not teaching. And getting a degree wouldn't have helped me advance at the store unless I wanted to sit in an office all day, which I didn't." Lenore reached over, took the sketches, and wrapped them back up. "Here. This will protect them while you're carrying them home."

The family was passing most of the presents around the room, so everyone could admire them. Lenore dropped the sketches down into Clara's tote bag. "Maybe it's one reason that I liked learning these seventeenth-century handwriting styles so much." A wide smile suddenly lit up her long, thin face. "Some of them are so elaborate that they are almost like drawing the words more than writing them. Every letter or filing that came to my desk because no one else could read it was an adventure."

She looked toward the double doorway leading into the hallway. Bryant was standing there, scowling at them. Her smile faded.

"I like *this* bridge. I like the way it blows in the cold wind when there is snow coming like tonight."

"You are a risk taker at heart, considering how many packages we are carrying. All right, we'll cross on the suspension bridge."

In the middle of it, Clara stopped.

"Brr," Wes said.

"We have another present, Wesley. One more than we opened at your mother's house."

"Hmmn."

Clara turned around, putting down her bag and circling his neck with her arms. "You have given it to me. In less than half a year, I will give it back to you."

She kissed him. "We are going to have a baby. I am sure of it, now. I have felt movement and also Kortney Pence said so, yesterday morning. So we will have all three of the purposes of marriage."

"What three purposes of marriage?"

"Oh, Wesley. I am not trying to convert you, like the up-time men who are going to class with Pastor Kastenmayer at St. Martin's now to be confirmed next spring, but I do wish you would at least *read* the small catechism. Every Lutheran knows that there are three purposes of marriage."

"Which are?"

"The procreation of children, of course. Which now we are doing."

"That's one."

"Mutual companionship and support, which we also have already. And I will need to bring a cradle to the consular affairs office after the baby is born."

Wes didn't blink. He could live with a cradle in the consular affairs office. And, obviously, would.

"That's two. What's three?"

She smiled up at him. "The third is that it is a remedy for lust."

"I can endorse that. We have been polite to a lot of people all evening. Shall we go home and remedy something?" This time, he kissed her.

Clara was quite relieved to discover that he would not expect them to forego the third purpose of marriage between the time he was notified of her pregnancy and the time she weaned the child. Some men thought that way. Apprehension about this possibility was one reason she had put off telling him about the baby as long as she reasonably could. So she happily kissed him back, for quite some time, in spite of the stiff wind that was blowing down Buffalo Creek.

"Is that actually your father and his Kraut woman making out on the suspension bridge, right in the middle of town?" Bryant Holloway asked.

"Looks like Dad and Clara to me."

"You weren't sucking up to her tonight, were you? Not a bit, of course. Insinuating yourself. Currying a little favor?"

"I like Clara. She's nice. She's nice to us. Really. She goes out of her way."

Bryant was looking at the couple on the bridge. "They should be ashamed of themselves."

"All they're doing is kissing each other." Lenore protested. "Wearing a batch of winter clothes. And they *are* married."

"Barely in time, if the gossip that Lola picked up is true."

"What gossip?"

"She went in to Leahy Medical to find out if she's pregnant."

"Pregnant?"

"What did you expect, the way they—"

"Act like married people in love? Clara turned thirty-eight a couple of weeks ago. We had a birthday party for her. You weren't back yet. If you really want to know, then—yeah, Chandra and I have been sort of expecting that a half-sister or half-brother would turn up one of these days. Or both. Or more, if they manage to squeeze them in."

She laughed. "I've got to grant that they've apparently been pretty efficient about it, though. I suppose we'll get the news officially in a day or so."

"I don't like that tone of voice. You're talking back. Again. You're getting to be more and more like your sister."

"What's Chandra ever done to you?"

"She spent at least an hour this evening trying to get me to talk about what Nathan has been doing in Frankfurt and quizzing me about why he decided not to come to Grantville for a visit. If he thought it was any of her business, he would tell her himself. And nagging me to tell her why he doesn't want her to go with him. He's given her his reasons, and that's actually more than she deserves. If he doesn't want her to come, then she should do as he wants and stay here without all this griping."

Lenore stopped walking. "Since when doesn't a wife *deserve* to know her husband's reasons for how he treats her?"

Bryant turned toward her.

She pushed the baby stroller so that it was between them. "We'd better get Weshelle home. I have her all covered up, but this wind is chilly."

Chapter 33

Grantville

"Because I don't really want to be at home, Veda Mae, if you want me to be brutal about it. Every time I turn around, I see another German, and not a servant, either. What is it about Lenore's family? They collect Krauts like cat hair on your best dress slacks." Bryant Holloway finished off his coffee. "At least Nathan Prickett had the sense not to come home for the holidays."

"You're acting like a fool about Lenore, Bryant," said Trent Dorrman.

Bryant glared at the other man sitting at the table. Brother Green had sicced Dorrman onto him. He hadn't gone to church, so Green had come around knocking on the door, saying that he hadn't been at services for a while. The pompous Reverend Doctor Albert Green.

Blasted preachers, wanting guys to come in for counseling, and then when he had refused, this "peer counseling by laymen" stuff. He'd been stuck with Dorrman all vacation. What did Dorrman know about marriage? He'd been divorced for years before the Ring of Fire and remarried even less time than Bryant had been married to Lenore.

Bryant said as much.

Dorrman spoke very softly. "I think that Brother Green thought that maybe I'm a little smarter for the experience of living through a broken marriage once. I count myself lucky to have Caroline. For a guy like me, it was sort of like hitting the jackpot. I don't intend to make the same mistakes again." He smiled. "New ones, maybe, considering that I'm a human being. But not the same ones."

"You're on a collision course, Dorrman," Veda Mae predicted. "She's got more education than you, just the way your first wife did. History repeating itself. The way Laurie tried to do to Gary. The way Lenore has more than Bryant. Mark my words, it's a recipe for disaster."

Dorrman looked at her. "'I'm proud of my wife and her accomplishments.' That's a place to start. That was my first resolution, this time, after she said she would marry me. To be proud of Caroline. Not to try to put her down or pull her down. To do a better job of understanding her interests than I did with Pam."

"Then go home and drool over her for a while, but leave me alone." Bryant had his suspicions about Caroline Jones. Caroline Dorrman, she should be now, but since the Ring of Fire, the women weren't changing their names when they got married because the Krauts didn't do it.

Jenny Maddox and those uppity women in the genealogy club were at fault, too. They said it was easier to keep track of people if they kept the same names. Lenore, though some people called her Mrs. Holloway, was still signing stuff as "Lenore Jenkins." If he was looking over her shoulder, she would add "(now Holloway)."

Maybe Caroline had put her uncle Simon Jones up to putting Brother Green up to this counseling stuff, somehow. Through the blasted Interdenominational Ministerial Alliance or something. She was almost exactly the same age as Lenore and they were friends. Methodist Sunday school together and all that. Maybe Lenore had been tattling. If so, she'd regret it. Whether Lenore had been telling tales out of school or not, Caroline was probably meddling.

He turned back to Veda Mae. "And I'm between assignments. Hell, I'm supposed to be on vacation for two weeks, between finishing in Frankfurt and going back to Magdeburg. Steve Matheny said that he didn't want to see my face at the fire department the whole time, so I don't have any place else to go except home or to my sister Lola's and she's working. 'Relax,' says the chief, 'relax, relax.'"

"You should talk to Jacques-Pierre Dumais. You really should. Even if you don't drink, you can talk to him at the 250 Club. Ken Beasley doesn't like him a lot. He calls his corner the 'dry table' and complains that he loses money on it. But that would give you someplace to be, evenings at least, where you can get away from Lenore."

"I talked to him a couple of times last fall."

"Well, talk to him again."

That was all he needed, Bryant thought. Another lay peer counselor.

Trent Dorrman looked at Holloway, frowning. Brother Green was probably right to be worried about him. There had been some kind of meeting that Brother Green had attended, with Mayor Dreeson and Steve Matheny, the fire department chief. About stress problems. That was when Brother Green decided to train lay peer counselors.

He'd taken apart an old fashioned alarm clock once, when he was a kid. After he had the back off, he'd taken the key and wound the spring inside so tight that it snapped. He hoped Bryant Holloway wasn't getting to that stage.

Scotland

"I agree. There's no direct connection with our greater purpose." André Tourneau gestured at Antoine Delerue.

His fellow silk weaver, Abraham Levasseur, made a calming gesture. "Guillaume is getting impatient, André. Here, we are planning. Focusing. Preparing various projects, such as the one we have already given to Abraham Levasseur. In Frankfurt, he and the others are merely waiting. These little enterprises will occupy their minds and give them something to do."

"I disagree." Delerue waved one hand at the report that had just come in. "They are only using the demonstrations as excuses to not make any real effort to carry out the assassinations we ordered. A piddling attack on a hospital. A minor action against a synagogue. What is the point?"

Ducos chimed in, very forcefully. "I don't intend to let them lose sight of the ultimate purpose. Reiterate my instructions to

Guillaume. Between the election and the transfer of power. No matter who wins the election, Stearns or Wettin. Think—the emperor, Stearns, and Wettin dead. All that welds these Germanies together gone. With Kristina dead, the new union of Kalmar, fragile enough at the best of times, will be broken. There is no other obvious heir in Sweden, either, so Oxenstierna and Brahe will be pulled out of Germany to handle civil strife and two generations of attempts by the Vasas to build a centralized kingdom will collapse. Poland will intervene, again. Which will tempt Russia to send another tentacle toward Poland. Which will distract both Wallenstein and Ferdinand III, opening a gate for the Ottomans."

Ducos sat back, in happy contemplation of the impending chaos. Armageddon would be welcome, if that was what it took to remove Richelieu from his post.

If only the lever he needed to move the world proved adequate to the task.

"Again, Antoine. Repeat my instructions in your reply. Remind them again. All five. On the same day. In the same place. As soon as possible after the election."

"Guillaume has brought up the difficulty of getting them all in the same place at the same time. Not to mention security."

Michel Ducos narrowed his eyes. "Guillaume, too, is a tool in the hand of God. I have seen a vision. He has done better, perhaps, than he believes. These demonstrations that he is planning—minor in themselves, just as you say—will occur in Grantville. If they should turn out not to be so minor? If the consequences of these actions should become greater? All five of our real targets might, by some happy chance, gather in Grantville itself. Leaving, necessarily, most of their excessive security apparatus behind."

Delerue clasped his hands behind his head. "I read the newspapers, too. On this 'Thanksgiving' festival, Stearns and his wife went to Grantville by plane. Leaving the sturdy Yeoman Warders behind in Magdeburg. Accompanied, the whole time they were in the town, only by a few soldiers from the SoTF forces who met them at the air field with a single truck. Standing for a period of time, quite out in the open, on the sidewalk in front of his house."

Ducos nodded. "An invitation, Antoine. A clear sign. An indication of the will of divine providence."

Grantville

What they called the "dry table" at the 250 Club wasn't exactly dry. That just turned out to be Ken Beasley's description for wine instead of 'shine or beer. The people who sat there seemed to spend a lot of time talking politics.

"I'm not going to vote for Wettin. No way." Bryant Holloway wasn't yelling, but his voice didn't give any hint of flexibility.

Dumais had received instructions directly from Rohan and from Locquifier via de Ron through Mauger to make contact with the up-time firefighter as soon as he returned from Frankfurt. For, of course, different reasons.

"Ah, but why, then? Although you oppose Stearns, you do not support his opponent?"

"Because Wettin is one more goddamned Kraut, Dumais. Surely you can figure that out for yourself. We're overrun with them. This stupid Stearns immigration policy. Come one, come all. Stay a while, take an oath of allegiance, and 'presto, you're a citizen now.' No standards at all. Good God, considering how long you've been working here, all you would have to do yourself would be walk down to the administration building, enroll in their little class, and bingo!"

Jacques-Pierre looked at Holloway consideringly. This was one aspect of his current assignment in Grantville that had not, for some reason, crossed his mind previously.

The man was steamrolling along. "Sure, Stearns is married to a Kraut, but at least he's an American himself. Wettin, even if he's changed his name, was born a Kraut nobleman and he's still a Kraut nobleman, no matter what he calls himself. He's married to another one. He's got a brother who is fighting us. He'd not be any improvement. Worse."

Dumais frowned. "Stearns is not married to a 'Kraut.' Rebecca Abrabanel is not a German. She is a Jewess. Her family was originally from Spain. She grew up in the Netherlands and England."

"I don't give a damn whether she's Jewish or not. I haven't met a half dozen Jews in all my life. Hell, except for the Roths, I've never actually met any as far as I know, and I don't have anything against Morris and Judith. Their boy was five years or so younger than me, so I didn't know the kids well, but they were perfectly ordinary people. Spoke English, went hunting. Americans, if you know what I mean. Not foreigners."

Jacques-Pierre pondered the matter. Mrs. Haggerty had, upon occasion, expressed similar ideas. Most of these Grantvillers, even the most unpleasant such as those who frequented the 250 Club tavern, truly did not seem to care whether someone was Jewish or not. There were a few exceptions, such as the man named Cooper, but most of them did not.

In fact, he thought, although there were some tensions, most of them did not care whether a person was of any particular religious persuasion at all, which was somewhat unnerving.

They did, many of them, seem to care whether someone was "foreign" or not. This was something he would have to pass on to Rohan.

The question for even the most dissatisfied among the up-timers, apparently, was whether someone was . . . *different* . . . or not. It was something to think about. What caused enough difference between people for an up-timer to take notice of it and to resent it? Was there such a word as undifferent? It couldn't be "indifferent." That was a word in the English language, but it had another, quite distinct, meaning.

Difference. He had been allowed to learn a great deal—more, really, than he'd expected—in large part simply because he said that he wished to become like them. Take, for example, his acquaintance through the Genealogy Club with Mrs. Sandra Prickett, who also worked for the Bureau of Vital Statistics. She had been so willing to explain how things worked. And then to show him how to look things up.

Most of the up-timers probably would not want to act against the hospital, either. How many of the down-timers living inside the RoF would have absorbed that attitude?

As he reflected on what might make a person completely "undifferent" in this town, he continued chatting. "You are returning to Magdeburg next week?"

"I was supposed to be," said Holloway. "Now, though, it looks like I'll have to run some other errands for high-and-mighty Stannard on the way. Halle for a couple of weeks. Naumburg for a while. It could be the middle of February before I actually get there. In fact, I might have to come back here first for a while."

Jacques-Pierre looked at him for a minute. "Do you have any 'spare time' when you are in these cities for your work?"

"Usually, yeah."

"You do work with down-timers, don't you. Even though you do not enjoy it?"

"No way to get around it. Most of the fire companies outside of Grantville and Magdeburg are all-Kraut. There are millions and millions of them in this stupid country, even in this state it seems like, and nowhere near enough of us to go around."

"So you have contacts. Could I employ you in your spare time? I need to hire some men. Day laborers, casual workers. Strong men, physically. 'Toughs' are okay. Hooligans; thugs, as long as they will do what they are told in exchange for their pay. Could you ask around for me? Not too many from any one city. They would need to be in Grantville by the first of March. A commission for each successful hire?"

"What are the Garbage Guys up to now? You must have a contract for some kind of big project." Holloway waved his hand. "But that isn't any of my business. How much commission?"

Part Six

January 1635

Winged with red lightning and impetuous rage

Chapter 34

Grantville
New Year's Day, 1635

"That was a pretty comprehensive defense of yourself for staying out all night with Ron on New Year's Eve, Missy," Chad Jenkins said. "Designed to drive your mother to maximum distraction, I'm sure."

"Then why are you laughing?"

"Because I was listening. Outside the door, but listening. That's a lot of what a salesman does. And through all of your pointing out that the two of you don't have to sneak around in hotel rooms or anything because Ron has a whole house at his disposal out at Lothlorien where you can do whatever you please in perfect comfort and have a kitchen in which to cook breakfast to boot . . . not once did you say that you actually were there."

Missy gave her father a lopsided smile.

"We were over at Pam's. Playing cards with her and Cory Joe. And a guy named Jean-Louis LaChapelle, who is a nephew of the man that Velma Hardesty married. He's really a student at the University of Leiden. If this was back home, we'd say that he was a hard science major, I guess, with a sideline in engineering. They're not as specialized here as majors were at Fairmont State or WVU. He's in town on business for his uncle and also learning what he can while he's here. He's been here several weeks and took the 'how to use a research library' training that we give out at the state library. Very, very, French, for a Calvinist who was born and grew up in the Netherlands. All charm. 'Oozing charm from every pore,' like the song said."

"How does this involve Pam?"

"Good grief, Dad. Naturally, he looked up the family of his new aunt-by-marriage. The first time this Jean-Louis saw that tow-blond hair on top of Pam's head, he went into meltdown. Also, she's in charge of the circulation desk at the State Library now and sometimes she gives the class. She taught the section he took, so when he found out that she works there, it gave him a doubled and redoubled reason to haunt the place."

"Is she flattered?"

"Part of her wants to melt back; part of her doesn't want to get a reputation like Velma's. The rest of her, which doesn't ever want to see Velma again, which she would probably have to if she got involved with her stepfather's nephew, is trying to referee. So until she decides what to do, the one thing she's absolutely sure of is that even though she wants to be with him, she doesn't want to be alone with him. So Ron and I told her that we'd play backup. That was before she knew Cory Joe would be here. His schedule between Grantville and Magdeburg is pretty irregular. Anyway, you can't play cards with three people, and Cory Joe didn't have a date."

She turned her head to the hall. "And you might as well come back in, Mom. I know you're there."

Debbie came back, having the grace to look a little ashamed. "Um. Is Cory Joe doing well in the army up in Magdeburg?"

"Cory Joe is on General Jackson's immediate staff and serving as his personal liaison to Don Francisco Nasi."

That stopped the conversation temporarily.

"Look, Mom. He'll be twenty-five in another couple of weeks. Pam splurged on a whole cup of sugar and is going to bake a little half-sized cake for him and Susan—her birthday was in December—before he goes back to Magdeburg. We're growing up. All of us. Time didn't stop when the Ring of Fire happened. That's something you've got to face. If we were back home in West Virginia, I'd be away from home, halfway through my first year of college."

Missy stopped, then started again. "And about Ron . . . This is important for you to hear."

Her mother looked at her.

"He isn't going to go away. No matter what happens between him and me. If anything ever does. Ron and Bill . . ."

"Bill?"

"Bill Hudson. Remember Bill? My cousin Bill? Your nephew Bill?"

Debbie nodded.

"While he was fighting that diphtheria epidemic down at Amberg last summer, he decided that when he got out of the army, he was going to work for Ron's dad. That it was more important in the long run to make the medicines that doctors can use than to be a doctor himself. Uncle Ray wasn't too pleased at first—he'd thought that Bill would go to the new medical school in Jena once he got out of the army, since he'd already gone as far as EMT.

"But now they've settled it that Ron and Bill, along with Reichhard Hartmann from Oberweissbach, will be setting up a subsidiary of the pharmaceuticals side. Right now, until they draw up formal papers, they're calling it 'Whatever Works.' I'm not sure exactly why—it goes back to something Tom Stone said, I think. Not just to reconstitute up-time drugs, but to figure out what can be developed from what people use here, down-time. Maybe, using modern analytical methods, come up with things derived from herbals that we didn't have before the Ring of Fire. The point is that Ron and Bill are going to be business partners, which means that Ron is going to be a sort of, um, permanent fixture as far as the family is concerned. Your side, the Hudson side, at least, no matter what Nani thinks about it. You might as well get to know him."

Ron walked down the front steps of Missy's porch. He knew that he could wait until tomorrow. There wasn't any special reason that he needed to tell someone this today rather than tomorrow, he expected. Mr. Jenkins' office wouldn't be open. It was probably not the right place, anyway. He was in charge of Consular Affairs, after all—Grantvillers abroad, not foreigners in Grantville. Otherwise, though, he wasn't sure even who was in charge of that stuff since Mr. Bellamy took a job in Magdeburg. He couldn't quite take it directly to Mr. Piazza.

Cory Joe would tell Don Francisco, but he'd be looking at things from the Magdeburg perspective. Broad brush, so to speak. That wasn't quite the same thing as local developments.

And if Ron waited until tomorrow, he'd have to make a special trip back into town from Lothlorien. Or try to explain it on the phone, which never seemed to work for him quite as well as face to face. Or try to explain it on the phone to some functionary who was trying to prevent cracked nuts from using up an important person's time.

So. He walked up to Missy's uncle's house and knocked on the door.

Wes Jenkins opened it himself. He smiled in a friendly enough way. In fact, he looked like he was in a really good mood. That was always better than catching a man in a bad mood. Not to mention, he seemed awfully wide awake for this early in the morning on New Year's Day.

Mrs. Jenkins seemed like she was in a good mood, too. Also wide awake. And she worked at the same office, so it ought to be all right to say everything in front of her.

Ron started talking. It was amazing how much a man could say during a whole night of playing cards. Particularly a man who was not entirely and totally all there because of a head of blond hair. Particularly a man who was trying to impress that head of blond hair with his family's connections and influence.

A man who apparently didn't have the vaguest idea that the half-brother of the blond hair was in military intelligence. That was interesting in itself.

It was surprising how much Jean-Louis LaChapelle had let drop in passing while they were playing cards the night before. How much Ron, in thinking back to Venice, had started to get the sensation of "*deja vu* all over again." People representing themselves as out of town Committee of Correspondence sympathizers trying to make contacts in Grantville. And . . .

"I've heard some of this at work, too, out at the plant. I just hadn't put it all together. Everything in Grantville isn't perfect. There are places, not just the 250 Club but other places, where up-timers and down-timers seem to rub one another the wrong way, sometimes. LaChapelle seems to know they're doing this. More of the 'who, what, when, where, and how' than I felt comfortable about, even though he didn't say anything to indicate that he's involved in it himself. Especially considering who he is."

"Who?"

Wes obviously didn't know. Well, there wasn't any obvious connection between the two names.

"LaChapelle is the nephew of the man who married Pam's mother. Velma Hardesty. That guy was—well, is, he's alive and well somewhere in the Netherlands, Haarlem I think—thick as thieves with this Jacques-Pierre Dumais. They spent a lot of time together while he was in town. And Dumais . . . Mr. Jenkins, I really don't want to say something stupid."

"Say it." Wes smiled. "As I recall, I thought your view of my mother's gravy boat was a pretty fair assessment of the item."

"Dumais makes a big thing about being Huguenot. It's one of the cards he plays, locally. 'I'm your heroic Protestant type Frenchman, no lackey of that evil Cardinal Richelieu.' The other, for the 250 Club people, is, 'I'm no Kraut,' which isn't quite the same thing. But in Rome, Ducos and those people who tried to assassinate the pope—they *were* Huguenots. And they were manipulating other people to do their dirty work. That included the Committee of Correspondence people in Venice."

Wes looked a little blank. He had had other things on his mind during the period of the embassy to Venice.

"Uh. The Marcoli family. My brother Frank's in-laws." Ron frowned. He *knew* that he didn't have all the connections, so not all of this made sense. "Ducos got away. He has to have gone somewhere. He has to have connections, ways to get instructions to his people. I don't have a thing to tie LaChapelle and his uncle to Ducos. But they do tie to Dumais, at least Mauger does, and Dumais is manipulating other people to do his dirty work. I don't have anything to tie Dumais to Ducos, either. It's . . ."

"You don't have to have a full picture when you bring something in," Wes said. "Every piece of the puzzle helps. There's staff up in Magdeburg who spend all day, every day, trying to fit the pieces together."

"Nasi's people, I know. Thanks anyway," Ron said. "If it hadn't been for the gravy boat, I might have let the whole thing drop, or tried something really roundabout like writing to Father Gus, since he and Frank are pretty good friends, and hoping that he would show it to Father Mazzare—Cardinal Mazzare, I should say. But I thought, if you were interested, this might be faster."

"If a couple of other people are interested in this, is there anyplace in town I can catch you later today? I know it's a holiday . . ."

"I was going back home. I suppose I could always go over and annoy Missy's parents by existing."

"I wouldn't, if I were you." Clara said. "Debbie has already sent Missy to go to sleep and called me to complain."

"Go over to Ben Hardesty's," Wes suggested. "Cory Joe has already been in touch with Arnold Bellamy this morning, early. He's waiting at Ben's until we get a meeting set up. I'll swing by for the two of you when we've gotten in touch with everyone who should be sitting in on this. At least, everyone who doesn't have a hangover. The administration of the SoTF has at least a couple of officials who seem to have partied harder than the rest of them." He grinned. "Ed Piazza among them. We'll brief them tomorrow."

Ron blinked. The principal? Well, the president of the State of Thuringia-Franconia?

"He's Italian," Clara said gently. "There was red wine. Annabelle says that at least New Year's Eve is not a wedding or a wake."

By a week or so later, it became clear that Bill Hudson was wasting an awful lot of time getting back and forth from Willie Ray's place to Lothlorien. Ron suggested that he might as well move in, since it didn't seem likely that his brother Frank would ever need his room there again.

They packed up the personal stuff that Frank had left behind when they left for Italy a year before into barrels and put those in a storeroom. Then they moved Bill's stuff with his father's team and wagon.

This involved meeting Bill's grandmother. Who was also Missy's other grandmother, the Hudson one, the one she called "Nani."

It was a sort of interesting experience. The kind of thing that made Ron glad that Missy had introduced him to her Jenkins grandmother first. That had to be saying something.

They were standing next to the wagon, waiting for someone to bring out another load of stuff on the dolly. She appeared and demanded fiercely, "Are you the young man who kissed Missy while she was riding a motorcycle last fall?"

Perhaps he shouldn't have answered, "Like this?" and demonstrated the procedure.

It certainly hadn't helped that Missy responded to the old lady's glare by throwing her arms around his neck and kissing him again. With considerably more verve.

Chapter 35

Grantville

"Good morning, Lenore. It's nice to have you back." Faye Andersen jumped up and gave her a hug. "We have an in-box waiting for you and can you work with Donella an hour or so every day? She's learning, but she hasn't had a chance to work in one of the down-time chanceries yet."

"Oh, Faye, it's so good to be back." Lenore leaned across the desk and gave the older woman a hug. "Hi, Linda Beth. Donella, I love your engagement ring. Catrina, oh golly, you have the baby right here. Isn't he a doll? I wish Bryant had let me do that after Weshelle was born. Where's Andrea? She said she still had some more forms for me to fill out."

"Meeting with the judges. You'll have to wait till that's over. All okay at your end? No child care problems?"

"Great, Faye. Chandra is babysitting for Weshelle, so everything is smooth at home. Your problems must be nearly over by now."

"Sometimes I think they're worse when you have teenagers. Toddlers at least have the good grace to stay where you put them, so to speak, until you come back and pick them up again. Brandon and Hanna have so many activities now . . ."

"Are you on your own, again?" Linda Beth Rush asked Lenore.

"Bryant left for Magdeburg again the first thing this morning.

He's got to make some stops on the way, though." Lenore grinned. "Give me some records to transcribe and I'll transcribe them."

"Back in the swing of things?" Chandra asked when Lenore knocked on the door to drop off Weshelle.

"Three days at work and it's as if I had never been gone."

"Did you eat breakfast?"

Lenore laughed. "You know me too well, Sis."

"Well, I'm hungry, and we have time. But I'm out of eggs. I've got to drop Mikey off anyway, and then Tom, so let's both walk downtown and stop at Cora's."

"When is she due?" Cora asked as she deposited the plates of buckwheat pancakes in front of them.

"Who?" Chandra broke a piece of hard bread in three pieces and gave one each to Lena Sue, Sandra Lou, and Weshelle to teethe on. She had dropped Mikey off at school on the way, but Tom was running around the table at a rate which made her yearn for the moment when St. Veronica's Academy would open its doors and receive him for the morning.

"Stop pretending you don't know who, Chandra. Your step-mother, of course."

"Um."

"When?"

"Late May."

"Didn't waste any time, did they?"

"Shoo, Cora." Chandra watched the proprietress head for another table, taking their coffee pot, and turned to her sister. "Cora Ennis has no shame at all."

"I think everyone in Grantville is asking the same question," Lenore answered. "And some of them are making bets on how long it took between the time they married themselves to each other and start of the pregnancy. I understand that the heavy money at the Thuringen Gardens is on fifteen minutes. The 250 Club types aren't conceding that the vows came first, on the grounds that German women are all whores." She blushed.

"Cut it out, Lenore. Why should you be sitting here blushing for Dad? We didn't have a thing to do with it."

"Except for your manipulating to send her over there in the first place. Let's hope for a week's margin. Early June."

"Kortney Pence gives them nine months to the day, and the story I heard from Mary Kat, who got it straight from Derek Utt, is that it was already well after dark when the kidnappers locked them into Ritter von Schlitz's pantry, so the money on 'fifteen minutes' may not be too far off the mark."

"Chandra! Stop it!"

"Oh, well. I guess I'd better write Nathan before he hears it from someone else. And you're going to be late for work if we don't get a move on."

Sandra Prickett, Nathan's mother, was happily demonstrating the workings of the Bureau of Vital Statistics filing system to an interested and admiring Jacques-Pierre Dumais. There really weren't a lot of people around who were interested in the nuts and bolts of how she spent her days. Since he mentioned that he had attended the wedding of Velma Hardesty to Laurent Mauger, she pulled out the master file card.

Jacques-Pierre looked at it with some interest for the content. Particularly the age of the bride. "It's accurate," Sandra said. "She's lived in this town all her life, so there wasn't any point in trying to fudge off a few years. I wouldn't put it past her, though, if she moves away."

His attention fixed on the meaning of the punched holes around the edges of each card.

"It's because we don't have computer systems available," Sandra answered. "Grantville wasn't maintaining its own vital statistics before the Ring of Fire. They were kept at state level. So when we set the bureau up, it was from scratch, and we did a system that was really old-fashioned back home. But it's one that any down-time office, all through what was the NUS, through Thuringia-Franconia, can maintain. We get the blank forms printed and manually punch the holes that code the data that is on each license and certificate. Each of the squares around the edge represents a specific fact."

She explained the retrieval system, saying that, for example, for statistical purposes, they could easily use this to track all up-timer/down-timer marriages, such as that between Velma and her husband. Returning the Mauger/Hardesty card to its place, she stuck her little wire rod through the cards in the drawer and pulled out all of the up-timer/down-timer marriages for the last four months, spreading them out on the table.

As it happened, this included the ceremony performed for Wesley Williams Jenkins and Clara Bachmeierin at the Methodist parsonage. The one that Jenny Maddox had filed personally and had not included in the weekly list sent to the newspaper.

Sandra picked it up and showed it to her guest specifically, simply because the ceremony had been performed by her brother Simon, with her sister-in-law Mary Ellen as one of the witnesses. "I've always been so proud of David and Simon," she explained. "My brothers were the first members of our family who ever went to college. Now David is a school administrator and Simon is a preacher."

"I'm sure that you are," Jacques-Pierre said in his oddly formal English. "Indeed, one thing that I have observed, here in Thuringia, that is not so true in France, is that many of the teachers and government officials in these small German principalities, also, are the first person in a family with a university education. Do you think it is possible that this similarity makes the cooperation between the up-timers and down-timers easier?"

This question obviously interested him. Sandra had never really thought about it, but she did her best to help him understand.

She thought that his request for a copy of the certificate, so he could study the way the system of punched holes around the edges worked, was presented almost as an afterthought.

As it happened, he wanted to study that, too. It seemed like something that would be useful for the record keeping system at Garbage Guys. Much of Jacques-Pierre's success was based on the fact that he really was interested in at least ninety percent of the topics that came up in his conversations with the residents of Grantville.

His conversations with the former Velma Hardesty excepted, of course.

"It's perfectly true," Veda Mae Haggerty said. "And him heading up that fancy initiative to make sure that all the marriages between Americans and Krauts are legal, too!"

"I knew it to start with," Willard Carson said. "I mean, I sure thought there was something funny about it."

"I don't really believe it," Lois Carson answered. "Nobody could have managed something like that."

"It was a regular coverup. Wes Jenkins and that Clara he calls his wife weren't married until they came back here in October.

All hush-hush, because Wes is one of Mike Stearns' cronies, I suppose. Did anybody else count from Stearns' wedding to that Kraut Becky of his and when their first daughter was born? I sure did." Veda Mae shook her head with righteous indignation.

"Do you know anything else?" Lois asked hopefully.

"Simon Jones did the wedding. Too bad it wasn't Mary Ellen; maybe we could have used it to undermine this female minister business. It was one of the United Methodist Church's biggest mistakes when that came in. She was one of the witnesses, though. Mary Ellen, I mean. Someone—I won't say who—found the copy of the marriage license in the Bureau of Vital Statistics files. Jenny Maddox signed as the other witness. She must have deliberately not included it in every week's listing of the licenses issued that the bureau sends out for the newspapers to publish, to make Wes Jenkins' Kraut slut look like a respectable woman."

Willard Carson said, "It's a conspiracy." His nose was quivering with excitement. "A real conspiracy, I tell you. Commies."

Veda Mae looked at him. "Get hold of yourself, Willard," she said firmly. She had her opinions, but she hadn't lost all grip on reality. "If there's anything that Wes Jenkins isn't, it's a Commie."

"But," Lois sputtered, "aren't all conspirators Commies?"

Veda Mae went back to the original topic. "Remember that I told you first. We've given a copy of the certificate to Roger Rude at the *Grantville Times*. It should be in the next issue of the paper. With a little highlighting, using that new color press that they're trying out."

Mary Ellen answered the first phone call. Then the second and the third. After that, she took the phone at the parsonage off the hook. So much for discretion.

Unfortunately, she couldn't leave it off permanently. They got too many calls that were really important. So she had to live through all the others that came in over the next week or so, because Willard Carson's conspiracy theory was generally taken up by the 250 Club types and then ricocheted all over town, which meant that nicer people kept calling up and asking her to say that it wasn't so.

She tried to explain, but the whole thing was complicated. Most Grantvillers didn't entertain themselves by reading comparative law. She reflected on everything that had been going on.

Wes went ballistic after he heard some of the insults to Clara's virtue that were being tossed around in the 250 Club. He insisted on publication of all the paperwork that followed the original marriage. Considering that the lawyer who was working for Andrea Hill over in Fulda, who had taken their affidavits after the event, didn't have any more interest in polite euphemisms than any other down-timer, the statements made generally interesting reading. Some women said that the English translation was almost as good as having *People* magazine back.

Victor Saluzzo sternly reprimanded the health teacher at the high school who assigned his students to take the affidavits and work through such events as timing of intercourse, progress of the sperm, fertilization, and implantation to obtain a more realistic estimate of the time of the start of Mrs. Jenkins' pregnancy than the "fifteen minutes" being bandied about at the betting sites. The reprimand went into the teacher's permanent record in spite of his protest that the project had done more to get the boys' minds focused on how all this really worked than anything else he had ever tried.

There were times she thought that if anybody opened one more phone conversation with, "My goodness, Mary Ellen!" she would stand there and scream.

Although Clara had been coming to church with Wes since they got back, she was still officially Lutheran, so Pastor Kastenmayer at St. Martin's wrote and issued a theological treatise on the Lutheran view of the matter, which came out from a press in Jena and was widely admired in scholarly circles. The pastor had served in parishes all his life, but now it seemed that he was starting to be seen as something of an expert on comparative up-time and down-time marriage law. The university invited him to give a guest lecture, which he had certainly never expected in his wildest dreams. Much less that Count Ludwig Guenther would appoint him to the *Ehegericht* for Schwarzburg-Rudolstadt. As Kastenmayer's wife Salome was telling everyone proudly, it was a real honor for a pastor to serve on the marriage court. Kastenmayer himself said to Gary Lambert, the business manager of Grantville's hospital, that he was not quite so thrilled about the prospect of spending a lot of his time for the next several years sorting through the debris of failed betrothals and marriages.

Given that West Virginia had not recognized common law

marriage, there was fairly widespread doubt among even the nicest of Grantvillers that the do-it-yourself ceremony was for real, no matter what the affidavits said. Over in Jena, Chip Jenkins, who was going to law school, wrote a treatise in English on the down-time legal view of the matter. That got published too. Down-timers admired it, but almost every born Grantviller who phoned Mary Ellen at the parsonage "figured that he owed it to his uncle, after all," so none of them were taking it very seriously.

Somewhere in the course of these developments, Veda Mae Haggerty said something about the various marriages of Willard and Lois Carsons' much idolized son Matt that caused them to declare her *persona non grata* in the dining room of the Willard Hotel. Common political prejudices will only take people so far and no farther. The Carsons considered Matt to be off limits.

Mary Ellen found that out the day she walked into Cora's and heard Veda Mae proclaiming that she guessed she was stuck with having to eat here again if she didn't want to pay the higher price at Tyler's, die of ptomaine at the greasy spoon, or make do with pizza, because she wasn't about to go to the Thuringen Gardens with all its racket and she'd always hated packing a lunch.

Cora didn't usually make the City Hall Café off limits to anyone, but she finally made an exception for Veda Mae Haggerty. Again. Much to the old hag's indignation, of course.

Veda Mae was extremely indignant. She was forced to go grovel to Lois Carson and apologize for what she said about that over-aged spoiled baby who was Lois' son Matt.

At least she still had a place to eat lunch.

Pastor Ludwig Kastenmayer looked at the up-timer standing in his study.

"It said so on the radio," Jarvis Beasley said. "In one of the stories about Wes Jenkins and that woman he married over in Fulda. Or, maybe, didn't marry over in Fulda. That you're in charge of fixing this sort of problem now."

That wasn't quite the way that Pastor Kastenmayer would have described service on a marriage court.

"The story said you wrote a book about it. It's no skin off my nose, you know. I'm free to come and go. But Judge Tito told Hedy to stay inside the Ring of Fire, so she can't go to church any more. She's likely to have the baby any day now. If she can't bring it to church, she can't get it baptized. She's afraid that if it isn't baptized and then it dies, it will go to hell. Can you do something? She thinks that she's being more trouble to me than she's worth."

Jarvis frowned, a vaguely disturbed look on his face. "She's not, really. Too much trouble, I mean. Hedy's good. Works hard. Doesn't talk all the time. Doesn't drink much. Doesn't flirt with other guys. Makes good stew, even if she does use a lot more mutton than I'm used to eating. Doesn't waste money. That's why we eat so much mutton."

Pastor Kastenmayer stroked his goatee, thinking. The man's effort to catalog the merits of his concubine—she was clearly a wife under Grantville's civil law, so perhaps it would be more prudent to refer to her as his wife in this conversation—had clearly strained his analytical ability.

Jarvis went on. "Vesta, that's my boss."

"Yes?"

"She says that if you came over into town, we could have the kid baptized the way Hedy wants it at the laundry. There's always plenty of water in a laundry. Walpurga, the girl who's got her eye on Mitch Hobbs who's the manager now, says she would be a godmother. Hedy thinks the baby will need one."

"And what tasks do you perform at this laundry? For your boss, this Vesta. Her name is?"

"Vesta Rawls. She was Vesta Eberly before she married Chuck Rawls. Well, I'm the maintenance man. Not for the machines. I sweep up. If someone breaks out a pane of glass, I put in a new one. I carry things around, or if they're too heavy for that, I push them on the dolly. Stuff. It's a good job. Regular. Not like picking up odd jobs."

Not an uncommon type, Kastenmayer thought. Designed by God, in the hierarchy of being, to live and die as a day laborer. In a way, it was comforting to know that the up-timers had those also. That not everyone among them was brilliant and understood the miracles of "technology."

The man's job was regular. His employer's suggestion was irregular. Highly irregular. However, no baby should remain unbaptized longer than necessary.

"Let me know," Pastor Kastenmayer said, "as soon as the baby is born. As for the other . . ." He sighed. "Sorting out matrimonial problems always takes time. Usually a lot of time. Judge Tito was probably right. Tell your, uh, wife, to stay right in Grantville. I'll start arranging for collection of the affidavits and depositions. I served parishes in Saxony until I received my first appointment in Gleichen about twenty years ago. I know something of the ecclesiastical ordinances in force there, but I'll have to review them."

Jarvis nodded. He had no idea what affidavits and depositions might be, much less an ecclesiastical ordinance, but it did seem like this guy was willing to try to help Hedy. Which meant that he was probably okay. Which meant that Buster might have the right of it about some of the things he'd been trying to tell him lately.

"I'll tell Hedy to stay in Grantville." Then he said. "Um. If you come downtown and baptize the baby, could I invite a couple of people? My grandma died last fall and Gramps is taking it kind of hard. It might cheer him up a little."

Pastor Kastenmayer thought that caution was in order. "Which of the Grantville churches does your grandfather attend?"

"He ain't a church member. Never has been. None of us are."

"Very well." *A third of them are heathen.* "Let me get all the information I need to start. Could you spell your name, please?"

Jarvis spelled his name. He spelled Hedy's name. The recollection of a newspaper article about a brawl and an attempted beating rose vaguely to the top of Pastor Kastenmayer's mind.

"Ah. Beasley. Are you any, um, connection of Denise? Denise Beasley." He remembered Denise well. She had been to church at Christmas with Gerry Stone and Minnie Hugelmair. The girl was unusual, but not hostile. "Or of Kenneth Beasley? Of the 250 Club?"

"Denise's dad is my cousin."

That was all right.

"Ken's my dad."

Pastor Kastenmayer sighed deeply. What was the phrase that Jonas had picked up from that extraordinary woman who worked for Herr Piazza? Liz, her name was. Liz Carstairs. "We do not have problems. We have challenges and opportunities."

He would have to include thankfulness to God for so many challenges and opportunities in his morning prayers. In his evening prayers. If he repeated often enough that he was sincerely grateful, he might come to feel gratitude more sincerely, as a habitude. The catechism was correct, of course. "We should fear and love God, that . . ." Sometimes the tasks to which God set his servants could be truly fearsome. While baptizing a grandchild of the owner of the 250 Club might not be equivalent to standing in defiance before the Holy Roman Emperor at the Diet of Worms, as Martin Luther had done, still . . . it might be an interesting event.

There was another of the up-time proverbs that Jonas had collected. "'May you live in interesting times.' They considered it to be a curse, Jonas said. They might have a point.

Chapter 36

Grantville

"What you are," Denise said, "is a dumb, filthy-minded old bitch, to say any such thing."

"And you are Buster Beasley's little bastard."

Cora Ennis was not happy. Gossip was one thing. A direct physical confrontation in her café was something else. Right now, it looked like Denise Beasley and Benny Pierce's Minnie were about to attack Veda Mae Haggerty with their fists and fingernails. Which, if it happened, would be about as one-sided a contest as she could imagine. Veda Mae's viciousness did not extend to fisticuffs—and both Denise and Minnie could physically handle most boys their own age.

"They have published the papers about their marriage, Frau Haggerty," Minnie Hugelmair said. "The affidavits. The expert opinions. It was legal."

"Forged documents!" Veda Mae sputtered. "Poppycock."

"Pastor Kastenmayer at St. Martin's has published a pamphlet explaining that even when the marriage and the church blessing happen at the same service, it is the couple themselves who exchange vows. It is consent that causes a marriage to take place, not something that someone else does. The part that goes, 'I, Somebody, take you, Somebody Else.' If they don't do that, having somebody official pronounce them man and wife has no effect at all. Mayor Dreeson can't walk up to any two unmarried people walking down the street together and pronounce them man and wife. Or, I suppose, he could, but it wouldn't mean anything. Gerry Stone sent Denise a copy that he bought at the bookstore in Rudolstadt. If you have not learned German, I will be happy to stand here and read it to you in English. Every word."

Minnie's voice was very calm, and her tone of voice remained even. "Then you will apologize to the Reverends Jones for what you said."

Joe Pallavicino had heard that tone in Minnie's voice many times in the past couple of years and recognized it as the start of trouble. He started to slide out of the booth where he was sitting.

"What is it to you, anyway?" Veda Mae went on the offensive.

"Benny Pierce goes to your church. He loves the Reverends Jones. And nobody is going to insult anybody that Benny cares about to my face. Not without having to deal with me. Not behind my back either, if I ever get to hear about it. And you are not supposed to be a nasty gossip. Your church says that is wrong. I've had to sit there with Benny enough Sundays in the winters, when I didn't want to walk all the way out to St. Martin's in the snow, that I've learned that much."

"Little Kraut vagabond."

"Listen to me, Mrs. Haggerty," Denise said, leaning forward. "You were thick as thieves with Velma Hardesty all last summer yourself. She married a down-timer too, so where do you come off being so picky nice-nice about Mrs. Jenkins?"

"Laurent Mauger isn't a Kraut. He's a Frenchman, from the Netherlands. The French and the Dutch were our allies in the war," Veda Mae proclaimed.

"The French aren't our allies," Denise retorted. "King Gustavus Adolphus is fighting Richelieu. That's France. They were part of the League of Ostend that killed Hans Richter."

"Not *this* war, you stupid little idiot. The *real* war. World War II."

"What was that?" Minnie asked.

"The war my daddy fought in. The war against the Nazis. The war against the Germans. The war against you Krauts. And we were allied with the French. So people like Velma's husband, or Jacques-Pierre Dumais, are ancestors of those heroes of the resistance. The Free French. Just like the Huguenots, here and now, like Laurent Mauger and Jacques-Pierre are resisting that Cardinal Richelieu. Huguenots are Protestant."

"Mr. Jenkins is a Protestant too," Minnie said. "At least, I think that Methodists are Protestant. Anyway, he goes to the same church that you and Benny do, you old witch, so if he isn't Protestant, neither are you. And you *are* going to apologize to the Reverends Jones. Whatever you may say about me, Mr. Jenkins is not a German and neither are they."

"No way is that Dumais guy some kind of James Bond hero. He's a garbage collector!" Denise yelled. "And he hangs out at Uncle Ken's 250 Club. I tell you what I'm going to do. I'm going to write to Don Francisco Nasi and ask *him* if that guy is some kind of resistance hero. And I'll publish his answer in the paper. If Roger Rude won't take it, I'll buy an ad. So there."

Behind the counter, Joe Pallavicino was poking phone numbers as fast as he could. Benny. Buster. The police. Henry Dreeson. Anybody. Cora was holding the phone book open in front of him. Then he slipped out into the aisle between the tables and the booths, hoping that he could defuse the situation before the girls got themselves into more trouble than they could get out of. Girl fights were one thing, but . . . Veda Mae wasn't well liked, but people wouldn't react well to having them go after an old woman.

Damned if I'll call her an old lady, even to myself, he thought. *Veda Mae Haggerty is no lady of any kind.*

Those two girls would beat the crap out of her, too. A raw and primitive side of Joe was urging him to let them do it. It'd sure be fun to watch.

"I told her I was going to," Denise said at breakfast the next morning. "And I did. Even though Benny showed up and coaxed Minnie into backing off."

"Did what, Princess Baby?" Buster asked.

"I wrote a letter to Don Francisco Nasi in Magdeburg. The Spook of Spooks for Mike Stearns. And I told him every single word that Horrid Hag Haggerty said about those two guys, Mauger and Dumais. And every other little scrap of information I could find about the people they've been hanging out with, asking around a bit yesterday."

"You think he's going to read a letter from a kid?" Christin asked.

"He'd better," Denise muttered. "If he knows what's good for him."

Saturday was almost always the busiest morning. It started a little later than most days, but then it never let up until after lunch. Cora looked out over the room. *Kaffeeklatsch* time. Every booth was full. So were most of the tables. And, just what she didn't need, Veda Mae Haggerty coming in the door. Coming back again. Life at the City Hall Café had been more tranquil while Veda Mae was patronizing the Willard.

A half hour later, all she could think was that Veda Mae sure was in rare form. She had started with comments on Wes Jenkins' marriage to Clara again, repeating her insults in regard to the roles played by the Reverends Jones and Jenny Maddox.

Cora glanced at the back booth. Jenny was in there. She'd been there before Veda Mae arrived, tucked in the far corner, having coffee with Marietta Fielder. Also with her sister, Maxine Pilcher. And Anita Barnes. Of the four, even if she looked that way, the only one Veda Mae would be able to see was Anita.

Veda Mae declaimed on. A follow-up about Tom Stone and Magda and something rude about the Stones in general. Then down to specifics: Frank getting married to an Eye-talian and everyone knew they had been allies of the Krauts; Gerry being in a down-time school over at Rudolstadt and planning to become a Lutheran Kraut minister; Ron dating Missy Jenkins. That brought her back to the Jenkins family again—something about Chip Jenkins going to the Kraut university in Jena and being for all practical purposes engaged to Katerina von Ruppersdorf who was one of those awful Kraut nobles which was undoubtedly why he had written that trashy pamphlet. His half-sister Anne Jefferson being married to some Kraut guy who had gone off to Russia and everyone knew that the Russians were Commies, a passing comment on the "little Kraut slut" who had been living with Chad and Debbie while she went to school, and ending up with a concluding proclamation that the Jenkins family in general, for all its money and prestige in Grantville, was "going native."

Someone stood up. *Oh, lordy!* Cora thought. Vera Hudson. Willie Ray's wife. Debbie's mother. Vera wouldn't give Chad the time of day, but she would never let anyone get by with put-downs on her grandchildren. Not that Vera was likely to say anything in defense of one of the Stones, since Missy and Ron weren't official yet, exactly, not but what it appeared to be high time that they should be, but she was bound to attack full steam in defense of Chip's young lady and Anne's husband.

Anne's husband, in particular.

Vera had kept Anne for a long time after Don Jefferson's death. First while Debbie finished high school, then during the four years Debbie was getting her degree at WVU, and when Debbie came back to Grantville to teach in 1978 on the grounds that the first couple of years were always so time-consuming for a beginning teacher and what they were paying Debbie really wouldn't cover decent day care. Back when Chad and Debbie married during Christmas vacation in 1980, Vera insisted on keeping Anne. At the time, Cora had thought it was a little odd. But Vera claimed that it would upset Anne to move in with them in the middle of the school year and the newlyweds needed some time to adjust to one another. At least, that was the story she told everyone. Debbie finally put her foot down that summer and insisted Anne live with her and Chad. Vera had not been a bit happy and the ten-year-old Anne even less. Afterwards Anne spent as much of her weekends, school breaks and summers with Vera and Willie Ray as her mom would allow.

As far as Vera was concerned, Anne could do no wrong.

Cora had a feeling that this was going to be one of those days that caused her to start her evening diary entry with, "A lively time was had by all." That was before the door opened again, admitting Inez Wiley and Veronica Dreeson, who—*oh, no, no*—had Denise and Minnie in tow. And Idelette, the Genevan girl, of course, but she was very well behaved.

After the last confrontation, Joe Pallavicino had talked to the two old biddies. Since then, they had been, as Joe put it, mentoring Denise and Minnie more intensively.

They came in just as Maxine scooted over and let Jenny out of the back booth.

"*So sehr wie eine Walküre*," an appreciative male voice murmured as Jenny stalked down the aisle toward the front of the café, lining herself up next to Vera.

Couldn't Inez and Ronnie have decided to mentor somewhere else?

Who needed an irritated Valkyrie in the City Hall Café?

Why was Veda Mae here instead of over at the Willard, anyway? Why had she been here the other day, for that matter? Was she on the outs with Lois again? About what, this time? Cora's natural curiosity perked up a bit.

The wad of little bells fastened to the front door jingled again.

The first person Clara saw when she came through the door was Jenny Maddox, whom she liked and admired. "Good morning, Chenny," she said. Then she saw Vera Hudson, to whom, as a connection of her husband's family, she should be courteous. She gave a little wave. "Isn't it gorgeous out, Mrs. Hudson? I have been walking around, up and down the hills, admiring the sun on the icicles. Up on the greenhouse, where the roof is warm and the snow water trickles down, they reach all the way from the eaves to the ground, like the stone formations in the *Feengrotten*. There are many snow men, Mikey Tyler has made a snow sphinx in his front yard. Isn't that interesting?"

Jenny stared at her. Then said, "Good morning."

No one else in the room was saying anything at all.

Clara had never heard such quiet in Cora's. She looked around for the cause just as Denise and Minnie tore themselves loose from their mentors and dashed to stand one on each side of her.

"May I have tea, please, Cora? The sassafras kind."

She reached out, putting one hand on the nearest shoulder of each of the girls. "Has she been making a fool of herself again, this malignant . . . pain in the donkey?"

Denise broke into giggles. "It's 'ass,' Clara, not 'donkey.'"

"Wesley told me that 'ass' is not a nice word."

"It's not, but 'donkey' sort of loses the meaning of the insult. Because one kind of an ass is a donkey but the other kind of ass is the one that has a pain in it."

"I don't know if she has been making a fool of herself right now, exactly," Minnie said quietly. "We just got here. But she has said such awful things, over and over again, about so many good people, that she should be ashamed of herself. Not just about you and Mr. Jenkins. About Chip, Gerry, Gerry's dad. Everyone."

"Why would it matter to Chip or Cherry what she says? Neither one of them cares what Grantville thinks, any more."

"Clara!" Jenny Maddox said.

"Well, it's true. Neither of them lives here; both have left this town behind. They are not likely to come back. They are both being educated, being qualificated—qualified—for responsible professional careers that will take them to far more important places than this. For them, now, this is only a small city in which they were born, far off the main trade routes. They have relatives here, but it will not be their home. Why should they care what a bitter woman says about them?"

"*Klug, diejenige*," the voice that had admired Jenny said into the silence.

"As for her . . ." Clara gestured at Veda Mae. "Do what the Mennonites do. Shun her. Do not acknowledge that she is present. Soon enough, if you do that, she will go away."

"Clara," Vera Hudson asked. "Clara, don't you *mind*?"

"Thirteen years," Clara said, looking around the cafe. "Thirteen *years* in my first marriage I was barren. I stormed heaven, I beat upon its gates with my fists. I prayed for a child as hard as Hannah prayed for Samuel. We consulted physicians, but still my husband died leaving no son to follow him. How can this old fool make me *mind* that in my marriage to Wesley I am blessed to be fertile right away? She cannot make me other than the luckiest and happiest woman in this town. She cannot make me other than the luckiest and happiest woman in the whole, entire, world. I will not let her make me other than that. I say only that she is being—has been—very, very, rude, from start to finish."

"That's one way to put it, I guess," Maxine Pilcher, who was still standing by the back booth waiting for Jenny to slide back in, said to Anita.

Clara grinned at her. "Don't you think that I do not know that your husband Keith has been betting when I have this baby? Like a lot of other husbands of you women here. It would be easier to make a list of who of them have *not* been betting when I have this baby. I will have it when God wills, like every baby is born. I am bound to have it some time, so I wish every bettor at the Thuringen Gardens a winning wager, but I dare you all. Make your husbands, whoever gets the winnings, donate them to the Red Cross once I have delivered and they know the date. That is only fair. The men have given Wesley much 'razzing' because he made me pregnant so fast and since his mother is the president of the Red Cross now, it is right that it should benefit from his suffering. So. And now I want my sassafras tea, please, Cora."

She plopped herself down into a chair between Inez and Ronnie, telling Denise and Minnie that they were both so skinny that they could share the fourth one.

"Well," Marietta Fielder said, raising an eyebrow. "What do you make of that?"

Jenny Maddox grinned at her best friend. "Clara thinks she is the direct beneficiary of a divine miracle and Wes Jenkins is God?"

Marietta managed to catch her cup before it broke, but not before she had splashed a considerable portion of the coffee onto the front of her sensible gray jacket. She was, after all, Wes' first cousin on the Newton side of the family. Before the Ring of Fire, Grantville had been a rather small town.

"What's interesting," Anita Barnes said, "is what she didn't say."

"Didn't?" Jenny asked.

"She didn't even pay any attention to the controversy over the—is 'legality' what they call it?—of whatever they did in Fulda. She blew it off. A marriage; then a baby right away. Whee."

" 'Validity,' " Marietta said. "That's the word they're using. 'Validity.' "

"Clara obviously doesn't have any questions," Anita said. "As far as she's concerned, it was legal. Valid. Whatever. At most, she's annoyed because Her Nastiness Veda Mae has been harassing Wes."

"Well, about the marriage," Jenny said, "keeping the wedding here secret was really Mary Ellen's idea. She persuaded Simon and Wes. Clara was standing there in the parsonage parlor that afternoon saying, 'I still think we should have had a party.' Looking back, maybe they should have. It would have cut the gossip off right then. And she absolutely did insist on inviting Wes' mother and Chad and Debbie. Put her foot down. Sort of hard. Practically a stomp."

"Wes sure hasn't reacted so calmly," Maxine said.

Marietta shook her head. "Wes has a temper—always has had, as long as I can remember. According to Debbie, he got mad because he thought the 250 Club types were trying to insult Clara's virtue. Which they were, of course. Debbie says that he's awfully protective about Clara."

"Personally," Anita said, "I think she can take care of herself."

"Agreed," Maxine interrupted, "I hope that Wes and Clara don't ever both get mad at the same time. Whether at each other or at somebody else."

Jenny giggled. "As for the 'razzing,' though, I sort of doubt that even Wes really minds. Do you all know any man who would really get upset about being teased about being so virile that he got his wife pregnant the first time he gave her a poke? If he's going to get razzed at all, that has to be a pretty tolerable reason, the way guys think."

Anita frowned. "Arnold Bellamy would get upset."

"Arnold," Maxine said, "is an exceptional case. A person has to wonder how he and Natalie ever produced three kids."

"But if Clara thinks the thing they did in Fulda was enough, however they did it, I wonder what she thinks the marriage license and the ceremony that Simon did were all about?" Anita picked up her purse and started to dig through it for change for a tip.

"What I wonder is who managed to get into my files and dig out that license. One of these days, I'll find out and then . . ." Jenny's tone was threatening.

Maxine lined up her knife and fork on her plate. When Keith got back from that trip to the Upper Palatinate, he had called Doc Adams, who ordered her to come in, gave her a checkup, and told her that she had to eat more. Then Keith told Cora, who wouldn't let her get away with ordering "just coffee" any more. "Decorations on the Christmas tree? Icing on the cake?"

"Huh?" Anita blinked.

"That's what she probably thinks that the wedding Simon did for them was. That would go with wanting to have a party."

"Let's ask Ronnie. She's more likely than anyone here to know how the down-timers look at these things." Anita didn't seem inclined to give up.

"No," Maxine said. "I will *not* ask Veronica Dreeson. No matter how curious I am."

"Bite off your nose, will you?" Marietta finished her coffee. "I've got to get back to work."

Chapter 37

Frankfurt am Main

"I really think he means it," Ouvrard said.

Locquifier had just read Ducos' repeated order to assassinate Gustavus Adolphus, Princess Kristina, Michael Stearns, Rebecca, and Wilhelm Wettin—all on the same day, in the same place, and as soon as possible after the election.

Ducos' orders were accompanied by a long disquisition from Delerue explaining precisely how they were to do this in such a way that the *derailment* of the smooth transition of political power after the election would, without question, be blamed on Richelieu. And an explanation of why the word *derailment* was now acceptable French.

"What does he intend to do?" Brillard asked. "Submit it to the *Académie française* once it is founded next month? If indeed, it is founded on schedule, so to speak, on the twenty-second day of February in the year of our Lord one thousand sixteen hundred thirty-five?"

Delerue had bored the remainder greatly with his enthusiasm about this epochal cultural development.

"To get their approval to place it in a dictionary?" Ouvrard grimaced. "One would hope he has the prudence to maintain silence in Michel's presence—keeping in mind that Richelieu founded it."

"Let me think about this," Locquifier said.

✧ ✧ ✧

Locquifier sat there for a long time, his forehead resting on his hands.

Michel must be mad. At the very least, isolated in Scotland, he must have no idea exactly what challenges the men in Frankfurt were facing. It would be hopeless, utterly hopeless, to try to organize those five assassinations.

For one thing, he had developed his own plan. One that was in his grasp. One that did not overreach. In his own mind, he had already allotted Mathurin Brillard to a specific project.

Brillard was the only really good marksman in the group. Something that Michel tended to forget. Something that Antoine Delerue frequently forgot. Or, at least, frequently ignored when the realities of life started to impinge upon his abstract and theoretical convictions.

"Budget," Ancelin suggested.

"Unfortunately, budget is not really a problem. Sandrart may have removed Milkau from our clutches, but we are squeezing enough other members of the Calvinist diaspora hard enough that we can't lament that we are poorly funded. Not, at least, with any pretense of plausibility."

"Personnel, then?"

"Better." Locquifier scratched his head. "We must reiterate, I think. Since Michel has reiterated his orders, we must repeat our reply. With just enough variance from the last time that he knows we did in fact read his letter. So, we tell him what? That we will stick with what we have already decided—namely to act against the Grantville synagogue, with the hospital as a cover for this."

"Ah. Publicity. Explain how useful the dual approach will be. If rumors surface, if Nasi gets wind of the project, etc., the focus of the opposition's attention can be 'blipped' either way as they say on the radio. Just a few well-chosen pamphlets, rapidly produced on our faithful duplicating machine."

"It is rarely a life-enhancing experience to tell Michel that a person cannot do what he wants. He won't be happy with demonstrations only, I suspect." Deneau crossed his arms over his chest.

"Pamphlets," Locquifier said with sudden inspiration. "More pamphlets, apparently from many different sources, repeating a variety of rumors that Richelieu is planning to have those five persons assassinated. Just *rumors* will have a greatly unsettling impact. Anger the Swede. Occupy the time and attention of the spymaster Nasi. Why, rumors will do almost as much good as actually trying to do it."

"Are you certain that Michel will see things that way?"

"Not certain, no. But it's better than nothing. Ah, actually . . ." He hesitated. Should he explain this? Or not? Probably better to explain it.

"I was rather intending not to inform Michel that we are producing the pamphlets about the rumors ourselves. Rather hoping that we could just send selected pamphlets to him, as they appear. We can put on false places of publication, of course—everyone does. Distribute them through the same network that Weitz's contacts use. I was . . . rather hoping that Michel and Antoine are so far away that they will never find out that we aren't actually working very hard to carry out his instructions."

"*Merde!*" Ancelin exclaimed. "Guillaume, that's . . . damned brilliant."

The others agreed.

"So," Ancelin said. "Is there anything else we can do to give Michel the right impression?"

"Analysis of alternate possibilities," Ouvrard suggested. "That usually works well in causing a discussion to veer off course. Send Michel a listing of every 'soft underbelly' in the USE that we can think of."

"Why limit it to the USE?" Deneau asked.

"Because that's where we are?" was Ancelin's practical answer.

"We're creating smoke and mirrors anyway," Ouvrard pointed out. "So, we say: The USE is worried, so security is tight and the targets are hard. But—let's think. Princess Kristina is unreachable, but what about the Danish prince to whom she is now betrothed? Or the up-time lady-in-waiting to whom she is said to be so attached? That one's betrothed, the ridiculous Imperial Count of Narnia? If we can't reach Gustavus, then what about his queen in Stockholm? If not Stearns, then his ally Piazza? Ableidinger? If not the Abrabanel woman, then her father? If not Wettin, then one of his brothers? The possibilities are endless."

"Don't become too fond of your brainstorming, Robert. If we list too many options, he will realize that we are just creating excuses." Locquifier paused. "Choose three of these possibilities you have suggested and write up an analysis of each. As if we were seriously offering them for his consideration."

"It's a pity to abandon the rest."

"Then just give them a passing mention at the end, as if you were blowing them off as unrealistic and unlikely."

"In fact, Mathurin, nothing will placate Michel and Antoine but an assassination. Not in the long run, though this ploy will probably work for the time being." Locquifier looked up. "Hold yourself ready. As the time draws nearer, I will provide you with a target. Only one, since I am a reasonable man. Under cover of the demonstrations."

Brillard nodded.

Soubise picked up his wine and looked at the latest letter from his brother Henri again. Meditatively. Besançon. An interesting choice. He had rather anticipated that he would be off to Geneva for negotiations with the good Calvinist city fathers. But . . . Henri de Rohan and Bernhard of Saxe-Weimar were old friends, of course.

Richelieu would not be pleased at all. This move would also make it somewhat more difficult for Henri to present his continuing protestations that he was unquestionably a loyal subject of Louis XIII in a plausible manner. A lot more difficult, even, considering that the cardinal had not approved a change of venue. Important men could not just wander around the map of Europe without the permission of their monarchs. Not even if the council of the Most Serene Republic of Venice had finally decided not to renew a particular man's contract with its army, which meant that, as an exile, most of his estates confiscated by the French monarchy, Henri was once more looking for a job.

And would love to get back into the field. A general could only write so many books before the activity palled.

Not that Soubise wouldn't like to be commanding a few ships again, himself. Or many ships.

Garrison commander in Geneva would have been good, Soubise thought. Not that Henri had asked him. His older brother was well into his fifties, not as young as he used to be. A comfortable municipal post from which he could face down the dukes of Savoy would have been—not bad, in Soubise's humble opinion. Which it was now too late to express.

He opened the second letter in the stack.

Cavriani's son was off to Naples. Leopold himself had discovered that he had urgent business matters in Strassburg.

Very few really urgent business matters, Soubise thought, involved conferring with history professors. Not that Matthias Bernegger at the University of Strassburg didn't have an interesting network of his own, but it rarely involved exalted financial transactions.

After Strassburg, Leopold anticipated that he would be passing through Freiburg im Breisgau. Then Basel. One might almost think that he had seen enough of Basel when he was there with the Austrian archduchess, but perhaps not. Basel, Buxtorf, and Wettstein. Then back to Strassburg. Then . . . Besançon.

Oh.

No particular reason for Henri to go to Geneva right now, if Cavriani wasn't there.

But. As a response to Henri's ploy, Richelieu would certainly start making life more difficult for the duchess and for Anne. For the girl—his niece Marguerite.

If Rohan was to continue as Rohan, they could not let Henri's daughter be forced into marriage with any Catholic peer.

Roi, je ne puis,
Duc, je ne daigne,
Rohan je suis.

No, they lacked the lineage to be kings. But they must remain themselves. "I am Rohan."

What they needed for Marguerite, as a husband for the Rohan family's only heiress, was, obviously, a Protestant.

Soubise frowned. He was not sure that Henri was wise to be considering a match with Bernhard of Saxe-Weimar so seriously. If the lineage was to continue, they shouldn't choose a man who would absorb Rohan into his own career and use its assets to further his own ambitions. They needed a man who would become Rohan for her. With her.

Soubise prayed that Marguerite would mature to have the same spirit as her grandmother, Catherine de Parthenay-Larchevêque, who had written to Henri from La Rochelle during the great siege, insisting that they must achieve "secure peace, complete victory, or honorable death." The old motto of Jeanne d'Albret, Henri IV's mother—never to be forgotten by the Huguenots.

Not if they hoped to survive in this world, at least.

Not for nothing did the Rohan descend from Isabelle d'Albret, aunt of that very queen of Navarre.

Grantville

Noelle threw the newspaper on the table.

"Would you like me to say 'damn' for you?" Eddie Junker inquired politely.

"I am so sick of how the Crown Loyalists are insulting Ed Piazza because of Barclay and that bunch." She looked across the table. "And you, too, Mr. Jenkins. I'm sorry about the whole thing. If we only could have stopped them."

Chad Jenkins put his toast down. "At least they aren't using it much in the campaign on the national level."

"I suppose that's better than nothing. But it still isn't what anyone could call good." She looked at her uncle. Who was married to the sister of Chad Jenkins' wife. She was still sorting out all the dozens of new relatives and relatives-by-marriage she had acquired when she officially became a Stull instead of a Murphy. Consanguinity and affinity, the church called it. "What do you think, Joe?"

She still hadn't managed to talk herself into calling any of them "aunt" or "uncle." Not when she called her father by his first name.

"You should have shot the Hungarian when you had the chance. Or at least shot into the barge instead of into the river. With any luck, it would have sunk in the Danube, right there at Regensburg. The garrison could have fished them out and sent them home, we could have tried them the same way we did Bolender's bunch, and we'd be done with it by now."

His wife Aura Lee looked at him, reproachfully. "Don't be mean to Noelle."

"It would have taken really a lot of luck," Eddie pointed out. "Considering Noelle's marksmanship. She was lucky to hit the river."

Chad Jenkins laughed. "No point in crying about spilled milk. Duke Albrecht and Kay Kelly are going to make the most of it in the campaign, and that's all there is to it." He leaned back. "I hear she's actually gotten Gustavus to order delivery of ten of those 'Dauntless' planes, just as fast as Bob can build them."

Joe, who was also the SoTF Secretary of Transportation, was on solid ground, now. He leaned back and began to summarize resources, warehouse space, how far the various companies that were starting to manufacture aviation engines had gotten, delivery schedules for parts and components, availability of skilled personnel, and testing procedures.

It didn't seem like Gustavus was likely to get those planes any time soon. He should thank his lucky stars if he got a couple of them in time for next spring's campaign.

"I don't think that Mom's really designed to hit the campaign trail," Missy told Ron. "Honestly, she hates it. She tries to hide it, but she just hates it."

"Well, your dad keeps her out of it, as much as he can," Ron said. "And you've got to admit that Willie Ray is in his glory. Your grandfather's having a wonderful time."

"Oh, yeah." Missy giggled. "Just like the old days, back when he was in the state legislature. He's having a ball."

"He and Dreeson make quite a pair."

Chapter 38

Frankfurt am Main

"The Vignelli machine is broken." Deneau looked up in annoyance.

"What did you expect?" Brillard put down the stylus with which he was making a stencil. Another stencil. One of the many deliberately amateurish stencils that Locqufier's group had spent their time making this winter. They offended Brillard's pride. He had been a properly apprenticed type maker, once upon a time. Before the lead type had been taken by de Rohan's soldiers, to make bullets. Before the dysentery that the soldiers brought to his home town carried off his master and fellow apprentices. Before he had been caught up in the first of de Rohan's Huguenot revolts and become a soldier himself, nearly fifteen years ago.

He started to count on his fingers. "First, the unfortunate machine has been asked to make hundreds of pamphlets opposing the practice of vaccination. For many reasons. Not only those set forth in the up-time materials that the man in Grantville sent to de Ron, but also for new reasons that we invented, such as that getting a vaccination indicates that a person is not meekly submitting to the will of God.

"Then, from the encyclopedia, Gui found out that the up-timers—not the ones now in Grantville, but their ancestors a century and a half before the time they came from—had opposed these new 'lightning rods' for much the same reason. So we requested of the poor machine that it be so kind as to produce hundreds of pamphlets opposing lightning rods.

"Plus Antoine's ordinary diatribes against Richelieu.

"Plus manifestoes for Weitz.

"Followed by the need for Guillaume's 'rumors of assassinations' pamphlets by the thousand. What did we expect? The poor machine is overstrained. 'Stress' that up-time reporter, Waters is his name, calls it in his 'American' newspaper."

Ancelin walked over and gave the roller a disgusted poke. "Whether it is stressed or broken, it will not produce any more pamphlets. We can still make the stencils ourselves, of course. But until Fortunat can find someone to fix it, we're out of the pamphlet business."

Locquifier shook his head. "We cannot fall behind now. There are printers in Frankfurt who have Vignellis. We must hire the use of one. Not give our stencils to him, of course. He might read them. We can't risk having the authorities discover the source of so many of the pamphlets in circulation. Just hire the use of the machine after the man's normal working day. We can demonstrate to him that you know how to work it, Fortunat. And find someone to fix ours."

Brillard shook his head. "No. One of us, at least, would have to go to the print shop. The man would know that we, the Frenchmen living at *Zum Weissen Schwan*, are producing masses of pamphlets. Just get the machine fixed."

"We can't have a repairman come here, either," Deneau protested.

Locquifier pulled on his mustache. "No, no, of course not. Find out if one of the printers knows someone who can fix it. We will take it to the shop."

"Mathurin is right. None of us should take it to the shop, either," Ouvrard said. "The printer will learn that the Frenchmen living at *Zum Weissen Schwan* have a Vignelli. None of us should ask about repairs, either. It might bring the attention of the authorities to us. We can't be too cautious."

Locquifier jumped up. "Have Isaac de Ron send one of his porters around to ask who can repair the machine. Put the machine in a box. Seal the box. Have the porter deliver the sealed box to the print shop and then bring it back again. But . . ." He banged his fist on the table. "Fix the machine!"

✧ ✧ ✧

The printer Crispin Neumann told de Ron's porter that he had a duplicating machine of his own and his apprentice was quite skilled in its maintenance.

So Locquifier told de Ron to have the porter remove the boxed machine from the back parlor and take it to Neumann.

Which made Emrich Menig very happy. He loved to fiddle with Vignellis.

Martin Wackernagel lounged lazily in the back room of the shop, watching Menig disassemble and then reassemble the machine.

"Stupid klutz," Menig muttered.

"What?"

"He's managed to get the silk from one of his stencils bunched up here." He jerked it out and threw it at his honorary uncle.

Who spread it out and read it. Not having anything better to do at the moment.

"Where'd this machine come from, Emrich?" Martin managed to keep his voice idle and bored.

"One of de Ron's porters brought it in. Over from *Zum Weissen Schwan*."

The bells tolled nine. Wackernagel stood up. "Appel should have the things he wanted me to pick up ready by now." He picked up the sheet of crumpled silk. "I guess I should be getting on the road again."

Which he did. After detouring to speak with David Kronberg's uncle in the ghetto.

Hanau

The rabbi sighed. Oh, the complications. Just because he helped arrange Kronberg's job in the Fulda post office and subsequent happy marriage to Rivka zur Sichel. Whose parents were now the sutlers in Barracktown bei Fulda. Where the redoubtable Sergeant Hartke and his now-famous wife Dagmar held sway.

"Give it to Utt," the Hanauer rabbi told Wackernagel. "He can not only radio the gist of the information you have collected about de Ron's connection to the pamphlets, but also give the silk itself to someone who can deliver it directly to Nasi. Not only directly, but quickly. After all, King Christian and Princess Kristina are coming to Fulda this week to deliver the medals to Dagmar Nilsdotter. There will be a plane as close as Erfurt."

The rabbi sighed.

"As it happens, I have a priority code. Nasi casts a very wide web."

Nathan Prickett picked up his pen.

Dear Don Francisco,

Jason Waters, the reporter who's here in Frankfurt, was in Crispin Neumann's print shop the other day. He met one of Neumann's clients, a man named Heinrich Hirtzwig. He's the rector of the gymnasium here in Frankfurt. That's not a sports place, but the most important high school for boys. The kind that sends a really high percentage of its graduates to the university.

Anyway, this Hirtzwig was born in Hesse and he also writes plays. In Latin, that is, because he's a kind of professor.

Anyway, the Crown Loyalists, especially the landgrave of Hesse-Kassel, have hired him to write some plays saying that Wilhelm Wettin is right and Mike Stearns is wrong. In a lot more words, of course. I just thought you might want to know.

Neumann, the printer, said to Waters that it's too bad that the up-timers with all their maps hadn't managed to arrive with all their maps fifty years earlier, because someone named de Bry would have been delighted. I have no idea what that's all about.

There was still half a page. And these steel-nib pens, even if a guy had to dip them, really were a lot handier than the quills had been.

There's a kid named Emrich Menig who works for Neumann. He was mixed up with those anti-Semitic pamphlets that came out in Fulda when my father-in-law Wes Jenkins was there. But he was just a kid and innocent, so Wackernagel brought him down to Frankfurt.

He's come out to Sachsenhausen a couple of Sunday afternoons to watch the militia drill. I've been showing him how the guns work. He's not particularly hot on shooting, but he has a real knack for mechanical stuff. If he wasn't working for a printer, Blumroder would love to have him.

Anyway, he was fixing a duplicating machine here in Frankfurt the other day and pulled a stuck stencil out of it that said a lot of the same things. But he lost the stencil, so I don't have it.

But being a kid, he was curious, so he went to talk to de Ron's porter. The porter says that there's a bunch of Frenchmen, five or six, who have been staying at de Ron's inn since last summer—July or so. That means they can't be hurting for money, given what de Ron charges. It's not some kind of a dive.

It looked like this was going to run over to another page of paper.

They don't just have this duplicating machine. They use paper by the bale. The porter has to carry the bales in and out, so he knows.

But it isn't delivered to them as bales of paper. It comes into the cellars of the inn labeled as shipments of wine from a company called Mauger's up in the Netherlands.

The guy guesses that they have some other way to get rid of the paper after they've printed things up, because they never ask him to carry it out.

Do you remember Ernie Haggerty, the guy Jason Waters brought to Frankfurt with him? He's made a lot of friends in low places. Sometimes he just sits in taverns, not looking like an up-timer. He can do that, because he's a scrawny little fellow who's going bald and his teeth aren't so good. His folks never got him braces—couldn't afford to—and he's a smoker. Of course, he broke the front one when he was a kid. His brother hit him with a softball. But the cap he has pops on and off pretty easy, so he can be snaggletoothed whenever he wants to.

Anyway, Ernie schmoozed up to the porter from de Ron's.

Vincenz Weitz, that guy who a lot of people thought was mixed up in planning the attack on the ghetto back when Henry Dreeson was here—remember him?

He's been visiting these Frenchmen at de Ron's and taking piles of paper under his arm when he leaves again.

The guy named Curtius left Soubise's house. He's not

gone back to England. Somebody told Wayne Higgenbottom that he was going to meet Soubise's brother in a town called Besançon, which I never heard of, but it's not around here.

Speaking of Wes, him and his second wife are going to have a baby. Chandra says that it's caused a fair amount of excitement in Grantville.

Best wishes,
Nathan Prickett

Grantville, late January 1635

Under the circumstances, Wes found it a little embarrassing that he was still chairing the initiative in regard to uniform statewide matrimonial legislation.

Solving the problems by simply declaring separation of church and state wasn't as simple as a person might think. Take the problems of Jarvis Beasley's wife Hedy, for instance. Even if down-time betrothal contracts were handled procedurally in the church courts, they still were included in the civil laws of the various territories as well. Even in the unlikely event that Saxony abolished its state church, its civil laws of marriage would still be in force in those Henneberg territories south of the Thuringenwald.

Until Gustavus Adolphus managed to do something definitive about John George, at least.

Unless the SoTF congress simply got rid of any variant marriage laws below the level of the province as a whole? Passed a law saying that this was a state-level matter and no longer the concern of the individual territories that had coalesced to create the SoTF?

Wes had never considered himself a radical. A conservative, rather. In no way a revolutionary. A caretaker. That was, in a way, why he had been interested in parks and such, originally. Once upon a time. Up-time.

But there were times when the thought of abolishing the whole diddly-squat mess and starting over, the way Gustavus had done with the new USE provinces in western Germany the previous June, was very appealing. Times like this one. Put the whole USE on a grid. Make it look like Kansas.

He shook his head. No. When you came right down to it, he was an old West Virginia boy. Hills and hollows, curves and bends. He'd lived with them all his life, geographical or jurisdictional. He'd figure something out.

Frankfurt

Nathan Prickett looked at the letter from his mother again.

You know, she had written, *I think that I caused a lot of trouble without ever meaning to.*

She explained the tour of Vital Statistics that she had given to Jacques-Pierre Dumais.

Everyone knows that's he's a friend of Veda Mae Haggerty, so I think that's the only way word of Wes and Clara's marriage could have gotten out. All the gossip seems to have started with her. But Jenny was so mad that I don't dare tell her. I don't know what I ought to do about it.

Nathan had a feeling that he knew what he ought to do about it. Had to do about it, really.

> *Dear Don Francisco.*
>
> *I'm enclosing a letter that I got from my mom.*

He finished up.

> *If you can think of some way to handle this without getting Mom fired from her job, I'd really appreciate it. Jenny Maddox will fire her if she finds out, but all Mom meant to do was show him how the system works and raising a stink about Chandra's dad's second marriage doesn't count as international sabotage or a plot against the USE, if you ask me.*
>
> *Wes was mad as hell, from what Chandra wrote me, but they are public records. There's nothing Top Secret about a marriage license.*
>
> *You might want to keep a closer eye on this Dumais character, though.*
>
> *Thanks a lot,*
> *Nathan Prickett.*

Chapter 39

Frankfurt am Main

"You might as well leave now, Fortunat."

Deneau raised his eyebrows. "Go where?"

"To Thuringia, of course. You, Gui, and Weitz, now that Boucher and Turpin have arrived from La Rochelle. Weitz has already contacted like-minded individuals in various Franconian and Thuringian towns. In fact, it is likely that the industrial towns on the south slope of the *Thüringerwald* will provide more people willing to take action against the Grantville synagogue than you will find in Thuringia. Certainly more people who will be qualified to find temporary work in Grantville than rural villages will.

"In any case, do not let any of the locals know that there is a Huguenot connection. Weitz and his associates are to do the recruitment. They are to be told of it in connection with the men in Frankfurt who were frustrated last fall. Assure, them, of course—have Weitz assure them, that is—that there is plenty of money available to back a major riot. They will expect recompense for the time they miss from work. Everyone has expenses, and many of them will have families to support."

"If Weitz is doing all the work, why are the rest of us going?"

"To ensure that he does the work that we want him to do. In the way we want him to do it. On the schedule we have laid out."

"Four supervisors to one laborer seems somewhat excessive," Brillard commented.

"There will be work for Fortunat and Gui when it comes closer to the day. Someone must draw up the charts that design who, holding what weapon, will stand where, in the market square."

Ancelin frowned, once more pulling out his map of the Croat raid. "There is no market square. Not even a market, as far as I can figure out." He spread it on the table. "See, we have gone over it before. The synagogue is one house over from a corner building. It fronts on a street, not a square. The bridges are nearby, but not immediately in front of it."

"I am getting very tired of that map," Brillard said.

"Memorize it," Locquifier advised him. "The day is coming when you will need to have the layout very clear in your mind."

"Very well."

"And do not worry about four supervisors. Fortunat will find out for himself very soon that neither Boucher nor Turpin could supervise a small child taking a bath, much less a complex undertaking."

"Small children in baths are very slippery. My sister has three of them, so I have some reason to know."

"What we are planning is very slippery, as well. You are preparing for your own part?"

"I spend some time every day at the shooting range. The owner knows me as one Matthias Bruller, from Alsace. A partisan, he suspects, for Bernhard of Saxe-Weimar." He smiled. "It was Michel's mention of Charles Mademann that gave me the idea to choose that particular pseudonym. Alsace is such a convenient place, the way French and Germans, Catholics and Protestants, intermingle."

"A job well done," Soubise said. "Thank you, Sandrart."

Joachim Sandrart bowed.

"A loose end. Perhaps not a crucial one. But it was d'Avaux who took Ducos to Italy, d'Avaux who did not control the man once he was there. Ultimately, therefore, d'Avaux who can be considered responsible for the entire Galileo debacle.

"It is amusing, in a way, that Mazarin arranged to send d'Avaux to Brittany. Of course, he is Italian. Perhaps, it did not immediately spring to his mind that the Rohan family does not lack influence there." Soubise drummed his fingers on the table. "My sister-in-law will see to it, then, that the count's tenure in his new position is unpleasant? More unpleasant than even Mazarin intended that it should be?"

"A more appropriate choice of word might be 'miserable.' 'Wretched,' even. A view in which your sister, Mademoiselle Anne, seemed to concur."

"Then, Joachim, we may rest easy that d'Avaux's life, henceforth, will be a lamentable experience. Even in the unlikely event that he should elude the watchers placed on him by the . . . newly naturalized cardinal."

"Your sister seemed quite enthusiastic about planning measures to ensure it."

Sandrart paused, then continued.

"It is a pity that Mademoiselle Anne was unable to marry. The travails of your family after the death of Henri IV prevented your mother from arranging a suitable match, I presume. She would have brought forth redoubtable sons."

"Anne does not perceive it as a misfortune. Aside from Catherine, may God rest her soul, my sisters chose not to marry. A choice more easily achieved, for a noblewoman, when, as in the case of our family, her father is long since dead by the time she reaches marriageable age. Henriette died ten years ago. She was a quite special friend of Catherine de Mayenne, the duchess of Nevers—Carlo Gonzaga's wife, in Mantua. They exchanged verses. When Catherine died in 1618, Henriette was devastated. Her spirits never recovered."

"Ah." Sandrart nodded his head.

"And you met Anne."

Sandrart inclined his head again. "She is quite impressive. Very learned."

"A remarkable woman. With my late mother, she was the soul of La Rochelle's resistance during the siege in 1627, the one marked by Buckingham's disaster on Ile de Re." Soubise turned his head. "You know la Gentileschi, do you not? You were traveling with her from Rome?"

"Assuredly."

"My mother as a young woman, scarcely twenty years of age, wrote a play which was performed at La Rochelle. *Judith et Holopherne*. I believe that Gentileschi has painted this theme?"

"Several times."

"Obtain one for me, if you would be so kind. If she has none available that she has painted as a studio project, commission a new one. Oil on canvas. Talk to my steward about costs." Soubise rose from his chair.

Missy's uncle Wes might think Ron was getting to be a pain. However, he supposed this might count as something consular. Approximately. Vaguely. At least, this time he was at the office and he'd phoned ahead for an appointment.

"I got a letter from Joachim Sandrart."

At least Mr. Jenkins' face looked encouraging.

"He's an artist who traveled with us from Padua to Frankfurt. He came up from Rome with Signora Gentileschi, Prudentia's mom. Jabe McDougal's girlfriend. Have you met her? Either one of them?"

Don't rattle on, he told himself. *He'll think you're nervous. Just because you are nervous doesn't mean that he needs to know it.*

"Joachim's working for Soubise, now, in Frankfurt. He just got back from a trip to France. But that's not exactly why I thought I should bring you the letter to read."

He reached into his pocket, pulled the letter out, and dropped it on the desk.

"He mentioned that Soubise's brother, the duke of Rohan, who is a very important man among the Huguenots, has left Switzerland and gone to Besançon. That's where Bernhard of Saxe-Weimar is setting up his new capital."

"So?"

"In October, on our way back from Italy, we stopped to see the duke. It was Joachim's idea," Ron inserted defensively, "not mine. Honest."

"I believe you."

"It's not been in any of the papers, the Besançon business, I mean. I read at least three different papers every morning, from beginning to end. Because of Dad's business. I pretty well have to. We ship internationally, of course, and there are so many variables. I start with the *Street* and then the *Times* and then whatever's the most recent one from Magdeburg that's been delivered to the office. Plus my secretary skims a bunch of others and makes me news clips."

Which actually embarrassed him. Both having a secretary and reading news clips. Frank was running a dive in a slum in Rome and Ron was sitting out at Lothlorien like some Wall Street penguin-type reading news clips, so he could make a reasonable decision on whether some offer that had come in was legit or not.

Not that his secretary was a bad guy. Actually, he was pretty efficient, considering that he was only a couple of years older than Ron. Muselius over at Countess Kate's had recommended Barthold Orban for the job, once it had dawned on Ron that he needed a secretary and mentioned to Jonas that the last thing he needed in the outer office was some guy with a lot of experience who would try to take over because Ron had hardly any.

"Anyway, when we stopped in Switzerland, the duke spent a whole evening talking to me, and gave me a couple of books he's written. I've read them. A little hard-hearted, maybe, but . . ."

He stopped.

"Uh. Could you just read the letter, before we go any further?"

Wes' first thought was: *way above my pay grade.*

"May I make a copy of this? I think I'll have to ask a few other people before I can give you an answer and I'd like to have one to refer to."

"Sure. Keep the original, if you want. I'll do fine with a copy. I can wait outside." Ron tilted his head at the door that led to the Bureau of Consular Affairs waiting room. "Or come back later this afternoon, before I go back to Lothlorien, to pick it up."

Wes looked at the letter again. "I don't want anyone else looking at this. If you have time, you can go back there"—he tilted his head at the back door of his office, which led into a file room—"and write the copy out there. If you would be so kind."

"Yeah. Sure." Ron stood up.

Wes, still sitting, looked up at the boy. Young man.

"Is there any other business that might possibly have brought you to the Bureau of Consular Affairs this afternoon? Something I can reasonably call Martina or Lucia in and ask her to take care of? To account for your visit? Something that's preferably reasonably complicated?"

Ron frowned. "You know, I really don't like to ask for special favors. But we have this guy out at the plant who comes from someplace up in the Baltic. He landed here because he was in the Swedish army, the Yellow Regiment that was stationed here under Kagg in 1633, but his sister was married to a Pole . . ."

"Sit down again, why don't you?" Wes started taking notes.

". . . and even though he's a Swedish citizen, he'd be willing to be naturalized here if that would help get his sister's kids out of the clutches of their wicked uncle on the other side of the family. Does the SoTF have a consular agent in Danzig?" That was where Ron reached a stopping point. Fifteen minutes later.

Wes asked, "Why hadn't you brought this up with me before?"

"Well, I really don't like to ask for special favors."

Magdeburg

Ed Piazza thought it was probably beyond his pay grade, too. He bucked it on to Magdeburg.

Where it ended up in a conference.

"The letter makes it quite clear, I think," Francisco Nasi said. "The duke of Rohan is not interested in corresponding with anyone in an official position in the USE government. Or in the Swedish government. Or in the SoTF government. He merely wishes to pursue an amicable exchange of opinions with a young man in whom he takes a friendly interest."

Hermann of Hesse-Rotenburg nodded. "Plausible deniability." He paused. "Additionally, Rohan may not feel that he can rely on having his letters treated with full confidentiality by the next administration . . . It could be a delicate position for him, if Wettin wins. Willhelm is, after all, Duke Bernhard's older brother."

Nasi nodded. "No risk of offending anyone in an official position by breaking off communication at that point."

"If Jenkins thinks Stone can do it . . ." Arnold Bellamy's voice trailed off.

"He wouldn't have forwarded the idea, if he didn't," Frank Jackson said. "Not that the thought of one of Tom Stone's boys conducting delicate diplomatic negotiations with a French ex-rebel doesn't practically make me fall flat on my face."

Bellamy nodded. "Then we'll need a regular liaison. Someone . . . inconspicuous."

Cory Joe Lang made a discreet coughing noise. As usual, the young intelligence officer was sitting somewhat to the rear, making himself inconspicuous.

"Yes?" Hermann cocked his head.

"If I have understood what you and Don Francisco have been saying, our network is trying to establish an inconspicuous connection, by way of Stone, to the duke of Rohan. And, indirectly, to Bernhard of Saxe-Weimar."

"That does seem to be the point." Don Francisco took off his spectacles and started to clean them. The action served to control any impulse to smile. Also as usual, Cory Joe was proving to be an excellent assistant. For all the world, the young man seemed to be wrestling with a brand new idea—as if he hadn't already, many weeks since, started working on this very problem.

"If the two of you are willing, I could do it. After all, I see Ron every time I'm in Grantville anyway."

Arnold Bellamy leaned back in his chair. "You do? If you don't mind my asking, why?"

"Pam Hardesty, my half-sister, is working at the state library. Through that she's friends with Missy Jenkins, who's about three years younger than her. So through that, I see Ron every time I'm in Grantville."

It was pretty clear that the connection was not computing.

"Missy and Ron are a couple. Not exactly official. Yet. But trust me. They are."

"I remember them," Jackson protested. "They're just kids."

"They're both nineteen, sir. They had birthdays just before Christmas." Cory Joe grinned. "They have birthdays just before Christmas every year, sir."

The general glared the ordinary adult level of indignation at kids who managed to grow up, apparently in an instant, while a person's attention had been focused elsewhere.

"It's a natural tie," Don Francisco commented. "Already friends. Already established, so not obvious."

Hesse-Rotenburg nodded. "It would certainly be far less conspicuous than for Stone to be reporting to one of the SoTF administrative offices regularly."

Cory Joe shrugged. "Not really, sir. Ron is normally in and out of the administration building two or three times a week. After all, he's managing the local end of the Farbenwerke. His normal business tends to take him into the various corners of economic resources quite a bit. Talking to people like Noelle Stull and Eddie Junker."

Again, Don Francisco had to suppress a smile. He had found it convenient to bestow those portions of his Grantville operations that weren't precisely police business in among the accountants and auditors, who always had a legitimate reason to be nosy. "Speaking of Noelle, while she is on my mind, do you know a young woman named Denise Beasley? She wrote me a letter, recently."

Cory Joe nodded. "Buster Beasley's kid. Friend of Ron's brother Gerry. She's a pip, that one. Even if she is just sixteen."

"I am, I suppose, delighted to hear it." Don Francisco loved ties of blood. The interconnections among the Grantvillers had turned out to be so charmingly intricate as he came to be familiar with them. "When," he asked hopefully, "is this coupledom—if there is such a word in English—likely to become official?"

Cory Joe paused for a moment, assessing the problem. Then: "I don't think it's a sometime thing, even though they may not be sure of that themselves yet. They've done Thanksgiving dinner at Missy's grandma's house. They've done Christmas dinner at Missy's house. You already know about New Year's Eve, because Ron and I both reported on LaChapelle from our own perspectives, independently. Ron's come face to face with Vera Hudson and survived the experience. According to my sister Pam, Missy has set up a pretty effective defensive perimeter, so to speak, so things aren't likely to slide for very long."

Jackson guffawed, but Cory Joe managed to keep a straight face. "Engaged by spring would be my best assessment, sir."

Frankfurt am Main

"Now that the others are gone, Mathurin, it is time for you to be on your way as well. Don't arrive so early that your face will have become familiar by the fourth of March."

"I am gratified to have been entrusted with your most confidential plans, Guillaume."

Locquifier narrowed his eyes. "No, you're not."

"Well, of course not. But one does what one can to maintain life's little courtesies. Do say 'ta-ta' to Robert for me."

Isaac de Ron duly reported to Soubise that Deneau, Ancelin, and Brillard were no longer at the inn *Zum Weissen Schwan*. Also that he had not managed to find out where they went, but that they had left with two other men, just a day or so after those had come into Frankfurt—newly arrived, as far as de Ron knew. They hadn't even stayed long enough to register their presence with the pastor of the Huguenot church.

Soubise sent the information on to his brother. Henri de Rohan replied that de Ron was to continue to observe but not, of course, to display any undue curiosity. Presumably, the "dear departed" would turn up somewhere. He would alert the remainder of the family's agents, particularly along the travel routes between Frankfurt and Scotland. They might well be joining Ducos.

In a flash of humor, Rohan added that they would probably not be showing up in Haarlem, since Mauger was presumably still enjoying his honeymoon. Both brothers had thoroughly enjoyed Dumais' report describing the man's courtship and marriage.

Since Locquifier and the others had always met with Vincenz Weitz elsewhere, de Ron had no reason to notice that Weitz, also, had left Frankfurt.

Chapter 40

Halle

"Pull those hoses straight! I mean straight! No kinks!" Bryant Holloway was shouting at the top of his lungs.

"You do realize," the warden of the Halle fire watch said, "that these men are mostly casual day laborers, *Tagelöhner* who at this season of the year find available jobs very thin on the ground. They may learn to handle the hoses today, but that does not signify that they will be available to handle the hoses the next time we have a fire. If I were in charge of this project, I would train only citizens of Halle. People who can be relied upon to turn out because it is in their own interest. Men who have wives, children, houses, shops. Whose idea was it to use so many extra hands?"

"Someone in the USE Fire Marshal's office in Magdeburg. I started with your citizens and shopkeepers, but it became pretty obvious, pretty fast, that they prefer to be in their warm shops doing their own work rather than out here slogging through a lot of cold, slippery, muck. It's one thing to join a bucket brigade when a fire's actually burning and your livelihood's in danger—"

He made a sudden dash for the pump. "No, no! Not like that!"

The head of the fire watch followed him.

"Pay attention, damn it! You have to work as a team."

The warden sighed. "These are fairly tough characters, mostly.

Boatmen, dock workers. Strong of body and weak of mind. Not the kind who find it easy to work together smoothly."

"Hell, maybe bribery will help."

"I doubt it. I know that man, though—the second one you have on the pump lever. He used to be a fairly good rope-maker, before his family died and he lost his business through neglect." The warden waved. "Klick, Friedrich Klick. *Hier!*"

A half hour later, Klick seemed to have grasped the purpose of the training drill. He went to explain it to the others. This involved standing in the cold, wearing boots that were far from waterproof, for another half hour. Bryant shivered.

Klick waved. "We are ready to begin."

"Fine, take your places."

They men moved. Began the drill. Bryant looked at the hose crew with horror. "No, no, not that way!" He ran over to the wagon to which the crew was trying to attach the hose end. "Don't force, it, for God's sake. You'll strip the screw threads. They're just wood—the wagon and the fasteners on end of the hose, both. Do it like this."

He looked around.

Klick was leaning on the pump.

The fire watch captain had disappeared. Back to his own warm shop somewhere in town, presumably.

He put his hands on his hips. Christ, but he hated Archie Stannard.

Bribery time.

"After you've gotten it right twice in a row, I'll buy every man here a beer."

That helped a little, but not much.

"Anyone who gets it right, I'll tell him about a job out of this cesspit of a town—give him the name of a man who's hiring for work a lot easier than this."

Sometimes it just took the right incentive.

By the end of the day, sixteen men knew how to work the wagon, pump, and hoses.

Seven of them left the next morning, heading south up the Saale to find Jacques-Pierre Dumais in Grantville.

Including Klick.

At least Dumais was paying a commission for every recruit he sent.

Bryant's feet were back in the wet and muck. "Pull those hoses straight. I mean straight. No kinks."

What did that guy say? Yogi Berra, maybe? "*Déjà vu* all over again."

Naumburg

"What does it take to get an idea across to you?"

Fortunat Deneau was not having a good day.

"Listen, Weitz. Yes, I know that you hate the Jews. That is why you are here. But you are going to have to do your hating someplace other than Grantville until March fourth. That is the crux date. On the fourth of March, you may go hate the Jews of Grantville. Until then, you may speak, rant, perorate, whatever you want to call it, in other towns in Thuringia, but *not there.*"

Weitz protested that the Jews of Grantville were the ones they had all come to attack. The excitement that enabled him to gather a couple of hundred volunteers was because they would be attacking the synagogue in the up-time town. Where they would all get to be in the newspapers after their triumph.

Deneau took a deep breath. "Until March fourth, I do not want a large demonstration. I want a few people, scattered in several towns around Thuringia. Badenburg, Saalfeld, Rudolstadt, here in Jena, over in Weimar—you can read a map, can't you? Preaching in the street. Calling out in the marketplaces. Making noise, but not doing anything. But they are to avoid Grantville. Avoid. Do you understand the word? Not go there."

"Why?"

Deneau wondered if it would be helpful to tear his hair. He had heard that it was a custom in some exotic locales. "I am trying to lull the people of Grantville into a false sense of security. I want them, their police, their mounted constabulary, their military forces to come to the point of thinking, 'Those rabble-rousers at least have enough sense not to come *here.*' I want them to send their constabulary and soldiers away, to Stadtilm, to Arnstadt, to Ilmenau, to Zella and Mehlis, for all I care. But far enough that it will take them some hours to get back."

Gui Ancelin shook his head. "I don't like that part of the plan.

Counting on someone else's complacency to do part of one's work is always a dangerous assumption."

Weitz ignored him, concentrating on Deneau. "And what are we to do, then?"

"Rabble-rouse. Agitate. Do what agitators do. But in small groups. And close enough to Grantville that your men can walk there in a day or two—quickly enough that the authorities won't have time to notice that the ranters have suddenly disappeared from everywhere else and wonder where they have gone.

"If there are any among you who have enough prudence to remain quiet for a couple of weeks, you can send them ahead. They can infiltrate into Grantville now, pretending to be day laborers, migrant laborers, temporary workers. But *only* those who have enough self-control to wait. Silently."

Eventually, Weitz agreed, although he was far from pleased.

That left Deneau with just one other important problem.

He had been trying to get Boucher and Turpin to do something useful ever since the group left Frankfurt. Without any notable success. He called them in and sent them to Grantville. They were to look up Dumais and be his errand boys.

Let Dumais deal with the hapless, hopeless, and helplessly inept.

Then, another thought crossing his mind, he called them back.

"Don't tell him that I sent you. Tell him that Laurent Mauger sent you."

A couple of minutes later, he called them back again.

"Don't mention Weitz. Don't mention Ancelin. Above all, do not mention Frankfurt. Or anyone in Frankfurt—not Guillaume or Robert or Mathurin. Or me. Or Jews. Or synagogues. Or . . . Don't tell him *anything*, understand?"

"If we don't say anything, he'll think that we are mute," Turpin protested.

Deneau cast his eyes up to the ceiling. "Very funny, Georges. Tell, him precisely, these words. 'We come from La Rochelle, like you. Laurent Mauger sent us to help you.' Do you think you can remember that much, my dear compatriots? Perhaps one of you can take the first of the sentences and the second of you the other one?"

✧ ✧ ✧

After they were gone, Deneau sat, brooding over his wine. "If Boucher and Turpin are an example of what La Rochelle's defense forces were like in 1628, my dear Gui, no wonder our great citadel fell to Richelieu's siege."

"There is a proverb, Fortunat. There is always a proverb. 'Against stupidity, the gods themselves strive in vain.'"

Grantville

"The man will pay me to do it," Friedrich Klick told his brother-in-law Jacob. "For just one day. Of course, I'll have to practice with him and the others. He insists that it is to be a 'controlled, orderly demonstration.' We will arrive together. We will carry placards made of stiffened paper attached to sticks, which we will wave in the air. We will shout slogans. He is very insistent, though, that we must not act like plebians. No looting. No . . ."

"Where's this happening?"

"In Grantville."

"That's a big city now—must be twenty thousand people there. How many of you are there, making this 'demonstration'?"

"He would like to have between seventy-five and a hundred men."

"Not enough to make much of an impression."

"We will all be concentrated in one place only. On a plaza they call a 'parking lot' in front of the hospital. The Leahy Medical Center. It is right on their famous tarred highway, Route 250, so we won't get lost in some maze of crooked streets, trying to find it."

Jacob Menzer raised his head. "Why is he demonstrating against the hospital?"

"Vaccinations." Klick pulled a handful of pamphlets out of his doublet. "See. Even many of the up-timers thought they were dangerous, but they are trying to force them on us and our children."

"Vaccinations?" Andres Scherf scoffed a couple of days later. "Why are they worrying about these 'vaccinations,' Jacob? Don't you know that they perform autopsies there? They desecrate the bodies of the dead, just as Dean Rolfinck does at the medical school in Jena. But Rolfinck, at least, limits himself to corpses of executed criminals that have been turned over to him by order of the city council." He laughed harshly. "Which, they say, does wonders for keeping down the crime rate in Jena. In Grantville, though—and I have heard this myself from a man who talked to the sister of the employer of the man who died—the doctors use the bodies of respectable citizens who die at that Leahy Medical Center for autopsies. Or want to. True, in that case they asked permission and gave the body to the family, undamaged, when the wife refused. Or so the man said. But who can tell how many times they have desecrated the bodies of people who came to them hoping for a cure?"

Jacob Menzer, grave and solemn, worried now, nodded his head.

"They call them 'anatomy lessons.' Yes, I know this. It is not a rumor. Hans Hessburger told me himself. He learned it from his cousin, who knows a man from Kamsdorf whose cousin Franz is studying to be a 'nurse' there. They expect Franz to stand around a table and watch while a surgeon cuts an arm or a leg into layers and pulls out the veins and muscles. 'Dissection' is what they call it. And then . . ."

Gabriel Kratsch paused for effect.

"Yes?" Thomas Klau leaned forward, anxiously.

"Then they will expect Franz to do it, himself. He went to work at that hospital as a respectable baker, providing food for their 'cafeteria' that feeds the staff and patients. But then one of the up-timers tempted him into becoming one of them. A respectable Lutheran boy from Thuringia, cutting up the dead. Sending them into the resurrection with mutilated bodies."

"Who did you say this is?"

"The boy? Franz Brohm, from Rottenbach. The man in Kamsdorf is named Heinz Bickel. You can talk to him yourself. He will tell you the truth."

"We will have to do something about it," Kratsch said. "Can you talk to Friedrich again, Jacob? Find out from him what day this 'demonstration' is going to happen. What time of day. All that information. Orderly protest—bah! We will let them know what we truly think of their blasphemy."

✧ ✧ ✧

Trent Dorrman, at Grantville-Saalfeld Foundries and Metalworks, bundled up the last batch of material they had found in the files that seemed like it might have anything, no matter how tenuous, to do with Jay Barlow, Caryn Barlow, Billie Jean Mase, and the other defectors to Austria. It had taken a while and involved a lot of overtime.

He put on a cover note to Preston Richards.

At the end, he added a postscript saying that the company had picked up several new temporary laborers lately. That was normal enough in this season, when a lot of casual laborers were having trouble finding work in their home towns, but he'd overheard several of them talking. It seemed like they'd been working heavy labor on the hoses and pump wagons in several towns nearby, and that Bryant Holloway had sent them down to Grantville to find work.

He couldn't help but think that it was sort of peculiar that Holloway, who was paid by the fire department, would send men away from the towns where they lived after he'd gone to all the trouble of training them for the fire watches there.

Since the Reverend Green always said that a Christian was supposed to put the best construction on everything, he'd called the fire chief Steve Matheny to check, because maybe Holloway had sent his best prospects to Grantville because the department was short of men, and they were just picking up work in Kamsdorf because they hadn't found jobs in Grantville yet.

Matheny said that none of these guys had showed up at the Grantville fire department as volunteers.

Preston Richards read the note and put it on his "sort of peculiar" stack. Which was a large one.

Jacques-Pierre Dumais, after trying several other options, set Boucher and Turpin to lettering signs. Even this had required quite a bit of explanation—especially the need for waterproof paint on placards that men would be carrying outdoors in a town where it often snowed, sleeted, or rained. Particularly in late February and early March.

He reminded them that the demonstration would take place on March fouth.

"Why not just wait for a sunny day, if the weather's bad?" Boucher asked.

"We have a set schedule to follow."

"It would be cheaper to wait for a sunny day. The paint mixed with lac costs more than twice as much as the plain tempera."

It occurred to Boucher that if they just brushed a little raw egg white over letters painted with tempera, it would look shiny, like lac paint. Dumais would never know the difference. What's more, they could scramble the yolks and eat them. And buy a couple of bottles of the local wine from Winzerla, up by Jena, to drink with the eggs, with the money they saved at the paint store.

Their living conditions improved.

"I don't know," Jacques-Pierre Dumais said to Friedrich Klick. "Holloway has sent me a number of people, just as he promised, but your group from Halle is the single largest. Even if everyone we've given a retainer so far shows up, there won't be many more than fifty men taking part in the demonstration."

"They are reliable, though," Klick said. "We have practiced with the placards and the shouts. They will do as you tell them."

Dumais nodded. "I just wish that we had a few more, though."

Totally forgetting the maxim that a man should be careful what he wishes for . . .

Scotland

"This is damnable—this latest report from Guillaume."

"It goes into considerable detail in regard to the desired assassinations of which we reminded him last time."

Delerue spat on the floor. "What has he done, really? The whole tenor of this report is that we should not be overly disappointed if the effort to destroy Richelieu by assassinating those major figures and attributing the actions to France should fail. He devotes five times as many lines to describing the strong security in place as he does to explaining how he intends to circumvent it."

"A thorough understanding of the obstacles in one's path is a virtue in itself."

Delerue snorted. "He's losing his edge, Michel."

"Let's not be hasty. I will read the report again."

✧ ✧ ✧

"What do you think?"

"Antoine is just being irritable. The security analysis that Guillaume sent is realistic. Therefore, it is useful."

"One thing caught my eye." Mademann picked up the report.

"Yes?"

"Here, Michel, on the seventh page. The mention of how insignificantly Gustavus Adolphus' queen features in all these security arrangements. She is living in Stockholm; going about her daily routine. No significant variations to throw off observers. No significant effort to avoid surveillance. Only the ordinary palace guards."

Ducos nodded. "Gustavus even allows her, it is believed, an uncensored correspondence with her brother Georg Wilhelm, the elector of Brandenburg. With whom he will soon be at war. That, in itself, shows how far she has been relegated to the margins of important political developments."

"It shows it to those of us who care. But, how many ordinary people really care? In Sweden or in the USE? They read the newspapers. The queen went here; the queen wore this; the queen held a reception. Or speculation. Will the queen visit Denmark? Will the queen soon join her daughter Kristina in Magdeburg? For public consumption, certainly, Gustavus Adolphus treats her with the greatest respect. How is this unlearned 'popular opinion' to conclude that she is supernumerary?"

"So you are suggesting? A trip to Stockholm, perhaps?"

"I would not be averse to the idea. Scotland is beginning to pall on me."

Ducos considered the matter for a moment. "At the very worst, if Locquifier should fail in the matter of Gustavus Adolphus and he survives, there is another possibility. It is irrational for a monarch who has only one heir, and female at that, to refuse to divorce a wife who can never bear another child. There may be some level of sentiment involved in his attitude toward Maria Eleonora. If Guillaume fails with him, but succeeds with one or more of the other targets, the death of his queen in Sweden would at a minimum demand his attention. Perhaps cause him actual grief."

"From a marksman's perspective, 'fuzz up' his focus on pursuing the culprits in the USE."

"There is always the possibility that you might be caught. What cover do you intend to use?"

Mademann smiled. "Why, none. In the case of such a misfortune, the capture of an Alsatian Lutheran subject of Bernhard of Saxe-Weimar should provide the Swedes with a nice red herring directing their intelligence forces away from the activities of French Calvinists." He raised an eyebrow. "*Non?*"

"True," said Ducos. "But be careful. Take no unnecessary risks, even if that means postponing any action. There is no need for this to be coordinated with anything else."

Chapter 41

Grantville

Pam Hardesty's apartment was a handy place to meet. Much more convenient than going out to Lothlorien, especially now that Bill Hudson was around so much of the time. Cory Joe had asked her to set something up the next time he came from Magdeburg. She was sitting on the end of the sofa now, frowning.

Missy was looking at Ron. She hadn't expected anything for Valentine's Day. She seriously doubted that Ron had even noticed that it was Valentine's Day. What she had just gotten had nothing to do with Valentine's day. He had made her an offer that was an honor in a way. He trusted her. But it was an honor that she would much rather refuse.

"You seriously want me to do that?"

"There's enough local rumbling about these anti-Semitic groups in a dozen towns around. We really need to know if they can be expected to try something in Grantville. Missy, honest, I hate to ask this. I tried to tell them that I didn't like the idea at all. I knew that it would not really be your thing. Your uncle Wes doesn't like it, either. It's Don Francisco Nasi's idea. He thinks that if you could pick up an acquaintance with this Dumais guy? Something superficial. Play 'ditzy sympathizer' for a while? Everyone knows that early on, your dad supported Simpson instead of Stearns.

"Yow," he protested against a ferocious attack with a sofa pillow.

"I'm not saying that Chad's a bad guy. Just that he did, back when, even if he's changed over, since then. Cory Joe says that it would give you 'plausibility.'" He looked at Cory Joe, hoping for assistance. "Or his boss says it, and Cory Joe is just passing on the message?"

"I am not," Missy said flatly, "all that much of a risk taker."

The sentence sat between them. It had come up in other contexts.

"I particularly do not want to take the risks that would come up if I had to deal with some of those guys who hang out around the 250 Club. I'm not a wilting lily, but some of them are really rough."

"I could go with you," Pam said. "Two would be better. And that way, we wouldn't even have to go to the 250 Club."

Cory Joe raised his eyebrows at his sister. "How?"

"Veda Mae Haggerty. The Willard. Dumais is there with her, sometimes."

Missy looked up with obvious relief. So did Ron.

"I could hack that, I think," Missy said. "Willard Carson is a stinkeroo, but the hotel is a perfectly respectable place. I could play a 'ditzy sympathizer' in the hotel dining room, I think. I don't even want to be *in* the 250 Club."

"I'll start with Veda Mae," Pam said. "You'll be with me sometimes. Is that better?"

"It's a lot better," Missy said.

"Don Francisco has sent some stuff for you to study. Basic guidance, more or less."

Cory Joe was feeling uncomfortable. This had seemed like a much better idea before it involved his sister.

He began to understand why Ron and Wes Jenkins had argued so hard against it before the others had voted them down. Back when they'd been expecting Missy to do it on her own.

"Ditzy," Missy said indignantly. "'Ditzy.' I'll get you for 'ditzy.'" She leaned down, made a snowball, and threw it at him.

He grinned, the snow all over his ski cap. "What about 'ditzy cheerleader'?"

They battled all the way from Pam's to St. Mary's, where a huge bank of snow had been thrown up behind the church. They climbed it, tossing snow all the way, and fell over into a little pit at the top, like a miniature volcano crater, with seven or eight inches of undisturbed fresh snow on top of that which had been cleared from the alley.

They were just kissing, to start with, enchanted by finding this magic little mini-world right in the middle of town, isolated from all the rest of it.

When they stood up, Ron took her hand. "I might make you cry someday. But not on purpose."

Shivering, they slid back down the pile. Missy picked up some snow at the bottom and threw another ball; they battled all the way to her house. By the time they practically fell through the kitchen door, they were sufficiently white that Debbie accused them of being a pair of yeti.

"Well," Missy said. "Look at it this way. We're considerate enough that we didn't come in the front door and aren't dripping all over the hardwood floor in the front hall."

"You're going to be considerate enough to mop the linoleum, too. Toss those things in the dryer. Ron can't walk out to Lothlorien with half his clothes sopping wet."

They started to strip, beginning with mittens and hats and continuing for quite a while. Winter in Thuringia during the Little Ice Age encouraged the layered look.

"How on earth did you get snow there, Missy?"

"Snow angels?" Missy offered, hoping her mother would not pursue the issue.

"Those ski pants, too," Debbie said firmly. "They're wet."

Ron looked at her. "They're the last layer before my boxers, Mrs. Jenkins."

In Debbie Jenkins' experience, epochal changes tended to turn around small things. "Toss them in. I'll get you an old pair of Chip's to wear while they're drying." She went upstairs.

When she came down, Missy was curled up on the floor, sitting with her head against the door of the dryer. Ron had the teakettle on. "She needs a cup of tea," he said. "With sugar or honey, if you have it."

"I'll make it," Debbie said. "I don't have any real tea, but I have some herbal concoctions. Use this to dry your boots."

"What's that?" Ron asked.

Debbie was startled. "It's a portable hair dryer. You can use it to blow hot air into your boots to dry the lining." She looked at the expression on his face. "Haven't you ever seen one before?"

"I didn't even know they existed," Ron answered. "I thought hair just dried."

"He didn't know about portable hair driers," Debbie said.

Chad turned a page of the newspaper. "Where would he have learned?" he asked. "There weren't any women out at Lothlorien while he was growing up. I doubt he ever read the ads for beautician's supplies in the Sunday paper."

"It's one of those things," Missy said. "WYSIWYG. With Ron, what you see really is what you get. It's just that every now and then, something a little unexpected surfaces. Something you haven't seen before.

"He says that according to his dad, a lot of the world's problems come from not cluing people in when you ought to. That's why he made me sit here and tell you what Don Francisco wants Pam and me to do. So we wouldn't have any misunderstandings."

Thinking, as she said it, that she was glad she had ratcheted the level of the project down to something she *could* clue them in on. The truth was that, "I'm going to be going with Pam to the Willard occasionally when she tries to pump Veda Mae Haggerty to see if the people she hangs around with have dropped any information about these anti-Jewish agitators" was something that her parents had swallowed, however unwillingly. "I'm going to go by myself to the 250 Club, pretending to be a fellow traveler, to try to pump information concerning anti-Jewish agitators out of a possible agent of Michel Ducos, who is the guy who tried to assassinate the pope" would have been thoroughly over the top. She could only imagine how they would have reacted.

"You really needed that tea," Debbie said.

"We ate at Cora's before we went over to Pam's. She doesn't earn enough that we can expect her to feed us. So it had been a while. And first contact with Don Francisco, even by way of Cory Joe, can be a bit unnerving. I'm going to bed."

She lay there, curled up.

She was so relieved that it hadn't come to that.

She wished so badly that it had.

No valentine from Ron. But a hand brushing her cheek, a voice saying, "No risks you don't want. It would be a pity if salty tears melted these snowflakes." Without those, the evidences of her virginity, as the down-time girls called it, would be in a snowbank behind St. Mary's this evening. She hadn't been going to push him away. She'd been pulling him down toward her.

She *sooooo* didn't need this kind of complication in her life right now.

"It's not very exciting," Missy said. "But it's odd."

"Everyone already knew that Dumais was dealing with Velma. He's the one who hooked her up with Mauger."

"It's those Theme things. But I guess you weren't back yet."

"What Theme things?"

"For a while before she left town, Velma was wandering around town talking about Themes and other sort of new age stuff."

"So?"

"About the only thing I've picked up so far is that she got those Themes from Dumais. So I sort of followed her trail. Where she repeated them. Picked up what she said from week to week. Tried to track them down."

"And?"

"And you're lucky that you guys picked a reference librarian to do this job. Not a 'ditz.'"

Ron had a feeling that "ditz" had really grated on Missy. She kept coming back to it.

"I really think you ought to bring it to Don Francisco's attention. Those Themes were quotations, almost all of them. Most of them from Seneca. Which makes it likely that Dumais has some kind of an academic background. That's not exactly typical for a garbage collector, is it? One of the things in the material that Cory Joe brought for Pam and me to study was to look for things that are out of character. If you ask me, Seneca quotations from a garbage collector are really out of character."

There was something to be said for the greenhouse at Lothlorien. For one thing, it was, for the time being, private. Over at the house, Bill was sitting in the living room studying an incredibly expensive herbal, or botanical manual, they had bought. The down-time cleaning woman, who did it as a second job and had no qualms of conscience whatsoever about working on Sunday afternoon, was racketing around with the vacuum cleaner.

Admittedly, the floor was brick. On the other hand, the air was warm. Part of Missy's pony tail had come loose, which was an increasingly common problem as time went on and the bands lost their stretch. The winter sun was catching it, making every individual hair glisten. They'd been here a while. The sun wasn't going to last much longer. Once it went down, that it was it for necking in the greenhouse. The artificial lighting would be like putting a spotlight on them.

Ron looked down. Her eyes were dreamy.

"What are you thinking?" she asked.

"That I'm getting positive feedback."

It wouldn't be a good idea to say exactly what he had been thinking. Which was that he had made out with a fair number of girls before Missy, but he'd sure never made out with one who appreciated his perfectly average and ordinary efforts at making love anywhere near as much as she did.

He had a suspicion that he wasn't likely to come across any other girl this appreciative in the future, either. Which meant that since he wanted continuing positive feedback, he ought not bring up other girls, past or future.

He might even be starting to get the hang of this.

His left foot gently climbed upward from the bare toes, started to explore her lower leg, and then pulled back from the barrier.

He had been a little startled when she climbed up into the Jenkins attic the day after the snow fight, went through several boxes of old toys that her mother had put away to wait for the day she had grandchildren to babysit, came down with a pair of fairly sturdy plastic handcuffs that still had their key, and put them on her ankles that evening. Plus quite a few following occasions.

"Revival of the chastity belt?" He had to laugh.

"Not exactly," Missy answered. "I'm the one who has the key. That makes it different."

He wasn't sure she was joking. At least not entirely. She kept the handcuffs in her jacket pocket, tucked underneath her gloves. And referred to them as "the accessory."

Not that there hadn't been a couple of occasions when the reminder had been useful.

Necessary, really, considering that even though Missy's mind really meant it when she said "no way," the subsection of primal instinct that had moved in on her was obviously starting to put up considerable argument on the point.

Sometimes Ron could kick himself for having pulled back when they were in that snowbank. He hadn't been violating Dad's precepts. By no means had it been a first date, by no means had he been forcing the issue, and Missy had been so willing. Or, at least, the part of Missy that was her body had been very willing indeed. Cooperating, responding, inviting, and encouraging every move he made.

But . . .

He had rolled himself off her, face down into the snow, which had been goddamned fucking unbelievably *cold* by comparison to the heat the two of them had been generating ten seconds before. Well, no male fantasy story he had ever read back up-time had recommended a snowbank in February as a desirable venue for seduction.

He had this suspicion that if her instincts took over before her mind agreed with them, he was the one she'd be mad at. Mad at herself, but really mad at him. Maybe mad enough to break the whole thing off. Even if it wouldn't really be his fault.

He knew that having Missy break it off would be a bad thing. Way closer to a catastrophe-type bad thing than to a nuisance-type bad thing. That was why, really . . .

Not that he could have explained to anybody else exactly what "it" was.

"It" was pretty amorphous right now.

They were spending more and more of their free time at Lothlorien, where the privacy and comfort seemed almost designed to foster temptation. But it also seemed to be almost the only place that they could really talk. They talked a lot when they weren't doing other things. Even while they were doing other things, sometimes.

Besides, Missy was helping him design a records management system and compile a procedures manual, so a lot of the time they spent there wasn't private at all, but involved wandering through the manufacturing plant with clipboards. As she said, it wouldn't be as good a system as if he had been up-time and able to hire a professional consultant, but it would definitely be better than no system at all.

She had told him that one of the nice things about Lothlorien was that none of the staff looked at them cross-eyed, unlike Nani and Gran, who definitely did. The employees, she said, were mostly as friendly and helpful as they could possibly be, even when she plopped herself down on a stool and spent two hours watching how a process was carried out. Then watched it six times more, trying to figure out what parts of it needed to be standardized and recorded and which ones didn't.

He definitely didn't want to do anything that would cause her to break it off before they were finished with the procedures manual. *Great Om, Stone, what a rationale.*

On the other hand . . .

Out of the corner of his eye, he could see a handy pair of pruning shears leaning against a potting table. If he didn't have *some* rationale available, he would take them to the stupid handcuffs. The things were only plastic.

He didn't want to do anything that would cause her to break it off at all.

He kissed her again. She also had an eye on that vanishing sunlight. There was a kind of equation. The less time remaining, the fewer restrictions. This was a really rewarding kiss. Sort of an improved, expanded version.

He could live with the accessory. It wasn't a good thing, exactly, but it was sure better than a bad thing. They might as well make the most of the last ten minutes.

Plus, there was always hope. Once her mind finally decided to agree with her instincts, she had the key. More accurately, in the unlikely event that her mind ever decided to agree with her instincts, she had the key. Hope springeth eternal . . .

Part Seven

February 1635

In dubious battle on the plains of heaven

Chapter 42

Magdeburg, February 22, 1635

"This is actually quite boring," said Rebecca. "I had not expected that. Whatever else I thought 'election day' would be in a republic, 'boring' is not it."

Her husband Mike smiled. "Well, back up-time it would have been quite exciting. Every TV station breathlessly reporting the latest results, precincts closing, exit polls, the whole nine yards."

Rebecca frowned. "I detest that expression. 'The whole nine yards.' It makes no sense at all." Accusingly, she added, "And you use it frequently, too. But—you have explained this to me yourself—in football one must carry the ball *ten* yards before it makes a difference. So why is it not 'the whole ten yards'?"

As much as he adored his wife, there were times when Mike thought she was just a tad too obsessed with precision and perfection. "I don't know the answer, sweetheart. But I do know—for sure, you betchum—that it's 'the whole nine yards.' Not 'the whole ten yards.'"

A slight cough drew his attention and Becky's. Against one wall of the large room in a rented building that served the Fourth of July Party for its national campaign headquarters, Melissa Mailey was sitting on a couch holding hands with James Nichols. The two of them had come up to Magdeburg for the occasion.

She had that certain look on her face, the one that Mike remembered from the days she'd been one of his high school teachers.

That certain much-detested look. The one that prefaced the ignorant student about to be enlightened by the oh-so-god-damn-her-well-educated schoolmarm.

And—yep—sure enough, she began it all with a slight sniff.

"That's because it's almost certainly not a reference to football in the first place." (Here she clucked her tongue. Mike remembered that detested mannerism, too.)

"No, no." (And—yep—always the double negative. As if simply telling a dumbass kid that he didn't know squat once wasn't enough.)

"So what is it, then?" asked Becky.

For a moment—a very brief moment—Melissa looked a little less than completely self-assured. "Well . . . nobody actually knows, for certain. It's a relatively recent expression, it seems. There's no reliably dated use of it prior to the 1960s, at least not in print, when it emerged into prominence in the space program."

Rebecca choked a little laugh. "I always find that so odd! 'No earlier than the 1960s'—which is to say, more than three centuries from now."

"But the most common theory is that it comes from military aviation and originated in the Second World War. The machine gun belts for most U.S. aircraft were twenty-seven feet long. So 'the whole nine yards' would have meant using up all your ammunition in a full and complete effort to strike at your enemy."

"Well!" Rebecca seemed to sit a little straighter. "Well, yes, that *does* make sense."

The two women shared a look of mutual esteem, for a moment. Then Melissa shook her head and made a face. "I have to admit, you're right. This is pretty damn boring, isn't it? James and I could have just as easily stayed down in Grantville, for all the good it did us or we're doing anyone else by coming here."

Nichols shrugged. "What the hell, it's a nice trip."

"It's February," countered Melissa. "It's cold in February."

"Not in that heated compartment on the train it wasn't. I admit, the barge kinda sucked, creature-comfort-wise. But I like to look at snow-covered countryside. Dunno why. Must be my African genetic background."

Melissa looked at him sideways. "It's very well-established in the historical records that almost all Africans brought over to the New World to be slaves came from either West Africa or Angola. Not a snow-covered patch to be found anywhere. African genetics, my ass."

James grinned, very toothily. "Well, sure. That's the *white* man's version of African history. The same rascals who deny that ancient Egypt was African, and that half the Greek pantheon and Jesus himself were black. In point of fact, I'm quite sure my ancestors were born and reared in the very shadows of Kilimanjaro."

Melissa rolled her eyes. James' grin widened still further. "Did I mention that Neil Armstrong was black, too? Yup. First man on the moon was a brother. Naturally they kept it under wraps and never let him out in public 'less he was wearing whiteface. 'Course, the whole moon expedition was actually a media fraud and it all happened in a studio somewhere in either Culver City, California, or Roswell, New Mexico, depending on who you ask. So I guess it'd be more accurate to say that the star of history's greatest and most successful fraud was a brother. But, what the hell. Prestige is where you find it. And speaking of which, Mike, how the hell *are* you doing in this election?"

"Who knows? I can tell you how we're doing in Magdeburg."

"We're winning by a landslide in the city," pronounced Gunther Achterhof, looking up briefly from the table in the corner where he and Spartacus and three young assistants were keeping a running tally of the vote results as runners brought them in. "The party will win by something like eighty percent. Otto Gericke will get over ninety-five percent as city mayor. Of course, he ran unopposed, so it's not really important."

Spartacus looked up also. "So far, we're doing almost as well in Magdeburg province as we are in the city itself. A little over seventy-five percent. Of course, the only precincts reporting in yet are the ones closest to the city."

Nichols shook his head. "Oh, whoopee. What a shocker." Half-scowling: "For Pete's sake, Gunther, the man in the moon knew we were going to win Magdeburg—city and province both—in a landslide. How are we doing everywhere *else*?"

"Stop pestering the poor man," chided Rebecca. "We have no way of getting results quickly, and you know it. It will be several weeks before we get the final results from all the outlying areas."

"We'll survive," said Mike, although he sounded perhaps just a tad doubtful. "After all, the Founding Fathers of the old USA had to do the same thing. Just wait and wait and wait till you found out who won the election."

"Would anyone like to play cards?" asked Rebecca.

Grantville, February 22, 1635

The Voice of America announced that on the basis of a survey of sample precincts, the Piazza/Ableidinger ticket had won in a landslide in the State of Thuringia-Franconia.

"Not," Arnold Bellamy said, "that it's exactly a big surprise."

Duke Albrecht of Saxe-Weimar went to the studio and conceded in a very gracious manner. Then, with a sigh of relief, he went home to Weimar.

The station once more brought on Count Ludwig Guenther of Schwarzburg-Rudolstadt, who had been providing political analysis throughout the evening.

At the national level, the Fourth of July Party did well in some regions. Again no surprise. Mike Stearns would be in Parliament again—as the leader of the Loyal Opposition.

On the basis of early returns, sample precincts again, radioed in from about anywhere a newspaper could put a radio, it definitely looked like the new state capital would be Bamberg. The heart and center of the Ram Rebellion. The symbol of popular democracy in Germany south of the Main. The . . .

Every reporter in Bamberg was having a ball thinking up new headlines.

Magdeburg, late February 1635

"A landslide, as I said." Gunther Achterhof sounded immensely pleased with himself, as if he'd just pronounced some dazzling new scientific theorem. "The Fourth of July Party won Magdeburg province by seventy-six percent."

He looked at Rebecca. "You won by ninety-eight percent, in your district."

"Well, yes. I ran unopposed." She frowned at the cards in her hand. "And now bridge is getting boring also."

"Start losing, for a change," suggested her husband. "That might perk up your interest."

"Do not be ridiculous, Michael," said Rebecca.

"Fat chance," jeered her partner Melissa.

Grantville, late February 1635

"Well, I've got to say," Joe Stull said, "that it's suddenly become a real high priority on everybody's list to push the railroad through Kronach and all the way down to Bamberg. I guess that's the main thing I'll be dealing with personally and it'll keep me more than busy. The rest of the cabinet will have to handle everything else."

"No question that you and Aura Lee are moving with us?"

"Nope. Billy Lee's going to stay here with Chad and Debbie, to finish high school, but we'll take Juliann. There'll be some school there to suit her. I already talked to Constantin Ableidinger when he was up here last week. Or correspondence courses. Or something. We'll deal with it."

George Chehab frowned. "The decision's going to be easier for some than others. A whole bunch of families who work for the SoTF government are starting to agonize about 'do we go or do we stay?' Especially if half the couple's a state employee and the other half isn't."

Ed Piazza spread both of his hands out on the table. "We're not going to be cutting them any slack."

"How so?"

"Every office moves, just as fast as we can find office space in Bamberg. And we're not going to dawdle on that. Ideally, I'd like to get the whole move done in six months. We're already negotiating for leases. New construction, where we can get it. Temporary buildings, if that's all we can get. *Vox populi*, and all that. The voters said that we go, so we go. Make it clear to the personnel office. So they can make it clear to everyone who comes in and whines."

Tony Adducci leaned back. "Yeesh—that's hard-nosed. We're going, of course. But where's everybody going to find housing?"

"The CoC people are helping with that—locating rental properties and such. Encouraging landlords to rent. Not that a lot of families won't be crowded into a lot less space than they're used to, next winter," Chehab said. "I'll be pushing electrification and telephones. Not the way they're available here in Grantville, but at some sort of minimal level. Not that we can't live without them, if we have to. Vince Marcantonio's staff have been, all along.

"Vince and the others who've been in the regional administration there since the fall of '32 are coming up to give orientation sessions on finding housing and schools. Janie Kacere's going to talk to the career people. Stacey O'Brien, Tom's wife, is going to talk to the wives and mothers." Ed laughed. "Do you think that this is the first redistricting I've overseen in my career? This is nothing compared to the grief an administrator gets every time the system redraws the school attendance boundaries."

"What's going to be left?" Vera Hudson asked. "After the government people go? Could someone pass the potatoes this way, please."

"It's not as bad as the doomsayers make it sound," Chad Jenkins answered. "Do you want gravy?

"The town's keeping the state library. It just doesn't make sense to split it off from the other libraries at the schools, or from the research center. So all the foreign visitors who use those will keep coming."

Missy passed the gravy boat, grinning as she thought of Thanksgiving dinner last year.

Chad kept talking. "And we're getting a sort of consolation prize. The Tech Center's being promoted into the SoTF Technical College, with a lot more faculty and an expanded curriculum. It's going to absorb the teacher training program that's been at the middle school. And the first two, maybe three, years of the Jena/Leahy medical training curriculum. Basic science and nursing through the RN, pre-med. That will be drawing a lot more students into town."

"A lot more rowdiness, it sounds to me like. Solid citizens leaving and flibbertigibbets coming in."

"Mother," Debbie said.

"The music people will stay here, too," Missy said. "A lot of them at least. For a long time. Because of the sound equipment."

"I don't actually see many of the businesses moving out, Mrs. Hudson," Ron said. "Not for years, at least. Especially not the ones heavily dependent on technology. Or electricity and telephones. Just think—the USE left the Federal Reserve here, even when it went national and not just part of the NUS/SoTF government. The Voice of America will stay here. Nobody can move the mine, either."

"What about you and Bill?" Willie Ray asked.

"Lothlorien isn't going anywhere. We'll be starting up branches in other places, sure, but it doesn't make sense to move our headquarters. Especially now that they're pushing the railroad network out, so travel's going to get a lot easier."

Eleanor Jenkins started to laugh.

"What is it Grandma?" Missy asked.

"I suddenly got this improbable vision of Grantville turning into . . . what should I call it? A university town, maybe. Like Charlottesville, or Raleigh."

Ron smiled at her with bland politeness. "The way Dad put it in his last letter was 'Berkeley, not Sacramento.' A hotbed of radical thought, avant-garde literature, art and social customs, and progressive ideas."

Chad spewed coffee all the way across the table. "And I'll be representing this hippie district in the state Senate?"

"How would you describe it, Ed?"

"Pretty much what we expected, back when we first talked about it last summer. There's a general sense of dislocation. It's not just that Grantville wasn't picked as the state capital. It's that it didn't even get picked as the regional capital for Thuringia. We came in as a respectable second to Erfurt, but really not all that far ahead of Weimar and Eisenach."

Chad Jenkins nodded. "Debbie calls it a malaise. That's sort of general. But with some people, it's more than that. People who feel that we've been thoroughly dissed. People who already had personal grievances and this just makes them worse. Take Bryant Holloway—my niece Lenore's husband. He already wasn't happy that she'd gone back to work. When she told him that she intends to keep her job and move to Bamberg when the state government goes, all hell broke loose."

"That doesn't make a speck of sense," Henry Dreeson said. "With Bryant's job, he's out of town more than he's here. He can see her and Weshelle just as often if she's in Bamberg as if she's in Grantville."

Ed shook his head. "Sometimes sense doesn't have anything to do with it. Sometimes I feel like I'm in the middle of one of those 'theater of the absurd' plays. I never liked acting in those."

Veronica Dreeson breathed a sigh of relief when Ed and Chad left. Finally, maybe, Henry would be able to get some rest. Dorothea and Nicholas' baby had turned out to be colicky, to the point that her incessant wailing disturbed Henry's sleep, even when he had his hearing aid out.

She was planning to segregate out a portion of her income from the schools, the payments received at the beginning of the second semester, and lease a trailer for them, just as soon as she could.

She would be very relieved to have a little privacy again. Perhaps most people would not consider a household of eleven persons to be private, but none of the remainder were—clingy—the way Dorothea often was.

She hoped that Nicholas got a promotion fairly soon. It would be very nice if he could pay the rent himself.

Magdeburg

"Cory Joe said I should see you, sir."

Frank Jackson looked up from his desk. Cameron Hinshaw, one of the army's radio operators, was standing in the doorway to Jackson's office. He was looking a little uncomfortable, and seemed to be fidgeting between standing at attention and a more relaxed pose.

Frank had to suppress a smile. He'd seen the same thing lots of times by now. One of the problems with being elevated to the august status of a "general" after the Ring of Fire, when you came from a small town like Grantville, was that most people in town had already known you—often quite well—back when you were just a coal miner and a local union official. Not to mention how many people in Grantville were related to each other, one way or another.

So, when they had to deal with you officially they weren't always sure how to go about it. Even if, like Cameron here, they were soldiers in the same army and had military protocol as a guide.

"What's your problem, son? The radio service getting you down?"

"No. Uh, sir. Not exactly. Do you remember that my mom, Laurie, was married for a while to Gary Haggerty? He's Veda Mae Haggerty's son."

Jackson nodded.

"Well, even though Veda Mae broke the marriage up, and Glenna Sue drowned last spring, we still have Duane to think about. He's my half-brother. So Mom talks to Gary pretty regular. Gary said something about this guy who works for him, a Frenchman named Jacques-Pierre Dumais. If you wouldn't mind looking at this last letter I got from Mom . . ."

Frank sent him on over to Francisco Nasi with it.

Chapter 43

Grantville

Lenore unlocked the door and pushed the stroller through, locking it again behind her.

There was a sound coming from the rec room. Surely she hadn't left the radio on that morning? Leaving Weshelle in the hallway, she slipped out of her boots and walked to the back of the house.

"Bryant?"

He was sitting on the sofa.

"It's me, all right."

"I hadn't expected you."

"Surprise, surprise."

"I'll go get Weshelle out of her stroller. I left her by the door when I heard noise back here."

He followed her. She ignored him as she pulled off the covers and unbuckled the complex of straps.

"Let me put her in the playpen. Then I'll start some supper." Lenore started for the kitchen.

"Since when is the playpen in the kitchen?"

"We keep each other company. I'm in the kitchen quite a bit."

Lenore suddenly remembered that she had left a large batch of papers from work spread out on the table. She'd been working on them evenings, since the report wasn't due until next week. If Bryant saw them . . .

"You can go back and finish catching the news."

"If you don't want me in the kitchen, then maybe that's where I'd better be. Trying to hide something. Maybe a boyfriend after the husband, like you had one before the husband?"

She looked back. "Not likely."

"If you're trying to hide the fact that you went back to work as soon as I left town, give it up. Veda Mae told me. Enjoyed herself, in fact. Like she's been saying, you couldn't wait to show off all that fancy education instead of staying home like a decent mother."

"Weshelle is perfectly fine with Chandra."

She started clearing the papers off the table in the breakfast nook, Weshelle still on one arm. Bryant picked up the transcriptions she had already completed and started tearing them to pieces.

"Stop that!" She grabbed for them.

He pushed her away.

She caught herself on the refrigerator, then backed out of the kitchen. He was still tearing up the papers. Once in the hall, she reached for the phone.

"Wesley is not here," Clara said. "He had to work late. There is a problem?"

"Clara," Lenore said. "I need Dad. I need help now. Bryant is here and he found out I went back to work. Clara, I'm afraid."

"I will come," she said. "I can get there more quickly than I can find him."

"Damn you for a Kraut bitch." Bryant's tone was threatening.

"I have told you nothing but the truth," Clara said stubbornly. "For what you have done, for what you have threatened, she should pick up Weshelle and come away with me now. Right now. This moment."

"She's my wife and it is no business of yours to interfere."

"Why is it not my business? She is the daughter of my husband."

Lenore stood a little helplessly. Clara had read Bryant the riot act. Now, he was starting to focus his generalized anger against Grantville's immigrants against her.

"She is my husband's daughter. She is family. I will call the police if you harm her."

Bryant clenched a fist.

Lenore shrank back. If Bryant hurt Clara, Dad would . . . Dad would be perfectly capable of killing anyone who hurt Clara. Dad had a temper and when it came to Clara he was . . . well, more that way than ever. Protective.

The doorbell rang. She ran so fast that her stocking feet slipped a little on the waxed linoleum in the hall. She saw her boots sitting there and slipped them back on.

Brother Al Green from the Baptist church. Caroline Jones' husband, Trent Dorrman. Standing there, clutching a supply of helpful pamphlets, back once more in another effort to do counseling with Bryant. They had been here before, around New Year's. She didn't have any hopes that their attempts would do any good, but she had never been so happy to see anyone in her life.

"Come in," she said. "Please, please, please, please, please."

The situation had been defused, if that was the word for it. Brother Green was walking Clara back home. Trent had stayed to supper. Nothing but scrambled eggs and fried apples. She hadn't had time to do anything more.

She left them at the table while she took Weshelle into the nursery to get her ready for bed. When she came back, Trent was just going.

She looked at him, thanked him, and asked how Caroline was. Caroline was fine, he said.

Once the door closed, she looked back at Bryant.

It had been the wrong thing to say. Something else to set him off.

"Caroline," he said. "Prim, prissy Caroline. Meddling Caroline. Caroline who sicced Dorrman onto me in the first place."

"I'm sure that she didn't have anything to do with it. She's a Methodist like me, not a Baptist."

"Who else would have? Miss Methodist who refused to obey my wishes and join the Baptist church? Tell me that."

"Maybe Brother Green thought of it by himself. I'll clear off and do the dishes."

He sat there at the table, watching her.

"I guess I'll go on, now. I'll sleep on the cot in Weshelle's room."

"No." He grasped her arm. "Damned if you will."

"Bryant, I don't want this."

"I don't give a fuck what you want."

"I guess I knew that already."

"If you think I'm going to let you near that phone again and sit through a rerun, think again."

"I do not want this."

"You gave up the right to 'don't want' the day you said 'I do.'"

She got up the next morning and got Weshelle ready to take to Chandra's. Got herself ready to go to work.

Chandra came to the door and looked at her. "I still have some cover stick," she said, brushing the small birth mark on her cheek. "If you want to use it. Silly to try to save it for special occasions. I don't go to that many parties. It's probably a little dried up already."

Lenore looked at herself in the hall mirror. "Maybe I'd better."

"You'd better," Chandra said. "You don't want to accidentally run into Dad looking like that. Or have someone tell him."

Bryant stayed in town a couple of weeks this time. He wasn't home much, though. He spent a lot of his time at the fire department, of course. That was why he had come back. For lunches, he was at the Willard, talking to Veda Mae Haggerty and that Dumais man.

As far as Lenore was concerned, that was fine. He was welcome to be anywhere as long as he wasn't home.

She really wished that he would never come home again. She wasn't even unhappy that he spent his evenings at the 250 Club.

He came home at night, though. But she had the cover stick.

He was *not* going to make her quit work.

She was glad when he went back to Naumburg, even though it would only be for ten days. He would be back early in March.

And she managed to avoid her father.

She managed to avoid Lola, too. Lola did not have the kind of temperament to go along with pretending that nothing was wrong. She'd have rung the curtain down, Bryant's sister or not.

"We ought to have done something right away," Donella Hardy said. She looked around at the small group of women who worked with Lenore. "We all suspected that something was wrong. Knew it, really. We ought to have told someone the first time. It's not as if we couldn't tell. Even with the makeup."

"Especially with the makeup," Catrina said. "Lenore doesn't

usually bother to wear any at all. Maybe if we had done something then, it wouldn't have come to this."

"So are we all agreed to be ashamed of ourselves?" Andrea Constantinault had a tendency to take charge of things.

"Yeah," Faye said. "But I think we ought to do something more than that. Let's talk to Judge Riddle and Preston Richards. Maurice Tito. There ought to be something we can do. We've got a couple of weeks to get something in place before Bryant comes back again."

"Preferably something that keeps Wes Jenkins out of it," Linda Beth Rush added. "Wes has a temper. He always has had. Personally, I think we ought to call Lola."

"Lola?" Andrea had been one of the guests at Tom and Rita Simpson's wedding, not someone native to Grantville. Even nearly four years after the Ring of Fire, she didn't always come up with the connections right away.

"Bryant's sister. She works for Jim McNally, the optician."

"Won't she be more likely to try to shield him?"

Linda Beth shook her head. "There were problems with Bryant, even when he was a kid. Torturing kittens kinds of problems. He seemed to be normal enough when he grew up, as far as I know. But he had trouble with a couple of his girlfriends over in Fairmont. Lola's a realist. She'll want Weshelle out of there."

Pastor Kastenmayer looked out over the gathering. It had ended up being a couple of dozen people, even though nearly half of them were his up-time catechumens and their girlfriends. A full half of them, counting sisters of the girlfriends. Walpurga Hercherin had arranged it.

Walpurga was perfectly capable of arranging such a thing. She would be capable of managing a household. A large household, with servants. That, of course, was what she had been expected to do, as the daughter of a village councilman, a *Vollbauer*. What she had been prepared to do, before the destruction of Quittelsdorf. She was standing behind Hedwig Altschulerin, a determined expression on her face.

The opinion she had expressed to the pastor had been utterly pragmatic. "What would you have had her do? An abandoned fiancée, working as a servant in Meiningen, considered fair game by half the men in the town, probably. Jarvis offered her a safe place. He was prepared to bring her here and marry her where it's legal. He's willing to work a job and support her and the baby as best he can. He is prepared to fight to protect her. He has shown that. He's willing to do things for her harder than that, such as going to talk to you. She figures she's well off. She *is* well off. Even with his father and brother making trouble for them, she's a lot better off than if she had stayed south of the *Thueringerwald*. Even if some day the law declares her a concubine rather than a wife, she is still better off."

He had told her that he would contact the chief of police and request riot protection for the occasion of the baptism.

She had looked at him then.

"Mitch and his friends have all been in the army, too. If there's more trouble, they can handle it."

He had repeated that he would call upon the police force.

"If the police handle it, that's well and good. If they don't . . ."

Pastor Kastenmayer had no doubt whatsoever that many of the witnesses to this baptism had come armed.

He had no doubt because Derek Blount had told Ursel Krausin who had told him.

Ursel said that the people at the 250 Club also had no doubt that many of the witnesses to this baptism had come armed. She said that, "the guys define this as a 'deterrent.'"

Thus far, the deterrent seemed to have worked. There were a few men gathered outside the laundry, shouting and making catcalls, but no sign of an attack. Possibly because several policemen were there also, watching them. The chief of police had proved to be most cooperative.

Otherwise, a contingent of Beasleys. The grandfather. Two cousins of the child's father. Everett and, um, Buster. Both with their wives. Everett's wife looked somewhat apprehensive. Buster's wife was very small for an up-timer, but did not look apprehensive at all. Denise, the daughter of this Buster. He had seen her before, at the Christmas Eve play. Accompanied by Gerry Stone, the young candidate for the ministry? She had been with him on Christmas Eve, also. What could the connection between them be? He would have to ask Jonas.

Another girl, the foundling child, Wilhelmina Hugelmair. Minnie, as they called her. Her adoptive father, Benny Pierce. The adoptive father's niece, who cared for the old man.

He would have to remember—he had a request on his desk to write to Dieskau and obtain all the information available concerning the circumstances under which she had been found abandoned. She told him that the "birthday" she had given the school, the only one she had, was neither her date of birth nor her date of baptism. It was the date on which she had been found.

She could not provide even the date of her baptism. The pastor at Dieskau, realizing that she was already several months old, had not been willing to risk the possibility of rebaptism, even conditional, since she would almost certainly have been baptized somewhere else, shortly after birth. Anabaptism was a grave sin, Pastor Kastenmayer acknowledged.

There would certainly be an entry about it all in the church books there, and there should be one in the city council records as well when she was bound out the first time.

Gerry Stone's brother Ron, with a young woman whom the pastor did not recognize. Otherwise, Jonas Justinus Muselius, Jonas' fiancée Ronella Koch, his own wife Salome and his daughter Maria Blandina.

He would not be surprised if the Beasley contingent was also armed. He had not been informed in regard to this, but he would not be surprised.

He began the liturgy. The father wished to name the child Viana, in honor of his mother. Lutheranism had no requirement for biblical names or saints' names, although they were customary. The infant would be Viana.

After the baptism, the party went to a tavern called the City Hall Café for food. Some of the police followed them. Two remained behind, out of sight. To "keep an eye out," the chief had said, in case anyone attempted to vandalize the laundry. This resulted in three arrests.

According to Jonas, the connection between Gerry Stone and Denise Beasley was "friend."

"Friend?" Pastor Kastenmayer cocked his head, thinking that many young men were diverted away from their academic aspirations by inappropriate . . . friendships.

Jonas nodded. "Gerry says that the last thing in the world that

Denise needs is one more guy hitting on her. That she gets too much of that already."

Jonas paused. "Ronella confirms this. She has heard it from the other teachers, now that she is at the middle school. Denise has very few friends. Only Minnie Hugelmair, really, and she has been in Grantville for less than two years. Gerry and Denise have known one another since they were small children."

"Very well," Kastenmayer said. "He is her friend."

"He is also," Jonas said, "or had the reputation of being, before his experiences in Italy, a very pugnacious young man. The up-timers believe that this is a quality often associated with red hair."

"I have not received any complaints about his behavior from the rector of the Latin School in Rudolstadt."

Nobody ever accepted public responsibility for the series of stink bombs that forced the 250 Club to close for business the evening after the Beasley baptism. The police located no clues whatsoever. Pastor Kastenmayer heard subsequently that most Grantvillers assumed that they were retribution for the effort to vandalize the laundry.

Opinion was divided on the merits of this action. But it did not seem to be divided very much concerning the most likely culprit.

Pastor Kastenmayer tried to reconcile in his mind the juxtaposition of "Gerry Stone, devout student," and "Gerry Stone, chemical saboteur." It was not easy.

Part Eight

March 1635

To wage by force or guile eternal war,
Irreconcilable, to our grand foe

Chapter 44

Haarlem, Netherlands

Velma stared out the window of the villa, down the driveway, into endless vistas of flat, flat, flat.

Her four resident sisters-in-law sat in a semi-circle behind her, chattering.

Laurent was away on business again, which meant that he would be eating things that were bad for him.

The baby was starting to become more real. The kind of real that required her to visit the necessary what seemed like every fifteen minutes.

The thought that if Laurent popped an artery one of these days, there was no guarantee at all that his family would provide support for the baby was becoming more real, too.

Much less that they would continue to provide support for her.

Aeltje was sympathetic, though. Aeltje understood about horoscopes.

Aeltje had also married into the faculty at the University of Leiden. And Aeltje's sons were studying science.

Everybody at Laurent's party had loved the lava lamps.

The high-ups in Dutch society might actually pay to have lava lamps of their own.

With hers as a model, the letter that she'd gotten from Pam

to help them, and the ability of Aeltje's sons to do things in laboratories, and someone to do the work, could she start manufacturing lava lamps?

A girl had to take care of herself, after all.

Frankfurt am Main

Isaac de Ron concluded that Locquifier and Ouvrard were gone. Which meant that all of Ducos' Huguenot fanatics were gone. Out of the inn *Zum Weissen Schwan*, definitely. Out of Frankfurt, probably. Out of the USE? Perhaps.

First he called upon Soubise. Who called in Sandrart.

Then, since Laurent Mauger was in town, they called in Mauger.

He was thoroughly shocked to discover who his real employer had been. Pleased also, of course, in regard to his new employer. Mauger was a man who respected status and nobody in the Huguenot diaspora had more status than Duke Henri de Rohan.

He didn't know much to tell them, however, beyond the instructions he had conveyed to Dumais in Grantville, which Soubise already knew about in any case.

Mauger agreed to continue to channel communications to Ducos in Scotland. If any more should arrive in Haarlem, he stipulated. All of the ones he had already transmitted had come from or been addressed to Locquifier, after all.

And he did not know where Michel Ducos was. The sailor who carried the letters back and forth from Haarlem just picked them up and left them at a drop point.

That provided Soubise with the name of a tavern in a Scottish port. Nothing more.

Grantville

Matthias Bruller, a guest at the Willard Hotel, presented himself as a pleasant and unobtrusive man. He was mildly disappointed that the room to which the desk clerk assigned him did not provide a view of the bridges, but it wasn't worth complaining about. He made only a couple of casual remarks about being a tourist—a man involved in the mutton trade from Strassburg to

Silesia. Not that he ever had been, but he had learned enough from Ouvrard during the years of their association that he could fake it, easily enough. In times of peace, when the economy was going about its business, the city of Strassburg, population about twenty thousand, approximately the size of Grantville now, figured on consuming about four thousand oxen per year. Grantville, given its up-time citizens' fondness for beef, slaughtered many more. By contrast, Strassburg slaughtered and consumed about a thousand sheep per day. Grantville, although the down-timers ate mutton, of course, slaughtered less than half that many. It was not a place of intense interest to sheep merchants.

He was a merchant, detouring from Erfurt, come to see the sights for a couple of days. He had no reason to go near the local slaughterhouses.

Jacques-Pierre Dumais was feeling reasonably satisfied. Grantville had become a medium-sized city for Germany. About twenty thousand residents. Many of whom, for all practical purposes, were transients. Not refugees, any longer, as they had been during the first months after the Ring of Fire. Those had either settled down permanently or, with removal of the armies from central Germany, gone home to save what could be saved of their former homes, farms, shops, or jobs.

Now there were transients, who came to use the libraries or take a course or two in the schools. Plus tourists, whose stays were even shorter. It was not conspicuous that a couple of hundred people were here today who had not been here two or three weeks ago. They merely walked in, one at a time, like any other persons looking for work, looking to buy materials, carrying out an errand for an employer.

Bryant Holloway had not only found many of them for him, but had also provided the unexpected service of reserving a block of spaces at the workmen's hostel, making the deposit under the pretense that there would be a batch of guys in town for training the last few days of February and first few days of March. Since the fire department had made similar reservations before, it did not attract any particular attention.

With that, Jacques-Pierre had been able to find places for the remainder to stay with reasonable ease.

Not, of course, with the people who frequented the 250 Club.

The people he needed to house were Germans. "Krauts." People whom they would not invite to stay in their homes.

Rather, he placed his recruits with people whom he had come to know on his regular garbage collection route. People who might have a spare room temporarily and be happy to earn a little extra money. That was better, in fact. The police watched those persons who regularly came to the 250 Club. They did not watch ordinary people, many of them down-timers themselves.

Sometimes it was rather difficult to make the most of all the different preferences and prejudices in this town. He could only do his best.

Jacques-Pierre reached into his pocket. He was not entirely certain why he had taken the course and obtained his citizenship papers, but he had.

Madame Haggerty was very proud of him. She had served as his witness when he signed the oath of allegiance.

That pride was why she had given him permission to store some materials of his own in her garage, along with the extra supplies for Garbage Guys that her son Gary, his boss, kept there. This was a great boon. Placards, especially when mounted on sticks and stiffened against the wind, were very bulky. He didn't have room in his own trailer to keep all the materials that would be needed to put on the demonstration at the hospital.

Veda Mae introduced Jacques-Pierre to the two young women sitting with her, Mademoiselle Hardesty and Mademoiselle Jenkins. He recognized both names and faces, of course, but appreciated the introduction.

To Mademoiselle Hardesty, he extended his most sincere felicitations upon the anticipated birth of a new sister or brother in the Netherlands.

Pam gaped at him. "Mom's pregnant? Again? At *her* age?"

He was mildly surprised that her mother had not already informed her. He had not thought that Madame Hardesty was a woman who felt that her daughter needed to be spared in regard to matters of such delicacy. The inheritance complications alone would, in the absence of a proper marriage contract, affect not only Mauger's children but also those of his wife.

For the rest, her reaction was so parallel to what his own had been that it was almost amusing.

"You're sure?" Pam asked.

"The arrival of the child is expected in August. Your stepfather is blissfully happy."

"I . . . Well, thank you very much. I'll have to let Cory Joe and Susan know."

"It makes sense, Missy," Pam said. "Where else would he be likely to hide his records that no one else would look?"

"In garbage cans?" Missy was very doubtful.

"He's a garbage man. And if you watch the Garbage Guys doing their collections, people mostly put their things out on the curb, they way they did up-time. But for some of the old people, who have trouble getting the cans out when there's snow and ice, the guy running along beside the wagon goes behind the house, wrestles the can out, dumps it, and takes it back. That guy is Jacques-Pierre. All he would have to do, if he wanted to hide something, is put a couple of extra cans with tight fitting lids behind one or two of those houses. Cans that he doesn't bring out and dump into the wagon. Who's going to go around town counting people's garbage cans?"

Missy looked at her friend dubiously, suspecting where this might be leading. "We are?"

"Not if we don't have to," was Pam's answer. "I was in class all the way through school with Marcie Haggerty. Her brother Blake's a couple of years younger, and he's a policeman now."

"Yeah. He graduated with Ron and me in the accelerated program."

"Let's tell Ron and Cory Joe what we think and see if Don Francisco can talk Preston Richards into letting Blake look in his grandmother's garbage cans. If that doesn't work, though . . ." Pam frowned. "If they won't assign someone else to do it, if they think we're nuts for suggesting it, or if there's nothing in those particular cans—then, yeah, I guess we are."

Blake Haggerty reported that there was nothing in the garbage can behind his grandmother's house except garbage. He had avoided all things associated with such formalities as search warrants simply by dropping by and offering to take out the garbage while he was there, which gave him a perfectly good reason to take the lid off her garbage can.

Then he said, "But."

"But what?"

"Dad has a whole batch of stuff belonging to the Garbage Guys stored in her garage. It's locked. I looked through the window. There are three more garbage cans in there."

"We can do it Sunday morning," Pam said. "That makes sense. Veda Mae does go to church every Sunday. She leaves in time to catch the nine o'clock brunch and say a few cutting sentences about people who aren't there. Then she sits in on the Bible class for adults to make sure that if Simon Jones says anything liberal that she doesn't agree with, she'll be there to correct him. Then she goes to the eleven o'clock service to check to see if the organist is playing any modern hymns. Then she goes out for lunch to make sure she has a chance to spread a little vicious gossip before she goes to work."

"Do I detect some sarcasm in your description?" Missy asked.

"Maybe a trifle. Veda Mae palls on closer acquaintance." Pam made a face at her younger friend. Missy could come up with an amazing number of excuses not to accompany her to the Willard and talk to Veda Mae. A little of Veda Mae had gone a really long way with Missy.

"But it's accurate. That's what she does. She'll be out of the way. Neither of us goes to church, so we won't be missed if we don't show up. It's a perfectly ordinary old garage. No foundation. Just posts stuck into the ground, and the weatherboarding starting to rot where it gets damp at the bottom. We sneak along the alley where the snowbanks are still piled up where people shoveled and make like Peter Rabbit. Wriggle, wriggle, under the boards. We could probably even pull one loose, if it's too tight a fit. She'll blame it on raccoons. People blame everything peculiar that happens in sheds and outbuildings on raccoons. It's one thing that the Ring of Fire hasn't changed."

Chapter 45

Grantville, March 4, 1635

"I called Ron and told him."

"Missy, this is one thing at least that we could have done on our own. You don't have to tell Ron everything. Do you phone him at bedtime and tell him you're brushing your teeth?"

"No. The upstairs extension is out in the hall, so it's not really handy for pillow talk."

Pam stared. As she often did, Missy had taken a purely hypothetical query at face value. If someone asked her a question, she would provide an answer. Or try her best, at least. Born to be a reference librarian. She'd found her niche. "Okay. Why did you tell Ron?"

"So somebody would know where we were going. I couldn't very well tell Mom and Dad that we intended to go digging around in Veda Mae's garage this morning, and you're always supposed to check in before you go somewhere, so people can find you if an emergency comes up. Just to say where you're going, who you're with, and when you'll be back."

Pam nodded. In spite of their genuine friendship, the chasm, the abyss, between the way Chad and Debbie had brought up Missy and the way Velma had brought her up yawned very wide at times.

"Ron thought it was sensible," Missy said a little defensively.

"He and his brothers were always expected to check in with their dad before they went off somewhere, too."

Pam stopped pulling on her boots. It . . . it actually *hurt* a little, somewhere, to realize that for all the reputation Tom Stone had as a hippie before the Ring of Fire, that even his kids had been more protected and sheltered and cared about than she and Cory Joe had been. Much less Tina and Susan.

She shouldn't have left home when she did. At the time, all she was interested in was self-preservation. She had to get out, she had to get out, she had to get out. Maybe—maybe if she had stayed, Tina wouldn't have turned into the kind of risk taker that the little sister who had drowned at the quarry last spring had been.

"Pam," Missy said. "Pam, what's the matter?"

She blinked back the tears. "Nothing, really. I was thinking about Tina, for some reason."

Missy gave her a quick hug.

Pam stood up. "Let's get going."

Missy stopped, her boots squeaking on the packed snow. "There are people in there!"

"There can't be. Why would anyone be there?"

"I don't know. But there are. Lots of them. Well, four or five, at least. One of them has a handcart out in the driveway and they're loading things into it." Missy braced one hand on Veda Mae's back fence.

"Blake did say that his father stores stuff there, for the Garbage Guys. Is it Gary?"

"I can't tell from here. We're going to have to get a little closer."

"Why don't I go out and walk on the street? That way, I can look down the driveway with a curious expression on my face. Sneaking closer from an alley is the kind of thing that's suspicious by definition, but walking down the street is something that anyone can do." Pam turned back the way they had come.

Missy stood there, wishing that she wasn't by herself. She thought of sitting down on one of the piles of snow, but the sun was warm enough that it was starting to melt on top. Ugh.

The men were still loading the cart.

✧ ✧ ✧

It seemed to be taking an awfully long time for Pam to walk around the block. The blocks in this part of town weren't all that big. Missy looked at her watch. After a while, she looked again. It was taking way too long for Pam to walk around the block.

Jacques-Pierre Dumais was feeling a certain amount of distress.

It was very unfortunate that Mademoiselle Pam, the daughter of that appalling Madame Hardesty, had come along just as Léon Boucher dropped an armload of the placards prepared for use at the demonstration against the hospital. She had paused, looked at the slogans, and said, "What on earth?"

Luckily she had not seen him, he thought. He had still been well within the garage. Compared to the sunlight on the snow, it was dark there. It was particularly fortunate since Boucher had panicked, run to the end of the driveway, and grabbed her, pulling the navy blue knit hat she was wearing down over her face. She had tried to jerk away, but her feet had slipped on the wet snow. Fortunately, she had not screamed. She had opened her mouth, but Léon, an experienced street fighter if not very bright, had jammed part of the knit hat into it with his fist as he dragged her into the garage.

Dumais dropped into the Rochellais patois of their childhood. No one else in this town would understand a word of it. "Fool. Idiot," he mouthed under his breath. "Her mother is a friend of the woman who owns this house. What did you think you were doing? You could have ignored her. Or said something casual and she would have gone on. You will be out of town by this afternoon. It wouldn't have mattered that she saw you."

"I do not believe in coincidences," Boucher answered.

"That is because you make them impossible. What could she have done? Now we must gag her and leave her here, because we have brought attention to ourselves." He gestured impatiently to the other three men. Turpin and a couple of the hired Germans. They had picked up the signs that Boucher had dropped and put them on the cart, but since then had been standing there like fish with their mouths open. Common day laborers, men with no initiative. "Finish loading the placards. I will be with you in a moment."

"We can start without you. At the end of the street, which way should we turn?"

"Toward the right."

He bound Mademoiselle Hardesty's hands firmly, placed an additional blindfold over her eyes on top of the ski mask, and pushed a rag into her mouth, leaving the knit hat in place over her mouth first. Then he dropped her on a pile of lumber and tied her feet. She would be secure enough until the day's activities were over.

Releasing her without either harming her or having her identify him would be . . . more complex. He would deal with that problem when the time came. If all was to go smoothly today, the demonstration planned for Leahy Medical Center needed to start very soon. He pulled the garage door shut and put the padlock back on as Boucher turned to follow the men with the handcart.

Missy looked at her watch again. The men were gone. She had seen the handcart and some men cross the far end of the alley, headed toward Route 250. Pam hadn't come back. Missy hoped that she hadn't slipped and fallen. The thin layer of melt that was developing on top of the packed snow was pretty treacherous.

She had better go around and see. Pam was more important than crawling into Veda Mae's garage in pursuit of some probably imaginary espionage papers. If she'd sprained her ankle or something, they'd have to get help. She started back up the alley, the way Pam had gone.

Nothing. No sign of her.

Pam wouldn't have had any reason to go beyond Veda Mae's driveway. Missy stopped and looked just as Dumais started to turn.

"Excuse me," she asked. "Have either of you gentlemen seen another girl? She was coming down this way and got ahead of me."

As quickly as possible, Jacques-Pierre faced back to the garage door and pulled down the ski mask he was wearing. Involuntarily, he closed his eyes and placed his fingers against his temples. Such a headache, *la migraine*, to have on an important occasion, the sun glaring on the snow and the day scarcely begun! He should have realized that where one of the girls was, it was only likely that the other would not be far away. He turned.

Léon, you fool! Don't go dashing at her like that! Don't make threatening gestures!

Too late.

Missy opened her mouth and prepared to shriek at the top of her lungs.

Jacques-Pierre could tell exactly what the girl was planning to do. Among other things he had done in the course of his time in Grantville, in an effort to understand these up-timers, he had attended recreational league sports events. He had observed Mademoiselle Jenkins' coaching. Her voice had carrying power.

"Léon, you idiot, stop it," he exploded, keeping his voice down in so far as he could. "We're going to be late." Embellished with considerable profanity. He dashed after the other man, grabbed his shoulder, and dragged him down the street in the direction the men had taken the handcart.

Missy stood there, feeling a little silly for having almost screamed. But she still didn't see Pam anywhere. She stood there for a moment, undecided. Then she walked up Veda Mae's driveway, cupped her hands on either side of her eyes, and waited a moment for her pupils to adjust so she could see inside the garage through the dirty windowpane in the door.

That was what she was doing when Ron came up behind her. She jumped about a foot when he asked, "Missy? What's going on?"

"I have never been so glad to see anybody in my whole entire life," she answered. "I think I'm a damsel in distress. Or, at least, Pam is. Help me rescue her. There's something really weird going on this morning."

Ron felt distinctly relieved. He had felt very foolish all the way as he ran from Lothlorien into town after she had phoned him, with every footstep that slogged through the snow suspecting that he would be greeted with, "What do you think I am, anyway? Some kind of an incompetent ditz?"

They looked at the padlock, decided it was substantial, and reverted to Plan A, which involved crawling into the garage from the back. Except Ron decided that by this time there wasn't much point in pretending to be a raccoon. He simply grabbed a couple of the old boards and yanked them off by main force, stripping the rusty nails.

"Pam," Missy was saying. "Are you okay?"

Pam swung her feet to the floor and sat up. "I have a mouth

full of acrylic fuzz that tastes like hair, that's how I am. What in hell was going on here?"

"I don't have any idea, but I think we ought to tell the police."

There weren't any police to be had. The dispatcher took the information when they phoned from Pam's apartment, but said that this was going to be very low priority. Probably somebody would get back to them tomorrow.

Chapter 46

Grantville

“There are twenty-five or so men gathered in the parking lot at Leahy Medical Center,” Gary Lambert said calmly to the police dispatcher, “with another group about the same size by the emergency entrance.” The business manager was reluctant to sound alarmist. “They arrived about nine o'clock this morning and have been there for approximately three-quarters of an hour now, yelling anti-vaccination slogans and waving signs. Thus far, they have not interfered with traffic into and out of the building.”

“If they have been there that long, why did you decide to call us now?”

“Because other people are joining them. The original group came together, had a leader, divided quietly, and appeared to be a disciplined protest. We don't enjoy that sort of thing, but we really have to put up with it. The regular police patrols swung by, took a look at the ones in the parking lot, and moved on. I assumed that this meant they shared my feeling that there was no immediate cause for alarm.”

“What has changed?”

“Quite a few additional demonstrators are coming now. Not in a single group, but in smaller ones, three or four together. They are not waving prepared signs. They already outnumber the original party and they are still arriving. Instead of clustering in one or two places, in the parking lot and by the emergency entrance, they are scattering out here and there around the exterior of the building. A half dozen by the main entrance; eight by the pathway from the laundry to the service entrance; about the same number by the pathway from the bakery to the service entrance."

"I'll send a couple of cars that way."

"Warn the cars that something is starting to happen. Several of the smaller groups that were still out on Highway 250 are coming together now, behind the original demonstrators in the parking lot. They are reaching under their cloaks and bringing out signs that protest the practice of doing autopsies as a part of medical education. The slogans they are beginning to shout include 'sacrilege,' of course, and predictions that as a result of these, at the time of the Last Judgment, people will be rising from the dead maimed and incomplete, denied the glorified bodies promised in the resurrection."

The police dispatcher squawked.

"This isn't something caused by Grantville. It was a controversy that existed between the medical schools and the yahoos downtime, before we ever arrived. That's why so many autopsies were done on condemned criminals. And why medical students were practicing grave robbing two centuries after the 1630s. It's an emotional thing. Emotionally very highly charged."

Gary paused. "Very bad theology, of course, but very highly charged."

"What's the estimated total number of demonstrators at the moment?"

"Let me check." He looked up from the phone. "What's the count, Maria? All sides of the building?" Then he spoke into the headphone. "Forty-three more within the last ten minutes. With others still coming along the highway. They are attempting to block the first patrol car you dispatched from entering the parking lot. The total is over a hundred and fifty now, including the original fifty or so, but they are moving around enough that it's hard for our people to get an accurate count."

"I'll notify Chief Richards right away. We'll get a full unit out to you as soon as possible."

"I think you should indicate that this may become urgent. I now have reports that a few of the newest arrivals are apparently preparing to take signs out from under their cloaks."

✧ ✧ ✧

Jacques-Pierre Dumais was seriously worried. This was to have been an orderly, planned demonstration. He had made that very clear to the hired demonstrators.

He had no idea who these other people were or why they had arrived.

Of course, there were always certain hazards when organizing this type of thing, given the sort of people one had to use. Even the two Huguenots Deneau had brought and assigned to assist him weren't the sharpest knives in anyone's drawer.

The miscalculation this time, although Dumais had no way of knowing it, was that two of the men contacted by Bryant Holloway early in his circuit of the towns of Thuringia were genuine anti-autopsy fanatics. When they had heard that there was to be a demonstration against the sacrilegious practices of the up-time hospital on a certain date, they had not only come to Grantville themselves, but had brought their friends.

Jacques-Pierre was cautious by nature. He found it prudent to withdraw from the scene. It was not as if his presence had been conspicuous to begin with. He had merely been standing among the rear of the first group in the parking lot. He crossed to the other side of Route 250 and stood back from the highway, near the corner of a building. Corners were good places to stand. In a pinch, a person could always go around the corner and emerge somewhere else.

From his location at the rear of the original group, he had been providing instructions to Friedrich Klick from Halle, who was playing the role of leader in the anti-vaccination demonstration. When Dumais disappeared without leaving any guidance as to what his puppet should do next, Klick began to panic. He had no knowledge about the additional men who were arriving, no contacts among them, and no way to get them organized. He slipped to the side of his group, walked backwards for several steps, and then ran. Several others of the original fifty or so followed him. Others surged forward to take their places.

By the time the Grantville police were fully in place around Leahy, there were an estimated two hundred fifty participants in the demonstration.

Two or three smaller bands had attempted to force their way into the building.

Inside, the staff was evacuating all patients into center rooms.

Outside, the police had taken ranks at all the entrances. The police dispatchers had contacted the fire department and advised them not to bring ill or injured people to the hospital. Traffic on Route 250 had been blocked in both directions. The trolley to and from Rudolstadt had to turn around several blocks to the east of the hospital and return from there.

Two hours after Gary Lambert's first call, the demonstration at the hospital had nearly the entire on-duty Grantville police force fully occupied. Not all of them. Jürgen Neubert and Marvin Tipton were down by the Y where the bridges came together, since someone had called in a disturbance in front of Cora's. One of those anti-Semitic ranters who'd been showing up in several nearby towns the last couple of weeks had finally made it to Grantville, it seemed.

Angela Baker, on dispatch, was contacting those off-duty to come in.

Police spokesmen with bullhorns attempted to persuade the demonstrators to disperse. A call for the leader of the group produced Klick. He came around from behind a parked wagon at the edge of the lot and was quite willing to speak to the police, but it turned out that his main wish was that they should get him away from the site.

As he said, plainly, he had, after all, been hired to come and do this. As had everyone who had come with him. He would be quite willing to tell the *Polizei* everything he knew in return for the favor of being removed from the scene. More than willing to do it. Happy to do it.

When the rest of the anti-vaccination demonstrators saw him being placed in a police car, they moved toward that side of the parking lot. This allowed the anti-autopsy demonstrators to take up a more central position, directly in front of the main entrance.

A shoving, pushing, and shouting match developed at the side. No one seemed to be able to get the idea across that Klick was being evacuated at his own wish.

"It looks to me," Bill Magen said, "that a batch more of these guys are getting ready to pull out their signs and start waving them. They're twitching at their cloaks."

"Moving forward, too," the officer next to him answered. That was Karl Maurer, who was scowling fiercely. "I don't like this. It's a good hospital. When my son was so sick in the winter, coughing, they brought him here. The physicians cured him."

A man moved to the front. "We demand that you surrender to us the surgeon who violates the bodies of the dead!"

Many of the demonstrators reached under their cloaks.

"Those aren't signs!" Magen called. "Those are guns."

Ralph Onofrio, the senior man on duty, moved forward to try to calm the situation.

The more aggressive autopsy protesters began to move forward from the perimeter, pushing the earlier anti-vaccination demonstrators who had not moved to the side already toward the hospital. One man lost his balance and fell forward. Several, trying to escape the readied guns to their rear, ran over him as they were pushed in the direction of the hospital entrance.

The smaller groups by the bakery and laundry moved toward the main entrance, pulling weapons as they came.

Then the whole crowd moved forward a few steps, several of the demonstrators readying their guns. Within five minutes, the demonstration had become an armed confrontation.

Onofrio was still calling orders when Maurer, the policeman whose croupy child had been treated at the hospital, fired. Most of the other down-time policemen, without waiting for orders, followed suit.

The Grantville police had notably more firepower than the demonstrators, not to mention better body armor. Still, it was not exactly a massacre. There were many more armed demonstrators than policemen and they did not hesitate to shoot back.

A significant number of the unarmed anti-vaccination demonstrators were caught between the two armed groups.

It lasted quite a while. Several of the armed demonstrators had remained around the edges of the parking lot. They sheltered behind vehicles, fences, landscaping, just as they would have done in their home villages if fighting a delaying action against a marauding mercenary band.

The firing continued for quite some time as the police attempted to disengage enough of their people ringing the building to get behind the scattered shooters.

As long as the shooting continued, it was impossible for anyone to try to deal with those who had fallen dead or wounded outside the building.

Several of the panicked, unarmed original hired anti-vaccination demonstrators, caught between the two sources of fire, managed to break through the police line, seeking refuge in the hospital's main lobby, which started a second sphere of action as the hospital staff attempted to prevent them from pushing farther into the building.

"Oh God, Marvin," Jürgen Neubert cried out to his partner, who was standing on the sidewalk by Cora's. "He's dead. It came in over the car radio. Ralph's dead. Angela, Angela, what is happening?"

"The demonstration. The one at the hospital. There were other groups, off to the side. Press is on his way over there. Marvin, I've got to tell you. We fired the first shot. Bill Magen is dead, too. I know that for sure."

Marvin Tipton grabbed the hand-held.

"Who fired?"

"Maurer. It was Karl Maurer who shot first. It's all so confused, still."

"Hang in there, Angela. We're heading over."

"What do you have, Franz?" Jürgen asked.

"Three more of yours, here. Besides Officer Onofrio. Maurer. And both of the Hansens. Shruer and Schultz. The two ex-mercenaries. The ones who were always together. There are several more wounded policemen. They have taken them inside the hospital, Erika Fleischer said. She is okay. Not hurt."

"Perps? Ah, demonstrators. How many?"

"Seventeen here."

Here was the morgue.

"Inside?"

"I am not sure. Many. Almost forty, maybe. There were others who could still run, and did."

Pam, Ron, and Missy came out onto the sidewalk in front of Pam's apartment when they heard a shot. Followed by lots of shots.

The gunfire wasn't really close, so they stood there, listening.

"Over toward the hospital," Ron said.

"I think I can guess why we're low priority for the police," Pam answered. "Should we grab our guns and head over there?"

"The dispatcher didn't sound flustered or say anything about getting the reserves out when we talked to her," Ron answered. "We'd probably be more in the way than anything else. Let's concentrate on writing up every single thing that happened to you girls this morning, in order. So you'll have it when they do get around to talking to you."

"Including that we were planning to sneak into Veda Mae's garage?"

"I think we can leave that out," Ron said. "We can tell that to Cory Joe, for Don Francisco, but as far as Preston Richards and the Grantville police force are concerned, let's start with Pam walking down the street and seeing the guys unloading the signs out of Veda Mae's garage."

Pam was about halfway through her part of the narrative when she stopped writing. "Do you know what we forgot to do while we where there?"

"What?"

"We forgot to look in the extra garbage cans. They're why we went in the first place."

"Well, we can't very well go back now. There are people swarming all over the place because of that shooting over by the hospital."

"Maybe we can try again next Sunday morning."

Ron and Missy looked at her. "Pam," Ron said, "by next Sunday, whatever was there is likely to be long gone."

"Then maybe we should go back now."

This time the other two looked at one another with the mutual unspoken feeling that Pam was maybe getting a little overinvolved in this project.

"I don't think so," Missy said.

Chapter 47

Grantville, March 4, 1635

The batch of genuine anti-Jewish fanatics whom Gui Ancelin and the Frankfurt anti-Semites had garnered from more than a dozen towns in the SoTF, mostly from Franconia, headed for the synagogue under the leadership of Fortunat Deneau. The action started as he had designed it, with a few people standing around a man who was giving a harangue on the pattern of those that the agitators had been giving in other towns throughout the SoTF in recent weeks. Harangues which the SoTF administration did not like but which it had to tolerate under its own free speech laws. The small group would then attract a few more spectators, gradually growing in size. The only thing that might make it conspicuous would be that all the spectators were male, but Deneau regarded that as unavoidable. Women in such crowds were ordinarily drawn from the town where the riot was to occur, but the public opinion in Grantville was such that if there were local anti-Semites, they did not ordinarily proclaim their opinions openly.

This harangue, unlike the ones that had been delivered in other towns, drew the attention of Henry Dreeson and Enoch Wiley, who were standing and talking outside of the Presbyterian church after the end of the eleven o'clock service. The service had run late because of communion. Enoch never saw any reason to abbreviate his sermon on communion Sundays.

As quickly as possible—which was no longer very quickly, in Henry's case—they walked over to stand in front of the synagogue door. As the harangue continued, both of them spoke to the gathering crowd. Henry, basically, tried reasoning. Wiley preached the seventeenth-century Presbyterian line, in no way variant from his own twentieth-century beliefs, that predestination was all and that if God wanted the Jews to convert, they would. Since they had not done so, this constituted evidence that they still had a part to play in the Divine Plan.

Deneau had not prepared for this development, having had no way to anticipate it. As he tried to think how best to proceed next, Léon Boucher showed up with a message from Dumais. The Grantville police force was now fully occupied at the hospital.

That was his signal. They would have to proceed. He sent in the remainder of the actual anti-Jewish fanatics, the ones Weitz had brought from Frankfurt am Main and other cities of the Rhine and Main rivers. A substantial number of them were veterans of prior anti-Jewish riots. He reinforced them with those from the nearby Thuringian towns who had been standing around as "spectators" up to that point. These larger numbers coalesced around the haranguer. Meininger, his name was, from Schleusingen.

By the time they were in place, however, the circumstances changed again. A number of men came running down the street shoving the table-and-chair pushcart that belonged to the Presbyterian Church. They had dragged it out from the education wing, with the piano from the old "yahoo shack" on it and Inez Wiley riding along.

They were followed by a group of women who, he noted, might for the most part be described as "advanced in middle age." The Reverend Simon Jones, had he been present, would have informed Deneau that they were "front-pew battleaxes." More specifically, they were the board of directors and a couple of committee chairmen of the Grantville chapter of the Red Cross, which had been starting a meeting in the Presbyterian church's education wing.

The men pushed the cart up next to Mayor Dreeson and Reverend Wiley. Once they set the brakes on it, Inez Wiley started to pound out a selection of hymns that she deemed most appropriate to the occasion. The Red Cross ladies started to sing.

"Ye chosen seed of Israel's race,
Ye ransomed from the fall."

Brillard stood on the bridge toward the rear of the demonstration, leaning on a balustrade and looking mildly curious. It had been his intention to carry out a simple act, precisely in accord with Locquifier's instructions. While apparently watching the man delivering the harangue, he had in fact been watching the mayor as he stood in front of the Presbyterian church. He had intended simply to shoot him there.

That his target had moved to the front of the synagogue was something of a complication. However, the opportunity was still reasonable, even if his line of shot was no longer quite so clean because of the cluster of women on the steps. Perhaps he could even add some confusion to the scene by killing the minister as well. Certainly, killing the town's Calvinist clergyman should serve to divert suspicion away from the Huguenots, while simultaneously cementing the idea that Richelieu, the persecutor of French Protestantism, was the instigator.

Brillard pulled an up-time carbine out from under his long cloak, took Dreeson and Wiley down with two quick shots, dropped the gun into the creek, and calmly walked away.

He disliked losing the gun. It was a marvelous weapon and had cost them quite a bit to obtain. But it would be too dangerous now to keep it. Even a small carbine was not so easy to hide, once a real search got underway.

Inez Wiley reacted to her husband's fall by crashing a chord on the piano and launching into *Jerusalem the Golden*. The attackers, fanatics and goons alike, pulled their weapons out from under their clothes. Few had guns. The fanatics had been told that the point of this attack was to do damage to the synagogue rather than to kill people. Nobody expected that there would be any significant number of Jews in the building on a Sunday at noon. It had generally been overlooked that this day was the fourteenth of Adar, 5395, the festival of Purim, which celebrated the deliverance of the Jews in Persia from the plots of Haman the Agagite.

The significance of the date had escaped Locquifier's attention entirely, since his main interest was not in the attack at all, but in using it as a red herring to distract attention while Brillard carried out the assassination of Dreeson. Neither Ducos nor Delerue nor their Huguenot followers had anything in particular against Grantville's Jews. Their hatred was focused on Cardinal Richelieu, who was to be blamed for the attack.

The date had not occurred to the fanatics, either, in Frankfurt or elsewhere. If it had, they might have harbored a few thoughts of satisfaction along the general lines of double jeopardy, that where Haman had failed, they would succeed in their attack. However, most of them were sufficiently ignorant concerning the objects of their hatred that they had no knowledge of the Jewish calendar whatsoever. The Book of Esther was rarely included in their favorite reading matter in any case, since it tended to portray the Jews in a far too heroic light. Quite a few of them suspected God of extremely poor judgment in having selected His chosen people.

They had therefore brought mauls, axes, sledgehammers, and other implements designed mainly to destroy material objects. One of the hired goons closest to the synagogue steps attacked the piano with a sledgehammer, mainly to get it out of the way. It was blocking a significant portion of their access to the facade. It was only a small spinet type, comparatively light and easy to move around on a dolly. His second blow was sufficiently furious to tip it over. It landed on one of Inez Wiley's legs, knocking her off the piano bench and pinning her down.

The remainder of the attackers launched themselves at the building, aiming first at the expensive glass windows. The men who had been handling the pushcart grabbed metal folding chairs from it, wielding them first as shields around the bodies of Dreeson and Wiley but then, on the principle of "let the dead bury their dead," moving over to try to keep the mob away from Inez and the Red Cross women.

The assault started to waver. These were hardened thugs and street rioters, but they had never previously experienced the form of aural assault created by a dozen or so American ladies with nasal twangs launching themselves into "We're Marching Upward to Zion" without a piano to keep them on key—not necessarily because they were objectively brave, but because Inez was pinned down by part of the shattered piano and the rest of them were simply too stubborn to abandon her. They kept going *a capella*.

Deneau came forward and rallied the attackers.

"What on earth is going on?" Minnie, having once more experienced the tedium of the morning service at First Methodist in company of Benny, Louise, and Doreen, had successfully made her escape to eat lunch at Cora's with Denise. They planned to go up to Buster's self-storage lot afterwards and pick up the bikes to spend the afternoon riding.

They headed for the bridge.

Minnie spotted the man tossing the rifle into the creek. She took her stance next to that balustrade, marking exactly where the gun went, determined to keep marking it. Denise dashed back into Cora's and called her daddy. After the fight between Jarvis and Jermaine, he had talked to her several times about the importance of calling him when it looked like things might be starting to go down.

Especially violent things.

"People are attacking the synagogue with axes and sledgehammers, Daddy. Somebody shot Mayor Dreeson and Reverend Wiley."

"Stay right where you are, Princess Baby," he said. "I'm coming."

Nothing much changed in front of the synagogue until Buster Beasley, on the largest Harley hog in Grantville, rolled down the highway, crossed over, and rode right into the middle of the riot. He did a wheelie, scattering the rioters as he went through them.

Then, calmly parking the bike with its kickstand, he drew a .45 automatic from his waist and started firing. He was a good shot and the range was pretty much point blank. Each shot took a man down, and all but one of them killed the man outright. The one exception would die from his wounds about six hours later.

Fortunat Deneau was the second target who came into Buster's sights. Pure happenstance; Buster had no idea who he was and didn't care anyway.

Deneau went down, killed almost instantly by a bullet that shredded one of his lungs and removed a piece of his heart.

Buster's stubborn traditionalism served him badly in the end, though. An old-style .45 like that only had seven shots. He'd started shooting so quickly that most of the rioters were still gathered around and still armed when he ran out of ammunition.

He didn't have a spare clip, just a pocketful of hastily grabbed shells—and he wouldn't have time to reload.

He didn't even try. The pistol butt worked fine clubbing down two more rioters, before someone grabbed his wrist and the wrestling started. Within two seconds, Buster had his buck knife in his left hand and that man went down too. So did the next and the next and the next, clubbed or stabbed or both. Buster Beasley was a very strong man and utterly ferocious in a fight.

But there were just too many opponents, and they were no strangers to street violence themselves. One of them finally got a clear shot at Buster with an ax. The ax took an ear off and a good part of his face. It was all over within a minute, after that, although Buster did take a last man with him. When he was on the ground he still had one of the rioters in a headlock and kept working on his throat with the buck knife even as he finally bled to death.

By that time, though, the attack was pretty well broken up.

"Where," Veleda Riddle yelled from behind the piano, "are the goddamned police?"

That question was not immediately answerable.

But Denise had not been the only person on the phones. An informal custom had developed in the town, in those businesses that operated seven days a week, that Jewish employees who were willing volunteered to work on Sundays, thus allowing church-goers to have the day off. Consequently, they were somewhat dispersed. The holiday had complicated matters, of course. Some holy days were bound to fall on the Christian Sabbath, but it was not a good thing to volunteer and then renege. As many as possible had been at the synagogue, but it had taken some time, nearly a half hour, to get all the members of the defense force together when the harangue began.

Once everyone arrived, though, the Grantville Hebraic Defense Force rather efficiently mopped up the remainder of the attackers clustered around Buster Beasley. Attacks on synagogues were not uncommon; the members of the one in Grantville were prepared. A few were briefly disoriented. None of them had before observed the phenomenon of people singing Christian hymns in order to *protect* a synagogue from assault.

Several assumed, at first, that the women were present to incite the mob. Not for long, though. Rafael Abrabanel, who had married an up-timer, let out resounding shrieks of, "No, you idiots!" and redirected their attention.

They did not use guns. After all, the Grantville synagogue was right in the center of town. Defense by firearms, conducted in the public street, would be as likely to hit innocent bystanders or the children in Frau Dreeson's academy across the street. An individual like Buster might not concern himself over that, but a standing organized defense guard couldn't afford to ignore the possibility.

It didn't matter. Short of guns, the defense force was quite well armed with swords and clubs—and given the prior conduct of the rioters, they certainly didn't have to worry of being accused afterward of using excessive force. By the time they were done, only four of the rioters who'd been reckless enough to stay around to brawl with Buster were still alive. And two of them would not be, within minutes. Like Buster, they'd bleed to death in the street.

Denise was the first noncombatant on the scene, when it was all over. By then, her father was dead. There wasn't any doubt about that. There was blood everywhere. His wounds were pretty ghastly.

So, she knelt by his side, holding the hand that wasn't completely mangled. She said nothing; did not weep. It was not the girl's way. Just stared at the hills above the town, not really seeing them at all.

Mathurin Brillard walked casually up to the trolley stop by the Central Funeral Home.

He could still hear shooting from the direction of the hospital, so he crossed the street, where he could catch one of the cars heading west, toward the intersection of Route 250 and the Badenburg road.

He decided he would walk from there, rather than renting a horse at the livery stable. No need to bring his face to anyone's attention.

Chapter 48

Grantville

Under the influence of Mary Ward, the mother superior of the English Ladies or "Jesuitesses" whom she had met during her Bavarian adventures the summer before, Veronica had started attending mass regularly. She could walk downtown with Henry, see him into the Presbyterian church for the ten o'clock sermon, run a couple of errands, fulfill her duty, which she now felt vaguely obliged to fulfill, and then be back to walk home with him after he and Enoch Wiley finished their regular Sunday chat.

It worked. She worried about having him walk by himself any more. She had changed her schedule at the school this winter. She had hired an extra attendant so she could walk with him to City Hall in the morning and return home with him in the evening. If he fell, it could do a lot of damage. Dr. Nichols recommended that he start using a walker instead of the cane. Henry referred to that as "the beginning of the end."

She wished that he would use the walker. If there had to be an end, she would rather have it not come for quite a while than have it come now. There was no reason to let him slip on a patch of black ice frozen on the sidewalk.

The walls at St. Mary's were so thick that they muffled all the noise. The parishioners spilled out into the middle of the after-attack activity down by the main bridge.

Henry? She started to run toward the Presbyterian church.

"Mrs. Dreeson?"

A man was waving at her, beckoning her to the front of the synagogue.

She knelt down by the two men who'd been shot.

She had seen death all too often before.

So had Annalise, who was suddenly standing behind her, Idelette Cavriani at her side.

Where had Annalise come from? They had left her at home, looking after the children. She went to early mass, came home and fixed breakfast, and was there when her grandmother and Henry started out. The cook and housekeeper had Sunday off. Martha would be out at St. Martin's in the Fields, still. Who was taking care of Gretchen's children?

"I checked," Annalise said. "As soon as someone phoned me. Thea and Nicol are at the house with Willi and Joey and the other children."

Veronica spared the couple the first kind thought she had given them since she had parted with them in Grafenwöhr the previous summer.

"Thea said that they'd been getting ready to have a romantic lunch to celebrate their first anniversary. Anniversary of what?"

Her grandmother was getting up off her knees, to get out of the way of the men who had come with a stretcher. "*Ganz ehrlich*," she said, looking at the two girls, "*braucht ihr beide das gar nicht wissen*."

Annalise wondered why on earth she didn't need to know that. Then she started counting backwards from the date of little Anna Elisabetha's birth and came up with a pretty good idea. Idelette, who had apparently been conducting the same exercise in mental mathematics, winked at her. They then turned their minds to the obligations of mourning.

Someone pried Inez out from under the piano. The next step should have been taking her to the hospital, but there was still shooting going on down in that direction. They could hear it. Jenny Maddox ran out of the funeral home, saying to bring her inside there. With the lower panel of the piano console serving as a makeshift litter, a half dozen men carried her in. Wilton Blackwell, who during more than forty years as a mortician had gained a very sound working knowledge of basic human anatomy, splinted her leg. Without anesthetic, unfortunately. His regular clients, as he said rather apologetically, never needed it.

"I don't, either," Inez said. "I'm not feeling anything, yet. Maybe it's shock. Maybe there's something cutting off the pain the nerves down there are trying to send up to my brain. It's not getting through."

Jenny looked at her, frowning with worry.

Ellen Acton, Wilton's daughter and their billing clerk, closed the doors between the front and back parlors. She thought that Inez didn't need to see the men carrying Enoch and Henry in. And Buster. Definitely. Nobody needed to see Buster until her pa had a chance to work on him a bit. For Enoch and Henry, at least, the shots had been clean.

She'd told them to put the goons in the garage. It was cold enough that they would keep for a while and the police might want to go over their clothes and things. They were sending the policemen who went down at Leahy over to Genucci's. Central Funeral Home was out of space.

Ellen touched Jenny's shoulder. "Will's back," she said in a whisper. "I don't know when he got into town, but Bob saw him last night. He was eating at Marcantonio's Pizza with Skip Hilton. Should I call over to UMWA headquarters to see if they know where he is?"

Jenny bit the nail on the little finger of her left hand. "I guess you had better, seeing as he's the only one of Enoch and Inez's kids who came through the Ring of Fire. Even though he's been on the outs with them for years. Since he was in high school. They can at least let him know about this before it goes on the radio tonight. Call the power plant too. Gina works Sundays as a regular thing. She has for years, so she doesn't have to face the issue of whether Reverend Curtis would humiliate her if she showed up at church. Have someone out there get Gina, so she can pull Brette out of youth group over at the Church of Christ and tell her about her grandpa. That will take a while. They'll have to call someone else in to replace her for the rest of her shift."

Jenny hadn't really expected Will to come. He had been a bad boy since his early teens. "Rebel without a cause" style, except that he had a cause, at least to start with, which was that his dad had been so unreasonably strict with him. Unlike John Enoch, who had turned into an Episcopalian monk in response to Enoch's Calvinist child-rearing techniques, Will had reacted by going wild and then wilder.

Inez had felt obliged to agree with Enoch, so Will had fought with her, too.

Jenny had reason to know. Will Wiley was only three years younger than she was. He'd run around with her twin sisters, the ones left up-time. Maybe more than run around with Donna Jae, both before and after she got married, at least while Lee was overseas during the Gulf War. Will had been working in Fairmont and going to college part time. That was over before he married Gina and luckily Lee had never found out as far as Jenny knew, but it was the sort of thing Will did. The sort of thing that finally caused Gina to blow up.

But here he was.

For good or bad, so was Gina. The power plant had sent her downtown in one of its trucks.

Brette was standing there, her hands behind her back. What was she, now? About ten? She'd only been three when Will and Gina separated. Four when they divorced.

Gina's brother Drew used to pick her up and take her over to Will's for visitation; then pick her up at Will's and take her back to Gina. Brette probably didn't remember ever seeing her parents in the same room.

The last time the two of them *had* been in the same room, probably, was in the courthouse in Fairmont. And the time before that, Gina had taken a shot at Will. She'd missed, but not intentionally.

That had been back when Velma Hardesty was starting to notice the arrival of middle age and was going through her "younger man" phase. As it was, Will insisted to the judge, swearing under oath, that it was accidental. Gina got probation for reckless handling of a firearm.

The judge had to have been a very trusting type of person. When was the last time he had a case in which a wife had accidentally let off a gun at her buck-naked husband who was in bed with another woman? In the other woman's trailer? How many cases like that did a judge ever get?

Jenny cleared her throat. Damn, but Will Wiley was still a good-looking man.

She wondered what Gina was thinking. She glanced over that way. From the expression on Gina's face as she looked at Will, probably the same thing as she was.

Jenny's mind clicked along. In a way it was too bad that Gina hadn't shot Velma when she had a chance, before she messed up a couple of other marriages, but then who would have taken care of Brette? The judge had probably realized that Gina wasn't a danger to anyone but Will. He'd put a restraining order on her along with the probation.

Why had the UMWA sent Will over to Brandenburg, anyway? He'd been there, in Berlin or somewhere near it, for months. Politics. Jenny didn't even try to keep up with politics.

It was finally Inez who said something.

"You'll have to go home, Will. Over to the house and get his other suit. The keys are in my purse. That's back at the church. Ask Idelette Cavriani to take you to the committee room where the Red Cross was meeting. She's in the other parlor, with Veronica and Annalise. You haven't been there since we remodeled it so much. You'll have to bring his other suit for him to wear."

After Denise made her second call up to the storage lot, Christin George rode down to the bridge on her own motorcycle, ignored the "pedestrians only" prohibition, and pulled up right in front of Cora's. By then, Denise was waiting inside the café. As soon as Christin appeared, she ran out.

"They took him into Central Funeral Home," she said. "For the usual reason."

Christin looked her over. Denise's clothes were pretty well blood-soaked. "Are you okay?"

"Yeah, Mom, I'm fine. The blood's all Daddy's. Well. Some of it's probably from some of the men he killed."

Christin nodded. Like daughter, like mother. She wasn't given to public histrionics either. "We'd better go find out how much it will be, then."

"Daddy didn't believe in funerals. He always said he wanted to be cremated. Or just put out in a garbage bag."

"Grantville never had a crematorium. They'd have had to take him out of town, even up-time. I don't think they have them at all around here. Or plastic sacks, either. We ran out of those a long time ago."

"I don't want to see him in one of those satin-lined things. He'd have hated it, Mom. You know he would."

"Jenny ran out of those a long time ago, too. It's plain wood boxes now, and linen sheets. We'll do the best we can to keep the frills off, but this is going to hit Johnnie Ray hard, especially with Julia passing last fall. I ought to at least ask him what he wants, since he's Buster's grandpa."

By mid-afternoon, the Grantville police appeared at the synagogue in force, if somewhat belatedly, after finishing up at Leahy. They rounded up the casualties—in addition to the twenty-two dead goons and four badly injured ones who'd been involved in the fighting with Buster and the Hebraic defense guard, there were twelve others who'd been wounded earlier. Not badly enough to die, but badly enough not to run away. They were being held by the informal posse of Jewish defenders.

Then, the police started scouring the town. They arrested any of the attackers still on foot who had not managed to get out of Grantville or go into hiding. There were about twenty of those, although three of them turned out later to be innocent vagrants and were released.

Six members of the synagogue had been wounded, but none of them very badly. Buster had been so savage that by the time the Hebraic defense guard swung into action there hadn't been much fight left in the rioters.

They'd all recover. None of them would even agree to go to the hospital. They'd patch each other up.

In addition to Inez, fourteen Grantvillers, a mix of up-timers and down-timers, were wounded. Mostly the men who had been wielding folding chairs in defense of the women on the cart. Only three had to go to the hospital; Jeff Adams' staff had worked on the others in his office and then sent them home.

Before the police arrived and while they worked, Minnie kept standing on the bridge, right next to the balustrade, stubbornly, well into the afternoon. Several times, she tried to get the attention of some of the police. They knew her, of course. How could they avoid knowing her, the way she handled that motorcycle?

They ignored her. Several times, one or another tried to shoo her away, get her to go home.

There wouldn't be daylight for much longer. They wouldn't be able to retrieve the weapon.

Finally, someone showed up who might listen to her. "Blake!" she called. "Blake Haggerty!"

He turned. "I can't talk now, Minnie. I'm working. We don't need gawkers. Go on home."

"Blake, I saw the sniper who killed them. I'm standing here marking where he threw the gun. It's down in the creek. They won't listen to me."

He was turning away, trying to concentrate on what he was doing, half-blocking her voice. Then what she was saying penetrated. He almost jumped back toward her.

"Please, Blake. If I leave, I'll lose a lot of what I'm marking. Can't you go into Cora's? Call Benny. Call Mr. Pallavicino from the school. If they come down and believe what I'm telling them, then maybe someone in the police will pay attention."

"I'm paying attention," Blake said. "Believe me, I'm paying attention right now." He paid more attention when she pointed and he could see, misshapen by the ripples of the water in the creek, the wavering outline of a gun.

His immediate superior dismissed it as "a fool girl trying to attract attention and get some publicity."

Blake wasn't supposed to go out of the chain of command. But he went over to Marvin Tipton, interrupted what he was doing, summarized the situation, and requested permission to go into Cora's and call Benny and Joe.

"For one thing," he said, "Minnie's half frozen already. She was dressed for noon and the temperature really starts dropping once the sun goes down. If nobody pays attention to her, she's prepared to stand on that bridge all night."

"Why?" Marvin asked.

"The mayor gave her that eye. Old Jim Dreeson's artificial eye from World War I, in place of the one she lost at that riot in Jena. As far as Minnie is concerned, she owed Henry. Owed him a lot."

Jacques-Pierre Dumais was truly very relieved when he returned to Madame Haggerty's garage at the end of the day to find that

Mademoiselle Hardesty had disappeared. If not mysteriously disappeared, given the hole in the back of the building. He wondered how she managed it. He stood there briefly, deciding upon the most prudent course of action.

Which would be the least conspicuous. He nailed the two broken boards lying at the back of the garage into place, rubbing some dirt over the new, shiny, nail heads. Then he moved the three garbage cans in which he was keeping his records. Not far. Just onto Madame Haggerty's enclosed back porch. It was not difficult to carry them. There were only one or two packets in each. Partly because he had sorted them by topic; partly because even he had no particular desire to try to wrestle anything as heavy as a garbage can packed solid with paper from one place to another.

Then he went home to his trailer to listen to the news on the radio. Tomorrow, he thought, each of the newspapers would publish a special edition. He would need to buy a copy of each.

As he listened to the reports, Jacques-Pierre's dominant emotion was annoyance. The whole thing had been poorly handled, from start to finish. During his time in Grantville, he had read every police procedural novel in the "mystery" section of the public library. He certainly understood how the local authorities felt, up-time, when the feds had moved in on one of their cases.

If only Locquifier had left it to him! He could have managed it all much better.

But, of course, if Locquifier had left it to him, there would have been no attack on the synagogue and no killings.

This was going to be a disaster.

To be fair, though, the miserable debacle at the hospital was his own fault. His own disaster. Somehow, he should have found out about the anti-autopsy group and prevented them from coming.

But the other. Didn't the fools ever learn?

Possibly not, it seemed. He would have to think about that.

He wrote up a report to send to the duke.

"The hard thing, sometimes," Pam said, "is trying to remember how much of what you have reported to whom. Just in case any of the recipients come around asking questions again."

"It was easier back when there were copy machines," Missy said wistfully. "Just put a sheet of paper on the glass, press a button, and there you were."

She got up and looked out the window, then turned around. "Do you know what, Pam? There are kids coming into middle school now who don't remember copy machines at all. The first year middle school students, the fifth graders, were only six or seven years old when the Ring of Fire happened."

Ron walked over and put his arm around her. "You two have diddled around with these reports for long enough, now. One version for Cory Joe, one for the police. They're as done as you're ever going to get them."

"I don't really want to do this," Missy said. "But I guess that I will." The thought of having to go to the two funeral homes, much less the morgue at the hospital, had been looming over her head all day.

"You will, though," Ron said. "Not because you want to. But because you have to."

Missy and Pam didn't recognize any of the bodies in the garages at Central Funeral Home. None of the bodies at Genucci's, either. Those were the men who had been in front of the synagogue. At the hospital, both of them were able to identify one of the anonymous corpses as one of the men who had been taking signs out of Veda Mae's garage and putting them on a handcart. He was the one who had dragged Pam into the garage and had rushed at Missy, but been dragged away by another man wearing a ski mask.

Neither of them, of course, had any idea who that man was. As Pam said to the disappointed policeman, all they knew was that he had been hauling signs out of Veda Mae Haggerty's garage and putting them on a handcart. She was sorry, but that was it. Although several other men were there when Pam came by, they had all been in the shadow of the garage, so she couldn't tell if any were among either the dead or the living demonstrators in custody. Missy said that by the time she caught up, there had been only two men, both had been outside the garage, and the second one had been wearing a ski mask.

Overall, the policeman was disappointed. He had been hoping for more. But, of course, it was only coincidence that the girls had been out walking the previous morning in any case, and it did provide a connection to Mrs. Haggerty.

Veda Mae simply refused to answer questions from the police. She said that she didn't have to. She challenged them to come back with a search warrant. For the time being, they left it at that. She wasn't likely to become a fugitive and eventually someone would be in a position to question her under oath.

When it crossed her mind that her grandson Blake was now a policeman, she refused to answer any questions he asked her, either.

She decided to warn Jacques-Pierre Dumais, the next time she saw him, that the police were asking about the signs he had stored in her garage.

Chapter 49

Magdeburg, March 4, 1635

The news about what was going on in Grantville reached Magdeburg, via radio, almost immediately. Even though it wasn't the best window, the radio people threw every bit of power they had, combined and consolidated, into getting out word of the incident.

From there, the news hit the streets almost at once. It was already being called "the Dreeson Incident." That was perhaps unfair to Enoch Wiley, who'd been the other man murdered, but most people assumed the mayor had been the target of the assassin, not the minister. Which, indeed, was true enough.

The other name spread widely by the news, of course, was Buster Beasley's. It wouldn't be long at all before Buster had become a national hero for those people inclined toward the CoCs or the Fourth of July Party, especially the youngsters. Not on the level of Hans Richter, perhaps, but awfully close.

Partly that was because he'd died in what all such people considered a good cause. By the spring of 1635, almost four years after the Ring of Fire, anti-Semitism and witch-hunting had become associated in the minds of just about everyone in Europe with opposition to the newly arrived Americans and the changes they represented. And that was true whether the person was a partisan or an opponent of Mike Stearns and his people.

If you were for Stearns and what he represented, then you were automatically opposed to anti-Semitism and witch-hunting, even if those two traditions had been deeply rooted in your family or craft or village. And if you were hostile toward Stearns and his people, then you tended—though not with quite the same rigor—to lean favorably toward anti-Semitism and witch-hunting, even if in times gone by you wouldn't have been.

Not very sensible, perhaps, but much of human social behavior is tribal and ritualistic rather than well-reasoned.

But, just as much, Buster's rapidly growing popularity as a folk hero was due to the sheer ferocity of his actions. This man was no "martyr," in the usual sense of the term. Yes, certainly, he wound up getting killed—but, oh, he took so many of the swine with him! Roland at Roncesvalles couldn't have done any better.

An interesting side effect of the incident was that, throughout the continent and in all of its many languages, the term "harley" became the commonly accepted term for motorcycle—despite the fact that most of the motorcycles in Grantville were actually of Japanese manufacture. And, even more quickly and thoroughly, the word "buster" became a term used everywhere to refer to a stalwart and upright fellow, not to be thwarted by miscreants.

By the evening, the word had reached almost every place else in Europe—not just in the USE—that had a receiver. The next day, the newspapers from Amsterdam to Frankfurt, to Paris, Venice, Prague, and Austria, were on the streets with it.

Almost the only places that had to wait for land communication were Spain and Poland.

In Stockholm, Charles Mademann studied the news reports carefully. Very carefully.

There was no chance now to carry out the planned assassination of Sweden's queen in coordination with the Grantville actions. Unfortunately, the weather had been uncooperative and Mademann's ship had been delayed in port. He hadn't been able to reach the Swedish capital until two days after the target date.

And there was no point in even considering the action at the moment, of course. Security had been tightened up considerably, even for someone like Maria Eleonora whom no one seriously thought was at risk.

So be it. Eventually, security would become lax again. Mademann would simply wait. He had enough funds to remain comfortably ensconced in this inn for months. He wouldn't stand out, either. The Swedish capital was full of men from the Netherlands and the Germanies and northern France, brought there by Sweden's burgeoning industries and commerce. Quite a few of them were Huguenots.

Stockholm was a dull city, and hardly the place Mademann would have voluntary chosen to while away his time. But at least it wasn't Scotland.

On a Train Running Parallel to the Elbe

The train, again. Another full, frustrating, utterly unavoidable day on the train. A day on the train with very little news—only what boys, at the various stops, ran alongside the cars shouting through the windows.

Gretchen was breathing fire. She was in full avenging fury mode.

If she only knew whom to direct it at.

How was her grandmother? How was Annalise? What about the children?

Someone had killed Henry.

Nobody knew who had killed Henry. About the only thing the police had concluded, pretty much for certain, was that it hadn't been any of the people directly involved in the demonstration against the synagogue. There had obviously been some sort of connection, of course. The general opinion that was forming—Gretchen's also—was that the vicious act was the responsibility of one or another of the USE's many reactionary extremist groups, all of whom were anti-Semitic to one degree or another.

She wanted vengeance.

All the more so because she was feeling quite guilty that they hadn't come back right after the election the way they had promised, to take the children.

That had been her decision. There had just been so much that she still had to do.

Jeff sat next to her, watching her stew.

Grantville, March 1635

"A state funeral of some kind," Ed Piazza said. "No, I don't know exactly what the protocol will be. We've never had a precedent for anything like this. Not a USE-level state funeral. Neither Henry nor Enoch held any office under Gustavus Adolphus. Never had. Never would have. Not really a province-level state funeral, either. Neither of them held any SoTF office. Never had. Never would have. But we have to give them some kind of public recognition."

He was pacing the floor.

"I've never organized anything like this."

"No help from me, either." Chad Jenkins shook his head. "If Simpson weren't still up north, he might have some ideas from when he was in the navy. Or Mrs. Simpson, perhaps? Just on general principles, that she knows how to pull off these ceremonial-type things?"

Preston Richards pulled his head up out of his hands.

"Ask Dan Frost if he can come down. Talk to Sylvester Francisco. We're going to have to do police funerals for the officers who went down. Both of them have been involved with those before. We could start with the protocol for that, maybe, and work something up."

That seemed like the best idea anyone had so far.

Preston nodded toward Ludwig Guenther. "We should lean on his advice, too. He does protocol stuff all the time—grew up with it. Between him and Dan, we can invent our own. A mix of what the up-timers and down-timers will expect. His steward can write it down, so we'll have it the next time we need it. Not that I want there to be a next time, God knows."

The count of Schwarzburg-Rudolstadt nodded deeply, indicating his willingness.

"Good idea," agreed Chad.

Inez then pointed out that Henry had been a Presbyterian and Enoch had been the Presbyterian minister. That didn't leave anyone to preach the funeral—either one of them. At least, not anyone obvious.

"So who's going to do the honors?"

Inez shook her head. "Charles Vandine and Gordon Partow are still in Geneva, being trained to succeed Enoch. We knew he wouldn't live forever. But they can't get back in time for the funeral. There's no Scots Presbyterian minister in Grantville. No other Calvinist minister of any persuasion, as far as I know, whether French, Dutch, Palatine, Swiss, Hungarian, or 'other.'"

"Who, then?"

Veronica stood up. "Elder Orval McIntire. Henry liked him. They were friends."

Inez concurred.

"At the church?"

"No. Even after the remodeling, there wouldn't be room for everyone who'll want to come. A lot of people will. There've been lines all day and nearly all night at the funeral home, for the viewing. And I don't want to be in the position of saying, 'you qualify to come inside, but you don't.'" Inez shook her head. "That's . . . invidious."

"Where, then?"

"At the fairgrounds, I guess. Outside, and hope it doesn't rain. If it does rain, the families will need to be inside. Mike and Becky are flying in. Ed and the rest of the SoTF officials—the department heads, Chad Jenkins, Ableidinger. The county board. The elders and deacons. Then let as many more people as possible inside. First come, first served. And borrow every umbrella in town for the rest of them."

Preston Richards put his head down on his hands again.

"I'm so glad Gustav Adolf decided he needed to stay in Copenhagen. Having the emperor here, too—sorry, the captain general—would have been a little much. At least we don't have to handle everything that would have been involved with having him here."

"Which reminds me. What about other prominent guests?" Arnold Bellamy gestured at Count Ludwig Guenther. "You'll be there, won't you? And your wife? The mayor of Badenburg, certainly; several other mayors are still 'maybes.' Jena, almost certainly; Erfurt, perhaps. People like that?"

The count nodded. "Duke Albrecht and his wife, as well. Plus, since Duke Ernst is in transit from the Upper Palatinate to Magdeburg in any case, his brother. Wilhelm Wettin will apparently be staying in Magdeburg. Unwise, that, in my opinion. But . . ."

Ludwig Guenther shrugged. "I suppose he had to keep from irritating his own followers. Duke Johann Philipp from Altenburg and his wife and daughter will be here. I'll have my steward furnish you with a head count."

Inez resigned herself to the inevitable. "We can borrow folding chairs from all the churches, I guess. And the American Legion and the lodges."

At the funeral, Veronica went through everything with a perfectly calm face. Then she went home and locked herself in their bedroom for a while.

Inez had to go through it all in a wheel chair, because of her injured leg, which was worse. She couldn't go home and lock herself in afterwards, because they took her right back to the hospital. Doctor Nichols thought he would have to operate on the broken leg, not that Wilton hadn't splinted it right, but because there had to be some injury in addition to the break. Inez still didn't have any feeling in it.

Will rode back to the hospital with her in the ambulance. He didn't leave right away, which meant that he was still there when Gina brought Brette.

When he looked up and saw them standing in the door of the room, he said, "The restraining order expired a long time ago."

Chapter 50

Grantville, March 1635

"Buster didn't belong to any church," Christin said, "and he definitely would not want to be buried by some preacher." Buster's grandfather Johnnie Ray agreed with her, considering that he had managed to live eighty-five satisfactory years without being a member of any church himself.

They ended up, the day after the state funeral, with this overfilled memorial service at the old movie theater downtown, conducted by Jenny Maddox. There was no way they could have fitted everyone into even the big parlor at the funeral home. Not even with the folding doors open and both parlors thrown together.

Jenny had written a nice statement about the boy, Johnnie Ray thought. The printed program called it an eulogy, which he sort of wondered how to pronounce. Now she got up and was reading it out loud.

Denise wished she didn't have to listen to it. Daddy had been alive and now he was dead. He was dead because she had phoned him. If she hadn't phoned him, he wouldn't be dead. He would be up at the storage lot, working at something. Probably working in his weld shop. He was—had been—one of the town's best welders. He would have been there at breakfast this morning, saying something rude about the fancy funeral they had yesterday where all the politicians got up and orated about Mayor Dreeson and Reverend Wiley.

If she hadn't phoned him, he would still be alive. Taking care of his Princess Baby.

From now on, she would be taking care of herself, forever and ever and ever.

Dealing with the boys at school, without the threat of Buster Beasley in the background. She might have to change the way she handled them. Mom wasn't . . . quite the same thing as Daddy.

She wasn't really too worried about that, though. Daddy had made sure that she could take care of herself.

Was this speech of Jenny's going to go on forever? After that, there was going to be music, because Johnnie Ray thought there ought to be. Even though Daddy would rather have been put out in a garbage bag.

"Let Benny pick," Johnnie Ray had said. "We've known each other all our lives. Old men. Way older than Henry and Enoch. Let Benny decide what's right."

Benny Pierce was sitting on the theater's little stage. Jenny had brought him a chair. Minnie stood by his side. She had a fiddle of her own, now, but she held it loosely by her side, waiting for him to play. Once he started, her voice joined in:

> *'Tis a gift to be simple,*
> *'Tis a gift to be free,*
> *'Tis a gift to come down,*
> *Where we want to be.*

That wasn't one of Benny's songs. Benny hadn't picked that. Minnie had! Minnie knew that she was a sucker for that song. How dared Minnie pick that? How dared she?

Denise hadn't intended to waste any of her energy crying. She could hear his voice now. "Don't get mad; get even."

Don't worry, Daddy, I plan to. Minnie saw the guy who started it. Killing the mayor and the preacher, I mean. The reason I had to call you. Don't worry, Daddy. I'm your Princess Baby. I'm your pip. Minnie saw him. We'll take care of it. Starting as soon as possible.

"Don't get mad; get even." Denise ignored her tears. But Daddy had never said anything about "Don't get sad," now that she thought about it. Maybe he wouldn't have minded. It had never come up.

Gerry Stone, who had walked all the way from Rudolstadt, loaned her a clean handkerchief. Then another. He had remembered to put a half dozen in his pocket that morning, he had said before the service. She had wondered why.

Minnie's voice went on.

After Jenny's people had removed the casket, Christin thanked everybody for coming. Especially Ronnie and Inez, considering the circumstances, and that the ambulance had to bring Inez downtown again.

There wasn't going to be a graveside service. Christin had told Jenny to take care of the rest of it without any fuss.

It had been a considerable shock to Christin's parents, Mike and Amina George, when they read the obituaries and biographies, to find out that she and Buster actually were married and had been for years.

They showed up at the memorial service. They waited in the lobby afterwards.

Christin was in no mood for a reconciliation. "If you weren't willing to accept me with Buster when you thought he was a live bum, you don't have any business trying to claim some of the reflected glory now that he's a dead hero."

"Mom," Denise said.

"Plus the first thing you'll say is that if I need to, I can bring the kid home and you'll support me. I know the business as well as Buster did and can damn well keep on running it myself. I don't need you, or anybody else."

She hadn't fought it, though, when Benny, with Louise and Doreen, and Minnie, had taken Denise over to meet her grandparents. Christin herself refused to have anything to do with it, but she hadn't fought it.

Benny introduced Denise to her grandparents, her aunt, and her aunt's husband Bob Atkins. She vaguely recognized her cousin Amina from seeing her at school, but she hadn't known that they were cousins. Amina was almost two years older and separated by three grades. She nodded at her cousin George Atkins, who was older.

It was all pretty stiff. It was unsatisfactory for everyone.

She didn't offer to shake hands. Both of her hands were hanging onto Gerry's elbow. Then she went back to Mom, who asked Minnie to please ride her cycle home, because she wasn't sure she could handle it safely right now.

Christin was perfectly calm. West Virginia women were not given to wailing in public.

"Do you need a lift?" Louise asked her.

"We'll be all right," Denise answered. "I have my cycle here. I'll take Mom home in the sidecar. But if you like, you could follow us and pick up Minnie after she drops Gerry off at Lothlorien and garages Mom's, so I don't have to bring her back to town. I'd—well, I'd really thank you for that."

The general Grantville reaction was of two minds. The ones who thought that Mike and Amina had meant well and that Christin's way of looking at it was a little bit skewed. The ones who thought that Christin had hit it right on the nose. Either way, it was pretty clear that she wasn't going to change her mind.

There wasn't a lot of "give" in Christin George.

Most people agreed that Denise had quite a bit of her mother in her, and not just the good looks, either. That was the consensus at Cora's, anyway.

Chapter 51

Erfurt, March 1635

Mathurin Brillard always enjoyed his morning paper.

This morning's was truly fascinating. Being a stranger to Grantville, he had not realized at the time that he had not merely assassinated the mayor of Grantville, precisely as Locquifier had told him to do, and the Calvinist minister, more or less as a bonus, but that it was significant that he had fired those two shots in the general direction of a dozen or so middle-aged to elderly ladies standing next to a rolling cart and on the steps of the synagogue. Given his marksmanship, the women really hadn't been in any danger. But he realized now that the residents of Grantville didn't know that, so their fury was all the greater than if he'd simply shot the two men.

The group of women included . . .

In addition to the Calvinist minister's wife: Annabelle Graham, the wife of the SoTF president, Ed Piazza; Eleanor Jenkins, who was now the SoTF Red Cross president, and her daughter-in-law Deborah, who was wife of the increasingly prominent industrialist Charles Jenkins who had just won election as West Virginia County's senator to the SoTF congress. It appeared that Jenkins' wife also ran the town's teacher training program and was the daughter of Willie Ray Hudson, well known as the first president of the Grange movement. Not to mention Veleda Riddle, the mother of the chief justice of the SoTF Supreme Court, who was also the president of the SoTF League of Women Voters and reorganizer of Grantville's Episcopalian Church; her daughter-in-law Kathryn, wife of the chief justice of the SoTF Supreme Court; Mary Jo Kindred, the wife of Grantville's senior newspaper publisher; Claudette, the wife of the Reverend Al Green of the First Baptist Church, and Linda Bartolli, organist at St. Mary Magdelene Catholic Church.

That was the purely factual information he gleaned from the most staid of the newspapers. The more gossipy added additional information, such as that Mrs. Bartolli had gone to early mass specifically in order to have time to attend the Red Cross meeting. And that Veleda Riddle, in the opinion of Frau Veda Mae Haggerty, was there because she was not about to let Eleanor Jenkins run anything without keeping her nose in the tent to make sure what was going on.

Brillard reflected as he ate his morning bread.

The Grantville powers-that-be were very angry. It was entirely possible that shooting the two men while they were near the women had been a mistake in judgment. Possibly he should have waited until the men moved somewhere else. But that was water over the dam. At the time, he had no way of knowing who the women were.

He paid his bill and started north on the trade route. Still walking.

Grantville

Press Richards looked like he hadn't slept for two days. For good reason. "I don't know where our training went wrong," he said. Again.

"Stop agonizing," Chad Jenkins advised him. "We're going to have to make the up-timers come to terms with the fact that for the town's new citizens, 'restrained response' to civil unrest is a relative term. Which most of them are doing. Yeah, Maurer shot first, out at the hospital. There aren't a half-dozen people in town who have complained. Just because a couple of bleeding heart liberals like Linda Jane Colburn and Rachel Hill have big mouths, it doesn't mean there's some kind of a 'groundswell of opinion.'

Not even Gerry and Tami Simmons are making a fuss. Forget it. Or call Dan Frost, talk to him for a while, and then forget it."

"Not to mention," Arnold Bellamy added, "that Maurer is dead. So's Bill Magen, who was the only person in the line who was talking to him right before it happened. Which means that there's not going to be any long-drawn-out investigation, agonizing about his motivation. That always helps. Least said, soonest mended."

The Grantville police kept on doing policelike things. Investigating. Arresting. Questioning. Putting people in jail. And, since this more than strained the capacity of Grantville's rather small jail, putting people other places where they could be watched.

"What I really wonder," Pam Hardesty said, "is where they ever got those slogans against vaccination. The ones that were on the placards at the hospital demonstration. The placards that they were hauling out of Veda Mae's garage. There's got to be some kind of a connection."

"I'll check through the reference materials and see what I can find out," Missy said. "But I sure don't remember that we have anything like it in the state library."

"Whereas I," Pam said, "will have another little heart-to-heart chat with Veda Mae."

"Hey. You volunteered. You don't like to look things up, remember? You're a people person. That's why you picked circulation instead of reference. Think of Veda Mae as a people. Well, as a person."

"That's a damned hard thing to do."

A couple of days later, they had the data. They gave it to Cory Joe who, on behalf of Don Francisco, filed off the serial numbers and gave it to Preston Richards. Who, in turn, sent Marvin Tipton to talk to John Daoud, the chiropractor, who fingered Jacques-Pierre Dumais as the only person he recalled who had come to him seeking information on the topic.

"I really wish," Preston Richards said, "that I knew how you do it."

"Oh," Cory Joe answered mildly, "Don Francisco has his sources."

Chapter 52

Magdeburg, March 1635

The election results were finally certified, for the nation as a whole and each of its provinces and imperial cities.

Nationally, so far as the popular vote was concerned, the Fourth of July Party had gotten forty-four percent of the vote; the Crown Loyalists, forty-eight percent; and the remaining eight percent had been divided among the various small parties.

So far as the provinces were concerned, there were not many surprises. As expected, the Fourth of July Party swept the Province of Magdeburg and the State of Thuringia-Franconia. In the case of the SoTF, it split the vote in alliance with the Ram movement.

The Crown Loyalists enjoyed equally lopsided victories in Hesse-Kassel, Brunswick, Westphalia, and the Upper Rhine.

They also won a majority in the Province of the Main and Pomerania, but the results were much closer. The Fourth of July Party won a similarly narrow victory in the Oberpfalz and a wider one in Mecklenburg.

Also as expected, the Fourth of July Party was very strong in the imperial cities. They won clear victories in four out of the seven: Magdeburg—that was another landslide—Luebeck, Hamburg and Frankfurt. They also won a majority in Strassburg, although just barely. The Crown Loyalists won the election in Augsburg and Ulm without any difficulty. No surprises there either. All of the imperial cities were actually small provinces, with a considerable amount of hinterland attached to the city itself. That was particularly true of Augsburg and Ulm, which meant the rural vote in those imperial cities was not really that much smaller, proportionately, than it was in most of the Germanies.

Although the popular vote was rather closely contested, the Crown Loyalist victory was much more pronounced in terms of seats won in the House of Commons. They would wind up with a clear majority of the seats. Not much of a majority—fifty-two percent—but enough so that they wouldn't need to form a coalition government with any of the small parties.

Again, that was no real surprise. The Fourth of July Party had a pronounced advantage in the cities and bigger towns, while the CLs enjoyed an offsetting strength in most of the rural areas. There were some exceptions, like Franconia and much of Mecklenburg, but not many. What that often meant, however, was that much of the FoJP victory in the cities was effectively wasted. It didn't matter whether a district was won by fifty-one percent or eighty-one percent, after all. Either way, it was still just one district.

So, often enough, the FoJP would win a single seat in a city by a landslide, only to see it offset by a much smaller margin of victory by the CLs in a rural district.

To some extent, the results were a reflection of the compromises that Mike Stearns had made with Gustav Adolf when the USE was created in the beginning, in the fall of 1633. The emperor had been able to force through a number of provisions that would obviously be to the advantage of the more conservative areas and sectors of the new nation.

Still, there was no point in complaining or crying foul. The fact remained that the Crown Loyalists had won more of the popular vote than the FoJP, even if they hadn't won an outright majority and even if the political structure of the USE favored them in terms of seats. They had every right under the democratic principles that Mike Stearns advocated and championed himself to replace him as the head of government with one of their own—and he said so in a short and gracious concession speech once the election results were finally announced. The speech was played live over the radio and reprinted in every newspaper in the nation.

✧ ✧ ✧

"We *were* planning to stay longer, this time, Ronnie. Honestly, we were."

"Still, you are going. Without the children."

"I'm willing to plead. I'm willing to grovel." Jeff grinned, in a desperate sort of way. "Gretchen has to get back. It's a crisis now, but it could get a lot worse. There's plenty of blame being flung around, and some of it's landing where it doesn't belong. Spartacus is trying to be a voice of reason. Hell, he *is* a voice of reason. But . . ."

Jeff stopped and started over.

"Nobody knows who had Henry and Reverend Wiley killed. Or why. So if it was just that, it wouldn't be too hard for her to keep a handle on it. But the synagogue demonstration was worse, because it wasn't a one-time thing. There's been agitation for years and it hasn't stopped. Whoever is churning those pamphlets out is still churning them. Somebody's got to identify those guys and put a lid on it. Pretty permanently. And it's not being made easier when a lot of the Crown Loyalist partisans keep giving interviews saying that as soon as Wettin comes into office, he's going to roll back this reform and roll back that reform. Not always agreeing with one another either. It depends on what he promised to whom, and when he did it."

"When are you going to take the children?"

"After the transfer of power, maybe. That's June. If the transfer goes smoothly. If it looks like Wettin can manage the guys who keep howling about 'backward, turn backward, O Time in thy flight.' If . . ."

"If you are not away in Gustavus Adolphus' great war on the eastern front. If you are not dead in his great and magnificent campaign. You are in the army. Which I have not forgotten. You could well be dead by then. If Gretchen has not been dragged down in this political crisis. If . . ."

Nicol reached out and put a hand on Veronica's shoulder.

"Tante," he said placatingly. "Tante, if those things should happen, then it is far better that the children should be here with you. With us. Not lost with them."

Veronica turned and left the room.

Francisco Nasi sat on the train. Reading. In spite of the rough roadbed that caused him to push his glasses up every few minutes.

While he was in Grantville, he would have to see McNally and get the frames adjusted. He made a note on a small pad.

Then he went back to reading. Ed Piazza was conscientious about sending all the information that the Grantville police had gathered. Magdeburg had some advantages, in the sense of being the center, for the time being, of his web of contacts. Sometimes, though, there was nothing quite as good as being on the scene oneself.

Chapter 53

Grantville

Bryant Holloway heard about it all, of course. He'd been busy at work, but no one could have missed it. It had been all over the radio and papers last week. He'd even been interviewed by a reporter in Naumburg, for the "up-time reaction" to it.

He'd told the reporter that his reaction was, "damn the Krauts." Attacking the hospital, attacking the synagogue, killing Mayor Dreeson and Reverend Wiley.

It was all the fault of the Krauts. Just like the vote about moving the capital of the State of Thuringia-Franconia to Bamberg.

For which he had received an official reprimand. Representatives of the USE Fire Marshal's Office should not say such things for publication.

"That's how Stannard would have it. Sure. 'The Krauts are our allies. The Krauts are our fellow citizens. The Krauts are our friends.' Talk about a party line. Talk about being expected to hew to the party line."

So here he was, driving back into Grantville in the fire department's pickup truck that he used on out of town assignments, and practically the first thing he saw was Lenore, coming out of the administration building, standing in the street, talking to one of them. A man. A young man. A Kraut. For a married woman, going to work was nothing but a chance to find men and a chance at extracurricular sex.

He would take care of that this evening.

Lenore saw Bryant looking at her as he passed. She remembered what she had promised, turned, and went back to the office.

"Almost everyone in the office is a woman," Lenore said. "Count them, Bryant."

"The Americans are mainly women. But that guy was a Kraut. This is where we came in, I think."

"His name is Nicholas Moser. He's married to Mrs. Dreeson's niece, I think. Or her first husband's niece. They have a baby; she's a few months old."

"Which is probably why he's looking for something on the side. I remember what it was like for us when Weshelle was that age."

"You're making things up. That's what it amounts to. You're looking for excuses to blame me for things that don't exist. I was congratulating him on his promotion. That's all."

"I'm not about to forget that someone was there before me. Since you did that, what's to say that there won't be someone there next to me, too? Especially with me being out of town so much. With the way your family collects Krauts."

"Stop using that word. It's derogatory. Like the 'N-word' was. I read that interview you gave and I know that Steve Matheny issued a statement repudiating it. Not just Archie Stannard. Clara doesn't deserve it. Neither does Katerina or Gertrude. They're . . . they're family now. Not aliens. Family. Almost family, at least, for Katerina and Gertrude."

Bryant started to get up and come toward her.

She moved. "Stay right there."

He was startled enough by her tone of voice that he sat back down.

She opened a drawer. He wouldn't have been surprised if she was dumb enough to pull a knife or something on him. She wouldn't get very far with that. She was tall for a woman, granted, but not unusually strong. It was very easy to turn a knife on the person holding it and create an unfortunate accident.

Instead, it was a little plastic tube.

She took off the top, turned the base, and set it on the kitchen table in front of him. "Do you know what that is?"

He shook his head.

"What it *was* was Chandra's cover stick. Probably the last one in Grantville. I used it in February. To cover the marks. To cover for you."

She leaned against the sink.

"I'm not going to do that again. We're married. I'm not going to argue the point right now, whether I gave up the right to 'don't want' when I said 'I do.' Maybe so, maybe not. I've been thinking about it. But one thing is sure. Look into that tube. It's empty. There isn't any more. I used it up. If you hit me while you're here this time, I'm going out into the street with the bruises showing. And if you try hitting me where it doesn't show, I'm going down to the emergency room at Leahy and strip."

"You can't do that."

"Oh, yes. She can," a voice behind him said. "And she will. Other people will go with her to make sure that she does."

He turned around. His sister Lola was coming in from the enclosed back porch. He remembered very well how Lola had reacted when Latham Beckworth got a little on the side. He would be damned if he would ever have dreamed that Lenore would have told Lola.

Lola seemed to be reading his mind. "She didn't tell me. Faye Dashefsky did. Right after you left town this last time. Then Faye and I came down and confronted her. Got her to say what happened."

"She can," another voice said from the porch. "And she will. I still think that she should pick up Weshelle and walk out of this house with me. But if she will not leave you, if she believes herself bound by her vows, at least this time, you will not hit her. Or you will suffer consequences."

Wes' trouble-making Kraut bitch. Clara.

She laid a piece of paper on the table. It had Maurice Tito's signature. Some kind of namby-pamby protective order, at a guess.

"I told Judge Tito about your two priors over in Fairmont," Lola said. "After that, he didn't have any qualms about putting his name on the bottom line."

"How sisterly of you."

"If you hadn't arranged the whole thing while the two of you were over in Rudolstadt, I'd have damned well told Lenore about them, too. Before she ever married you."

"Neither one was my fault."

"Two beaten-up ex-girlfriends?" Lola snorted. "Not your fault? Tell me another fairy tale, little brother."

"They provoked me. Tried to ditch me before I was through with them."

"And Kiki's little boy provoked you?"

"He tried to get in between us."

"One more word," Lola said. "You won't hit Weshelle, any more than you will hit Lenore. You won't threaten to hit Weshelle to make Lenore do what you want. You won't touch Weshelle. You will not lay a finger on Weshelle. Do you understand us, Bryant? Your boss Steve Matheny knows about those two priors. So does the police chief, Preston Richards. Whoever we figured needs to know, does know. Touch either of them and you get thrown out of this house. Out of this town, if we can manage it."

"I still think," Clara said, "that she should come with me. Now."

After they left, he looked at Lenore.

"I'm sleeping in the nursery," she said. "I've moved all my things."

He went into the bedroom and slammed the door.

Damn those women. Damn all of them. If Faye Andersen had been involved, then so had probably every other one down where Lenore worked. Which was one more reason why married women shouldn't work. It gave them a chance to form alliances against their husbands.

Willard Carson didn't need to find Commies to have a conspiracy. All he needed to do was look around every day. Women. Sneaking, plotting, conspiring to get their own way. Not doing what they were told.

Vincenz Weitz arrived in Grantville from Halle scarcely a week after the shootings. He was directed to Jacques-Pierre Dumais by Bryant Holloway.

Business, he said, had unavoidably detained him from participating in the events of March fourth.

By this time, Jacques-Pierre had heard from Soubise, via de

Ron, with a lot more information about what had been going on at *Zum Weissen Schwan*. Weitz confirmed, inadvertently perhaps, that Locquifier had never meant the hospital demonstration to be more than a distraction.

In Weitz's opinion, although he was certainly displeased that the hoped-for effects of the attacks on both the hospital and the synagogue seemed to be backfiring, he said that he thought that Locquifier might be able to pull something worthwhile out of it yet.

Dumais found Weitz a little startling. The man was really, genuinely, indignant.

Right now, Weitz was pointing out at great length that, except for the little problem of the anti-Semitic riots, Fettmilch's 1612–1614 revolt in Frankfurt had really stood for a lot of things that Mike Stearns was trying to introduce to the USE now. A greater voice for the average citizen in the deliberations of the council, so that the old patricians who had adopted a near-noble lifestyle wouldn't have it all their way any more. Citizenship for the Calvinist refugees. An end to financial corruption. The riots against the Jews had been the least of it, and didn't happen for a couple of years after the revolt started. A man could sort of understand why Matthias, the Holy Roman Emperor at the time, had declared the actions of Fettmilch and his followers to be treasonous. Why he'd had them executed. Thirty-eight people of them tried; seven of them executed. But you'd think that if the Grantvillers meant all the stuff they went around saying about the will of the people, they ought to appreciate their pioneering efforts of Fettmilch's followers to bring democracy to one of the great imperial cities rather than heaping their heads with scorn.

"Their heads. Literally. Not one of the up-timers who passed through Frankfurt"—as far as he knew, at least—"has ever said a word about taking the heads down from the bridge tower."

"What heads?" Dumais asked. "What bridge?"

"The head of Vincenz Fettmilch, of course. Konrad Gerngroß, Konrad Schopp, and Georg Ebel. A gingerbread baker, a carpenter, a tailor, and a dyer from the suburb of Sachsenhausen. Just the kind of people that these up-timers claim ought to get involved in politics instead of leaving them to the great merchants and patricians. But they leave their heads up on the bridge."

Dumais let him rant.

Weitz claimed—genuinely, Dumais thought—to know nothing at all about who carried out the assassinations of Dreeson and Wiley. That didn't prevent him from having opinions. No matter who shot the men, their deaths might be useful. He directed Dumais to duplicate a flyer he had drafted, accusing Veronica Dreeson of harboring anti-Semitic beliefs because she had not been standing on the steps of the synagogue next to her husband the way Inez Wiley was Standing By Her Man. Dumais was to make some extra stencils for him to distribute in other towns. Plus doing a run of the flyers from one stencil right here and now.

Jacques-Pierre did so with great efficiency. That very afternoon. Not because he sympathized with the man's views about the Jews, but on the theory that the sooner Weitz left town again, the better. Strangers really were attracting a lot of official attention in Grantville right now.

Weitz took the stencils and left immediately. As soon as he had distributed the stencils to his contacts, the flyers would appear in multiple locations on the same day. He told Dumais that was one of Locquifier's favorite techniques, now.

It was astonishing in a way that even now, after the assassinations, Weitz managed to drop the flyers themselves, piles of them, at various points inside the Ring of Fire without being caught.

That evening, Dumais wrote a really long report for Duke Henri de Rohan and sent it out of Grantville in four copies—two to Benjamin de Rohan in Frankfurt and two to the duke himself in Besançon. In each case, one by the postal system and one by courier. At least one of them should get through. He hoped. It should be enough to enable them to make sense of all the newspaper reports, which were totally confusing, even right here in Grantville where it had all happened. They must be worse elsewhere.

Bryant Holloway certainly found the flyer completely confusing. He waved it at Jacques-Pierre. "But the attackers were the ones who were anti-Semitic. Weren't they?" he asked. "Not Ronnie Dreeson?"

Dumais admitted that they were, while wishing that Holloway had not brought up this topic in the dining room of the Willard Hotel. Luckily, no one was at the nearby tables.

"You *were* working with them, weren't you?" Holloway peered at him suspiciously. "The demonstration out at the hospital and everything? You had me find those men for you."

Dumais granted this also. Only as far as the hospital went. But it was probably too much to hope that even Holloway would swallow the argument that the occurrence of two riots and two assassinations on the same day had been purely coincidental. At least, not that the two demonstrations had been coincidental, considering that he had directed Weitz to Dumais.

"But then, if someone goes around saying that Ronnie Dreeson hates the Jews, that would make it seem like she's on *your* side, wouldn't it? Why would you want that?"

"I do not hate the Jews," said Jacques-Pierre mildly. All he needed—or didn't need—at that point was for Veda Mae to start insisting to Bryant that "we" are anti-Kraut; not anti-Jewish. With Holloway agreeing that the point of the whole thing was that they did not like having all these Kraut immigrants in Grantville.

Holloway was now digressing into a diatribe against his father-in-law's wife. Again. He was irrationally hostile to the woman, for no apparent reason that Jacques-Pierre could determine.

Veda Mae started out, once more, on the issue of the baptism of the Beasley child at MaidenFresh Laundries. Adding, this time, a new grievance: that Vesta Rawls and that manager of hers, Mitch Hobbs, who was marrying a Kraut girl, had given that Kraut preacher permission to come down and hold services in the entryway every Sunday afternoon, so Jarvis Beasley's Kraut wife, the bigamist, could go to church.

"This is just the thin edge of the wedge," she insisted. "Watch and see if I'm not right. Pretty soon, there won't be Kraut churches just on each side of town. Pretty soon, there'll be one right in the middle, with all of the proper ones, like the Baptists and Methodists. The Catholics, even."

Dumais drew a deep breath, trying to sort out the tangents into which the two of them could fly at the slightest passing thought from the essentials of the issue in regard to Mrs. Dreeson.

He patiently pointed out that propaganda did not have to be true to be effective, but just have the tiniest element of plausibility. He pointed out that from his reading of American history, he had concluded that enough of the up-timers would be inclined to assume that almost any German had covert anti-Semitic tendencies that the fact that Mrs. Dreeson was not there, combined with her lack of publicly displayed grief, should be sufficient to drive a wedge between the up-timers who held positions of authority in Grantville and the SoTF and the USE and the Richter family.

Or, at least, to begin the process of undermining the status of Hans Richter as national hero and the influence of Gretchen Richter as a principal organizer of the Committees of Correspondence, which would have a very anti-German effect.

That was what the pamphlet was really about. Anti-Semitism was purely coincidental.

Frau Haggerty and Herr Holloway seemed somewhat happier after this illuminating exegesis. Not a lot. Dismissing the flyer in regard to Frau Dreeson, Holloway returned to his diatribe against Clara Bachmeierin and Veda Mae resumed her complaints against Mitch Hobbs, his Kraut girlfriend, and Lutheran church services at MaidenFresh Laundries.

By the end of supper, Jacques-Pierre had *la migraine.* Badly.

Headache or not, he could still think clearly enough. It was not good that Mrs. Haggerty had said these things. If she continued to say them in public, it might cause questions. Bring people to ask where she had encountered the ideas.

Jacques-Pierre began to consider retirement. Seriously.

For the second time in his life.

The first time, Velma Hardesty had caused the thought to cross his mind.

He started to make plans to leave Grantville. Quite quickly, if necessary.

Not yet, however. There were still a few things to be done, such as arranging for the disposal of some records and papers. Records and papers in regard to Mauger's channeling the money that had financed the demonstration at the hospital that had gone so miserably awry. For the time being, they were safe enough where they were, in Madame Haggerty's enclosed back porch. She rarely used that part of her house and, unlike most Grantvillers, was far too cantankerous to have taken in boarders. But disposal was turning out to be more difficult than it might seem. He was almost certain that he was under surveillance.

Perhaps Holloway could be of assistance. Dumais understood that he would be remaining in Grantville for another three weeks before starting his next assignment.

Chapter 54

Grantville

"Do something revolutionary," Ron recommended. "The Committees of Correspondence approve of doing revolutionary things. We're in the middle of a nationwide purge or something. So kiss me good night here in the hall, instead of going out on the sidewalk. The temperature is dropping and you'll get your ears cold again."

Missy thought about it. Right inside her own house? That would . . . change things, somehow.

As a kind of temporary compromise, she put her arms around his waist and her face against his. "Could you talk to your manager Kautz in the morning?" she asked. "I know that your dad trained him and that he knows what he's doing, but he doesn't seem to be into sharing. It's as if he's convinced that 'we hold these truths to be self-evident.' Can you persuade him that if he rolls over dead one of these days, they won't be so self-evident to anyone else now on the payroll? Your dad isn't really in a position to come all the way back here, just to train someone else."

"I'll give it a try."

He took his hand and moved her chin. "You'll get your nose cold, too, if you don't kiss me right here. And your feet wet and very cold. The rain is changing to sleet."

The impish electrons that had been residing in her kneecaps and hip sockets all winter perked up at the thought of being able to take advantage of a kiss that would take place in a warm, dry, and generally comfortable environment for a change. With the result that the requested kiss not only occurred, but incorporated what amounted to a crotch grind.

"Wow," Ron said. "Very enticing. A new addition to the repertoire. Where has this been before?"

"If you think I would do that outdoors where people could see us . . ."

"I'm crazier than you think I am." Ron moved his hands down where they could encourage the electrons to do it again. "Wish I didn't have to go get some work done."

There was another distinct pause before the front door opened and closed.

Missy came back into the living room and looked at her parents, who were valiantly attempting to give the impression that they hadn't heard every word. Not to mention counted the duration of every interval between the words. And that they had been born middle-aged.

Chad finally gave it up as futile.

"What's with the self-evident truths?" he asked.

"We're working on a formal procedures manual now. They've been winging it without one. Most of the staff is pretty cooperative."

"But some of it isn't." Chad grinned. "Business as usual. But why his business and not mine?"

"I don't know, exactly." Missy stood there. "Actually, a lot of the stuff that I learned Saturday mornings, over the years, racketing around in your office, has been pretty helpful. I guess I should say 'Thanks.'"

"You'll have to deal with it some day, you know," Chad said. "My business. Businesses. Chip certainly isn't going to."

She put her hand on the corner of the piano.

"Nothing urgent," he said. "Nothing to interfere with getting your education for the next few years. But eventually. That's something to tuck away in your mind. Fit into your schedule as time goes on."

"Damn it, Tino! No." Ed Piazza was close to exploding.

"The county board had to do something about replacing Henry. We couldn't just let it hang. Not with everything else that's going on. I got the most votes in the county board election last year, so they picked me as interim mayor. I'll finish out his term."

Chad Jenkins stood up. "You will not fill out his term. The county charter provides for a special election. That's what we'll have. Whether you and Frisch like it or not."

Tino stomped out. Chad tuned to Ed. "I'd feel happier about it if we had any idea who ought to succeed Henry. I've talked to Willie Ray and to several others. All we come up with is blank minds. The Crown Loyalists will nominate either Tino Nobili or Hartmuth Frisch, I suppose. I just can't predict what our caucus will do."

"The meeting will now come to order." Willie Ray Hudson, as local party chairman, banged the gavel.

He looked around. The auditorium at the middle school was packed. There must be fifty copies of *Robert's Rules of Order* in the room. At least three-quarters of them in German.

"The floor is now open for nominations."

About a hundred hands went up.

One of them belonged to Orval McIntire. The rest of them belonged to a caucus of women all sitting together over on the left side.

Well, the majority rules. Especially under these circumstances.

He motioned. "Inez."

She didn't stand up. She couldn't. She was still in a wheel chair.

"We're together," she said. "All of us. Ronnie's going to speak."

Veronica got up.

"Not everybody's going off to Bamberg," she said. "Somebody's got to take care of this town. We've got a candidate. She was the executive assistant to the Emergency Committee, right after the Ring of Fire. She was executive assistant to Mike Stearns when he was president of the NUS. When he went off to Magdeburg and Ed Piazza took over, she stayed here in town and she's been working for Ed ever since. She knows how things work."

"Not to mention," Veleda Riddle muttered, loudly enough to be heard by almost everyone, "where all the bodies are buried."

Ronnie was still reading her prepared speech. "She is civic-minded. She has been an active member of the League of Women Voters ever since it was founded. Her husband's business is here, so she's going to have to quit her state job. So, we . . ." She stopped and waved at the group. "All of us. We nominate Liz Carstairs to run for mayor of West Virginia County on the Fourth of July Party ticket."

"Well, I'll be damned," Ed said. "If that didn't come at us right out of left field."

Chad Jenkins nodded in agreement.

Annabelle and Debbie looked at each other, wondering once more at the innocence of the male of the species about so many things.

"Not," Annabelle said, "if you really sit down and think about it."

"Can Liz win?" Joe Stull asked. "Against Frisch?"

"Yes," every woman in the room said at once.

Veda Mae Haggerty was sitting in the Willard Hotel dining room again—for lunch, this time—when she said what she said about Veronica Dreeson. Again.

It was pretty much what she had read in the pamphlet. About how all Krauts were anti-Jewish and Ronnie hadn't been there with Henry when he was shot, so she had probably been a supporter of that mob of Krauts who were attacking the synagogue.

She said it very loudly. A lot of other people were listening.

The popular disapproval was general. Except, of course, among those people who thought there might be something in it.

She gave her lunch partner a copy of the pamphlet and assured her that Jacques-Pierre Dumais could explain what it all meant.

Pam Hardesty had not realized, in advance, how many incredibly boring, unpleasant people an apprentice spook had to be nice to. She went home, wrote up her longest report so far, even longer than the one about the garage, and sent it to Cory Joe.

Don Francisco was pleased. It was so nice to know more or less what one was looking for. It enabled one to concentrate on the needles and ignore most of the haystack.

"That's the best description that I can give," Minnie said.

"It is admirable," Don Francisco said. "You should not criticize yourself."

It *was* admirable. The girl had recalled many nuances that an experienced observer might have missed. But how to record them, make them permanent, distribute them?

"I sure wish," Preston Richards said, "that Grantville had an Identikit setup. But we didn't."

Explanations followed.

"Lenore can do it," Wes Jenkins said.

"Do what?" Richards asked.

"Make sketches from Minnie's description. You should have seen the sketches she gave Clara for Christmas, that she did from Mom's old family photos."

"Lenore?" Don Francisco asked.

"My older daughter."

"Can you bring her here?"

"She is here. Well, not right here, but downstairs and in the other wing. She's a records transcriber for Chuck Riddle's setup. We can take Minnie down there."

"Someone take her, then. Not you. I have more questions about the Fulda end of things." Don Francisco looked around the room for a surplus participant in the meeting. "You do it, Stone."

Lenore understood almost right away. She listened to Minnie go through her descriptions, again and again. She produced a set of sketches. Not just a "mug shot" but also full length views of the sniper from various angles, showing what he was wearing and how he held his body. It was amazing what her idea of placing the railings and balustrades of the bridge behind him contributed. Height, set of shoulders, angle of the head.

It took quite a while. As Minnie and Lenore worked, Ron wandered around the office.

As they were getting ready to leave, he pointed at the prints up over Lenore's desk. "What are those?" he asked.

"A classical Greek temple. It's called the Erechtheum."

"I mean, the women who are standing there where you'd expect a column to be."

"They're called caryatids."

"Cool."

Ron looked at them again, more closely. "I've never seen anything of the kind, before. I'm impressed."

He was impressed. They were absolutely magnificent.

The reminded him of Missy. Hairdos. Faces. Shapes. Posture.

Maybe that was why she got to him so. What kind of a guy would make do with "cute" or merely "pretty" when, with a little luck, he could have stupendous?

Lenore was her cousin, but didn't look a thing like her.

"You know," he said. "I don't think I've ever seen Missy in a dress. She says she doesn't look good in dresses. But she would look wonderful in a dress like that."

Don Francisco was delighted with the sketches of the assassin. The etcher whom he employed to make the plates did an excellent job. The pictures appeared in every newspaper in the USE with facilities to duplicate them. Often as cruder woodcuts, to be sure, but still showing the essence of the man's appearance.

He hoped that Locquifier and Ducos would be profoundly annoyed.

He was quite impressed with the competence of the girl Minnie. Plus, he had that letter from Denise Beasley. The Grantvillers told him that the two were close friends.

Chapter 55

Haarlem, the Netherlands

Don Francisco sent Cory Joe Lang off to the Netherlands to try to deal with the various threads that led to Laurent Mauger.

In the course of gathering information, Cory Joe looked up his mother, even if reluctantly, and then went up to Leiden to talk to Jean-Louis LaChapelle again. He also met Mauger's half-niece, LaChapelle's half-cousin, Alida Pieterz.

Alida reacted to the tow-blond hair on top of Cory Joe's head much the way Jean-Louis LaChapelle had reacted to his half-sister Pam. A reaction which Cory Joe fully reciprocated. Cory Joe wondered with some amusement whether there was actually a chemical reaction between members of the Mauger and Hardesty family lines—one that could be measured by someone like Bill Hudson if he had the chance and the proper set of calipers.

Jean-Louis had been delighted to receive the letter and lava lamp report from Pam.

Laurent Mauger was amazed and totally bewildered when the two young men announced that they wished to initiate marriage negotiations with the stated purpose of strengthening the business and personal ties in the new family alliance between Grantville and Mauger's enterprises.

He certainly had no objections, since this might ameliorate the objections that the children of one of his half-sisters and one of his sisters might raise in the future in regard to the inheritance status of the child that his adored Velma was carrying.

There were no guarantees of that, but it might help. Additionally, Lang was prepared to be most accommodating in the matter of Alida's nonexistent dowry. In fact, Lang said that he didn't give a damn whether she had one or not, if she was prepared to live on what he earned.

Alida, who had been a "poor cousin" for nearly fifteen years, since her father and mother died, declared that she was perfectly prepared.

Cory Joe warned her that this wasn't going to be a Cinderella story. That she would be exchanging a life of sharing an attic room with her sister Madeleine, wearing hand-me-downs, running errands for her employer, and eating at the second table, for sharing an efficiency apartment in the Magdeburg officers' quarters with him, buying at thrift shops, finding a job, and eating a lot of bean and barley soup, which she would have to stir herself unless he could get his sister Pam in Grantville to find a crock pot at a yard sale. He even went so far as to warn her that there was a good chance he'd have to move to Prague in the not-so-distant future.

Job-related reasons, he explained. He drew the line—right now, anyway—at explaining to Alida the complexities of his professional relationship with Francisco Nasi. Cory Joe figured he'd been honest enough, for the time being. He saw no point in piling on the fact that his real job was assistant and bodyguard to a Sephardic spymaster soon to be in private enterprise in what had to be one of the shadiest and riskiest businesses in the world.

Alida took into account that Version One of a fairly Spartan continuing lifestyle did not include Cory Joe, whereas Version Two did. She repeated that she was perfectly prepared, while thinking that she would deal with figuring out what a crock pot was later.

Consequently, the lawyers went to work.

In the case of LaChapelle, unfortunately, Jean-Louis proceeded without notifying Pam in advance. He assumed that since her older brother and stepfather were both present and agreeing to the provisions of the marriage contract, all would be well with Pam when he returned to Grantville with the happy news that they were betrothed.

Jean-Louis was a young man with an immense amount of self-confidence.

Laurent Mauger saw no reason to bother his darling Velma about the negotiations for her two oldest children's marriages until all the provisions of the marriage contracts had been satisfactorily resolved. Worry and concern might mark the unborn child. Better for her to remain quietly at the villa, without a concern in the world, sheltered and protected by his sisters.

Grantville

Before Grantville's law enforcement staff was ready to move, all paperwork and authorizations in hand, Jacques-Pierre Dumais left town.

The Garbage Guys, Duck and Big Dog Carpenter and Gary Haggerty, told the powers that be that he quit his job and was going to the Netherlands on the grounds that his good friends Laurent Mauger and his wife Velma had invited him to come be godfather to their baby and take over the day-to-day management of a new startup company, which would be manufacturing lava lamps.

As Veda Mae said to Willard Carson and Pam Hardesty, all of them at Garbage Guys were quite proud of his success. It went to show how much an immigrant could accomplish after he had been exposed to that good old American spirit of get-up-and-go for a little while.

She was sure that he would be spreading that spirit up there among the Dutch. After all, he had taken out his citizenship papers here in Grantville. She had sponsored him herself.

Frankfurt am Main

Soubise read the latest letter from his brother for the third time. His valet was already packing.

Henri was quite right, of course. This had been Ducos again.

The man was simply creating too many problems for the remainder of the Huguenot diaspora. Locquifier and Ouvrard had gotten out of town, before the authorities could apprehend them. Before even de Ron knew that they were gone. Leaving him stuck with the last three weeks of their bill, which had made him rather snappish to deal with recently.

Deneau was in a morgue in Grantville, unless someone had paid for his burial.

Ancelin was in Grantville's jail. Thus far, taking full advantage of the prohibition on judicial torture that the congress of the State of Thuringia-Franconia had enacted at the insistence of the up-timers—a thoroughly wrong-headed law, in Soubise's opinion—he had said nothing. But Francisco Nasi was no slouch; and neither, from what Soubise could tell, was Grantville's police chief Preston Richards. Between the two of them, if they didn't know already, they would figure out that Ancelin was a central figure in the plot. It was safe to assume that the officials of West Virginia County would keep him as their unwilling guest for a long, long, time.

Brillard? Nobody had seen Brillard for a couple of months. They would probably find him with Ducos. When they found Ducos.

Which was the critical thing. Soubise was leaving for England. From there, he would go to Scotland. *Noblesse oblige.* He looked at Joachim Sandrart, who would be traveling with him. "We will take care of our own."

Sandrart laughed. "If, as Ron Stone would say, somebody hasn't beaten us to it."

Magdeburg

Francisco Nasi reviewed the several reports that Cory Joe Lang had sent from Haarlem, along with copies of the draft marriage contracts for himself and Alida Pieterz and for Jean-Louis LaChapelle and Pam Hardesty. The young man had remarked blithely in the accompanying letter that this way, he should be in an even better position to keep an eye on what his stepfather was up to with Dumais. Not to mention, of course, that Alida was one really scrumptious girl, and he couldn't imagine why someone hadn't married her long before now. That accomplished, he and Jean-Louis would be leaving for Grantville.

✧ ✧ ✧

"Sometimes," Don Francisco said to Mike Stearns, "perspective is everything."

"Just what does that comment pertain to?"

"I have contemplated the latest reports from Grantville with some disbelief. Particularly the one about Dumais' citizenship papers. Which, however, checked out in the records at the administration building."

"It does seem a trifle farfetched."

"Of course, if one studies the Christian scriptures, it becomes quite plain that the Saul of Tarsus who became Paul made a very good thing of being a Roman citizen. Under the circumstances. It certainly improved the circumstances under which he was imprisoned here and there."

Mike nodded.

"Indeed," Don Francisco continued, "if one looks at the Christian scriptures from the right perspective, one might classify them as being among the ancient classics."

"Different viewpoints, though."

"Certainly. But there are common elements with the thought of Seneca." He paused. "I need to make a trip to Grantville, I think, if you can spare me for a few days."

Mike wondered what on earth Francisco was up to now.

Grantville

"If you would be willing, of course," Don Francisco said. "There is insufficient evidence to indict Frau Haggerty for treason or anything else of a serious nature. Perhaps unfortunately, being a loathsome and vile human being is not, by itself, a criminal offense. The prosecuting attorney is profoundly frustrated."

Pam looked at him.

Talking to Veda Mae, as a short term thing with a specific purpose, had been bearable. But . . .

"Frau Haggerty appears to be quite loquacious whenever she has a sympathetic listener. She so rarely has one, given her personality. The way she saw him, Monsieur Dumais was a thoughtful, concerned man. Now that he has left town, she is not going to have her 'sounding board.' And you have been talking to her already. She will not cooperate with the police, but who knows how much incidental information she picked up over the past few months? If you could keep listening to her and collecting the things she lets drop . . . You are better suited to do it than Missy Jenkins. She has difficulty in disguising her feelings about people."

"Growing up with Velma," Pam said, "I got a lot of practice disguising my feelings about people. I was home the night that Gina Goodman shot at Will Wiley. I was sixteen. In the next room, doing homework. The newspapers said that they were in bed together, but actually, by the time she let the gun off, he had jumped out and was standing up, trying to talk to her. The slug came through the wall and went about three inches above my head. Walls in mobile homes aren't very thick. I didn't have time to have hysterics. Tina and Susan were asleep in the room beyond mine. I walked out into the hall, looked into Mom's bedroom and saw the three of them, suggested to Gina that I thought it would be a really wonderful idea if she put that gun down, walked on into the living room, and called the police. If I hadn't disguised my feelings, I would have reverted to monkeydom and been hanging from the ceiling by my tail, gibbering."

Don Francisco wondered what monkeys had to do with it. "We will pay you an hourly rate."

"I don't believe this," Pam said. "I'm a spook. An actual on-the-payroll spook. Just like Cory Joe."

"Your brother," Nasi said piously, "is in military intelligence. That's something quite different."

Pam reacted to the news of her betrothal with even greater disbelief than she had reacted to the discovery that she was a salaried spy. And did not bother to disguise her feelings.

"The least you could have done was *ask* me!" she shrieked, to the general interest and entertainment of everyone in the state library's main reading room. "Cory Joe, what in hell were you thinking?"

"Err . . . I assumed that he had. It didn't seem likely that we would be drawing up a marriage contract if he hadn't."

"But . . ." Jean-Louis protested. He had come with Cory Joe. It was their first stop upon getting back to Grantville. They had come to break the happy news. "Don't you *want* to?"

She stared at him. Of course she wanted to. She knew it. He knew it. They knew it.

"You could have *asked* me first, you creep. You really could have."

She sent him back to Leiden without a "yes."

For one thing, it was obvious that Jean-Louis was having real trouble getting his mind around the concept of marrying a bastard after Pam brought it up.

Jean-Louis couldn't seem to help feeling like that. Down-timers' minds worked that way, most of them.

Sometimes you had to wonder if their heads were screwed on straight. What could a kid do about what his parents got up to before he was born? Or she was born?

After he left, Pam cried herself to sleep.

The next morning, she discovered that he'd left a poem in her mailbox.

It was pretty expressive. Descriptive of her charms. Both the ones he had seen and the ones he hadn't. As to the latter, Jean-Louis had a very good imagination. She hoped he wouldn't be disillusioned when confronted with reality.

Sometimes she could almost strangle Jean-Louis. Just when she was maddest at him, he would do something like that.

It was probably just as well that she'd started learning French. And Dutch.

She'd better read through the marriage contract, too. Cory Joe had left it on her desk at the library.

Besançon, the Franche-Comté

Henri de Rohan finished his letter to Francisco Nasi and sealed it. He would have it sent off on the morrow.

Most likely, of course, Nasi would not be the USE's spymaster for much longer. But Rohan was not concerned about whoever the incoming prime minister Wettin might appoint to the post. Even if that person was competent—a chancy proposition, given the way the Crown Loyalists seemed to be handing out posts as a reward for past favors rather than skills—he wouldn't know enough to be a problem.

Nasi was the one to worry about. He and his somewhat

frightening master, Stearns. Best to move quickly to deflect suspicion, by being open and honest about almost everything. Hopefully, the old ploy would work again: make a full confession unnecessary by freely offering a partial one.

Needless to say, the duke of Rohan had not seen fit to inform Nasi that Jacques-Pierre Dumais, now known to be employed by Mauger's expanding subsidiary in Leiden, was actually his own agent. There was the unfortunate matter of the riot at the hospital, to which the SoTF authorities might take exception.

He had warned Jacques-Pierre not to become overconfident. "Always prepare for a fall when fortune puffs you up, for it is then that peril comes closest."

Haarlem, the Netherlands

"Ah, Madame Mauger," Jacques-Pierre said, kissing her fingertips. "What an unexpected pleasure to meet you again."

And again, he thought. Very probably, again, and again, and again.

He had thought he was rid of Velma.

Now he held a position in her husband's firm. Quite a responsible position, in fact.

What had the duke warned him? "Do not become overconfident. Always prepare for a fall when fortune puffs you up, for it is then that peril comes closest."

So. Clearly, it was Meant, possibly even foreordained by divine providence, that Jacques-Pierre should endure this woman's conversation, *la migraine* or not.

"I was desolated when our pleasant conversations in Grantville were necessarily ended by your marriage."

"Me, too, Jacques-Pierre," Velma said. "Have you met Laurent's sisters, yet? Marie and I work on interpreting our horoscopes when she comes to the villa."

Ah, monsieur le duc de Rohan, he mused. *The things that a man must endure for the good of the Huguenot cause. Little do you know the travails to which you subject me.*

Grantville

"You know," Wes Jenkins said to Clara. "It's really getting harder and harder to define this whole war as a nice, neat conflict of 'us' against 'them.'"

She nodded.

He continued. "There was a comic strip, up-time. *Pogo*, it was called. 'We have met the enemy and they are us.' Or at the very least, it seems, they're our relatives. Our in-laws."

"Of course," Clara said. "It will come to be more so, the longer that Grantville is here in the Germanies. Perhaps it will help the up-timers understand better how someone like Wilhelm Wettin feels about his brother Bernhard and what is going on in Swabia and Alsace."

Part Nine

April 1635

Farewell! happy fields,
Where joy forever dwells! Hail, horrors! hail
Infernal world!

Chapter 56

Grantville, April 1635

Every guest who lived inside the limits of Grantville proper climbed somewhat inelegantly out of the back of Ray Hudson's flatbed farm truck, which was doing Easter Sunday taxi service today. Vera Hudson was waiting at the front door. "Where is Missy?" she asked, as she surveyed the guests.

Debbie went into the hall and concentrated on putting her coat on the rack, trying not to look at her sister Aura Lee's face. Easter was April 8 this year, not really an early date for it, but the weather was still chilly. "I told you that she was going to dinner at Wes and Clara's, Mother. I told you that last week."

"She should have come with you."

Debbie concentrated on taking deep, regular, breaths. "I also told you why. That since you preferred not to include Ron and Gerry Stone in your Easter, she has chosen to have dinner at a house to which they had also been invited."

"I had no obligation to invite those boys."

"Nani," Bill Hudson said, turning around from his immediate preoccupation with Jessica Booth, who was simultaneously Vera's apprentice as a master gardener and his own fiancée. "If you don't want to acknowledge that there's something between Ron and Missy, that's your business. But Ron is, in fact, my partner. I am living in his house right now."

"Mother," Aura Lee said.

Her brother Ray, Bill's father, touched her shoulder. At the kitchen door, his wife Marty was making "keep the lid on" gestures behind Vera's back. She and Ray did, after all, have to live with Vera on a day-to-day basis. The rest of the family—with the exception of Willie Ray, of course—could pick and choose how often they came out to the farm.

"For that matter, where's Joe?" Vera was momentarily distracted.

"At the fire department, of course. I told you last week that he had pulled volunteer duty shift this afternoon. Most of his VFD shifts fall on holidays now that he holds the exalted title of Secretary of Transportation of the State of Thuringia-Franconia." Aura Lee seemed to find it very interesting that she was wearing gloves, which she would need to pull off one finger at a time. "And that Billy Lee would be going with him. He's a cadet there now that he's sixteen. With Eric in Erfurt, it's just Juliann and Dana of the kids today. Besides Bill, of course."

She didn't add that her thirteen-year-old Juliann hadn't really wanted to come. Or that Ray and Marty's Dana hadn't really wanted to come, either, if Missy wasn't going to be there. Those two cousins were the same age. "Juliann and I need to leave early. We're meeting Joe and Billy Lee at Eden's for supper."

"Making an extra trip for Ray, I suppose." Vera went back to her original grievance. "You should have put your foot down and told Missy to come, Debbie."

Chad Jenkins cleared his throat. "Mom went to Wes and Clara's too. So she's having dinner with one of her grandmothers."

That earned him a withering glare.

Debbie clenched her jaws and with her right thumb and middle finger, twisted her wedding and first anniversary rings back and forth on her ring finger, knowing her mother would notice it.

Chad put his arm around her. She looked perfectly calm, but he could feel the tension in her shoulders. "Vera," he said. "We could go to Wes and Clara's too. It's not too late. They aren't eating until two o'clock. Ray could drive us back into town."

"Vera," said her husband Willie Ray. "Let it be. This time, let it be."

"It's too bad that Bryant had to work today," Eleanor Jenkins said. "It seems that he hardly ever comes to family occasions."

Lenore, Chandra, and Clara all looked at one another.

"Perhaps some other time," Lenore said.

Missy had an uneasy feeling that this was not the best thing to be talking about. She knew that Bryant was under observation in connection with the demonstration at the hospital, but she hadn't learned it from them. Ron had it from Cory Joe, and that was so she would know what to say in case anything about Bryant came up during her and Pam's conversations with Veda Mae and Dumais.

Distraction, distraction, my kingdom for a good distraction.

"Gran," she said. "I was looking at your picture wall the other day. Why isn't Mom and Dad's wedding photo there?"

"Because they didn't have one," Eleanor Jenkins said rather shortly.

Uncle Wes winked from across the table. "Actually," he said, "they did. I'm sure that Debbie still has it somewhere. But it was a Polaroid. If it had been up on the wall all these years, exposed to daylight, it would long since have faded away. Maybe you could have her get it out and make a sketch from it, Lenore. That would last a lot longer."

Missy looked at him. "There has to be a story in this somewhere. One that nobody ever bothered to tell Chip and me."

"I was down in Charleston, then," Wes said. "I'd been working there ever since I graduated from WVU. Chad called me and asked whether, if they came, Lena and I would put them up while they waited out getting the license and all. I told him that I could do better than that. I knew people around the courthouse by then. If they gave me a date, I'd have the judge prepped to waive the waiting period for good cause, so they could get it all done in one day. That's what they did. Drove down Friday, starting the first thing in the morning, the day after Christmas. Got the license. Married in the judge's chambers with Lena and me as attendants. The judge's secretary took the Polaroid of the five of us. That was always his present to couples he married."

"They didn't even have the courtesy to call and tell us that they had done it," Gran said. Missy thought that her voice was the embodiment of "miffed."

"*I* called and told you," Wes pointed out.

"That's not quite the same thing."

"I called and told Willie Ray and Vera. I even called and told

Bruce and Lily Jefferson. For that, I should have received a decoration for 'heroism above and beyond the call of duty.'"

Missy had a suspicion that there was more to this story than Uncle Wes was sharing with her.

From the expressions on Lenore and Chandra's faces, they had the same thought.

All three of them looked at their grandmother.

"I'm not going to tell you," she said. "If Wes wants to, he can, as far as I'm concerned. Keeping in mind that it will be from his perspective, of course."

Clara nodded, encouraging him to go on.

"Bruce and Lily, Don Jefferson's parents," Wes said. "Ever since he was killed, they had been trying to suck the life out of Debbie. Acting like vampires, trying to turn her into a white marble statue on his tombstone, labeled 'The Tragic Young Widow.' A perpetual monument to a dead boy. Willie Ray fought them; got her back into school. Backed her on going for a teaching certificate. But they weren't giving up." He frowned. "Vera and Lily were best friends. Vera sort of agreed with her. I'm pretty sure that for eight years, Debbie never went out on a date. It wouldn't have been worth the grief they would have given her."

Wes' frown was suddenly replaced by a wicked grin. "I don't know exactly what Chad did to persuade her that he was worth the grief they were undoubtedly going to give her. He wasn't quite that confiding in his big brother. But I beg leave to doubt the official explanation he made at the time, which was that the big bad spider enticed the dainty little fly into his web by offering to let her look at exploded diagrams of the brand new 1981 model year engines in place of the traditional etchings. They did not have the hypnotic effect of the up-to-date WVU Economics Department bibliography of readings on international trade policy I would have used in the same situation. But . . ."

"Dad!" Lenore said.

Her father wrinkled his nose at her. "Whatever it was, it worked and you now have an Aunt Debbie.

"In any case," Wes went on, "Let me figure. He graduated from WVU in December 1979, a semester early, and came back to Grantville to manage the garage after Dad's stroke. It was just before Labor Day in 1980 that he called to say that Debbie had agreed to marry him. That's the way he put it. Not that they were engaged. You've probably noticed that she doesn't have a traditional engagement ring. Don's parents made it very plain that she would offend them grievously by wearing one and Vera didn't think it would be 'appropriate' when Debbie had removed Don's rings so very recently."

"Look," Missy said. "I've always known that Nani didn't like Dad, but this is simply off the wall. Where did Mom get the ring she wears?"

"Chad got it for their first anniversary," Eleanor said. "Amethyst for her birth stone surrounded with opals for his. A wraparound for the wedding ring. Considering that he was salting away most of his money to be ready to buy the dealership when Lou Prickett got to the point he had to give it up, it was providential that both of them had stones that were reasonably affordable. Chad didn't have a lot of spare cash at the time."

Wes nodded. "The way Bruce and Lily, and Vera for that matter, reacted was more than a little 'off the wall,' to use your phrase. Sure, he was younger than Debbie, but not all that much. Three and a half years. Three years and eight months, to be exact. They went on about it as if it was a lot more. Debbie was a kid the first time she got married.

"They were intending to get married over Christmas, so as to have at least a few days of honeymoon, given that she was teaching. So they started trying to schedule a wedding at First Methodist in Grantville. Nothing before Christmas would work, according to your Nani. There was Anne's school program. There was Anne's Sunday school program. There was Anne's holiday piano recital. Debbie couldn't possibly miss a one of those, of course. At least not according to Vera."

Missy thought, *Anne again*.

Wes went on. "Then they started trying to find a day between Christmas and New Year's. Nothing suited Vera. So nothing was set. My personal opinion is that Vera and the Jeffersons were hoping to drag things out until Chad gave up. Which led to the Charleston expedition. Lena and I had been intending to take them out to dinner, so they would have a little celebration, but the truth is that by the time the ceremony was over, the two of them were so tense that they practically twanged each time they touched. So instead, we took a phone number where we could reach them in case of dire emergency, told them to come back on New Year's Eve and we would take them out to dinner then, and I wished them good night. Even though it was three o'clock in the afternoon."

Wes' grin took on an even more wicked slant. "I have to say that by the time they reemerged into public view five days later, they were a lot more relaxed."

His mother frowned at him disapprovingly.

"Be calm, Mom," Wes said. "Clara doesn't shock as easily as Lena did."

Chandra giggled.

Missy blushed. This was a new way of thinking about her parents. Very new.

Wes' expression changed to regret. "Unfortunately, I didn't put in a separate call to tell Anne. I wished that I had, later, even though she was only nine. Vera and Lily had a week to work on her before Chad and Debbie got home. And they were both absolutely convinced that the marriage was a mistake. That there was no way it would last."

Saluting his mother, he added, his voice a little ironic, "I know you didn't think that it would any more than they did, but at least you never tried to revoke a signed treaty."

Missy glanced quickly at Ron and Gerry, wondering how they would take a conversation that had turned serious about family business.

"I thought that Debbie was bringing him more . . . complications . . . than any twenty-three year old man really needed," Eleanor grumped.

Missy nodded. "Thanks."

She had a lot of new information to process. As family dinners went, this one had been a doozy.

Chandra dropped the kids off. With about six cubic feet of equipment, she thought.

"You know, Aunt Debbie, this is really nice of you. Back when I asked you, of course, I didn't know that Clara was expecting yet. But now, I sure wouldn't feel right about asking Dad and her to keep them when she's so far along."

"I've had it on my calendar since Thanksgiving, honey bun. Between Gertrude and Missy and me, it's no problem to manage four of them for a few days. I know this situation with Nathan has been eating at your mind."

Chandra didn't quite smile. "I guess that's what you can call it. At any rate, it's been going on long enough. I can't put it off any longer."

"How are you getting to Frankfurt?"

"I bought a passage on the regular freight wagon as far as Erfurt. It's slow, but it's reliable. Those oiled canvas covers keep rain off a lot better than anything a person riding a horse can wear. And Heinz has put cushions on the passenger seats. He got the idea from the pews at church. From there, I'm riding with Martin Wackernagel. The courier, you know. He comes down to Grantville regularly."

Debbie laughed.

Chandra caught her ride.

Debbie hadn't exactly forgotten what it was like to have four small children in her house. Except for brief occasions when they came as guests and then went home again, she had never before had four small children in her house at one time. Plus the dishwasher broke and the repairman said he was going to have to have a part fabricated by the one-off shop behind the hardware store.

Gertrude would have to get up for school in the morning, so Debbie had sent her to bed.

Which was why she and Missy were washing dishes at eleven-thirty p.m.

"Why don't you have a wedding photo, Mom?" Missy asked. She had finally gotten up enough nerve to tackle research in the primary sources. She wanted her mother's version as well as Uncle Wes' version. "It's about the only thing missing from Gran's wall."

Her mother almost laughed. Or almost sobbed. It was hard to tell.

"We wanted to get married at Christmas so we could have a sort of honeymoon, even a few days. It was that or wait until school was out. We were scheduling a wedding, or trying to, around Anne's school play, Anne's Sunday school program. With your Nani, to tell the truth, really wishing we weren't scheduling a wedding at all. Your Gran too, I think. I'm sure, even though she kept her mouth shut. To me, at least. I have no idea what she said to Chad. I think, even now, that I'd rather not know, just in the interest of amicable relations. Anyway, it couldn't be before Christmas; it would have to be after, everyone insisted.

"That was long before Simon Jones became minister at First Methodist, of course. The man we had then was inclined to listen to Nani. She was taking on as if the remarriage of a widow were something shameful. Equivalent to the woman taken in adultery. She didn't even want us to hold it in the sanctuary. She wanted us to go to the parsonage. Street clothes. No attendants. No guests. No reception. She didn't want Anne to be present; Don's parents agreed with her. If it had been possible in our culture back then, I think they would have hired mourners, the way the down-timers do now to follow the hearses through the streets.

"Finally, believe it or not, with nothing procedural decided here in Grantville, we drove down to Charleston the day after Christmas, got the license there, and got married at the courthouse, with Wes and Lena as witnesses. Wes knew people there because he'd been working in Charleston for several years, ever since he graduated from WVU. He persuaded the judge to waive the waiting period, so we didn't have to perch somewhere for three days. We've never had a church ceremony.

"It isn't as if we launched ourselves into marriage to the sound of joyous celebrations, surrounded by legions of well wishers. So no wedding photo for the wall. In our dresser, I have a snapshot. I can show it to you. The judge's secretary took it. The four of us with the judge, in his chambers. It's really faded, even though I've kept it in an envelope. If it had been up on Gran's wall, exposed to the light, it would be entirely gone by now."

"Mom," Missy asked. "If things were like that, why did you marry Dad?"

Debbie looked up frowning. "Your father can be very persuasive when he sets his mind to it. And he was persistent."

That wasn't much help. "Come on, Mom," she said.

Missy could almost see her mother counting up the birthdays and deciding that Missy was old enough to hear this now.

"Nobody ever said that I had a full figure and it's a lot fuller now than it was then. Before we were married, Chad had never seen me undressed. He'd seen me in tee-shirts and shorts, of course, driving me between WVU and Grantville for two years. Anyway, after we started, well, sort of dating, I thought about letting him see more, like me in a bathing suit. Two piece. I wasn't, um, all that sure that he was prepared for stretch marks."

Debbie fiddled with the dishcloth. "But any occasion that I was wearing a bathing suit, he would have been too. I wasn't quite ready to deal with that much . . . uncovered physique yet, the summer before we got married."

Missy gave her mother one of those looks.

"Well, all right. Being a young schoolteacher in any small town has the wonderfully inhibiting effect of being the under watchful eye of not just your current students' parents but also that of all your former students' parents and future students' parents, as well as anyone in the school administration, as well as all the students from your school. Adding Don's and my parents was just frosting on the cake. Both of us all but nude in public when we *started* kissing, word would spread like wildfire."

Her mother would obviously rather not have said that. Perhaps as a slight revenge, she added, "Which is something that you might want to keep in mind in regard to Ron Stone, now that spring is coming. Considering how far the two of you apparently managed to strip in a snowbank in the middle of February."

"That," Missy said a little stiffly, "was a one time aberration."

Debbie's face clearly expressed her doubts. "Keep in mind how far aberrant you would have been by the end if you hadn't started out wearing parkas," she admonished. "You both had melted snow in your underwear and I did not buy the 'snow angels' explanation for one second.

"Anyway, Chad had to have been able to tell, by looking and feeling through my clothes, that he wasn't getting 'lush.' And when the time came, he seemed happy enough with what there was of my body. Ah . . . Well, it wasn't very impressive, but it worked fine. All the parts were in order. I got pregnant with you kids and all that."

Missy took a very deep breath. "What went wrong? Nobody explained it to me, back then. Nobody explained anything."

Debbie looked at her. "Long run or short run?"

"Both. If you will."

"Long run, I couldn't shut the door. Sometimes you have to shut a door. I couldn't admit to myself that the way things had worked out, for all practical purposes, Anne was my younger sister rather than my daughter.

"I don't want to blame anyone else. Don's parents would never have liked it that I was marrying again. Bruce and Lily might, just barely might, have accepted my remarriage if I had chosen a man fifteen or twenty years older than I was, well established, and they could have persuaded themselves that I was marrying again for the sake of security. Stability. Something like that.

"But Chad was just getting started, he was younger than I was, and he was, ah, obviously very, very healthy. Which didn't really give them much leeway for fooling themselves that there wasn't a physical attraction component involved in my decision to marry him. Which, as far as they were concerned, was adultery. Betrayal of Don. Even after nearly ten years.

"Maybe, even then, they would have tolerated it better if I had given Mom and Dad custody of Anne. But I didn't. Wouldn't. I did still want to hang on to Don, in some way, through Anne. Even though, by the time I remarried, it was really too late for that. The first few months of our marriage were the easiest, before I put my foot down and insisted that Anne was going to live with us.

"By the time Anne reached her teens, things were very, very difficult. The year after you were born was one of the worst. She was rebellious, Chip turned from three to four and was incredibly active, I was dealing with a baby. The next year was almost the same, except that Chip turned from four to five and I was dealing with a toddler. I was tired all the time, like the energy was draining out of me.

"I kept telling myself that if I could hang on until Anne started college, everything would calm down. In 1991, she was scheduled to start WVU. Tuition paid, board and room paid. Three days before she was supposed to leave, she announced that she had changed her mind. Didn't want to go. Wanted to stay with Nani and Pop and commute to Fairmont State, instead. Nani said yes. Pop put his foot down and said no. He thought she needed to learn to live independently. Don's parents got involved. Anne blamed me. Us. Chad. She went to WVU. But she made us regret it. Not academically. She did really well. But the tension built up and built up.

"By then, I was staring forty in the face. Exhausted all the time. Not that . . . responsive to Chad. Starting to feel, really feel, that I was quite a bit older than he was. One thing led to another."

"You mean," Missy said, "that he had an affair and you threw him out."

Debbie's face turned pale.

"It's true," Missy said. "Nobody explained anything to me at the time, but I found out later. Could you really expect that I wouldn't?"

Debbie shook her head. "I suppose not."

"Why did you take him back?" Missy had decided to press the issue. This might be the best chance she ever had, with her mother a captive audience at the sink. "Why did you take him back. After he had done that?"

"Once I realized that my wounded pride wasn't worth it." Debbie stopped. "That isn't quite true. It's only a tiny part of the truth, though I guess it had to come first. We didn't plan that meeting as leading to a reconciliation. Just that we finally had to get together and resolve some issues. We couldn't leave the separation hanging forever. We had to decide something. I hate to say it, but before Chip went to live with Grandma Jenkins, he wasn't dealing with the situation well at all. By then though, he and your Gran were getting along well enough that I started having nightmares about having him live with your Gran any longer. Nightmares about having my experience with Anne repeated. We had to come to some sort of closure."

Debbie laughed suddenly, a little bitterly. "In a way, we owe the reconciliation to Anne, I suppose. I asked Gran to take you for the day so your dad could come over to the house without the extra emotions that you'd bring into the situation. I was surprised when she said, 'About time the two of you got this mess settled.' I didn't tell Mother and Pop he was coming. Anne was living with them again and working at the clinic in Fairmont.

"Chad and I were sitting on opposite sides of the living room, sort of talking around what to do, the way we had every time we had tried to come to some kind of a resolution before. Then I heard a key in the front door and Anne came in. I didn't know she was coming. It was a Saturday morning, she should have been at the clinic, but she'd exchanged shifts with another nurse who wanted a weekday afternoon free for her child's teacher conference. When she saw Chad there, she started to spout Mother's lines, which I had been hearing for nearly two years. 'Time to get rid of him. What is he doing in this house? Pull the plug, take off his rings, get a divorce.'

"First, I pointed out that it was his house, really. Which it is. This is the old Williams place. We bought it when it came on the market because he had a sentimental attachment to it and I adored all the oak and walnut woodwork. It's where your Grandma Jenkins grew up. Her parents moved into it after her grandfather died and your father used to visit them here. After Grandpa Joe died, Grandma Esther eventually went to live with your Great-aunt Elizabeth and sold the house. It's not the easiest house to keep, even after all the remodeling we did, but that's fine.

"Then I said that I had taken off her father's rings long after his death, but Chad was still alive and we were still married.

"Finally, I guess, she pushed me too far. I stood up and said, 'I don't want a divorce. I *want* him to come back to me and have things right between us again. More than anything else in the world.'

"I've never seen Anne look so shocked.

"But not much more than Chad did, honestly.

"Not that I even knew he would be willing to come back. He'd never said so. I kept thinking to myself, the whole time we were separated, that he was probably waiting for me to get to the point where I would cut the knot and set him free to get on with it. He wasn't quite forty, yet. He could have started his personal life over, easily enough.

"Just saying that had brought me to my limits. I couldn't do or say anything else, right then. I was standing there, shaking like a leaf. I couldn't believe that I'd said that.

"Anne opened her mouth to say something else.

"Chad got up and put his arms around me.

"Then he laid down the law to Anne in no uncertain terms. The first time since we married. He told her that she was an adult woman and a registered nurse now, not a ten-year-old child. So she had two choices. The first was to go home, think about the fact of our marriage in a reasonable way, and come back in a couple of days when she was prepared to talk and act rationally. The second was to go home and not come back at all. And he added that if she went wailing to Vera and Lily and sicced them down on us before we were ready to deal with them, the first option would drop out of the picture.

"She stood there looking at us for a little while. Then she left.

"The next week was worse than when we told our families we were getting married in the first place. Chad's father was dead by then, so the only oasis of calm was provided by Wes and Lena. They were back in Grantville by then. Wes had left the state government and taken the job with Marion County Parks and Recreation.

"I don't know what Wes said to your Gran, either, but I know he said something, because I know that Chad didn't have a chance to talk before we officially broke the news to her. She heard the news, nodded her head, called Chip and then stood stiffly with her lips closed tightly as Chip started bringing all the boxes of his stuff down from his room. They were already packed. She didn't like it, not one damn bit, but knew that if we'd settled it between us, it was better this way. She's one tough lady."

"Why *did* Dad come back?"

Her mother looked at her. "I don't know, really. For the sake of you and Chip, I suppose. Chad never said. I'd said that I wanted to have things right with us again. Once we decided to get back together, it seemed to me as if asking more questions would be like picking at a scab. That things might never heal over if I kept trying to examine them under a microscope. Even if they weren't quite entirely right, that was better than an open sore.

"Of course, I never really understood why he married me in the first place. Why he wanted to. He told me he loved me, but guys always say that. He could have dated any girl in Grantville. Any girl in Fairmont or Clarksburg, for that matter. Someone he had met in Morgantown. And he did date a lot of different girls, up until the day in May he told me we were getting married. Out of a clear blue sky. Actually, it was cloudy and started to pour rain almost right away. So he could certainly have married someone younger. Someone without all the tribulations and problems I brought him. Anyone he wanted. Someone with whom things would be simpler. I always realized that."

Missy nodded. She had a lot to think about.

She wished that she had the guts to ask one more question. *Were you ever in love with him? Did you love him, Mom?* But she didn't. Not right now. She had a feeling that she'd pushed her mother about as far as she dared. *It sure wasn't because you wanted to be Mrs. County Commissioner. Or Mrs. SoTF Senator. You hate the politics. Why did you marry him, Mom?*

Chapter 57

Grantville

It was finally the block of reservations at the workmen's hostel that provided unambiguous evidence of Bryant Holloway's participation in the events leading up to the hospital riot, once they started looking. Steve Matheny had made it quite plain that the fire department had not had any training project under way the last week of February and first few days of March, and had known nothing of the men who had been billeted there with Bryant's name on the ledger.

"We've got to deal with it," Wes said. "There's no way to pretend that he wasn't involved."

The rest of the people around the table looked at him with considerable relief.

"It's going to put you somewhat on the spot, Wes," Ed Piazza said. "He's your son-in-law."

"He was involved with it. He was actively, heavily, involved with Jacques-Pierre Dumais. He was recruiting the thugs the man used. Mostly for the attack on the hospital, as far as Don Francisco can find out, but a few of them were in the mix at the synagogue. He's as culpable as the attackers themselves."

"The question now," Arnold Bellamy said, "is not whether we deal with it, but how we deal with it."

"We need to show that the judicial process does not play

favorites because of family connections. Arrest him. Try him. Lenore doesn't know, yet," Wes said. "I wish she would never have to find out. That's what I wish as her father, at least. But there's no help for it."

"Lenore is a big girl now," Clara said. "She should not have any illusions about Bryant left. If she ever had any to start with."

The men looked at her.

"She does not know what he was doing in this matter. I am sure of that." Clara paused. "She will have no reason for surprise that he was capable of doing it, I think. I will accept the task of telling her, if the rest of you prefer."

Cory Joe Lang, representing Don Francisco Nasi, simply said, "Thanks." This relieved the other men around the table from the obligation of saying anything at all.

"Then," Cory Joe said, "the next thing is to see about getting Holloway into safe custody. Preferably before the more radical local CoC people find out what he was doing, catch him, and decide to string him up in public without considering what the consequences for Lenore and the rest of the Jenkins family might be. They're prepared to live with a judicial process, I think. Isn't that really what you were saying, Wes?"

"I have people looking," Preston Richards said. "They haven't found him yet."

The phone rang early. Bryant grabbed it.

One of the clerks at the workmen's hostel owed him a favor. So now he knew that the police had taken the record book containing that block reservation and that Matheny had been right there saying that it had not been for the fire department.

So it looked like it was about time to get out of town.

But he was going to do a few things before he did.

He went across to the nursery and looked at Lenore on the cot. She had slept right through the phone ringing, the lazy bitch. The first order of business was to make sure she stayed available until he got around to her.

He had her more than halfway tied before she woke up. The rest was no problem. In his job, a guy had to keep himself in good shape.

He walked right past the crib. If the other bitches said that he wasn't to lay a finger on Weshelle, then he wouldn't. The kid could lie there all day in her stink as far as he was concerned.

Item the first. Wes Jenkins' German woman who had tried twice to get Lenore to walk out on him.

She worked with Wes, at the Bureau of Consular Affairs. Bad example. Maybe she was why Lenore had gone back to work, too. He'd always thought that old-time women had been domestic. Docile. Big miscalculation. These Krauts. Rebecca. Gretchen. Clara. Wannabe Amazons, the whole batch of them. Some of them could make an outright American feminazi look like a piker. Like the women out in the fields, when a guy drove by, working like men. Or someone like Bibi Barlow, who outranked him.

Item the second. Lenore. Damn Lenore.

Item the third. Those papers Dumais had told him to get rid of. If Dumais had wanted him to get rid of them, they must have some value. That was why the three garbage cans were still on Veda Mae's back porch. He hadn't ever bothered to put them out at the curb to be dumped.

Can't make that item the third. No way to move them. Item the third. Transportation. Pickup truck from the fire department lot. That was what he got when he went places on detail.

Then item the fourth, get those papers.

Somebody, somewhere, in the SoTF bureaucracy had decided to issue drivers' licenses to operators of motorcycles and dirt bikes.

Separate from drivers' licenses for four-wheeled vehicles. Not to be obtained by mail. Granted only between the hours of eight o'clock a.m. and eleven o'clock a.m. in the Department of Internal Affairs office in Grantville. Required to be obtained by April fifteenth. Subject to administrative penalties. Identification required.

For various reasons of combined nostalgia and *Schadenfreude*, Grantville had continued to use April fifteenth as a deadline for all sorts of measures that its citizenry was likely to dislike.

In any case, Christin George was in line. Followed by Denise, Minnie, Ron, and Missy.

The line was going nowhere.

That was exactly what Christin had predicted when she had first insisted that all of them show up early. It was a reminder of the importance of keeping your paperwork in order. And of the fact that in order to do so, a person had to outwit a lot of bureaucratic inertia and incompetence.

The deadline had come and the deadline had gone. This was their fourth appearance at the licensing window over the past two weeks.

At the moment Christin was predicting that the person behind the counter, if that person ever took notice of their presence, would insist that they needed some other item which had unfortunately been omitted from the public notice published in the newspapers, that nobody had told them about on their prior appearances, and with which they would have to return another day. Which would mean that they would all have to pay a fine for being tardy and would not legally be allowed to ride for several days until they got the mess straightened out, at which time some incompetent clerk would not realize that it had been straightened out and send them a bill for another fine, which would require another visit to the Department of Internal Affairs.

The person behind the counter, who this morning happened to be Arnold Bellamy's daughter Amy, waved from behind the barrier, cheerfully calling out to Missy that she would get to them in no time.

That was when someone down the hall started screaming. The five of them turned and ran, followed by Amy, who leapfrogged over the counter.

Consular Affairs. Christin had been last when they left the queue, but somehow she was first through the door. She took a running leap, landed with her arms around the man's neck like a spitting cat, and began to kick the backs of his knees and jam her knees into his kidneys while letting her full, if not very impressive, weight press against his windpipe.

Ron paused a moment in surprised admiration. When it came to plain old dirty fighting, of no particular style, Denise's mother was no slouch at all. She could probably open up a martial arts studio of sorts. Then he reached over her head, grabbed the man by his hair, and yanked backwards.

Missy thought of trying a tackle, but didn't. She had a feeling that she was too likely to get hit by Christin's flailing feet.

The man had a knife. Amy reached up and handed Denise a vase of dried flowers that was on top of the filing cabinet.

Denise brought it down hard on that hand. The man yowled, turned, and ran out into the corridor, jerking away from Ron and bowling over the security guard who was running up the stairs.

Christin dropped off his back. “Damn,” she said. “That guy is strong.” She ran after him, Ron following.

Missy thought vaguely that she probably ought to chase him too. Instead, she dropped onto her knees. “Clara, are you all right?”

Clara Bachmeierin crawled out from under the desk. “Yes. I would not let him hurt my baby. I drop under the desk onto my hands and knees and scream and scream and scream.”

“The scream was pretty impressive.”

Christin came back saying, “He got away. But not for long or very far, I think. The security guard is calling the cops. What became of the knife?”

“Over here, Mom,” Denise said. “That was Bryant Holloway. What is going on?”

Missy’s automatic reaction to any question was to try to provide an answer. This was not the best orientation for a covert operative, as Don Francisco had concluded to his sorrow. In this instance, preoccupied with getting Clara back on her feet and making sure that she was in fact uninjured, she covered the essentials in four or five pungent, cogent sentences.

The only part that really interested Denise was Holloway’s involvement in setting up the distraction at the hospital that drew the police away from the synagogue on March fourth.

Ron came back, following Christin. “Missy,” he said. “That’s, ah, privileged data.”

“It’s just us. And Clara knows anyway.”

“There’s going to be practically dozens of people here any minute. Uh . . .”

“I,” Christin said, “am going to get back in line to get the drivers’ licenses. Amy will go back and issue them. Right now. Denise and Minnie will come with me. And Amy will give me yours and Missy’s as well as ours. It’s an ill wind that blows nobody good. We weren’t here, anyway.”

“Ah,” Amy started to protest. Then she decided it would be better to say, “Yes, ma’am.”

So by the time the police arrived, those four were back at the other end of the corridor, inside another door. With Minnie writing up detailed notes concerning an event at which she had not been present, officially speaking.

And Clara was asking, "What about Lenore? If he comed—came—to hurt me, what about Lenore?"

"There isn't any answer," Missy said.

"Maybe he didn't come here," Ron said. "The garage door is open."

"That doesn't make any difference. Bryant and Lenore don't have a car. Not even bicycles. She walks everywhere and he uses fire department vehicles when they send him out of town."

"Now what?"

"I think we ought to break in," Missy said.

"Why?"

"Because Lenore ought to be at work and Weshelle ought to be at Aunt Debbie's since Chandra went to Frankfurt this week. I don't know what happened, but Weshelle is here. I can hear her crying. And crying. And crying. If she was sick and Lenore stayed home with her today, if Lenore was here, if she was okay at least, she wouldn't let that happen."

Ron came up the walk. "Do we actually have to force our way in, or does she hide a key somewhere?"

"She does, now that you remind me. Under the kindling pile. There's a fake rock. It's hollow."

"He didn't kick me," Lenore said. "He's strong. If he had kicked me, I would probably be dead."

"Then," Ron asked, "what are these marks?"

"He hit me with my boots. My winter boots. That's what he used the last time, too. I wish I hadn't put them back on, that night when Clara and Trent Dorrman and Brother Green were here. I wish I hadn't gone into the bedroom still wearing them. I wish that I had left those heavy winter boots right there in the hall, by the door. I wish that they hadn't been so handy."

"What night?" Missy said, as she came in carrying Weshelle. "I got her changed, gave her a sippy cup of milk and now she's chewing on toast. So she's happier."

"Back in February."

"Lenore, what happened in February? I know that Bryant was recruiting for Dumais, and Clara said, when she sent us over here just now, that she and Lola and the other women at the court had gotten a protective order for you, but what else is going on here?"

"I'm too ashamed. I'm too ashamed to tell anybody else. Too many people know already what he did."

"This time, in another half hour, you would have been too dead to tell anybody else." Ron thought it was only reasonable to point this out. "It might have gone faster if he had kicked you, but he was definitely making progress when we turned up."

"I didn't *do* anything," Lenore moaned. "I didn't *do* anything to make him so mad."

Missy looked at Ron. "What next? We can't leave Lenore alone with Weshelle and we can't stay here. At least, both of us can't. One of us has to go back and tell Chief Richards and Don Francisco and all those that Bryant was here and what he did and that he ran."

"I'll go, but they'll need you too, if we're going to make sense out of this. Is there anyone else you can call to help?"

Missy stood there, holding Weshelle and thinking. Uncle Wes was at a meeting somewhere and Clara was busy with the police at Consular Affairs and anyway, if Uncle Wes saw Lenore right now . . . That was not a good thing to think about.

"I'm going to call the Reverend Mary Ellen. I don't ever go to church any more, but Lenore does. That's the best idea, I think. She'll come. And the hospital. Some medical type has to take a look at Lenore. We'll need an ambulance anyway, to move her. She sure can't go anywhere by herself. You go now. After other people get here, I'll come after you. Mary Ellen can take care of things here and send the police to catch up with us later to tell them what was going on."

"No," Lenore said. "I'm not going to cry for a love gone wrong, Mary Ellen. There wasn't any love between Bryant and me, from start to finish. Neither of us ever thought so."

She looked up. "And I'm not going to cry for anything else, either. I didn't try to fool Bryant. I am angry, though. I've thought about it, and what I'm feeling is angry. Miserable, degraded, but angry, too. When we married, I was willing to give him an honorable effort to make the best of things in a world that isn't perfect. He wasn't willing to give that much back."

Mary Ellen looked down. None of them had tried to lift Lenore off the floor. All of them thought that had better wait for the EMTs.

"I thought he was, at first. If I hadn't thought so, I wouldn't have agreed to marry him. He wasn't, but I'm not going to cry about that. I'm not going to cry. Not ever."

"Lenore," Mary Ellen asked. "If the EMTs say that you don't have to go to the hospital, is there anyone that I can get to come over and stay with you after I leave? Someone you are willing to have? The kind of friend who would come and ask no questions?"

Lenore smiled for the first time since Bryant had come back to the house that morning. "The only person I can think of I would want is Caroline Jones. Dorrman. Which isn't going to work, considering what you just told me."

Mary Ellen smiled too. About nine o'clock in the morning, Simon's niece Caroline had phoned the parsonage to say that the baby was on its way.

Chapter 58

Grantville

Wes came back from his meeting over at the legislative chambers. There were police all over the place around the administration building. As soon as he saw the expression on the security guard's face, he knew that something was wrong. Specifically wrong, for him. Not generally wrong, politically.

"Ah, sir. I am sorry. Truly I am. I had no way of knowing that I should not admit him. I hadn't been notified. He wasn't on my list. And he is a member of your family."

"Who is 'he'? And what has 'he,' whoever he is, done?"

"Mr. Bryant Holloway, sir. He came into the building. Quiet enough, when he came in. He went up to your office. To Consular Affairs. Where he tried to knife your wife."

At the expression on Mr. Jenkins face, the guard turned pale. "Ah, she's perfectly fine, sir. Ms. Bachmeierin, that is. She's upstairs, talking to the police. She yelled, so other people came."

The guard had heard any number of people say, from time to time, that Mr. Jenkins had a temper. He'd never seen any sign of it before.

The policeman talking to Clara was Preston Richards, who had sent Ron and Missy into another room to be interviewed. He also carried out the unpleasant task of letting Wes know that Bryant had gotten to Lenore and beaten her very seriously.

The guard looked up. The way Mr. Jenkins' face had looked on the way up did not even start to compare with Mr. Jenkins' face on the way out.

Ms. Bachmeierin came running after him. Running down those steep old-fashioned stairs, as close to her time as she was. Running, her short legs trying to catch up with her tall husband.

"Look, Ed," Preston Richards said. "If Wes lays hands on Bryant Holloway, the man's life expectancy is going to be very short. And while I don't give a damn about Holloway, we'd still have to arrest Wes for murder. Second degree, anyway."

"Then," Arnold Bellamy answered, "we must find the best way to save Wes from himself."

Ed Piazza didn't answer right away. He was thinking.

Arnold was right, of course.

Arnold could be an uptight pain in the ass a lot of the time, but he was frequently right.

Michael Dukakis had probably been right too, back up-time, when he answered that question about his wife Kitty. Right in an abstract sort of way.

Natalie Bellamy hadn't been among the women standing on the steps of the synagogue the day of the assassination. No one had shot at her. Ed wondered vaguely how Arnold would have reacted if she had been there. Or if someone had tried to knife her this morning. Or if someone beat up his daughter Amy. Amy would be how old now? Nineteen already? She'd been a freshman in high school the year of the Ring of Fire.

This coming spring, a class would graduate that had never attended the high school while Ed had been principal. *A whole new school generation*, he thought, formed during their freshman year by Len Trout but mostly under Victor Saluzzo's leadership.

"I'm sure you're right, Arnold," Ed said. "Do you have any suggestions?"

"Not really. I was hoping that Preston might."

Ed's thoughts kept wandering. Lots of people sort of wondered about Arnold and Natalie. It was lucky that Amy hadn't been involved in this at all. She worked right here in the building. Who could tell how Arnold would have reacted?

"Ah," Arnold was saying. "Preston, while I have your attention, I think I'd better let you know that several other people were involved in pulling Bryant Holloway out of Consular Affairs than your men found when they arrived on the scene. Amy says . . ."

"That must have been a sight," was Preston Richards' comment when Arnold had finished his summary. "I guess I had better talk to Minnie and Denise. Minnie has a really amazing memory for things she observes."

Arnold rearranged the papers in front of him into three neat piles. "Amy thought you ought to know. No matter what Christin George's opinion was."

Ed blinked. Amy *had* been involved in the fight. And Arnold's reaction was—somewhere between perfectly calm and mildly concerned?

Arnold was continuing. "At least she phoned me once she got rid of Christin. She's a lot like Natalie, you know. Amy, that is. Came equipped with a mind of her own from the day she was born. All the paternal guidance I have been able to muster over the past two decades has not sufficed to persuade her that 'Damn the torpedoes. Full speed ahead!' is not necessarily the most appropriate response in every single circumstance that may arise."

He rearranged the three piles of paper. "I really do wish that she were a little more cautious. I thought that working in Internal Affairs would offer comparatively little risk, since she has no desire to teach. Compared, say, to working in Economic Resources or going to Franconia." He frowned. "Minimal risk is difficult to achieve these days, though. Natalie was teaching the day of the Croat raid, and Amy was at school. I had just transferred to the Department of International Affairs, so I was downtown. I was very concerned about their safety. With all the other things that had to be done, and all the confusion, it was almost three hours before I was able to confirm that they had come to no harm."

Clara insisted that Lenore and Weshelle must move in with them, at least temporarily, rather than having Lenore try to find a health aide and stay by herself here, where it happened.

Mary Ellen backed Clara up on this. "The EMTs are still here; the ambulance can move you. Wes and Clara can take Weshelle, and I'll send Simon and Sebastian over to bring your things and hers. They can use a dolly from the church."

"There's a crib there already," Wes said. "And a playpen. On the sun porch. Just for grandchildren."

Lenore was shaking her head.

"You should have come the first time," Clara said. "Like I told you to. Or the last time, like I told you to again."

Wes' head came up. First time? Last time?

He learned about February.

"Why in the name of God didn't you tell me then?"

"Because you would have killed the man. Just as right now you are on the verge of killing the man if you lay hands on him. And I did not want to see you hanged before you saw our baby. Well, not to see you hanged at all."

"She's *my* daughter. You had no business taking that on yourself."

Clara stuck her chin out. "I exercised my best judgment."

Then he learned about March. Faye, Lola, Andrea, Chandra, the protective order that had been in place since Bryant came back. With Clara involved again.

"Dad," Lenore said. "Dad. It wasn't . . ."

Her attempt to intervene didn't do any good.

Chandra? Both Clara and Chandra had known, but hadn't told him?

Wes and Clara were yelling at each other when the ambulance arrived. Still yelling when Mary Ellen left in it, with Lenore, carrying Weshelle herself.

Still yelling when they got home after locking up at Bryant's house.

Just yelling, though.

Mary Ellen sighed and left them to it, wondering how long it had been since anyone in Wes' family had stood up to him. Probably, if the stories she had heard were true, back when his mother tried to talk him out of marrying Lena. Which hadn't worked.

Wes would never have thought of himself as a domestic dictator. And, to give him credit, she thought, if that rubric applied in any way, he had certainly been the most benevolent dictator ever born in the human race. His efforts to elicit a point of view from Lena had been practically superhuman. He had nobly refrained from playing the heavy father to Lenore and Chandra, even when he clearly hadn't been pleased with the choices they made.

But still. He was pretty short on experience when it came to give and take on the home front. Lenore and Chandra hadn't had to fight for their choices. Wes had stood back and deliberately let them make them, which was a different kettle of fish.

Faye looked up from the phone. "That was Mary Ellen Jones," she said.

"Is it true?" Linda Beth asked. "What we heard that Bryant did to Lenore this time?"

Faye nodded. "Bad enough that she's going to have to be off work for several days."

"What do you think? Like your friend Bernadette Adducci says, Andrea, it's really hard to help someone who won't help herself."

"Personally," Faye said. "I think that Lola and Clara were right. She should have gotten out. Not that a protective order would have prevented him from hunting her down at Wes' house. But it sure would have made it less convenient for him to get to her if she had been living somewhere else, with other people around."

"Why on earth didn't she?" Catrina asked.

"She's a masochist?" Andrea suggested.

Linda Beth shook her head. "You have to know something about her family to understand, I think. I'm the same age as her grandparents. Lenore has been surrounded all her life by folks who are pretty nice. Not perfect, but the Jenkinses and the Days, both sides of her family, are basically good people. Lenore and Chandra are both alike, in that way. At some level, they simply expected to be—what's that word in the wedding vows?—yeah, to go on being cherished when they got married. Without even thinking about it. They'd been cherished since the day they were born, after all."

"Maybe you're right," Faye said. "That is sort of what it was like when Lola and I talked to her. When it came right down to it, I'm not sure she actually believed what was happening to her. That Bryant was completely off the deep end. Not even though Lola warned her back in March that he'd gone off it a couple of times before."

Wes said he would set up a folding bed for Lenore downstairs on the sun porch, next to the crib, so she could be with Weshelle.

Clara brought sheets, blankets, an extra pillow, all from the linen closet.

While he was doing that, Clara moved her things out of the master bedroom.

Lenore wasn't going to be able to climb the stairs for quite a while. No one but themselves would know that she was sleeping on the single bed in Chandra's old room.

Not even if she cried herself to sleep at night, feeling . . . a little bit lonely, at times.

After all, she could scarcely stay in the master bedroom. It had been wonderful to sleep in Wesley's arms when his favor had been resting upon her. But she could scarcely perturb him with her presence when it was not.

When Wes came up that evening, he stopped at the door of the bedroom, a little startled. Whatever he might have expected to happen as the next stage in this disagreement with Clara—it wasn't this.

He hadn't really expected anything specific. He had never had a fight with Clara before. Some minor arguments about this and that, but no fights.

He had never had a fight with his *wife* before, for that matter. Lena had been compliant. Sometimes to the point that it tried his patience, but most certainly compliant. Lena had not been one to stand her ground.

On the other hand, if Lenore had picked up Weshelle and walked out, that night back in February, as Clara had advised her to, it would not have come to this.

Sometimes Lenore was so much like her mother that it was uncanny.

He stood there. *Bitte, geh doch nicht weg. Bleib bei mir*. It had been so . . . forlorn. But now, *she* had gone away. There had to be something that he wasn't understanding. Some piece of this puzzle was missing.

He looked down the hallway. All the other doors were closed. He wondered which room Clara had chosen.

Chapter 59

Grantville

"I hate to say that I'm relieved," Preston Richards said. "But I am."

Ed Piazza nodded.

According to the latest reports, Bryant Holloway had left town in a pickup truck stolen from the Grantville VFD lot.

"Wes Jenkins might have killed him if he had caught him here in town. He isn't likely to go chasing him down, however. Not with Clara's pregnancy so far advanced." Richards sighed. "I suppose part of it's the stress. Cumulative. That's what the Reverend Al says, at least. There's been more violence in Grantville in the four years since the Ring of Fire than we'd have expected in twenty or thirty years, up-time."

"Considering that we've got more than five times the population we did before—" Ed started to say.

"Do you have any idea where he might be headed?" Nasi asked.

Arnold Bellamy answered. "Steve Matheny—that's our fire department chief, if you haven't met him, Don Francisco—says maybe towards Frankfurt. He was over there some time back. Stayed with Chandra's husband, Nathan Prickett."

Don Francisco frowned slightly.

"Surely," Ed Piazza said, "Nathan isn't going to take him in after what he's done to Chandra's sister."

"How's Nathan going to know?" Richards asked. "Unless we radio to him. Which wouldn't be the most prudent thing, right at the moment. Without a SoTF consulate, the USE radio setup in Frankfurt isn't exactly confidential. Or reliable, for that matter."

"Additionally," Don Francisco said, "according to information I have obtained, it would appear that the man is carrying potentially important evidence with him. He was observed, on the way out of town, loading packets of papers into the truck."

"Dare I ask observed where, and by whom?" Arnold asked.

"Preferably not. But it would be desirable to get the papers back. Based on information received, some of them may well be pertinent to the trial of the various hooligans the police rounded up after the demonstration at Leahy Medical Center."

"What can he be planning to do with them?" Ed Piazza asked.

"At present, of course, we don't know. He might be trying to return them to Dumais. It is possible that he intends to try to use the material to make a plea bargain of some kind. Or, of course, he simply may not be thinking clearly."

Those who were sitting in on the meeting purely in the capacity of providers of miscellaneous factual information tried not to wiggle and twist on their chairs.

"How long do you think they're going to be looking at it from all the angles?" Missy asked at coffee break.

"For a long, long time, the way things are going. I must say that when Mike Stearns is around, things get decided faster than when he isn't." Ron grinned.

"It seems to me," Missy said, "that when you narrow down what they're saying, they'd be willing to do without Bryant, since he was sort of peripheral, but they really would like the papers that Pam saw him picking up behind Veda Mae's house."

Ron nodded. That seemed to be the essence of it. "Is there any reason that we can't chase him down and get them? Don Francisco is probably pretty much right that he's heading for Frankfurt. Even if he isn't, pickup trucks are still noticeable in rural Thuringia."

He didn't want to hear himself say that. It was the kind of thing that Giovanna's father had been prone to say, down in Italy. Very Marcoli-ish.

"Chase him down? What can we use to chase a pickup?" Then Missy's mouth formed into an "Oh."

"Are you game?"

Missy took a deep breath. Time to take a risk. "As long as I'm going with you."

"They're fueled up," Denise said. "And the sidecars have gas cans, as many as I could fit in."

"If we run short," Ron said, "we should be able to get more gas in Erfurt. I hope. Plus in Fulda and Frankfurt."

Denise shook her head. "If he's actually going to Frankfurt. You're not going to be able to get more in Podunksdorf, so keep an eye on your supplies. You don't want to be pushing these babies home. Some oil. A toolkit."

"Be careful not to overbalance," Minnie said seriously. Neither Ron nor Missy had a lot of experience with the sidecars yet, especially not on unimproved roads.

"I called Pam," Missy said, "and begged a really big favor of her. To let Mom and Dad know where I've gone after we're well out of town. And to tell Mrs. Bolender and Marietta that I need to take a few days for a family emergency. And to tell Cory Joe."

"The joys of true friendship," Denise said.

"Do you need to check in with anyone?" Missy asked Ron.

"I called Fischer at the Farbenwerke and told him to hold three or four upcoming things until I get back. Otherwise, no." Ron looked a little startled. "I, uh, don't have to ask anybody if I can go. I, ah, still consult with Edelman on marketing, of course; he knows more than I do in that field. And if I wanted to do something radical like change a whole product line, Dad and Magda and my brothers would have to vote their shares and I'd have to persuade them, in order to get a majority. Like I did when Bill and I wanted to add the Whatever Works project. Otherwise . . . Well, actually, I'm the boss."

Missy looked at him, even more startled than he was.

"I like the lab work, but I don't know it the way Dad does. It would take years to master all that, since I don't have any special talent for it. And I don't really need to, so long as I understand what's going on. Someone like Bill belongs in the lab, over at the school, learning, or at Lothlorien, working. He shouldn't be spending his time worrying about resource allocation and stuff like that."

"I get it," Missy said. "That's why we've been spending so much time on records systems and such."

"You see," he said. "A business isn't something like the technical stuff you're learning at the libraries, or studying to be a doctor, or even a pastor, like Gerry. It's a different kind of thing. Management, I mean. Once you have a normal, basic education, either you can do it or you can't. And it seems like I can. So I do. It's not very glamorous, but it's the least I can do for the people who are actually accomplishing some real work. It feels a little odd, considering that a year and a half ago I was still checking in with Dad and Magda if I wanted to go somewhere in the evening. But these things happen."

"What do you think?" Minnie asked.

"Honest? I wouldn't put it past them to get into trouble," Denise answered. "I think we ought to go after them. Four heads are better than two. We have Daddy's hog."

That had slipped a lot of people's minds. After the events of March fourth, the police had duly returned Buster's motorcycle, which had been only slightly damaged, to Christin. Minnie and Denise had since repaired whatever damage there was. It never hurt to have a spare on hand.

"Especially," Minnie said, "since I don't think they remembered to take any serious weapons. Missy hardly ever carries a gun, except at work. All the librarians have to be armed when they're on duty, of course. And she didn't ask us for a loaner before they left."

They stood for a minute, meditating upon this serious omission.

"You're right," Minnie said. "We'd better go after them. From what we heard in Clara's office, this Holloway guy seems like a real freak. I'm not sure they can handle him."

"Not to mention," Denise added, "that he's one of the guys I promised Daddy that I'd take care of. At his funeral."

"Do we check with Mrs. Dreeson and Mrs. Wiley first? The mentors?"

"No way. We want to go, don't we?" Denise paused. "They'll want to know why we can't be more like Annalise and Idelette. Sometimes those two models of perfect young-ladylike behavior piss me off, even at second hand. If Mrs. Dreeson and Mrs. Wiley had any idea some of the things those two get up to while they're looking like butter wouldn't melt in their mouths, they'd freak out. I'll tell Mom, though. She can call Benny later and tell him not to worry." She paused again. "Mom has her head screwed on straight about things like this. What does Mrs. Johnson in home economics call them?"

"Priorities," Minnie said. "Your mother has a pretty good grip on what's a priority and what's not."

Before they left, Denise got the M-1 carbine her father had bought for her as a hunting rifle a few years earlier. It was a powerful enough gun for deer hunting while being small enough for a girl her size to handle—and, best of all under the current circumstances, it was easy enough to carry on a motorcycle.

After loading her jacket pockets with extra ammunition, she handed the carbine to Minnie, who'd be riding in the sidecar. Minnie held the weapon the way she'd have held an ax or a hoe. Solidly gripped, of course—not the sort of thing you want to see flying loose—but not as if it were really a weapon. She'd never handled guns as a kid, and now with only one eye she didn't see any point to learning.

Chapter 60

Frankfurt am Main

Chandra sat in the waiting room at the Frankfurt post office. Not a room, really. A sheltered porch sort of thing in front of the building. No benches; she was sitting on a keg with someone's freight in it.

She had stayed too long to catch the turnaround on Wackernagel's trip out. He wouldn't be back for at least two weeks. That was his schedule. Nathan hadn't given her any money. Wackernagel would have trusted her to pay him back after she got home, but a stranger wouldn't. As soon as someone else came through with available space in a wagon or cart, she would pay him for a ride back home. Whether she had ever seen him before in her life or not. At least, if the postmaster said he was reliable. She thought she had enough for that. She was closer to having enough for that than she was to being able to pay for a room at an inn for two weeks.

She wished she could start out walking, but she couldn't. The roads were still not safe enough for an unaccompanied, unarmed woman to go walking alone. If nothing else, there were feral pigs that went hunting in the night if she was outside the walls of a town, and she couldn't afford inns for all the nights it would take to get back to Grantville any more than she could afford an inn here. She had responsibilities. She had the kids. She had to get home safely for them. She had to sit here and wait for a ride.

She felt so miserable.

Nathan had been mad when she showed up, but she'd expected that.

First, he had claimed that he was angry because she came in spite of the civil unrest resulting from the assassinations, because she had put herself in danger, because she had risked the possibility that she might leave the children motherless. He had tried to make her feel like she was an irresponsible fool.

She'd stood her ground, at least. Pointed out that there would have been plenty of time for her to come before the assassinations, if he would have let her. Maybe she hadn't just stood her ground. She'd pushed him.

So now she knew. Well, she knew already that he hadn't wanted the third pregnancy. Now she knew that he considered it the end. From now on, he intended to conduct their marriage on an absentee basis. "To eliminate temptation," he said. It was the "best plan."

He hadn't even offered to let her stay at his place until she could find a ride back.

He hadn't even offered to arrange for her to stay with one of the other Grantville men in Frankfurt until she could find a ride back.

He hadn't even asked whether she had enough money to pay for a ride back.

He would rather that she had never come. Coming hadn't been one of his plans. So she wasn't here, as far as he was concerned.

He had told her not to come. That had been his plan. For her to stay in Grantville forever more, like a good little girl, asking no questions.

"Ask me no questions, I'll tell you no lies."

She was sick and tired of Nathan's plans. All of them.

Bryant Holloway drove the pickup truck he had stolen from the fire department lot in Grantville off the road to the right, behind some trees and brush, about a mile outside of Frankfurt. Around a curve going to the right, sharp right, and then double back a little. No one coming in the direction from Grantville toward Frankfurt was likely to see it. It wasn't the best place to leave it, but there weren't any better ones. He got out and headed into town. He had to get to Nathan's. Once he got to Nathan's, he should be safe enough for the time being. He could come back and get the stuff later.

✧ ✧ ✧

Neither Missy nor Ron noticed the place where Bryant had driven the truck off the road. The road surfaces were naturally pretty rocky and bumpy. Not something on which a truck left obvious tracks—but something which did require all their attention to keep the cycles upright. Assuming that he was headed into Frankfurt, they continued right into the town.

Just inside the walls, Missy braked the motorcycle more sharply than she should have. What on earth?

Ron, hearing her stop, slowed and then turned back.

Chandra? Sitting at the post office?

"Get on," Missy said. "We'll explain later. Something blew up after you left Grantville. Once we take care of it, I'll take you back home with me, if you don't mind riding behind. Not the most comfortable way to go, but a lot faster than a horse and wagon."

Chandra nodded. Any way to get back home was better than staying here, sitting outside the Post Office, waiting.

Ron and Missy proceeded through Frankfurt pretty sedately. She figured they didn't want to attract a lot of attention. At "sedately," they would just be a couple more of those oddball up-timers, doing oddball up-time things that involved oddball up-time machines. The inhabitants of Frankfurt were used to that by now.

Chandra hadn't expected that their business would take them directly to Nathan's.

Nor that, as they pulled up, Bryant Holloway would burst out of the back door and make a run for it, heading toward the east side of town.

It took them a while to explain things to Nathan. Particularly since Ron and Missy didn't want to explain one bit more than they had to.

Particularly since Chandra had left for Frankfurt before Bryant had beaten Lenore up. Explaining that caused quite a bit of delay all by itself. First to Chandra, who was horrified. Horrified, but not surprised. Missy looked at her rather sharply when she noticed that.

"He beat her up in February," Chandra said. "We managed to hide it. He wasn't so bad to her when he came back in March. We sort of hoped that the worst had blown over. Maybe he was just biding his time."

Then to Nathan, who was righteously indignant that Bryant

thought he would provide him with any kind of refuge after he had pulled a stunt like that.

Nathan didn't much want to ride behind Ron, but he did. They headed back, in the general direction in which Bryant had been running. There was only one real road going east from Frankfurt. They came to it from behind the post office.

"Look!" shouted Minnie, pointing to something on the side of the road. Looking over, Denise saw the unmistakable tracks of truck tires heading off into the woods.

Minnie might have trouble with depth perception, with just one eye, but there was nothing at all wrong with the eye itself.

They set off in pursuit. Buster would have chewed Denise out, if he'd seen her driving a motorcycle like that over such rough terrain, especially a bike with a sidecar.

But Buster was dead and Denise thought she finally had one of his killers tracked down and cornered. Some part of her mind understood, probably, that Bryant Holloway hadn't been directly involved with her father's killing. But that was a very small part of her mind and one she'd already brushed aside.

Buster had had a favored expression, when he wanted to describe someone in a really dark fury. "He's feeling Old Testament," he'd say.

Denise Beasley was feeling very Old Testament that day. Who cared whether Bryant Holloway had been directly responsible for her father's death? Had the God of the Old Testament cared about the fussy details when he slew all the firstborn of Egypt?

Not hardly. If it was good enough for God, it was good enough for Denise.

They found Holloway's truck, but there was no sign of Holloway himself. Denise took the carbine from Minnie and climbed into the truck bed, then stooped so she could get a better look at the papers he had in there.

"*Look out!*" Minnie shouted.

Two gunshots. They shouted like pistol shots. Nine millimeter, maybe.

Denise sprawled flat and then peeked over the side of the truck, in Minnie's direction. She could see Minnie's feet sticking out from behind a different tree, where she must have gone for shelter.

Movement to the left. She looked and saw Holloway, rising from behind a bush. He must have heard them coming and been waiting in ambush.

He saw her at the same time, aimed in her direction, and fired two more shots with his pistol.

Both of them went wild, as far as Denise could tell. But she wasn't paying much attention to that. She was getting up on one knee and the carbine was coming to her shoulder and she was a damn good shot and her soul was now well into Leviticus.

Bam! Bam! She didn't even feel the recoil.

Holloway was down, sprawled against another tree. There was blood all over his chest.

There were a lot of chapters in Leviticus, none of them kindly and forgiving. And there were fifteen rounds in the magazine of her M-1 carbine.

Which her Daddy had given her, for her twelfth birthday.

She went through the entire clip. Only the last two shots missed. By then, finally, Denise Beasley had started crying and her aim got a little wobbly.

She didn't cry for long, though. By the time Minnie came up, she was dry-eyed. In fact, she was starting to reload.

"You going to keep shooting him?" Minnie asked.

Denise thought about it. "I guess there's not much point, any longer."

Minnie shook her head. "No. He's dead. I don't think anybody in the history of the world has ever been deader."

Shots, in the distance. One, two. Then another two. Then another two. Then a whole fusillade.

They came around a curve. From this direction, it was easy enough to see where Bryant had driven the truck off the road. The spring growth of the plants along the way was still a little squashed.

Better to be cautious. They stopped and cut the engines. Nathan and Chandra got off. Missy and Ron pushed the cycles. When they reached the cutoff, each of them followed one set of the truck tracks.

Not just the truck. Another motorcycle.

A motorcycle, pretty obviously, whose rider had been more skilled than Ron and Missy. And who had a second rider on the pillion who had spotted the truck on the way into Frankfurt. Who had stopped to investigate.

Denise and Minnie were, quite calmly, putting Bryant Holloway's body into the cab of the truck, behind the steering wheel.

With Denise, in a most businesslike manner, advising Minnie to use a handkerchief to roll down the window. "Just in case they've heard of fingerprints or one of the Grantvillers in town tells them, we'd better not leave any. There's probably not a lot of crime detection going on. We can hope, anyway."

"What about his gun?" Minnie asked.

"Take it. No reason for anyone to know he dropped it here, and one more can always come in handy."

That was about the time they saw the others coming.

They didn't panic in the least. Just finished what they were doing and waited until the others came down toward the truck.

They gave a quick description of what had happened.

Ron looked into the truck. There wasn't as much blood as you'd expect in there. Probably because Holloway had already bled out before they muscled him into the cab, as many times as he'd been shot.

You could recognize him, but just barely. Two of Denise's shots had hit him in the face.

Ron and Missy looked at one another. It was perfectly clear that the girls were of the opinion that they had not done anything wrong. As they saw it, Bryant Holloway had helped bring into Grantville the demonstrators who killed Denise's dad, had helped the people who arranged the killing of Mayor Dreeson, who gave Minnie her eye.

Minnie was pretty Old Testament herself. She reached up into the socket, popped it out, and held it out for them to look at. None of the others had ever observed this phenomenon before. It did have the effect of taking their minds off Holloway's death for the time being. "I owed him," Minnie said.

"No different from killing a mad dog," was Denise's summary.

The four others stood there, wondering if there was any way to salvage the situation.

Minnie and Denise looked at one another. There was no telling how long the others were going to stand around. With the possibility that someone else could come along any minute and find them there. Shots tended to attract attention. Since they were of the opinion that the papers were now available to the people who had gone looking for them and that they had already taken care of the rest of situation quite adequately, they climbed back on Buster's cycle and started for home.

"See you later!" Denise called over her shoulder.

For one thing, they were cutting school. They saw more of the truant officer than they wanted to even without side trips to Frankfurt. Mrs. Dreeson and Mrs. Wiley would be pissed. Mrs. Dreeson and Mrs. Wiley had a tendency to compare their behavior at considerable length to the far more responsible and thus infinitely preferable manner in which Annalise Richter and Idelette Cavriani approached life.

Having a mentor could be a real pain.

"I don't believe it, quite," Missy was saying, "but he has Dumais' papers thrown in the back here. Just tied up in bundles with red tape around them. Without so much as a camper cover. What if it had started raining?"

"He wasn't thinking straight when he left Grantville," Ron answered. "That's pretty obvious. Reach over the edge of the truck bed and lift them out. Try not to snag your sleeves or anything. Pack them into the sidecars. I hope there's not more than will fit."

"There's more than will fit into one. I think that we can put the rest into the bottom of the other one and then the full gas cans on top. But we can't leave the empty gas cans here."

"Give the empty cans to Nathan to carry," Chandra said. "He might as well be of some use, for a change."

"That's it, then. Let's get out of here before someone shows up to investigate those shots. Prickett, we're going back to your place." Ron started his cycle. On the way out, he was once more careful to follow one of the tracks that the truck tires had made on the way in. Missy followed the other one.

Nathan Prickett was sulking, insofar as an adult could be said to sulk. That kid Ron had started giving him directions. Notify the Frankfurt authorities where he found the vehicle; say that he found Bryant dead in it; had no idea who'd killed him; say that he had gone looking because he knew that his brother-in-law was coming and he was getting worried because of the delay; remind them that Bryant had been here before on that firefighting detail.

Ron ran through it again. "Tell them that you were expecting him again and were getting worried because of the delay. Tell them you saw tracks where the truck ran off the road. Before you notify them, hide the empty gas cans—and make sure that you send them back to Denise and Minnie when you get a chance, because they are practically irreplaceable. Let the authorities worry about what to do with the truck next. It has a fire department sticker on it, so that will back up your reminder that Bryant was here in connection with that the last time."

"At least," Missy said, "I'm Chandra's cousin. It may make some minimal sense that I would have come to give her a ride back home. If anyone asks you why we were here. If nobody asks, don't bring it up."

Then she glared at Nathan.

"Which reminds me, Prickett you prick. Exactly what did you think you were doing leaving Chandra to sit there shivering in front of the Post Office, waiting for some way to get back home, not having the slightest idea when a ride would come along? What were you expecting her to do if none came along today? Sit there all night?"

"I told her not to come," Nathan said sullenly. "I've told her that all along."

"He doesn't want us to live together any more," Chandra said. "He doesn't want any more children. It's not in his plans."

Ron turned around and stared. "You know," he said. "That is really stupid. You could always take a couple of weeks off. Go back to Grantville for a few days. Go to Dr. Shipley and get a vasectomy if you really want to go back home. Or if you want to have Chandra and the kids come here. Unless you're so attached to keeping the family jewels as an option, even though you *already* have more kids than you want, that you're willing to ruin all of your lives."

"Look, Stone," Nathan said. "None of this is any of your business at all."

"Chandra is Missy's cousin."

Nathan blinked. "What does that have to do with it?" He had a strange feeling of being out of the loop. Why should it make any difference to the Stone kid that Chandra was Missy's cousin?

Missy interrupted. "And, now that the possibility of doing something about it has been pointed out, if you tell her to go have her tubes tied instead so you can keep the jewels, I personally will tell the whole world that you're willing to risk her life unnecessarily. That's abdominal surgery. Something they can do these days, if they have to. But no joke. Way too high risk, compared with your option. You're not worth it to her. Believe me, you are not. She doesn't have to put up with you. She has people around who love her."

Ron kept going. "Face, it, Prickett. It's one thing for couples who want kids, but not yet. Or still want more kids, but not right now. They have to deal with the whole spacing thing. Timing thing. Inconvenient timing thing. But where are you getting off on this? The whole point is that you don't want any more at all. If you don't intend to do anything sensible, you at least ought to have the common decency to ask your wife for a divorce and let her get on with her life. Talk about being a dog in the manger."

Chandra looked from one to another. She had not wanted to come quite as far as that word. *Divorce.* At least not yet. She'd thought around it, of course. Back last fall. Talking to Paige Modi. Talking to Aunt Debbie at Thanksgiving. Skipped around it. Skirted around it. Never quite looked it in the face. She hadn't quite wanted to think that it was something that could happen to her.

Divorce. Now Ron had said it for her. With Nathan in the room. She couldn't pretend that it didn't exist. Not any more. Maybe she was as bad as Nathan, in her own way. It wasn't something she had planned on.

Nathan's reaction to Ron's unsolicited advice was far from favorable.

Particularly when Ron expressed the opinion that in all probability he was just using this as an excuse—that if he didn't have it, he would be finding some other reason to skip out on his responsibilities.

"What in hell do you know about it?"

"If someone wants to dump his kids—or hers—he will. Or she will. He'll find a reason. Or she will. What did you want? Not real sons, apparently. A couple of little wind-up toys to pat on the head at the end of the day?"

✧ ✧ ✧

Missy flinched. This wasn't just about Nathan and Chandra. For Ron, this was about him and his brothers. About abandonment. About children left without a father. Or a mother. Even if Ron wasn't conscious of it himself.

Missy decided that she couldn't calm the situation down. She had no idea how to do that. But she could bring it to an end.

"Stop it," she said. "Both of you. We've got to get going. If we don't leave now, we won't make any decent time today at all. We don't want to get stuck out on the road somewhere."

Nathan Prickett stood outside his house, looking at the vanishing motorcycles.

Damn Ron Stone's multiple last-minute instructions. Most of which, Nathan granted rather grudgingly, made sense. All of which Nathan distinctly resented having to take from a kid. Much less one of that hippie Tom Stone's kids. As if he wouldn't have been able to manage things himself.

But he had taken them. Because, probably, it would turn out to the best way to handle it all from the don's point of view. If it wasn't, at least it would give him a little maneuvering room. But the don would need to know exactly what had come off here.

He'd done the best he could, under the circumstances. He couldn't very well have said, "I'm one of Francisco Nasi's agents in Frankfurt, so you can leave the stuff with me."

One of the agents, he was sure. He was certain that Don Francisco had others here. If he didn't have a couple of down-timers in place, at least, he wouldn't be competent enough to have the job he did.

Dear Don Francisco.

He concentrated on the report. Better to think about that than to think about how he felt when he saw Chandra leaving, riding pillion behind Missy.

A lot better to think about what Don Francisco needed to know than about the other things Ron Stone had said. The things that Missy had said.

Chandra had not been in his plans. He'd done his best to fit her into his plans. He really had. For a long time now, he had done his best to fit Chandra into his plans.

Part Ten

May 1635

Hurling defiance toward the vault of heaven

Chapter 61

Grantville, May 1635

"Made it," Ron said, as they rolled onto Route 250.

It was very late dusk, almost dark. Even with headlights, they didn't want to be riding these hogs on anything but asphalt after dark. Too many chances of unexpected ruts leading to untimely death.

"Grantville, here we come."

They couldn't find Ed Piazza. He wasn't in his office. It was after regular office hours. They couldn't find Preston Richards. He wasn't at the police station. And, they were told by the people who were in those places, the phones were down. All the phones. The whole phone system, as far as anyone knew.

They couldn't find Piazza or Richards at home, either. They were at a meeting. Somewhere.

They couldn't very well do a room-by-room search of the SoTF administration building and the Grantville city hall.

"What next?" Missy asked.

Neither one of them was on the best of terms with Tino Nobili. The city council had picked him to serve as interim mayor until the special election in June. Actually, they weren't on any terms with him at all and it was a given that Liz Carstairs would beat him next month, so it was hardly worth bothering to try.

Ron was prepared to brave Arnold Bellamy in a good cause, even though he didn't have a sense of humor, but he was at the same meeting. Somewhere.

"You can take the stuff to Dad," Chandra suggested. "At home."

That struck them as reasonable. That would work. Wes had been in on the conversations that sent them off on the expedition to Frankfurt in the first place.

Inez Wiley arrived at Benny Pierce's house by wheelchair, pushed by Veronica Dreeson, who was muttering under her breath. Something about *where was a healthy young archduchess when you could use her?*

"Open up the door, Minnie!" Veronica yelled as she pounded on the screen. "We know that you are in there!"

Minnie opened it. "How's Mrs. Wiley going to get up the steps?" she asked. "Do you need help? If so, Mr. Pallavicino is here. And the Reverends Jones."

Joe Pallavicino and Simon Jones hauled the wheelchair, with Inez in it, up the steps. Inez realized once more that Grantville was not a handicapped-accessible town in general. There was an occasional ramp, here and there, but generally it was a problem.

Once Inez was settled, Denise looked at her. "We're in trouble," she said. "But how did you find out?"

Inez looked back. "Generically, you have not been in school since Tuesday. Specifically, several people saw Ron Stone, Missy Jenkins, and Chandra Prickett coming back into town along Route 250. On your motorcycles."

Christin George crossed her arms over her chest. "I can't do anything for Minnie," she said. "But I can and I will write an excuse for Denise. I can and I will say that she had permission to loan her cycle to Missy Jenkins. I can and I will say that she had permission from me to take Buster's cycle."

Joe Pallavicino frowned at her. Her stance was reducing the meeting to something of a standoff.

"Take Buster's cycle where?" Inez asked.

Christin looked at her. "Just to take it."

"Looks like they went somewhere," Benny Pierce said. "So the better question might be where they went and why they went there."

"Where did you go, Minnie?" Veronica asked. "Why did you let Ron Stone borrow your hog?"

Minnie shook her head. "I can't tell you. I really can't. Not either one. We're all back safe now."

Veronica started to say something.

"I can't tell you," Minnie repeated. "But it was important. I promise you that. If you ask me to, I'll swear upon the eye that Mayor Dreeson gave me that it was important."

The time that Minnie Hugelmair spent at First Methodist did not appear to be making much impression on her overall world view.

A flash of light reflected on the ceiling. Inez looked out Benny's front window. It was Gina Goodman, the headlights of a power plant truck shining at the house, sticking her head out and yelling, "If you're still trying to find Ron and Missy, they're at Wes Jenkins' house! Chandra's with them."

She paused. "Christin, there's someone up at the storage lot who needs you ASAP to get something out."

Gina took off. So did Christin.

Breaking off the recriminations, the mentors and mentees refocused on the immediate concern. Getting the girls' motorcycles back. They headed for Wes' place, Denise and Minnie running ahead while Veronica pushed Inez's wheel chair.

Benny, Joe Pallavicino, and the Reverends Jones shook hands and assured one another that they would have another try at straightening this out tomorrow.

A half block from their goal, Inez and Veronica saw Chandra running out toward the girls; then right back in again, Denise following her. Minnie headed back toward them.

"Clara's having the baby. With no one to help her except Ron and Missy and Chandra. Chandra has to keep an eye on Weshelle because she's learned how to climb out of the playpen and Lenore can't keep up with her. Weshelle took a long nap this afternoon and is probably good to go until midnight. Lenore keeps trying to phone for help, but she can't get a dial tone anywhere."

"My mother was a midwife," Inez said. "I've delivered plenty of babies. Just get me to her."

Veronica started to push the wheel chair faster. Minnie grabbed the handles, which definitely picked up the pace. Once they got to the house, Ron and Missy carried Inez, wheelchair and all, up the front steps.

From the vantage point of the front hall, they looked up an

intimidating flight of stairs, too narrow for them to stand on either side of the wheel chair.

Lenore called from the other end of the hallway, where she was trying to fasten a wriggling Weshelle to a tether, that Clara was upstairs by herself, that there was no way that Clara could possibly come down, and that somebody had to do something *right now*. Like, preferably, getting hold of Kortney Pence, who was scheduled to do this delivery. And getting hold of Dad, who had called before the phones went down to say that he had scheduled a late meeting down at the legislative chambers, in the senatorial office.

Ron and Missy formed a chair with their arms and carried Inez upstairs to where Clara was. Ron ran back down for the wheel chair.

Denise, spotting her motorcycle next to the front steps, grabbed the stacks of paper someone had stuffed into the sidecar, dumped them into the playpen that Weshelle had obviously outgrown, and headed for Leahy. If she couldn't get Kortney, she could get *someone* medical at the hospital.

Kortney, thank goodness, was there. Denise had a funny feeling that there wasn't much time to spare. Kortney picked up her own baby, loaded her into a chest sling, and grabbed the kit she used for home deliveries.

From the things Clara was saying, loudly, clearly, and entirely in German, it was obvious that she had a firm grasp on who she held ultimately responsible for the whole situation.

"Minnie," Veronica said, "Go downtown and find Wes. Get hold of Wes Jenkins, somehow. I don't care how. Legislative chambers, senator's office. Now."

To Minnie, the obvious solution was the other motorcycle. She dumped the second set of papers out of the sidecar into Weshelle's abandoned playpen.

Minnie braked to a stop. Thinking back briefly to the obvious ire with which several policepersons had viewed her motorized dash through the "pedestrians only" section of town, she decided to take the motorcycle into the building with her.

Its arrival was not greeted with a smile of welcome by the security guard.

To whom she said, "Stuff it, dimbulb. Make sure none of the law and order types haul it off, either. Mrs. Jenkins is having a baby right now and I've come to fetch her husband. Where is he?"

Leaving them both, man and machine, in the overfull hallway, she pelted up the stairs and right into the middle of a rather large meeting of political higher-ups before the guard could verbalize his protest.

Her arrival got their attention. Her statement riveted it.

"Clara is fully dilated according to Mrs. Wiley, she's at home because Lenore couldn't get anyone on the phone, and Mrs. Dreeson wants Mr. Jenkins to come before the baby does, so cough him up. Denise went off to Leahy to get Kortney Pence. Ron Stone and Missy Jenkins are helping Mrs. Wiley, since she's still in a wheel chair, and Chandra is chasing Weshelle."

Wes dashed out the door. Minnie followed him.

"Not exactly a cast of thousands," Ed Piazza grinned, "but it seems to be mounting up. Reaching, at least, a level equivalent to the number of extras in a Jesuit outdoor drama."

"I do believe he forgot his briefcase," Arnold Bellamy said. "First time in his life, probably. I've always enjoyed working with Wes. He's so methodical."

"Well, put it in his office so he can pick it up tomorrow," Ed said.

Arnold frowned. "Is this kind of thing getting to be a habit? First Anita Masaniello in the middle of a field, now Clara Jenkins in the middle of a phone outage? It can't be good for the public image of the Department of International Affairs."

"Fascinating," Francisco Nasi said. "Relevant information only, arranged in order of importance, and condensed into a terse report. And she's the same one who provided the splendid description of the assassin. Who *is* that girl?"

Chapter 62

Grantville

In the sidecar of Minnie's hog, Wes was having the first motorcycle ride of his life. He profoundly hoped it would be the last.

By Minnie's standards, it was quite sedate. Of course, because of the artificial eye, she had only limited depth perception. Even though she compensated very well, as Buster had told her when he was teaching her, it still added a certain something to the way she approached stop signs, other vehicles, and pedestrians. Especially after dark.

Halfway there, she leaned over and said, as she slowed slightly for a stop sign, "By the way. You can forget that Holloway guy who beat up your daughter. He bought it."

"I should have done something, considering how he treated Lenore."

"You'd have blown a fuse if you'd caught him, Mr. Jenkins. Pardon my saying so. You'd have messed it up. Let it go."

"What happened?"

"You know he was mixed up in what happened at the synagogue? Or, at least, in what was going on at the hospital that pulled all the police away?"

Wes nodded; then realized that she couldn't see him. At least, he hoped she wasn't going to glance down at him while she was steering this mechanical beast through the dark at the speed to which she had now accelerated. So he said, "Yes."

"Denise didn't get mad. She got even. And he started it."

Wes nodded. Then he remembered again that Minnie couldn't see him and said "Yes."

Somewhere, back in college, he had read a play. *The Furies.* Three women. Bringers of retribution. Three of them. Gretchen Richter, so tall and blonde. Denise Beasley, so tiny and brunette. And one-eyed Minnie Hugelmair, who had started to sing.

> *"His chariots of wrath the great thunderclouds form,*
> *And dark is his path on the wings of the storm."*

He shuddered a little. He had sung that hymn a hundred times in the Methodist church. He had never understood it until now. It sounded different when Minnie sang it.

Bryant Holloway had been far from the only person "mixed up" in the events that had led to Henry Dreeson's assassination and Buster Beasley's death. He wondered how even Denise and Minnie intended to get.

"Thanks, Ron." The boy had enough lab training that Kortney had found him to be the most practical help of all the people here when she called for this and that out of her bag. Inez's mobility was still pretty limited. "That's it."

Kortney handed the baby off to Inez and, with Veronica's help, went back to taking care of Clara, who was still hearing and speaking only German. Veronica stubbornly repeated "*gesundes Kind*" and deftly evaded "*ein Maedchen*" until Kortney waved a little sponge under the new mother's nose. In Veronica's opinion, every new mother wanted to hear "healthy child," but "it's a girl" was the kind of news best delivered by the father. Who wasn't here yet.

Inez, who was no slouch herself and fully cognizant of the general speculation about the precise nature of Missy Jenkins' and Ron Stone's intentions toward one another, drafted Missy to help with the process of cleaning up the newborn. Once that was done, she literally left her holding the baby, with Ron peering over her shoulder with great interest.

"Hang onto her until Clara is ready," she said brusquely. "God only knows where they've put the cradle. It isn't in here."

"It wouldn't be in here," Missy said. "This is Chandra's old room, here right at the head of the stairs. That's why there's only a single bed. I wonder why Clara is in here. She must have been trying to go down to Lenore and then realized she couldn't make it." Suddenly, she fell into helpless giggles. Abruptly, she handed the little pile of blankets to Ron. "Take her. Before I drop her."

"What on earth?"

"On Thanksgiving." Missy was sputtering. "I'm sorry. I can't help it. On Thanksgiving, after dinner, Gran called me 'littlest granddaughter.' I told her that I'd outgrown it. That she'd have to promote one of her great-greats. But . . ." She giggled again, a little hysterically, reacting not just to this but to everything that had gone during the past week. Death and birth. "Just look. I've got another girl cousin. Gran has a 'littlest granddaughter' again."

Wes came running up the stairs, ignored the rest of them completely, and headed straight for Clara.

"She's perfectly fine," Kortney assured him, all the while muttering technical things to Inez about hard contractions, pulse rates, the baby coming faster than was ideal for an elderly primipara, pulse rates again, and a little tearing to be sutured.

He started to turn pale.

"Wes! Everything's okay. All right?"

"But?"

"She's a little out of it. I gave her a whiff. We don't have any locals anymore, really, and she's been through enough this evening. Let me get these stitches in. She'll be back with us in a jiffy. I don't want to use a second dose if I don't have to. Ether on a sponge isn't exactly scientifically measured anesthesia."

Wes wiggled himself onto the narrow bed, on the side next to the wall, and slid an arm under Clara's shoulders. Kortney spared enough time from what she was doing to give him an odd glance.

"She'll want to be held when she comes to," Wes said. "She always wants to be held when it's over. It's the only favor she's ever asked. 'Please don't go away. Stay with me.'"

Ron was distinctly feeling that he probably should not be here, that he should definitely not be hearing this, and that Missy's Uncle Wes, if he was paying any attention to anyone except Clara, would be of the opinion that he absolutely should not be here. But he couldn't really go away, because he was still holding the baby and nobody else seemed to have any interest in taking it.

Kortney snorted. "If that's the only piece of heavy baggage she carried with her out of that first marriage, you're a damned fortunate man. Okay, stay put. Her blood pressure is stabilizing nicely now."

Wes didn't care who else was there. As far as he was concerned right now, all of Grantville could be in this room, as long as Clara came through in good shape. Even if she did see things her own way. Even if she did argue with him now and then. Even if she had moved down the hall for a while. He tightened his arm around her a little. She was beginning to regain consciousness. He leaned over and kissed her.

Missy stood next to Ron, almost paralyzed. That wasn't the kind of kiss she would have expected of Uncle Wes. She wouldn't have thought him capable of it. If she had really thought about it at all. And Clara was, um, kissing him right back. Not quite awake and after everything that had been going on here. And after the big fight everyone knew they had after Bryant beat up Lenore.

They were old. Her mind went back to the birthday party. Clara was thirty-eight. That was old. Exactly twice as old as she was herself. And Uncle Wes was way older. Older than Dad. Older even than Mom.

She didn't remember much about how things had been before Mom and Dad separated. Except that Anne was always a pain. Anne hadn't ever wanted to be part of their family. Didn't want to be a big sister. Did want to go to Nani and Pop's by herself. She hated it when Chip and Missy came too.

Then Mom and Dad had separated. Gotten back together. And she had learned the why of it when she was twelve. Since the reconciliation, they had always been . . . matter-of-fact . . . toward one another. At least out where she could see them. But somewhere, way back at least, they must have, uh, done something of the sort. Mom had hinted at it, back in April. That is, she and Chip were here, after all. There had been a time when they were really preoccupied by something of the sort. That was, ah, definitely what Uncle Wes had been implying at Easter. Something like what Uncle Wes and Clara were doing right now.

Uncle Wes was still kissing Clara like that. Right in the middle of their having a baby, so to speak. Well, of course, kissing each other like that was probably what had led up to the baby. Which was probably why the guys downtown had been running Uncle Wes through such a gauntlet.

Which meant that a person didn't get rid of feeling the confusing stuff she felt about Ron. There wasn't a day when you suddenly woke up and were a grownup and all that was behind you. Which, at some level, she had been hoping that there was.

Mom must have done it with Anne's father when she was, uh, way younger than Missy was now. Mom? Irrationally, absurdly, the old TV commercial ran through her head. *Mom, what on earth were you thinking?*

She grabbed onto Ron's arm rather hard.

Clara came back to full consciousness, ascertained that Wesley really was there rather than a dream, closed her eyes again, and went to sleep.

Through the fog of her thoughts, Missy heard Mrs. Wiley saying something to Kortney.

"In a way, hospital deliveries take place in a sort of artificial setting. They limit the ways that people behave.

"Since most of the immigrant women won't go near the hospital to have their babies, it really couldn't hurt for you to suggest to Beulah and Garnet that they might bring some of the older midwives, Germans and Grantvillers both, into the curriculum. To talk to the new nurse-midwives like you whom they are training."

Missy glanced up. Mrs. Wiley was looking at Uncle Wes and Clara.

"Sometimes, when you're doing a home delivery, there's really no way to predict exactly what you'll run into."

For a minute, Missy suspected that Mrs. Wiley was teasing Kortney. But her face was as placid as her voice.

Wes looked around. Where was the baby? Ron Stone was looking back at him, trying to shrug his shoulders without disturbing the little bundle of blankets.

"Want it?" Ron asked.

"Not yet, I think."

"Uh. Then, if you have a minute, Mr. Jenkins?"

Wes looked at the boy. He might as well. He really didn't want to look at what Kortney and Inez were doing to Clara right now.

"Ah, we got the stuff. You know. What we went to Frankfurt for. It's downstairs, I guess, wherever Denise or Minnie put it when they went to get you and Mrs. Pence. And, I expect, someone ought to do something about it as soon as possible."

"Are the phones still down?"

"As far as I know, yeah."

Wes glanced around the room. "Veronica?"

"*Ja*."

"Is Minnie still here?"

"*Ja*."

"Send her down to the legislative chambers again, will you? To bring Francisco Nasi back here. She'll find him in the same room where she found me. I've never seen that young man flustered." He paused. "I think he *deserves* to spend some time in the sidecar of a motorcycle that has Minnie Hugelmair at the helm."

Don Francisco came and went, taking the materials that would go down in the history books as the "Playpen Papers."

Veronica Dreeson took Denise and Minnie away with her.

Weshelle finally went to sleep, so Lenore went to bed too.

Chandra stayed downstairs watching Kortney's baby. She hadn't seen her own kids yet since they got back from Frankfurt. They were safe at Aunt Debbie's and could wait until morning.

"We're done," Kortney said. "I'm going to nurse my own little lady and then go lie down. The motto of the midwife. 'Never miss a chance to take a nap.'"

Clara moved restlessly, half asleep, trying to turn over toward Wes.

"What?" Kortney asked sharply.

Wes put his other arm over the top of his wife. He looked at Kortney a little apologetically. "She wants my leg over hers, too."

"Well, keep the weight on her ankles. Below the knees, at all costs."

Wes leaned over and kissed Clara again. She settled down.

Kortney glared at them briefly. She then disappeared down the hall, thinking to herself that those two were at least indirectly responsible for the "little lady" she was about to nurse. After they had spent the Christmas party in Fulda last year dripping their uncontrolled sex hormones all over everyone else, blast them, she and Fred had duly escorted her mom and Clara to the upstairs apartment in the house Fred rented, gone down to Fred's rooms, and proceeded to forget about proper operating procedures for the remainder of the night.

Talk about an embarrassing outcome for one of Grantville's prime banner carriers for birth control. Jared was eight and she and Fred had only ever wanted one child. But he had already been in Fulda when Susannah Shipley really got the "Snipley" campaign going. Once he got back home, that was damn well going to be his first port of call.

Blast them both, again. Mom had thought it was so funny that she nearly had hysterics and been very flattered when she and Fred named the little lady Andrea Rose.

Chandra was coming upstairs, carrying said Andrea Rose. "I've locked up," she said. "If you don't need anything else, I'm going to sleep. It's been a long day."

Inez Wiley looked at Ron. "Sit there," she ordered.

He thought he was probably sitting on a toy chest. Missy sat down next to him.

"I don't hold with that early bonding mystique. As long as the baby is asleep, she'll be as fine with you as with her mother. Human arms, human body temperature. Don't disturb her, but the minute she wakes up and starts to want to eat, have Missy rouse me so I can get Clara up. I'll be next door with Kortney, on a folding bed in Lenore's old room. I do believe in getting them on the breast right away. You can't miss it. She'll open her mouth, start to make noises like a little sump pump, and then start rooting at your chest like a piglet."

"Yes, ma'am," Ron said.

Mrs. Wiley rolled down the hall in the same direction that Kortney had gone.

Ron sat there, thinking about adults.

That there had been something in the life of the calm, cheerful, competent, confident Mrs. Jenkins of Consular Affairs—the serene, unflappable Clara who had blown off every old cat in town by proclaiming that she was the luckiest and happiest woman in the world—something that led to her wanting, when things were over, to have her husband wrapped around her like a cocoon while she slept, warding off whatever things that went bump in her own personal night.

That Mr. Jenkins did it for her.

That growing up the way he had, on the commune, Ron probably didn't know much about husbands and wives. Dad might: he hadn't grown up on a commune. He and Magda got along great. But they kept things between themselves pretty private, and they were in Italy, anyway.

Missy put her head down on his shoulder.

Chapter 63

Grantville

Chandra stirred and looked at the alarm clock. Six-thirty. Somebody was going to have to get up and make breakfast for whoever was still in the house. That somebody was probably her. She showered and headed for the stairs. Mrs. Wiley was sitting with Dad and Clara, who was holding the baby. Presumably, at some time during the early hours, her new half-sister had decided that it was meal time. Mrs. Wiley made sshhh-ing gestures, so Chandra tiptoed down.

She paused at the open double doorway that led into the living room. Ron and Missy were sound asleep in the recliner. In order to fit into the limited space, they had assumed a position usually associated with words like "consensual." Chandra grinned. Either Aunt Debbie's direst suspicions were fully justified or else Missy had a *lot* more confidence in Ron's powers of self control than she had ever had in Nathan's back before they were married.

She knocked on the doorpost. Ron roused first, shook his hair back, and briefly looked down at Missy with an expression of such sharply intense delight that Chandra thought, *Okay, girl. If he looks at you like that very often, we can forgive you for going totally bonkers over a kid who doesn't demonstrate many of the attributes of a Prince Charming clone on other counts.*

It only lasted a couple of seconds. Then he shook Missy and

said in the ultracasual tone of voice that he usually produced when in the presence of her relatives, "Hey, it's morning. Wake up, Dumpling. We're going to have to coordinate to spring ourselves out of this thing."

Chandra stood there, wondering. He had not been using those mannerisms the day before. Not at all.

A crash at the end of the hallway, followed by several more, indicated that Weshelle was awake. The noise would come from her tossing all the ample contents of the crib onto the floor. Weshelle seemed to have a hunch that Noah's flood might recur during any night. If so, she intended to take her worldly possessions with her as she floated away.

Thinking that in another week, Weshelle would be able to get out of the crib as well as the playpen, Chandra started that way. The crashes stopped. Weshelle must have run out of ammunition. A loud thump, followed by a wail, indicated that her prediction as to the date of successful crib escape had been off. Lenore's voice, half asleep, offered comfort and consolation. She didn't sound panicked, so presumably Weshelle hadn't done herself any damage. The kid was one of those natural climbers.

Kortney appeared at the top of the staircase, carrying her little lady and asking if anyone had seen Wes' briefcase. Then asking if Ron and Missy could get Inez downstairs. Chandra yelled first "no" and then "yes."

The doorbell rang. Ron, still barefoot, got it. It was Aunt Debbie and Gertrude with Mikey, Tom, Sandra Lou, and Lena Sue. Mikey and Tom wanted to know why Chandra hadn't come home to see them the night before. She hugged them and said that it was because they were having a new aunt and she had been busy.

This led to a foray up the stairs, as soon as Missy and Ron finished carrying Mrs. Wiley down, to see Grandpa and Clara. And the new aunt. Wes, who had taken a perch on the toy chest, showed them the baby.

That was an aunt? Mikey and Tom were sadly disillusioned. Aunts were, by definition, old enough to take kids to the park. Each of the three girls began to assume that defiant "*I'm* the baby" expression.

Kortney called for Ron and Missy to bring Inez's wheelchair back upstairs so they could move Clara and the baby into the master bedroom.

Chandra sighed. One of these days she would have to try to decide, in a methodical and analytical way, sensibly, practically, what to do about Nathan and their marriage. Some day when she had time. Probably about the same time the cows came home. She headed for the kitchen.

The phones were still down, which was only a mild hindrance to circulation of the news of the Jenkins' blessed event. Starting at Cora's during breakfast, where it was announced by Veronica on her way to work, with a secondary source at the administration building once the offices opened and Don Francisco confirmed the outcome, and tertiary sources at the middle school and high school courtesy of Minnie and Denise, it simply flew.

"Fifteen minutes" was designated as the winning bet. It had a flair that attracted bettors. The more academic conclusions reached by the health class at the high school were a distant third. They had been based on "fifteen minutes" as the starting point, anyway, which was part of the reason that Vic Saluzzo had been so annoyed by the project. This meant that there was no single large winner to take the pool. "Fifteen minutes" had been the most popular odds by far.

An intransigent coalition of Grantville wives obtained the book that Irv Sonderman had been keeping at the Thuringen Gardens and forced the winners to pay up to the Red Cross.

Outwardly, the happy grandmother accepted the donation graciously. It was a substantial amount of money and the organization had a lot of obligations.

Inwardly, Eleanor Jenkins ground her teeth.

Preston Richards looked at the rest of the people around the table. Politics. Politics was always a problem when it impinged on what should be straightforward police business. But here were Ed Piazza and Don Francisco Nasi, who said that Mike and Rebecca were waiting at the other end of the radio connection to put their two bits in. Arnold Bellamy. Not Wes Jenkins. Someone might need to express an opinion that it would be too hard for Wes to hear. Not to mention that he had a new baby at home.

The issue, once again, was how to deal with the Bryant Holloway situation. More specifically, how to handle his death. The death, obviously, had to be announced. How much of the circumstances had to be announced seemed to be negotiable. The only outsiders who definitely knew about it, Nasi said, were Nathan and Chandra Prickett.

In other words, the State of Thuringia-Franconia could attempt to minimize external interest in Holloway's role. Now that he was dead, to what extent would justice be served, Don Francisco asked, by making a federal case of it? Literally. Since the papers were safely in hand, his role could be perceived as entirely local. An unwitting dupe. A sympathizer who ended up holding the bag. That would be enough to explain why he headed out of town.

Which was why the other side of the table was occupied by Veronica and Inez. Also Christin George. The widows. Ed Piazza insisted that they should be asked, at least, whether they would find it tolerable if one of the guilty parties, being dead, should be allowed to escape with an, if not unscathed, at least only minimally scathed reputation. If there was such a word as scathed.

"Are you sure that Nathan and Chandra will keep their mouths shut about that chase down to Frankfurt?" Veronica Dreeson directed the question to Don Francisco.

"There is very little certainty in this world," Don Francisco admitted.

"The people who would be most harmed by puffing up Holloway's importance in it all are Lenore and Weshelle. I can't believe that Chandra would want to hurt them," Inez Wiley said. "And he really wasn't that important."

"I agree," Don Francisco said. "All the information that I have is that Mrs. Prickett's relationship to her sister and niece is close and loving. There does not seem to be any immediate reason to assume that she would not prefer to protect them."

"This doesn't cause problems from the perspective of your department?" Ed Piazza asked.

"No new data about the incident is likely to be gained by 'plastering the information all over the place,' as Mike Stearns said to me earlier," Don Francisco said. "It may in fact be preferable to let things rest and remain with the story that Holloway was shot by unknown hands while driving to Frankfurt to visit his brother-in-law. Without adding anything about why he was driving to Frankfurt. Possibly someone else will become careless."

✧ ✧ ✧

Don Francisco still wished to avoid letting even Bellamy and Richards know that Nathan Prickett was one of his agents. The man's present usefulness in Frankfurt, watching for sales of arms to the enemy, was still high. Additionally, he had serious hopes that someone would become careless. The "Playpen Papers" that Ron Stone and Missy Jenkins had retrieved had been very illuminating. He had done some fuzzing of the context as to how he got them, managing to leave people with the impression that the playpen had been in the kitchen at Bryant Holloway's house, no longer used because Weshelle had learned to climb out of it and gradually coming to serve as a general catch-all.

The story did have the merit of maintaining the connection between the papers and Holloway, at least, while avoiding uncomfortable questions about Frankfurt. Provenance was important and that origin tied them to Dumais. Not that a precise provenance was crucial. Many of the records were financial in nature. Payments to and by Dumais. Duplicate copies of his itemized expense accounts. The instructions and reports turned out to be encrypted. Time-consuming, but not a surprise. The financial records were not.

Of course, as far as the politicians and Preston Richards were concerned—as far as everyone at the table except Don Francisco himself was concerned—Holloway had indeed been shot by unknown hands. One thing that Ron, Missy, and Chandra agreed on completely was that nothing in the world was to be gained by letting anyone else know that Denise and Minnie did it. None of them had told a single soul.

Don Francisco knew because Nathan Prickett had duly reported the sequence of events. He had therefore ensured that Ron and Missy were not asked to attend this meeting. He wasn't certain what would happen if their former high school principal asked them point blank. They might tell him.

Inez Wiley cleared her throat. "I don't think we need to say anything about why he was driving to Frankfurt. People will be ready to assume, I believe, that he was leaving town for personal reasons. Especially since his sister Lola is the one going over there to Frankfurt to make arrangements. Not Lenore."

"What Inez means," Christin George said, "is that a lot of people already know that he flipped out, showed up at Consular Affairs where he tried to kill Clara, and then beat Lenore up real bad. The women down at the court were not happy about what he did. They kept their own counsel back in February and March, so Wes Jenkins wouldn't find out, but this last time, believe me, they did not keep their mouths shut. No reason, since Wes couldn't be kept out of the loop. So that's public knowledge now. The fact that he went postal would also account for your department poking around, Preston. Quite aside from any minor matters like being involved in setting up the assassinations."

"Yes," Preston Richards said. "Yes they did, that is. The ladies down at the court made it very plain that they were upset. Beyond that, the question of why he took a truck can be fuzzed—at least if Steve Matheny is willing to cooperate, since he nabbed it off the fire department lot. As far as I know, nobody saw him loading Dumais' leavings."

"This does leave open the possibility," Bellamy said, "that it may blow up in our faces one of these days if Nathan Prickett ever decides to become obnoxious and disagreeable about it. Remember what happened when they tried to keep Wes and Clara's Methodist ceremony secret. That backfired badly. And though I hate to say it, there are stories going around that Nathan and Chandra's marriage is in trouble."

"It's a risk," Ed Piazza admitted. "I still think that it's probably the best that we can manage at the moment."

Don Francisco kept his own counsel.

"Well, I don't see," Veda Mae Haggerty said, "why everybody is going around feeling so sorry for Lenore Jenkins. If you ask me, Bryant was the one who deserved some sympathy. He went into the marriage and through it knowing that some other man had been there first. And Lenore wasn't a divorcee, as you know perfectly well."

"Ma," her son said. "Ma, I really don't think you really ought to have said that, right here and right now."

"Well, why not? You may not have any standards, marrying Laurie with that little bastard of hers, but that doesn't mean that I shouldn't. It's a disgrace, the way the Reverend Mary Ellen is going around saying 'poor Lenore.' If you ask me, she didn't get anything that wasn't coming to her."

Veda Mae was in top form, her voice echoing through the dining room at the Willard Hotel. People at the five or six surrounding tables had turned their heads to listen.

Gary Haggerty stood up. "I've had it," he said. "It's too late to salvage anything, but I'm going to go find Laurie and throw myself face down at her feet. I'm going to apologize for everything you put her through and everything she put up with. Ma, you are the most disgusting excuse for a human being I have ever come across."

He started to walk out.

"That doesn't change a thing!" Veda Mae screeched at the top of her lungs. "Miss Oh-So-Prissy Lenore Jenkins of the Oh-So-Prissy Jenkins family was not a virgin when she got married and she wouldn't even tell Bryant who it had been when he asked. And after that, everyone makes such a fuss about her."

Gary turned around. "What about your friend Velma?" he asked.

"Velma wasn't my friend."

"Somehow," he said, "I'm not surprised."

Veda Mae sniffed. Then she looked at Pam Hardesty who was also sitting at the table with her. "I expect you'll be walking out in a snit, too."

"Actually, Mrs. Haggerty," Pam said, "I know my mother pretty well. It's not easy to be friends with her. I'm sure you tried your very best."

She hoped Don Francisco would be proud of her.

"Oh, God, Mary Ellen," Lenore said. "I'm so sorry. First Dad and Clara's marriage. Now this. I wouldn't be surprised if First Methodist would be ahead of the game if you and Simon just struck the Jenkins family off the membership rolls and had done with it."

Out in the yard, a German girl Clara had found was chasing around after Weshelle.

"Do you want to tell me about it?"

Lenore shook her head. "Not really. I think Dad would have been okay with it, but I know that it would have been a problem for Mom. Not that she would have acted up, but she would have been miserable and very brave about trying not to show that she was miserable. So that's the way it was."

"Why?"

"Jay was from India. Sanjay was his full first name. We were both fairly traditional products of our own cultures. Even telling each other's parents about us would have been a major step."

Lenore stopped.

"I met him when I was taking classes at Fairmont State, of course."

Mary Ellen nodded.

"It's funny. Dad actually saw us together once. He was walking through the student union with a batch of other parks and recreation officials who were there for a conference. We were at a table with our study group. One of the girls said, 'Hey, Lenore, there's some old fart staring at you,' and when I looked over there, it was Dad. He just smiled and waved and went on."

"Do you think he connected the two of you?"

"There wasn't really anything to connect, back then. We were friends for a couple of years before anything else. On Friday nights, if I didn't have to work at the store, we'd eat take-out while he finished up at the department and then go to something. There was always something free to do on campus on Friday evening, if you looked hard enough. Once we went to a lecture on control and eradication of multiflora rose."

She blinked.

"Then it got to the point that we realized that there would be something else. Something more. One night, we were about to leave the lab. There were sirens outside, police cars and a fire truck in the parking lot. We'd already switched the lights off. We were standing there, looking out the window, wondering what was going on. Jay put one of his hands on the back of my neck. I took his other hand and put it against my collar bone. Nothing flashy. But we knew.

"I did all the sensible things. Went to the clinic, got the pill. A couple of months later, there was a terrible storm. I called home from his lab and left a message on the answering machine that I would stay overnight with a friend rather than try to drive from Fairmont to Grantville with a risk of flash flooding and mud slides. And I did stay with a friend."

Lenore swallowed hard.

"When I got home the next evening, Mom was very unhappy. She had called the dial-back number and got the telephone tree for the chemistry department, so she didn't *really* know where I was the night before if she had needed to reach me, she said. And, and . . . Dad told her that she should at least be glad that it wasn't some honky-tonk bar. He was teasing, but she didn't see that he was being the least bit funny."

Mary Ellen wasn't quite sure what to say. Lena had never really been known for having a sense of humor.

"Good God, Mary Ellen. We were both twenty-five! What do people expect?"

"I think, maybe, it's that you were always such a perfect lady, Lenore." And, she thought to herself, also that every guy in Grantville knows perfectly well that it wasn't him, which adds some intrigue to the speculation.

"When the Ring of Fire came, we'd gotten to the point that we were thinking and talking about that when he finished his MS at Fairmont, if his application to WVU for the Ph.D. program was successful, I might stop living at home and working and taking classes part time. That I might move to Morgantown, go to college there, and we would live together. And I wish that I had been in Fairmont with Jay that Sunday afternoon. He wanted me to come."

Mary Ellen held Lenore while she finally cried. Not for Bryant, not for Weshelle, not for herself, not for her injuries, but for a young man left up-time, for whom she had never let herself grieve because no one else had even known he existed.

"I'm sorry, Lenore," Jeff Adams said. "But what you were thinking is right. You're pregnant."

She looked at him. "February," she said. "I didn't want a second baby. I really didn't."

"It's a little late. But I can deal with it, if you want me to. Under the circumstances."

She sat there.

Then she shook her head. "It isn't the baby's fault what Bryant did."

"Under the circumstances . . ."

"Would you go out and shoot Cory Joe and Pam and Susan, just because Velma Hardesty is the pits?"

Adams looked at her again. That was where the spirits divided. For Lenore, this fetus fell into the same category as those three young adults. Was just as much a person. He'd known that the minute she referred to it as a baby.

He hoped that she knew what she was doing. But, given that viewpoint, if she was to come through this sane . . .

"I've learned something, though."

He raised his eyebrows.

"Sometimes the proverbs we were brought up on are wrong.

Sometimes stoical endurance isn't the right response. No, 'you made your bed and now you have to lie in it.' No, 'no use crying over spilt milk.' I've learned that Clara has a point, the way she approaches things. Sometimes it makes sense to run away. But sometimes the right thing to do is to scream and scream and scream until someone comes to help you deal with it."

Lenore stood up and picked up her purse.

"I hope it's another girl," she said. "I think I'd have trouble dealing with a boy. Especially when he started to get older. Under the circumstances."

Apparently she did know what she was doing. At least she had the kind of family that would rally around her.

He sighed. It was her call, after all. No matter what he thought about the wisdom of her decision, it was her call.

Frankfurt, May 1635

Lola climbed off the freight wagon, asked the postmaster for directions, and walked to Nathan Prickett's office.

She was the last person Nathan had expected to see. Except, of course . . . funeral arrangements. She was Bryant's sister, his nearest kin inside the Ring of Fire. Except for his cousin Shannon, and Lenore and Weshelle, of course, about his only kin.

Bryant was on ice, in a cave not far from town, waiting for someone to do something about him. It was just as well she had come.

"For public consumption here in Frankfurt," she said, "Lenore hasn't recovered from her 'accident' yet. Not that everyone in Grantville doesn't know what actually happened."

"Ah, yes. I'll take you over to the mayor's office. That's where you will need to pick up permits and such."

"I'm not paying to take him back," Lola said. "And I'm not dumping a bill for it on Lenore, either. It's not as if there's a traditional family cemetery or anything. Our parents were still alive in Clarksburg when it happened. Uncle John and his wife were left up-time, too. Our grandparents are still alive. They agree with me. There's no reason to take him back."

"So why did you come?"

"To make arrangements here. To do whatever is necessary to get him into the ground, given that he doesn't belong to any church that prevails around here."

"There's a kind of potter's field. For beggars and vagrants. People they don't know what religion they are."

"Okay. That'll do. Take me to the mayor."

"For that, I think the city clerk will do. And the sexton at the church. He's in charge of the cemetery. Grave digging and such."

"Take me to the city clerk, then. You know your way around Frankfurt. I don't."

"Where are you staying?"

"With you. If you think I'm paying for a room when you have space, you're crazy. Jim McNally pays a reasonable wage, but I've got two kids to feed."

"Doesn't Latham pay support?"

"When he's in the mood. Which he rarely is, now that he's moved to Magdeburg and doesn't have to look me in the face. He's not been what you could call an involved father since I threw him out. It's not anything I can rely on. When it comes, I put it in savings. For emergencies. Medical expenses and things. The regular bills come out of what I earn and I make sure there aren't more than I can cover."

"I'm not sure it will look right, having you stay with me."

Lola glared at him. "I have news for you, Nathan. I don't care how it looks. Either you let me in your front door and provide me with a place to sleep or I'll crawl down through the chimney like old Saint Nick. I have had it about up to here with this whole mess."

The arrangements took most of the day, which annoyed him. He had several tasks on the list of things he intended to get done today. Now they would all have to be pushed over into tomorrow. Plus what he had scheduled for tomorrow. Some of which would have to be rescheduled for the next day.

He hadn't planned to spend today dealing with Bryant Holloway's leftovers. But he supposed that he had known he would have to do it one of these days. Today was as good as any.

He sat on the bench, his elbows on the table. Lola had cooked some supper. Nothing fancy, but hot. Seventeenth-century stir fry.

A little bit of chicken, lots of onions and cabbage. The apples had given it a good flavor. He usually just had a cheese sandwich at night, along with the second beer he allowed himself.

"What are you doing for politics?" he asked. "Now that you're missing the American idols?" She had named her children Clinton and Hillary.

She was washing up the dishes. Looked at him. Turned back to the dishpan. This house didn't have a sink.

He made another crack. Just couldn't resist it. They'd always argued about politics.

She turned around and started to blast him for a fool. Apparently Missy Jenkins had talked to her.

She blasted him more devastatingly than Ron Stone had done. As an ex-girlfriend, she knew him well enough to manage to hit him in places where it really hurt.

She pointed out that there had been a while between the Ring of Fire and the conception of the twins. Like about nine or ten months. During which he could have done something about it. She had a few choice words to say about the fact that during any one of those months, he could have betaken himself off to the doctor. To Adams or Nichols, if his masculine sensitivity was too delicate to patronize Susannah Shipley.

As far as Lola was concerned, there were no self justifications allowed.

Although when she finally reduced him to, "Because I'm a wimp?" she did laugh.

She blew steam out of both ears for about two hours.

The dishes were long done by then. Mostly he just sat there, looking at his hands.

Finally she said, "Look at me!"

He did.

"Are you going back to her?"

He looked back down at his hands.

"You married Latham before I married Chandra."

"It was several months after you got engaged to her. Are you going back? Bringing her here?"

About fifteen minutes later, he reached the answer. "No."

"Why not?"

That took more time.

"She was just a kid, Lola. As naive a kid as could possibly

have existed in the United States of America in the last decade of the twentieth century, the way Wes and Lena brought her up. A really good kid. She had no idea what she was doing to me. Standing there in her modest little blouses and skirts, her not-by-any-means-too-tight jeans and her plenty-loose-enough-to-pass-Lena's-scrutiny tee shirts, radiating enough come-hither to drive a man mad."

"She *was* a good kid," Lola agreed. "She's grown into a nice person, too. Friendly. Capable. No nonsense. Funky sense of humor. I really like her better than Lenore, to be honest. Not so passive."

It occurred to him suddenly that Lola had probably seen a lot of Chandra while Lenore was married to Bryant. Whom they had buried today. While he had been down in Frankfurt, most of the time. For the last couple of years, she would have seen a lot more of Chandra than he had.

"She doesn't deserve for me to cut her off to handle four kids alone."

"She's not going to be any more alone with them from now on than she has been for the last two years almost. Look at it straight. She does deserve better than to be tied to you long distance forever. 'Irreconcilable differences' covers a lot of ground."

"All I could think of, when she came here to Frankfurt, was that I had to get her away before it started up again. Even though she really had come just to find out what was going on. Even though she didn't come down with the slightest intention of . . . When I saw her leaving with Missy on that motorcycle, all I really felt was relief.

"Chandra . . . wasn't really ever what I had planned on." He looked at Lola a little helplessly. "Not even what I had hoped for. She just happened to me."

"It's about time you faced up to that," Lola said. "That you haven't always been in control of things."

Then she took him to bed.

It was safe. She'd had her tubes tied when she divorced Latham. She had the sense to realize when she had enough on her plate.

And God only knew, it had been a long enough wait.

Chapter 64

Grantville

The phones were still down two days later. That made four days without phones. Grantville did not have a decent messenger system. Naturally. When it had working telephones, it did not need one. Even the messengers it did have, for delivering packages, were summoned by phone.

Don Francisco Nasi frowned. He would need to find Wes Jenkins himself. He needed the man. This meeting might be critical and Jenkins knew more about the situation around Fulda than anyone else available. Jenkins was probably at home. Impatiently, he started walking.

Walking was so slow.

The first motorcycle ride with that astonishing girl, though . . . That had been glorious, utterly glorious. He would have to do it again, as soon as possible. The ride back, with the extra weight of all those papers, had been less interesting. She had been going more slowly, balancing carefully for fear of tipping over.

"Upstairs," the young woman who answered the door told him. He recognized her, vaguely. One of Jenkins' grown daughters. Chandra or Lenore. He had trouble telling them apart, both so tall with light hair and long faces, and the house was full of children, so he would not try to guess which one it was. He thanked her.

Jenkins was not in the room to which he had been taken the night the child was born. That, when he opened the door, was empty. There were voices farther down the hall. Jenkins was sitting on a very wide, very long, bed. Larger than any Don Francisco had ever before seen. Jenkins was tall, of course, and not a poor man. Perhaps he had once had it made especially for his comfort?

The remarkable Clara was propped up on pillows. Jenkins had the infant on his lap. Eleanor Maria, they were calling her, in honor of both grandmothers. Most appropriate.

Don Francisco listened with amusement. According to Jenkins, there had never been such a perfect infant, right down to her fingernails and toenails. He was spreading out the little fingers and toes, showing these off. He was telling his wife that daughters were wonderful. He was saying that no man in his right mind, having been presented with such a splendid child by his wife, could possibly wish that she were a son instead.

Don Francisco had to give him credit. It was a spectacular performance. *Bravura*. Quite convincing. Perhaps Jenkins would ultimately achieve a higher rank in the diplomatic service than he himself had expected. If Nasi had been a wife rather than a man, he would probably have believed every word. Many of them, at least. It was almost too bad that he would have to interrupt. However.

"Wes," he said from the doorway. "Wackernagel has come in with more information from Frankfurt. We need you at a meeting right away."

Clara waved at him. "Tell our favorite courier Hi! for me," she said. He looked up, a little startled. The tone of her voice did not match the normality of her words.

Clara thought that the little speech had been very nice of Wesley, particularly on this third day after the birth, when she ached all over and felt so wretched and weepy. Her milk was coming in. She had been doubtful of the wisdom of permitting the child to suckle the pre-milk, but Kortney had insisted that the up-time physicians found it of value. Putting Eleanor Maria to her breast, she admitted to a certain feeling of smug satisfaction as to how single-mindedly this particular baby, so far superior to all other babies, devoted herself to nursing. The child would be strong. That made up for the way her breasts hurt. Or it ought to.

A wife should believe her husband. But in her heart, she admitted, she did not believe one word of what Wesley had been saying. She sat there thinking that she *would*, definitely would, give Wesley sons yet. She shifted uncomfortably. Before this day, she would not have believed that a human bottom could hurt so much. Buttocks were usually so squishy and bland, causing one no trouble at all. She cradled her daughter a little closer and briefly, fiercely, wished that every man who fathered a child should be required to produce a bowel movement the size of a baby on the same day it was born.

Even Wesley. Especially Wesley, who had gotten up off this bed quite nimbly and walked down the stairs with Don Francisco without feeling any pain at all.

That would be only fair of God.

Gently, she stroked Eleanor Maria's cheek. "*Kindlein so suess*," she crooned under her breath. "Sweet baby, sweet baby."

She should have known, of course. God had told her. "Your desire shall be unto your husband. In pain shall you bring forth your children." God knew everything. He had given her what she prayed for, and she couldn't claim that He hadn't warned her.

Her desire was unto her husband. She had never been quite so happy as when she woke up, after the birth, to find that she was back in Wesley's arms. Without apologizing for having used her own best judgment.

But. Desiring him didn't mean she had to take all of his statements at face value. Every man wanted sons, no matter what he said. That was a truth more certain than anything taught by either religion or science. More true than any article of faith, truer than the movements of the planets. There was time. For now, they had this wonderful baby. Wesley was right. Eleanor Maria was incredibly beautiful, unbelievably adorable. But Wesley would have his sons, too.

She would have to have a word with God about it. Maybe praying for the blessing of children hadn't been specific enough. Maybe God thought that she hadn't cared whether the baby was a boy or a girl.

Next time, she would leave no margin for error.

"Why aren't you taking this up with your Nani?" Willie Ray Hudson asked.

"Because I don't think she would tell me," Missy said honestly enough. "She's ticked off enough as it is, because of Ron. Remember last fall? Remember Easter dinner, when she wouldn't invite him?"

"And you got some of this stuff from Eleanor?"

"Yes, Pop," Missy said as meekly as possible.

"Including the comments about the women in your mother's family?"

"Yes." Missy nodded.

"I may have to have a conversation with that gossipy old lady one of these days. But, since she's opened it . . ."

"I opened it, Pop," Missy said. "I told her I had counted from when she and Grandpa got married to when Uncle Wes was born."

"Girl, you may have more guts than any Jenkins born in the last century to do that. Or more Hudson than Jenkins in you." He paused. "Did you get an answer?"

"One thing led to another. 'Another' was a rather deft change of topic from the behavior of members of the Jenkins family to the behavior of female members of the Hudson family."

"Sounds like Eleanor." Willie Ray paused. "Well, okay. I suppose you also counted from our marriage to your mother's birth?"

"Yes. But you might say that it was within the realm of plausible deniability. Especially given how little Mom is. From June 27 to February 2 is sort of what you might call marginal."

"Take it from me. Debbie was full term. You might consider your mom part of a joyous ongoing celebration of the fact that I'd made it back from Korea all in one piece."

Missy nodded.

"Vera wasn't nearly as young then as Debbie was when she married Don Jefferson, of course." Willie Ray paused. "I'm not going to talk to you about your mother's personal life. That's between the two of you—however much she wants to tell you. Or not."

Missy nodded again.

"Then, if that's understood. Vera and I were both twenty-two when we married." He smiled. "What gave your Nani nervous prostration for several weeks was that I wasn't out of the army yet, which meant that for a while we weren't sure that the wedding could be scheduled to come off as promptly as it did. Vera was the kind of person who would have been awfully embarrassed to be showing when she walked down the aisle. Her sister Bonnie, Keith Pilcher's grandma, cut it a lot closer to the deadline and she'd had to be a bridesmaid with Bonnie bulging, so to speak."

"Oh."

"Yep. It was one of those 'heads only' engagement photos for Bonnie and Bert. And then for the wedding, a picture of them seated, with the attendants standing behind them. It's amazing what a few strategically placed artificial ferns could do for a girl's public image."

"Mean, Pop," Missy said.

"After we got married and I got out, we spent the next couple of years in married students' housing at WVU while I finished my degree on the GI bill. Vera worked as a secretary and got what they called back then her 'Ph.T.'—'Putting Hubby Through.'"

"Cutesy," Missy said. "Really cutesy."

"It was a different time and a different way of looking at things," Willie Ray said. "Though I can't say that I thought much of it myself at the time. Sort of a consolation prize. Your Nani has a sharp mind."

"So you graduated when?"

"In June of '57. The second baby was supposed to be the boy, since we already had a girl with Debbie. 'Tea for two and two for tea, a boy for you, a girl for me.' You can't believe how spitting mad Vera was when it turned out to be your Aunt Aura Lee. Luckily, Ray was born eleven months after that, so Vera had an absorbing new interest and never really took it out on her. But the truth of the matter is that Vera's 'mothering' focused on Debbie and Ray. As long as Aura Lee kept her head down, Vera was pretty oblivious to what she did."

"Does that lead to what Gran was implying?" Missy asked.

"In a way, I suppose. Every now and then, Vera would perk up. The summer Aura Lee was fourteen going on fifteen, before her freshman year of high school, she came home one evening from Nat Fritz's house. Vera went into a tirade because during the afternoon, several people called to say that she was sitting on the creek bank with Joe Stull instead of being at the library, where she was supposed to be," Willie Ray said. "And reminding your Nani that Joe was two and a half years older. Plus not exactly from the cream of the crop, socially."

"Sounds like Grantville."

"Aura Lee pointed out rather firmly that since all Nani's informants agreed that that the two of them had been sitting on the creek bank talking, in plain sight of everyone, not touching, each one of them throwing a pebble into the water every now and then, her mother didn't have much to complain about. Which was true, as far as it went."

"Didn't it go far enough?" Missy asked.

"Well, I bothered to do what Vera didn't. I asked Aura Lee what they'd been talking about, and she answered, 'kissing frogs.' Specifically, that most boys were frogs and that very few frogs turned into princes when they were kissed by princesses. So that, overall, there wasn't much point to kissing them. All of which seemed to derive from some kid who was going to be at the Fritzes' that evening wanting to kiss my daughter. She never did explain exactly how or why she called Joe in as a consultant on the point. But basically they concluded that she was going to put off kissing anybody at all until she got a year older, at which point they'd meet there on the creek bank again and discuss matters in more detail."

Missy giggled. "That is so funny."

"Except that a year later, we had one of the worst gully-washers ever. It was raining solid sheets of water, the creeks and branches were up. Joe came along in his mother's rattletrap of a car and, just like he expected, found Aura Lee in a yellow slicker huddled up next to the guard rail, with the creek rising fast and water lapping the toes of her flip-flops. Holding onto the post. As stubborn as a little mule. So he piled her into the car and headed out here to bring her home. They barely made it across the ford at the run. Dashed into the house. Headed into the kitchen. Of course, Aura Lee was hungry. The girl was always hungry. For someone so tiny, she ate incredible amounts. So I found them sitting at the table. She offered me her specialty, a peanut butter and banana sandwich. I made a face. Joe said that he'd opt for straight peanut butter on toast. That sounded pretty good, so I took it. Just then the phone rang. Vera, with Debbie and Anne, saying that she couldn't cross the run and was going back to spend the night in town. I told Joe to call his Ma with the news. So he ended up staying the night."

"With or without hanky-panky?"

"Without. Aside from a reasonable amount of flirting on the

porch while they stood there after supper and watched the rain come down. Presumably talking out whatever they were scheduled to talk out on the creek bank that afternoon. But it was clear that they were eyeing each other meaningfully, so to speak."

"You were willing to live with that, Pop?"

"There's not a lot of point in trying to make the rivers run upstream."

"You didn't do a thing?" Missy sounded scandalized.

"The next morning, with the water going down, I walked him out to his car and asked him what his plans were. He said he was leaving high school right then, after junior year, and going into the army. I said I trusted that Aura Lee would not have any serious reason to regret his departure. Joe was eighteen. A kid too, when you came right down to it. He had the guts to look me in the eye and tell me that Aura Lee featured in every possible future he drew up for himself, if she was willing to be there. And the sense of humor to tell me that he didn't have any intention of making a serious move until she had outgrown putting bananas in her peanut butter. 'First things first,' he said.

"So he went off to basic training a few weeks later, then to Leonard Wood, and Aura Lee spent her sophomore year of high school getting excellent grades and still not kissing frogs. Though I suspect that she kissed Joe more than a few times before he left, whether he thought she was too young or not. All things considered. Just to make sure that he'd remember her. She grew up a lot that next year."

"This leads to what Gran was saying?" Missy asked.

"That next summer was the one after Debbie finished high school. I was determined she was going to WVU and living on campus—that she should have a chance to grow up. Vera was equally determined that she wasn't. Let's put it this way. Both of us were distracted and not paying a lot of close attention to Aura Lee. Who by that time had the firm reputation of being a good girl who kept herself to herself and was in no way a troublemaker. I never even told Vera that Joe had been here that rainy night. The only other person who knew it was Juliann Stull, who kept her mouth shut."

"So nobody was watching Aunt Aura Lee?"

"Not closely. As long as she was home by curfew, she was pretty much on her own. Part-time job at the grocery store, six hours a day, for pocket money. Driving one of my old rattletraps that was barely good enough to get her to town and back. So when Joe got back on leave, she had time on her hands."

"Where was there to go in Grantville those days?" Missy asked.

"Hardly anywhere. That first evening they ended up in a booth in the pizza place, Joe catching a half dozen of his own friends up on army life. Until she reminded him that her curfew hadn't been extended indefinitely and he had to take her home. The rest of the time . . . I did ask her once during those two weeks if she had taken up kissing frogs. She gave me a look and said, 'Joe's not a frog. He just looks sort of like one to people who don't have enough sense to tell the difference.'"

"I can almost hear her," Missy said.

"We could have tried keeping her on a shorter leash those couple of weeks, I suppose. But nobody can be in two places at once. He sat with her in church. The first Sunday, Vera and I had a political reception in Fairmont in the afternoon. When we got home, Debbie was playing with Anne down by the run—she'd stayed home to babysit because Anne was always grumpy if a person waked her up from a nap—and informed us that Joe and Aura Lee were in the back yard, not particularly in a mood to have a two-year-old jumping up and down on them, so we should honk the horn, whistle loudly, sing off-key, rattle a few chains, or otherwise make noise before rounding the corner. Talk about simplicity in pursuit of privacy. I'm sure the last spot any of their friends would have thought to look for them was at our place.

"He always got her home by curfew. Telling her not to see him would have gone nowhere. We'd already had your mother marry before she finished high school." Willie Ray smiled ironically. "I was clinging to a certain glimmer of hope that Aura Lee and Joe had more common sense than Debbie and Don had at the same age. Which, in the long run, they did."

"You mean that she stayed home, finished high school, and went to the university?"

"Basically. She'd been very partial to Joe since the first day she noticed that people came in two genders," Willie Ray said philosophically. "In fact, it wouldn't surprise me if she was looking at him when she noticed it. Even though no one would be likely to describe him as a good-looking boy or a handsome man. She never so much as went out on a date with anyone else. Not even to a church party or school dance. But I have to say that they managed to keep everyone guessing about exactly where things stood between them for the next two years, which was hard to do in a town this size. Which meant that Vera didn't have anything substantial to complain about. After Aura Lee started WVU, they didn't even try to pretend. They stayed reasonably discreet. Those are two different things."

"How?"

"That first year she and Debbie were sharing that apartment in Morgantown, your dad dropped your mom off here one Friday evening in the spring. Vera complained that she'd been trying to call the apartment all day and wasn't getting an answer. Debbie said that Aura Lee had caught a ride over to Baltimore at noon to meet Joe there. Spend the weekend. Go to a preseason game; they were a lot cheaper than the regular Orioles games. Tour the harbor. Just relax a bit before she started cramming for finals. Vera got all upset. Debbie answered that it wasn't hurting her a bit. And it wasn't. If Vera hadn't pushed, she'd never even have known that's where Aura Lee was that weekend. Much less any of her friends at First Methodist knowing about it."

Willie Ray leaned back. "One more thing for you to think about, girl."

"What?" Missy asked.

"It's a little hard to tell, since Joe was around. Maybe he was blocking Aura Lee's view, so to speak. On the other hand, he was a thousand miles away for months at a time those first few years they were more or less a couple. Years when she was very young. She had plenty of time to look around. No matter what Eleanor Jenkins was implying about the Hudson women, I think that if Joe didn't exist, Aura Lee would have ended up as uninterested in men as Chad's cousin Marietta Fielder at the library. Not hostile to them. Not a man-hater, or anything like that. Just . . . not personally concerned with the topic. For her, all the rest were frogs—the ones she grew up with here in Grantville, the other students in Morgantown while she was at the university, all the men she met while she was working in Charleston. There are some women who will look at a half-dozen or so men with reasonable interest while they're growing up, and depending on circumstances could be happy in a different way married to any of those possibilities. Not your aunt. Single-minded."

"I see," Missy said.

"Do you? You might want to give a thought to whether you're enough like her that Ron Stone is the only man you're ever going to be interested in that way. If he is, that maybe ought to affect your calculations. Whatever you're trying to figure out at the moment, if it's so, it had better affect your calculations. Weigh them."

"I'm not like that. I dated a half dozen guys before I started dating Ron," Missy protested. "Kissed them, too, some of them. More than once."

"With what result?"

Missy looked at her Pop for a while. "They all stayed frogs," she finally admitted.

Willie Ray leaned back. Point made. No reason now to bring up how relieved he and Vera had been every month things stayed on schedule for quite some time before he'd left for Korea. It embarrassed Vera to remember that, even after they'd been married for fifty years.

The fact remained that Eleanor had pegged one thing right. Missy was more like the Hudson women. Which meant . . .

He didn't believe that he was the only person still alive in Grantville who had been surprised when Eleanor Newton actually settled down and made John Jenkins a good wife. She had been as wild as they came when she was a girl. And if she continued to make a nuisance of herself, he wouldn't hesitate to remind her. He'd appeal to her better nature first. But if that didn't work, he wouldn't hesitate at all to remind her that she would probably prefer not to have Missy asking a lot of questions. He couldn't be the only person who remembered the stories and Missy would find one of them who was willing to talk, eventually. She was bound to, as tenacious as she was.

"Was it true, Mom? What Gran said—well, implied—about Aunt Aura Lee? I've learned to take some of the things that she says with a grain of salt." Missy pulled her feet up onto the glider.

"The summer of '74?" Debbie asked. She tapped her fingernails on the porch railing a minute while she thought about her mother-in-law and the way she tended to put things. "That's thirty years ago. Your Gran was telling the truth *if* she simply told you that Aura Lee and Joe were already an item the summer she was sixteen going on seventeen. As Elaine Bolender said then, he was cradle robbing, a bit. But there wasn't anything anyone could have done about it. Not short of locking one of them up. Or, more likely, locking both of them up, with guards posted twenty-four hours a day."

"I took it from Pop that he and Nani didn't lock her up?"

"Joe hitchhiked over from Fairmont when he got back on leave that Saturday, dropped off at Stevenson's Groceries, went in, said 'Hi, Boyd, where's Aura Lee?' Boyd said, 'in back stocking canned goods.' Which is where they went public, so to speak. A fast hug, her head on his shoulder, him saying he was on his way to his ma's and what time was she off so he could pick her up, she saying that she was driving Pop's old Studebaker and he'd have to follow her out home so she could drop it off and get her weekday curfew extended an hour or two. With enough interested spectators to get the report circulating." Debbie grinned. "And enough nicely chosen words in it to make plain that there was nothing going on behind her family's back. She hadn't spent several years as a politician's daughter for nothing."

"I suppose," Missy said, "that it's at least some comfort to learn that the Hudson women weren't dumb. Which Gran managed to skip over. Whatever else they were."

Debbie leaned back against the porch banister. "If she implied . . . or tried to imply . . . that Aura Lee ever had any interest in anyone except Joe, you can forget it. Things went on from there. The next day, Sunday, your Pop and Nani left for Fairmont right after lunch. Political reception. Ray was out in the barn, banging on something mechanical. I stayed behind with a napping Anne, curled up in an easy chair in her bedroom looking through WVU orientation stuff. I heard Joe pull in—it was pretty impossible to miss the noise of his ma's car—and didn't hear anything more. I'm sure they didn't know I was home. Aura Lee had gone outside before we decided not to wake Anne up."

"How does that song go?" Missy asked. "'The sound of silence?'"

"Close." Debbie smiled. Well, sort of smiled. "About an hour later, I looked out the back window. They were in the back yard, lying on a sleeping bag. Not, at that point, even touching. She was on her back with her arms up over her head; he was propped up on one elbow, lying on his side, looking at her. I couldn't see his face, his back was toward me, but I could see hers. The first thing that I thought was practically blasphemous. You know that hymn? 'Have thine own way, Lord, Have thine own way. Thou art the potter, I am the clay. Mold me and make me, After Thy will, While I am waiting, Yielded and still.' Okay, that's how she was looking at him. Even if they hadn't done anything irrevocable yet, it was clear that they would. It was a done deal. Sooner or later. She was just waiting for a cue from him.

"It didn't last that long. In a couple of minutes she said something that made Joe start laughing, they both sat up, and he grabbed her around the shoulders for a regular 'kiss and cuddle' session. They were clearly enjoying themselves, so I went back and finished reading my orientation materials."

Missy frowned.

"Yes," Debbie continued. "I did just decide to ignore them. When Anne woke up, I took her out the front door and down to the run. I thought about letting her go out to the sandbox and bounce up and down on them. 'But that would be wrong,' to use a quote from that era. Funny as could be, but wrong."

"Did Nani and Pop catch them at it?"

"When Mother and Pop got back, the car made enough noise that by the time they drove around to the garage, they found the two of them sitting on opposite sides of the sleeping bag, their hands around their knees, looking thoughtful. Like those statues of monkeys contemplating a skull. Not that I expect our parents believed that they had spent the afternoon discussing Darwin."

"I can't believe that Nani and Pop just lived with this!" Missy exploded. "You and Dad wouldn't have. Ah. You still won't, really, even though I'm nineteen."

"I'm not my mother. Joe and Aura Lee got up, rolled up the sleeping bag, tossed it back in the closet on the back porch, and said that they were going to meet friends for pizza. Much to Mother's relief, I think. She sure didn't want to be put in a position where she almost had to invite Joe to stay for supper. She had been willing enough to see that Don and I were . . . very close. Not even really upset that I quit high school to marry him. She didn't want to see Joe. As long as she didn't acknowledge that she saw him, somehow he wasn't really there. So she didn't invite him to stay for supper. Any more than she would invite Ron to Easter dinner. Not even though, if she had, Aura Lee would have been right under her eyes all evening, instead of wherever they ended up. It went that way for his whole leave."

"Why?" Missy asked.

"I can't read your Nani's mind, Missy. As for Pop . . . He said once that there were worse possibilities in Grantville than Joe Stull, lots worse, even as rough around the edges as he was then."

Missy shook her head.

"So things kept going," Debbie continued. "Once, when we were at WVU, Chad came to pick me up one Friday evening. He came into our little hallway and asked, 'What's with the lifelike VE Day double statues in the corner?' I said, 'I'll tell you later.' Once we got out into the car, I explained that when Joe came in and dropped his duffel bag, they did that. Just stood there for a while with their arms around each other's waists, not moving. You could sort of multiply 'how long has it been since we saw each other' times 'how much of a hassle have things been since we saw each other' to get an answer as to whether this would last ten minutes or a half hour.

"Eventually, though, they would let loose and Aura Lee would say something on the lines of 'Pop sent ground venison and I'm making stroganoff' or 'I bought stuff for a cheese omelette with green peppers.' Food was always their next thought, once they were reassured that the other one was still really there. At least it was Aura Lee's next thought, and Joe's not one to refuse a meal.

"And the last thing they did before he left was go to the laundromat. On Sundays, when Chad dropped me off again, I'd come back to a big pile of clean towels and sheets, all folded with military precision.

"To be perfectly honest, I don't claim to understand Aura Lee and Joe. Like when she had that cancer diagnosed. Joe was like a rock for her and the kids, the whole time, but if she hadn't beaten it, I think he'd have gone under."

"What cancer?" Missy asked.

"She was diagnosed in the summer of '95. You were only ten, then. They operated at the university hospital in Morgantown. She was back and forth for radiation and chemo for a long time. She had to take leave from her job for nearly a year. Joe was still working out of Morgantown. He rented out the house in Fairmont and moved them all up there into an apartment so she wouldn't be faced with driving back and forth all the time, or finding someone to drive her if she was too nauseated. Got an older woman to live in so she didn't have to worry about constantly finding sitters for Juliann or where Billy Lee would be after school."

"How did I miss all that?"

Debbie sighed. "There were other things going on here at the time. And we didn't see them all that frequently anyway, so you may not really have noticed the difference. Aside from being sisters, Aura Lee and I didn't really have the same friends, the same acquaintances, by then. It had been over fifteen years since we shared that apartment while we were at the university. She was in Charleston for seven years and then had her own concerns the first few years after they got married. The doctors had to take both Billy Lee and Juliann by C-section and neither pregnancy was what they call uncomplicated."

"I've been getting so much news lately," Missy said, "that I sort of feel like one of the guys who were under the gun in the 'Charge of the Light Brigade' poem."

"If you think about it," Debbie said, "mostly our families only saw one another when all of us were out at your Pop and Nani's for a holiday. You and Chip were enough older than Billy Lee and Juliann that you were set to watch them more often than you played with them, really. The two of you had Eric and Dana to play with. Bill was a bit older. In fact, half the time he watched the little ones while the four of you played. He's always been very responsible."

Missy leaned forward, her elbows on the table. "And Dad and Uncle Joe don't really get along all that well. I know. Anyway. Is she okay now? Aunt Aura Lee, I mean?"

"As far as I know," Debbie said. "I certainly hope so. Because if the cancer recurs, down-time, there's not going to be much anyone can do about it."

"Yeah," Missy said. "Bill and Ron go on and on about that sort of thing when they're talking to one another out at Lothlorien. On and on and on. That the kind of research they're trying to do will be of more help to our children and grandchildren than to our parents and grandparents."

Chapter 65

Magdeburg

"You're sure about that?" Mike Stearns took his gaze away from his office window and looked back over his shoulder at Nasi, sitting in a chair next to his desk. The spymaster had just returned to the capital that morning and had requested an immediate meeting with his boss.

"Yes," said Francisco firmly. "I have weighed the matter carefully, and for many hours. Double-checking myself to make sure I did not overlook any piece of the puzzle."

Mike looked back down at the Elbe. With such a nice sunny day, he had the window open, so he could enjoy some fresh air. "It seems a little incredible, though."

Nasi smiled, a bit ruefully. "Yes, I suppose. But it's not, really. I was only able to unravel the plot myself through a haphazard series of chances. However preposterous the overall logic of their scheme might have been, Ducos and his people carried it out quite well in the details."

Mike nodded. "Yes, I understand. Still . . . *Nobody* knows?"

Nasi made a face. "Well . . . I wouldn't put it quite that strongly. Cory Joe Lang knows the truth, of course, and perhaps his sister Pam. But both of them have every personal reason to want the matter kept secret. Ed Piazza and Wes Jenkins—perhaps Arnold Bellamy also; always hard to tell with him—understand much of the plot, at least at it impacted directly on Thuringia and Franconia. But I spoke to both of them and they are agreed that no good purpose would be served by making the matter public. It's quite clear that Laurent Mauger had no idea that he was actually working for Ducos' fanatics, nor did he know what they had planned in the way of the attack on the synagogue. He was, as you say, a 'cat's-paw.' Or a 'patsy,' if I understand that term correctly."

He shrugged. "So why make his role public? Or that of Dumais, who was his agent on the spot? That would only have the immediate effect of damaging the personal situations of Velma Hardesty's children, Cory Joe and Pam and Susan, who are certainly blameless in all respects. And, in the long run, it would be foolish. Far better for us to have a lead into some of the inner circles of the Huguenot political exiles, which we now have through the Mauger connection. Not to mention . . ."

"Yes, I understand. Duke Henri de Rohan will be quite careful to stay on good terms with us, from now on. Lest we drag this mess involving Dumais out from under a rock and beat him with it."

"His brother Soubise, as well. Both are quite capable men, and who can say what alliances might be valuable in the time to come? As it stands, Rohan sent me a letter recently assuring us that he had no knowledge whatsoever of Ducos' intentions. He also provided me with some details of the plot that had previously been obscure, that his agents had uncovered themselves. I think that's a connection that will prove valuable in the future, especially given his close ties to Bernhard of Saxe-Weimar."

Mike turned away from the window and resumed his seat behind the desk. "Okay. And I'm not really worried about Ed and Wes anyway. But what about the kids? They've got to know most of it."

"Oh, yes. But the four who are critical—Denise, Minnie, Ron Stone and Missy Jenkins—have every reason to keep quiet also." Nasi raised his fist and coughed into it. "Not, you understand, that I was so coarse as to threaten to press murder charges against the two girls. I made no reference to the matter of Holloway's killing at all. Still, they have every reason to, as you say, let lying dogs sleep."

"It's 'sleeping dogs lie.' But I see your point." Mike chuckled softly. "Not that they'd really have much to worry about. No jury in Grantville would convict Denise of murder. Hell, not even manslaughter. Not after what Holloway did before he beat it out of town, and not after what her father did at the synagogue. But she's only sixteen, and the kind of kid who takes it for granted that her relationship with the authorities will always be a contentious one."

He closed his eyes for a moment, thinking.

"And no one in the leadership of the Committees of Correspondence knows anything," he mused. "Like everyone else, they're assuming that the killings were carried out by one or another of the anti-Semitic outfits."

"Exactly." Nasi chuckled also, much less softly than Mike had done. "It's amusing, in a way. Ducos' people did their job too well. By keeping their own role hidden and using anti-Semites and other fanatics as their . . . ah, forward men?"

"Front men."

"Yes, front men. By doing so, they completely failed in their ultimate aim. I doubt if there is a single sane person in the Germanies who suspects Cardinal Richelieu of the deed. Instead, everyone is blaming our homegrown reactionaries—who were actually not much more than patsies themselves."

"Vicious, stinking, filthy patsies," said Mike, reopening his eyes. "And soon to be very dead patsies, many of them. And good riddance."

He sat up straight. "All right, Francisco. We'll do it. Is Gretchen back in Magdeburg yet?"

"She's supposed to arrive tomorrow."

"Fine. Pass the word quietly to Spartacus that I'll want a private meeting—very private—with the two of them, as soon as she returns. Um. Better include Gunther Achterhof in the invitation also. For something like this, it'd be pointless not to involve him from the start."

Nasi nodded. "And which of the lists do you want me to have ready for them?"

"All of them," said Mike grimly.

Nasi's eyebrows went up. "You are certain?"

Mike nodded. "Yes, I am. Every last scrap of information you've put together on the USE's anti-Semitic outfits."

"You understand that means, essentially, every extremist reactionary group in the nation? In the nature of things, anti-Semitism is their common coinage even if most of them don't actually do much about it."

"Yes, I understand. Ask me if I care. We'll use the vicious murder of a nice old man by Huguenot fanatics to rid the Germanies of a plague that's been a problem for centuries in this universe and, in at least one other universe, produced a holocaust. Set up the meeting, Francisco."

Chapter 66

Grantville

Missy lay in Ron's arms, shuddering, her face down on his shoulder. "What in hell was that?"

Ron stroked her hair, then started rubbing the back of her neck. "You came. All the way. Not because we were doing it, or even anywhere close. Not even heavy petting. Not even really making out. Just lying here with all our clothes on the way we always do—well, mostly do, kissing and hugging, and wanting. Damn it, Missy. We're so ready for prime time that it isn't even funny any more."

She left her face right where it was and nodded.

He slipped his hand between her sweater and her blouse. His knee came up between her legs. Then he realized something.

"Where's the accessory? Want to get it?"

"It's prom night. I loaned it to Gertrude, just in case."

He thought about that a minute. "I take it that's not an open invitation to further advances. 'Greater love hath no woman' than to take a risk for the sake of her 'kid sister.' Because she loves her."

"I . . ."

"What?"

"After I gave it to Gertrude, I went and saw Kortney. And she. She said to tell you."

Missy stopped.

"Tell me what, Miss Missy?"

She had her face buried all the way in his sweater. He pushed her chin up.

"That it's the biggest sponge she could squeeze in the way things are so you'll have to be careful not to poke it through the cervix because they're a pain to get out all in one piece and don't do any good anyhow unless they stay on this side. And I'm to come back and get a bigger one next week, if . . . if it turns out not to be a one time thing."

Her face went right back down into his sweater. What little skin he could see around the edges of her hair was beet red.

Any guy who would hang around a girl for six months waiting for her to agree to do it and only want to do it once would have to be some kind of pathological . . . Normal guys didn't wait that long in hopes of a one night stand. But he'd never exactly said anything about long-term. Long range. Whatever. They'd talked about everything else on earth, but when it came to sex, all they'd ever said was, "No way, not now." And it was Missy who kept saying that.

Even here in Grantville, right in the high school, there had been a couple of guys who did whatever it took to score and then dropped the girl the minute she was on their card.

There was something skeptical that was part of the basic Missy. She never made assumptions. She didn't take anything for granted. "No risks you don't want" from him didn't quite cover the case of risks she did want.

The day her mind decided to agree with her instincts, she had gone to see Kortney, who could and did ask the most embarrassing questions imaginable. Then she had come out to Lothlorien this evening and walked right into his arms.

"You'd better plan on going back. And getting a large-sized bottle of that solution they dunk the sponges in."

He stroked her spine for a while. The little bit of her face he could see was returning to its usual color. While he thought. Once she decided, she had walked right into his arms. Without a word of commitment from him. Even though the last thing in the world she wanted to do was have a baby. Even though she knew how iffy anything Kortney could give her was. Even though she had thought about the possibility that it might be a "one time thing" for him.

"Miss Jenkins, would you do me the honor of bestowing your hand upon me in matrimony? And all that?" The fancy words were good. If she wasn't at all interested, they could pretend it had been another bit of joking and go on from there.

"But . . ."

Joking wasn't good enough. "I mean it, Missy. Let's clear things up before we get ourselves into a situation where we feel like we have to, and it comes up as a grudge in every fight we have for the next fifty years."

"I want to be a librarian, not . . ."

"Be one."

"If we get married. If we don't have to stop and think about what we're doing in advance every single time, because it will be so convenient . . ."

He tilted her chin up again. "Is your Aunt Clara going to be a Little Miss Perfect Housewife?"

"No. She's going back to work after six weeks off."

"Think about it. Why? How?"

"Why? Because she wants to. How? Because with Uncle Wes and her both working for the consular service, she can afford a nursery maid to do the scut stuff and handle the baby while she has meetings and things at work. And another maid to keep the house, so supper's ready when they get back home. And they send the laundry and stuff to MaidenFresh." She pulled herself up, sat back, and grinned. "Clara really isn't into housework. She knows how to do it, cook and bake and stuff, and she's run a house before, but she would a lot rather be doing something else."

"So pull your mind-set out of up-time middle class. Dad used to talk about this, sometimes. What happened in the nineteenth century was that there was this push on for everyone to follow bourgeois values. But most families didn't have the money to hire the staff that it required back then when modern appliances weren't around, so for most families, the mom turned into the maid and the nursemaid, too. Doing scut work and changing diapers all day and then expected to dress nice and make like the lady of the house in the evening so her husband wouldn't notice that her hands were all rough and chapped from scouring pots."

"I never thought of it that way."

"Bourgeois hypocrisy, Dad used to call it. 'Boor-jwah!' But there's no reason for you to, Missy, any more than Clara does.

Get real. As weird as it still seems to me—my Dad, too, even more—the fact remains that in the here-and-now the once scruffy and disreputable hippie Stones are fast becoming one of the richest families in Europe. Outside of royalty, for sure. If there's any couple our age in Grantville who'll be able to afford all the household help they'll ever need, it's us. And we don't need to do the upstairs/downstairs thing, either. Just hire employees at home, like we hire the people at the plant."

He abandoned the fancy words. "Marry me, Melissa Marie Jenkins. No matter how unlikely it seems, we'll make a good team."

Missy wrapped her arms around her knees and looked down at him. "We'll make a good team" wasn't exactly, "You are the light of my heart and the love of my life," she thought. But she wasn't going to get flowery declarations from Ron. No lacy valentines. No poems. Probably not chocolates, either. If there ever were sweet, smooth milk chocolates again. No bouquets on anniversaries. No . . . flimflam, except as an occasional joke. No "I adore you and will until my last breath."

But she'd never said those things to him, either. He wouldn't know what to do with them if she did.

"Mom and Dad separated for a couple of years, did you know? She caught him running around with another woman. Anne was already away at nursing school. Chip lived with Grandma Jenkins and I stayed with Mom. Later on, Mom forgave him and took him back."

Ron shook his head. "I guess we weren't that close to most of the people in Grantville back then. I never heard about that."

"They didn't explain any of it to me when it was going on. I found out the reason a couple of years after they got back together. At a picnic out at Pop's. I was being a 'little pitcher with big ears,' eavesdropping on Nani while she sniped at Gran about Dad."

He looked up. Missy's cheek had marks from the texture of his sweater. Her gray eyes were bleak. She had pulled her hair back that morning, fastening it in a twist. She was magnificent. He wondered how she had ever come close to disguising herself as a cheerleading ditz. Maybe it had been the uniform.

"I wouldn't forgive you and take you back if you did that," she said quietly. "I would kill you, instead. I would find the heaviest long-handled cast iron skillet in our house. I would take it in a two-handed grip and bring it down on your skull as hard as I could swing it. Then I would sit there and howl over your corpse until I died of grief."

Ron reached up and took one of her hands.

"I don't remember ever seeing my mother. She took off when I was too little. Here's my own promise, separate from anything your family's ministers at First Methodist will ask me to say. I won't run around on you, if you say yes. Never, ever. I won't run off from you, the way Nathan did from Chandra without telling her what was going on. If I do have to go somewhere without you, you'll know why or I won't be going. No matter what."

In the back of her mind a little voice wailed for the last time. *I soooo did not want this complication right now.*

Missy took his other hand. "Done."

Ron pulled her down against him again. "It's going to be okay, Missy. Really it is. Honest."

Chad could not entirely believe that he had just received a formal request for his daughter's hand in marriage.

Accompanied, reasonably enough, by a separately delivered warning from the daughter in question that she and Ron would be getting married with or without her family's approval, even though they would rather have it. *Nope, can't begin to imagine where she gets it.*

Not to mention that he was examining a set of tax returns. Chad shuffled the papers in his hands. Apparently growing up on a hippie commune made Ron less sensitive than ordinary Grantvillers when it came to talking about practical things. The kid was almost down-time that way. And even though the rumor that Tom Stone refused to make a profit on the pharmaceuticals turned out to be correct, he was at least enough of a businessman to break even on them. But it hardly mattered, since the profits from the dye-making business were well-nigh astronomical and the business was expanding explosively.

Interestingly, the "improvident hippie" Stones were plowing most of the profits right back into the business. Their own income was quite modest, given what it could have been. Still, Ron received a reasonable salary for the work he was doing. It was a lot of work, too, even aside from setting up the new subsidiary with Bill Hudson. The dye works. Stone had incorporated, with his sons as minority shareholders. While the Venice-based enterprises . . .

Ron and Missy would not be suffering deprivation, to put it mildly.

Ron had the makings of a very good businessman, actually. Perhaps because money as such really didn't mean much to him, he had the knack of seeing ways to make it grow. He also had ties to the Committees of Correspondence, not to mention Don Francisco. Those would gave him entree into a lot of other things.

Debbie would be okay with it, he thought. At least not surprised, by now. Willie Ray would be okay, too. He'd gotten to know Tom Stone pretty well through the Grange activities since the Ring of Fire. Chip wouldn't really care. He and Ron had the CoC in common and he seemed to get along well with Gerry. That left . . .

Vera and his own mother.

He couldn't do a thing about Vera. Missy had made her primary allegiance pretty clear at Easter already. For that matter, the first appearance of Ron on the Jenkins family's horizon was Missy's spirited defense of him against Vera, way last fall. It might be that Vera had finally met her match. Which would be hard on Debbie, if neither of them backed down. Let Willie Ray handle it.

He looked back down at the tax returns, folded them up, and handed them back to Ron.

"Should we expect to be grandparents?"

Ron studied the ornate wallpaper border that someone had applied all the way around the room, about a foot below where the walls met the ceiling. "Not any time in the next few months, if that's what you're asking."

Chad nodded.

"We'd actually rather put that off till after Missy finishes her library training, if we can. Even though Eleanor Maria is cuter than either of us had ever really thought a kid might be. But the best thing anyone can say about down-time birth control is that it's fallible. That's one reason why we thought we'd get married. So if Missy does get pregnant one of these days, all we'll have to cope with is a baby instead of a crisis. If you know what I mean."

"I'm a little surprised that the formality of a marriage means that much to you."

"To me?" Ron raised his eyebrows in surprise. "It doesn't, really. I'd be perfectly happy to go on from here with the promises we've made each other already. But I'm not the only person involved and you and your wife brought Missy up differently."

"Give me a week, will you?" Chad asked. "Before you make it public? To bring my mom around."

That sounded like a paternal blessing to Ron. At least, closer to one than he had been expecting.

He thought of his few meetings with Eleanor Jenkins since the dinner last Thanksgiving. She hadn't been really thrilled when Wes and Clara had invited Missy and him to be Eleanor Maria's godparents.

She particularly had not been thrilled when Gerry entertained the christening party with a description of the day that Magda, finding out that her stepsons had never been baptized, had taken care of the matter. In the Lothlorien Farbenwerke greenhouse. With a garden hose. On the grounds that, after all, only water and the Word were necessary.

Clara had thought it was hilarious. Clara and Magda would get along great if Dad and Magda ever got back from Italy. They had a lot in common.

If Missy's dad could bring the old lady around in a week, then he had to be as good a salesman as he claimed. Though even Chad hadn't said anything about bringing Vera Hudson around.

"Ah," he said. "Um. The things that Missy's grandma was saying last Thanksgiving. All that stuff about handing china down in the family for generations and such."

Chad nodded.

"I'm not going to lie to you. I don't have that. We have the best dad any boys could ask for, but growing up on a commune, you don't have that generation to generation stuff."

"People have wondered, sometimes."

"Dad's always made things plain to us. He's Frank's father, biologically. He's not Gerry's, no way. For me, it's sort of iffy. There was opportunity and our blood types don't rule out that he's my father, but we don't know for sure. Nothing ever made it important to find out, up-time. It's never made any difference to him. He's always been there for all of us when we needed him, and that's enough."

"That pot-growing hippie in our family!" Eleanor Jenkins said. For about the tenth time.

Chad got up and wandered over to the wall with the family photos, standing with his hands folded behind his back. "Tom Stone is not a hippie anymore, Mom. Not a poor one, at least. He's made a lot of money. Legally. In fact, today he's easily the richest man in Grantville or anywhere nearby. And I've worked a couple of deals with his father-in-law. No flies on him or his daughter."

He looked at the picture of his grandfather Newton. "It's not like Ron is in a hillbilly band, traveling cross-country in a bus. I wonder what Great-grandma Williams said when Grandma told her who she wanted to get married to."

"That was different," his mother said primly, her arms folded across her slim chest. "Besides, it's pretty obvious that Ron, or young Gerry at least, isn't . . ."

"Hold it right there, Mom," Chad interrupted, turning towards her. "What Tom Stone has been for those boys ought to be enough for us too, I think. There when they needed him. That's exactly what Dad always was for Wes and me, and you told me once that he was the finest man on earth. Emphasized it with a slap, as I recall. I figure you had reason to say that. Right?"

Chad pinned his mother with his eyes, glaring at her until at last she turned her head away. "I'm not asking you to clasp Ron Stone to your bosom. Just don't make Missy miserable. She loves you."

She started to shake her head.

"In the Bible, Mom. About casting the first stone. I'm not going to cast it. I know I haven't been perfect. I let you get away with bossing us around a lot because it's easier and most of the time I don't give a damn either way. But not this time and if you can't see your way clear to accepting Ron and his family, you're going to be seeing a lot less of the rest of us.

"Sure, having china being handed down through the generations is nice. So is having a lot of family photographs. But it's not worth spit if you're a miserable human being. I don't care if Tom Stone doesn't have a plate or bowl older than a week.

He's brought up three good sons, Mom, no matter what else he's done. Three decent, honorable, boys. Even if only one of them was 'his' son, the way some people might see it. That was what Ron said to me. 'He's always been there for all of us when we needed him, and that's enough.' There's stuff in the Bible about pride going before a fall. Get over it."

Eleanor sat silently in her chair. Then she raised her head and in a calm, clear voice said, "You may as well get the quote right. It's from Proverbs. 'Pride goes before destruction, and a haughty spirit before a fall.' I'll drop my objections except for those I reserve mentally. Not that I can tell what Missy sees in the boy."

"That's it?"

"Yes. I want her to be happy. I'm far from sure that this is the best choice for her. But I guess she's old enough to know her own mind and make her own mistakes. Just like you thought you were old enough when you married a woman with a nine-year-old daughter when you were only twenty-three yourself. Not that I think Debbie was a mistake now," she added hastily. That was a battle that had already been fought. "Back then, your father over-ruled my objections. Which you seem to be doing this time."

"Wes likes him," Chad said. "For what it's worth, Wes likes Ron Stone a lot."

"He would scarcely have asked him to stand godfather for my littlest granddaughter if he didn't. As absurd as that was. For that matter, Wes would probably enjoy knowing Tom Stone. Wes remodeled himself quite a bit over the years in order to become the kind of man with whom Lena would be happy."

Eleanor relaxed a little. "The quirky, sardonic sense of humor that has been showing up this winter is more or less a reversion to normal. He never quite managed to stamp it out, but he controlled those tendencies pretty firmly for nearly thirty years. With Clara, he can be himself." She smiled wryly. "I do wonder what will become of him."

Part Eleven

June 1635

Each in his hierarchy, the orders bright

Chapter 67

Magdeburg

"This is madness," hissed Amalie, the landgravine of Hesse-Kassel. Her hand on her husband's arm tightened. "What is Wilhelm Wettin *thinking*?"

Her husband, Landgrave William V, looked out over the huge crowd celebrating in the great hall of the new imperial palace in Magdeburg. "What difference does it make? Wilhelm can't control this. I doubt if anyone can."

He shook his head. The landgrave—some primitive part of him, at least—understood the riotous mood of the celebrants perfectly well. The last few years had been deeply unsettling to any member of Germany's elite classes, and sometimes terrifying. Now . . .

It is over! The troll is dead! Sanity has returned! We are back on top!

Unfortunately, the troll was not dead. Defeated, yes; dead, no—and perhaps the worst of it was that the troll had predicted the defeat himself. Predicted it, quite matter-of-factly, and gone about his business.

That was because he was not a troll in the first place. He was a man, and a particularly cunning and astute one, when it came to politics.

Far more astute, William suspected, than the leader of the Crown Loyalists, Wilhelm Wettin. The brutish troll, for instance, knew when his reach was beginning to exceed his grasp; knew the difference between real allies and fellow travelers of the moment; perhaps most of all, knew when he could safely compromise and when a bargain led into an abyss.

William sighed. There had been too many promises made. Too many unwise trades, for the sake of immediate gains. And now, all of the people with whom Wettin and his Crown Loyalists had bargained had come to Magdeburg to enjoy a raucous celebration of their victory—and to demand payment in full.

And Wettin would pay them. He had no choice.

Or try to pay them, at any rate. Whether he could succeed or not, remained to be seen. The landgrave was becoming increasingly dubious.

He came to his decision. "We shall leave, Amalie. We have no choice, I think. We must place Hesse-Kassel first."

"I agree," she said firmly.

On their way out, they were intercepted by Hieronymus von Egloffstein, who was one of the central figures in Wilhelm Wettin's personal staff. Egloffstein was not himself an elected or public official. His capacity was that of what the Americans called a "political operator."

"Surely you aren't going!" he protested. Grinning gleefully, he waved a goblet of wine at the crowd, spilling some of it on the floor. "The festivities are just starting."

William disliked the man. Amalie positively detested him.

"Surely we are," she said coldly. "Half the nation is in mourning over the murder of an old man and seething in anger—and you choose to rub salt into their wounds? Well, you may be idiots, but we are not."

The landgrave cleared his throat. "Tell Wilhelm we've returned to Hesse-Kassel. Where we will handle this situation quite differently."

They left, then, with Egloffstein gaping after them.

"It's starting already," William said an hour or so later, as their carriage neared Magdeburg's outskirts. He let the curtain fall back into place over the window and leaned back in his seat. "I can't see very much, of course, in the darkness. But it's obvious the city's Committee of Correspondence is mobilizing its forces.

And I could see that many of them are armed. With flintlock rifles, too, not just hand weapons. They look like military issue. I wouldn't be at all surprised to discover they came from the army's own arsenals."

Amalie's hand went to her throat. "Oh, my God. Surely you don't think . . . William, he *can't* be that rash."

"Stearns?" Her husband shook his head. "It won't be anything as reckless as an assault upon the palace. No, certainly. Those imbeciles will be able to celebrate as long as they want, quite unmolested. If nothing else, Stearns won't want to risk bringing Torstensson and his regular army units into the city."

He barked a grim little laugh. "Assuming that Torstensson would even do so—given that no one really knows how the army would react in such a situation."

"Do you really think the CoCs take their orders from Stearns?"

The landgrave cocked his head, considering the question. "It's . . . not that simple. Take orders from him? No. He is not their commander, nor even part of the central leadership the way Gretchen Richter or Gunther Achterhof or Spartacus are. In some ways, in fact, I sense that there is considerable distrust on both sides. Stearns, that the CoCs will behave foolishly; the CoCs, that Stearns is too much the politician, too much the compromiser. But they *listen* to him, Amalie, you can be sure of that."

"Yes, I suppose." The hand at her throat began to massage it gently. Then, much more softly, she laughed herself. "And can you blame them? Whatever else, he's a canny bastard."

She leaned forward, drew aside the curtain on her side with a finger, and peered into the darkness. "What *do* you think he's told them?"

"I have no idea," replied her husband gloomily. "But, as you say, whatever it is, it will be canny."

When he wanted to be, Gunther Achterhof could be as ferocious as any man alive. No trace of his usual sardonic humor was in evidence here and now. The hard face that gazed upon the subordinate commanders gathered for their final instructions was that of the refugee who, years earlier, had fled from his destroyed town to Magdeburg across half of Germany—and left a trail of dead and mutilated mercenaries behind him. He'd come into the city holding a bag full of their severed noses, ears and genitals.

"Remember, the known anti-Semites and witch-hunters only—and the line has been clearly drawn. All of you have your lists and you must stick to the names on those lists. Any column which violates that directive will be severely punished."

Gretchen Richter spoke then. For a wonder, this time she was a mollifying voice.

"Look, fellows, we know you'll find it hard to resist striking all of the reactionaries." She threw a disgusted glance at one of the windows in the building. Even at the distance—they were about half a mile from the palace—the sounds of the Crown Loyalist celebration could be faintly heard. "And it's not that the swine don't deserve it. But they won this victory playing by the rules, so if we go after them we'll just make ourselves look like criminals or would-be tyrants. Neither of which we are."

She paused, scanning the faces to see if anyone seemed doubtful or questioning.

But no one did, so she continued. "So you don't touch them—well, at least not unless they attack you first and it's clearly a matter of self-defense. But so long as a nobleman keeps his armed retainers quiet and the city patricians and guildmasters do the same with their militias, we will leave them alone. We will not even so much as snarl in their direction. Just tip your hats politely and go about your business. Instead, we will destroy the illegitimate arm of reaction, that no one tries to defend openly, but which all the reactionaries lean upon, even if only as a veiled threat. Within a week—well, two or three, in some of the provinces—that arm will have been amputated."

One of the column commanders grinned. "By the day after tomorrow, in *this* province."

That drew a chuckle from a number of the men. Of course, in some ways it was an empty boast. Magdeburg province hadn't had much in the way of organized anti-Semitic groups or witch-hunts in quite some time. The city, none at all.

Gretchen smiled. "You'd best leave, then. Some of you have a long way to go."

After they were gone, a side door opened and Francisco Nasi emerged from one of the small rooms adjoining the big central one. He hadn't been hiding, exactly. Given the nature of the lists that every one of those commanders had been given, only a very dim-witted one would have failed to understand that Richter and Achterhof had the quiet support of Stearns and his spymaster. True, the Committees of Correspondence had their own lists of known anti-Semitic organizations and prominent activists. But those lists were nothing compared to the meticulously detailed records that Nasi had compiled over the past year and a half.

Still, good habits were worth maintaining for their own sake.

"Mecklenburg?" asked Gunther.

"The orders have been transmitted," said Francisco. "To Pomerania as well, although that'll obviously take more time to unfold."

The orders had already been sent to all the other provinces and imperial cities. But Mecklenburg and Pomerania required more circumspection. They also had army radio posts, with reliable operators. But since both provinces were directly administered by the Swedes, with the emperor himself as their duke, they had a higher proportion than usual of Swedish soldiers. In fact, the provinces were used as training areas where the up-timer soldiers could train Gustav Adolf's own forces how to use the new technology.

There were not very many Swedes in the Committees of Correspondence. Swedish soldiers were not actively hostile to the CoCs, as a rule. They just didn't find them particularly relevant to their own situation. There was no great social unrest in Sweden. In fact, the emperor—just a king, to the Swedes—was quite popular among his countrymen.

"It's done, then," said Gretchen. Her expression suddenly became rather disgruntled. "I wish I were out there myself."

Nasi smiled. "Surely you're not *that* bloodthirsty?"

She gave him a cold look. "Henry Dreeson brought some real happiness—well, contentment, at least—to my grandmother. Who needed it, if ever a woman did. And now, she's a widow again. So do not presume to think how bloody I might like to be, if I could have all my wishes."

Achterhof made an impatient gesture. "Cut it out, Gretchen. You're needed here, at headquarters, and you know it perfectly well."

He was right, and she knew it. But she still wished she could be leading one of those fierce columns, beginning to spread across the Germanies. Many, from the capital cities of the provinces. Some, from other strongholds.

By dawn tomorrow, there would be no known anti-Semitic agitators or groups in Luebeck or Hamburg. By dawn of the next day, none within fifty miles of those cities. A week from now, none within a hundred miles or more.

There weren't very many in Thuringia, anyway. But whatever there were would all be gone by then also.

Franconia would take longer. Anti-Semitism had deep roots there. But the Ram had more experience with armed struggle than the usual CoCs, and quite recent experience. Franconia would be scoured clean, soon enough—and probably scoured more thoroughly than anywhere. Constantin Ableidinger and his closest associates were handling the matter directly.

Elsewhere, the process would be more ragged. In some places—Hesse-Kassel and Brunswick—the local committees had been instructed not to push matters to an open confrontation with the official authorities. Just . . . strike some hard blows, and then pull back and see. It was quite possible that Landgrave William and Duke Georg would decide to finish the job themselves, once they realized the peril of doing otherwise. The landgraves of Hesse-Kassel had never allowed anti-Semitism much leeway anyway, not for centuries. And Duke Georg was now far too reliant on Jewish financing for his booming new petroleum industry to have any truck with the anti-Semitic swine either.

But, however long it took, and however it was done, it would be done. That long-festering boil in German politics would be lanced, finally. Crushed; shattered; destroyed; drowned in its own blood and gore. Reaction would have to make do thereafter without that sturdy support. And the same with witch-hunting.

And—best of all, from Gretchen's viewpoint—by the time it was all over the Committees of Correspondence would have been transformed. For the first time, that often fractious and disorganized movement would have acted coherently, in unison, on a national scale. And in a directly military manner.

There was no way to know what the future might bring. But whatever came, the CoCs would be ready for it.

Francisco still had his doubts. But . . .

First, he did understand the reasoning, as Mike Stearns had laid it out. Harsh and cold that reasoning might be—even cruel, you could fairly say. Within two weeks, the Germanies would have several thousand more corpses than they would have had otherwise.

But Francisco didn't question the reasoning. Like his employer, Nasi had now spent a great deal of time studying the history of another universe. Not, as many foolish people did, because he thought he could predict the future in this one, but simply to find the underlying patterns. The logic of developments, as it were.

One thing was clear. Anti-Semitism had always played an important role in European politics, but the phenomenon could be quirkier than it looked. Francisco had been quite fascinated to discover, for instance, that during the Holocaust the two safest places for a Jew in those parts of Europe under the Nazis had been Italy and Bulgaria—both of which had fascist governments themselves.

He still didn't know the reasons for that, beyond the fact itself, in the case of Bulgaria. Grantville's records concerning Bulgarian history were essentially nonexistent, and even that seemingly endless fount of historical knowledge Melissa Mailey had admitted she knew hardly anything on the subject.

But Grantville's records on Italian history were quite good. Not surprisingly, given the high percentage of its inhabitants who came from Italian stock. And the logic in the case of Italy was quite clear, once you knew where to look.

In Germany, anti-Semitism had become a tool of the emerging nationalist movement and became an integral part of it. One of the early nationalist leader Father Jahn's complaints against the foreign tyrant Napoleon had been that the French bastard prevented the Germans from indulging in their ancient custom of pogroms.

The logic developed in an opposite manner, in Italy. There, anti-Semitism was seen as a tool of the papacy—and it was the papacy and the papal states who were the principal internal obstacles to Italian unification. As it emerged, therefore, Italian nationalism was deeply hostile to anti-Semitism. Where Germany's Father Jahn had stirred up anti-Semitism, one of the first acts of the revolutionists in the great 1848 revolution in Rome had been to tear down the walls of the ghetto.

So. Who was to say that the rise of German nationalism in *this* universe couldn't develop in a nicely Latin manner?

Not Francisco Nasi. Who was, after all, himself a Jew.

He began humming a tune.

"Catchy," commented Achterhof. "What is it?"

"Oh, it's an up-time melody. Composed by a fellow named Verdi."

And then, of course, there was the second reason. Whatever doubts Francisco might have had were simply overwhelmed by the delightful possibility that opened up in the course of the final discussion between himself and Stearns and the CoC leaders.

"We need a name for this operation," Gretchen had said at one point. "Something striking and memorable."

Mike scratched his chin, thoughtfully.

It came to Francisco, in a flash. And by the sudden change of expression on Stearns' face, to him as well. They exchanged glances, and much as the poet said:

Looked at each other with a wild surmise—
Silent, upon a peak in Darien.

"I have it," said Francisco. "You should call it 'Operation Krystalnacht.' "

"Absolutely," said Mike.

Gretchen and Gunther and Spartacus rolled the name around.

"Krystalnacht," mused Achterhof. "I like it. It's catchy and memorable. 'Crystal Night.' It doesn't make any sense, but I like it."

" 'Krystalnacht' it is, then," said Gretchen.

Later, when the two of them were alone, Mike shook his head. "I can't believe we did that."

"Don't be silly," said Francisco. "It's perfect."

Chapter 68

Kassel

The first thing Landgrave William did upon his return to his capital city was summon his military commanders.

"Here," he said. He placed a small sheaf of papers on the table in the salon where they'd gathered. "I want every man named here—every member of every organization named here—arrested immediately. And I don't care what level of force you need to use to bring them in. Dead is fine. I'll have a fair number of them executed anyway."

One of the officers picked up the list and studied it. By the time he got to the third sheet, his eyebrows were lifted.

"If you don't mind me asking, Your Grace, where did you get this list?"

"It was handed to me on the border of the province, as we passed across," William said grimly, "by the commander of a large force of the Committees of Correspondence. A large and well-armed force. The same flintlocks provided for the federal army—and better guns than most of our own soldiers have. They seem quite well disciplined, too."

The officer's eyebrows lifted still further.

"Just do it, Colonel. I don't need to see anti-Semites and witch-hunters hanging from gibbets in Hesse-Kassel, or lying by the road where they were shot by firing squads. I saw quite enough of that already on our way here from Magdeburg. The best way to keep out the CoCs is to make them unnecessary."

He sat down heavily in a chair by the table. "I'm sick of those bastards anyway."

"Stinking CoCs," agreed the colonel.

"Not *them*," said the landgrave. "The anti-Semites. The witch-hunters. As if we didn't have enough trouble!"

The worst bloodshed was in Mecklenburg. The nobility in that province was still solidly in place, and it had long been the most grasping, piggish and narrow-minded in the Germanies. The reason for the Fourth of July Party's popularity in that largely rural province was due to the aristocracy's greed, in fact. The peasantry hated them.

The Mecklenburg nobility actually had very few ties to anti-Semitism. They were an impoverished, hardscrabble sort of aristocracy. Really, more in the way of what in England would have been considered country squires or, at a later period in Russian history, the class of rich peasants known as "kulaks." There just wasn't a lot of blood to be squeezed out of the turnip of north German agriculture—which meant the aristocracy squeezed very hard. But it also meant they tended to rely on the Jewish populations in the towns for a number of needed services. It was actually among the peasantry that anti-Semitism had traditionally been most deeply rooted.

But, as often happens, social customs were trumped by politics. Everyone in the Germanies except village idiots understood perfectly well that the Committees of Correspondence, in Operation Krystalnacht, were using the anti-Semites and witch-hunters as scapegoats—in another of history's little ironies. When one of their columns marched into a town and rounded up known anti-Semitic agitators or known witch-hunters and summarily executed them after a summary trial, what they were really doing was baring their teeth at the establishment while, simultaneously, making clear to their own supporters what was henceforth to be acceptable or unacceptable conduct. Directly, they didn't threaten the noblemen or the city patricians or the guildmasters, no. Achterhof's orders on that subject had been crystal clear and fairly bloodcurdling as to the consequences if they were disobeyed.

But who was fooled, really? Hardly anyone. So, often enough, the CoC columns were cheered as they marched through a town by the same lower classes of people who, for generations, had actually provided most of the members of lynch mobs. And were glowered upon, from their shelters behind fancy windows, by people of the upper classes who were in fact often quite guiltless of persecuting Jews or hunting witches. It just didn't matter. The CoC leaders had ordered Krystalnacht as a combined mass education for their own followers and form of intimidation toward their enemies. That was the essence of it, not the several thousand anti-Semites and witch-hunters across the USE's provinces and imperial cities who wound up being killed in the process.

In every other province, even Pomerania, the nobility as a whole was shrewd enough to step aside and let the CoC columns do their work. Except those of them who were directly part of one or another anti-Semitic organization on the CoC lists, of course. But most noblemen were not. Almost none, in some provinces.

Mecklenburg was the exception. There, the pigheaded nobility rose to the bait. They didn't care in the least about the anti-Semites being shot by the CoC columns. They were simply by-damn and by-golly not about to tolerate the CoCs operating openly in *their* territory.

The result amounted to an outright civil war.

The noblemen had the upper hand, at first. The CoC columns who first appeared in the province came from Mecklenburg itself. Mostly from the towns of Wismar, Rostock and Schwerin. They were well-armed but not very numerous, and they were caught off guard by the fierce reaction of the local aristocracy.

It was the sheer ferocity of the reaction that carried the field, at first. It certainly wasn't any splendid organization or discipline on the part of the nobility. The truth of the matter was that Mecklenburg's aristocracy was a sorry lot. For generations, not having the English custom of primogeniture, they had been dealing with the poverty of their rural estates by sending their more competent sons out to earn a living by serving in the armies and bureaucracies of more powerful rulers, while keeping the dumbest ones home to administer the estates. As breeding systems went, this was counterproductive.

Nor did Mecklenburg's aristocracy have the luxury of maintaining large bands of well-armed and well-trained retainers. Most of the Mecklenburg nobility didn't have any "armed retainers" at all, in the sense that an Elizabethan era English duke would have understood the term. What they had instead were their huntsmen, their stable hands, their household staff—the steward, the butler, a few footmen, the driver for the family carriage. And while many of the huntsmen, stable hands, and household staff, given the situation in the Thirty Years War, had military experience, most of them by this time who'd been in one or another of the armies had left because of some kind of physical problem that made continuing military service impractical.

So, there it was. The small CoC columns who moved incautiously into the Mecklenburg countryside were driven back into the towns by mobs of often one-armed butlers and one-eyed dog-trainers led by profane and semi-literate "noblemen" whose clothes were likely to be filthy and who almost invariably stank of drink.

Had the peasants come into the fight at that stage, things would have been different. But while the peasants might be sympathetic, the peasant militias—quite unlike the situation in Franconia, where the militias worked hand-in-glove with the Ram movement—were not coordinated with the CoC columns. The peasants armed themselves; but having done so, the militias simply guarded their own villages. Leaving the outnumbered CoCs to fight the nobility's private forces in the field.

Very quickly, the CoCs were driven back into the towns. In fact, the noble bands started following them into the towns, intending to scotch this snake while it was still small.

But then the army reacted. More precisely, the air force, which had a large base in Wismar. The air force's three warplanes assigned to the province began bombing the aristocracy's armed bands in the field, and even carried out bombing raids on some of the most prominent noblemen's estates.

They did so in complete defiance of military law, of course. They did not even have the excuse, as so many army regiments did, of being largely composed of soldiers recruited by the CoCs. Unlike the army, there was not much in the way of direct CoC influence in the USE's air force.

What there was instead, however, was a much higher degree of direct American participation. Half the air force's pilots were still up-timers from a small town—and they were furious about Henry Dreeson's murder. They'd known that kindly old man all their lives.

So, their commanders looked the other way, while "training flights" used up a preposterous quantity of munitions.

That was enough to produce a stalemate, for a week. And a week was all that Gretchen Richter and Gunther Achterhof and Spartacus needed to bring in reinforcements.

CoC columns started pouring into Mecklenburg from everywhere. By then, two weeks into Operation Krystalnacht—which actually lasted more than a month, not a single night, despite the code name—the CoCs were finished with their task in most of the provinces.

It all came to a head in what became known as the Battle of Güstrow. Seven CoC columns converged—more or less; it was a rather ragged affair—on the town and clashed in a field just to the south of it with approximately eighteen hundred armed retainers led by dozens of noblemen.

Numerically, the forces were pretty evenly matched. But it wasn't much of a contest. With their military-issue flintlock muskets, the CoC forces were far better armed than the semi-feudal retainers. They even had three six-pound cannons, whose provenance remained mysterious.

They also had radios, and were provided with constant information on the movements of their opponents by the planes flying reconnaissance overhead. (Although the aircraft weren't dropping bombs any longer. The air force's commander Jesse Wood had finally been pressured enough by Torstensson to order a stop to that.)

Within two hours, it was a rout, and the rout turned into a slaughter. Any CoC member who'd been captured by the Mecklenburg aristocracy in the early stages of the fighting had been murdered, often quite sadistically. So the CoC fighters were in no forgiving mood, now that the tables were turned. They wouldn't be taking any prisoners either. The only reason that several hundred of the enemy survived was because the battle only started in the afternoon. So, they escaped come nightfall.

As word of Güstrow spread, a peasant rebellion erupted across much of the province. The now-weakened aristocracy found themselves under siege. Their schlosses and estates were burned; they and their own families were massacred, if they were reckless enough to stay and try to put up a defense.

Torstensson might have finally felt compelled to intervene with the army, then. Try to, at least. But Gretchen had foreseen the danger and had already arrived in Wismar to take charge of the CoC forces in the province. Because Achterhof had been shrewd enough to keep her from indulging in pointless expeditions earlier, the CoC's most famous national leader was available when she was really needed.

The CoC columns now placed themselves at the head of the peasant rebellion. Informally, if not formally. The peasants were willing enough. They had no great familiarity with the CoCs themselves. But by now, Gretchen Richter was famous across most of Europe.

Gretchen made no attempt to actually lead the struggle in military terms. She was not a soldier. She was a political organizer, with the experience of the Amsterdam siege to guide her.

The key thing she brought was a new slogan.

Long Live the Duke!

It was well-known that Gustav Adolf, the duke of the province along with his greater titles, had clashed frequently with the pigheaded Mecklenburg nobility.

So, *Long Live the Duke* it was. Preposterous, that slogan might be, looked at from one angle—certainly if you knew Gretchen Richter's attitudes towards dukes in general. But it was under that slogan that the nobility of Mecklenburg was for all intents and purposes expropriated and destroyed as a class. Most of its members survived, to be sure. But they would henceforth be living as refugees in the mansions and castles of their relatives elsewhere. Mecklenburg had become as plebeian-dominated a province as the SoTF or Magdeburg, and every bit as much of a stronghold for the CoCs and the Fourth of July Party.

Emperor Gustav Adolf would be flooded with petitions in the time that followed, demanding that he do something about the horrid state of affairs in Mecklenburg.

But . . .

The Mecklenburg nobility really *had* been a monumental nuisance for him. Given their preferences, which they continued to express with extraordinary tenacity at meetings of the Estates even after Gustav Adolf became duke, the nobles of Mecklenburg would have turned the duchy into a mini-Poland with its duke having no more financial or military authority than Wladyslaw IV. So he always found reasons to delay doing anything about those petitions, iguring that, as the years went by, the disgruntled older Mecklenburg noblemen would start dying off and their younger kin start blending in elsewhere.

There was very heavy fighting in the Province of the Main, too, although it never assumed the scale of the civil-war-in-all-but-name that it did in Mecklenburg. The critical difference was that the nobility and the town elites stayed out of it, at least as organized groups.

The Rhineland had been the hotbed of anti-Semitism in the Germanies going back well into the Middle Ages. Anti-Semitism was common everywhere, but it was among the urban artisan classes that it developed the most fervor and violence, and no other part of the Germanies was as urbanized as the Rhineland.

That meant the CoC columns were clashing with people from the very same classes that provided most of their strength and support—and were doing so in areas where the CoCs themselves hadn't yet sunk the very deep roots they had in provinces farther to the east. To a large degree, what was happening in the Province of the Main and the neighboring areas amounted to a civil war within a civil war. The Committees of Correspondence were establishing in towns up and down the Rhine and the Main—by force, when need be—the same authority among their own supporters which they had established in the eastern and central Germanies over a longer period, using only persuasion and moral agitation.

To make the situation still more chaotic, the neat lists of "agitators" and "groups" and "organizations" that Francisco Nasi had provided the CoCs were more a reflection of the needs of efficient record-keeping than the actual reality on the ground. In the eastern and central Germanies, as a matter of self-defense if nothing else, every political movement no matter of what stripe or persuasion had begun adopting the rigorous organizational methods of the CoCs. Which had, in turn, been heavily influenced by the habits and attitudes of the Americans, accustomed as they were to the level of social and political organization common to advanced industrial societies of the late twentieth century.

But the Rhineland, for the most part, was still in the past. Anti-Semitic "organizations" were really more in the way of loose associations that formed and disintegrated in response to specific impulses. As a rule, those impulses were provided by a particularly effective or charismatic individual agitator, who would be the one to actually incite the violence.

These men were usually clerics of one sort of another. Low level clerics, at that. Itinerant mendicant friars, in Catholic areas; junior clergy looking to make a reputation and get a permanent parish assignment in Lutheran regions. Such were the names that appeared in Nasi's lists as "leaders" and "central figures" of anti-Semitic "groups."

The reality was quite a bit more fluid—which made for a very fluid sort of armed struggle. Typically, these anti-Semitic agitators would react to the approach of a CoC column by inciting a mob of locals, who would in turn form themselves into a militia—not infrequently, they *were* the town's official militia—to sally forth and meet the invaders in a small battle.

A small and quick battle. These hastily formed military bands, even the ones who constituted formal militias, were simply no match for the CoC columns in an open battle. The CoCs were, first, better organized and more disciplined; second, they were far better armed; third, many of their troops and the majority of their commanders were veterans of the recent wars. Almost a third of the column commanders, in fact, had been at the great battle of Ahrensbök.

Soon enough, their opponents realized they couldn't match the CoCs in straight battles, and they fell back on the standard tactic used by town and village militias for centuries when facing more powerful regular troops—which amounted to urban guerrilla warfare.

That would have been savage fighting under any circumstances. It was made still more savage by the harsh attitudes of the CoC soldiers.

By now, in the central and eastern Germanies, the political program of the CoCs had assumed the proportions of a social crusade for its members and supporters. There was more at stake than simply this or that specific issue, this or that specific grievance. What was ultimately involved was the very soul of a new nation coming into birth.

And they were fiercely determined that that nation would be "modern," as they understood the term. A term which was of course heavily influenced by American ideas and attitudes but which stemmed still more from long-gestating German ideas and long-festering German injustices. What the Americans had brought through the Ring of Fire was really not so much their "new ideas." What they mostly brought was the deep and abiding confidence that those ideas *worked.* That, so far from being airy and impractical, they were vastly more practical than the notions and methods advocated and used by the existing rulers of the Germanies.

So, all that was medieval and barbaric and primitive was to be destroyed. First and foremost, those two prominent and long-standing traditions in the Germanies of anti-Semitic pogroms and witch-hunts. Traditions which, in fact, were very closely related not simply in spirit but in the persons who carried them out.

The fact that many of the CoC soldiers didn't know any Jews or care about Jews—even, in plenty of instances, were themselves prejudiced against Jews—was neither here nor there. Some of them even still, somewhere deep inside, probably believed in "witchcraft." Half-believed, at least.

That didn't matter, anymore than it mattered whether this or that soldier in Sherman's army burning its way across Georgia in the march to the sea liked or disliked black people. The Confederacy was an abomination, a gross act of treason to the republic, and the Confederacy would damn well be destroyed. Period.

So it was with the attitude of the soldiers in the CoC columns fighting on the Rhine and the Main. The ancient customs of anti-Semitic pogroms and witch-hunting were damn well going to be destroyed. Because so long as they remained they would keep the nation shackled to barbarity and medievalism.

Not compromised with; not alleviated; not diluted; not "reformed."

Destroyed. Razed to the ground. Turned into rubble—and if the bodies of the defenders of medieval barbarism lay bleeding to death beneath the rubble, not a one of those fighters in the CoC columns cared in the least. Good riddance.

It had taken several years to entrench those new attitudes in the central and eastern provinces of the USE. The CoCs planned to finish the job in the western provinces in a few weeks.

And . . .

For the most part, they succeeded. Mike Stearns had predicted they would.

"It's simply a myth," he told Francisco Nasi, "that social attitudes are so deeply rooted that they'll last for generations under any circumstances. And the reason it's a myth is because attitudes in the abstract require actions in the concrete in order to remain solid and well-entrenched. It's not enough to 'feel' or 'think' this or that bias or prejudice. To keep those biases and prejudices solid—give them meat and blood and bone—you have to be able to *act* on them. And you've got to be able to do it frequently and regularly and in the public eye. Destroy the ability to act, and you will—very quickly—see the attitudes crumble and fade away. That's because you can't dragoon everybody else into tacitly supporting you, any longer."

He studied the Elbe from the window, for a moment. "I've seen it happen in my own lifetime. Well . . . most of it actually happened while I was still a kid, or hadn't even been born yet. Americans don't like to talk about it now, but the truth is that there were as many lynchings of black people in America in our not-so-distant past as there are lynchings of Jews and so-called 'witches' in Germany in the here and now. Yet by the time I was an adult, the lynchings were over. In a few short years, a social habit and custom that had lasted for centuries and had seemed as deeply ingrained as any had just vanished."

He swiveled his head and gave Francisco a fierce, hawkish look. "And you want to know how it was done? Forget all that vague twaddle about changes in so-called 'social consciousness.' Yeah, sure—those changes did happen and they were both real and important. But it's what lay beneath them and anchored them solidly that really counted—and that was as crude and simple as it gets."

He transferred the hawk glare to the river. "There was a time in America when you could lynch a black man with impunity. And then the time came when if you did so, you would get your ass handed to you. Often enough, by a black man wearing a badge and carrying a gun."

His smile managed to be wry and savage at the same time. "It's amazing, Francisco, how quickly 'deeply ingrained attitudes' will change—when the consequences of not changing are so immediate and obvious and detrimental to your health and well-being. Oh, yeah. It's really amazing how fast that can happen."

✧ ✧ ✧

The CoC columns that marched up and down the great rivers of the western provinces for several weeks shooting and hanging anti-Semites and witch-hunters, and burning down their homes and shops if they fled, did not really care whether anyone liked or disliked Jews or believed or did not believe that witches were real. That was a private and individual matter, by itself.

What they did care about was forging a modern nation. And that meant all medieval and barbaric public behavior—*especially* if it was done by the classes of people who provided most of their own support—was now at an end. A complete and total end. There would be no compromises, no bargaining, no dickering.

The murder of an old gentile had been the last straw. The Dreeson Incident was going to be the end of it.

It was over. Period.

Start a pogrom, you die. Burn a witch, you die. Accept and yield to the demands of a modern nation or be buried in the rubble of its medieval past. That is the only choice we give you.

Often enough in the past—the Fettmilch revolt in Frankfurt had not been particularly exceptional—the mobs who carried out pogroms against a town's ghetto were also hostile to the town's patricians. Yet that brought little or no comfort to those same patricians, as they watched, day after day, while the CoC columns established a new law and a new authority in their towns on the Rhine and the Main.

Today, they posed no threat, true. You could even, if you squinted really hard, fool yourself into thinking they were protecting you.

But this did not bode well for the future. Especially if—some of the more farsighted began rethinking their plans—the Crown Loyalists were reckless enough, now that they were in power, to try to force through all the provisions in their program.

As for Vincenz Weitz, he made his escape from the State of Thuringia-Franconia and headed for Bavaria, only to be caught up in the CoC's sweep of the Oberpfalz. He and a dozen or so of his followers and associates tried to find refuge in Nürnberg, the independent city-state completely surrounded by USE territory. But the authorities in Nürnberg wanted no part of the madness. They denied Weitz and his people entry into the city.

In the end, they died at a crossroads just north of Amberg, hunted down by a detachment from a CoC column.

Weitz was no coward, so it was a fierce little battle. But a short one, also. Afterward, Weitz and his men were shoved into a shallow mass grave in a nearby meadow.

By then, he'd been identified. But there was no marker placed over the grave, and never would be. By the time the bones started weathering through, many decades later, the local village legends would place him and his men as a lost unit of mercenaries from a much earlier period. It was an understandable confusion. The weapons in the possession of Weitz and his men at the end had been quite antique.

When it was all over, and the peculiarly-named affair—why "crystal night"? it made no sense—had entered Germany's history books, Gretchen and Achterhof and Spartacus summoned all the CoC columns into the capital city.

They came, some twenty thousand combatants by then, and paraded in an orderly manner right through the city. The CoC even set up a reviewing stand in front of the parliament, on Hans Richter Square.

Prime Minister Wilhelm Wettin and the entire leadership of the Crown Loyalist Party found reasons to be absent from Magdeburg that day. But Princess Kristina—overriding the advice of all of her ladies-in-waiting except Caroline Platzer—chose to accept Gretchen's offer to join her on the reviewing stand.

It was hard to know if the child really understood all the political subtleties involved in the heir to the imperial throne accepting that invitation. It was quite possible, though, that she did—well enough, at least. Kristina was almost frighteningly precocious.

But, perhaps there was nothing more involved than the emotional enthusiasm of an eight-year-old girl who knew that those thousands who marched past the stand would be very friendly and would return her cheery waves with roars of applause and appreciation.

(Which, indeed, they did. Another great large stick to shove up the rumps of the Crown Loyalists.)

General Torstensson came to watch also. For understandable political reasons, however, he felt it would be unwise to watch the parade from the reviewing stand. So he satisfied himself with a good view from the steps of the palace.

"Nicely done," he commented to one of his aides. "They don't march as well as real soldiers, of course. But it's still quite impressive."

He glanced back at the parliament building. "I do hope Wettin and his people have learned some prudence from all this."

The aide was a Swede, like Torstensson. So, like his commander, he felt a certain detachment from all this messy German business.

"I wouldn't count on it, General. I really wouldn't."

Chapter 69

Grantville

"Weren't the fireworks that the Farbenwerke put on great?" Denise was reliving every minute of the celebration. "Where did they get so many so fast? There were only three days between when the Jenkinses announced Ron and Missy's engagement in the paper and the picnic up at Lothlorien."

Minnie shook her head. "It wasn't fast. Lutz Fischer in seventh grade is the son of the facilities manager there. He says the union had figured for months that this would be coming up, so they bought a case every time they had a chance and had them stashed away in advance."

"I think it's exciting," Denise said. "Especially that maybe they're engaged, sort of, because we taught Missy and Pam to ride, so we had something to do with it. They wouldn't have kissed each other up at Lothlorien that afternoon if Missy hadn't been on your hog and given Ron a lift."

Minnie nodded. "Yeah. But I sure can't tell what she sees in him." Having thus defined romance as *a priori* irrelevant to this betrothal, she reconsidered the matter from a practical perspective. "And coming from the kind of family she has, she doesn't need to marry him for money, either."

She was, however, willing to grant that a groom was a prerequisite for putting on a wedding. Ever since the announcement of the engagement, she had been spending her spare time in Mrs. Johnson's home economics room, reading a dozen or so tattered copies of up-time bridal magazines that had found a final resting place there. "I bet Missy's mom is going to insist on a big wedding, whether Missy wants one or not. Or her grandmas will. If so, do you suppose she might ask us to be bridesmaids because we helped things along?"

Denise shook her head. "She'll probably ask her cousins. Or someone she was in the same class with at school. Brides almost always do. Vanessa Jones, that's the daughter of the Reverends Jones, asked Caroline and Ceci. When Mary Kat Riddle got married last winter, her brother's wife was the matron of honor and she didn't have any other attendants at all. Gerry will probably get to be best man, though, if the rest of Ron's folks haven't come back from Italy by the time they get married."

The expression on Minnie's face was seriously disillusioned.

"But she might invite us to serve cake and punch at the reception," Denise offered as a consolation prize. "Or whatever people are using now instead of cake and punch."

"That's better than nothing. I guess."

"We did already get invited to Gerry's confirmation." Denise held out an elaborately decorated printed sheet. "He mailed yours to me, too, because he wasn't sure of Benny's address."

Minnie took her copy. "I guess Doreen would be willing to go with us over to Rudolstadt. I don't think that your mom goes to confirmations."

"It's going to be here at St. Martin's. A real big deal. We can go by ourselves if none of the grownups want to go with us. What do you wear to a confirmation?" Denise asked. "I've never been to one."

"Your best dress. Not a prom dress, but if you have a good dress to wear to daytime things, that would be right. Like the one I wear when I go to church with Benny, Sundays when the weather's nasty and I don't want to walk out to St. Martin's."

"Good jeans?"

"I don't think so. Maybe nice slacks, though, with a matching top."

"I wore my good jeans to the Christmas play at St. Martin's."

"That was at night, and everyone kept their coats on, you said, because the church was so cold. You could ask Mrs. Reading what to wear. She'd know what's right. Your mom can afford to buy you one, can't she?"

"Yeah. I think so. She'll wonder what I need a dress for, though."

Minnie frowned. "Is Gerry better now? Less upset about what went on down in Rome?"

"Yeah. Maybe that's why he's being confirmed here instead of over at the school. He really likes this pastor. It's funny, Minnie."

"What?"

"Here we are, all three of us sixteen. When I look at Gerry, I start thinking that we've really got to start deciding what we want to do with our lives beyond skipping school whenever we can get away with it and riding motorcycles."

"And being bridesmaids, if Missy would ask us." Minnie looked wistful. "I would love to have a green bridesmaid's dress. Doreen picks my new clothes out and she never picks anything green. With one of those skirts that's slim at the top and flares out below, like an upside-down lily."

"It's a little discouraging. Gerry is so absolutely sure of what he wants to do. He's not bothered a bit by knowing that he'll be going to school for years and years and years more."

"It's that atonement thing. He's still really bothered about killing that Marius guy."

"I know," Denise said.

"Why did it bother him so much? Why does it still bother him so much? What did that book we looked up at the library call it? A crisis of conscience?"

"Well," Denise suggested tentatively, "maybe he got so upset because he did it by accident. On the spur of the moment. To a guy who wasn't really right, mentally. It wasn't something that he knew needed doing and decided to do."

Minnie nodded her head. That seemed as good an explanation as any they were likely to think of. They settled down to catch up on the homework they had missed while they were out of town.

Mrs. Dreeson and Mrs. Wiley had really been pretty annoyed with them. So had Missy and Pam. Mentoring. It wasn't as if they were so dumb that they had to be in class every day in order to get decent grades.

When they got their diplomas, they knew, they had some interesting things coming to them from the locked cubicles at the storage lot. Buster had left a letter covering it in his safe deposit box, in case anything happened to him.

Denise's dad had believed in keeping his paperwork in order.

"I still think," Minnie said, "that it would be more fun to be a bridesmaid and walk down the aisle carrying a bouquet than it would be to serve cake and punch. Junior bridesmaids, maybe? One of the magazines had an article about those. Do you suppose we could hint?"

Don Francisco put down the report currently in front of him.

The news from the Netherlands was that lava lamps bade fair to become the equivalent of the tulip craze recorded in the encyclopedias from up-time. There appeared to be every reason to believe that Laurent Mauger, his wife Velma Hardesty, his LaChapelle nephews in Leiden, and Jacques-Pierre Dumais were on their way to a fortune that would dwarf Mauger's original very prosperous business enterprises. A fortune which, being prudently kept in the names of Velma, the two nephews, and Dumais, would be unaffected by the civil agreement Mauger had made with his sons and other nephews before he remarried.

This might have significant potential for increasing Mauger's influence in the circles of recalcitrant, irredentist, Huguenot opponents of Cardinal Richelieu. Even more, it would signify that Madame Mauger was likely, some day, to be found in the role of an influential and wealthy widow.

Dumais, he heard, was retiring from the trade to concentrate upon becoming an industrial magnate. A pity, in a way. He'd been a competent man. Francisco would have preferred to turn him, if possible.

Well, you couldn't win them all, as Mike Stearns often said. And, if the rumors of a possible betrothal between Dumais and the sister of Pamela Hardesty's suitor were true? The man had, after all, taken out Grantville citizenship. So who knew? That was a matter for the future. It would be useful to have a competent agent inside Laurent Mauger's various enterprises and not just rely upon chance.

Sighing, Nasi looked at Wes Jenkins and asked, "How much do you know about the circumstances of your son-in-law's death?"

"Beyond what has been discussed within the administration? Or beyond what you may know beyond that?" was Wes' cautious answer.

Respond to a question with questions. Yes, Jenkins might rise farther than he had expected in the diplomatic service.

"Stalemate?"

"I feel certain that you have agents in Frankfurt. Its products are much too important to the war effort that you would not."

"You are correct." Nasi thought back to the last letter he had received from the up-timer he had placed in Frankfurt. Nathan Prickett. Awkward, that he was Jenkins' other son-in-law. All the people in this town were so interrelated that it sometimes made things difficult. Fascinating, always, but sometimes difficult. When he first encountered Grantville, the interconnections had not been so clear to him.

"I don't need to know who they are."

Don Francisco found that something of a relief, under the circumstances. "I received a quite detailed report from one of them who was on the scene at the time the death was discovered."

"Probably didn't tally very well with the official story."

Don Francisco sighed. He had been afraid of that. Perhaps a circumlocution was in order?

"I would appreciate your advice."

"On?"

"Suitability. I have been considering speaking with Christin George and Benny Pierce in regard to those two girls with the incredible motorcycles. Ah. I can never thank you enough for arranging that first ride with Minnie for me. Marvelous."

Wes smiled. It was generally known that Don Francisco now had a new interest in life. He had purchased Buster Beasley's Harley from Christin George, for a price that no one else in Grantville even wanted to think about.

"Minnie told me that Denise didn't get mad; she got even. That he started it. She didn't offer any details and I didn't ask for any." That was as far as Wes originally intended to go. But. "That I would have lost my temper and messed it up."

"You feel no obligation to bring this to the attention of the authorities?"

"I was quite prepared to let the authorities deal with his treason." Wes paused. "That's political. Threatening Clara, beating Lenore—that was different. Personal. Denise and Minnie didn't do anything that I wouldn't have done if I had caught up with him. That was personal, too, for them. For Buster, for Henry. They only did it better."

"I think, then, that I will arrange a coffee. The two parents. Mrs. Dreeson. Mrs. Wiley."

"I'd suggest that you invite Joe Pallavicino, too. You might get some good input. He knows them as well as anyone in the school system does."

Don Francisco nodded his thanks.

"I know," Don Francisco said, nodding at the three widows, "that for you it was a tragedy. A great personal tragedy, and I do extend my full sympathy to you all. But in the larger picture, both for the USE and for Grantville . . . You do realize, I hope, that as a result of the reaction against the assassinations in front of the synagogue, particularly against that of Herr Dreeson, anti-Semitism as an organized phenomenon will almost vanish from the United States of Europe. So will witch-hunting. For a number of years, at least. Individual prejudices, of course, are a different matter. This may even extend to any kind of outright reactionary political formations in the USE, because, given the nature of the situation, all of them had been dabbling heavily in the anti-Semitic efforts."

Veronica nodded. "So be it. Henry hated all that viciousness. And . . . he would not have liked being an invalid. Not at all. And, as Doctor Nichols had told him, hip replacements will remain a 'thing of the future' for a long time yet."

"As for Grantville itself," Don Francisco began.

This time Inez Wiley nodded. "Yes, this has brought the town together again. It is more . . . more *cohesive* . . . now than it has been since right after the Croat raid. We were cracking apart. People are so tired, so overworked. So many men have taken jobs elsewhere, the soldiers have been stationed in other places for so long, so many families have been split again. First losing relatives to the Ring of Fire, then to other towns and cities. And so many new people coming in so fast, taking their places in some ways, but not quite. I hate to think that it took the deaths of Henry and Enoch to reverse the breakdown, but since it did and I'm sure it was not the intention of the assassins that it did, God has granted us justice."

She blinked. "So, that's all right. Even if most people won't ever notice how it happened. Otherwise, it's been a little tempestuous since Enoch's funeral. Will and Gina are going to marry each other again, so maybe I'll have more grandchildren yet. Gina's only thirty-three." Her voice caught in her throat, somewhere between a laugh and a sob. "If she doesn't shoot him first. I sure hope he's learned his lesson. The power plant is designated safety-critical, so ever since the Ring of Fire, she's been real conscientious about keeping up her target practice at the police range every week."

Don Francisco nodded his respect. He could not have said himself whether the respect was for Inez or Gina. Grantville's women were . . . astonishing. Spiritual sisters of Judith and Jael. Now for the next part.

"Your daughters," he said. This time he gestured to Benny Pierce and Christin. "They are growing up."

Yes, Don Francisco granted to himself, these girls were dangerous. Would continue to be dangerous as they matured. As dangerous as any man such as Harry Lefferts, he thought. More dangerous, perhaps, because people did not see it so quickly in females. His mind drifted back briefly to the City. To the *Sultana Valide*. He must, if possible, have them. It would be far better to have their potential harnessed than left to run loose.

He hoped he would never have to tell the old man and Denise's mother what Nathan Prickett had written to him from Frankfurt. There was certainly no reason to do so right now. And there was no hurry, of course. Perhaps he should let them finish high school here in Grantville first. However . . .

"The girl Denise," he began, "wrote me a very interesting letter some time back, containing extremely valuable information that she and Minnie had compiled. Combined with other data, it was extremely helpful in tracking the instigators of the attack on the synagogue and the motives for the assassination. Additionally, at the time of the Jenkins child's birth, the girl Minnie delivered an impromptu emergency report that was a model of brevity and relevance. It is time, perhaps, that they should be considering their future careers. I will be starting up a private practice that continues much of my previous work for the government. I believe what you up-timers would call a 'consultant' sort of thing. I will always have need of . . ."

Benny Pierce smiled. "That Mrs. Simpson," he said, "you've heard of her?"

Don Francisco agreed that he had heard of Mrs. Simpson.

"She's invited me go come to Magdeburg this coming summer.

To 'anchor a folklife festival,' she said." Benny started digging through a pile of mail stacked on the arm of his chair. "There's a letter here about it. I'd thought, with Minnie trying to catch up in school and all, that I'd probably have to pass on it. But if you would have some kind of stuff for her to do there, too . . . She's sixteen, after all. I quit school before I was that old. It wouldn't be such a hard trip, now that a person can take the train."

"That would certainly work for a few months," Francisco said. "Not, perhaps, in the long run. I have decided, for a variety of reasons, that it would be best to relocate to Prague."

Nasi cleared his throat. "Of course, Wallenstein is said to be an enthusiastic patron of the arts as well. And Prague is world-famous for music."

He and Benny smiled warmly upon each other.

Joe Pallavicino smiled too. "Actually," he said, "in many ways, both Minnie and Denise would benefit from starting to gain broader experience now. Outside of the Grantville school system. Particularly since both of them are old for grade. And there are such things as correspondence courses. No reason why they shouldn't go ahead and get their high school diplomas while receiving additional training in your office, Don Francisco."

If he pulled this off, Joe reflected, then some day, when he appeared before the pearly gates, he could hand St. Peter a letter of recommendation from Victor Saluzzo. The high school principal might even pay for sequins on his wings.

Whether Don Francisco Nasi would provide one for him by then would be another question, of course.

Epilogue

Don Francisco took his motorcycle up the curvy hill on Route 250, enjoying the feel of the wind on his face.

Magdeburg would do for the duration of Benny Pierce's summer folk festival appearance. That was fine. It would take Francisco a few months to move himself and his enterprise to Prague, anyway.

Nasi pulled out onto an overlook. The hills, at least, he could see without his glasses. They were far enough away.

So. It should all work out quite nicely. Morris Roth had established a coeducational university at Prague and Judith . . .

He laughed to himself. What had Judith Roth ever done to him to deserve his bringing Minnie and Denise to her, like a matched pair of burnt offerings?

Cast of Characters

Abrabanel, Rebecca	USE parliamentary delegate from Magdeburg Province from February 1635 onward; USE government, envoy to Frederik Hendrik, summer 1633–late autumn 1634; wife of Mike Stearns
Achterhof, Gunther	Leader of the Committees of Correspondence
Altschuler, Hedwig	Wife of Jarvis Beasley
Ancelin, Gui	French Huguenot fanatic; part of Michel Ducos' organization
Bachmeier, Clara	Wife of Wes Jenkins; SoTF government, consular service 1634–1635
Beasley, Clark "Buster"	Father of Denise Beasley; nephew of Ken Beasley
Beasley, Denise	Daughter of Buster Beasley
Beasley, Jarvis	Husband of Hedwig Altschuler; son of Ken Beasley
Beasley, Johnnie Ray	Retired miner; grandfather of Buster Beasley

Beasley, Ken	Owner of the 250 Club tavern; father of Jarvis Beasley; uncle of Buster Beasley
Bellamy, Arnold	SoTF Department of Internal Affairs 1632–1635
Boucher, Léon	French Huguenot fanatic; part of Michel Ducos' organization
Brillard, Mathurin	French Huguenot fanatic; part of Michel Ducos' organization
Carson, Willard	Hotel owner
Cavriani, Idelette	Developing businesswoman, apprentice to Hartmuth Frisch; bookkeeper for St. Veronica's Academies 1634–1635; daughter of Leopold Cavriani
Delerue, Antoine	French Huguenot fanatic; part of Michel Ducos' organization
Deneau, Fortunat	French Huguenot fanatic; part of Michel Ducos' organization
Dreeson, Henry	Mayor of Grantville; husband of Veronica "Ronnie" Schuster
Ducos, Michel	Assassin; Huguenot fanatic
Dumais, Jacques-Pierre	Agent for Henri de Rohan, double-agent spy for Michel Ducos via Laurent Mauger; employee of Garbage Guys in Grantville
Ennis, Cora (Parker)	Owner of City Hall Cafe and Coffee House (aka "Cora's")
Gentileschi, Artemisia	Artist
Gentileschi, Constantia	Daughter of Artemisia
George, Christin	Wife of Buster Beasley; mother of Denise Beasley
Green, Albert "Al"	Baptist minister
Haggerty, Blake	Grantville police officer; grandson of Veda Mae Haggerty

Haggerty, Gary	Owner of Garbage Guys; son of Veda Mae Haggerty
Haggerty, Veda Mae	Nursing assistant 1631–1635
Hardesty, Pamela	SoTF State Library, trainee for circulation desk manager; daughter of Velma Hardesty
Hardesty, Velma	Wife of wealthy merchant
Hartke, Dagmar	Wife of sergeant in SoTF forces, Fulda Barracks Regiment; chair of Barracktown Council
Hartke, Helmuth	Sergeant, Fulda Barracks Regiment
Hercher, Walpurga	Laundress, MaidenFresh Laundries; part-time cleaning woman
Hesse-Kassel, Amalie Elisabeth, Landgravine of	Noblewoman, wife of Wilhelm V of Hesse-Kassel
Hesse-Kassel, Wilhelm V, Landgrave of	Ruler of Hesse-Kassel, ally of and military commander for Gustav II Adolf
Hesse-Rotenburg, Hermann, Landgrave of	Half-brother of Wilhelm V of Hesse-Kassel; Secretary of State of the USE under the Stearns administration
Higgins, Jeffrey ("Jeff")	Lieutenant, USE Army; husband of Gretchen Richter
Higgins, Wilhelm Richter	Son of Gretchen Richter
Hill, Andrea (Decker)	Employee, Department of Internal Affairs of the State of Thuringia-Franconia (SoTF)
Hinshaw, Cameron	USE Army; radio operator on Frank Jackson's staff 1634
Holloway, Bryant	Lieutenant, fire department; husband of Lenore Jenkins
Holloway, Lola	Optician's assistant; sister of Bryant

Holloway, Weshelle	Daughter of Bryant Holloway and Lenore Jenkins
Hudson, Vera	Wife of Willie Ray Hudson; grandmother of Missy Jenkins
Hudson, William Raymond ("Bill")	Pharmaceutical researcher, Lothlorien Farbenwerke, partner with Ron Stone in "Whatever Works"; grandson of Willie Ray and Vera Hudson
Hudson, Willie Ray	Farmer, Department of Agriculture advisor; husband of Vera
Hugelmair, Minnie	Singer and violinist; high school student; adopted daughter of Benny Pierce, friend of Denise Beasley
Jackson, Frank	Colonel, USE Army; adjutant to General Lennart Torstensson
Jenkins, Charles Hudson, Sr. "Chad"	Prominent citizen in Grantville; political figure in the State of Thuringia-Franconia; husband of Debbie Jenkins; father of Missy and Chip Jenkins
Jenkins, Charles Hudson, Jr. "Chip"	Student, University of Jena, 1632–1634; CoC organizer and university docent, law student 1634–35; brother of Missy
Jenkins, Deborah (Hudson) "Debbie"	Head of Teacher Training Program in Grantville; wife of Chad Jenkins; mother of Missy and Chip Jenkins
Jenkins, Eleanor Anne (Newton)	Red Cross president; grandmother of Missy Jenkins
Jenkins, Lenore	SoTF government, Court System, transcriber of records; daughter of Wes Jenkins, wife of Bryant Holloway
Jenkins, Melissa Marie "Missy"	SoTF State Library, Information Librarian in training; daughter of Chad and Debbie Jenkins
Jenkins, Wesley Williams "Wes"	SoTF government, Consular Service director; older brother of Chad Jenkins

Jones, Mary Ellen	Methodist minister; wife of Simon Jones
Jones, Simon	Methodist minister; mission to Venice 1634; husband of Mary Ellen
Junker, Egidius "Eddie"	SoTF government, Department of Economic Resources; assistant to Noelle Murphy/Stull
Kastenmayer, Johann Conrad "Cunz"	Consulting counsel to the county board 1635; son of Ludwig Kastenmayer
Kastenmayer, Ludwig	Lutheran pastor, St. Martin's in the Fields, Schwarzburg-Rudolstadt
LaChapelle, Jean-Louis	Student, University of Leiden, 1634; nephew of Laurent Mauger
Lambert, Gary	Leahy Medical Center, hospital business manager
Lang, Cory Joe	USE Army, military intelligence; Frank Jackson's liaison to Don Francisco Nasi; son of Velma Hardesty
Levasseur, Abraham	French Huguenot fanatic; part of Michel Ducos' organization
Locquifier, Guillaume	French Huguenot fanatic; part of Michel Ducos' organization
Mademann, Charles	French Huguenot fanatic; part of Michel Ducos' organization
Magen, Wilhelm	Grantville police officer
Mailey, Melissa	Political adviser to Mike Stearns
Matheny, Stephen "Steve"	Chief of Grantville Fire Department
Mauger, Laurent	Wine merchant, indirect agent for Michel Ducos; husband of Velma Hardesty
Maurer, Karl	Grantville police officer
Moser, Nicolas, "the Younger"	Employee in city clerk's office, husband of Dorothea Richter

Nasi, Francisco	Head of intelligence and political adviser for Mike Stearns
Nobili, Agostino "Tino"	Pharmacy owner; prominent citizen of Grantville
Ouvrard, Robert	French Huguenot fanatic; part of Michel Ducos' organization
Pallavicino, Joseph "Joe"	ESOL teacher, and guidance counselor for transferring former ESOL students, 1631–1635
Pence, Kortney	LPN, going for specialized RN as nurse-midwife
Piazza, Annabelle	Teacher; wife of Ed Piazza
Piazza, Edward "Ed"	President of the State of Thuringia-Franconia
Pierce, Benny	Retired miner; musician; adopted father of Minnie Hugelmair
Pietersz, Alida	Niece of Laurent Mauger
Prickett, Chandra	Wife of Nathan Prickett; daughter of Wes Jenkins
Prickett, Nathan Garson	Sales representative in Frankfurt-am-Main for Blumroeder's gun business; secret agent for Don Francisco Nasi
Richards, Preston "Press"	Chief of Grantville Police Department
Richter, Anna Elisabetha "Annalise"	Assistant manager of St. Veronica's Academy; high school student in Grantville; Gretchen Richter's younger sister
Richter, Dorothea "Thea"	Wife of Nicolas Moser; cousin of Gretchen and Annalise Richter
Richter, Maria Margaretha "Gretchen"	Leader of the Committees of Correspondence; Wife of Jeff Higgins
Riddle, Veleda	League of Women Voters, founder; Red Cross committee member

Rohan, Benjamin de, Duke of Soubise	French nobleman; prominent figure among the Huguenots; brother of Henri
Rohan, Henri II de Duke of Rohan	French Huguenot nobleman; general, diplomat
Ron, Isaac de	Innkeeper in Frankfurt-am-Main; wine merchant; secret agent for Henri de Rohan
Ruppersdorf, Katerina von	Noblewoman, estate owner and manager; fiancée of Chip Jenkins
Saluzzo, Victor	Grantville high school principal
Sandrart, Joachim	Artist, painter
Schwarzburg-Rudolstadt, Emilie, Countess of	Wife of Count Ludwig Guenther
Schwarzburg-Rudolstadt, Ludwig Guenther, Count of	Ruler of the county of Schwarzburg-Rudolstadt; Prominent political figure in the SoTF and USE
Stearns, Michael "Mike"	Prime Minister of the Unites States of Europe; husband of Rebecca Abrabanel
Stone, Elrond "Ron"	Manager of the Lothlorien Farbenwerke and Stone pharmaceuticals operations; son of Tom Stone; brother of Frank and Gerry Stone
Stone, Gwaihir "Gerry"	Youngest son of Tom Stone; brother of Frank and Ron Stone
Stull, Dennis Robert	Military procurement in Erfurt; father of Noelle Stull
Stull/Murphy, Noelle	SoTF government, Department of Economic Resources, "gray ops" for Ed Piazza and Mike Stearns
Stull, Aura Lee (Hudson)	SoTF Government, Department of Economic Resources
Stull, Joseph Harlan "Joe"	SoTF government, Secretary of Transportation

Thierbach, Joachim von "Spartacus"	Leader of the Committees of Corresponence
Tito, Maurice	Grantville court system, chief judge
Torstensson, Lennart	Swedish general, commander in chief of USE army
Tourneau, Andre	French Huguenot fanatic; part of Michel Ducos' organization
Turpin, Georges	French Huguenot fanatic; part of Michel Ducos' organization
Utt, Derek	Military administrator for the Fulda District
Wackernagel, Martin	Courier
Waters, Jason	Newspaper reporter
Weitz, Vincenz	Anti-Semitic agitator
Wettin, Wilhelm	Politician, leader of the Crown Loyalist-party in the USE (formerly Saxe-Weimar, Wilhelm IV, Duke of)
Wiley, Enoch	Presbyterian minister; husband of Inez Wiley
Wiley, Inez	Presbyterian church secretary, organist, and general factotum; wife of Enoch Wiley
Wiley, William Lyman "Will"	Son of Enoch and Inez Wiley; SoTF government, Department of Economic Resources